DEMONWITCH

(A Novel of Good and Evil)

by Robert Arvay

DEMONWITCH

(A Novel by Robert Arvay)

This is a work of fiction.

Any similarities to actual persons is purely coincidental.

Cover art by

Mario John Borgatti

ISBN: 978-0-6151-3948-7

To my daughter, Sandra.

DEMONWITCH

(A Novel by Robert Arvay)

Introduction

"We're being watched," Miril whispered to her playmate. Her tone had suddenly changed, from childhood merriment, to one of fear.

Veelos quickly looked up from where they were squatting in the sandy soil. The two girls had been playing with homemade dolls. But now her gaze shifted alertly toward the edge of forest nearby, there to join with Miril's in search of whatever lurked for them.

"I feel it, too," she breathed nervously, afraid to make any loud sound. In all their lives, neither girl had ever sensed danger, not real danger, and certainly nothing as ominous as this. Now they both felt a sense of dread, the kind that warns of impending doom. It chilled their spines.

The girls were not just imagining their fears. For, perilously nearby, concealed by the shadows of trees and brushy undergrowth, two sets of eyes narrowed with sinister intent. Not one creature, but two, lay in ambush at the border of the forest, intently observing the girls. Beneath furrowed brows, their serpent eyes glared with hunger and ferocity. But although they were predators, it was not hunger for flesh which attracted these two creatures to the edge of the village. Their craving was not of the earthly sort. For these two beings devoured not bodies, but souls. And to them, the utmost delicacy was the soul of an innocent.

"We'd better go tell," Miril uttered. "If it's wolves, they'll soon hurt someone."

"You know very well that they're not wolves," Veelos replied, almost scolding the other. "But let's get away from here, before something awful happens to us." With that, the two girls abruptly stood and fled toward the safety of the village.

"Look!" the creature named Luur grunted excitedly, "they're escaping. We've got to stop them."

"We dare not," retorted Mok. "Restrain yourself. Our instructions are only to survey them, to make sure that these are the ones."

"Clearly they are," Luur said. Its fierce eyes remained focused on their fleeing quarry, and it only barely suppressed the urge to leap from concealment, and to lunge toward the helpless girls. Had its impulse become compulsion, the beast would have roared ferociously, and would have chased the girls down before they could make good their escape. But the creature named Luur well knew the penalty for disobedience to the master, and so it restrained its murderous instinct.

"None among mortals have auras of such destiny," Mok said almost in awe. "None except these two. So they are indeed the ones. Very well, then, we have found them. That's all we came for, to confirm the master's suspicions, that the prophecies are finally coming to pass. At long last! Our day cannot be far away anymore. Let's return to Thorgar and tell it what we've seen."

But Luur still seemed anxious. "Can't you see?" it said. "One of them must be the priestess of prophecy, the one we are warned about. This is our chance to prevent her from ever wearing the silver ring, to forestall her from destroying us. We must kill her, and now."

"We must not," Mok said. "We must not interfere with the anti-prophecy. True, one of them is indeed to become the priestess of the orb, but we cannot know which one. And remember also, that the other child is the foretold demonwitch. It is she who will slay the priestess, not us. No one can destroy the demonwitch except the priestess. And none can slay the priestess, but the demonwitch herself. Our work here is done. Let's go quickly."

The two girls were running as fast as they could toward the center of the village, when Veelos suddenly grasped Miril's arm. "Stop."

But at just the same time, Miril stopped also, of her own accord. "They're gone," she said.

"What were they?"

"How should I know? If I did know, then so would you, and already."

Veelos was still catching her breath from their brief sprint, when she said, "We've just got to tell, Miril. We must. Whatever they were, they were evil, not just dangerous, but very, very---"

"We can't tell," Miril insisted. "No one will believe us. They'll just say that two silly little girls wandered too close to the forest, and became frightened. That's all."

Veelos reluctantly nodded in agreement. "And besides, they'll punish us for straying too far from home. You're right."

Miril glanced back in the direction from which they had just fled, to reassure herself that, after all, nothing was pursuing them. "They'll be back, you know. Either them, or their ilk. Today was not their day. But they're not finished here, not yet."

"And they'll come back just--- for us," Veelos said. "They didn't care about anyone else here, did they, but only us."

Miril shuddered slightly. "Yes, only us. But why? Why should they single us out?"

Veelos hesitated, unsure of whether to voice her thought. Then she said, "I know this may sound a bit odd, but Miril, maybe it was because--- do you think that maybe they were just a little bit like--- like us?"

"No. Not at all like us. Not even close."

"I don't mean it that way. We're not evil. They are. Unspeakably. But what I did mean was--- Miril, they, like we, can sense things that others cannot, just as you and I do. Whatever they want from us, it has something to do with our special sense, the secret we no longer speak of to anyone. Think about it"

Miril gave it a few moments of thought, then admitted, "Perhaps you're right, Veelos. They do have powers. Strange powers. But so do we. We have powers too, Veelos." She paused, as if announcing the solution to a great mystery. "And they knew that, didn't they? That's why they didn't pounce when they had the chance. Could it be that they fear us--- as we feared them? I think so, Veelos. Then let's not fear them at all. Instead, if they come again, let's find a way to fight back."

Veelos scoffed. "They have tooth and claw, and those are not their worst weapons."

"True," Miril said. "But we have something more powerful than that. We have each other."

Veelos scoffed again.

But Miril persisted. "They care only for themselves, and for no one else. They cannot stand together for very long, certainly not long enough to lay down their lives, not one for the other. That is our power, Veelos, the power that you and I do have. If you and I stand together against them, then they can never hurt us. Not if we stand together, as we always have."

Veelos felt strangely comforted by those words. "It's true," she said. "We have always stood together, you and I. And," she added, "we always will. Always."

It was the year of the wolf, and the two girls were six years old. They had not yet become mortal enemies.

* * * * *

"What are you doing here at so late an hour?" Jen-Aga asked. The temple library was darkened, with but a single candle to illumine the dusty, ancient scrolls of the innermost chamber.

"Searching," replied the high priestess. By her manner, she seemed hardly aware of the presence of the younger priestess. An urgent task preoccupied her.

"Searching for what?"

Soniya was annoyed by the distraction. "The truth," she replied. "What else does one seek among the scriptures?"

With that answer, Jen-Aga decided that she had no further choice but to retreat. The hint could not have been stronger. "Very well. I shall not disturb you more than I already have. By your leave."

"Wait," Soniya said. She had not meant to be so abrupt with the young priestess. Her tone softened, almost in apology. "This concerns you more than the others. You need to know."

Jen-Aga had begun to turn away, but now she stood facing Soniya, her hands clasping each other at her waist, a gesture of submission. "To know what?"

Soniya sighed. "Jen-Aga, you know some of it already. Surely you must have thought about what it must mean. Very well then, I'll tell you. All three of the high priests, myself included, are growing old. That much is obvious. But what does it mean? Soon we will be unable to tend the orb. We won't be able to keep watch over the priesthood, nor to confer upon others the silver ring. And all this is coming to pass just at a crucial time, a time when it will be more difficult than ever before to protect the priesthood."

Jen-Aga showed confusion on her face. "Protect? From what?"

Soniya continued to fumble among the scrolls. "That," she said, "is just what I'm searching for." Then pausing, she said solemnly, "Jen-Aga, I was not going to say this tonight, or here. But I suppose that this is the time and the place for it, after all. So brace yourself for some shocking news. For you,

Priestess Jen-Aga, are one of the three, whom we have chosen, to replace us when we must give way to youth."

Jen-Aga took a moment to absorb the impact of what the high priestess had just spoken. Her astonishment was profound. "Me? Are you serious? Me? To become a--- but High Priestess! You cannot mean that. There are others older than I---"

"Yes," Soniya said. "Older, and more wise, and more strong, and more blah blah blah. I know. I said much the same when I was appointed over my seniors, many years ago. Do you think that we would appoint someone who aspires to power, someone who seeks authority? May God forbid."

"But High Priestess, I am not merely less wise, I am not prepared for such---"

"Nonsense. Your very denial of worthiness, the sincerity, the intensity, confirms that you should be a high priestess. Jen-Aga, you embody the very essence of the priesthood: to be an instrument of the divine will, not of our own will, but His."

"But I could never wield the powers as---"

"Hush now. You know full well that we never wield the powers."

Jen-Aga lowered her gaze. "I did not mean it that way."

"I know you didn't, but we must be careful when we speak. There are many who envy power, and there are even some who would seek to obtain the orb of power itself. They simply don't understand that its power is not like the power of a sword or a potion, to be mastered and wielded. They cannot grasp the concept. And when we tell them that we simply let the power flow through us, they disbelieve. When we tell them that it is not our own will we seek to do, but rather God's will, they dismiss us as secretive and conspiring. A careless word could incite them to demand that we work miracles for them."

"I know," Jen-Aga said. "But what I meant is that I am afraid, afraid to have such power at my fingertips. And the responsibility of guarding the orb--- High Priestess, I am afraid."

"Have no fear. God Himself will guide you, as He has guided us three who now serve before the high altar."

Jen-Aga trembled in as much fear as if a panther had suddenly appeared. For Soniya had, obviously, with the other two high priests, already decided the matter beforehand. She could refuse, of course.

But Soniya had already anticipated that possibility as well. "And if you try to wiggle out of this, I'll shadow your every move, until you accept the post just to be rid of me."

Jen-Aga felt a slight smile hint upon her face, for she had never seen the normally stoic high priestess speak with such affectionate humor.

But then Soniya's tone darkened. "We need you, and the two priests whom we have selected. We need you desperately. For the times call for younger instruments, three new high priests, who will be able to confront the evil now invading the world of men."

Jen-Aga felt her fear return. "An invasion?"

"Of sorts. Jen-Aga, have you ever heard the legend of the demonwitch?"

Demonwitch: the very word unnerved Jen-Aga, almost as if Soniya had spoken a profanity. Amid the purity of the temple, among its ancient scriptures, could such a word be uttered? But then, after all, the answer to Soniya's pointed question was in the affirmative. "Yes. I've heard the story. The minstrels sing of it. But it's only a legend, is it not?"

Soniya replied, "It's time to look into that legend, time to ask how much of it is mere fable, but also to ask, how much of it is true after all. Tell me what you've heard from the minstrels."

Jen-Aga hesitated for a moment, then spoke almost reluctantly. "There was a woman. She was a princess, who became a priestess. But then she turned against God, and commanded a legion of--- of--- demons. Her name was Kattaroon. There was a warrior named Tarok, who was a barbarian, a savage, who loved her. But when Kattaroon turned to witchcraft, Tarok sided with the angels whom God sent to oppose her. His army defeated hers in battle. And then, Tarok faced an agonizing choice."

All the while, Soniya had continued her search for the ancient scroll, one in particular. Then, even as Jen-Aga was still speaking, the high priestess finally found it. Carefully, she extracted it from behind many others, where it had lain unopened for centuries. Carefully, almost ceremonially, Soniya held the scroll across both hands and turned with it to face Jen-Aga.

"Here," she said to the mortified young priestess. "Take it, and read."

"But---"

"Obey me," Soniya commanded. "For you and two others will soon bear a great burden. And we three shall not be at your beck and call to teach you, nor to instruct you. You will be on your own, you three, with an overwhelming responsibility. For the demons have not given up their yearning to seize God's creation, and to turn it forever into corruption and evil. Just as they themselves have transfixed their own souls into irreversible abomination, so also, they would do to our world."

Nervously, Jen-Aga accepted the proffered scroll. "But what are we to do? Can we hope to stop them?"

"You can more than hope."

"But how? How does one stop a demon?"

Soniya answered, "Read the scroll. Perhaps it contains the secret. Read between the lines, and perhaps you may unlock the answer to your question. A thousand years have passed since the time of Tarok and Kattaroon. And even though they are dead, yet there are lessons to be learned from their story. Learn those lessons well, for you will need them against the new demonwitch who is soon to arise."

"A new demonwitch?" Jen-Aga shook her head, almost in tears. "Soon to rise up? I beg you, High Priestess. Do not place this burden upon me. I am nothing against the dark forces of a demonic witch. Please!"

"You'll not be alone," Soniya assured her. "For there will also soon arise one to stand against the demonwitch. This time, however, it will not be a mighty man of the sword, not a male warrior, such as Tarok was, but instead, a woman, one who is called the Priestess of Prophecy. Only she can slay the demonwitch. Your duty is but to serve her. But be careful, Jen-Aga. For remember, the demonwitch Kattaroon was herself once a priestess. And another name for the Priestess of Prophecy, as she is spoken of in the hidden scriptures, is the Unrecognized Priestess. Yes, your highest powers of discernment will be needed, Jen-Aga. And your utmost wisdom. For you, and your two brother high priests, must be able to detect who is the priestess of prophecy, and who is the witch."

Jen-Aga shook her head. "But I can't. I'm just not up to this."

Soniya smiled warmly. "None of us is," she said. "But remember, God does not expect you to succeed. Victory is His alone, and He will win it for you. All you need do is to seek His will. And remember that, with God, all things are possible."

PREFATORY CHAPTER
The Legend of Tarok and Kattaroon

According to the Hidden Scroll

The next day, Jen-Aga found a secluded room in the temple study. There, alone with the ancient scroll, she carefully unrolled the parchment. It was stiff with age, but because the keeper of the library had moistened it with special vapors and ointments, it did not crack or break.

The ink was slightly faded, but legible. The characters were of a language no longer spoken, written with symbols primitive and yet aesthetic. But foreign though the writing was, yet the priestess had studied well, and remembered the lessons she had learned in her early years of arduous study.

Her hands trembling slightly, Jen-Aga began to read. The scroll was taking up the story where an earlier text had left off. And it started immediately with a chilling picture of the darkmost demonwitch in a rage.

"Where are they?" she demanded to know. Her mere presence darkened the room, and her voice seemed to chill the air within its grey, stone walls.

"When I send for my advisors, I expect them to appear at once. How dare they tarry at such a moment as this!"

The slave girl cowered in dread beneath Kattaroon's seething rage. And well she did, for no rage is as deadly as that of a demonwitch cornered in her lair, even if that demonwitch is temporarily reduced to mortality. For, in such a one as this, even mere earthly evil undertakes its most dread and potent form.

But mercifully for the trembling slave girl, she did not have to speak in reply, did not have to be the bearer of the bad news which would surely enrage the already dangerous woman. The guardsman answered the question instead. "Your sorcerer, Kharakh, ascends the spire stairs even now, dark madam. And the serpent Thilgol is not far behind him. They will both arrive shortly."

Kattaroon turned her attention from the terrified maiden, and faced the armored guard. She glared in reply to his report, his most unsatisfactory report. "Only two?" she raged. "And what of the others? What delays them?"

"Death," answered the guardsman. "Death delays them. For all your other advisors lie dead beneath the sword of Tarok. Of all your commanders and conjurors and potionists, only these two remain alive, Kharakh and Thilgol." The guardsman's tone was emotionless, with a fearlessness only the dead themselves could achieve. For dead he was, bewitched by the curse of a witch who could trust no armed man within sword's reach of her blackened heart.

But the witch herself was anything but emotionless. Her smoldering impatience burst into the flame of outrage at this further, bitter news. "Dead, are they? All of them burning in Hell, no doubt. Not for their sins, but greater damnation yet, for their failure."

The demonwitch had all but snarled as she whirled to face the window, toward the radiant sunlight which shone inward from it. The window was the only vantage point afforded by the stone enclosure, the turret, atop the tall spire into which Tarok and his armies had forced her retreat. Then, the witch spoke with a quiet fury, but quiet with the menace of a serpent. She uttered a curse that terrified her maiden into tremors. And she concluded it with the words, "Damnation be upon that warrior--- and upon all who follow him. Wretched souls they are, and wretched shall they be."

As she spoke, Kattaroon stepped with angry cadence toward the windowsill, and reaching it, looked downward upon the military spectacle far beneath. Rows and columns of enemy soldiers surrounded the castle in formidable array. The air bristled metallic with their spears and swords. Colored banners fluttered in the breeze, seemingly as numerous as the blossoms of a meadow in full bloom. Bright yellows and brilliant shades of red were punctuated by darker blues and regal purples. But if each battle-flag were a flower, it concealed beneath its single bright petal, thorns of deadliest poison. For each banner marked a separate regiment of swordsmen and archers.

Such a sight would have struck fear into any ordinary mortal so besieged. But Kattaroon knew no fear. Proud and contemptuous, as cold and as hard as the castle itself, she fended off all spears of doubt. The witch's upper lip contorted into a sneer and her eyes darkened with vengeful malice. "Enjoy your puny victory while you can," she spoke with quiet defiance, knowing that none below could hear her even had she shouted. "But soon your exultation will turn to terror, your battle-cries to lamentation, and your hopes to despair. For here I make my final stand, a wounded lioness, defending her last redoubt. By day your victory seems certain and ordained. But be assured that, when nightfall comes, my powers, which were spent in killing your comrades, will return to me. And then you will share their fiery fate. All of you."

At this time, the slave girl forced herself to speak, though her blood seemed as water and her bones as straw. "Dark madam," her voice wavered as she forced each word. "Please, step back from the window, I beg you.

Surely they have archers, and even atop this tall spire, their arrows can reach with brutal force. I fear for your safety."

Of course Kattaroon knew that the slave girl had no fear at all for the safety of her evil mistress. What the girl did fear, was not to feign concern. For well the maiden knew that her unwilling duty was to tend a dangerous nightcat, one that devoured its servants at the very first and very slightest hint of their disloyalty.

Even though the maiden's pretense was transparent, it was necessary. For, to remain silent would unmask the slave girl's fond, desperate hope that the demonwitch would fall mortally wounded, releasing the spell of terror that bound the maiden more tightly than any chain ever could. To remain silent was to evoke a deadly curse from the hand of the demonwitch, a clawed hand that had power and willingness to kill, even without sorcery. So the maiden did obeisance and pretended to fear for Kattaroon's safety.

The witch knew it was a lie. But for Kattaroon, lies were sweeter than truth.

Just then, an arrow did indeed clatter off the stone near where Kattaroon stood, cracking violently at the edge of the window. The deadly missile would have surely been her death, except that the slightest breeze had wafted it astray in its failed quest for her evil heart. The once hawk-like arrow, broken and frustrated in its mission, fell harmlessly like a wounded dove, to the ground far below.

Begrudgingly, the witch did step backward a pace, away from the daylight, into a safer, more familiar refuge, becoming a shadow among shadows once more. Ordinarily, no arrow, no spear or sword could have touched her. But the earlier battle at Gur-Molkn had required her to exert all her powers, powers of darkest sorcery, in a futile attempt to defeat Tarok's army. There, treachery within the ranks of her own troops had proved fatal to her hopes, and with her forces decimated, retreating and scattered, Kattaroon had barely escaped alive into Castle Ki-Rori, where now she must make her last and final stand against mighty Tarok. Here, this day, this night, one or the other of them must reign victorious. For the loser, death awaited, death or worse, infinitely worse.

With a sound of wood scraping against stone, the oaken door, which sealed the turret from the spire stairway, yielded. The man who stepped through the semi-oval opening seemed almost as lifeless as the armored guardsman who ushered him in. Lifeless this new arrival was, but through no curse of any witch. A sorceror curses himself first of all. And no more powerful curse has any man, than that by which he curses himself.

"Kharakh!" the demonwitch uttered to him who entered. "Do you dare tarry when we are encircled by the armies of our foe? I should---"

"Have patience with me!" the sorceror pleaded. "You can see that I have suffered this day. I am weakened, as you are. Only Hell's favor has spared me alive. All my conjurors have met their doom, and I alone remain."

Kattaroon spat in disgust. "And what delays that serpent Thilgol? Does that lizard fancy itself immune to my reproach?"

The sorceror gave a slight shudder. "Do not contend with Thilgol this day, my lady. Rage has seized its heart. And as you know, when Thilgol is enraged---"

The witch's sudden display of her own rage silenced the sorceror. "Do you dare entertain the thought that I might ever fear that mere reptile? Even with my powers spent, sorceror, even then, my evil is more than sufficient to dispatch into Hell anyone who dares trifle with me. Anyone, or anything. Would you care for a proof?"

The sorceror shuddered again. "By no means--- no, my lady! I had only meant---"

But just then the oaken door swung open once more, as a bloodless guardsman gave way to what now slithered into the confine.

"Depart," Kattaroon commanded her slaves. The handmaiden gratefully scurried from the turret and down the spire stairs, followed by the blind, obedient guard. The door closed, and the three evil ones were alone.

Kharakh, the sorceror, had a weathered face upon which the centuries had writ an evil tale. But even that grey, fierce countenance conceded supremacy to the serpent.

For if Kharakh's face had witnessed much evil, Thilgol's eyes had seen the very flames of Hell itself, and its ears had heard firsthand the shrieks of the damned, the moans of agony of the eternally lost. For Thilgol was older even than Kharakh, indeed, older than mankind himself.

* * * * *

Jen-Aga set down the scroll, reluctant to continue. All her adult life she had lived amid gentle souls, among servants of the divine will. But the scroll was mentally thrusting her into a world of evil. And although she had always known about that world, it was one which she had never thought that she must one day confront. It was a world not only of violence, but worse, one of malevolence and ferocity. To read of it, to consider that she might one day venture into it, was a fearful prospect. Yet, despite her reluctance, the priestess knew that she must continue reading.

Atop the castle's tallest spire, enclosed within its lofty turret, the evil woman held council with her sorceror Kharakh, and with the serpent-embodied demon, Thilgol.

The sorceror, with his nervous countenance, his sweaty brow, and his slightly quivering lip, betrayed fear, an emotion he had not felt in many years. But now, fear stalked him, as the wolf stalks the wounded stag. Kharakh, proud master of the deadly black arts, had become a man with no safe haven remaining in which to hide. Vengeance well deserved, and justice well dreaded, were close upon him. He could all but feel their breath.

As for the demon, it with its wrathful glare revealed despair, a deep, wrathful despair not known by it since its expulsion from heaven. A similar defeat now seemed imminent once more. Yet it knew no fear. Wrath and despair, rolled into one, this was the reaction of a demon to impending damnation. It was not a human reaction. Nothing the demon did was as humans do.

She alone, the woman, stood strong and proud between them, man and demon, and yielded neither to fear nor to despair.

"Why quiver you with fright?" she demanded of the sorceror. "Yesterday you were so proud and haughty, so ready to cast others into Hell's most cruel anguish. Now where has your arrogance fled? Soon Tarok will stand within this room, armed and armored. If he finds you cowering, finds you unarmed, devoid of your powers, unable to meet cudgel with curse--- if so, then he will deal with you as you have dealt with orphans and widows--- with neither mercy nor conscience. Summon forth your spells, sorcerer. Your very life depends upon them."

Then, more afraid of his mistress Kattaroon, demonwitch, than of her enemies' clamor below and all about, the sorceror struggled to regain his composure. He would require it, at least a measure of it, to wage this one last battle, lest death might finally cast him, dismembered, into that unspeakable doom, that never-ending horror, into which he had cast so many others. Only dimly, was he aware that this last, fleeting moment of opportunity was being lost in Kattaroon's shadow, that moment of repentance, by which he might otherwise yet be saved.

Aware of it keenly, however, was Kattaroon herself. For her part, she would never repent. Nor would she permit the sorceror any time for thoughtful reflection upon his impending eternity. And Kharakh had not the courage to defy her.

Nor ever timid to confront demons, Kattaroon turned now to face its hideous incarnation, and taunted it. "And what fruit does your impotent wrath bear, Thilgol in dragon's disguise? Does your wrath offer to us some dark force, that might of hatred itself, succeed against Tarok, where swords of helliron failed us? In heaven, your hatred was defeated by the flaming swords of otherwise gentle angels. Will it prove any more potent a weapon against violent men? Mankind, him, whom you snared for doom--- upon his womankind now you depend--- upon mere woman, to wreak your wrath against God. I am that woman, Thilgol. I am the Darkmost Demonwitch foretold in your anti-prophecy. Then desist from your useless wrath, demon, and heed my command."

These last words were audacious, for demons of rank heed no mortal, nor yield to any earthly authority. The very thought of doing so was an unbearable humiliation.

And indeed, the demon's fierce rage was not assuaged, but rather inflamed the more. It spoke in a voice ghastly with otherworldly tones of moaning, sounds echoing from fallen souls (souls of both men, and of the fallen angels), souls in never-ending torment. "Deem you yourself worthy to command me?" it bellowed. "I was before time, woman, before earth, and before sun and stars ever did shine. Fought I against mighty Michael himself, and against all his angelic legions! Fought! Yet last fell I, last! last after all the others." (It lied.)

Kattaroon sneered with contempt. "If so, then it was treachery, not courage, made you last to fall. For behind your comrades-in-arms you hid, hid in fear, deceiving and betraying even your kin. Men, upon whom you look down in loathing, they at least have courage true, Thilgol; even this wretched sorceror can conjure it forth when needs be. Demons have none of courage true, but all they do have is that counterfeit of courage: treachery."

"Treachery!" the demon Thilgol sneered disdainfully, "serves better than that noble imprudence which mortals call courage. Once more I have survived, while all about me perished. I, of all which were dispatched from Hell, and who invaded earth, I last of all stand, sole survivor. Treachery always defeats courage, always.

"Proof lies in this: At Gur-Molkn had we victory, mortal woman. At Gur-Molkn we stood victorious against Tarok, against his priests and warriors, and even against his allies, those puny angelic soldiers. Victory was in our grasp, ours by the courage of our human warriors. Or so it would have been.

"But in the end, treachery ruled the day. For when earth's realm was almost within our grasp--- alas!--- we could almost taste the sweetness!--- when we thought victory sure, and deemed the battle but a ritual--- then did thoughts turn from the hunt, blackrobed woman, and turned instead to greed."

In this much, Jen-Aga knew, the demon spoke correctly. For none among demons was content with only its apportioned share, but instead, they fell into quarreling among themselves. As the battle seemed about to be won for evil, then did each demon become suspicious of the others. For each demon desired all, not only all, but more than all, and each desired only for itself. And each employed treachery against the others. Only then did the demonic armies know defeat at the hands of mortals and angels. They had defeated themselves, and done so with their only weapon, the dark sword of evil.

"But my own treachery, not manly courage, ruled that day," Thilgol boasted. "For even in grimmest defeat, did not we survive, we three, and our few servants and footmen? For of all treachery, mine proved greatest. Far superior is it to any courage, whether in hearts mortal or angelic."

To all this, the sorceror replied with contempt. "Treachery, yes. Well it served you, demon Thilgol, but served none other. By your own words, demonically wise, but humanly foolish, you have proved your treachery to be our undoing."

"It saved your life, sorcerer!"

"How so?" Kharakh rebutted. "For, if not for your treachery, Gur-Molkn would have been ours, and with it, all this earthly realm. But treachery undid us at Gur-Molkn, disarmed us, and gave hope and strength to our enemies."

"It led us safely here," the demon insisted.

"Safely?" Kharakh shot back. "We are trapped in this fortress, surrounded and besieged. Think you to escape? Hope you to elude Tarok by this, your only weapon? Of what avail will be your strongest treachery against

Tarok's weakest courage? Does not all the power of universal darkness yield before the light of one dim star in heaven? And how are we, this darkmost witch and I, to regard your treacherous nature? Will you dispatch us (into doom) as casually as you did your brothers?"

To which Thilgol retorted, "Do you question me? Do you doubt that I will slay Tarok? Then do battle with him yourself, courageous one. Gird yourself with potion and curse, and conjure forth your weapons from the outer darkness. Conjure forth those lost mortal souls which lust for breath; summon them forth, and then hurl them against Tarok as men hurl spears into the flesh of their enemies. And then? Then what will you, potionist? For Tarok will fling them back into your face. And they, those evil spirits whom you conjured from Hell with promises of satisfied lust, they will vent their rages instead upon you."

But the sorceror, though finding himself confronting a demon more ferocious than any beast of the forest, found courage enough to plot and scheme. "Neither my powers, nor your wrath, mighty demon, can undo Tarok. In battle he has proved his mettle, resourceful when outnumbered, and when superior quick to press advantage. But now is not battle of sword nor of curse, demon, but rather, this is a battle of cunning. For even now, below us, they hold council, this warrior and his priests and angelic guardians, to devise our undoing without further loss of life among them."

Yes, Jen-Aga said to herself, indeed. Even Kharakh had known that Tarok would not sacrifice a single soldier if that were avoidable. Even one lowly footman would he spare from sacrifice--- at great risk to himself--- not as the evil ones, who casually sent thousands to their deaths for scant advantage gained, deeming those deaths as no cost whatsoever, and scant gain being gain enough, worth any number of lives cheaply spent, except their own.

"Plot they," the sorcerer said, "so also plot we. And who better to combine raw force with subtle guile than woman? And what woman both more forceful and more subtle than witch of demonic power? So counsel us, witch. What would you? How most potently combine our triune evil?"

Kattaroon's eyes had darkened, and her gaze had appeared to penetrate deeply into some empty, endless tunnel. Then, awakening from this dream, she spoke carefully. "I myself," she seemed to conclude, after a timeless search through corridors unseen, "I, in myself, am Tarok's undoing. Alone I will slay him."

For a moment, neither man nor demon spoke, so uncanny was Kattaroon's demeanor, so assured her speech, despite that more preposterous words they had never heard uttered in such earnest.

"Slay him yourself?" Thilgol asked, all but amused. Then rage returned to its serpentine voice. "What treachery plan you, not at Tarok's throat, but our own?" Its cold, inhuman eyes glared suspiciously at Kattaroon.

The glare in her own eyes was colder yet. "Do you distrust me, demon?" No fear weakened her voice.

"I warn you," Thilgol growled with venomous anger. Its reptilian eyes were red with flame, its nostrils flaring as wisps of steamy breath escaped them. "Assuredly, even in so dreary a moment as this, in darkest defeat foredoomed, know you this: I would drag you with me into Hell itself, with your writhing corpse impaled upon my vengeful claws. Now tell me, what trick are you scheming against me? Dare you hope to betray the master of treachery itself? This?"

To this, Kattaroon retorted with a mixture of calm and of threat. Her menace was no less intense than the demon's, and scarcely more human. "If it is my treachery you fear, then fear it demon. For you have no choice now. Did our defeat at Gur-Molkn teach you nothing? We were nearly killed by your schemes. It was I who brought us safe into this, our final redoubt, where stand we reasoning against Tarok. It was I who saved us from the bitter fruit of your treason. So what will you do this time? Will you again unleash your suspicions to work their poison against us, Thilgol? Are you truly willing to forfeit everything? If so, then let me feel your fiery breath! But if you would rather scorch Tarok, then listen, while I lay out to you my plan."

Kattaroon turned her back, as none other would dare in the near presence of demonic savagery. Calmly, but with assurance borne of power, she paced about the confine of the turret, her arms folded, her dark eyes staring into---nothing. Then she whirled and faced demon and sorceror once more, her eyes as intense as burning coals, and as fierce as those of any predator. "For such a plan you could never devise yourself," she announced. "It is more than a plan, it is a masterful deception, a plan not merely for our survival alone, but for victory. Yes demon, victory! What was done to us at Gur-Molkn will be undone at Castle Ki-Rori, here, this day, this very night. Ask yourself, demon, would subjection to Tarok be sweeter than dominion by me? Would death by his sword be sweeter than life by my curse?" This last she spoke with sarcasm, for otherwise Thilgol would never have yielded her this necessary moment of solitary command.

"Be it done, then," Thilgol relented (grudgingly). "For with potents secret I am not within your power to betray." It was angry that it had no better plan, and angry that once again, this woman riding the beast of anti-prophecy had outmaneuvered the creature from the underworld.

"Then go you," Kattaroon commanded it, "into the dungeon of this castle, a natural abode for your kind. There wait--- await both me, and him whom I deliver to you. And take with you this sorceror, there to prepare for Tarok a fit welcome."

But in fear, the sorceror cast his furtive glance at Kattaroon, and distrusted what met his eyes. Well he knew that the witch would betray him at the first convenient moment. "Witch, born of fallen earth," he said, "made evil by Hell itself! You plot now as surely against us, as against our common foe, Tarok. How can we trust you?" His objection was less defiant than tremorous, more fearful than brave. "What better moment than this desperate hour, to seize all for yourself, even at greater risk of utmost loss?"

But Kattaroon's sneer this time showed the sharp, pointed tips of predatory fangs. Her eyes flickered with hellish flame. "Were my plot against you, sorceror, scarce could you stand against it. But if you dare, then strike me now, and discern which of us is the more deadly foe. Else with the demon take your stand. For when I convey Tarok into the dungeon, not in chains will you find him, but in my gentle embrace. If he finds your energies spent, then he will surely kill you. Conserve then, your powers for him alone. Need you more lecture than this, sorceror? For delay will bring us the lecturer himself: mighty Tarok."

But the sorceror yet distrusted Kattaroon. "What illusion deceives you?" he challenged. "Are we to believe, as you surely must, that Tarok will be seduced once more by your dread beauty, as once he was so long ago? Your physical charms might disarm any lesser man, but not Tarok. He is a man who discerns beauty true from beauty false. For well Tarok remembers what beauty once you were, soft and gentle submissive. And when now seeing that beauty fled, and in its place beholds this beauty proud, cruel and venomous, all affection will depart him. He will halve you with his swift sword before scarce one beguiling word you could utter."

"He loves me," Kattaroon whispered but aloud. Her eyes narrowed as that of a serpent coiled to strike, daring the sorcerer to deny her claim. And the sorceror knew not how near he stood, to sudden, violent death.

"Loves you, yes," he said, "but with a love you comprehend not. For Tarok, barbaric savage that he was, formerly enslaved by lust, is no longer the man who once desired you. He has instead given himself, in willing servitude, unto the one true God. There, a new kind of love he has discovered, not a love such as yours: violent, dark and selfish. Instead, the warrior has found a love which is never cruel, never envious, nor boastful nor arrogant, and which never wounds. He has discovered God's love for his wayward children. And alone this, no other love, dwells in Tarok's heart. Win you his love, you may, but only by casting from your own black heart this self-love which possesses you, as it possesses all who are evil."

Once again, Jen-Aga set down the scroll and pondered. How tragic, she thought to herself, that this man Kharakh, who had been so wise, so discerning, and yet was so tragically devoted to evil. Even though he had recognized its self-destructive nature, yet even then, he served evil, not good. What folly consumes men, the priestess wondered.

"He sins yet," Kattaroon retorted, "as all men must, until death, death at last, decides their eternal fate. And never more tempting sin will he find, than in my embrace to sin once more, and in doing that, to sin forever."

"His inclination is indeed toward sin," the sorceror agreed, but he agreed only in part. For he continued, "But now his sins are mere of a moment's duration. Thereafter falls he into repentance (or ascends into it as the angels say). He weeps, and fasts, and offers sacrifice, not merely to appease an angry God, but more so, to wash away brash, unintended sin with deliberate, intended love. Yet no such love know you, nor can, nor wish to discover."

But Kattaroon's word was final, and her command inalterable. Her countenance hardened, and the shadow of death darkened her gaze. "Tarok," she pronounced in words that permitted no dissent, "loves me yet. It was I who lured him from the temple, when youthful and ignorant he cowed before the altar of God most high. It was I whom other women envied, with their covetous tears and frenzied weeping, when he chose as me as his consort, chose me to be his forbidden love, rather than choosing them as regal brides. And me Tarok loves yet, though he remembers it not. He knows my love even yet, yes he does, a love lost in some memory distant from today. But that memory I shall awaken in him, much to his delight. His yearning for me shall be rekindled, and with its heat, his blood will boil once more for me as once it did those many years gone by. Once more his lust shall burn for me alone, all others to disdain. All else shall he hate save one object, that throne of evil which we will share, he and I, in eternal embrace, while at our feet all this world entertain us with its shrieks of agony everlasting."

* * * * *

Mightier a sword than Tarok's, no arm ever wielded, nor even scarce could lift, but his own. Bronze though it was, it had defeated swords of helliron in battle fierce.

Yet now it lay sheathed in leather, at rest from its day's labor, a tool unfitting the task at hand, the task of planning, the task of holding council.

"Their end is come," Tarok addressed his peers. "Not even their denials deny this. Up there, within that darkened tower, beneath heaven's bright blue sky, a demon is soon to fall into eternity below us, beneath this green grass: one final, eternal fall from which it can never again ascend. Even now it senses its certain fate, but seeks neither peace nor truce, but only to wreak one last vengeance, futile though that be. And in its service, a sorceror, false priest of false gods, knows that his doom also draws near. Yet unlike the demon, which is already transfixed into eternal sin, this priest might yet confess, and humbling himself before God offended, would find forgiveness and love, salvation freely given by God, gentle and mighty (in one word expressed). Yet, fears he rather her, than God, serves he doom, not hope, and if repenting not, begins this day horror unending."

Having paused, ambushed by emotion, Tarok spoke more. "And she. Whom once I loved as young men can love but once, unable ever after to regain first love's irreproducible bliss, but must starve for it afterward until death a greater love unveils--- she. Aloft that tower she crafts her wicked art, desiring not Tarok that was, but Tarok that would be hers, a man more cruel than even her, a man more cruel than even she could wish for. If only she knew, if only Kattaroon could see the end of her fatal course!"

Spoke next the priest beside him. His name was Thuurik, once gone astray, he was formerly a priest of pagan gods (which are disguised demons). Demonic he had been, until there had come to him one day an angel of heaven, bringing to him a message of redemption. Whereupon ever since, Thuurik had cast aside his former self, and labored night and day repenting of his wasted, demonic worship. At Tarok's feet he had lowered himself as lowest slave. But God had lifted him up to high priesthood, and entrusted him with Tarok's very soul to guard.

"Love well spent, was your love for Kattaroon," Thuurik mourned. "But that love was returned to you spoiled, ruined not by flaw of Tarok, but black soul, desecrated by her, who received love's golden treasure and debased it. Well you mourn for love's death, Tarok. But beware! That loves is now not only dead, but it is death itself, lurking for you in the dark crypt of a witch's soul. Its pierced remains are more foul than any corpse could ever be. So bury it. Even as lovers must entomb their departed lost loves, so also, this is your task. Then shed the tears, and sing the dirge, but fail not to seal the tomb. For nothing is gained from evil love, which is all she now offers."

"Well you speak, high priest," Tarok assented, for how could he not agree? "But who to roll so heavy a stone as must seal Kattaroon's tomb, her sweet form ever to enclose, sweetness howbeit fouled by curses vile? Who to pierce her stony heart with brass or bronze, to quench forever that fiery breast which loves with love so foul? Who but me, who loved so true, so long, but in vain? None other could I launch to this bitter task. No. Kattaroon must die, for death alone can now free her from the slavery that is witchcraft. But death must come to her by no hand other than this, which bears Tarok's terrible sword."

To this, replied the angel, martial spirit, in earthly appearance, his name was Imerius. "Know you this," he warned. "Kattaroon is witch most potent and dread. Nor in her any sweetness resides, all light turned dark, all love to hate. Think not to choose which man slays her, for slain she is already, by no hand other than her own. What yet resides lives not, but only death remains. Suffer not yourself to work this final deed, for it is you whom she awaits; her trap is set, nor spared she from its jaws any venom of earth or Hell. For well she knows your one desire, and strong she smells your ardor. You would save her soul, if you could, she knows. Herself she holds as bait. Then yield her not this single morsel, your gaze, which she longs to behold. Send instead a warrior crude, the like which merits no praise, a man who thoughtless swings his mace, and crushes skull, and remorses not. Send him. This is your one best hope to save her soul, though scant that hope may be. For seeing how her plan has failed, her plot foiled, her hope dimmed, only then might enter into the black empty abyss of her heart that pain which flowers sweet, repentance its blossom, submission to God its fruit. This is your sole hope to share with her the streets of gold above the clouds. But alas, her fate, her destiny, is hers alone to decide."

Tarok glanced upward at the castle tower, and then facing Imerius once more, replied, "Dear angel sent by God most kind, whose servant I should make myself--- but you permit me not to serve you. Instead, it is you who serves me, even though I am a sinner, and you are blameless. I am hobbled by my sin, while you are free to fly upon wings of noblest virtue.

"Well spoken your counsel, Imerius of Heaven, well spoken beyond any skill of mortal to refute, for God's own light illumines angelic wisdom. But I must dispute. In my fallen nature, I must dispute your wise counsel. For I live not by flight of angelic wing, but by stumbling of human foot upon temporal, stainful soil.

"So I must go, into that stony spire, where waits perhaps my doom, or perhaps instead, I dare to hope, my utmost earthly bliss. I will go, in one hand bearing the rose of love, but in the other, my two edged sword of death. For well I know her, authoress of my broken heart, crafter of my jealous rages, she who prides in my humiliation, temptress, seductress, betrayor. But despite all that she has done to me, despite all her treachery and evil, yet I cannot bring myself to hate her. Even so, I must end her evil. And how does one put an end to witch's evil? How does one put an end to witchcraft? I shudder to think of it. For there is only one means of doing this: by putting an end to the witch herself. For short of death, she would never yield back her hellish power, nor with it, its hellish delight. With every breath, she would continue to exhale evil--- evil words, and evil spells.

“And so, this sad task I must perform. It must be the work of love, but also, a savage deed. Savage am I. This day, surely, Kattaroon will die. Only her eternal abode is in doubt, and only she can choose between God’s sweet heaven, and demonic flames of hell."

Imerius, saddened by these words, knew not how to dissuade mortal folly; if able, then never had Adam sinned. But he knew his duty, and this now he offered. "Into the dungeon, even now, goes Thilgol, who once was an angel, as I am, in heaven, but who chose instead evil and demonicry, and who warred against God. Now, once more in battle I shall face Thilgol's hideous form, for it would otherwise ensnare you hostage, and imprison you in Hell for ages to endure until Messiah God Himself makes you free. I go now into the dungeon of Castle Ki-Rori."

Tarok raised a gentle hand to dissuade Imerius. "Remain here, my friend and fellow servant. Remain with my men, and among your angelic swordsmen. For Thilgol is fiercest of their warriors, and more treacherous than any among demons. Even for you, mighty slayer of demons, I fear what Thilgol might do against you. Let me send a battalion in your place."

"No, fear not, my friend, my brother, my fellow servant, fear not." Imerius spoke not with bravado but with serenity seemingly unfitting a warrior. "Fear not for me. For evil has no power over us, angels. Thilgol is no threat to me. If only it, that crafty serpent, understood how powerless it stands, even against God's weakest warrior, it would despair. But it comprehends nothing except its own treachery, its own vain desires.

"Even now it plots, devising schemes, first against you, second against its own sorceror, and even so, against Kattaroon herself. It intends to betray even its own demonwitch. But it, it Thilgol, will I vanquish final, into depth from which there is no upward path, nor any hope of escape."

Then Imerius's tone changed from one of unshakable assurance to one of great caution. "But even when Thilgol is vanquished," he said with quiet intensity, "trust not your own fate to beautiful Kattaroon. For demonwitch she is, and demonwitch she remains. Though your soul she cannot harm, she would seduce it to do harm upon itself, as she has blistered her own soul, scorched it, stained and scarred it. Beware, beloved comrade, fellow creature of innocent God eternal. While Demonwitch yet breathes, beware."

The priest Thuurik listened, and implored Tarok to heed this wise angelic counsel. "Send any emissary, but not yourself to do this. Dispatch even me. For receiving you is Kattaroon's fondest wish, receiving you into evil if she might enthrall you, but into death if not, and either result pleasing to her. Not only are you endangered, but all the world if perhaps she unleash her one last strike against God's fair earth. Go not!"

But Tarok gave his final word, as mighty hand grasped mighty sword. "My duty is to go. If she will but hear me speak a single word, who knows? Perchance she might feel that healing salve called remorse. And if a single part of her shall heal, thereby may heal the whole? No, I dare not hope, but dare not despair. So trusting this sword I go, fearing to die, fearing more to kill, but hoping soon to see her weep, and this sword to become a plowshare."

* * * * *

Upward but twisting, the stairs of spire led him. And not alone he found himself, confronted now by dread enemies. For in his path grim warriors stood, their mistress to defend, their swords against his own sword clashed, as each one met his fate. Bloodless fell they, bloodless they died, those whose souls had long since fled.

As death released them from their curse, their swords fell to the stone. Helliron swords, invincible, as light to the wielder as a feather, but against whom wielded, as weighty as a mountain crashing down. Helliron shields, impenetrable, yet no heavier than a thought to the arms which bore them. Helliron not base, but more precious than gold, and those who thought to possess such wealth, were by it possessed, who thought to wield such might, were by it wielded instead.

Now fell these to the stone, men and metal, dead by Tarok's arm. Men to dust, and metal to rust, as all illusion must end.

At last he stood, sweating, his breath heavy, bearded, helmeted, sword poised. The top step was at last behind him. The door before him was wooden, sealed shut.

He could smell her…

...not with scent borne by air, nor breath of nostril, nor any such. But near beyond the door she lay, he sensed, and she sensed him also, he knew, sensed him with that same uncanny perception which only lovers have for each other.

A thousand thoughts assailed him then. The fierce warrior felt a sudden urge to flee, to run away as cowards do upon first sight of an enemy. But the fear which tore at him came not from any cowardice, but rather, from the wisdom of his soul.

But soon among the swarming thoughts, a single one emerged, not thought but felt, not felt but known, and never known but it moved him, some mighty force, yet gentler than the dew which greets the thirsty, wakened fawn.

Love.

Could love be yet so strong? Could Kattaroon's mere presence, diminished by the thick oaken barrier between them, could it awaken desire---forgotten, fond, forbidden desire? If so, then how much more, how stronger yet, would that love be found, through a doorway opened wide?

Then Tarok's mind returned clear. Once more was his the mind not of a lover yearning lost love, but renewed, the mind of a warrior. And well for Tarok it was, for before him lay not love's flowery bed, but battle's barren field.

One rude kick, the door fell from its leather hinges, leather not of beast but of man (desecration abounded here), mighty oak shattered as would splintered pine, destroyed by Tarok's wrath. Into dust it fell, into swirling dust stepped Tarok, his sword raised, dooming whatever ambush might lurk amid the musty cloud and debris.

But worse than helliron awaited him there.

Soon the heavy, dusty air settled. It obscured his vision no more. Although purity here was foreign, he could see at last. The turret round encircled him, and a bright tunnel of light through a window led directly to her figure. She lay there.

No more thousand of the thoughts remained, which previously had swarmed; all thought fled, abandoned him. He beheld her beauty. Reclined upon her couch, a silken gown caressed her slender form. Tarok beheld soft black silk, long ebony hair, deep dark eyes. Not more than a moment had passed, but already the trance was deep. Yet, despite its crushing grip, the trance was not as that which enthralled the enslaved dead, (such as those which he had dispatched along the twisting spire stairs). No. Tarok's was the trance into which men desirous fall, desirous remain, whereby woman rules that of man which she might.

He awakened to her voice, remotely heard, yet as familiar to him, despite years passed, as ever it had been, a voice more sweet than song. But within that sweet voice, lurked unheard, the hiss of a serpent.

"Always as ever," her laughter was as soft as the blossom of deadliest fruit. "Tarok! Strong and bold, yes, but never cautious. You tested not the door, nor any lock barred it shut." No fear showed in her eyes, none at all. "Is it by this, violence so rude, you deal with us, who resist you not?"

Grimace contorted his face. Barely suppressed rage lifted high Tarok's sword with murderous intent; how dared she mock his anger? "Die you now!"

But the sword did not descend, not just yet. Some part of him wondered, why? What stayed his hand? Was it her physical charm, or perhaps her final reserve of conjury, or alas, his stubborn denial? Love?

"Die?" she breathed. "Of course, my love. What joy holds life for me? See what wretchedness has overtaken me, once a princess, once a priestess, now defeated, slave to evil, impoverished by that which once I thought enriches, but late discovered ruins. Die? How sweeter take leave of life than last to gaze upon your manly face, hear deep your voice, feel the might of your arm against my flesh, even if no other embrace but death your pleasure is to favor me. Yes, death, sweet death, delay no longer dear Tarok. You are the only love I ever knew. And now your love is lost to me forever, lost by my own wickedness, evil and folly. Delay not, but slay me quick, before weeping I plead one last kiss denied."

Still aloft, Tarok's sword awaited eagerly the command of his arm for swift descent. For the wisdom crafted into that sword was sublime when the wisdom of mind prevailed not.

But instead Tarok spoke urgently: "This moment I despair, Kattaroon dearest, that another breath might I spare you to inhale. I cannot. Fool that I was, to hope so vain, that ever might you turn aside from evil. But now I see that it can never be, never while you breathe. None other than God beloved Himself should now ever stay my hand another moment. Nor will He, dare I hope. But even as Hell, just now, opens wide its maw to swallow you (into agony more profound than ever can imagination encompass), yet one last moment I do grant you to escape, not to escape death, but to spare yourself from Hell. Ask God for mercy, Him whose mercy is infinite. Even to His surrendering enemy He has grace, as generous as if to His own beloved child. To ask sincere is to receive bliss eternal, to pridefully disdain Him earns torment beyond measure. Repent, Kattaroon, but for one instant repent, and in that instant know joy eternal. For there will be no next instant lived in which to sin, never another instant lived in which to fall again. Repent!"

Kattaroon winced. The power in that awesome sword, in that bronze hawk, hovered close above her, she its prey, it hungry for her black blood (for such is the blood of any true witch, blacker than night), she thought not to live another breath. If Tarok slew her not, yet would his sword, this unliving creature, of its own volition. It would make her also unliving. With a will of its own, Tarok's sword weighed heavy, demanding that for which it was fashioned, death, none other.

She winced, then said, "Why haste, dear love? See me now, a venomless adder--- if striking, dry of fang, or if a lioness, deprived of fang and claw. How much weaker am I than you! A witch, her powers spent, is nothing more than shadow. You know that. Truth be told, if thunderbolt I possessed to hurl, then hurl it I would already have done, your comrades to slay; their corpses would in flames burn even now upon the ramparts. But no. They live, and I die, my powers already spent in battle defeated, a woman disarmed."

Then Tarok made his fatal error, to believe Kattaroon. Knowing as he did, that even a truthful word, uttered from the mouth of evil, is sent only on a mission of deception, as much a lie as falsehood itself--- knowing this as he did, Tarok failed. He saw her then not as she was, but as he wished to see her (as she wished him to see), helpless and pitiful beneath his upraised sword. For true she had spoken the words. A witch, her powers spent, is shadow, not more. And spent indeed were Kattaroon's evil powers, powers hurled that morning in desperate battle's fury. But one more truth unspoken remained, though Tarok should have known, would have known, had not desire his reason suborned. Nightfall replenishes her power.

So she entranced him; the witch entertained her love the hours of daylight, caressed his face, wept into his beard, prayed with him, confessed her sin, renounced evil and witchcraft all. She revealed to Tarok that an ambush awaited him in dungeon Ki-Rori!

"I sent the sorceror and a demon there to ambush you," she confessed. "Oh, how I hated you, Tarok! I was so angry. But I can't let them harm you. Not now. Not ever. For your sake, I will betray them to you, and you will slay them. Then you will know how truly I do love you!" She lied.

But one truth Kattaroon did speak, though all else was lie, or else truth told as lies. Yet one truth, even Kattaroon permitted it, her tongue and lips to utter.

"I love you," she said to him. "Is it not written? Do not even the evil love their own?"

"And I you," Tarok confessed.

By sunset, Tarok had not returned to Thuurik. He had not descended the spire, had not displayed his sword aloft; its blade was not darkened by blood more black than night. By darkness, Thuurik knew, and mourned. But quickly he assembled the warriors to make their second plans.

Next day the mighty battle was fought, priests against potionists, warriors against bewitched footmen. And great was the shedding of blood, the blood of Tarok's loyal comrades. Victory for those who worship God was costly.

There was less courage in the world when finally that battle ended, for there were fewer brave men at day's evening. And though there was also less evil, the price was high. The consolation of many widows, the comfort of many orphans, was this: lost was the legion of Hell, and Thilgol had been cast by Imerius into depths from which never to return. Nor walked upon the face of this earth any witch. This was the consolation of weeping widows and hungry orphans.

Victory for Thuurik was costlier yet. For, in vain he searched for Tarok, searched, but never did he find him, never while Thuurik lived.

Into the dungeon Tarok had descended, in the embrace of his Kattaroon. There, he had expected (as she had promised him) that she would betray Thilgol and her sorceror to Tarok's sword.

But the demon had already been destroyed, by Imerius. The sorceror, having witnessed the destruction of Thilgol by an angel, had hidden himself in the darkness. There, through his own powers of sorcery, he had overheard Kattaroon reveal his hiding place to Tarok, and so had discovered her treacherous plot.

Kattaroon brought Tarok to him, to Kharakh, just as she had promised, not in chains, but in her gentle embrace. When the sorceror emerged from hiding, he ambushed Tarok with sorcery, but his curses were aimed also at Kattaroon.

Him Tarok slew.

Kattaroon had been standing behind him, behind Tarok, while he supposed himself to be shielding her from sorcery's furious revenge. There, at night and in that darkness, Kattaroon's powers had returned, returned even as the sorceror fell cursing to his death, cursing not only Tarok, but more so, cursing Kattaroon who had betrayed him to their enemy.

Nightfall shadowed the earth, and with it, Kattaroon's venom had been renewed. For Tarok, understanding came an instant too late. Before he could turn his sword against her, before he could command his arm to forget that he loved her, the demonwitch had overpowered the warrior of God.

Then, with her prisoner in chains, and accompanied by all who remained alive of her coven of the damned, herself and few women, witches all, Kattaroon descended ever deeper into the dungeon. Into depths known only to Kattaroon herself, there, she and her coven of witches carried Tarok, Tarok chained no longer by love, but by witchcraft. There him they tortured.

And when Tarok, overpowered captive, though helpless, chose love of God before love of Kattaroon, making final his defiance of evil, then him did Kattaroon at long last slay, long after the battle above had already been lost by evil, long after there remained no purpose, no possible gain to her. Him she slew.

Nor remorsed she for it.

Chapter 1

The First Tremor

A thousand years had passed. Four children had been born and reached the age of sixteen years, two boys, and two girls.

The peasant girl had not yet become a priestess. Her dearest friend had not yet become a witch. Their village had not yet been attacked by pirates. But all of that was to take place.

They lived in a small village, solitary and quiet; its name was Har-Keem. Nestled between the forested hills and the stormy sea, the dreary little village awaited, unknowing, its moment of destiny. For lifetimes, peasants and fishermen had dwelt there, passing their tedious, joyless lives amid toils and labor, enduring silently the inherited curse of Adam's sin.

There they lived, in small wooden cottages built drab and squat, scattered about in careless disarray, so much driftwood, as it were, strewn along the shore of a destiny which had passed them by. Or so it seemed. For today would be different. This day, destiny was to alter its course. Four lives, four paths, four people, would be changed, and through them, the world.

Destiny could not have chosen a more obscure crossroads. For, in Har-Keem, inconspicuous and remote, there was nothing elegant. Even the colors of the village were the faded greys and browns of weathered wood. The cottages, all alike, bore no sign of rank or privilege among them, for none there was. Nor was there even so much as rustic beauty to commend them. With corners not quite square, walls off plumb, and floors never level, they must have seemed carelessly slapped together, ready to collapse at any moment or breath. But the cottages, sturdy enough to have withstood many storms, merely witnessed to the peasants' complete unconcern with nicety. The sorrowful struggles of daily survival commanded their attentions instead.

On any morning, smoke rising from dirty, ashen forges would aspire toward the open sky above, much as the stained souls of men flee the travails below and seek the lofty heights, if only in their dreams, if only at last in that longest dream of all.

Each morning, at the first hint of daylight, a small fleet of fishing boats would set sail from the pier, coursing eastward through the arrowhead-shaped inlet, and from there, would venture out upon the dangerous ocean. At evening, all would return. (But sometimes, which all fishermen's' wives dread, sometimes in the evening one would not, would not return, would never again return from the dangerous sea. And then would much weeping be heard in the village Har-Keem.)

By day, those who remained ashore in the village, the women, children and craftsmen, these attended their toilsome chores. Their day would be long and arduous, and life itself would weary them. At evening, the ships would yield back their crew to family, to their small wooden cottages, to yet another night's rest hard earned. And so would one day end, so would another soon begin.

This had been so, this grinding unhappy existence, for as long as any could remember. Remote and isolated, Har-Keem's cadence and patterns had proceeded undisturbed, year after year, generation after generation. There, in Har-Keem, the months passed into years, and the years into lifetimes.

But patterns do break, and rhythms do cease. And so it came about. On one particular morning, a number of seemingly detached events, connected only by destiny's subtlest pathways, came to a crossroads all at once. This day, the relentless dreariness would be broken.

* * * * *

Kl'aarn asked his father, when the traveler had departed from their cottage, "Father, was that a mead peddler you were trading with?" Emphasis was made on the word "mead," an emphasis that carried a tone of disapproval. It was spoken as if the son almost dared to admonish his own father. But if so, the admonition was carefully kept just below the surface. For the boy's manner was respectful, in no wise fearful, but rather, revealing a respect borne of love, not of the rod, a respect therefore all the more sincere. Yet, despite that respect, the very slightest hint of reproach found its way into Kl'aarn's voice.

L'aarn simply shrugged. "Yes." His gaze remained fixed on the scroll which lay open upon his roughly hewn desk. He had detected the delicate rebuke in his son's voice, but was in no haste to judge, just yet, its meaning. For the moment, a direct question merited a direct answer, and patience. For L'aarn knew that Kl'aarn's curiosity would not be still for long, and that the boy would soon reveal his true motive.

A single candle lit the darkened study.

Kl'aarn's question was more than one of mild curiosity. He was puzzled, disturbed. "But father. Haven't you always told me that strong drink destroys strong men?" Now it was his turn to allow silence to invite a response.

The candle glowed orange amid the rolled books which filled the room's every nook and corner. Sharpened quills awaited their masters' hand, and vials of ink stood ready to become words.

"Indeed it does, son," L'aarn replied, not looking up from the ledger he was analyzing. "Strong drink is fit medicine for some, but deadly poison for others. And the tragedy of its misuse is multiplied, by those whose lives are touched by the lives so destroyed."

The flickering flame seemed to chase the shadows, which always managed to elude the light, as if in an eternal game of hide and seek.

The boy's perplexity only grew. "Then, why, father, did you do business with one of the mead peddlers? Are there no copper sellers, or carpet weavers, for us to trade with, that we must now make our living in commerce with peddlers of mead?"

Despite himself, L'aarn chuckled. Always he had kept his son under strict discipline, and the boy had never before challenged his father. But he was sixteen now, ready to begin thinking of running his father's business. And it was good to see him taking to heart the lessons his father had so earnestly taught him, not merely the lessons of writing and keeping accounts, but also, of keeping to a higher law. The boy's intensity arose not from disrespect, but rather from zealous commitment to that law.

"Now," L'aarn said, "don't go weaving long rope from short fibers, son. Yes, the man was a mead peddler. And yes, I was conducting business with him. But it was not mead we were trading in."

"Of course not--- not us," Kl'aarn objected. "But in any case, he will peddle it to others. No doubt he's off to Sholok's house, even now, to sell his evil potion. (How that family suffers!) Why should we enrich the man who sells ruin to them?"

Sholok was the village metalsmith, and the worst of the village drunkards, the worst by far.

L'aarn carefully rolled up the scroll which he had been discussing with the mead peddler. Doing so gave him time to consider his reply. "I was doing no such thing," he said at last, "enriching him. What is this questioning? Have I become your servant that I must explain each move I make? Far be it from me!"

Kl'aarn could tell that his father was not angry, despite his firmly chosen words. "Not explain," Kl'aarn said, "but only teach, that I may do as you do."

Again, L'aarn chuckled. "Well spoken, dear son. But don't think to use flattering words on me, the sort which we use when we barter and trade with those who would cheat us. To answer your question, and perhaps your doubts, the peddler was bringing me the news that I had asked him for, when last he departed here for Shi-Raq. And yes, I paid him for his valuable service."

"Which," Kl'aarn asked hesitantly, "was?"

L'aarn sighed. "I had given him a message to deliver to certain ship captains that here, in Har-Keem, we have skilled tradesmen with abundant goods. Among them, of course, is Sholok, whose metalcraft is inarguably masterful."

"When he's sober," Kl'aarn interjected. "Which is rare."

L'aarn nodded. "Sholok is indeed in the grip of a demon. How else can we explain his slavery to his self-destructive fascination with drink? But perhaps he will escape this demon. Maybe this mead peddler's service to us will yield an opportunity to help Sholok to become sober at last."

"Opportunity?"

"Yes. Opportunity. There is nothing more can we offer Sholok in his miserable state," L'aarn answered. "You see, the mead peddler brought word that one of the ship captains has taken an interest in my letter. He wishes to stop by, here in Har-Keem, to see for himself what we have to offer. His cargo ship was scheduled to depart Shi-Raq for Kiriath-Ben-Gor, let's see, four days ago. That would bring him to our shore sometime today, if I have estimated it aright."

Kl'aarn's demeanor changed from one of troubled perplexity to astonished delight. His eyes brightened in anticipation of a promise not quite made, but assumed nonetheless. "A merchant ship? From Shi-Raq? (The great city, Shi-Raq! Such a thing we've never seen in Har-Keem, but only our own small fishing boats.) Do you suppose they'll bring merchandise to trade with us? Silks, perhaps, and spices and oils? And fruits, moist fruits from---"

L'aarn laughed out loud. "I've no idea what they might have aboard, nor even if they'll steer out of the sea lane to test our waters. Our small port seems uninviting from a distance. But if they do visit, if they do so only this once, I am persuaded that they will return again and again. After all, we do have a safe harbor here, small though it is. And the fishing pier would accommodate the loading and unloading of a cargo ship. Har-Keem's always been overlooked by outsiders. Perhaps we can change all that."

Kl'aarn's mind swarmed with the many thoughts that competed for attention. But among them, one caught his notice. "There is a chance the ship might turn away, as you say, discouraged by appearances. But we might be able to greet them at the mouth of the harbor, persuade them to stop here, and show them the way in. I could take Uncle's skiff--- he never uses it anymore---"

"Whoa," L'aarn said. "You have your lessons to do today."

"But father! How am I to concentrate my mind on numbers and letters when there's a merchant from the great city? Besides, I've been imprisoned in the study for days now. I need some fresh air and sunshine."

L'aarn gave it some thought, and gradually agreed, but only reluctantly. "The last time I let you out on your own, you returned to me with a bloody nose and black eyes. And the time before that it was the same."

Kl'aarn gestured dismissal of his father's fear. "It was nothing. A little unpleasantness with Shalar, that's all. Nothing I can't handle." Shalar was Sholok's son. The boy was as brutal and vulgar as his father.

"Don't say it was nothing," L'aarn lectured his son. "Shalar uses his fists heartlessly on boys his age, as heartlessly as he beats metal into submission at the forge. Do you think I cannot feel your wounds, or suffer at your injuries?"

"A man must learn to fight," Kl'aarn said. "I'm soon to be a man. And mark my words, Shalar will not always prevail against me."

The older man became saddened at hearing Kl'aarn speak these words, for there was more cost to his son than mere bruises of the flesh. He sat, and bid Kl'aarn to sit with him. Then he said, "Kl'aarn, I know that you are leaving your boyhood, and embarking upon this thing called manhood. And I know that among all boys your age, one great sign of manhood is the ability to fight. To fight and win. But Kl'aarn, you have to accept the fact that you will never be able to fight, and least of all, to fight Shalar. He's like his father, Sholok, a brute of a man, as metalsmiths tend to be. But you, my son, will never have such stature. In your infancy, as you know, you were very sickly, and only our prayers saved you, our prayers, and the potions of that blessed lady, the healer, Valen Elder. But the frailty of body, which came upon you from those days, that will never leave you. You will never have the physical strength of a fighting man. It is not your path, most assuredly not the path which God has ordained for you. Accept that. And accept that there is no dishonor in avoiding fights. Don't think of it as running away. Think of it as wisdom."

Kl'aarn hesitated to speak. Then he said, "Father, you're beginning to sound like mother."

"No," L'aarn said. "It's just that, when boys fight, the worst of it is bruises and bloody noses. But when men fight, it is to the death. It may seem brave to take a beating to avoid the infamy of cowardice. But you are approaching manhood now. And your mother and I want you around to look after us in our old age."

Kl'aarn pretended to consider his father's words, and pretended to agree. But what mattered to him was that, in the end, he had his father's permission to take his uncle's skiff into the harbor.

Neither of them knew that more than just a ship would arrive in Har-Keem that day.

* * * * *

Shalar was the son of Sholok the metalsmith.

Shalar's father, Sholok, despite his low esteem in the village was, none the less, renowned at his trade. At least that much, no one denied him. The man could work any metal from tin and copper to silver and gold. But the pity was, Sholok was a drunkard, and even when sober a violent man. Having wasted his family into poverty, he lived with them in a small shed atop a hill overlooking Har-Keem. No one ever dared venture there, up that hill, except upon need of Sholok's skill with metal, a skill sadly exceeded by the vices of its owner.

As for Shalar, he was like his father in many respects, both in his skill at the forge, and with his reputation for meanness of spirit. He had barely enough discipline to respect his elders, and none at all for his peers. Other boys avoided Shalar, and for good reason. Not one in Har-Keem dared to confront the son of the metalsmith. He beat all challengers, not only beating them, but moreover, beating them down, mercilessly humiliating them in the process.

And so it was that as, one morning, Shalar was prowling the dusty street which ran through the village, he was alone--- all alone and friendless, and this at a time of his need.

This particular morning Kl'aarn had found an excuse to be away from his lessons. And once again, as he had before to his father's chagrin, in the sandy lanes of Har-Keem, he encountered the bully, Shalar.

At first, Kl'aarn felt the icy chill of dread. From experience, he now expected the usual beating. For just as L'aarn had said to his son, Kl'aarn was indeed frail of body, a mere leaf against the oak which was Shalar. Kl'aarn's gangly stature revealed a weakness which no amount of exercise seemed to be able to banish from his thin bones. He stood no chance against the brute who now faced him, no chance that he could possibly prevail in battle against him.

But neither would Kl'aarn run from the bully, a stubborn practice, which had always made Shalar all the angrier, and all the more brutal, whenever in the past they had fought. Because of that, Shalar had always given Kl'aarn an extra punch or kick beyond what was needed for victory. Upon encountering Shalar this day, Kl'aarn expected more of the same, and dimly wondered which he feared more, the beating, or his father's, "I told you so."

But this time, something would be different. The pattern had broken. This day, Shalar did not demand tribute, did not taunt Kl'aarn, nor did he perform any of the juvenile rituals which normally precede a duel of fists between boys. Indeed, Shalar seemed uncharacteristically placid this day.

At first Kl'aarn was suspicious, for Shalar was known as well for his devious tricks as for his brutal bullying. But if Shalar had some devious motive for his placidity, he at least did not hide it, not this day.

"I need to borrow a boat," he told Kl'aarn frankly. "And no one will lend to me."

Kl'aarn was perplexed, not only at the request itself, but at the fact that Shalar would even speak to him in words that showed no hostility. Something was surely strange this morning.

"A boat?" Kl'aarn found himself asking. "Of all things! Why?"

Shalar appeared uneasy, indeed embarrassed. But he wasted no words. "There's been little food in my house for days," he admitted. "My father's handed over all our money to the mead peddlers." This was a shocking confession, even though everyone in the village already knew. "He's passed out now in a drunken stupor." Shalar had never been so forthright in all his life, at least not as Kl'aarn could remember. "But my mother and I are hungry. We won't beg, but we'll pay for the use of your boat, and a fishing net. We'll share half the catch with you." His eyes dull with despair, Shalar awaited refusal. "So what do you say?"

So that was it, Kl'aarn reflected. Shalar was desperate enough to try his hand at some honest labor for a change. It was amazing how hunger could focus one's mind. And on this strange day, Shalar was more focused on conducting business than on fighting. For a moment, Kl'aarn was too astonished to reply. But he quickly recovered his wits and said, "What a coincidence. I'm on my way to make my uncle's skiff ready. We hope to meet a merchant ship coming in today."

Taking this as a proposed offer, Shalar seemed almost to plead. "I'll bring it in at first sight of sail. I promise. I'll venture no further than---"

Kl'aarn interrupted, sparing Shalar the embarrassment of begging. "Agreed. And I'm sure I can borrow a fishing net from old man Koto. But one thing I demand, Shalar."

Suspicion arched Shalar's brow. "Demand what?"

"I'll go with you," Kl'aarn answered. "You can't handle oars and net all at once. You'll need an extra pair of hands. And I need a pretext on which to stay out all day, one that will satisfy my father. Of course you'll testify in my behalf, if he questions me. So. We'll fish together on the bay. Agreed?"

Shalar seemed hesitant for a moment, unsure and suspicious. For the demand made by Kl'aarn was most unexpected. But then he replied, "I have no choice, do I? Very well, then. It's a deal."

Kl'aarn felt a tinge of astonishment at all this. Dimly, he wondered if he were embarked upon some foolish venture, one which he would soon regret. But no, he decided. There was something in the air, something uncanny. First, word of a ship from Shi-Raq, and now this, Shalar all but begging for food. Already, Kl'aarn sensed that this day would long be remembered.

* * * * *

The next event at the crossroads was that the two maidens, Miril and Veelos, had gone to gather kindling wood.

Their escapade had not eluded the notice of two of Har-Keem's wives, observant to a degree some might consider a fault, who watched the girls depart the village upon a forest trail. Both of the women were grey of hair, and wrinkled with a lifetime of toils, the kind which age one quickly. "Look at them," the older one said, with almost pompous disapproval. "Away from their mothers, as if they were still but little girls left to play in the street. How disgraceful! Why, they're nearly grown women, those two. We should hold them here, for their families to come get them."

The younger woman was less inclined to censure. "But look, Karina, those two girls are not misbehaving. They are Veelos and Miril. They are only going to gather some wood for the fire. What is the harm in that?"

"Oh, how much you have to learn," the older one said. "It's just a ruse to get themselves away from adult eyes. It's something the girls without families do, when they've arranged some rendezvous with boys, bad boys, and sometimes even with the good ones, to ruin them. Miril's and Veelos's parents should keep better watch over their daughters. And they don't. It's a disgrace, I tell you."

The younger woman took a different view. "Veelos and Miril will do no such thing," she remarked assuringly. "It's just that they enjoy being carefree, in their innocent way. Don't begrudge them these last few days of their childhood. It does a heart good to see them running free, while they still can. As it is, they'll be married off soon enough, just as we were at their age. Don't we two wish we had some fond memories to bring smiles to our faces now and then? And besides, they're good girls, virgins true, both of them. I wish I could trust my own daughters to keep their virtue as those two have."

It was the custom in that time and place, indeed a very strict rule, very strict, to keep young girls at their mothers' side at all times. This was partly to protect them from dangers, and in no small part, to preserve their value as brides. For marriages were all arranged by parents, and a young virgin bride would bring a good dowry from the family of the groom. (Whereas one without reputation would become both a burden and a dishonor to her parents.)

However strict the rules, though, however carefully designed, yet even then there could be (for the crafty) allowances made from time to time, certain exceptions to those rules. Such exceptions were rare and few, but Miril and Veelos had an uncommon knack for finding them. The key, they had discovered, was always to be polite and reserved.

Perhaps Miril and Veelos were a bit too unobtrusive that day, and perhaps on purpose. For as they gathered kindling from the forest floor, they strayed a bit farther than they were accustomed to doing, indeed farther than two girls should.

And when they did, they roamed toward the final event at the crossroads.

* * * * *

We began this list of convergent events with mention of a ship from Shi-Raq, a cargo vessel awaited by the merchant L'aarn, and more eagerly so, by his son. The ship was supposed to have reached Har-Keem that day. But it never would. For, during the night before, the ill-fated vessel had fallen prey to pirates.

One of these pirates was a man named Trook, as murderous a cutthroat as any of his ilk. With his crewmates, he had slaughtered the unfortunate passengers and crew of the merchant ship, and plundered its freight.

When mead had been found among the cargo, the pirates had quarreled between themselves over it, breaking more of the earthen jugs than they drank, but getting their fill nonetheless.

Amid the drunken chaos, a torch had been carelessly handled. A fire had started, and quickly spread. Soon, it had been burning out of control, destroying the cargo ship, and threatening to engulf the pirate ship as well. Men had fled in panic from the flaming cargo vessel to their own warship, abandoning the merchant, and leaving it a funeral pyre upon the vast, dark, watery wilderness.

Somehow, in the jostling and commotion, drunken Trook, pirate and murderer, had fallen overboard.

Floundering in the waves, he had cried out desperately to his crewmates for help. But help was not to come. Perhaps it was because his shipmates did not hear him. Or perhaps they were too drunken themselves to respond. Or then again, what concern had any of them, murderers all, for the others? None. In any case, whether from cowardice or from culpable indifference, none among the pirates had paid their frantic shipmate, Trook, any heed, none at all. They had sailed off, into the night, without him.

Clinging desperately to a floating, empty jug, embracing it to keep from sinking, Trook had spent the night in terror, expecting either to drown, or else to be eaten by sea creatures every bit as ruthless as he was. All the night long, the derelict pirate had struggled for just one more moment of survival. Life had never seemed so precious, until now, when its extinction seemed so certain.

But just before sunrise, the pirate, unexpectedly, had found himself washed ashore upon a forest beach near a fishing village. As soon as he had felt sand at his knees, the pirate had frantically clambered from out of the threatening sea. And finding himself on dry land, he knew not where, Trook became, once more, a threat himself.

He gave no thanks for his reprieve, neither to idols nor to God, but simply tossed all gratitude aside as thoughtlessly as he cast aside the empty jug to which he owed his life. And immediately forgetting his despair, Trook had turned his mind to evil once more.

All this had happened during the night before.

And now, on this fateful day, the events of destiny's diverse paths were to diverge no more, but to converge, nay, to collide, a collision which would ultimately shake the world.

Oh, yes, add to all these happenings yet one more. One more.

Though its importance would become clear only later, a distant event would also this day play a role, a very great role indeed. Far away, in a cursed place, a long-slumbering demon awoke. It stirred. It sniffed about, and then spoke, its voice a snarl, a serpentine hiss. It said to itself, "She lives. She breathes. Indeed, as Hell does have flames, at long last, she breathes."

* * * * *

The skiff was by no means a seaworthy vessel. It had never been intended for the rough waves and strong currents of the open sea. So the boys dared not venture far from shore. Kl'aarn rowed, and Shalar let out the net to trail behind the boat. They did not expect to catch much. All Shalar hoped for was a meal, or perhaps two. And Kl'aarn, for his part, was satisfied merely to be away from his studies. At first, neither of them spoke.

"I know what you're thinking," Shalar said after a long, tense silence. Indeed, their arrangement had been most awkward from the beginning; just how awkward, they were only now beginning to appreciate.

Kl'aarn shrugged. "Know my thoughts, do you? Then tell me--- what is her name?"

Shalar scowled at the sarcasm. "This is not a matter for lame jokes. Do I seem amused? For that matter, do I seem, to you, at all the same as ever before? Do you think Shalar would on any day be seen with the merchant's son except in combat? Then why, today, of all days?"

Kl'aarn had to admit it was peculiar. For the first time, he had begun to wonder what had gotten into him, that he would have trapped himself in so vulnerable a place with his lifelong enemy and tormentor. Now, it occurred to him that Shalar had been questioning the matter also.

"Very well," Kl'aarn said, not flippantly this time. "Tell me. What am I thinking?"

"You're thinking," Shalar said, "that I did not bully you today--- and you assume this to be your fortune--- because I need your uncle's boat, and that because of my need, I spared you."

"So?" Kl'aarn responded. "And what more am I thinking, Shalar? That I would expect you to be somehow grateful if I lent it to you? Am I so foolish to think that? Let's not try to kid each other. For once in our lives, we both have something to gain by helping each other. I have a brief respite from my studies. And you have use of a boat and net, which have already gained two small fish for your table. So each of us gains something. But we both know this: that tomorrow, everything will once more be back to being the way it was, to being the way it really is."

Shalar had released the last of the net. Now they circled about to gather it in again. While Kl'aarn rowed toward the other end of the net, Shalar sat and faced him. "Will it?" he asked. "Will tomorrow be like yesterday?" Then, after some thought, he said, "Time passes; people grow wiser. The truth is," he paused, and then said pensively to Kl'aarn, "I'm not as stupid as people think I am, even though I can neither read nor write, nor tally numbers. Everyone regards me as only a bully, and like all such, a dullard. And who can blame them for thinking so? For as long as I can remember, I've picked fights with you, and won them all. I've blackened your eyes and bloodied your nose more times than I can count. But I am no dullard, Kl'aarn. It has occurred to me that it cannot go on forever this way." Shalar studied Kl'aarn, waiting for a reply, and then prompted, "Do you get my drift?"

Kl'aarn shook his head. "Not exactly."

With a hint of impatience, Shalar explained, "The fact is, I've always been nervous about you, Kl'aarn. Don't laugh, it's true. The other boys our age either run from me, or else they pretend to be my friend, only to avoid beatings. You do neither. I've whipped them all, and not one of them stands up to me, not one. You're the only one who even tries."

Kl'aarn continued rowing. "I can't say that I've had any success at it."

Shalar answered, "What I'm saying, Kl'aarn, is that however weak you are in body, you're not a coward. You never run away, never hide, never avoid me, no matter how many times I beat you. You always stand fast against me, even in defeat, always. And why? You are no dullard, to do such a thing, so why would you do it?"

Kl'aarn shrugged. "Continue."

Shalar gave a look that was partly a sneer, but partly respectful. "I know why you do it," he said. "I've unraveled your riddle. It's because you know things, things that other people don't know, can't know. But I, Shalar, village dolt, dirty and unwashed, I have solved your puzzle. I understand the source of your courage."

Kl'aarn began to show signs of boredom. "Is there a point to this?"

In the past, such a remark might have been received by Shalar as an insult, a provocation to do battle. But this time, Shalar took no offense, but simply answered the question. "You understand true enmity," he replied. "You understand what it is to be an enemy of someone with whom you can never make peace, but to whom you can never surrender. And now--- now I know it, too. But you have somehow seen beyond that. You have seen the outcome of our lifelong enmity. I have seen it, too. One day you'll beat me, Kl'aarn. No, not with fists, and not over some boyish challenge, either. No, you'll pick your time and place. And when you lay me low, it will be over something that counts, something that truly matters. Now tell me, am I right or wrong? Have I solved your puzzle?"

Kl'aarn shrugged. "You've obviously thought this through, Shalar. I've never considered it."

"If you haven't, then consider it now," Shalar urged. "It's bad luck that I got into desperate straits just when I did. Because even if I had not needed your boat today, I was going to ask a pact with you. Truly, I was."

"A pact?" Kl'aarn asked, barely suppressing a laugh. "A pact? This sounds so formal. What kind of pact?"

Shalar responded somberly. "This covenant I offer you now: I'll not beat you anymore, nor will I demean you anymore, nor will I allow others to do you any harm, or if they do, I will avenge you. That will be my part of it. Acceptable?"

"It has a good sound to it," Kl'aarn admitted. "But what's my part?"

"Only this," Shalar answered. "That you will never seek revenge against me for all that I have done to you in the past. That you will lay aside our enmity, and forget that ever we were enemies, even though your soul should cry out for my blood. Then, one day, on that day when at last you find me under your power--- that day, you will spare me."

Kl'aarn pondered this strange request, with no small wonderment at what had wrought this uncharacteristic depth of foreboding by Shalar. For, indeed, he was commonly thought to be a dullard. Then Kl'aarn replied, "I was not going to seek revenge anyway, Shalar. God forbids vengeance. Not that I'd expect you to understand that. And I cannot imagine ever having the upper hand against you. Such a thing could never come about. But! But if you will swear to such a pact, then I will swear to it also. So let us both make our vow. And let him who first breaks it suffer a just penalty, whatever God will deem that penalty to be."

Then they both swore it, a formal vow of honor, that neither of them would ever harm the other, despite all the enmity that had been between them, and despite whatever enmity might otherwise in the future have set them against each other. And although it would prove a difficult vow to keep, neither of them would forget this day.

* * * * *

As Miril and Veelos tied up their freshly gathered bundles of kindling wood, Miril happened to catch a glimpse through the trees of the two boys in the skiff. "Veelos!" she called. "Come over here. Quickly! Or else you'll never believe this."

Veelos let fall her bundle and, crouching beneath the foliage, made her way to Miril's vantage point, their cheeks all but touching in the close confine. Pushing apart the branches of the bush which hid them, she peered with Miril past the shoreline and upon the bay. Not far away, L'aarn's skiff carried both L'aarn's son and Sholok's.

"You're right," Veelos said. "I would never have believed it. They're in the same boat and not fighting."

For a little time, they watched in silent fascination. Then Miril said abruptly, "Isn't Kl'aarn the handsomest boy in all the world?"

Veelos suddenly pressed the branches back together as if closing the curtains on someone else's privacy. Then with a jerking motion, as if to emphasize her embarrassment, she turned away, her gaze downcast.

"What is it?" Miril responded with mild indignation. "We're just looking."

Veelos faced her then, and answered reprovingly. "It's one thing to look," she said, with a slight shake of her head. "After all, the whole village will be amazed by the sight. But it's quite another thing to stare. And I know that you were staring. Don't deny it."

Miril scoffed lightly. "And why should I deny it? And you! Don't pretend you've never looked at boys. I've seen you doing it--- more than once, and at more than just one boy."

"Be careful how you speak, Miril," Veelos said, as her cheeks blushed red. "We could get into a lot of trouble."

Veelos was right to be concerned. For there was no such thing as a minor infraction when it came to matters of sexual purity. Even a careless word, if overheard, could bring down the most terrible punishment.

But Miril's answer was every bit as incautious as her open admiration of Kl'aarn had been. Perhaps it was because they were away from the village, and out of earshot of their stern and unforgiving elders. Or perhaps it was that this day was unlike other days. "It isn't fair, you know," Miril complained. "Boys get to go out into the world and do things. No one keeps them locked up, the way girls and women are kept. But as for us--- very soon, you and I will have to braid our hair and don veils. We'll have become women. And then what? Then we'll be sent from our homes to some man's house, some man chosen not by us but by our fathers. And there confined, we'll spend our lives cooking and cleaning and bearing up children for them. Don't tell me you've never resented that."

"What gets into you?" Veelos asked. Her discomfort was obvious. "Would you be a man? Absurd!"

"I wouldn't be a man," Miril answered. "I would be a lady, a very fine distinguished lady. I would have a man to protect me and provide for me, of course, but he would also treat me well. He wouldn't let me scrub and sew and chop. And whenever I decided to go for a walk, I just would, that's all. He wouldn't try to stop me, either."

"And do you have such a man in mind?" Veelos asked. She already knew the answer, of course.

Miril spoke it anyway. "Kl'aarn. He's not just handsome, you know. Have you noticed how polite he is? And very gentle. I hope to be given to him in marriage. And you know me. I'll find a way. Somehow, I'll have Kl'aarn for husband, and he will have me as his wife."

Veelos shook her head. "I know how you feel about him. You've made that clear to me, if to no one else, for a very long time. But Miril, don't get your hopes up so high that, when they are fallen, your heart will break."

Miril made a dismissive gesture. "Veelos, Veelos my dear sister. Listen to what you are saying. Why shouldn't we get our hopes up? We are young!

We have rich lives ahead of us. All we have to do is dare to hope--- to hope, and then to act on those hopes."

But Veelos replied, "While you're hoping and acting, Miril, don't forget to face reality. Your father won't give you to L'aarn's son. Your father won't care how good-looking Kl'aarn is, or how gentle or how anything. Our fathers will marry us off to tradesmen, men whose fortunes can be trusted to their hands, not to the changing whims of trade and barter."

But Miril was irked. "Why should we have to depend so entirely on what our fathers will do? Boys get to tell their fathers which girls they like and don't like. And their fathers listen. But nobody listens to girls."

Veelos hoisted her bundle upon her back. "It's time to go," she said. "We'll be punished if we delay any longer."

* * * * *

Now Trook was in a weakened state. After a long, sleepless night adrift in the sea, waiting endlessly to be torn apart by some shark or other creature of the deep, without food or fresh water, he should have been thinking only of finding sustenance and shelter. When he had found himself washed ashore in the pre-dawn darkness, he should have thought only of concealment and escape.

But when he chanced upon the two girls alone in the forest, his murderous lust was immediately aroused. And casting aside all thoughts of the morrow, Trook rejoiced, in that, he needed share his sensual fortune with no accomplice. For even despite his feeble condition, despite his hunger and thirst, he knew that he could easily subdue two young maidens. They were far enough from the village that their cries would not be heard through the muffling forest, cries neither loud nor long, and no one would find them until Trook had fled to safety, fled far from this place, and far from the vengeance of bereaved fathers and brothers.

Without warning, without thought, Trook sprang.

At first, Miril and Veelos were so taken by surprise that they did not even comprehend what was happening. But an instant later, comprehension, swift and terrible, invaded their senses with a sudden brutality that neither of them had ever imagined. Rough arms surrounded each girl at the waist, rough, strong, and without regard for the pain and terror those arms inflicted. The girls felt themselves being dragged toward the forest depths. And they knew, with terrifying certainty, that they were being carried to their doom, much like geese to the chopper's block. But this, they knew, would be even worse than that. Theirs was to be a fate utterly unthinkable.

Reacting to their sudden sensations of horror, the two girls began screaming and kicking as furiously as they were able. But, despite their fiercest resistance, it was obvious from the very beginning that the two of them could only delay the inevitable, and at that, delay it for only a short time.

But for that short time, if only that, the girls resisted.

At first, there even seemed to be some scant hope that one or the other of them might be able to break loose and run away. For they fought against Trook's greedy arm-hold with a fury all out of proportion to their size. Their desperate burst of biting and gouging caught the pirate off guard, at least in the first moments. For, despite their terror, neither girl fought for herself, but only to free the other. Each expected to die, and each implored the other to run, to save herself while yet she could. And indeed, either one, but not both of them, could have saved herself, saved her own life at the cost of the other's. But for each of them, that was a price too high to pay, far too high. And so they fought, each dooming herself, each doomed in the futility of opposing this human monster who meant to consume them, and then, evil upon evil, meant to destroy them.

At first, it confused Trook. For the pirate had never encountered such folk, and as a consequence, had some initial difficulty in securing the upper hand. Whenever he directed his attention at either of the girls, the other would savagely attack, biting, scratching and kicking, forcing him to attend to her. But when he did, then the first girl would likewise distract him again. It was maddening to a fighter who expected his opponents to sacrifice each other, not themselves.

But they were, after all, only girls, and he an experienced fighter. The outcome, however valiantly the girls struggled, was never in doubt.

Deciding, at last, to make an end of this troublesome fracas, Trook determined to draw his dagger. At first, the pirate had not even imagined he would need it, and had thoughtlessly left it in its sheath. After all, who would have thought these girls could be any trouble at all, any, much less such a handful? Make that a double handful, at that. But now Trook's mind focused on the deadly weapon, and his right hand crept toward it.

Because Veelos was clawing at his eyes, making it difficult for him to see, Trook put his left hand on her face. At first, this was only meant to push her away. But when Veelos stubbornly refused to relent in gouging at his eyes, Trook's hand found an easy grip on her neck. As if of a mind of its own, but a mind which Trook did not dispute, the hand tightened its grip. Then, as if by happenstance discovering that Veelos was now trapped, he began to choke her with the one hand. The other hand continued to grope blindly for the blade at his belt. Finding it after no little difficulty, Trook finally grasped its handle.

But as the pirate was withdrawing the dagger, Miril noticed what he was doing. She needed no training in the art of the fight to understand the fatal consequence, if Trook gained control of that lethal blade. Miril was not strong enough to wrest away his hand from it. There was only one thing she could do to save Veelos's life. In desperation, Miril bit at Trook's right thumb with all the power and violence her jaw could muster.

Unbearable pain shot like a bolt up Trook's arm and into his shoulder. He sensed, that in another moment, the thumb would be completely severed, unless he could quickly withdraw it. Reflexively, without thought, he balled his hand into a fist and jerked it outward and upward as hard as he could. Thrashing in desperate fury, the fist caught Miril fully beneath the jaw, and with a sickening impact, knocked the girl backward onto the forest floor, where she fell on her back. There, she lay motionless.

Trook had rescued his thumb, but in doing so, had lost the dagger. The sudden, explosive action of his wrist had caused the dagger to go flying beyond where Miril lay. It fell onto the sandy ground some distance away.

It made no difference. Enraged by pain and frustration, Trook turned his undivided attention to Veelos. He still had her by the neck. He intended to choke the life from her. His grip tightened again. Slowly, the pirate watched Veelos's face turn dark as the girl lost consciousness.

"Hey!"

Trook jerked his head upward at the sound. As if from nowhere, two village boys had appeared on the shoreline, and were racing toward him.

The swifter youth was but a boy, Trook saw, thin and gangly. He was armed with an oar, which he bore clumsily, almost wrestling with it as he stumbled along through the shrubs and bushes. It was too heavy for him to use as a weapon. Trook had no fear of this one, no fear at all. He could, with a single stroke of his dagger, kill the smaller boy. And he intended to do just that.

But there was another boy, somewhat slower at running, but much larger than the one with the oar. And this one carried, as his makeshift weapon, a fisherman's spearhook, a common enough implement, but as dangerous as a woodsman's axe in a brawl. This boy was to be reckoned with. Instinctively, Trook recognized that Shalar posed a real danger.

Letting Veelos collapse from his grip, which she did, Trook turned and lunged for his dagger, which had flown from his hand when he had struck Miril. But much to his surprise, Miril had regained her wits, and in her fear and desperation, she was racing him for the weapon. For Miril saw that Kl'aarn would soon be upon the pirate; she knew, with icy dread, what would surely happen if Trook became armed once more. He would disembowel Kl'aarn with hardly a thought.

The two of them, Trook and Miril, threw themselves at the dagger. They reached the fallen weapon in the same instant, and for a brief second, both of them grabbed for it in a blinding struggle, a cloud of sand marking their furious groping for the weapon. Each of them knew that his or her life depended on getting control of that lethal, sharpened blade of hammered bronze. For a brief second, the desperate struggle raged, and for an instant, the outcome remained in doubt.

But Miril could not hope to overpower the murderous Trook. The pirate took only a moment of delay to wrest the dagger from the girl. And as soon as he possessed it, he aimed his first slash at Miril's throat.

But that moment of delay was all Kl'aarn had needed to close the distance. Using the massive oar as a club, he caught Trook in the back with it, and toppled the pirate onto his right side, pinning his dagger arm beneath him. That alone saved Miril's life.

Stopping in his tracks, Kl'aarn stared down upon the fallen, stunned pirate, not knowing what to do next. Trook glared back at him with a scowl so fierce and so murderous that, by its ferocity alone, it forced Kl'aarn backward a step. Under any other circumstance Kl'aarn would not have lived a moment longer, not against so deadly a foe.

"Bash him again!" Shalar bellowed from near behind. "Kill the bastard!"

Trook, who would in another instant have severed both of Kl'aarn's jugulars, heard Shalar's swift, cursing approach, and realized that the larger boy would soon be upon him with the spearhook. Suddenly surrounded by more enemies than he had bargained for, Trook's resolve evaporated into panic. He jumped to his feet and ran.

Confused, an utter novice to deadly combat, Kl'aarn was still flabbergasted when Shalar rushed past him. Trook had wasted no time in fleeing into the bushes and trees. But Shalar just as quickly ran between Miril and Kl'aarn in pursuit of the pirate, calling to Kl'aarn, "He's getting away! Let's kill him!"

Kl'aarn hesitated, wondering why Shalar would be chasing the brigand. The pirate had, after all, run away, had he not? Therefore the fight was over, was it not? Was not the danger past? To Kl'aarn it seemed eminently foolish to continue a needless fight. Was it anything more than just a fight? But then, remembering the vow he had made just minutes before, Kl'aarn decided he should be chasing along with Shalar just the same. This he resolved to do.

As he started, however, he heard a hideous outcry from Miril. "Oh my God!" she screamed. "Veelos is dead!"

Kl'aarn turned, and saw Miril kneeling over Veelos's limp form, trying vainly to pull her upright. Miril was crying and frantic.

Kl'aarn stared blankly. He could never have imagined Veelos dead. Never. But now he was chillingly able to do just that very thing. For, indeed, there was no sign of life in her, none at all.

Then Miril glanced about through her tears, seeing as if in a heavy rainstorm. And finding Kl'aarn in the midst of that waterfall, him only standing there, she screamed at him with a terrible rage, the rage of agony and desperation. "Do something! Help her!"

Overwhelmed and confused, Kl'aarn stepped quickly forward, but with no idea what to do. He knelt beside Miril and, blankly, watched her struggle desperately to lift Veelos up, as if trying to raise her from the dead. Kl'aarn's hands reached forward to help, but wavering, they opened only into indecision.

"Damn you!" Miril cursed Kl'aarn. "Help us!"

For yet another painful moment, Kl'aarn wavered, paralyzed both by dread and disbelief. Then, suddenly, he noticed something. "Just like that!" he said. "Hold her just like that, Miril. She breathed when you straightened her neck!"

Now Miril had heard a terrible sound escape from Veelos's throat. But however awful to the ear, however wretched the noise, that sound had been the sound of a breath. A breath! Miril struggled frantically to reposition Veelos in that same posture, praying feverishly for just one more awful sound of life from Veelos. But this time there was no response. Veelos remained limp.

"Here," Kl'aarn said. He moved quickly to Veelos's other side, opposite Miril. Reaching over Veelos's waist, and placing one hand under the girl's neck, he pulled her up, so that her back rested on his knee.

Once again, there came that sound, the sound of life, an agonized wheezing, but welcome. It came again, and then yet again once more. It continued. Air was at last moving in and out of Veelos's lungs. She was not dead after all. She was alive, and breath was sustaining that life, however precariously. Veelos would not die, at least not yet.

"You did it!" Miril cried. "Thank God, Kl'aarn! Thank God! You've saved her life."

But Kl'aarn's face was a grimace. "I can't hold her this way for very long," he grunted. "My back is breaking." Indeed, he was balancing in a very awkward posture.

"We need help," Miril said. "I'll get Shalar." And in that very moment, she had already stood, turned, and run, from him and Veelos, into the forest.

Vainly, Kl'aarn tried to call her back. "You fool!" he shouted. "You'll be killed!" But Miril seemed unconcerned that she was running after the very danger which she had so narrowly escaped just moments before. In a burst of speed, she was gone.

Kl'aarn found himself struggling to keep Veelos breathing, and wondered when or whether Shalar and Miril would ever return to help him. Gritting his teeth, he settled into his back-wrenching chore.

* * * * *

All was black. There was nothing but a vast, empty blackness. It stretched on, forever, with no end to it.

Somewhere, far off, at a very great distance, Veelos could hear the sound of someone struggling to breathe. It was an awful noise, painful and disturbing. Veelos wished it would stop. But it continued, a harsh sound, repeating across the vast, empty blackness.

Dimly, Veelos knew that the sound was herself, her own labored breathing, her own desperate struggle for life. Yet, despite knowing this, she felt no connection to it, no personal concern with the sound. On the contrary, it was very annoying. But Veelos knew also that, soon, those terrible sounds would indeed stop, and that when they did, they would not resume again, not ever. She would be completely dead, then, a permanent resident of this no-place, this no-time, this nothing, into which she had suddenly found herself transported.

But it was not mere nothingness, after all, Veelos began to notice. The dreamscape which imprisoned her was a wasteland, a fantastic, macabre wasteland shrouded in fog. There was no sky, unless the eternal darkness all about could be thought of as a night sky, but a night sky with neither stars nor moon. All about were dead, gnarled trees. Their branches were twisted, as if they were arms reaching out in the agonies of death, a death unto eternal despair. Barren rocks were its only other features, aside from the trees and the fog. The rocks were scattered among the dead, tortured trees, rocks too large to be gravestones, and fiercely jagged, as if sculpted by some malevolent force. All of this was pervaded by thick fog, which was no earthly fog, but a sinister, swirling mist. And everywhere there was silence, dead silence, except for that distant, annoying sound of tortured breath.

At first Veelos felt, not fear, surprisingly, but only gloom. It was time to die, she knew. But that knowledge evoked no fear, a fact which should have astonished her, but did not. Her dreary life had come to a sudden end, as had the lives of so many of her kindred before her. She felt nothing, no emotions, neither astonishment nor fear, but only gloom, a dull gloom that numbed her to any emotion, any sense of hope or dread. Veelos prepared to spend eternity in that despairing, emotionless state.

But just as she had begun to resign herself, to accept the fate of passing her existence forevermore in this condition, a condition even more dreary than her life had ever seemed--- Veelos noticed a movement in the mist. Something dark was out there, and not far away, but disturbingly nearby. It seemed to slither through the shadows, across the large, jagged rocks, between the gnarled dead trees, and through the swirling mist. It was coming for her. Then did Veelos understand that there were predators here. Even here, in this place of the dead, there could be a doom more fearsome than death. Eternity was not to be dreary, after all. It was to be far worse than mere dreariness and gloom. It was to be unending horror.

Veelos felt the urge to scream in sudden terror. But in this no-place, neither was there any breath by which to cry out. Afraid, she wanted to run and hide. But whichever way Veelos turned, there was no route of escape, but only the sinister mist in which to hide, mist which held only more fear and worse dread.

Then another sound came to her, not a fearsome sound, but rather one of hope--- not a sound of dying, but the sound of one living. From across a vast abyss, it penetrated the fog and found her. "Veelos," it called her name. "Hang on. Help is coming. You're going to be alright."

Then, at the sound of that gentle voice, it was the dark, shadowy figure which felt fear, not Veelos. She saw its long, serpentine form slither swiftly away into the vast, endless darkness, barely eluding the sunlight which now dimly invaded her dream. Even the fog began to recede, as if escaping. The faintest hint of daylight showed through, into what had seemed impenetrable darkness. Veelos guessed, then, that she had left the morbid netherworld, that dark, outer wasteland, and returned into her own world. Even so, all was yet a blur, not yet focused.

But one thing was clear. Someone was cradling her. Veelos knew that she was in the arms of someone who cared.

* * * * *

Trook had not run far into the forest before he slowed to rest. It was then that he heard the sounds of Shalar's pursuit. For a moment, Trook could not believe his ears. For he was used to others running from him, not after him. The pirate considered resuming his flight, but quickly changed his mind. His condition was too poor to sustain a prolonged dash through the trees and bushes. He would soon become exhausted. Trook knew better than to let his pursuer catch him too tired to fight.

So, standing in a small clearing, Trook turned to make his stand.

Then Shalar burst into the clearing. As if meeting an invisible wall, the metalsmith's son stopped still. He was confronted by the sight of Trook's burly form in fighting stance. The pirate was squared off, his feet planted just so, his dagger at the ready, knuckles down, blade up. Many a man had died by its swift, upward slash.

But Shalar had not blundered into the ambush. At the edge of the clearing, he had stopped, and had instantly assumed his own posture of combat, with the spearhook held level, at just below shoulder height, and pointed straight ahead. Then, slowly, he advanced.

Trook laughed. He did so without compromising his ready position. "Aye," he taunted his adversary. "The village bully be ye? The village brute, now. Well, brute ye may well be, that you are, but no killer for sure. A far difference there is, and any killer knows that. Well, then, come for it if ye've a mind to. I'll nay tarry for yer mates to help you. Ye're on yer own, boy. Come for it!"

If Shalar understood any of Trook's dialect, he gave no sign of hearing. His eyes remained focused on his target. Careful step by step, he continued to maneuver toward Trook.

Trook soon realized that he was not going to be able to distract his opponent by taunts or threats. This boy was not going to run away, nor be hurried into a careless thrust of his makeshift weapon. He would have to be fought, not merely slaughtered.

"That look in yer eyes," Trook said. "Aye, but I've seen that hateful look, seen it often and enough in many pairs of eyes. But always it was in the eyes of me mates, boy, me own shipmates. It's the glare of hate now boy, isn't it? Do ye be hatin me boy? Not me, to be sure now. No, ye can nay be hatin me, for never have we two met, and hate needs blood to give it life. It's someone else ye're hatin, not me--- but I'm in his place now. It's him ye mean to kill, not me. Was yer folks killed by pirates be it? No! It's not the hatred of pirates breeds such a baleful glare. Someone else ye hate, and me to take his blame. Be it so! Let's finish it, then. Come now, with a weapon like that ye get but one chance and no more. One chance--- kill or die. Have at me then."

Trook knew that he would have to get past the tip of the spearhook to use his dagger. But doing so was not all that difficult, not against inexperience and undiscipline. A long, jabbing weapon could be thrust only once before being grabbed away. Then the dagger would do its deadly work. All Trook needed to do was to feint, to draw off the aim of his opponent, and then, to disembowel him. He had done it often enough before, and once again he executed the maneuver masterfully.

With a quick motion, Trook feinted left, and when he saw that his opponent had prematurely committed to the thrust, Trook reached to grab the shaft of the spearhook.

But something didn't seem right. There was a feeling of ice in his chest. Dimly, Trook became aware that his opponent had not been deceived by his ruse. With an explosive snap of his arms, Shalar had thrust the spearhook straight forward, neither to the right nor to the left, and had done so with stunning force. Its cold, bronze blade was wedged firmly and deeply inside Trook's chest.

Trook's face showed surprise, then pain, and finally terror, a wild, knowing terror. Before that look left him, his spirit had already fled his body, and was beginning its eternal torment. There was the laughter of a demon.

* * * * *

Miril had been running full speed along the trail. When she reached the edge of the clearing, she stopped suddenly, stunned by what she saw.

Shalar was gripping the shaft of a spearhook. At its other end dangled a dead man. Although the man was limp, lifeless, Shalar was lowering him slowly to the ground, giving the illusion that he was forcing the corpse unwilling to its natural supine position. When finally the dead man was flat on his back, Shalar leaned forward, putting all his weight into a final, vengeful thrust of his weapon. Then, releasing the shaft of the spearhook, he stepped backward a pace, as if admiring the skyward pointing monument to his victory.

Miril gasped in horror. "Shalar!" she exclaimed. "Look what you've done. Look! You've murdered him!"

Shalar turned suddenly to face Miril. She had expected to see him snarling and fierce. But instead, he unnerved her with an expression that was calm and serene. "He's dead," Shalar told Miril. His voice was informative, nothing more. "The bastard is finally dead."

Despite her pains and injuries, despite her fear, despite Miril's urgency to help Veelos--- Miril stared in disbelief at Shalar's calm demeanor. "Well of course he's dead, you fool. You killed him. Aren't you the least bit--- don't you even care?"

Shalar's unnatural calmness suddenly vanished. In the next moment, he was his old self once more. "I didn't do it!" He spoke defensively, denying the obvious. Then, regrouping and maneuvering for advantage, he said, "I mean--- I did do it, but it wasn't my fault. He tried to kill me. You saw it. I had no choice!"

"No choice?" Miril accused. "You chased him down!"

Then Miril suddenly remembered why she had run herself raw through the thick bushes which had torn at her already bruised flesh. "Never mind that now," she said. "Veelos is choking. She'll die if we don't get her to help. We need you to carry her. Now hurry!"

* * * * *

Veelos's eyes tried to focus.

Kl'aarn's face hovered close above hers. Through the blur, she could make out his eyes, pained, but concerned. Veelos became aware that he was holding her in his arms, holding her just so. He was giving her breath, breath and something more than breath. He cared enough to reassure her. "It's going to be alright, Veelos," he said in a voice that was gentle, yet strong. "We're going to take you home now."

There was a hypnotic quality in that voice, the more so for lack of any deceptive intent.

Veelos found comfort then. She was in manly arms, supportive and compassionate. Kl'aarn's gentle voice was convincing. He was going to take care of her, he had said. He was taking her home.

Chapter 2

Metalsmith

Sholok felt himself shaken from his stuporous sleep. The pain, which he had earlier felt, was by this time numbed from hours of unconsciousness. But the ever-present anger was as strong as ever. With a vengeful sweep of his arm, he struck out at whomever it was so rudely rousing him.

His wife Lev-Wan deftly dodged the predictable blow, then renewed her attack with determination. "Sholok, damn you, wake up! Shalar's gotten into some kind of trouble."

Sholok raised himself upon one elbow. But his intent was not to get up. It was to find a target for his vicious next strike. He would strike, then he would resume his escape from the frustrations and indignities of his brutal, indifferent world. "So what?" he bellowed, his eyes squinting but searching. "That damned kid's always in some kind of trouble. You bothered me for this?"

"But this time it's serious," Lev-Wan urged, moving out of range of Sholok's clenched fist. "The entire village is in the street over this. I heard someone say two girls were raped. And one of them is dead."

As the words registered, Sholok quickly forgot about sleep. The rage which had contorted his lip relaxed. His expression became one of cold, thoughtful premonition. "Shit," he said after a long time. "If Shalar's killed one of them damned sluts, they'll lynch him. Hell, they might even come after us."

Lev-Wan reached forward and grabbed her husband's wrist pleadingly. "Sholok, I'm afraid. What will we do?"

Sholok crawled to his knees on his way to a staggering, standing position. His hand rudely brushed aside Lev-Wan's clinging grasp, denying her any reassuring touch. He made his way to the window of his shanty, and tried to make out what was going on in the village at the foot of the hill.

Obviously, there was some very great disturbance. Everyone was out---men, women, children, everyone. They were making for the pier, which he could not see from his vantage. Whatever had happened, it had something to do with the pier.

"If he'd attend his work like I told him---"

"Please!" Lev-Wan cried out. "Don't let them lynch him. He's all we've got, Sholok!"

Sholok glared at the village. He knew that there might be no stopping them, once they got into the madness of bloodlust. Despite Sholok's massive frame and brawling nature, a frenzied mob would not fear him. He might break the bones of a few, but eventually they would have their way.

"Yeah," he said at last. "I'll see what I can do. Get my clothes."

* * * * *

Sholok forced his way through the crowd. With powerful arms he pried apart every pair of bodies which blocked his path. Finally, he broke through to the other side.

The sight which met his eyes was a staccato of impressions. Confused, Sholok tried to sort them out.

Two girls were the center of all the attention. Sholok recognized them.

They were from respected families, not at all the sort with whom Shalar was accustomed to consorting. But on the contrary, they were the type who would need a little convincing to submit. And indeed, they had been brutally beaten, that much was clear. One of them was hanging at the edge of death. Valen Elder was working her potionist's craft on that one, for whatever that would be worth. The other girl seemed in no danger of dying, but even so, she was bloodied and bruised, and her clothing torn to ribbons. She was crying and hysterical.

Sholok cursed silently. If Shalar had wanted to rape, why had he raped girls with families? There would be a vendetta over this, surely there would.

Indeed, Shalar was being interrogated by the male elders of the village, who had cornered him on the pier. Sholok devised a scheme to get his son loose.

"Shalar!" he barked. "What in hell have you done?"

Suddenly the crowd fell silent, and all eyes were upon Sholok. So far so good, Sholok thought. Even Shalar himself suddenly turned cold with fear. For well he knew the unreasoning brutality in his father's voice.

Then Sholok spoke to the crowd. "Whatever my son has done, it will be paid for. But vengeance will come to him from my hand, not yours."

After all, no one was dead, at least not yet. At worst, Shalar might be required to marry the two girls and support them, and pay a dowry to their families. But that could be worked out later.

Sholok stepped forward to retrieve his son.

But just as he did, he found his way blocked by the imposing figure of old fisherman Koto. Koto himself had a reputation as a brawler. But these two had never had occasion to face each other, since one kept to his forge and the other to the pier. Sholok sensed the beginning of a brutal fight.

But before it could come to anything, Koto said, "Your son's done no wrong, metalsmith. Much as I dislike you both, that's the truth of it. A stray shipwrecked pirate tried to do in these two innocent ladies. Your son and L'aarn's came to their rescue and saved them. And before the vermin could get any pleasure from his crime, Shalar killed the bastard."

Sholok was suddenly and uncharacteristically silent, as he tried to absorb this latest, incredible piece of news. "Killed a pirate?" he mumbled. "Shalar?"

"Killed him dead," Koto said. "Miril herself saw it, and her word is gold."

Sholok glanced at Shalar. "Is that right? You killed a pirate?"

Uncertainly, Shalar nodded.

After a moment, Sholok chuckled. He had been worried that Shalar had cost him all he had. To his relief, that was not the case. Then he said, "So. How did you manage to do that?"

Shalar seemed hardly to know how to answer. But he knew better from experience than to delay answering his father. "Spearhook," he said. "Got him with the sharp tip."

Sholok laughed with relief. "Lucky throw, huh?"

"No!" Shalar protested. "I didn't throw it. I stabbed him. In the chest."

Sholok frowned. "Are you trying to make it sound as if you went toe to toe with a fighting man, a wild murderer--- face to face--- and did him in with a spearhook?"

"Yeah," Shalar said. "I did."

Koto injected, "That's how Miril tells it, too, Sholok. For once, the boy's not lying."

But Shalar did not hear. He was occupied with looking into his father's face. He was puzzled by the strange expression he saw there. To be sure, he had seen that look in other men's eyes, but never in his father's; it seemed out of place there.

Yet there it was, unmistakable and undeniable. There, in Sholok's eyes, was pride in, and respect for, his son.

Chapter 3

Secret Love, Secret Hate

In Har-Keem, the village elder was an old woman named Valen; she was a healer, and also a devout worshipper of the One True God. It was Valen Elder who was called upon to administer the potions and ointments by which to nurse Miril and Veelos back to health.

Miril, despite her serious wounds, healed quickly. At least, she was soon able to hobble about, wincing with each painful step, suffering the soreness of bruises that would remain for many more days. But, at least, she was assuredly out of danger of death.

As for Veelos, it was not the same. Her injuries were much more serious. For a time, there was even a question whether Veelos would survive after all. The injury to her throat would seem at times to worsen, and her family feared she might stop breathing again. After Valen had tried all her potions, all that remained was prayer.

And so, Miril learned to pray.

She had, all her life, been a believer in God, at least in a general sense.

From the legends and scriptures, Miril knew of the God who, in the beginning, created heaven and earth, who planted the Garden of Eden, who created man and woman, and against whom humanity had rebelled so grievously. But Miril's belief had always been only casual. She had never given prayer much thought until, at Veelos's bedside, Miril knew that a miracle would be required, to bring Veelos back to health.

And so Miril prayed, as never before.

At first, God seemed to her distant and cold, an abstraction, a cosmic principle, some mystic force. Her prayers were to this God, the magistrate god, the rule-maker god, the god who was cruel and indifferent to human suffering unless appeased. Miril sought to appease Him.

But as she prayed, as she witnessed the miracle of healing in Veelos begin to take place, Miril experienced a miracle of her own. The God who answered her prayers was no abstraction. Nor was He distant and cold. Nor did He demand appeasement. Instead, He was real. He was close by her. And He suffered with her. He was the God who is, the God who loves without condition.

One night, in a dream, the spirit of Tarok visited Miril. She would have worshipped him, too, but Tarok forbade that. "See to it," he urged her, "that never you worship any, but only the one true God. He alone, and none other--- none other--- is worthy of worship."

But so awestruck was Miril--- for indeed the dream was unlike any dream--- that she prayed to Tarok in his presence.

He replied to Miril. "God has already met your need. Your sister in spirit, Veelos, will be healed. Her health will return. God has prepared for her a path to follow, and she will be set upon that path. And likewise for you, Miril. For well does God know your heart, and your love for Kl'aarn, son of the merchant, L'aarn. For God has put it into the heart of your father, and Kl'aarn's father, to give you to Kl'aarn in marriage. And you shall be his wife, and he shall be your husband, until death do you part."

Miril wept with joy. "Praised be the name of God," she said, "who has given me this day not one, but two, miracles of love: first, that my kindred of the spirit, Veelos, should be healed of her wounds and restored to life, and second, that the one true romantic love of my heart, Kl'aarn, will be husband to me. I know not why God should be so merciful to me. For never have I served Him. But I shall. From this day forward, I shall make myself a servant of the village shrine, and a slave to the one true God. Heaven and earth are filled with His glory!"

Tarok was pleased by these words. But he had more to say. "God is indeed merciful and generous," the ancient warrior spirit said. "But fallen man lives in a fallen world. And so he is subject to suffering, suffering which in man's limited view is not the work of man, but the work of God, and the wrath of demons. But do not be deceived. Miril! Your time of choosing will come. And when it does, you will see set before you a table, a table of suffering. When you see this, remember me. For the demon will seek your soul, to turn you away from your path, the path which God has set before you. It is then, Miril, then, that your gratitude to God will be measured. See to it, that it is then, that you worship God, and God only, and none other."

Miril answered. "I will," she said. "For already, God has given me all that ever I asked of Him, all, and even more. What suffering, then, could turn me from Him? None. I will serve God forever, God only, and none other. This I swear."

* * * * *

Although Veelos lay in bed several days, she seemed to rest but little. Although she slept, she did so fitfully. Those who attended her, especially Miril, who remained night and day at Veelos's bedside, noticed her troubled dreams.

But no mere dreams robbed Veelos of rest.

As the mists swirled about her, she recognized the desolate wilderness in which, once more, she found herself. It was here that she had stumbled across the no-place between life and death, when her life had been all but choked from her. Here, the ground beneath was hard and barren. Here, the only sign that life had ever resided was provided by the trees, gnarled and long since dead. But even in death, their wooden corpses seemed tormented.

"Where am I?" Veelos asked aloud. "I'm not dead, not yet. Am I? So, why? Where am I, and why am I here?"

"Don't be afraid," a voice said from behind her.

Veelos whirled to see what man spoke, so gently, in such a harsh land as this. He stood not far off. His leather armor, studded with nuggets of bronze, made him seem more sturdy than he was. But he was frail, very frail.

"Kl'aarn?" Veelos asked. "Can that be you?"

The young man shook his head. "No," he answered. "Only a dream."

But Veelos was unconvinced. "No," she insisted. "This is not but a mere dream. This is very real, however much like a dream it may seem. And you are no illusion. You are as real as I am. It is indeed you, Kl'aarn. Don't deny it. Is it your death which brings me here? Did you die? You tried to save my life. But now I see, that it must be, that we both died, killed by that pirate. And now we're here. For surely this is a place of the dead. Oh, Kl'aarn. I cost you your life! I'm so sorry. So very sorry!" Veelos held out her arms to him.

But the image of Kl'aarn stepped back from her approach. "I'm only a messenger," he said, "not the message. And you are not dead, though true, you are at the edge of the land of the dead. Now you must listen, Veelos. Hear the message which I bring. Because none of what is happening has been by chance. There is evil afoot, evil come down to earth. We are all in great danger, not only you in the world of substance, but also us, in the world of spirit."

Warily, Veelos glanced about. Whatever danger might lurk in such a wilderness, it must surely be dread, she thought. She remembered the black serpent which had slithered toward her, until daylight had chased it away. But this time, daylight would not intrude into the black nothingness of this land between life and death.

Then Veelos looked again at the image of Kl'aarn. She looked to him for protection. At his side was strapped the sword of a warrior. But it was too bulky for his thin bones. He could never wield such a weapon. Yet, he had indeed saved her life, defending her against a murderous pirate, an act which surely must have taken both strength and courage.

Then it occurred to Veelos that she was seeing Kl'aarn, not as he appeared, but rather as he really was. However weak of body, however frail of stature, Kl'aarn did have the heart of a warrior after all. His was courage unlike mere bravado. It was staunch and true, and would never retreat from battle.

"If there is danger," Veelos said, "you will protect me. I know you will."

But no. "Veelos, I am not who you think I am. I am not Kl'aarn. I am only as this fog which encircles us, but which has no substance. You must understand. I speak not of the kind of danger you encounter in your own world. You are being warned of another danger, a danger the like of which you have never imagined."

Veelos straightened herself. "If you are not Kl'aarn, then why is it that I see you as Kl'aarn? Why do I not see you as another?"

The figure who appeared as if he were Kl'aarn, but who denied being Kl'aarn, seemed to seek for an answer. But he did not give one.

"You are a warrior," Veelos said. "And so, in his heart, is Kl'aarn, albeit a very different manner of warrior than you are. You have courage, and so does Kl'aarn, even if his is not the courage of battle. And you are a kind and good man, true to your word, gentle, loyal, and Godfearing. And all these are attributes of Kl'aarn as well. Is it any wonder, then, that Miril loves him so?"

The image seemed for the first time to express discomfort. "Yes. Miril does love Kl'aarn. She has hidden that from everyone except you, from whom she hides nothing. But--- but there is something more--- that needs to be said about this."

Veelos felt a cold chill, a chill of the soul, as she guessed what words the image was intending to speak next. "Yes?" she prompted. "But what?"

"Miril has not hidden, from you, her love for Kl'aarn. But you, Veelos, have hidden something from Miril. Have you not?"

"No!" Veelos said. "I would never do such a thing. Never! And least of all to Miril, who lay down her own life for me, her very life, and offered herself as a sacrifice so that I might live. I would never fall in---- "

The image was compassionate, but relentless. "In what, Veelos? In love? With Kl'aarn?"

Veelos wanted to turn and run, to hide her embarrassment and shame. But of course, that was impossible. There was no--- no where. "How could you say that of me?" she demanded. "What is this, that you torment me with? I've done nothing to come between Miril and Kl'aarn. Nothing. And I would never, never, never wish to take him from her. Never!"

"I know that," the image said. "But it is not I who have chosen to appear to you as Kl'aarn. It is you who have imposed that image upon me."

Veelos shook her head. "It's just that he saved my life. He held me in his arms, but only innocently, only respectfully, and only to save my life. That's why I see his image upon your own."

"In this place," the image said, "truth cannot be concealed. Even when things are not as they appear to be, yet they reveal what is."

Veelos felt tears upon her cheeks. "And what good does it do to bring such ugly truth to the surface? Did you think to do some good by this? For I can see that you are no evil spirit, bent upon mischief. Yes, I am in love with Kl'aarn. When did it begin, I don't know, nor wish to. When first I noticed it, this tiny flame, I crushed it, snuffed it out and buried it--- and forgot. For Miril had already spoken her affection for Kl'aarn, and as far as I was concerned, that was the end of it. The end of it. I would never desire him again, never. But now, now this. You, a spirit, come to me disguised as Kl'aarn, giving fuel to this flame, casting its light upon my innermost, darkest secret. To what end, good spirit? To what purpose? Now cast me into death, so that I might never have to remember this, might never have to bear this awful burden again."

But the image spoke. "I did not come to you to embarrass you, nor to bring you pain or grief. Quite the opposite, Veelos, I bring you the message that God loves you, and has great plans for you. I come to encourage you, to embolden you, to give you the faith to stay upon the path which God has set before you, and which it is His plan for you to follow."

Veelos bowed her head, then, and wept in shame. "Then why?" she asked. "Why is it Kl'aarn's image I see now? If it is not truly you, Kl'aarn, then why do I not see the image of another?"

"There is a reason," the image said. "For the one who sends this message is too fearsome for you to look upon."

Veelos dried her tears. "Let me see him," she said. "Show yourself. For Kl'aarn's image is too painful for me to behold."

The image hesitated, then nodded in assent. Kl'aarn became a mist, and then vanished, to be replaced by another warrior, a man most surely a man of battle. Tall of stature and thick of bone, his ancient armor a double sash of bronze-studded leather, his sword was more than two men could wield.

"Tarok!" Veelos whispered.

"Then you know of me," the man said, with mild astonishment.

"Oh, but of course," Veelos said. "The legends are yet told of you. That you fought on the side of the angels, against the demons cast from heaven. That you drove the demons and their sorcerors and witches from the earth. And that you yourself were slain by the demonwitch Kattaroon. Did she herself cast you here? Are you imprisoned in this---this hell? Are we in Hell, Tarok?"

"This is not hell," Tarok said, "although Hell is what I deserve. God spared me. My torment, instead, is to see a world, which I had the opportunity to make blessed, to see it suffer. For instead of conquering the demons in victory final, I myself was seduced, seduced for but a moment, by evil. In that moment, Kattaroon took from me my life, and with it, my power to cast demons from the earth. Even so, the demons were vanquished, conquered, and forced from the world. But they are vanquished only for a season. They sleep. But not for long, I fear.

“For once again, the demons are to launch themselves against the world. Once again they are to raise up sorcerors, and a demonwitch. Would that I could oppose them as once I did! But this time, there is none such as I to defeat their armies by the sword. No. This time, the one who is sent to oppose them is no man, but a woman. A priestess."

Veelos all but forgot where she was. "The Priestess of Prophecy?" she uttered. "Are we to see her in our own lifetime? But why do you tell this to me? Who am I to hear such words?"

"I tell you these things," Tarok said. "because you are no ordinary maiden. You have special gifts, special talents, special powers. And because of these, you have a great role in the events that are soon to come upon this world."

Veelos dared not breathe. “But I am not she. I have not the calling to priesthood, not at all.”

“No,” Tarok answered. “Yours is not the role of priestess. That is for another. You are called to a different path, not to the temple. That path is soon to be revealed to you, and that is why I am here, so that you will know that this path is of God. And so you will be emboldened to follow it. For it is a path of great importance.

“But, Veelos, pay careful attention to what I am about to tell you. For there is a demon which seeks your soul. I come to warn you. I come to urge you. Seek out the path which God has ordained for you. It will soon be revealed to you. Do not turn away from it. Do not reject it. Follow your path, and do not stray from it."

"And what path is that?" Veelos asked.

But Tarok only replied, "It will be shown to you."

Veelos, though awed by the presence of the warrior, was not afraid. "I've made a fool of myself,” she said. “I have loved a man who does not love me, a man who belongs to my dearest friend. What shall I do with my perverse feelings? Will they never go away?"

Tarok seemed troubled. "I am but human myself. I, too, was slave to unwelcome love. It destroyed me. At least in your case, you love one worthy, and your love is innocent. May you never know the fire which consumes but does not illumine. Even as Kl'aarn is not meant for you, Veelos, yet there is one other."

Veelos lowered her gaze. "And this man--- is he such as will make me forget Kl'aarn?"

Tarok replied. "Even as you dream, Miril is being formally betrothed. To Kl'aarn. And even as you dream this, your father is arranging a husband for you. The time of your childhood is at end, Veelos. Your womanhood is set before you."

"But who---?" Veelos had lifted her gaze once more. Tarok was gone. And the mists which engulfed her drowned out her question. Soon, she would awaken.

* * * * *

"Shall I be jealous?"

It was Veelos's first conscious thought, once the fever had left her. "Am I truly in love with Kl'aarn, as I dreamed? Or was it all just an illusion? Will I wince when they tell me that Miril is now Kl'aarn's? Will Miril notice, if I do? And will we still love each other? Could anything at all, anything, ever cause us to part from each other?"

But when the news was given to her, Veelos felt none of that. On the contrary, she rejoiced that Miril's romantic attractions to Kl'aarn had not ended in bitter disappointment.

As for her own feelings, they had, after all, Veelos told herself, been only the fevered imaginings of one near death. In a dream, one could imagine anything, however absurd. And after all, Veelos reminded herself, "I only loved Kl'aarn in a dream. Is that any love at all?"

Then, too, Veelos remembered that in her dreams, she had been promised by Tarok, a husband of her own. She wondered who it might be, and whether her joy would be as great as Miril's.

But it was not to be so.

If Veelos were awakening from a dream, it was only to find herself in a nightmare. For as soon as she was well enough to hear it, the unthinkable words were forced upon her. The man to whom she had been given in betrothal was not the romantic fantasy she had envisioned.

There were several young men in the village for whom Veelos would have settled. And there were some with favorable qualities in nearby villages as well. Indeed, one or two of them came to mind as more than merely acceptable. In their arms, Veelos might forget that ever she had noticed Kl'aarn at all.

But for Veelos, there would be no life of wedded bliss. For Veelos was horrified to discover that her father had promised her in marriage to Shalar.

Shalar.

Never before had Veelos shown disrespect. Never before had she dared question her father's authority. But in this matter she wept and pleaded for him to change his mind.

"I know that you dislike him," her father said. His name was T'Oren. "But he is a good tradesman. And once he opens his own shop, apart from his father, Shalar will be a good provider to you. You will never know hunger in his house, not even into your old age."

But Veelos became, for the first time in her life, outspoken. "Father," she said, "how could you have done this to me? I don't merely dislike Shalar. I loathe him, utterly loathe him. Shalar is vulgar, crude and dirty. He consorts with prostitutes, and is also a bully." (How often, she almost said, has Kl'aarn borne the bruises of Shalar's cruel injustices?) "The very thought of living with Shalar and his family fills me with dread. I would rather die."

But T'Oren's decision was final. "Some day," he said, "you'll look back and thank me for what I've done for you in this matter. You'll see."

Veelos knew then that it was no use trying to change her father's mind. "What does he know of such things?" she asked herself. But Veelos understood Shalar all too well. She knew that marriage to Shalar would be the most horrible fate imaginable.

So, from the very first moment, Veelos vowed to find an escape. She promised herself, "I will never marry Shalar. Never. Never. And again, never! Whatever the cost, whatever the price, whatever the pain, I will find a way out of this. Whatever the ransom, I will pay it. Any price, any pain, any loss, but Shalar's lips shall never know my kiss. Never!"

Chapter 4

False Priestess

One morning Veelos awoke early and announced to her father that in her dreams, she had received a calling to the priesthood.

She had said it just as succinctly as that, unable to maintain any lengthier pretense. As it was, Veelos was barely able to maintain eye contact with her father long enough to deliver the few words which comprised her lie.

T'Oren, for his part, reacted with surprising calm. He sat down, at his work table (for he was by trade a cabinet maker), and bid Veelos do the same. Then he said to his daughter, "This is quite a bit of coincidence, isn't it? For several days now, you've been brooding about having to marry Shalar. And now, out of the blue, this. Could the timing of this calling have been more convenient for you? I think not."

"I know it seems that way," Veelos said. This was not going to be as easy as she had hoped. "It does sound suspicious, I know. And I was wrong ever to have questioned you, oh so very wrong. I realize that, now, father. But, really. I had a dream, father. And in that dream, I was told by Tarok himself that I have special powers, and a special calling. These dreams began many months ago, not recently. At first I tried to ignore them. But there is no thwarting the will of God. We all know that. I have learned it, too. So now, I want to give my life to God. I want to serve only Him."

"And well it is that you do," T'Oren said. "Everyone should serve God. But as for the priesthood, there is more to it than merely wishing. It is very sacred. Priesthood is reserved only for those who are given the calling. And a very special calling it is. It would be a grave sin to make up a story about having been called, especially just to escape a marriage."

"I know, father," Veelos persisted. "But it's not like that. Wouldn't it be just as grave an error to deny someone who was called?"

T'Oren sighed and nodded. "Yes, it would. But first we must be sure whether your dream is genuine. We shall put this to the test," he decided. "I will send you to Valen Elder. She is wiser than anyone in such matters. If she gives her blessing to this, then--- then---"

"Then what, father?"

T'Oren composed himself. "Veelos, if this is truly of God, then I will lose you to the temple in Shi-Raq. When would I ever see you again?"

Veelos felt tears come to her eyes, then. But she suppressed them. She wanted to speak the truth. She wanted to admit that it was all a lie, a scheme to escape the horror of marriage to Shalar. She wanted to tell her father that all he need do was to retract the betrothal. After all, no dowry had yet been paid, nor any vows exchanged. Veelos wanted to plead her case, even to tell her father she would rather become an old maid, like Valen Elder, than to marry Shalar.

But she knew that persuasion was impossible. Veelos's father had prayed fervently over his decision, and no logic, no emotional appeal could reverse him. Deception was the only way out.

"Send me then," Veelos begged, "to Valen Elder. She will discern the truth of it. And if my calling is not genuine, then I shall marry as you command." And silently, Veelos added, "Or die."

* * * * *

"I don't believe it!" Miril exclaimed when Veelos told her.

They were at the small river, which flowed from the hill into the bay. Several other women were nearby, washing clothes, just as Veelos and Miril were doing, beating the soil from them with specially made striking-sticks. Amid the busy laundry-day activity, the two girls could speak without attracting undue attention.

"You don't?" Veelos asked, a look of worry taking over her face. "You don't believe me?"

"Well, of course, you I believe," Miril said. "What I meant to say, is that, well, it's just such a shock. I mean--- I just can't believe all this is happening. What could it portend? First, Tarok came to me in a dream, to reassure me concerning you. And now, he has spoken to you! And you tell me that he has been visiting your dreams since many weeks ago. Yet you said nothing to me of all this until now. When did all this happen? Why didn't you share it with me before?"

Veelos's hands shook. She had never lied before, not to her father, and least of all, to Miril. But what, she asked herself, was she supposed to do? Being truthful had not produced the desired result.

"I meant to," Veelos said. "I wanted to share it with you. Really. But you've been--- well, I mean, your betrothal to Kl'aarn--- you've been so busy."

"Well, yes," Miril said. "But I'm never too busy to listen to you. Especially on so momentous a thing. How could you not have told me? I'm hurt, Veelos, truly hurt."

"I'm sorry."

"What does your father say? You are his only daughter. He must be either very pleased, or else--"

"He's not happy about it," Veelos said. "Not happy at all. He wants me to marry--- someone. I can't say who. Nothing formal yet."

"Wants you to marry? Can't say who?" Miril replied, as if offended. "You can't tell even me? What is all this? First Tarok comes to you in a dream, and oh, Miril can't be bothered with such trivial things. And now your father has selected a husband for you, and--- well, who is this Miril girl anyway? Why tell her anything? Veelos, what's come over you? You were never this way toward me."

"I'm sorry, Miril. I know how hurt you must feel. But I just can't. I just can't say more. And besides, it's not important. I'm not going to be married anyway, to anyone. So what does it matter with whom my father has been negotiating? The important thing is, I have to go before Valen Elder. I must persuade her to endorse my calling. And I'm asking you to go with me, to be at my side. I need you to do this for me. No one else would do, only you."

Being so invited, Miril seemed to be consoled, at least a little. She struck the bundled shirt she was cleaning, struck it with a bit more force than mere cleaning required, forcing its wetness from it in bursts of spray, along with the soil from between its fibers. Then, raising her hand for another such strike, Miril suddenly halted. Looking at Veelos, she raised a brow, as Miril always did when she recognized the importance of some subtle point. And few subtleties ever escaped Miril's notice. Nor did this one. "The way you said that," she remarked. "What was it? To go before Valen Elder? To persuade her? You make it sound like an inquisition. Why?"

Veelos already felt that she was enduring an inquisitor's interrogation. Miril was being barely more cooperative than her father had been. Indeed, if anyone could detect Veelos's lie, it would be Miril. Veelos wondered why Miril had not already discerned that Veelos was adding lie upon lie.

"Inquisition," Veelos said. "Yes. That is how I feel about it. Miril, I know that Valen's always been like a grandmother to us. But this time, she's going to sit in judgment over me, in judgment over the most important thing in my whole life. Oh, Miril, if she withholds her blessing from me, I won't be allowed to go away to the temple in Shi-Raq. And if she does that--- I'll just die, I know I will."

Miril took Veelos's hands. "But Veelos. Think of what you just said. You're asking me to lose you! I don't want you to go away. If you go to Shi-

Raq, when would we see each other again? It could be months, years--- a lifetime! I can't imagine spending so much time without you, much less a lifetime. I just can't bear the thought of it."

"But I have to go, Miril," Veelos wept. "I must! Please, you have to help me. You just have to. I can't be married to--- I can't get married and be a priestess too. I--- I---"

Miril gripped Veelos's hands tightly. "I can't say no to you. You know that. But dear God, why? Why take you from me? Oh, would that I, too, could receive the calling! Then we could both go to Shi-Raq together."

Veelos tried to laugh through her tears. "But pity poor Kl'aarn, if that were to happen. I mean, he's been so elated these last few weeks. I've never seen either of you so happy. You are truly meant for each other."

Through her own tears, Miril tried to be as brave as Veelos. "Then maybe Kl'aarn would be called, too. We could all become priests, all of us together. I could love him celibate as much as--- well, you know."

"Then you will help me," Veelos said, pleased. She dried her tears. "Tell me. What kinds of questions do you think Valen Elder will test me with?"

* * * * *

Valen's cottage was as coarse as any in Har-Keem. She was poor. Her craft as a potionist earned for her a living, but little more. For potions could be costly, and Valen would dispense them without thought of who could pay and who could not. Besides which, she dealt only in potions of healing, not in potions of harm or of sin, even though some folk, by so doing, became wealthy.

Always before, when Valen had greeted Veelos at her door, Veelos had felt that she was being ushered into a haven of love and comfort. But this time, it was very different. She felt she was entering into a dark cave, a lair within which lurked uncertainty, and her worst fears. Visiting Valen had always been a joy. This time it was an ordeal.

Valen greeted the two of them with her customary cheer. Hugging them both, she said, "Welcome, and come in. Come inside, and be seated at my humble table. Veelos, relax! I'm not going to bite you. However much like a hag I must seem, at least I haven't enough teeth anymore to take much flesh if I did bite you. What could make you so fearful of me? Do come in, now, both of you, and share my little feast. I've prepared some bread and honey for us, and a very nice tea, which I'm sure you'll like. Come in, now, and let us hear this good news which your father tells me."

They sat upon stools at Valen's rough-hewn table, and partook of the delicacy she served. It was finer fare than Valen could afford, better by far. But her generosity was never limited by what she could afford, rather only by what she had at hand.

Veelos, however, was impatient to be done with the visit, one way or the other. She barely tasted the sweetness of the honey. "I want to be ordained as a priestess," she said abruptly. "But my father won't let me go. Unless, that is, you give me your blessing. Will you?"

Valen chuckled. "Well, not so fast dear little one. This is a matter of the greatest moment. Priesthood! Oh, how many years I prayed that I, myself, would receive the calling. For that reason I kept myself from any man. But the calling never came to me. Now, I sometimes imagine the grandchildren never to be, and I wonder---. Ah, but this is about your calling. Then tell me of it. What is it like? How does one know she has been called?"

Veelos tried not to shake, as she recited her lie. "I cannot speak of it," she said. "I have dreams, but I cannot recount them. I just know, that's all. And I need for you to tell my father to let me go to Shi-Raq."

"Oh, my," Valen said. "Oh my." Suddenly, it seemed as if she might faint, and fall from her stool.

"Is something wrong?" Veelos asked, alarmed. She and Miril both grasped Valen by the arms, to support her.

But just as suddenly, Valen was lucid once more. "Oh, not wrong," she said, reassuringly. Her tone was that of one awakening from a dream. "It's just that, well, how can I describe it? The most peculiar thing just happened.

It swept over me like a tidal wave. Then it passed. Oh my. Miril, have you also been called to the priesthood?"

Miril shook her head, slightly puzzled. "No."

"Are you sure?"

Miril shrugged. "I'm betrothed in marriage. It's too late for me to be called. I'm no longer a single woman, exactly. Kl'aarn and I have already exchanged first vows. A year from now we will exchange final vows."

"Hmm," Valen said thoughtfully. "Oh my. This is a very remarkable sensation I'm having."

"What is it?" Veelos asked. A look of worry had stolen its way upon her face once more. Was Valen going to see through the story?

But Valen's answer gave no indication of that. Instead, she spoke in words that sounded cryptic to the two girls. "Destiny," Valen said. "Great destiny is in this room. Oh, would that I could fathom it. But the perception just came to me, as surely as the wind blows in from the sea. All praise be unto God!"

"Valen Elder," Miril ventured. "Are you sure you're well? Perhaps Veelos and I should leave for awhile."

"Oh, by no means," Valen chuckled. "Don't leave now. On the contrary, I have been blessed by your presence here, greatly blessed. By both of you. You are talented young ladies, I tell you, with great spiritual gifts to bestow. Great power resides within you, within each of you."

For a few moments, Miril and Veelos glanced curiously at each other. They had never seen Valen Elder act so peculiarly. Then Veelos remembered again what task had sent her.

"And the blessing?" she asked. "Will you bestow it?" She wondered if she had sounded overly eager, perhaps even greedy.

Valen paused. "Of a truth, I cannot discern the matter," she said. "There is a fog, and I cannot penetrate it. Is it my sin that clouds my vision? Or is it, that, it is being purposely hidden?"

For a moment, Veelos's heart fell. Had Valen Elder seen through her pretense? Was she going to withhold her blessing? Despair began to sink its icy claws into Veelos's heart.

But Valen continued. "What else could it be, though? Oh, there is a great destiny for you, Veelos, whatever path you have been given. And for you, too, Miril. Yes, my blessing is upon each of you. Do as God leads you. Follow your paths."

Veelos remembered that those had been the words of Tarok to her, in her dream, to follow the path she had been given. But what had Valen Elder meant by repeating those words? "Are you," Veelos asked, unsteadily, "commending me to the temple in Shi-Raq?"

Valen answered. "I tell you, that in this room is not merely a priestess, but a future high priestess, a priestess more blessed than any has ever been."

Veelos wished to leap in exultation upon hearing Valen's words. It had been so easy! But Valen had yet one more thing to say.

"A warning," she said. "A warning to both of you. Dark forces have been aroused once more in this world, just as they were in the days of Tarok. You know his story. He was a mighty warrior, and he led the armies of godly men, alongside the angels of light. Together, they defeated the armies of ungodly men, and the armies of demons. Oh, but there was one weakness which Tarok had, and that was for the beautiful princess Kattaroon. She had had a calling to be priestess. But instead, she answered the calling to witchcraft. Tarok cornered her in her lair, and it was his duty to slay her. But he could not bring himself to do it. Night fell. Kattaroon's spent evil powers were regenerated. And then she used them against Tarok. He died terribly. Oh, so terribly.

"I remind you of this, Veelos, not to discourage you, but to strengthen you against the temptations which will surely arise. You, too, Miril. For you two girls are very pure, beings of light, powerful forces for good. Follow the path which God has set before you, and you will find the only true happiness there is. Never depart from your path. Never."

Once again, Veelos was reminded of the gravity of her sin. Once again, she considered recanting. It was not yet too late to disavow her false calling.

But instead, Veelos thought to herself, "If this lie will spare me from marriage to Shalar, I will tell it."

And so it was that Veelos received Valen's blessing.

* * * * *

Veelos had thought she would be given more time to say her farewells. But with shocking abruptness, her departure was set for the very next day. When called by God to His priesthood, one did not tarry.

The following day seemed more like a dream than like reality. Veelos saw it through tears, not only her own tears, but also through the tears shed by Miril, by her mother, and through the unshed tears of her own father T'Oren, who could only barely disguise his great sorrow.

"You will send letters to me," Miril wept. "The priests will write them for you."

"But of course," Veelos answered. "And I'll send all the more, once I've learned to read and write myself. And you. You'll write to me through Kl'aarn?"

"Better yet," Miril said. "I'll have him teach me to write. What were you thinking, that you would become smarter than me?"

"You will teach her, won't you, Kl'aarn?"

"Miril has a quick wit," Kl'aarn said. "I'm learning from her already. She'll be writing her own letters in no time."

"Sun's up," the driver said. Veelos's transport was but a horsedrawn cart. The village could afford nothing better. "We'd best be going, now."

Veelos and Miril could barely tear themselves from each other. It seemed nothing could dry their tears.

But just then, Veelos caught sight of Shalar. He stood at the edge of the small crowd, which had gathered for the farewell, seemingly out of place, an intruder as it were, prowling the outer grounds, as might a thief. Veelos was surprised that the metalsmith's son had bothered to show up at all. Why had he? she wondered. Could he know?

Surely, Shalar must have known that their fathers, T'Oren and Sholok, had been negotiating. But that in itself meant nothing. The negotiations had been only preliminary. T'Oren would not have made any promises until Sholok had placed a suitable dowry on the table. And it was doubtful that Sholok had, in so short a time, gathered more than a few meager tin coins.

Even so, Shalar's appearing was more than coincidental, Veelos knew. It had to be. For Shalar had never been one to be sociable, not even sociable enough to stand at the outer edge of an informal gathering in someone's honor. And there was a strange look in his eyes, very unlike anything Veelos had ever noticed. One could almost sense his thoughts, as if the boy were standing precariously atop some narrow ridge of decision, unable to break his balance of thought toward one alternative or the other. Sometimes, it seemed that Shalar was about to step forward, to approach Veelos. When Veelos noticed that, she shuddered with dread. What if he tried to hold her hand in farewell, as Kl'aarn and Miril had done? The mere thought that he might touch her caused Veelos's skin to crawl.

She felt almost angry that she had noticed Shalar at all. It was as if the metalsmith's son had deliberately infringed on this delicate moment, just to spoil whatever sweetness this farewell could console her with.

But just as, once more, Shalar appeared on the verge of approaching Veelos--- just as it seemed he had decided to take some assertive step--- Veelos felt the wagon lurch forward. The large, wooden wheels began to trundle over the rocky pathway that began at the edge of the forest. For a few steps, the crowd followed after, first Miril, then Veelos's parents, and after them, the others. But the driver prodded the horse, and it moved just faster than the crowd could follow.

As the trees obscured Har-Keem from her view for the last time, Veelos caught a final glimpse of Miril. She had fallen to her knees in weeping.

Chapter 5

Dark Prophecy

Miril wept and would not be consoled. Her grief was as that for someone who had died.

In the days that followed, Kl'aarn did his clumsy best to comfort her. His intentions were good, but he seemed often to say or do the wrong thing. It was not his fault. Miril's despondency was not the ordinary grief of separated friends. There was a darker aspect to it, a sense of foreboding that not even Miril herself fully understood.

Kl'aarn tried not to seem upset that his formal courtship with Miril was now being dominated by Miril's weeping over Veelos. But he could not help thinking that the two of them should be enjoying the happy and carefree moments shared by young lovers. This was a time for uninhibited laughter, punctuated by the subtle, knowing smiles which are so expressive in the unspoken language of youthful romance.

As was the custom, their courtship was a matter of form and formality. Their daily walks, together, along the beach, and through Har-Keem's sandy lanes, were closely chaperoned, one day by the two fathers, another day by the two mothers. Each day, the chaperones would drift just a bit farther behind the engaged couple, but never out of sight. It was what, in those days, passed for dating.

"I'm sorry," Miril apologized to Kl'aarn. Seagulls cried overhead as a salt breeze swept through her unbraided hair. "This should be a time of mirth for both of us. You must find me quite burdensome."

"Yes," Kl'aarn answered. Then, when Miril seemed astonished that he would say such a thing, Kl'aarn explained, "Yes, there should be joy for both of us, not just for me. I'm happy whenever I'm with you, Miril. Truly happy. But I would be even happier if we both were cheerful. You seem so moody. I wish I could lighten your spirit."

"But I am as happy as you are," Miril answered. "Just as oil does not mix with water, so it is that, my tears for Veelos don't dilute my joy, my delight, of being betrothed to you. Don't think that I'm unhappy. Please?"

"It's not what I think that matters," Kl'aarn answered. "It's how you feel, and how you try to hide those feelings of sadness. It might help, Miril, if you would just open up. You can tell me of your pains. We should share them."

Miril nodded. "But it's no secret. I miss Veelos desperately."

"Of course you miss her, more than any of us do. All your life, the two of you were as twin sisters, sisters if not by blood, but surely of the spirit. Now don't start crying again. Your mother will think I've said something awful to you. Or have I? Am I a boor?"

"No," Miril answered, drying her tears on her sleeve. "That is what makes you so very different from all other men, Kl'aarn. You're--- don't be offended--- you're less mannish than they are."

"Thanks a lot, Miril."

"Don't pretend to be offended, you know how I mean it. The other boys are always trying to be tougher than the others, to be more rugged, more--- more boorish than each other. If they take a liking to a girl, they don't confess that to each other. They pretend that all they want with her is--- you know. But not you, Kl'aarn. You're not like that. You've never spoken of me like that to other boys. (And don't pretend you have!) You're gentle, and softspoken, well mannered. I---"

"Enough," Kl'aarn said. "Thank you. You surely aren't reticent when talking about me, now are you? Will you speak your mind so frankly after we're married a few months, after you've grown impatient with me?"

For the first time in days, a small smile graced Miril's features. "I won't grow impatient, not with you."

Kl'aarn, noticing her smile, said, "That's more like it. Now you look more the Miril I've always admired from afar, always secretly yearned for, but never dreamed to claim as my own: soft, sweet, and gentle."

But a few steps later, Miril's smile began to fade once more. "Maybe what attracts me to you is that you're so much like Veelos," she confessed. "I mean, you know, patient and understanding. Veelos and I could always talk to each other, without worrying that we might misunderstand each other. We shared everything: our brightest hopes, our grimmest fears, and our most intimate secrets. Together, we rejoiced in each other's good fortunes, and mourned in each other's sorrows. But now, it seems that a part of me is missing, torn from me, and with so little warning! I have a deep wound. My only consolation is to know that she has found happiness, the happiness of her calling."

Kl'aarn tried to encourage Miril in this thought. "Veelos has joined the company of the compassionate," he said. "She will, from now on, be dwelling among kind and loving souls. And no soul could be kinder and more loving than Veelos's."

"It is a soothing salve to know that," Miril said. "But not even that salve can erase all the pain. I must be so very selfish, to feel this way."

Kl'aarn sighed. "No, it's not selfishness. Or if it is, it's only that noble selfishness, that sense of loss we feel when someone we love dies, and is taken into God's chamber of sweet dreams. We wish them back among us, even though the departed in heaven are happy to be where they are. And indeed, you mourn Veelos as we mourn our departed loved ones. But, as you say, she has found her happiness by answering her calling."

"Has she?" Miril asked.

The question startled Kl'aarn. "Well, of course she has. Look about at our surroundings, and compare these to what we've heard about the temple of the Orb, in Shi-Raq. I've heard that it's a place of splendor, of polished white stones put in place by angels, kept immaculate by human hands. And the high priests have great wisdom, illumined by the Great Orb itself. We can only imagine such a thing, but Veelos lives there, awakens there each morning, lays down to sleep there each night. She must be in rapture."

Miril's demeanor remained tinged with a cloud of apprehension. "If--- if she is truly there."

Kl'aarn stopped in his tracks. "Now Miril. What can you mean by that? Of course she's there. We've already received word from the temple that she arrived safely."

"Well thank you, Kl'aarn." Miril's voice had become slightly sarcastic. "I'm too dull to remember that."

"Oh, Miril. What's come over you? Now you're not just sad, you're angry with me."

She did not answer, but quietly wept.

Kl'aarn began to recognize that there was more than mere sadness in Miril's weeping. There was shadow, a dark emotion, one that was not diminishing with the passage of time, but growing darker. His concern gradually became alarm. And although Miril wished not to speak of her feelings, at last he pried them from her.

"You must share it with me," Kl'aarn urged. "I know that your relationship with Veelos was very close, but---"

"Is," Miril corrected. "Don't say was. Say it is--- is--- a close relationship. Very close. It remains so, even though we are apart. Always. Once, long ago, as little girls, we vowed to each other that we would always stand together. And we did so, against that evil pirate. We always will, Kl'aarn, always."

"I should almost be jealous," Kl'aarn said, trying to lighten her mood again. "But no, in truth, the two of you were, in spirit, twins all your life. Everyone knows that. Veelos's calling came as a shock to us all. I can understand your grieving over her loss. But I think it goes beyond that, Miril. Your grief seems something more than just grief. It distresses me that I can't put my finger on it."

"You're right," Miril conceded. "For her loss, I merely grieve. But more than grief burdens my heart. I worry for her, Kl'aarn."

"Worry?" Kl'aarn asked. "For her safety?"

"Yes. I suppose one might say that. For her safety."

"But--- but what about that letter from the priests? It says that Veelos has arrived safely. She is in their loving and able care."

"I know that," Miril said. This time, the sarcasm had vanished. But the dark foreboding remained. “But you’re missing the whole point.”

"I see." Kl’aarn’s tone was just short of patronizing.

"No," Miril retorted. "You don't see. You're thinking to yourself, oh, how silly women are, to get all upset over nothing, to worry, when there is no cause for worry."

Kl'aarn would not admit it, but he had been thinking precisely along those lines. "Well, you are worried. And Veelos is safe."

"See? You do think I'm being silly."

"Then tell me," Kl'aarn replied with mild exasperation. "What am I missing here?"

Miril's tone revealed the urgency of her discomfort. "I don’t know, exactly. Some misfortune has befallen Veelos," she said darkly. "I fear for her. I don't know how to say it any better than that."

"Misfortune?" Kl'aarn asked, puzzled. "Are you saying that some harm has come to Veelos, after the letter was sent? But even if that were so, how could you know---"

"I could," Miril answered curtly. "I could know it, and I do know it, just as Veelos would know if something amiss befell me. It was always that way between us. And it always will be."

"Alright. Very well. But what kind of misfortune? She is safely cloistered in the temple."

"I know all that," Miril said. "It isn't that kind of misfortune. I can't put my finger on it, and that's what troubles me so. But, Kl'aarn, Veelos is in danger, some different kind of danger, something strange that none of us can fathom. Some great evil is afoot in this world. There are fierce beasts on the prowl, not wolves or panthers, but beasts more ferocious than anything that hungers for the flesh. They hunger for her--- and for all of us as well. Their breath is cold upon Har-Keem."

But Kl'aarn said, "Listen to yourself! You sound like a prophetess. But can a young maiden prophesy? Your dark mood is only depression, Miril, not prophecy. Of course you miss Veelos, and it makes you sad. You won't rest easy until you see for yourself that she is--- now there's a thought. Miril, how about this? After we are married, we shall pay a visit to Shi-Raq. Yes, we shall travel there, you and I, as soon as our vows are final. Once you see Veelos in the vestments of priesthood, once you hold her hands, kiss her silver ring, and hear her voice, then all your fears of evil will vanish."

At last, Kl'aarn had said something which lightened Miril's mood. "We will!" she smiled. "That's what we'll do. Promise me, Kl'aarn. Promise me that we'll see Veelos again, and that when we do, she will be wearing the vestments of a priestess. She will, Kl'aarn. I can see them now, white robes and hood, all trimmed in blue. We shall see her wearing them! Yes, Kl'aarn, sometimes a maiden can prophesy. And I just did."

And indeed, Miril had prophesied well.

Chapter 6

Druuk's Demonic Plot

In the middle of Har-Keem, at its center, there was a small shrine. It was a simple clay dome, too small for more than one worshipper at a time. But it held, within its confined space, one of those rare jewels known as the lesser orbs.

In the days when angels had walked the earth (before the wars of the upheaval), the angelic jewels had been common on the face of the world. But so delicate were they that, by this time, it was considered a miracle that any of them at all remained. To merely touch one was to destroy it utterly, for they were made not of substance, but of a quiet power which no one understood but the priests themselves.

After Veelos had gone, Miril had remembered her vow to Tarok, to tend the shrine and its small garden. But beyond that sense of duty, Miril felt more and more drawn to the shrine. Her visits there became more frequent, and she found herself praying there often. It was the one place where her sense of foreboding was replaced with comfort and courage. It was in the shrine that

Miril most strongly sensed the presence of a towering man, strong and barbaric, yet gentle and serene. And Miril knew that Tarok himself, in his spiritual form, was keeping watch over her, and assuredly, over Veelos as well. There could be no doubt of it.

For many weeks, it was these prayerful visits with the lesser orb, which kept Miril from melancholy. Its quiet, spiritual radiance comforted her during those difficult days. But even this much comfort was only temporary. For something evil was indeed afoot, just as Miril had spoken to Kl'aarn in the depth of her darkest foreboding. More than that, the evil was ever more sinister than Miril imagined.

In a foreign land, far from the quiet solitude of Har-Keem, in a land even farther away than Shi-Raq, an event was occurring that was soon to change Miril's life forever.

* * * * *

As far away from Har-Keem as one could go, on the opposite end of the continent Wirik, there was the kingdom ruled by Druuk. He was a ruthless man, who had conquered all the kingdoms surrounding his own. His conquests had carried him to the shores of the sea on three sides, and to the Lands of Demi-men on the fourth side.

Kingdoms of men, Druuk had conquered with ease. But the Lands of Demi-men were another matter entirely. Druuk was warned of their curse, warned that none who set foot in those savage realms could ever hope to return alive.

But Druuk had defied that curse. And in his doing so, a heavy price had been paid.

He had sent a legion, his best army, across the border, and into the un-mapped wilderness beyond. For weeks afterward, no messengers had returned., nor came any report of how fared the legion of one thousand elite warriors. By this silence, it eventually became obvious that disaster had struck. But no one knew what form the tragedy had taken, nor what mighty creatures could have defeated so powerful an armed force.

When news did come, it was in a fearsome form. For finally, one day, a single survivor did straggle back into the king's court. He was one of the soldiers, a swordsman, of the famed and feared legion, Druuk's best, which had vanished into the cursed land of demi-men. His report made it clear that he was the only one left alive. And at that, he was himself reduced to being only a bloody, tormented wretch, all that remained of a once-proud soldier. He babbled incoherently of fierce creatures, part man and part beast, which fought with claw and with sword, and which had eaten the flesh of all Druuk's mighty legion. Then, his story told, the man died.

Druuk brooded, and wondered how he might ever fulfill his destiny to rule all the world. For not even his strongest sorcery could pierce the curse which forbade him the conquest of the Lands of Demi-men. Nor could his most skilled conjurors overcome the magic by which the oceans swallowed up any ship which attempted to sail past those fabled, forbidden lands of curse.

But Druuk did know, through sorcery, that beyond the Lands of Demi-men lay east Wirik, and that it was defenseless against his plundering troops, if he could but reach it.

One day, a sorceror came into his court.

Now Druuk himself knew something of the black arts, and he had killed many an impostor. They would come working tricks of illusion, and Druuk would discover them and kill them most horribly. Even when they came working true, demonic magic, Druuk would test the power of their magic against the power of his sword. And always, the sword proved stronger. Each time, the sorceror paid with his life.

But one day there came a man named Peresor, and Druuk sensed that, within this man, there lurked a sinister power, a dark, terrible force which even Druuk dared not scorn.

This Peresor was covered head to toe in brown robes. His face was concealed by a hood, with the front opened only in a narrow slit, an opening into which none dared peer. For within was the lair of death itself. A mere glance at Peresor's hands was enough to make one retch at the thought of what his cadaverous face might be. For the hands were as those of an unburied corpse.

"I am an ancient man," Peresor told Druuk. "I was born well before the last great upheaval, that glorious war. I was one of Kattaroon's most feared weapons, a sorceror, left for dead at Gur-Molkn, but I died not, though the battle was lost. But despite our loss, even though we failed to conquer the earth for evil, neither did the angels prevail, for there is even now the power of evil in this fallen world. And there yet remains the anti-prophecy, the utterance of demons, by which we, the evil, will reign supreme over all the earth.

"And now the cycle is complete once more, King Druuk. Another great upheaval is beginning. Only this time, the winds of destiny are upon you, my lord. It has been revealed to me. The demons, which rule the world of spirit, have need of their equal to rule the world of substance. They send me, my lord, to beg you to take your place upon the eternal throne, so that the anti-prophecy might be fulfilled."

Now Druuk knew somewhat whereof Persesor spoke, for he had read of these anti-prophecies. So he tested Peresor concerning these things.

"But why?" Druuk asked, his dark eyes glaring with threat of death. "Why would the demons seek a man? For is it not true that they always use a woman to do their work? Have they not always sent before them a witch?"

Peresor replied. "Yes. And so do they, once again, my lord. This demonwitch, woman of demonic evil, is already upon this world, residing in a land far from here, as far from Gur-Molkn as one can travel. And indeed, a small faction among the demons do rely upon her, placing their hopes in her evil, in her power, in her destiny."

Druuk grew angry. "Then, if the demons have their witch, why do they send to me, your undecayed corpse?"

"Because, my lord," Peresor answered, "the demons are not of one accord. Do they not betray each other, even their own kin? Indeed they do. So it is, that some of them send forth a witch, as always they have done in the past.

"But," Peresor continued, his breath frosting the air, despite that it was a warm day, "others of the demons reject the errors of the past. They accuse their former leaders of repeating the ancient blunders, errors which have never led evil to its ultimate victory, but instead, have always and repeatedly resulted in our defeat and in our humiliation. These renegade demons, the fiercest and most evil of all--- these send forth a conqueror, a mighty man of evil, a man such as yourself. It is you, my lord, whom these demons have chosen, chosen to rule this fallen world--- for all time to come."

Druuk pondered these words, then said, "Wisely you speak, sorceror. For just as you say, the dreams have come unto me. And just as you speak, so it is written in the unholy texts which reside in my dungeon, far beneath us. But if the demonwitch, as you say, is already upon this world, then surely, she will seek my death. She will not tarry to eliminate her rivals. Even now, she will be moving against me."

"Not yet," Peresor replied. "For the woman is yet but a maiden, and as of yet, innocent of witchcraft, ignorant of demonicry. She has not yet donned her darkmost mantle, nor yet learned the practice of her powerful craft. This is your advantage, mighty king. For you shall strike first. If otherwise, then it will be as you say. For if you strike not, the demonwitch will soon learn of you, and of your great destiny. And if so, then what will she do, when she learns that Druuk is her rival? She will seduce and slay him, as her predecessor did seduce and slay her rival, the mighty Tarok himself. Unless, of course, Druuk is mightier and swifter than she. For although she has not yet power, soon she will."

Druuk's evil glare only intensified. It menaced with death. "So far," he said, "you give me only a message by which to fear. Think you to find power over me thereby? Others have tried before you, to intimidate me into submitting to their schemes. They all lie in rot, some yet alive in torment, in my deepest dungeon. Think you to fare any better than they?"

But Peresor had no fear. "Judge me, mighty king. If I deceive you, then slaughter me as it pleases you. But know you deep within your soul that I speak the truth. Then let me teach you the ways of uttermost evil, that none may survive your wrath, who oppose you. No, neither priestess nor witch, my lord, shall defeat you."

Druuk leaned forward. "The priestess. Speak of her."

The sorceror did so. "Just as the demons are not of one accord, but war against each other, so they war also, against the powers of heaven. Just as the demons have always sent before them a witch, this time the angels send not a man to lead their armies, but a woman. These things you already know, mighty king, though you are shrewd enough not to have spoken them. But you know, for the dreams have come unto you. If not, then slay me, and I shall die."

But Druuk had indeed had the dreams. "This priestess. Is she more to be feared than the demonwitch?"

Peresor replied, "You need fear neither. For although both of them, the Priestess of Prophecy and the Dreaded One Foretold, that is the Demonwitch, although they shall both seek your life, mighty Druuk, but instead they shall wound each other. Then you shall slay them both. This is my prophecy."

Having heard all that Peresor had to say, Druuk then brought forth his own sorcerors, that he would test their powers against this foul presence which had entered his fortress. Druuk set his own sorcerors in combat against Peresor. And one by one, Peresor slew them all with great torture, as it pleased the king to watch. And after all this slaughter, then the king sent swordsmen, his fiercest gladiators to dispatch Peresor; Druuk watched in amazement how impotent is the power of sword beneath the true and ruthless power of sorcery, as without effort, Peresor murdered each and every swordsman arrayed against him.

Then did Druuk accept the counsel of Peresor, and made him chief over all his council.

And so it began, their sinister and evil plot. Druuk and Peresor plotted it together, how they might destroy the temple in Shi-Raq, destroy it forever, and then master its Great Orb. But they would employ this great orb, not as a force for good, not for the purpose for which the angels had given it unto men, but rather for a different purpose altogether--- as a power unto evil.

Druuk was more than eager to launch this war, to invade as quickly as possible, and with all his remaining armies. He would have quickly launched a second invasion into the Lands of Demi-men.

But centuries of living had taught Peresor more patience than that, and also more subtlety and guile. They would indeed attack, he assured Druuk. “But not with legions,” he cautioned, “at least not at first.”

Peresor taught the king, taught him in the wiles and intricacies of evil, not merely of earthly evil, but of a darker and more foul evil than the earth could contain. “We must take a lesser orb,” he urged. “Our first aim shall not be the Great Orb itself--- not at first--- but rather one of its minor siblings, must be our present aim. For a lesser orb is required, so that from it, we might gain the power to seize--- and then to master!--- the Great Orb of Power itself. For such is the unspeakable power of a great orb, that unless carefully mastered, it could bring us ruin instead of victory.”

It was no easy task to restrain Druuk from action, from action immediate and brutal, action devoid of any art or delicacy. But Peresor was persuasive, and in the end, Druuk heeded the sorceror’s evil counsel.

"Very well,” Druuk acceded. “But where," he asked, "is there such a lesser orb to be found? For none of my sorcerors or potionists have ever found, in my kingdom, an orb which survived, so much as a mere touch of their hand. They have destroyed them all. Where, then, can we obtain such a thing?"

Peresor had a ready answer. "There is one,” he said. “There is a lesser orb available to us. It is enshrined in a small fishing village by the sea. But as you say, it is not in your own kingdom. Better yet, it is to be found in the land where the priests rule. The name of the village is Har-Keem."

Chapter 7

The Metalsmith, the Warrior, and the Demonwitch

Normally placid Har-Keem had become disquieted. First, there had been the nearly tragic circumstance connected with the marooned pirate, and soon after, the supposed calling of one of their own to the priesthood. None in Har-Keem was without an uncharacteristic sense of excitement.

But for Kl'aarn, the only excitement he noticed was his betrothal to Miril. It had transformed him almost overnight from the last of boyhood into the first of manhood. For never had he thought to acquire so desirable a bride as Miril. Always he had noticed her, and always before he had secretly found her attractive. But never before had he appreciated her beauty and charm as now he did, as now he dared.

Suddenly, the importance of his lessons was magnified, as the prospect of supporting a family of his own was a soon-to-be reality. For the first time, Kl'aarn studied the skills of the merchant with adult urgency.

Amid all this, Kl'aarn had all but forgotten Shalar.

Things had changed for the metalsmith, too. For one, Sholok treated his son differently than he had before. He no longer beat him as he always had, no longer cursed or humiliated him in public. Some people said he even felt some fear, yes fear. For Shalar was not only strong, but also, he had proved that he could kill.

When Veelos had gone away to Shi-Raq, Shalar had been spared one embarrassment. For, no one but his father and Veelos's had known anything about the talks between them, the negotiations, such as always preceded any betrothal. No one had known, and no one would, for one did not make public such matters until an actual dowry had been placed and accepted.

But although this left Shalar eligible once more, a bachelor, able to seek and take a wife, he did not escape entirely without embarrassment. For, as time went by, there was no sign of interest from the fathers of other daughters. It became an awkward thing to explain, then, that no suitable bride was found in Har-Keem for Shalar. No one had seemed eager, not even willing, to present his daughter to the family. And without a suitable dowry to purchase a woman from some other village, Shalar was without immediate prospect for a wife.

For his own part, however, Shalar did not seem embarrassed over this; indeed, he seemed unconcerned.

But if Kl'aarn was paying little heed to Shalar, at least he observed that Shalar was keeping his part of the pact they had made. Shalar had ceased to bully Kl'aarn. Theirs was hardly a friendship, but at least they could pass in the sandy lanes of Har-Keem without Kl'aarn having to brace himself for yet another brutal pounding. So, despite any actual camaraderie, Kl'aarn was pleased with the arrangement just as it was.

This being the case, Kl'aarn went one day to Shalar's smithy on an errand, seeking Shalar's skill at the forge.

Now the smithy was near the top of a small hill overlooking Har-Keem. Normally, Sholok's family could spot anyone who approached. But this day, Shalar was busy at the forge, his mother was in the village, and his father was abed ill. And so Kl'aarn innocently caught Shalar unawares.

But although Kl'aarn was innocent, Shalar was certainly not. His back to the entrance of the workshed, the young metalsmith was busily melting some silver coins. He was thoroughly engrossed in his secret task.

For a moment, Kl'aarn could not believe what he was seeing. Without thinking, he blurted out, "Shalar! How did you come by so much silver?"

Shalar spun about so quickly that he nearly had a catastrophe with the searing hot molten metal. The next thing Kl'aarn knew, the other had a hammer in his hand. Shalar was holding it, not the way one holds a tool, but rather as one wields a weapon. His eyes fixed fiercely on Kl'aarn, the metalsmith stepped menacingly forward.

Kl'aarn froze in fear. "My god, Shalar," he said hoarsely, then swallowing hard. "Are you going to kill me?"

Shalar halted. He glanced downward at his hand, as if surprised to see the hammer there. Then he glared at Kl'aarn. "What was the idea of sneaking up on me like that? Who sent you? Who put you up to this?"

"What are you talking about?" Kl'aarn replied with a slight tremor. "I just came to check on the sea chest you're making for my father. It's been over a week now."

Shalar struggled to compose himself. He let drop the hammer. "You've caught me red-handed, damn you. Now what?"

For a moment Kl'aarn was too perplexed to answer. But he quickly discerned the truth of it. He shook his head in dismay. "All the thievery these past months. Was it you?"

"Don't play the fool," Shalar answered. "Where else would I get silver?"

A coldness gripped Kl'aarn. "If the elders ever discover this---"

"Quit sputtering around," Shalar said. "The only way anyone will know is if you tell them. Well hell, I can't stop you. Even if I thought to kill you, what would be the use? I couldn't explain your death. No one would believe anything I said. They never do anyway. So tell me, merchant. What's it to be with you? What role will you play in this: the noble citizen, or the thief's accomplice?"

For a moment, Kl'aarn hesitated. He had a duty to report what he had seen. But in so doing, he would certainly condemn Shalar to a hideous punishment. Unused to such quandary, Kl'aarn hesitated to answer. Then, accepting the obvious, he said, "Damn you, Shalar. I can't let them cut off your hands. No, I won't tell what I saw. But why, Shalar? How could you betray your village?"

Shalar shrugged. "Maybe I was assembling a dowry."

Kl'aarn's perplexity was growing with each exchange of words between them. "Dowry? Are you betrothed?"

Shalar surprised them both with a laugh. It seemed out of place. "Betrothed?" he sneered. "I was only being sarcastic about the dowry, Kl'aarn. I'm not the sort to marry and settle down, in case you've never figured that out. Look, I'll show you what I'm up to."

But Kl'aarn stepped back. "No. Don't show me. I don't want to know. Shalar, you've got to return this silver to its owners."

"Owner," Shalar corrected. "I stole it all from Koto. Yeah, old senile Koto. He doesn't even miss it, Kl'aarn. He's had it buried in his garden for so many years he's forgotten he had it. As for whoever has been stealing whatever else, it wasn't me."

"Then you have to give it back to Koto," Kl'aarn said. "However senile he's become, he's entitled to the fruit of his own labor."

Shalar sighed. "Return it? That would be more dangerous than the stealing, Kl'aarn. Old Koto's as mad as he is senile. He would kill me for sure. What's done is done, Kl'aarn."

Kl'aarn was exasperated. "We have a pact, you and I. You're abusing it. Now I want an oath from you, Shalar. Swear that if I keep silent on this, you'll never steal again. Swear it."

Shalar nodded. "If that will soothe your conscience, then I swear it."

"On your life, Shalar."

"I swore it," Shalar spoke as one insulted. "Did I ever break an oath?"

Kl'aarn exhaled nervously. "Alright. Now tell me. How are you going to spend this silver? Everyone will know you stole it."

Shalar chuckled. "That's the best part. I'm not going to spend it. That's what I wanted to show you. Come look."

With his curiosity piqued, Kl'aarn stepped closer to the forge. As he did, Shalar reached into what was, it became obvious, a secret compartment, hidden behind a rafter of the shed. From there, with great care, almost with reverence, Shalar withdrew from concealment an item worth more than the purloined silver coins, over which Kl'aarn had become so incensed. Proudly, Shalar held up the bronze object which he so prized.

"Why, that's a sword!" Kl'aarn said with awe. "A warrior's sword--- a weapon of battle. I've never seen such a thing. Did you make it yourself?"

Shalar shook his head. "It will be a long time before I can craft a blade this finely balanced. No, I can't make such a beautiful thing, not yet anyway. No, I got it from a mead peddler. Don't ask me how. And don't tell anyone I have it. If my father finds out---," Shalar's voice became quieter, "he'd quickly guess what I've been plotting."

"Plotting?" Kl'aarn asked.

"Yes, plotting. To run away. I'm tired of this kind of life, Kl'aarn. And I'm not wasting my years searing soot ever deeper into my pores at this forge. There is a big world beyond the edge of Har-Keem, a world with lots of good things in it. And I mean to have my share of them: wine, women, song, and adventure. And this sword is the way to do it. The mead peddler told me. A fellow like me, with a sword like this, can easily find work as an armed escort. Every caravan needs them. Your father hires them, doesn't he? Well, that's the life for me."

But Kl'aarn shook his head. "My father used to hire them, Shalar, before I was born. He doesn't anymore. These warrior escorts are not the adventurous sort you imagine them to be. They are little better than the thieves they fight against. In fact, most of them are thieves themselves. My father has lost much to the very men he hired to protect his merchandise."

"I won't be like them," Shalar swore. "Sure I'm a thief now. I admit it. I stole Koto's silver and I shouldn't have. But even so, I had a reason for it. See? I'm using the silver to plate the hilt of this sword. Now that may seem an odd thing to do, but silver is good luck. Does it not symbolize strength and purity? Well, a man like me will need all the luck he can get. Go ahead, laugh. But some day you will hear tales of a warrior with a silver-hilted sword. It will be my sign and symbol. Men will know my name, and they will seek me out to lead their caravans through bandit country. All Wirik will know me, Kl'aarn. I have great dreams to fulfill, great dreams."

Kl'aarn hardly knew how to answer. Finally, he said, "I thought I was the dreamer, not you. But if you've set your mind on this, well, I just pray it turns out well for you."

At last, Shalar seemed at ease. Telling someone had lifted his burden. Suddenly, he said, "You know, Kl'aarn, this will sound queer to you, but think on it. You'd be just the sort to accompany me."

Kl'aarn laughed. "I couldn't fight my own shadow."

"Maybe not," Shalar said. "But you've got a good head on your shoulders. That counts for much. You've a good sense for business, for sensing who can be trusted, and when a deal is good or bad. And you've got a heart that doesn't melt in the face of danger. The two of us will be one hell of a team, Kl'aarn."

But Kl'aarn answered, "I'm betrothed to the woman of my dreams, Shalar. Not all the good things in the world can turn me from her."

"Bullshit," Shalar said. "Women are plentiful. A man gets tired of just one. Trust me. A year from now you'll have had your fill of Miril."

"I consider that an insult," Kl'aarn said.

"Alright, alright," Shalar said. "I take it back. But remember me. And if you ever find that she's put a ring through your nose, I'll be easy to find."

* * * * *

Nearly a year had passed since Veelos had left Har-Keem. During all that time, Miril had sent letters. For Kl'aarn had taught Miril how to write. But Miril had received no reply, none at all. Each day she awoke hoping for, expecting, a scroll to arrive from Shi-Raq, a scroll bearing the temple seal. And each evening, she lay down to sleep, disappointed and concerned, for no such scroll had appeared.

"Something is terribly wrong," Miril complained. It was considered proper, at this point in their courtship, for the two of them to be together and converse. (But of course, any more intimacy than that was out of the question, until after marriage.) "Veelos would not just ignore me," she told Kl'aarn. "If all were well with her, she would make sure to send letters to me. I know she would. She knows how I worry."

Kl'aarn tried to ease Miril's fears. "There are lots of reasons why we've not heard from Veelos," he said. "To begin with, she's cloistered. They're very strict in the temple, I've heard. Even if they give her time to write, she would be too exhausted. All that studying, day and night. And the chores. And finally, even if she has sent letters, they might never arrive. You've heard the visiting merchants--- the seas are becoming more and more plagued with pirates. Why, even the hills of Wirik are home to roving bandits. Be assured, Miril. Veelos is safer than we are."

But Miril was by no means relieved. "You're so logical," she said to Kl'aarn. "But there is no logic in this. A man cannot see what a woman can see. The day that pirate set upon us, Kl'aarn, that day was the beginning of change for us. Veelos and I, you, even Shalar--- we all changed that day. None of us has been the same since. Up until then, Veelos and I were so close, Kl'aarn, so very, very close. Why, we even had the same dreams at night! We hardly needed speech to know what the other was thinking. Often we could answer a question before it was asked, could feel each others' pains, warn of dangers to come. No, never did I know how close we truly were to each other, not until after Veelos was gone. Oh, but how I know it now, this sorrowful heart of mine.

"But here is the strange part, Kl'aarn: even before Veelos left Har-Keem, even before, already I felt that there had come something between us. It was so strange, I--- I dismissed it, at the time, as nothing, thinking that matters would just return to normal of themselves. But they never did. And now, now I know. I should have paid it more attention."

Kl'aarn tried to understand, but could not. "All I can say," he offered, "is that in a few days we'll celebrate our wedding. After that, we'll arrange a trip together to Shi-Raq, just as I promised. Once we've had a visit with Veelos, you'll feel much better."

* * * * *

On the night before his final wedding vows were to be taken, Kl'aarn was awakened from his sleep by Shalar.

He had come to the window of Kl'aarn's room, causing Kl'aarn to reach in fright for a dagger he kept beneath his sleeping mat on the floor. Upon recognizing that the shadowy intruder was Shalar, Kl'aarn became indignant. "What mischief are you up to now?" he demanded. "Of all nights!"

Shalar seemed more afraid than Kl'aarn. "Ssh! Quietly!" he urged. "I'm in big trouble, Kl'aarn. You're the only one I can turn to for help."

"You have lots of friends," Kl'aarn replied with irritation in his voice.

"None that I can trust but you," he whispered hoarsely. "Listen. Koto is on to me. He's been digging about in his garden, looking for his silver, and making threats about me if he can't find it. So I decided to return some of it. I have some left over," he explained. "But in doing so, I toppled over that idol he worships in his garden. Help me right the statue, Kl'aarn, or else he will accuse me of trying to steal the silver he hoards beneath it."

Kl'aarn was in no mood for this. "Damn, Shalar. That's not even a good lie. Admit it. You were trying to rob the old man, again, and now you want me to save your skin. On the night before my wedding!"

"This is no time for a trial," Shalar pleaded. "We share an oath of friendship, don't we? And Koto is mad enough to murder me, isn't he? Isn't that all that counts? You've got to help me, Kl'aarn. If the tables were turned and you needed help, would I abandon you?"

Kl'aarn sat up. "Well, I won't get any more sleep until we right that statue. But I'll get my pound of flesh from you over this, if anything goes wrong. Friendships like this I can do without."

"You won't regret it, I swear," Shalar promised.

Together, the two boys sneaked through the night shadows, toward Koto's hut. Now Koto had gone almost totally deaf in the past year, so that he would not likely hear them. But he was also slightly mad, and if provoked would become truly dangerous. And he had a crossbow.

Koto's garden was surrounded, and protected by, a tall fence, made of vertical poles, each sharpened at the top, like so many spears. When Kl'aarn looked upward at it, he hesitated. "How do we get over?" he asked.

"Here," Shalar said kneeling and forming a stirrup with his hands. "Step."

Kl'aarn did, and before he knew what was happening, Shalar had lifted him to the top of the fence. By reflex and momentum, Kl'aarn threw one leg over the fence. Just as he did, he felt Shalar let go of him. For one precarious second, Kl'aarn struggled to maintain his balance without becoming impaled on the spikes.

"Come back down! Hurry!" Shalar urged.

Almost slipping, Kl'aarn managed to retrace his path, and fell clumsily to the sandy ground beside Shalar. "Damn you!" he cursed. "Getting me killed on my wedding eve is bad enough. But you almost castrated me."

"Quiet!" Shalar whispered.

At first, Kl'aarn feared that Koto might have awakened, and have stepped from his hut with his crossbow. But Shalar was not behaving as if afraid. Instead, he had the look of a night animal searching the shadows.

"What is it?" Kl'aarn asked. He kept his voice muffled.

Carefully, Shalar pointed in the direction of the pier. They were not far from it.

In the dark of night, Kl'aarn made out a shadow at the dock, which fishermen used by day, to unload their catch. There, almost indiscernible, was the silhouette of a ship. There was neither light nor sound from it, surely a sign of something wrong.

Kl'aarn's first thought was that a pirated derelict had drifted in. Sometimes the currents would bring in the carcass of an unfortunate merchant ship. On rare occasion, a survivor or two would still be aboard.

But from a distance, it was difficult to see. The two boys went closer, quietly, to investigate.

Unfortunately, they were not quiet enough. As they stepped onto the narrow plankway connecting the shore to the pier, a volley of arrows whipped past them in a staccato of rapid hisses. Astonished at this, the two boys quickly hid in the shadow of a trestle.

From the end of the pier came voices speaking in a dialect never before heard in Har-Keem. "Did we get them?"

"Can't see. Nothing moving. No sound. Not running away."

"Dead then. Form up the men."

"They are pirates!" Shalar whispered. "We've got to do something fast." Then, thinking quickly, Shalar commanded Kl'aarn, "Run quietly back to the village and warn them. I'll stand against them on this plankway, and hold them off with this spearhook, for as long as I can."

But Kl'aarn whispered in reply, "No. You run back. You'll have to sound the alarm. But not until you reach the village. The first sound you make will bring more arrows. Get well inside the village before you call out. I'll stay here, and hold them off for as long as I can. Give me the spearhook."

"Don't be a fool," Shalar answered. "You can't hold them off. Now do as I say, and run for it."

Kl'aarn answered, "I can't, Shalar. I can't even walk well. I'm arrowshot."

Shalar glanced down at Kl'aarn's leg. An arrow had lodged in the thigh; both ends of the wooden shaft were fully exposed. Clearly, Kl'aarn was not going anywhere.

"Damn," Shalar cursed. Then, "Alright. There's no choice. You'll have to try to bottle them up while I get help. Look, you can do it. If anyone can, I know it's you. What do you say?"

"One thing," Kl'aarn answered. "See that Miril escapes into the forest. Swear it."

Shalar swore it. Then, as if placing a gift into a coffin, he pressed the spearhook into Kl'aarn's hand, and bade him final farewell.

* * * * *

Running low and swiftly, Shalar made no sound until he reached the village. He hoped that perhaps the pirates might delay, and that Kl'aarn might yet be spared. When he reached the alarm bell, Shalar sounded it, and raised a loud cry. "Pirates!" he shouted. "Fight for your lives!"

The village came awake. Men stumbled from their cottages and huts into the darkness. They grabbed shovels and picks, axes and hoes, whatever makeshift weapon was at hand. In confusion, they shouted orders at each other. Women gathered up their children and, screaming and crying in terror, began to run for the forest.

"They're at the pier!" Shalar shouted. "A shipload of pirates at the pier!"

Then, remembering his vow of moments before, Shalar made for Miril's house. If he could not save Kl'aarn, he could at least keep his promise to see to Miril's safety.

But as Shalar ran toward her house, he met Miril on the street, for the girl was already running in her nightclothes toward the pier.

Shalar seized her, and demanded, "Where do you think you're going? Get to the forest!"

"Let go of me!" Miril cursed him, and struggled to unloose his grip from her arms. "Kl'aarn's been hurt. He'll be killed. I've got to get to him! Let go!"

"What are you talking about?" Shalar replied, spinning her about. "Kl'aarn's not hurt. He sent me to get you. He's in the forest, waiting for you. Now hurry, or you'll only get yourself killed."

But Miril screamed at him. "You're lying, Shalar. Kl'aarn's at the pier. He can't run away. His leg has an awful wound! He told you to get me to safety, but he's badly hurt. Now let me attend him!"

Shalar was astonished. It was almost as if Miril had seen the entire event on the plankway. "Alright," he admitted. "I lied. Kl'aarn is on the pier, and he is hurt. But how in hell did you---?"

"I dreamed it," Miril answered.

"Alright, alright," Shalar said. "But Kl'aarn made me swear that I would get you to safety. And until I do that, I can't go back to help him. Do you understand? Now how long will we argue about it? You can't win, you know."

After one more desperate attempt to throw off Shalar's iron grip, Miril relented. "Very well," she breathed in exhaustion. "You're right. I'll only make it worse. Then you must vow to me, also, Shalar. Bring me Kl'aarn. Swear it."

"Of course I swear it," he said.

"On your life, Shalar."

"On my life. Now hurry. To the forest!"

Miril hesitated. "Don't fail me, Shalar."

"Run!"

So Miril finally relented, and ran with the other women and children into the forest. There she hid beneath a thick bush.

* * * * *

Shalar ran first to his smithy, and ensured that his parents were not still there. Then, he retrieved his sword, and made straight for the pier. There seemed little chance that he could save Kl'aarn. But there are some sorts of promise that even one such as Shalar would honor. And this was one such.

But by this time, the battle was all but decided. For, unknown to Shalar, or any of the peasants, the pirates were not pirates at all, but a disciplined company of professional soldiers. Against them, the villagers and fishermen were no match.

Shalar did not consider this. He knew nothing of battles, or formations, or strategies. He knew only to fight. Raising aloft his sword, he charged straight toward the invaders.

The martial officer was supervising the cutting down of the last of the village men, those who had tried to oppose him with their pitiful tools. It was too easy. But even so, the officer was careful to maintain discipline, keeping his swordsmen aligned abreast, just so, at precisely arm's length, with the spear carriers one step behind them, so that they could jab between the swordsmen at any peasants who did not fall before the slashing swords. And behind these, the archers felled those who retreated toward the forest.

All was going predictably, until the martial spotted a peculiar sight. In the firelit night, amid blazing buildings set afire, a young boy ran straight toward them. He was wielding a warrior's sword. That he had no military training whatsoever with such a professional implement of war was obvious. As to how he had come by such a weapon, the soldiers could not guess.

"Gilereab," the martial called out to his corporal of archers. "Drop him."

Gilereab notched an arrow, and standing, took careful aim. The target did nothing to evade, but made straight for him.

Suddenly the arrow sprang, and almost before the bowstring could hum its death song, the arrow buried itself deep into Shalar's chest.

The metalsmith's son stopped as if hitting a brick wall. His upraised arm went limp, and the silver-hilted sword fell from his grasp. Then, like a tree, the metalsmith toppled backward, crashing into the sandy soil. His breath went out of him.

Gilereab laughed derisively. "So shall die all the heroes of this land."

* * * * *

Peresor was among the warriors, and he gave but one command. "Find her. Kill her."

The martial officer, who up until then had given all the orders, resented this challenge to his authority. "Her?" he asked.

"You know of whom I speak," the sorceror replied.

"Of course I do," the swordsman said. "But are we not sent for two? Why, then, do you ask for only one?"

Peresor sighed. One could not tell from the sorceror's tone whether he felt disappointment, impatience, or any other emotion at all. "Sometimes I forget that mortals cannot--- very well. Only one of the two girls is here. The other has fled long since. No matter. She will fall to our swords when we invade the temple of the priests. As for this night, one of the girls yet abides nearby. Find her. Kill her. But as for the others, do not kill them, except as you must. Instead, carry whomever has survived to our supply ship. It will serve as our slave carrier."

"Slaves," the martial intoned. "We have no need of slaves from this distant land. We can get them much more cheaply by raiding our outlying provinces."

Before, Peresor's voice had shown no emotion. Nor did it this time. Yet despite that, a chill rage seemed heavy in the air, dangerous with sinister hatred, as the sorceror spoke. "The king always has need of a more entertaining gladiator for his arena, and always an appetite for a more exotic concubine to grace his bed."

The swordsman snorted. "It was not in my orders."

Peresor turned to face his adversary much as a gladiator might turn to size up a foe newly emerged from the dungeon. "It has become necessary," he explained coldly, "to make tonight's slaughter appear as if pirates had done all this. And since there is nothing worthwhile here for plunder, then slaves shall be their presumed booty."

Even now the martial officer was openly displeased. "Why all this skulking about and disguising our work? We are an elite company of the king's warriors. Why should we make our work seem to be that of mere brigands?"

This time there was no mistaking the sinister authority with which the sorceror spoke. "Then consider this, brave warrior. The temple priests in Shi-Raq are not fools. They will learn of this massacre. And they will learn that one of their dreaded orbs has vanished from their hand. What do you suppose they will think, when they learn this? If they believe it to be but the work of mere pirates, then they will rejoice, for among cutthroat pirates, there is none with the delicacy or finesse to secure for himself any orb. Such brutes would foul grasp it, and in the blink of an eye, the treasure would cease to exist. These jewels are not of mere stuff, but as much made of thought as of anything, destroyed by the merest touch of unskilled evil. Now, if Har-Keem lies desolate to the rising sun, all its inhabitants dead, then what gain? What gain? This shall be the question the temple priests will ask. What was gained for so much work? By whom? By whom indeed? For even pirates do not take all this trouble to gain nothing. And when temple priests ask, well it is within their power to gain an answer, and the correct answer, none other. Tell me, martial. What will the priests of the Great Orb, the mighty orb, do if they suspect that their lesser orb has fallen into capable hands? If they believe for a moment that Druuk possesses even the least of one of their orbs, then they will work out the truth of the matter. They will know of a certainty what we plan to do, to seize their greater orb. And knowing that, they will most assuredly turn their mighty Orb against ourselves. We could not survive such wrath as they would hurl against us. So therefore, warrior, what will you? To rebel against me?"

So the soldiers did as Peresor had commanded them. With none in the village left alive, save the dying, and while Har-Keem burned to the ground, the soldiers methodically began making their way into the hiding places of the forest, seeking whatever slaves they might find, and most especially, seeking Miril.

While they did this, Peresor stepped into the humble clay shrine at the center of the village. It was the only house remaining unburned this dark night. Peresor entered in. When he did, some of the soldiers heard a sound which they could not identify, nor did they wish to. For each of them, in his heart, knew well what it was, the sound of angels weeping.

* * * * *

By sunrise the soldiers, with their newly captured slaves, returned from the forest. The martial felt no small sense of fear as he presented the unwelcome news to Peresor. "We could not find her. Neither a priestess nor a witch is among our slaves, not, unless, she is well disguised among these women."

But if the warrior had feared that Peresor might become wrathful, his fears were quickly allayed. The sorceror seemed weary, judging by his stance (for none cared to look upon his face, well hooded it was). Yet to the warrior, the evil man seemed almost elated, though even in elation subdued, as if by rigor of death. He held close to himself a small chest, specially crafted and encased in gold foil, gold and other metals not known to mortals. Within that beautiful prison was encased the lesser orb of Har-Keem.

"No," Peresor breathed. "Not among the slaves, she is not. She has eluded us, then. An omen! For even though not yet has she assumed the mantle of her calling, yet even now she has powers and potents already. This one has a destiny. We will not lightly dethrone her."

The warrior, who rarely paid any attention to matters other than of the sword, felt a slight tremor within himself. "Perhaps we should go back into the forest, and seek for her again, if indeed she poses a future danger to us."

Peresor seemed to scoff at the suggestion. "Not even I could find her after tonight's exhausting labors. Nor would we now wish to do so. For she is a leopard, wounded and cornered, defending her mate. She is to be feared. Yet, fearing her this night, we shall not fear her forever. For there are two girls of destiny, not one. And although both have powers of spirit beyond compare, yet we have this thought to comfort us. They are become enemies of each other at our doing. One shall slay the other. And then, the survivor wounded, her we shall impale with the demon's claw."

Within the hour, the invaders were departing once more for the land of King Druuk. They sailed away in two ships: a warship bearing the victors, and a cargo vessel, now become a slaver, bearing the doomed.

* * * * *

Miril had hidden in silent terror all night beneath a thick, strong bush, never questioning how any bush, however thick, could have saved her from the evil which surrounded her. Indeed, throughout that long, black night, she had been tormented by the sounds of murder and rape all about her. Each moment, she had expected to be discovered, defiled, and brutally killed. Somehow, though, she had escaped, and the brutal men from the sea had, at long last, departed.

At first, Miril hoped that, in their departure, she might find some faint cause over which to rejoice. She hoped for someone with whom to celebrate unexpected survival. But when, by light of the morning sun, she could finally see, Miril counted her survival not as blessing but as a curse, a fate more cruel than merciless death.

For Har-Keem was no more. Only ashes and corpses remained of it.

For the next few minutes, Miril was barely aware that she was walking through ruins, wandering as if in a dream between ashen mounds which of so recent had been homes, and stepping, staggering about, among corpses which only hours before had been people she had known, and had loved.

It was in the depth of her grief, in the pit of sorrow from which not all emerge alive, it was there that Miril gradually became aware of Kl'aarn's scent. Nor was it any physical sense which told her, but told her with no room for doubt, that Kl'aarn was yet alive. It began when she could feel the pain of an arrow in her thigh, although she herself was untouched. Somehow, she knew. The pain, real but not her own, not a wound of her flesh but of her soul, told her of a certainty. It was Kl'aarn's pain she felt. Kl'aarn was in physical agony. This made Miril weep with grief. And yet in his pain she found cause to rejoice after all, after all that had befallen her. Because if Kl'aarn were in pain, then he was surely alive.

Desperately hoping against hope, doubting her own certainty, Miril ran toward the pier. What led her there she knew not, but knew that there, had Kl'aarn suffered the wound which now tormented his flesh.

Death was all about her. The rustic cottages and huts which once had been the homes in which she had so often visited, these, were now but heaps of rubble. Dead bodies littered the sandy street which so often she had trod. People whom once she had greeted each day were now lifeless, lying discarded amid the ruins of their life's work.

But Miril paid them no heed. Her eyes were focused on the distant pier, behind which the sun was rising, and which was blinding her to any detail. She stepped past the clay dome, which was the shrine in which she had so frequently prayed. She saw it not, but only the pier. She stepped past the form of once proud Shalar, lying on his back, with an arrow in his chest. Beside him lay a sword, the hilt of which was plated in stolen silver. Miril paid him no heed.

Finally, having completed her journey through the smoldering wreckage of her life, through the shattered remains of her dreams, Miril at last reached the plankway which led to the pier, the plankway on which Kl'aarn had made his valiant but futile stand against the barbarians who had murdered Har-Keem. "Please, God," she prayed. "Please let me find him alive. Please!"

There, on that narrow plankway, was a dead man.

Miril gasped, not daring to look, unable to endure seeing death in the eyes of her beloved. But neither could she turn away. A brief but fierce struggle within Miril subsided, and when it did, she gazed into the eyes of death.

He was a foreigner, one of the invaders, somehow left behind where his body had fallen into a cleft of the pier, unnoticed in the dark and hasty retreat. Miril peered deeply into his dead eyes. Some powerful sense told her, that, the last sight those eyes had ever seen, the last earthly sight, had been the sight of Kl'aarn with a spearhook, leaping unexpected from behind the trestle. A moment later, and those eyes had seen their last of this world.

Desperately, Miril cast about to search where Kl'aarn himself might be. She searched every possible place of concealment, and searched twice. But he was not on the pier.

Afraid now, fearing the worst, Miril found that her gaze was drawn sea-ward. First, she looked downward upon the waves lapping the shore. A dead man lay there, too. Old man Koto.

Then as if by some sudden, violent force, Miril lifted her gaze sharply to the horizon. Her eyes focused instantly.

There, in the distance, almost as far away as the rising sun, two ships were barely visible. Even so, Miril needed not see them clearly, to know the terrible truth they professed. One of them was a galley of warriors--- not of pirates, but of trained and disciplined men of war. Their ruse could not deceive her, not even at so great a distance. The other vessel, a slave ship, carried a cargo of suffering and despair. It was that one which bore her beloved Kl'aarn.

Miril could perceive his breath.

"Kl'aarn!" Miril cried out so loudly she thought surely to be heard. But the ships could no more be turned back by her outcry than could the tide be turned by mere wishing. Of that there could be no doubt. Miril had never felt such desperation in all her short life. She thought to plunge herself into the sea and to swim after him. It mattered not to Miril whether by doing so she would live or die, but it mattered only that she could narrow the distance, which relentlessly and mercilessly increased between herself and the object of her love. For it was that distance which had become more painful even than death.

Miril's next thought was of the shrine.

In recent days she had prayed there often. And each time, she had felt the near presence, the spiritual presence, of the Holy Warrior she had come to know as Tarok. Now, now in this dark and desperate hour, Miril felt his urgent summons. He was calling to her, urging her toward the shrine. From the shrine he beckoned, and to the shrine Miril fled on feet made swift by sorrowful hope.

Stepping once again past the corpses with familiar faces, stumbling, running, and stumbling again, Miril made her way along the sandy stretches which led to the center of Har-Keem's remains. Soon, she found herself at the small entranceway. For just a moment, for but a mere instant, she felt fear, the deep down trembling, which always accompanies the near presence of the supernatural. For surely, Tarok's presence was so powerful as to be clearly felt, even from outside the small shrine. Miril feared. But desperation was greater within Miril than all her fear. Quickly gathering her courage, Miril plunged forward into the holy place.

Within the small clay dome she beheld him.

Tarok stood there, as if in the flesh. Just as he had once appeared in life, so now he was visible to Miril. Tall, muscular and thickly bearded, Tarok stood before the terrified young girl. His ancient leather armor was studded with bronze, and his sword was as heavy as any battle-axe.

Immediately, Miril fell to her hands and knees. Then, bowing her head to the floor, she wept, "O Mighty Tarok! May God bless the angels who carried you to this place. Forgive me, Holy Warrior, forgive me that I have nothing to offer you, nothing, not even so small a thing as a proper greeting. But you see before you my woe and my unspeakable grief. I beg you, Mighty Tarok, I implore you---! Intervene for me, rescue my husband, and avenge our dead families."

Tarok did not hesitate to answer. "Indeed," he said. "I am sent by the angels of God Most High, sent to you by their compassion, and by their divinely given wisdom."

"Oh, yes!" Miril wept. "I know that, Great Warrior. I only fear that you will find me unworthy, and that you will turn away from granting what I ask. Forgive me if I beg haste. But please, the ships are bearing him away, and I so fervently wish him in my arms! Please hasten him to me. Please!"

"Alas," Tarok said. His voice was strong and yet compassionate. But next he spoke words which Miril found painful to hear. "Alas! I have no power to wield earthly force anymore. That power, the power of the living, I squandered by my sin, and was slain from mortal life. But despair not, Miril. For another power do I yet have. It is greater even than that for which you ask. For mine is the power to reveal to you the path which God has set before you."

In response, only dimly comprehending, and unwilling to give up hope, Miril tried to bow even lower than she already had. "I beg you, Tarok, intervene for me. You, who led the armies of the priests against the legions of Hell, you can spare me from this unendurable torment that has befallen me. Rescue my Kl'aarn and return him to me. If nothing else, do for me at least that much, and in return I will scrub temple floors all the days of my life."

Tarok was deeply moved by Miril's grief. But he was also wise beyond earthly wisdom. "Only follow the path laid before you," he commanded, "and set no conditions. Your obedience to God will bring you more happiness than ever I could win for you in battle. As for Kl'aarn--- his path is at end, Miril. This day--- he will rest with his ancestors."

"No!" Miril cried out, lifting up her tearful gaze and stretching out her arms as a very small child would to its father. "No! Please! He must not die. I beg you. I cannot bear to live without him."

"It is God's will for him," Tarok replied. "No, this cannot be easy, not easy at all. So I will remain with you in your grieving. But neither can it be shunned. If you love him---"

But Miril persisted in pleading for Kl'aarn's life. "What would you ask of me?" she cried. "Name it, and give me back the one who is taken from me. Just name it, and I will suffer it for his sake. Anything. Anything at all!"

But Tarok answered in this way: "I am sent to you for a purpose. For you are a woman born to destiny. I am commanded to reveal to you, that a great evil has arisen in your world, an evil more sinister than the one which has destroyed all you hold dear. For the demon would do this much, and more, to all the world, and to all the worlds beyond this one. Its demonwitch is soon to arise," he said. "And only the Priestess of Prophecy can defeat her. You must choose wisely, Miril. This is the time of your choosing. I have tried to bring you gently to this moment for many weeks now. You closed the thoughts from your mind with which I implored you, as now you implore me. But delay is no longer possible, Miril. It is time. You must choose your path."

For long moments, Miril was silent. Her deep breathing began to relax, and her weeping subsided. Slowly, even her tears began to dry. Finally, gingerly, Miril brought herself to her feet. She stood wavering for a time, but soon even her wavering was conquered by a reserve of strength, by an ability from deep within herself to stand fast, to stand steadily despite all that had swiftly and suddenly fallen upon her.

Miril stood facing Tarok. She spoke again. But this time, her voice was not that of a weeping child. It was cold. "Is that your final word to me?" she asked. Her eyes burned with a quiet, distant rage. "Have I no hope, no hope at all of melting your heart? Has all my weeping been for nothing? Has my anguish been answered with your indifference?"

Tarok answered. "No, no. I am not at all indifferent to your pain. On the contrary! Well do I know the---"

"Then give me justice!" Miril demanded. Her voice now was almost a shout. "Will empty words bring back my Kl'aarn for me? Kill his enemies, destroy his captors, and deliver my husband back to my embrace. Will you do that, Tarok? Will you?"

"Your anger is fierce, child. And I can understand that. But I sense a danger within you, Miril. Vent your anger, to be sure. But let it not go beyond mere anger."

Miril glared defiantly into Tarok's eyes. "I see. More empty words. If you detect in me some danger, then I also sense within you something, too, Tarok. But it is not danger, at least not a danger to any who have slaughtered Har-Keem. No. What I sense in you, Tarok, is weakness. Do you think that I have none other to pray to than you? It is not so, Tarok. If you will not give me Kl'aarn, then I will take him by other means," she said. Then, almost with a sneer, Miril continued, "Do you think I make an idle threat? I do not. For I know of a demon, Tarok, a demon recently awakened. Or did you think yours the only dreams which by night robbed my sleep? Its lair is not so far from here that I must rely solely upon you."

Tarok shook his head sadly. "Yes. I know of this demon, and well do I know that it has given you nightmares. Do not yield to it! Even to contemplate such a thought is a terrible sin. Turn from it now, Miril, while yet you can."

But Miril's reply was a snarl of rage. "You'll not have my service, Tarok. Nor shall you have my own Kl'aarn. Who are you, that asks so much, and offers so little? You say you have no power. And I see the truth of it within you. You squandered your power in the arms of Kattaroon.

"But I, Tarok," Miril continued, "I feel strength and destiny within me. I feel a power you have not known since Kattaroon slew you those many centuries ago. Mine is power stronger than even your own. Now yield to me, Tarok. Give what I ask while yet we can reconcile, you and I. Grant me this one favor, or else--- or else on that terrible day, I will surely destroy you."

Then it was that Tarok recognized who Miril really was. In all his might, yet he seemed to step backward in horror. Then he prophesied to Miril, saying, "You have made your choosing. So be it. I can see now what you have become, and become not by wile of the demon, but instead, by your own inclination. For God did not forsake you, nor did the angels abandon you. On the contrary, great power and great destiny were made yours. But how to employ those powers, upon which throne to rule, and with what destiny--- these choices were given unto you to make. And a terrible choosing you have made. You, whom even Valen the Elder thought good, you have taken up the war, not against demons, which you might easily have defeated, but instead, you will do battle against the angels of heaven. You have harkened not to them, but to a fallen spirit, an evil and malevolent creature of Hell. But you will not prevail, Miril. You will not. For weak though you deem my power to be, yet no force beneath heaven can withstand my sword when, on that terrible day, it will once more be unsheathed. When next we meet, Miril, then shall there be no more demon to protect you from my wrath." And with those words, Tarok vanished from Miril's sight.

She stood, then, trembling, alone, and suddenly unsure. After a few moments, Miril considered that she might have spoken too harshly, that her emotions might have clouded her reason. So she called after Tarok. "We can make a deal," she offered. "We can compromise. It need not be like this."

But Tarok had departed utterly from her. The shrine was more empty now than Miril had ever known it. Absent its orb, and with its spiritual guardian driven away, the shrine was no longer a consecrated place.

Miril's mind swirled as she considered her options. She might give in to Tarok without condition, as he had bidden her. She could repent and serve God. Surely, if she did that, a thousand angels would rejoice, and Tarok would instantly forgive her outburst.

But the thought fled before it could fully form. "I cannot bear to live without Kl'aarn," Miril confessed to herself. "I must find a way to have him, even if I must visit into evil to accomplish it. I make this plan: first, I will ask the demon to spare Kl'aarn's life, and then I will see what it does. If the demon cannot give me what I wish, then perhaps I will return here and serve God after all, even as Kl'aarn's widow. But first, I will do all that I can do, without God, to save Kl'aarn for myself. And who knows? Perhaps I will succeed."

And so saying, Miril left Har-Keem behind her, and set out for a place called Demon Point.

Chapter 8

The Demon in its Crypt

The raiders from the sea had taken no plunder but slaves. Nor had they bothered with livestock. Because of this, Miril was able to find a horse which had survived the pillage. It readily approached her, and soon Miril had bridled and mounted it. Then, knowing that she had little time, she whipped the beast mercilessly along the forest path which led from Har-Keem.

If Miril prodded the horse to cruel speed, perhaps it was because she was mindful that she was in a race for Kl'aarn's life. Not far to her left coursed the ships, just beyond a few forested hills. Their route would be long and slow, but they would not stop for rest. Nor dared Miril. Such was her speed that, should the horse have stumbled, it would have been death for both of them. But Miril was driven by a fear greater than death.

The sea lane would take the warriors through the perilous waters of Demon Point, which even the fiercest pirates avoided in fear. Miril knew. And at Demon Point she intended to be, when the ships would pass nearby. She intended to be waiting for them, waiting in ambush.

The horse which carried Miril served loyally in its purpose. After hours of tortured galloping, with not so much as a moment of rest, being prodded whenever it slowed its pace by even a single step, the mortally weary horse brought her painfully to the gate of Demon Point. There, the animal collapsed in death from exhaustion, having not even the strength remaining by which to draw breath. Without a backward glance at it, Miril stepped away from the worn out carcass, her gaze fixed in awe upon what lay before her.

The sun was almost directly overhead when at last Miril stood before the ancient metal gate which separated cursed ground from a world merely fallen. Yet, though it was noon, here a darkness dwelt.

On sailor's maps, Demon Point was drawn as a curved promontory of land, a half-crescent, which jutted claw-like into the sea. It was well feared by mariners, both the good ones and the evil. For at the foot of its towering cliffs were boulders and currents which had ravenously devoured many a ship. Any vessel which dared pass through the waters near Demon Point had to offer human sacrifice--- and many did, or else they perished. And perish, many had.

Stepping away from the dead horse, Miril approached the gates, and leaning against them, pushing as hard as she might, launched herself against the ancient, rusted portals. After a time, they finally gave way to her, but only reluctantly, groaning their complaint at this unwelcome disturbance in their ages-long slumber. As soon as there was a gap, just barely wide enough for her, Miril slid through it to the other side.

There, for just a brief moment, she paused. A cold chill gripped her, a chill not of the flesh, but of the soul. For the first time in centuries, human feet once more trod the shadowy realm of that ancient and mighty demon, that fierce creature of hell, which went by the name, Thorgar.

From Thorgar's gate there led a trail. It wound its way back and forth, almost snake-like in appearance, both enticing Miril to follow, and at the same time, warning her to flee its deadly venom. The winding trail ended abruptly, at an unnaturally darkened horizon, not terribly far away. Miril could see it. There, as if in a dream, a restless disturbed dream, stood a shrine, unmistakably demonic. Unmistakably. Its spires were as fangs, curved and pointed, all but snarling at the heaven. Its base was claw-like, gripping the earth with vengeful purchase.

The approach to that shrine was littered with bones, with the skulls and ribcages, of humans. Here and there a pelvis lay among them. From within these ancient bones, Miril sensed the monitions of lost souls shrieking beyond the mists of eternity. Turn back, they warned her, flee, run, escape from this snare, while yet you can. For also came we here, came seeking favors, and promising in return, our service to the demon. And now, see, indeed we serve it! But we serve forever, with our eternal agonies unrewarded. We have no favor from the one we serve, no pleasure to ease our suffering, no gain to replace our loss. For us, all is lost, lost forever and for naught! Just as it cheated us, so will it betray you, also. Turn away! Go back! Run!

Miril ignored them. She pressed onward, ever onward, toward the sinister abode, where aeons before, the demon Thorgar had betrayed its own worshippers. The echoes of that ancient treachery reverberated, even now, in the gloom and shadows of this earthly domain of unearthly evil. There had been an orgy, a frenzy of debauchery too wicked for words. Perversion and excrement had dominated it. The worshippers had devoted themselves, and their children, to Thorgar the demon. Thorgar! They had bowed down before it, and had given themselves over to it, sacrificing the children of abduction, and burning also their own young as well. And then--- then, at the very height of their malecstasy, the demon had suddenly and without warning cursed them all. In its own orgy of violence, it had seized them, tortured them, and one by one, killed each and all, every last one. Even now, it tormented forever their wicked souls.

For a brief instant, Miril wished to heed the dire urgings of the damned, wished to retrace her steps, and thought to depart this foul and murky world, into which she had thoughtlessly rushed.

But then another side of her, as if a part of her being, a part newly discovered in the hidden corners of Miril's soul, asserted its own voice amid the clamor of the shrieking, moaning damned. It sneered. It was as if it had sneered at the pleading, which rose up from the moldering bones of a vanished generation. Fools! it scorned them. Did they think Miril was merely one more among the many, who had ventured here unwarned? (Indeed! Miril thought to herself. Is that what they think? Did they not recognize her special power, her great destiny? If not, then the worse for them.)

Prompted by this newly discovered courage (it had to be courage, had it not?), and despite her misgivings, Miril ignored the warnings, dismissed all the feeble cautions. And instead, enlivened by her newfound bravery, even stepped upon the frail skulls, which stared helplessly upward from the dust. (Could a skull express terror? Miril wondered. What terror could contort even a dead skull?). She stepped forward, crushing them into dust, as she made her way ever further, ever deeper, into the demonic realm, into which she had so boldly intruded. Nor did Miril relent along her journey, but continued on, even as the ghosts of the demonic cult fled back into hell for fear of her.

At long last, Miril reached the end of the trail.

At the tip of the winding pathway, at the head of the serpentine road, Miril arrived at the chill, forbidding monument to evil, the cold, damp, demonic shrine, which encased the living corpse of the treacherous one. Merely to stand so near to it was to shiver, to shiver not only with cold, but with fear. Up close, its towering, looming reality was ever the more sinister, ever colder, and dreadfully more terrible than from a distance. Miril noticed the masonry blocks of which it was made. They were stones not of rock, but rather of bone, the skull bones of humans, and also of creatures frighteningly human-like, but not human, after all. Not quite.

There, Miril hesitated.

For an instant she felt, once more, a terrifying sense of danger. The tormented souls which had tried to warn her, she now knew, had been correct after all. It was indeed a trap. Miril wanted suddenly, desperately, to turn and run, to flee with the cold breath of death upon her back. She wanted more than anything to reach that iron gate, before the demon could swiftly pursue her as a lion leaps for the gazelle, before it could chase her down and catch her in its bloody claws.

This was what so many before her had done. They had panicked and run. But none had escaped. Not one had lived to tell of their final, futile terror. Only their bones now testified to Thorgar's bloodlust.

But the moment of sheer terror passed. At its worst, it had risen to a heart-pounding crescendo. But despite it, despite her terror, the peasant girl would not flee. Instead, Miril struggled to gather her courage. What, after all, she reasoned, was there to run to? A life without Kl'aarn? No, Miril decided. Whatever terror the demonic temple might hold for her, it could not be any worse than the depth of sorrow at the bottom of a life without Kl'aarn. What worse fate could there be than to live without him?

With renewed resolve, Miril pressed herself against the twin doors of bone, the doors which some demonic artisan had crafted from the remains of those sacrificed to Thorgar, the doors which sealed the malevolent being in its tomb. They were sealed more tightly than the iron gates which had barred her way onto the desecrated grounds. They would not open with mere effort, nor did they respond to her tearful entreaties. It was only when, in anger and frustration Miril cursed them--- and cursed them with a fearful curse--- only then did the doors yield to her determined assault.

For the first time in ages, those doors gave way. And then it was that Miril entered fully into the presence of pure evil.

But when those cadaverous doors came open, there rushed from within the crypt such a noxious odor that Miril was driven backward before it, driven into retreat as if by an army of freshly exhumed corpses, their stench unleashed after a century of entombment. Her empty stomach convulsed in a desperate effort to vomit. Every atom of her body was filled with dread: the natural forces living within her rebelled against the unnatural death within the tomb.

Miril vomited bile. She gasped for breath, struggling to overcome the rebellion of her viscera. Collapsing to her knees, she wondered if the palpable fumes of death would themselves consume her, leaving her unconscious, leaving her dead.

But even the revulsion of Miril's own body could not long delay her. Delay was the one thing she could not permit. For the ship which carried Kl'aarn prisoner would not be long in passing from her reach. Glaring angrily at the foul crypt, which lay open before her, Miril determined not to fail again.

Enslaving her own body to the will of her darkening soul, Miril stepped once again into the evil pit. Despite every effort of her body and soul to resist, she strode forward, if not boldly, then at least with grim and final determination. And then, with mere and few steps, Miril had done it. She was inside Thorgar's stronghold.

She could not see.

Even with the doors wide open, no light entered Thorgar's crypt. Light dared not. Herself blinded, Miril felt something crumble beneath her feet, some several things. She knew they were bones, bones ancient and bones human. And bones half-human too, not more, nor less.

Then, without warning, the doors closed behind her. She heard their damp thud, and with that sound there vanished all trace of hope. The peasant girl was sealed inside, unable to see, and utterly cut off from the outside world. There was no longer any exit, no possible escape, and strongest of all, there was the sense of utter finality.

Trembling in fear, hardly daring to breathe, Miril waited. Even blind, her eyes cast about in search of light, but found only more blindness. She listened intently for a sound, any sound; she waited for an acknowledgment of her presence, perhaps even for the killing touch of lethal claws. But there was nothing. Nothing. Darkness and silence ruled this outcrop of hell. Darkest darkness, and deafest silence: these were the only law in that place of eternal curse.

Finally, although fearing to break the cursed silence, Miril dared to speak. "I know you are here," she said into the emptiness. Her voice was weak with foreboding. She paused, listened, but there was no reply. Then, trying not to sound too nervous, Miril continued. "I know that you are expecting me. It is the time once more of your awakening. The cycle is full, Thorgar. Another upheaval has begun." Again, she paused to await a reply. But once more, there was only the heavy deafness pressing inward upon her ears. Miril's nervousness gradually began to turn into annoyance, and then into something resembling defiance. "If you think to toy with me, Thorgar, I warn you. If I get not what I have come for, then I will never serve you. Never."

Silence. Darkness. Death. Eternal gloom.

"Very well," Miril said. Despair had at last crept into her voice. The bitter taste of hopelessness, of doom, began to moisten her eyes and to sadden her heart. Who, after all, she thought, could hope for anything good from a demon? Tarok had been correct after all. God's will was too powerful to be thwarted. And now, she had shut God out forever, and left herself to the nonexistent mercies of an all too existent demon.

"Then let it be so," Miril wept. "I have lost everything." Then, with bitterness, and with the last remnant of her defiance, she added, "But also will I give you nothing, Thorgar."

A deep, rumbling sound began to make itself felt, felt more than heard. It was the sound of amused laughter from the throat of a predator fondling its helpless prey. It grew louder, and deeper. A faint red glow began to fill the chamber, a dark, shadowy redness. Blood colored shadows slowly took form, and dimly, Miril began to make out the stony features of an idol. But this was no ordinary stone. For in this one was life, if life indeed one could call it.

It spoke. "What disturbs Thorgar in its abode? It calls herself Miril of Har-Keem. She thinks itself clever and courageous. But it is fool of all fools.

For it damns herself for the flesh of a man, flesh which even now writhes in agony among the corpses of its family. Fool! You have lost all for none."

Miril had trembled upon hearing the demon's utterance. For its voice was a terrifying growl, more terrible than that of a panther springing suddenly upon its helpless prey. But just as before, when Miril had vomited bile, and yet regained her resolve, so now again she drove out her fear. "Indeed you are the treacherous one," Miril retorted. "But this time your treachery will betray only yourself. For I am the one you first smelled when you stirred from your slumber. It is of me that you said, 'She lives.' And now, would you pretend not to know me? Don't underestimate me, Thorgar. I am clever enough to know that you need me, as much as I need you. But before I give you what you wish, you must first grant me the favor that I seek. Or else. Do you think I would not turn against you? Listen, Thorgar. This very morning, I stood before Tarok himself, Tarok in the flesh--- and cursed him. So will I do also to you, if you refuse me as he did. Indeed I would do worse. For I would hand us both over to our enemy Tarok, rather than yield to you. Hurry and decide, Thorgar demon. For soon it will be too late, too late, for the ships are swift. So I demand of you, now, the return of my Kl'aarn. If you let pass the slave ship from your realm, if it escapes doom while you tarry, then I swear I will betray you, even at the loss of myself, just to spite you. For why would I want to live without Kl'aarn?"

Now Thorgar had indeed expected Miril, awaited her arrival, just exactly as she had said. Quite so, it had awaited her a thousand years. But the demon was clever and treacherous. Not even other demons had ever trusted it. It had tried to pretend that Miril was of no value to it, to see how much she would offer Thorgar, in return for the favor she had come to ask. The demon had delayed, in order to see how small a favor Miril would accept, in return for her life.

But now the demon saw that Miril's powers were much stronger than it had imagined. She could not be easily cheated of her birthright. Another time, Thorgar would have been murderously enraged at the slightest hint of insolence against it. But this was another matter. Instead of being disappointed, the demon was pleased. For Thorgar had use of a mighty demonwitch. Its pleasure, of course, was not for Miril's sake, but rather, its delight lay only in what Thorgar desired for itself. Miril's talents for evil were strong, stronger than Thorgar had hoped they would be. It had plans for her.

"You are already prepared," Thorgar told Miril, "to don the mantle of demonwitch. When you do, then even greater shall be your power. Far greater. But in human ways, you remain but a child, encumbering yourself with childish distractions. You imagine that you love this boy Kl'aarn, and that you would surrender your throne, rather than to lose him."

Miril answered quickly. "I would. I would lose anything but his love. Even the throne of evil, I would cast it aside for Kl'aarn's kiss. If Tarok had given him back to me, I would have served Tarok and warred against you, even unto death. Only when Tarok refused me did I turn to you, only then. But refuse me he did, and so now I turn upon one last, desperate hope. And this time, I will not be denied, Thorgar. Kl'aarn is mine. I mean to have him. Else never would I endure your sickening stench."

"Very well," Thorgar said, impressed at Miril's tenacity. "You shall have him, this boy Kl'aarn. Why would I want to take him from you? He is nothing to me. You shall have him for as long as you desire him. But hear a great wisdom, peasant girl, so that you will carry yourself with the dignity befitting your title. Let me ask you, in all wisdom, what is it of Kl'aarn that you love? Is it his appearance? His mannerisms? His smile, his touch, his laughter? All these you can have. You can conjure them from any man you choose. Such was the power of Kattaroon, that she seduced Tarok himself. And greater is your talent than was hers. This being so, then why constrain yourself to love but this one man, a frail peasant boy at that, when you could have any prince of any realm at your beck and call?"

Miril spat in disgust. "Wisdom? Do you dare try to pass off to me this leaden foolishness as golden wisdom? I come before you driven by love, yet you know nothing of it. And how could you? What wisdom has a demon concerning matters of the heart?"

"Wisdom to know," answered the demon, "that when a woman loves a man, she loves either that of him which she can have, or else that of him which she can never have. She loves either that of him which she can master, or else that of him which masters her. Most women are born to servility. That is their curse. But you are a woman who can command the love of any man. Do not choose, then, to be commanded by one."

But Miril proved herself of a single mind. "What I love of Kl'aarn is the happiness which he willingly bestows upon me," she answered. "He loves me, and he loves me with a love which could never be commanded, but which springs forth of its own. Not in all your ancient cleverness can you imagine such a thing. I will hear no more. The ships which bear my Kl'aarn to his death, now approach. Show me not your wisdom, Thorgar, for even Tarok did that and failed. And his wisdom is clearly greater than yours. But wisdom has this day proven to be cold comfort to my grieving soul. Show me instead what I asked of Tarok, and he could not provide. Show me, demon, your power."

Upon hearing these words, Thorgar was pleased to relent. For it knew that Miril was already at war with Tarok. It was a war that had begun a millennium earlier. It was a war in which Tarok would seek both Miril and Thorgar with his wrath. And Thorgar knew that if Tarok were to win, the demon would never have another opportunity.

"It will be as you ask," Thorgar told Miril. "Go, then, go to the farthest tip of Demon Point, where the land pierces the sea. Stand atop the cliff, and taste for yourself the power known so bitterly to men, but so sweetly to the mistresses of dark forces. Taste it. For the power will be not mine, but rather your own. Yes! I will draw it from you, and cast its cutting edge upon your enemies. But you shall know that it was your evil, not mine, which works its magic this day. For if you become choked with compassion for those who will die, then witchcraft will be useless in your hands. Are you ruthless? And if so, Miril of Har-Keem, then ask yourself this: are you ruthless enough?"

Miril affirmed it. "Whatever must be done," she swore, "I will do it. In the end, I will shrink from nothing except the loss of my beloved."

The demon had instructed Miril to stand atop the cliff of Demon Point, to stand, and from there, to see the ships which had destroyed Har-Keem, and to witness the power of her own evil. And although she could not understand this talk of power being drawn from herself, Miril obeyed. For all that she cared was that Kl'aarn would be returned to her from the ship which now imprisoned him.

The shrine doors opened. Blinding sunlight burned at Miril's eyes, causing her to wince in pain. But urgency prodded her onward, to run without being able to see, to run swiftly in the direction where, Miril knew, lay the ocean--- and the precipice overlooking its rocky shore.

The moment had at last arrived. There would be no more delay. In a few moments, Miril knew, Kl'aarn would either be hers, or else be lost to her forever. In either case, there would be no more doubt. It would be settled.

Blinded by sunlight, Miril's sight returned just as she reached the very edge of the cliff. Another step and she would have fallen to certain death. But the abyss would not have her, not this day. Recovering from the darkness of the tomb, Miril found herself atop Demon Point's highest ridge, the very tip of the claw of land which tore at the sea. Far, far beneath, giant boulders studded the waves like the teeth of a giant, hungry shark.

Wind whipped Miril's tattered nightclothes, and streamed through her unbraided hair. The sky above was cloudless.

But Miril's eyes focused instantly on the two wooden ships, their hulls, their sails and their oars.

The war ship carrying the soldiers was farther out to sea than the slaver, as if jealously protecting its mate from the pirates which infested those distant waves. From it, came faintly the sound of mannish laughter and revelry, the celebration of an easy victory, an almost bloodless triumph, and the capture of a priceless jewel. A sorceror, a platoon of soldiers, and a crew of sailors,

Miril hated every one among their number. But she knew better than to waste her hatred on these. For it was the other ship which carried the prize Miril envied.

It sailed defiantly close to her, as if mocking her, as if its crew were taunting Miril with the one thing she loved most, the man whom they had stolen from her. Of course, they did not even notice the girl, far above them atop the ridge. But that in itself was insult.

From the slaver came sounds also. But these were the sounds of weeping, the groans of the dying, and the jeers of cruel whipmasters. "Soon you'll be sport," they taunted their captives. "Gladiators for the arena, and whores for the brothel."

Miril cursed at them, a long, loud shrieking curse, filled with rage and bursting with vengeful wrath. "May you all burn in Hell!" she cried out at the end of her outburst. But they did not hear. For even the clamor of wind and waves were more self-important than Miril's pain, and they paid her no heed.

"Are you ready?" The voice rumbled from within her.

"Quickly," Miril said impatiently. "They are in your waters now. Work your craft."

But Thorgar said, "No, work yours, Miril. Let your hate become substance; let your anger become fire. Bring it forth. Give life to your evil, Miril. Inhale your lust for vengeance, and exhale the flame of hatred. Then curse those who lie helpless before you."

But Miril cursed the demon instead. "There is no time for lessons in witchcraft. You promised me, evil one. Now show me the power of evil. Show me."

The sky was still blue overhead. But from nowhere came a black cloud. It grew. Then, as a swirling cauldron, the dark cloud formed itself into a single, downward pointing claw. Quickly it descended toward the slave ship, whirling and howling with unearthly rage. Its tip reached the uppermost part of the mast, and tarried there, toying with its victim, as the leopard toys with the gazelle.

The sounds of weeping and moaning, which before had come from the ship, these sounds had quickly turned to screams of terror as the dark, cloudy doom had descended. The jeers of the whipmasters had turned to curses, and then to frenzied prayers to their idols. Desperate for escape, they began throwing slaves overboard in heavy chains, as sacrifice to appease the demon, into whose domain they had trespassed.

But Miril's eyes narrowed with intensity. Her stare focused on the slave ship. She felt hatred well up within her as never before she had felt any emotion. With fiery anger, she sent forth a thought, a curse, which took control of the spinning dark talon, and drove it suddenly downward onto the vessel, as a poniard into a sacrificial victim.

The mast snapped, tearing the sail to shreds. The hull of the ship began to spin in the waves, groaning and cracking its timbers.

Miril glanced momentarily downward. Far below her, white-crested waves swirled furiously between the sharp tips of huge boulders which jutted toothlike from the ocean floor. "Devour!" she cursed.

Suddenly, the ship was gripped by the lethal force which impaled it. No longer spinning, its bow was pointed directly at Miril's feet. Then, thrust by the wind, the ship lunged forward.

It moved with impossible speed, almost skimming above the water. Even before it hit the rocks, it was being torn apart. Then it collided with the jagged boulders.

A terrible mixture of sounds burst from the splintered vessel, the sounds of shattered wood, and the cries of a hundred terrified souls being spilled into the churning sea, a sea foaming with maddened bloodlust.

Desperate men crawled over each other, pushing others beneath the waves, in a futile attempt to cling to the razor edged rocks. Those who won this bloody contest did so only to be ground flesh from bone upon the rocks, which they had regarded as their hope of survival.

Valiant men struggled to save their kinfolk from the crushing waves. But they were themselves pulled beneath the waters, waters which by now ran red with blood, and brown with the dust of ship's timbers.

Then, as suddenly as the cloud had appeared, it vanished. The storm fell silent, and the waves became eerily calm. Miril felt her windblown hair settle once more upon her shoulders, at rest. It was as if it had all been but a dream. Only the stained water proved that a ship had been there, proved with red foam that it had borne aboard it human lives. In the distance, the war ship scurried for the relative safety of the high sea, already having escaped beyond Thorgar's reach.

Miril looked upon what she had done.

"Where is he?" she asked anxiously.

But there was no answer. Had the demon also been but a dream? Had any of this been real? she wondered. Could there have been any hope from the beginning?

"You let me kill him, didn't you?" Miril wept as she spoke. "Kl’aarn is dead with the others. I should have known. I should have discerned your nature. Your pleasure was to cause me to kill everyone, all of them, the evil and the good alike. That was the test, was it not? To show no compassion, not even for the innocent? But you wanted Kl'aarn dead, too. You were jealous of him. And in your jealousy, you thought that if he died, that I would blame God, and serve you. But no, Thorgar. Of that, you were in error, a most costly error. I will not. I'll not serve you. For without Kl'aarn, I have no desire to live. Do you doubt me? But I leave you now, Thorgar. I go to join my beloved. If we cannot be together in life---" and lifting her foot, Miril stepped forward.

But just as she would have plunged to her death, Miril saw him, and drew suddenly back. There Kl'aarn was, staggering half-drowned from the sea, limping badly on one leg, the shaft of a broken arrow piercing his thigh through and through. But he was alive.

Miril knelt, pressing herself as near to the edge of the cliff as she could, and cried out to him. But the sound of the surf drowned out Miril's cry, and Kl'aarn did not hear. He crawled onto the beach, and there he collapsed, vomiting sea water.

Quickly, Miril cast about for any ledge which might lead her to the bottom of the cliff. Having thought him lost forever, she no longer could wait to hold him in her arms.

"What are you doing, Miril?"

Miril replied from within her distractions, "You have kept your promise, Thorgar. And now as it is written, I owe you a debt of servitude. It is a debt which I shall gladly repay. Six years, is that not the prescribed law? Six years I will serve you, Thorgar, six years of bondage to you as demonwitch. But first I must see to my husband. He is hurt."

Thorgar spoke again. "Soon you will find your way down there. And then? There you will embrace him. And knowing his embrace, you will kiss him. And knowing his kiss, you will be unable--- and unwilling--- to tear yourself from him. An hour will pass, then a day and a month, then a year and six all told. Nor will I stop you, Miril. If go to him you must, then do so."

Miril ceased from her distractions, and addressed the demon. "What are you saying?"

"Witchcraft, Miril. You owe me six years of witchcraft. But it is a debt which not even I can enforce. For if you come not willingly into the den of evil, how then will you wage the war which even now begins taking shape? If you love not evil, then love at least its fruit--- love your Kl'aarn. Love him six years. And then, when Tarok comes for you--- but you will have had your six years, at least."

Miril hesitated. "This is a trick, Thorgar. You gave me Kl'aarn. Now you would take him from me."

"Would I? Or would I wish you to taunt Tarok with him?"

"I distrust you, Thorgar."

"Very well!" Thorgar boomed impatiently. "Then go. Your argument is not with me, but with Tarok. Let him deal with you."

Miril contemplated. "Yes. Deal with me. That was Tarok's parting promise to me, a threat he made not idly. Indeed, it was him who told me that Kl'aarn's path was at end, that my beloved was this day to sleep with his ancestors. But see, Kl'aarn will not die now. He lives. I snatched him from the path which Tarok had said was God's path. Now Kl'aarn is upon a different path, one which God never intended. Yes, well you speak, Thorgar, though I dread to admit it. Well you speak. For now, if I embrace my beloved, it will be just as you warn me. Never could I tear myself from him. And then, as surely as the sun sets, Tarok would catch me unprepared. And no demon would protect me from his wrath."

Thorgar spoke. "And yet, even knowing what you must do, you hesitate to do it. You fear to make final your choosing."

Miril shook her head. "No. No doubt assails me now. Too many lie dead for me to turn away from what I have done, dead not only whom I hate, but them whom truly I did love in life, dead now by my own hand.

"No, Thorgar, no doubt hinders me now. Yet a paradox taunts me. For consider it: if I am to have Kl'aarn," Miril said, "then I must become a witch. And if I become a witch, then Kl'aarn will turn away from me, for he worships the God of angelic beings. So it seems that I have dealt treacherously with myself. In order to regain what I had lost, I had to lose what I have regained. Is that not paradox? I have defeated myself. I have become my own fool, my own enemy."

"No," Thorgar answered. "You are no fool, and you will never be defeated. See for yourself. You have taken Kl'aarn from the path which his God had ordained, just as you said. Now another path he will wander, until he finds your path. Give him six years, Miril, the same six years you give yourself. For time, as you well know, makes all men evil. All of them. Six years I will protect him for you, Miril. After that, your beloved Kl'aarn will be yours for all time. Forever."

Miril understood. "I cannot hope to have Kl'aarn for more than a brief moment of joy--- unless I fight for him. And I sense now that Tarok is not my only enemy. There are others, as well, enemies who would take him from me if but only they could."

"You have many enemies," the demon told her. "Tarok and Druuk are fierce enough. But the worst of all your enemies, the one who would most surely take Kl'aarn from you, is the Priestess of Prophecy. As you are now, you could never hope to stand against her, for she has power to rival your own. It is because of her, not only Tarok, that you must let your love for this man wait. It must be this way."

Miril snickered. "Veelos. She has a hand in this, somehow. Her God, her Tarok--- and her love for Kl'aarn, they have now set her against me. Even my once dearest Veelos now wages war against me, her, for whom once I would willingly have died. She would kill me this moment if but she knew. And she would take Kl'aarn from me, if only she could. What power would she not use against us?"

Thorgar answered. "Trust in your own power. Veelos will not take Kl'aarn from you. I will put it in his heart to avoid her, and she will not know that he lives. As for you, you must master fully the black art, which today you but tasted for the first time. Hide from your husband, woman, hide while you serve Thorgar a mere six years. What is six years in eternity? Thereafter, Kl'aarn will be yours forevermore. You shall rule over all the world. And your enemies: Tarok, Druuk, and the Priestess, they will all lie dead at your feet. Dead, or worse."

Miril knew then what she must do. She must become more magical than Tarok, more cruel than Druuk, and more powerful than the Priestess of Prophecy. In this, then, Thorgar's counsel was the only wisdom. Alas, it was so.

With great sorrow, Miril relented. "I love you, Kl'aarn," she whispered to him. "Somewhere deep inside you, I know you can hear me. Even now, the seed is planted within you, and you know that we will be together once more. Always, you will know that. Go, then. Live as a man lives in this world. I will forgive anything. Only do this one thing for me, my dearest. Live. Live six years, and then await me."

Then, turning back to the crypt of the demon, Miril entered therein, shed her clothes, and donned the blackmost garments of witchcraft.

A new demonwitch now stalked the world. The Dreaded One Foretold had made her choosing.

Chapter 9

The False Priestess, Reprised

When Veelos had first arrived in Shi-Raq, the high priests had known right away that her calling was suspect. Of the three high priests, the woman Jen-Aga was the strictest. She had stood at the temple door, beneath its towering arch, amid its gleaming whiteness, with her brother high priest, a man named Emo-Luk. Closely observing the frightened peasant girl disembarking from the horse-drawn cart in which she had arrived, Jen-Aga had sternly commanded, "Send her away."

But Emo-Luk, a high priest as well, had questioned this command. "Without even a meal? We feed even murderers here."

"Then feed her," Jen-Aga had replied with irritation. For well she knew how difficult her brother priest could be. "Feed her, clothe her, give her gold for all I care. But after all that, send her from this place."

"And why, may I ask?"

"Why? You see it as well as I do. This is no prophetess called to the priesthood. She is a rebellious adolescent running away from the rigors of womanhood. How many times must we extend the hand of welcome to those who abuse us? Show her the charity we are obliged, but then rid us quickly of her deceitful presence."

"Indeed," Emo-Luk had answered. "We must not abide her. After all, are we not awaiting the soon arrival of the one who will be called the Priestess of Prophecy? The one of whom it is said, she will come from farthest east? The one of whom it is said, 'She will not be recognized. They will not call her Priestess.'? Oh, it would never do to have a peasant girl from Har-Keem sullying up our purity when the Unrecognized Priestess arrives, now would it? To be sure, this one is not called to the priesthood. Anyone can see that. For she is not nearly as pompous an ass as we are."

Jen-Aga had replied, "Must you always torment me with sarcasm and ridicule?" Then she had added, "But you are right about one thing, Emo-Luk. The cut of her clothes speaks of Har-Keem. Is it not the point of Wirik farthest east?"

Then, troubled by this, Jen-Aga went to the third high priest, the black-skinned man named Lar. "We have all felt the tremors of a great new evil," Jen-Aga said to Lar. "And now a runaway peasant girl from the east comes to us, pretending to the priesthood. Is this not an omen? Tell us then, is it a portent of blessing, or of danger?"

"It is indeed a mysterious omen," Lar had agreed. "For while the Priestess of Prophecy shall be sent to us, unrecognized, from farthest east, the demonic anti-scriptures are said to predict that the Dreaded One Foretold shall also arise from there. So what are we to do? Would we risk admitting the demonwitch into the chamber of the angelic orb? I understand your fear. So I leave the final decision with you, Jen-Aga. Shall we send this girl back to whatever torment drove her from Har-Keem? Or shall we equip her with the spiritual strength to conquer those pains?"

So in the end, Jen-Aga had agreed with her brothers, and Veelos was admitted to the temple. There, she began to study for the priesthood.

Chapter 10

Rebellion of the False Priestess

Veelos was brought to a young priestess named Keesha, and was commanded to obey Keesha in all things. Now Keesha, as did her high priests, also perceived that Veelos was not called to the priesthood. She could see that Veelos only pretended to be called. But Keesha herself had come from a life of suffering, and did not judge Veelos, but instead offered to instruct her in the ways of the temple. In the end, Keesha knew, the matter of Veelos's calling would be decided by a wisdom far transcending her own, or Veelos's, or even the high priests' themselves.

Temple life, as Veelos quickly discovered, was very harsh. Candidates for priesthood worked from sunrise to darkness, as would a slave. At night, Veelos was tutored by Keesha in the scriptures, and instructed in the disciplines of the ascetic life.

Many an impostor had visited the temple through the years, pretending to be called to the priesthood. Most of them had been runaways, transients or deluded fools. A few had even been sorcerors, deigning to glean the powers of priesthood, scheming to turn those sacred powers to evil.

But in every case, the grueling labor and tedious, unrelenting studies into the late night, had revealed each, for whom he was. Within a week or two, the most determined impostor collapsed in exhaustion, or else rebelled in anger, or as many did, ran away into the worldly pleasures of the great city, which was Shi-Raq.

But not Veelos.

She was an enigma. Although she bore none of the marks of one called to priesthood, yet everyone in the temple marveled at how steadfast Veelos was in enduring the regimen of temple life. And they were amazed at how quickly she learned to read and write, and to speak the ancient tongues. And they were astonished at how thoroughly she memorized entire scrolls of scripture.

But alas, when it came to understanding the soul of the priestly life, they found Veelos an abject failure. She could repeat much, but when asked to interpret, it was as if she had never studied at all. For some things cannot be taught, nor are they learned with the mind alone.

And so at last, after a year of patience, a year of hope, a year of effort, the three high priests considered again whether to expel Veelos after all from the temple. For they had concluded indeed that Veelos was not meant to be among them.

They voted on it, as was their custom, by sealed vote, the three of them in a darkened chamber. When their votes were unsealed, each was astonished to discover, that the other two had voted with a white stone, that is, to ordain Veelos with the silver ring of priesthood. For none had wanted to vote against her, even while each thought the other two would expel Veelos.

They took this as a sign. And so it came about that Veelos, despite receiving no calling, was ordained into the priesthood after all.

"She has the power now," Lar commented when it was done. "May she use it according to God's will."

* * * * *

Whatever joy Veelos might have felt at her ordination into priesthood, it was quickly dashed. For terrible news reached Shi-Raq, the worst news possible. Har-Keem had been destroyed by pirates. Not a survivor could be found.

The high priests mourned with Veelos. But amid their tears for her, amid their meditations and prayers, more than sadness burdened their hearts. For they discerned that Veelos had been spared from the fate of her fellow villagers not by mere chance, but rather for some important purpose. It was yet another omen connected with her, and they prayed that it might be for the good.

For a month, Veelos mourned her family and her friends. She grieved for the loss of Miril, and regretted that she had never answered any of the letters which Miril had so regularly sent. Those letters had meant so much.

But one for whom Veelos did not weep at all was Shalar. Even at the thought of his death, she could not think kindly of him. Had it not been from him she had fled? Had not he torn her from Miril? Was not he her dark secret, of which she could not speak, not even to Keesha?

"And now that at last I have escaped him forever," Veelos wept, but to herself alone, "Shalar has taken with him all, all to which I had hoped to return. He has taken from me my Miril, my family, my village--- taken them, with him, from this world. Thief that he was in life, thief in death he shall always be."

Then the name of Kl'aarn crossed Veelos's mind. For an instant she remembered his face, hovering close above hers, his breath entering her lungs, his gentle voice saying, "Don't fear. I'll get you home."

It was only an instant of thought, a thought which Veelos purged quickly from her mind. "He is with Miril now," she reminded herself. "They are together." And she vowed never again to think of Kl'aarn in any way, except as Miril's husband.

Eventually, the worst of Veelos's pains had begun to lose their mastery of her tears, no longer able to command her abject weeping at the slightest evocation of a painful, or even pleasant, memory. Those pains had seeped into the depths of her soul, never to lift from her their burden of sorrow. But the time came when Veelos no longer resided in their constant shadow.

It was then that Keesha began taking Veelos along on her frequent forays into the city, to help her minister to the crippled, whom Keesha loved. And Veelos was an eager apprentice, more than pleased to help Keesha tend to the needs of the weak, the halt and lame.

Even so, after all her learning, Veelos still had not learned the heart of priesthood, that heart without which priesthood is but a lifeless husk of ritual and show. Her failure to learn was soon to cost her dearly, very dearly indeed.

It began when Keesha mentioned that her favorite person to visit was a young girl named Shier-Bek. Now Shier-Bek's legs, as Keesha described them to Veelos, were twisted, deformed since her birth. Shier-Bek could not walk, not at all. But otherwise, she seemed a beautiful young girl. She was a weaver of carpets, renowned for her skill at the loom. There she sat all the day, weaving the works of artisanship for which she was nearly famous. Shier-Bek had even designed her own, unique looms, which her brothers built for her, looms by which she crafted fabrics which were a trade secret, shared only with her family. Shier-Bek's produce was much in demand. But even so, she was not becoming wealthy. She weaved quality goods, but not cartloads of them. Each item completed was a masterpiece, and such work takes much time.

Keesha intended to teach Veelos how to minister to such as Shier-Bek. The first lesson was to avoid undue pity. "God has chosen Shier-Bek's path," Keesha explained. "To us it seems a cruel one to travel. But God has given us to assist Shier-Bek in her journey through life. And listen to this mystery: it is Shier-Bek who leads us."

For a time, Veelos accepted what Keesha had said, and ministered to the emotional and spiritual needs of those whom they visited. But none among the afflicted were as dear to Veelos's heart as this one young girl named

Shier-Bek.

One day, alone, Veelos visited with the crippled young maiden. The family lived in a modest clay house in a quiet part of the city. But they were away on the day's chores, having left Shier-Bek by herself to work her craft in solitude.

As Veelos entered the abode, she noticed its faded elegance. Once, plush tapestries had adorned the walls, and thick, soft carpets had lain upon its floor. Now brick and stubble lay bare. The echoes of laughter and cheer seemed distant and faint, all but drowned out by the more recent ghosts of weeping and lamentation.

All this, Veelos took in with an inner sense which, since her ordination, had grown ever more keen day by day.

Shier-Bek's father had, from an early age, shown talent in accumulating honest wealth. But he had lived in a world that, for the most part, valued honesty only in word. While Shier-Bek had been yet in her mother's womb, her father had journeyed afar with a small caravan of goods to sell in distant cities, which had never known such craftsmanship as his. His return had become overdue. Days, then weeks, and finally months had passed, before word of him had finally arrived: that his return was never to be. The precious work of his hands, and of the hands of his sons, had become the loot of murderous bandits upon some distant forest trail.

His widow and orphans had struggled to live upon what wealth had been stored for them. But other merchants, not so honest, had defrauded the trusting family, and soon, there had nothing been left but the house itself, and only the walls and rafters thereof.

It was then that Shier-Bek had been borne, her tiny legs hideously deformed. Money that could have been fruitfully spent on healers for her was now in the hands of those who cared nothing for her suffering. By age 12, her leg bones had hardened into twisted, useless appendages. Her fate had been sealed.

Keesha delighted in her visits with Shier-Bek, and had eagerly introduced Veelos to her. It had been the more delight for Keesha to see these two bond so quickly with each other. Whatever Veelos's shortcomings might be, Keesha had thought to herself, at least lack of compassion was not one of them. None was more compassionate than Veelos.

This day was the first in which Veelos had come to visit the girl by herself. Veelos felt nervous. Part of her wished to embrace the smiling child tightly, to never let her from her arms, to shelter her forever from the world--- the callous, indifferent and often barbarous world--- into which her adolescence was emerging.

Another part of Veelos wished to flee, to recoil in horror from Shier-Bek's affliction.

It wasn't fair, Veelos told herself. This young maiden, so vibrant, so exuberant, so innocent. Her girlish face would soon become that of a woman, clearly that of a beautiful woman who could command the love of any man--- indeed, of any princeling of Shi-Raq.

Except for the legs.

A dowry of fortunes had become forfeit because of all which had happened. The bandits, the dishonest merchants, the mercenary healers, an entire city bereft of charity when it could have made a difference, these had all conspired to bring about this evil, this injustice, this unfairness. Now those ugly legs annulled all that was otherwise beautiful in Shier-Bek. The beautiful face, the charm, the wit, the strength of character, none of these would now entice any man to take Shier-Bek as wife.

No man would have her.

Yet this day, Shier-Bek announced the betrothal of her older sister, and casually wondered what kind of man she herself would be given to in marriage some day.

It was not until then--- until Shier-Bek had spoken that innocent remark, that naïve question--- “I wonder what kind of man I will be given to in marriage?”--- that a long-suppressed urge in Veelos finally rose to the surface. What kind of man indeed, Veelos asked, but asked angrily. What kind of man would Shier-Bek ever have as husband? None!

But the urge which rose in Veelos's breast was not merely anger. At first, its warmth had been but tears in her eyes. But the tears soon dried, and the thing that had begun as warmth, soon became heat.

"Why do you act so?" Shier-Bek asked when she noticed something amiss. She had never seen Veelos seem so angry before. It was disturbing. "Have I misbehaved?"

Veelos's angry laugh was but an abrupt snicker. "Misbehaved?" she asked sarcastically. "Of course not. But that's the whole point, isn't it?"

Shier-Bek was not soothed by such strange talk. "What can you mean, Priestess?"

"Uncover your legs for me," Veelos said.

Shier-Bek glanced upward at the strange request. Something in Veelos's tone began to frighten her.

"It's alright," Veelos reassured her. "I want to see if there is something I might do to make them better."

"Oh, it's quite useless to try," Shier-Bek said.

"I know. But please. Let me try."

"Well--- but only because you are Keesha's friend--- and mine."

It was a sight Veelos had never grown accustomed to. There was always a shock, a revulsion, whenever she had chanced to look upon those tiny, contorted branches of flesh. But this time, the revulsion was more than just that. The priestess felt indignation.

Anger. Could a merciful God do this to otherwise so beautiful a child, an innocent and helpless orphan? How? Why? Indignation became a burning rage.

"No!" Shier-Bek cried. "What are you doing?"

"Let me put a blessing upon you, Shier-Bek. Just a gentle touch, that's all. What are you frightened of? This won't hurt."

"Are you sure? I'm afraid, Priestess. Why do you have that look in your eyes?"

"It's just love," Veelos answered. "Just love caught fire. Look. See? This doesn't hurt. Tell me if it does."

But Shier-Bek only watched in fascination, as the parts of her body she had never known could be like those of other people, began slowly to change form.

* * * * *

For the two years before this visit with Shier-Bek, Veelos had lived among the priests of the temple. For two years she had endured their sternness, endured their special brand of sternness, which was never cold, but always demanding of her best. For two long years (but years so swiftly fled!) she had enjoyed their unstinting love, their boundless generosity, and their relentless kindness. They were a people who would embrace poverty without regret, giving away all their excess produce and more, never counting who owed them or how much. And they were a people who forgave, whether the debts of outsiders, or the sins among their own brothers and sisters.

But this was different.

Veelos was on trial. She had violated their law. She had broken her priestly vows. And having done that, Veelos saw, for the first time, a side of the priests that she had never imagined would confront her. For a trial had but two purposes: to judge the accused, and to set punishment for the guilty.

"You have committed a high crime," Lar accused her. They were gathered in the chamber of angels, the large central dome, which housed the Great Orb of Power. All eyes were upon Veelos. Even Keesha's gaze seemed pained with disappointment.

"What crime?" Veelos demanded. Her voice echoed stonily through the hall, and aside from Keesha's faint gasp, was the only sound. "What wrong have I done? Whom have I harmed?"

Astonished murmuring erupted among the onlookers. Keesha's countenance withdrew behind the white hood of her vestment. For no one, no one dared address the high priests with such defiance. The high priests themselves remained silent, passive, weathering the storm.

"I healed her, yes," Veelos continued. "So? Is it a crime to heal?"

"No," Lar answered. "It is not a crime to heal. But priests are supposed to do all things according to scripture. This, you did not do. The offense of which you are accused is a serious one, a most serious crime. But I see you are impatient to speak your defense. Very well, speak it."

Lar had barely completed his words before Veelos thoughtlessly continued her tirade. "Shier-Bek was born crippled," she complained. She glanced quickly about the hall, seeking any sympathetic ear. "Her father died, even while she was yet in her mother's womb. Afterward, swindlers and dishonest merchants cheated her mother out of all the family's wealth. There was nothing left, no inheritance, no fortune, not even money enough to hire the physicians who could have healed her. Nothing! There was no hope at all for Shier-Bek--- none that is, except the power of the silver ring. I took pity on Shier-Bek, and not just the kind of pity that one finds in cold scripture, or in a recited verse, or in a rotely memorized chant--- but the kind of compassion that demands action. That was what I felt, not some holier-than-thou advice for Shier-Bek to suffer in silence what we ourselves do not suffer. So! With this ring of ordination I healed a crippled, helpless child. Tell me, where is the crime in that?"

Lar waited for the emotion in Veelos to subside. Then he answered. "Do you think you have healed Shier-Bek? Is this truly a healing? Do you think yourself wiser than God, who set her upon her path? Do you? Because of you, Shier-Bek no longer walks the path which God gave her. Instead, she walks a path which you gave her. Have you so mastered life that you can chart anew its course for others? Can the blind lead others through life's ambushes?"

But Veelos had an answer. "What good is all your spiritual insight, if it abandons innocent children to a path of pain and deprivation?"

"None," replied Lar. "My spiritual insight is nothing more than the babbling of an idiot in a drunken rage. Nothing. But fortunately, Veelos, we need not rely upon our own insight. We rely upon God's revealed truth.

Whether one's path be one of riches or of privation is of no account. Whether it is God's path or not--- that is of sole importance. For we always know where God's path leads. But where will your path lead Shier-Bek? Will your path carry her to heaven? Or will Shier-Bek run nimbly on healthy legs into Hell?"

Veelos's defiance began to waver--- but only slightly.

"When you accepted the power of the silver ring," Lar continued, "you accepted it on its own terms, not yours. You became its servant, not its master. Oh, the rings do confer power on the wearer, Veelos--- greater power than you can imagine. For centuries that power has sustained us as rulers of all east Wirik, without ever once our wielding it of our own. We have never turned the Orb against our enemies, never, though they are many and powerful. We have never used it to turn lead to gold, nor to make ourselves immortal, nor to do any of the other things that worldly men would do, if only they could master these powers. Never have we wielded this power. We have never needed to. No! For the power of good lies not in our power, but in submission to God. Yes, it is a paradox. But is not all holy scripture paradox? In them, do we not find life in death, and freedom in slavery? Are not the humble elevated and the proud brought low? So also it is with power, Veelos, a paradox more sublime than any riddle. The Orb radiates its power as passively as a breath enters the lungs. So also do the bearers of its ring radiate God's message by example, not by force.

"But you have taken this ring, which was given to you for the sake of good, and you have used it instead for evil."

Then Veelos blurted out, "It was not evil. Even if I were mistaken in what I did--- which I was not--- but even if I were, how could you say I did evil? Was not my intention for good? Was not my motive compassion? That is what matters."

"What matters," Lar replied, "is whether it was God's will. That is what separates good from evil. That alone. Have you not learned in all your studies, not even so simple a lesson as the difference between good and evil?"

"Good is what brings God's blessing," Veelos answered. "And evil is the opposite of good. Is it not? Then what did I do to oppose good?"

But Lar's answer silenced her. "Your concepts of good and evil are those of worldly men, but not those of servants of the priesthood," he told Veelos. "Men say that good and evil are opposites of each other. But that is not true."

Veelos was perplexed. "Then what is evil, if not the opposite of good?"

"Its counterfeit," Lar answered. "Evil is that which pretends to bring about blessings. But instead, it leads to death. Evil is but death disguised as life, pain wearing the mask of pleasure, a leaden coin made to seem as gold. For it is plain to us that good has no opposite. There is good, and there is absence of good. But absence is not opposite. Otherwise, this room is the opposite of everything that is absent here, and that is preposterous. And if good has no opposite, then evil is not the opposite of good. Evil is but counterfeit."

Veelos absorbed the words as if struck. Slowly, she began to comprehend, however dimly, that the ring on her finger represented a vast, complex power which she was incapable of understanding, much less of wielding. She felt like a child entrusted with fire.

"What you did to Shier-Bek was the counterfeit of good," Lar explained. "She will walk her new path, and many will think it a good one, because now her legs are strong and beautiful. But it is an evil path, Veelos, a counterfeit path. It is not the path ordained for her by God, but by you. And many will follow her upon it."

For the first time, Veelos did not merely memorize a lesson of the priesthood. A cold chill gripped her heart, and she felt the first faint tinges of regret for what she had done. For indeed, she had interfered in a human life. She had rushed in foolishly, seeking to salve her own feelings, but not considering that for Shier-Bek, the stakes were very much higher than mere feelings. Veelos knew, then, that she had set a fire she could not control.

"We find you guilty," Lar told her with grim finality. "We judge you guilty of the one crime which alone can destroy the priesthood. With great remorse we regret that ever we did ordain you. For from the very beginning, you were indeed a false priestess, just exactly as Jen-Aga warned us upon seeing you for the first time. You deceived us. Now, you must depart from among us."

For a long, terrible moment, Veelos stood. "Depart from you?" she gasped. "Am I being cast from the temple?" For long moments, Veelos found herself uncomprehending, unable to believe that she was truly being cast out from the priesthood. Then, slowly, the terrible reality of it imposed itself upon her senses. They were going to force her out of the temple, never again to return. Never.

"What will I do?" she asked pleadingly. "Where will I go? I have no money, no skills, no home. I will starve."

Lar answered. "We are not without compassion. You may come to us with your petitions. You may come as do others, to ask of us from our produce. And you will find us no less generous to you than we are to any others who ask from us. Indeed, we will take a special interest in your welfare. Perhaps, at our expense, you might even apprentice yourself to a healer, a healer of the physical sort. Only, you must first surrender to us your ring of ordination, and exchange your priestly vestments for worldly garments."

Veelos trembled. The finality of it all was unendurable. For long moments she stood before the assembly, humiliated and afraid. Veelos thought she might collapse. But then, in the next moment, she gathered herself, stood rigidly, and spoke.

"Take from me what you will," Veelos said. "Take my pride, my hope. Imprison me. Kill me. Do whatever your law allows. But one thing I know of your law: your law does not allow you to take from me what is my self. And what is my self? It is no longer, maiden of Har-Keem, for Har-Keem is no more. It is no longer daughter of the family of T'Oren, for that family is extinct. What am I? I am the Priestess Veelos! She I have been these two years. And Priestess Veelos will I be to my dying day; this I prophesy. Now I turn the matter to you. Does your law permit you to take from me this ring? These vestments? If so, then take them. Otherwise, I will never surrender them."

The silence of those in the hall was again broken. Once more, a murmuring sound filled the domed chamber, as priests discussed quickly with each other what they might do. Some glanced toward the orb atop its pedestal, as if from there might come an answer.

The three high priests consulted quietly among themselves, obviously disturbed by what was happening. Then, finally, Lar turned to Veelos and spoke again. "You vex us, woman, as no one ever has. What mist is this that prevents our discerning who you are? And now you quote to us our own law, and we have no answer. No one has ever taken from us the ring and vestments without our blessing. No one has deigned to keep them when cast from among us. But we cannot oppose you. Go, then. Go and never return to this temple. If God allows this thing you do, if your ring and vestments do not themselves flee from you, then who among our number will take them by force?"

And having found Veelos guilty, the priests expelled her from the temple.

And so came into being the one known in Shi-Raq as the false priestess.

Chapter 11

The Healing Begins

There was no ceremony of expulsion. Being cast from the temple did not warrant circumstance. Veelos simply went to the sleeping quarter which housed the priestesses. There, she gathered up her few personal effects: a comb, a candle, the letters from home. Wrapping them in a cloth, Veelos lay the bundle across her shoulders. She took one last look about. Then she left the womens' wing, and walked back into the domed hall of angels.

At its center lay the Great Orb of Power, nestled in its cradle atop the pedestal. A circle of steps led up to it. Delicate as a breath, the priceless jewel was utterly vulnerable. There it had stood since the days when angels had walked the earth, chasing in battle the retreating demons, which had been cast from heaven. There it stood even now, pure, perfect and uncorrupted.

"What are you?" Veelos asked of it. "So much a thing of divine beauty, yet so handily the instrument of evil in hands such as mine! What else can you be except love itself?"

* * * * *

Veelos passed through the arched doorway of the temple. It was the only entrance, the only exit. It led onto a pier. There, the men priests kept fishing boats, by which much of the priestly diet was obtained. A squat, low cargo ship was approaching, its merchant hoping to sell whatever goods he bore this day.

Veelos walked from the pier and turned into the temple garden. There, priests and priestesses tended the fragrant flowers, herbs and fruits which grew so abundantly. The workers paid Veelos no heed, none at all. As if invisible to them, she walked past them in the silence befitting an outcast.

Soon, Veelos had stepped beyond the temple grounds, onto the dusty roadway which separated the temple from the city. And across the road, she entered the noisy, clamorous bazaar.

It was done.

For a few moments, Veelos stood, as hawkers and buyers pushed rudely past her, engrossed in the pressing business which ruled their lives, the business of acquiring wealth.

It was done. Veelos was alone now, utterly alone. In a few hours it would be night. If she could not beg her way into a safe home, she would be sleeping on the street. And city streets were dangerous.

Veelos sighed, and pressed forward into the crowd. Just then she felt a touch from behind. She turned.

It was Keesha. For a moment they simply looked at each other. Despite their nearness, Veelos had never felt so distant from Keesha in all the time they had known each other.

"You'll need this," Keesha said. She held forth a small purse of coins.

Veelos reached for it, then suddenly pulled back the hand which so eagerly sought the prize. "I can't," she said. "But thank you."

"Don't be stupid," Keesha said. "This city will not be as kind to you, as you are to it. This isn't much. A few copper coins, a silver or two. But it will see you until you can get a trade started."

"Really," Veelos said. "You're too kind."

"Not me," Keesha said. "Jen-Aga sends it."

Veelos swallowed. "Really? But she---"

"She told me not to tell you it's from her," Keesha said. "But sometimes I'm not very obedient." She pressed the purse forcefully into Veelos's hand. "Now hear me," she said. "There is a healer in the west quarter of the city. His name is Jagmoor. Go apprentice yourself to him. As long as you have this, as you call it, 'compassion, not to be found in cold scripture,'--- was that how you phrased it, this urge to heal---? you might as well learn to do it, in accord with the way which God has provided."

Veelos absently tucked the purse into her vestment, while she gazed at Keesha. "Am I going to see you again?" she asked.

Keesha nodded. "I minister to the lame, don't I?"

Veelos felt a tear coming on. "Have I ever said that I love you Keesha? I was so afraid, today--- afraid that you--- that you would---"

Keesha grasped Veelos's hands tightly in her own. Then, gently pushing her away, said, "God and His angels be with you," and turned, and ran back toward the temple.

* * * * *

The west quarter of Shi-Raq was near the harbor, but away from its noise and bustle. Here were the homes of fleet captains and shipping contractors, of money lenders and landlords. Priests rarely ventured here.

The sign, above a modest shop, caught Veelos's eye. The lettering spelled out the name, "Jagmoor." Next to that was the word for "Healer." And across the bottom, in faded strokes, was the inscription, "Skilled with scalpel and herb."

Veelos wandered closer. From without there was no sign of activity. She wondered what sort of man this Jagmoor might be, that Keesha had sent her to him. The building was of clay and brick. No doubt it served as both workplace and home for the healer and his family. The door was of sturdy wood, but it gave way easily to Veelos's touch.

Curses greeted her.

A sailor lay upon the wooden, surgical table, barechested, hairy. He was covered with the sweat of much pain. Two other sailors held him down for the healer.

Seated on a stool, the plump old man (Jagmoor, Veelos guessed) was bent over the sailor's outstretched arm, carefully threading shut a gaping wound.

"You'll be watching your language now," the plump surgeon said without looking up from his work. "We've a priestess in our company." Then, to one of the shipmates of his patient, he said, "Give him another sip--- and none for yourself, mind you."

Veelos wandered from the doorway into the shop, morbidly fascinated by the bloody wound of the man's forearm. Although she wanted to turn away from it, the grotesque scene commanded her unwilling attention. Between two long, tapered chunks of red meat, there glistened the whiteness of exposed bone.

"What ails you, lady priest? Something worse than this? Or can it wait?"

Veelos heard herself reply weakly, "I can wait."

"Good," the healer said. "Because this will take a bit more time, as I am sure you can see with those big saucer eyes of yours. Take a walk."

But Veelos felt an urgent need to sit down. She leaned toward an empty stool beside her. Her stomach felt sour. There was a shrill, high pitched ringing in her ears. Dimly, she became aware that she had missed the stool. Everything went dark.

Veelos awoke on her back, lying on another hard table not far from where the cursing sailor filled her ears with his drunken oaths. "I'll find that cheating bastard and gut him from his chin to his---"

"Another word and I'll sew your lips," the healer threatened. "Now keep this wrap on it, mind you. It keeps out the poisons. We have enough one-armed beggars already. So if your arm rots off, don't come to my door for alms. And if you do find the one who did this to you, send him to me. Unless, of course, he sends you again. Now out with you. Go."

Jagmoor's self-asserting authority cowed the sailors into obedience, despite that they were hulking figures of brawn. He rudely ushered them out the door.

When they had gone, Jagmoor turned to Veelos. She lay dizzily on the table.

"Ah, yes," Jagmoor said, his voice a preamble of sarcasm. "The lady priest. Don't care to see the inner man, do you?" He chuckled with amusement at his own joke, then continued. "Lucky he caught you, that ugly one. You'd have got a nasty gash on the head if you'd hit my brick floor. I doubt you could afford my services, too. So. What ailment brings you to Jagmoor Healer?"

Veelos slowly pushed herself to a seated position on the edge of the table, taking time to regain her balance.

"Well?" Jagmoor prompted. "What is it? Oh, I see. Something for a priestess to be ashamed of. Well, you wouldn't be the first one. No matter. I don't believe in all this religious claptrap you people sell. If you've violated your vows, you can tell me. But if you've suddenly got cold about it, there's a midwife not far from here. Her patients seem to do well."

Finally, Veelos steadied herself. "Nothing ails me," she said. "I'm not pregnant. Nor am I here as a patient."

Jagmoor showed puzzlement. Then, deciding what Veelos might mean, he said, "I see. Well, I don't need your blessing, thank you, and especially if there is a fee involved. Now back to the temple with you. There are prayers to be said."

"I'm not here to rescue your soul," Veelos said. "The way I feel at the moment, you could go to hell right now, for all I care."

Jagmoor's face went blank for a moment. Then he broke into laughter. "I like your gods," he said. "Not that I'll offer any sacrifice, mind you. You'll get no money from me. Now tell me what your business is, or out with you."

Veelos stood. "I want to learn to heal."

Jagmoor turned away from her, and picking up a bucket of water and a sponge, he began washing off the table which his last patient had blooded.

"Go away, lady priest. I can't support an apprentice."

"I'll work for nothing," Veelos offered.

"You'll cost my time," Jagmoor replied.

"I'll pay for your time."

Jagmoor turned once more and faced the priestess. "Go see the midwife. She teaches. Or Karf, or Halerd. They are respected men of the profession."

Veelos stood unmoving. "Why do you refuse me?"

Jagmoor sneered as if she had asked a stupid question. "It is my right to refuse," he said.

"It is your duty to teach," Veelos answered back. "It is the duty of every healer to pass on his knowledge. Do you deny it?"

Jagmoor replied with sarcasm. "I already taught you a valuable lesson. I taught you that the sight of blood renders you incompetent to heal. That is your lesson. Pay up."

"So that's it," Veelos said. "You are willing to teach, but only if it is without effort. That has always been your excuse, hasn't it? And no one has ever measured up to your requirements. You'll see to it that no one ever does."

Jagmoor showed anger. "Take your sorcery elsewhere, woman. You'll not sway me with your clever divinations."

"Sorcery?" Veelos shot back. "You have no idea. Did you hear tell of a mob last night, a mob at the temple gate?"

"I heard some mention of it," Jagmoor admitted. "What of it?"

"They demanded miracles. Miracles of healing."

Jagmoor grunted a laugh. "Yes, now I remember overhearing some banter. Ignorant worshippers. Some rumor about a miracle healing stirred them up. They demanded more of the same, for themselves. Some charlatan priestess started it all."

Veelos stepped from where she stood, and moved in front of Jagmoor. She looked into his eyes wordlessly, but with a look that conveyed only one meaning.

Jagmoor was not long in discerning that meaning. "So it was you," he said with disgust. The casual humor that had seemed to be part and parcel of him was gone, replaced by a scowl. "I see your game now. Get out of here. If there is one thing I cannot abide, it is a charlatan healer. Get out now, this moment."

But Veelos's hand snapped forward and clutched Jagmoor's sleeve, forcing his attention. "Turn me away the charlatan I am," she challenged, "or else train me and send me forth as healer. Which will you put on the street, Jagmoor? One whom you made a healer, or one whom you continued a charlatan?"

For a time, Jagmoor was silent, trying to find some clever response to Veelos's demand. "By the gods," he said at last, "you are a persistent lady, aren't you?" He was silent again for a time, then continued, "Alright. Your spell has worked. I'll give you a chance--- only a chance, mind you, but a fair one. But you must abide by all my rules, understand?"

"And what rules are those?" Veelos asked.

Jagmoor shrugged. "I'll make them up as we go along. And just now I thought of the first rule: every patient pays. Is that clear? Merchant or orphan, warrior or widow--- pirate or priest--- they all pay at the door. Agreed?"

Veelos nodded. "Everyone pays. In advance."

Jagmoor nodded. "Excellent."

* * * * *

For the first few days, Jagmoor did his best to overburden Veelos with the duties and lessons of healer apprentice. The sooner she became discouraged, he reasoned, the sooner she would be out of his hair. But he had not reckoned with her tenacity.

After a few days he told her, "You haven't taken up my time, as I feared you would. You've even saved me time. Here's the money you paid me for tutelage. Take it back. And buy yourself some commoner's clothing, or you'll ruin that fine vestment."

The days passed quickly.

During them, Veelos absorbed everything that Jagmoor could teach. "See this patient's skin," he instructed her. "It is the key to everything a healer does, the body's living parchment, upon which is written all that transpires within. Notice its warmth, its moisture, its hue and patterns. These are its language. Every ailment from within shows itself upon the skin."

And a few days later: "Urine. Have you ever tasted urine? Just a drop of course, as small a drop as your tongue will taste. I never said this would be pleasant."

Again a few days: "Press your ear to his chest, Veelos, as you would to your lover. Listen. Do you hear that tone when he inhales? Memorize it. Ignore his throat sounds. Now listen to him exhale."

Days later: "This man is dead, Veelos, a beggar. No family. It's not right that I do this. But it's my sin, not yours, so watch carefully." Jagmoor's scalpel opened the cadaver. "This is what you're feeling when you feel a belly."

And after many weeks: "You have done well, Veelos. No teacher could ask for a better student, no master for a better apprentice. To be honest, I don't know how you do it. You learn quickly, and forget nothing; not even the slightest detail escapes you. If I were inclined to believe in gods, I would explain you in terms of magical powers."

* * * * *

"You don't look well, Jagmoor." Months had passed, and Veelos had not slowed her pace. Already, Jagmoor had learned to trust her judgment.

"It's my wife's spicy cooking," Jagmoor said. "Majra is a bit too liberal with the peppers."

Veelos replied, "Your skin does not say spice."

Jagmoor laughed. "Don't be foolish, Veelos. As much as you've learned, you are still new at this. I have forty-four years of experience. I know when I've overdone the spices."

"You have fever, Jagmoor."

"It's just the spice, Veelos. Now attend your chores. The shop needs cleaning."

* * * * *

The physician named Halerd momentarily glared at the woman who stood in his doorway. "You're interrupting me," he said. "I'm reviewing my accounts." Then he absently remarked, "Your master Jagmoor is wise to demand payment in advance from his patients. My patients are sending me into poverty. So state your business quickly."

Veelos did. "Jagmoor is ill. The bulb of his bowel is poisoned."

Halerd stood from his table, obviously concerned. "He told you this?"

"He denies it."

"Then whose words?"

"Mine," Veelos answered.

Halerd cocked his head. "He's boasted for you of your talents. But I find it hard to believe that you have already mastered the touch of the belly. Are you truly that good?"

Veelos shifted nervously. "He won't let me touch him."

The healer snickered. "Then how do you know he has a poisoned entrail?"

"Come see for yourself," Veelos said.

Halerd sat down again, and returned his attention to his account books. "Go away, woman. I've no time for your foolery."

Veelos had known it would be awkward. "You are a believer, Halerd, are you not? I've seen you at the temple."

"A believer in God, yes. But not in your skills at healing."

"I am not an ex-priestess, Halerd. I still wear the silver ring."

"Then go pray for him," Halerd said.

"If you are a true believer, and not the sacrilegious pretender I see before me," Veelos said with voice slightly raised, "then you'll at least come and examine your friend, rather than let him die, while you decide which of your debts to collect first. If I am wrong about him, then I will pay you for your time."

"Priestess Veelos, with all respect due your station--"

"Now!" Veelos insisted. "I command it."

Halerd glared at her. "You are a false priestess, cast from the temple. You don't have the authority---"

"Are you sure of that?" Veelos challenged. "And what if you are wrong? Will they cast you also from the brotherhood of believers? With how much impunity can you defy my command?" It was an empty threat, Veelos knew. But Halerd might not know that.

Halerd stood angrily. "Indeed then. It's clear I'll have no respite from you. But after visiting Jagmoor, I'm going to the high priests and have something done about you."

* * * * *

Halerd immediately noticed that Jagmoor was ill. With intimidation from Halerd, Veelos and Majra, the three of them forced Jagmoor upon a table long enough for Halerd to perform the touch.

Then, without looking into Veelos's eyes, Halerd confessed, "Priestess, I owe you an apology." Then turning to Jagmoor's wife, he said, "Lady Majra, please go get Karf. He has more experience at surgery than I do."

"Oh no you don't," Jagmoor said, struggling up from the table. "No one is cutting me open. Majra! You come back here. Damn you! And damn you too, Veelos, you meddlesome wench. Look at all the trouble you've caused. You're fired. Get out. And get Majra back here!"

By the time Karf arrived, Jagmoor was moaning with increasing pain. Karf quickly agreed with Halerd's diagnosis. "We'll have to get him drunk."

Jagmoor had resigned himself to his fate. "I'll agree to the blade," he conceded. "But under one condition."

"What's that?" Karf asked.

Jagmoor looked at both Karf and Halerd with the intensity of deep conviction. "Veelos must do the cutting."

Halerd laughed grimly, and said to Karf, "He's not even drunk yet."

"It's the fever," Karf agreed.

"I'll drink not a drop--- I'll fight tooth and nail until I have your word on it," Jagmoor insisted. "Veelos, swear to me--- swear you'll not let them do the cutting."

Veelos shook her head. "Jagmoor--- I can't."

"You must! You will."

"Jagmoor, these men have experience."

"Use their experience. But you do the cutting, Veelos--- you and none other."

"Jagmoor, no."

"Damn you, Veelos. Remember my rules. You agreed."

"Within reason," she answered back.

"This is reason," Jagmoor pressed. "Three of four who get these pains die from them. I've seen what is the difference between those who live and those who die. You have it. I've seen you work. You have a sense for things unseen, a feel for forces and powers. Can anyone see the poisons at work in me now? No. But you can deal with them, I know. I'll do whatever you ask. I'll worship your gods if you do this for me."

Halerd turned to Majra. "Your husband has gone delirious. We may have to ask you to leave the shop."

But Majra replied, "Veelos is clean. She keeps the poisons from her touch. And all her patients do well, very well." Then she turned to Veelos, her expression one of desperate plea. "I can forgive anything, anything but that you did not try. I beg you."

Veelos swallowed hard. "I'll need candles," she said, "and boiled water."

* * * * *

It was very late night before the final stitch was in. Veelos reeled with fatigue. The sounds of Jagmoor's shrieks still rang in her ears. She felt Majra's guiding hands grasp her shoulder. "You'll stay the night," Majra said.

Karf and Halerd exchanged words as they departed. Veelos overheard them just as she fell off to sleep. "I can't believe I allowed that. I've never seen such inept surgery."

"Don't feel guilty. He was too far gone in any case. I give him two days at most. Poor fool. Two days if that."

* * * * *

Three days later, Jagmoor hobbled about his shop, bent over and with pain, but with his usual jovial spirits having returned. Karf and Halerd were recovering from their embarrassment.

Karf said to Veelos, "You could almost make me a believer. I never saw anything like it. But be honest with me, Priestess. How much of all that was of the healing art, and how much was ceremony and ritual? I mean, the candles and the purified water--- those are mere religion, no?"

Veelos shrugged. "I don't know. To me, it was all ritual, even the cutting. But could it do harm to clean the skin before putting the blade to it? Does it hurt to pass the blade through flame before using it? To boil bandages before using them? If nothing else, they made me feel comfort. The Lord of the universe knows I needed that."

Jagmoor interjected, "In any case, let none ever call Veelos charlatan. Never. You are a true healer, Veelos, as true as any ever lived. And I will sign my name to that, so that all will know."

Veelos bowed her head. She remembered a girl named Shier-Bek, and wished that as healer she had attended her, rather than as sorceress. She prayed silently, "Perhaps at last, dear Lord, I have met the test of priesthood."

But there would soon be a more difficult test.

* * * * *

The old woman said she had no money. The old man's face spoke of death. It was night, the street was cold.

"Come inside," Veelos invited them. And when Jagmoor glared sternly at her, Veelos placed ten copper coins on his ledger.

"He was healthy just today," the old woman told Veelos, "chopping firewood in the hills. It's our meager living: chopping wood, carrying it and selling it. Suddenly, Kirok couldn't push the cart. And I'm too old to do it all by myself. We live only meal to meal. What will we do? How will we eat?"

"Open his shirt," Veelos said. She pressed her ear to the frail, bony chest. The skin spoke of malnutrition, of a lifetime of poverty and labor. The heart spoke of impending death, the lungs of feeble breath. Veelos lifted her head, and looked sadly into the old woman's eyes. "I'm sorry," she said. "We can only ease his passage."

The old woman's eyes went wide with fear and disbelief. She turned pleadingly to Jagmoor. "You have many years of learning. You will save him."

Jagmoor brought himself to the table, and repeated Veelos's examination. Then he told the woman in his trained, somber voice, "There is nothing can be done. We are sad."

"But you must!" the old lady cried. "We have no children left to care for us. Our sons were all lost at sea. We have no one. If Kirok dies, then I am left all alone, a wretched beggar. I see potions upon your shelves. Try them."

Veelos answered. "The potions will not save him. They will not help." She could not bring herself to tell the woman that the potions were rare, difficult to obtain, and were reserved for cases which had some hope. Nor could Veelos tell the woman that the potions cost much gold.

The old woman noticed Veelos's hand. "You bear the silver ring," she said. "You wear no vestments, but you are a priestess, aren't you?"

Veelos nodded. "Yes."

"You can heal my husband."

"No."

"Yes you can. You have the power. This is well known."

"Kirok's path is nearing end," Veelos said. "I know it is difficult to hear that. But---"

"You must heal him!" the old woman begged. "We are believers in the God of angels, Kirok and I. When we had money, we gave it to the poor, just as the scriptures tell us to. We practiced all the virtues and devotions. We said all the prayers and obeyed all the divine commands. We did all that the priests told us to. Now that we are in need, where is our prayer from you?"

Veelos looked down upon Kirok's dying face, then back into the terrified, mourning eyes of his soon-to-be widow. For just the shadow of an instant, Veelos felt the beginnings of a warmth in her hand, a warmth meant to become heat. It was the same feeling which had grown into the healing spell she had cast upon a crippled girl named Shier-Bek. But in the next instant, Veelos had rejected it. For she knew better than to think it came to do good. It came not from the ring, but rather from some sinister force which imitated the ring. Veelos sent it back from whence it came.

"I will try," Veelos told the old woman. "I will pray."

Then, placing Kirok's hand into her own, Veelos prayed. "Dear God in heaven. You are the God of mercy and love. Hear our plea. Look upon the suffering before you, and take pity. You know the anguish of loss. You know the emptiness of loneliness. You know the indignity of poverty, the nightmare of hunger. Bestow your mercy upon this humble and devoted servant who lies helpless before you. Spare his wife this wretched fate. I, your unworthy servant, beg this of you."

But two hours later, Kirok was dead.

* * * * *

"Well, I'll grant you this much," Jagmoor said. Veelos was leaving for her rented quarters, wearied by the extra hours she had spent in arranging for Kirok's burial. "You tried. You gave it your very best. Here, take back your ten copper coins. You put me to shame."

Veelos refused. "It was you who made the rule," she said. "You must abide by it."

Jagmoor had learned to recognize when Veelos could not be argued with. "I'll split them with you. Five for each of us. No, don't push them back at me, or it's to be an ugly fight between us. Take them."

Veelos's face wearily gave way to a faint smile. And she needed the money.

"Too bad," Jagmoor remarked. "You gave her your money, and your best prayer. But she was ungrateful. She blamed you. Now isn't that something? It wasn't your fault that the prayer failed."

Veelos turned in the doorway, half in, half out. "I prayed for mercy," she told the healer. "Mercy for both of them. What made you think that the prayer failed?"

Chapter 12

The Persistence of Falsehood

"I heard rumors you were still alive," Keesha jested. "I came by to see if they were true."

Veelos laughed with joy. It had taken her but a moment to understand what Keesha had meant by her greeting at Jagmoor's door. Then, "Has it been so long?" Veelos asked.

The months had slipped by so quickly that Veelos had hardly noticed them. Where once the temple had kept her occupied night and day, now the labors in Jagmoor's clinic did so. Early each morning she arrived, and late each night she departed for her own rented quarter. The wages Jagmoor paid her, she spent on those of his patients who could not afford him.

Then, this day, to Veelos's astonishment and delight, Keesha had showed up unannounced.

"Since you never send word, I thought I'd visit with you," Keesha said. "Will Jagmoor give you the day off?"

He did, and very soon the two priestesses were strolling together along the street, toward the market. But as much as Veelos enjoyed Keesha's companionship, something did not seem right. Hesitantly, she asked, "Being seen with me--- will this get you in trouble?"

"Trouble?" Keesha asked. "Trouble for what? For visiting with you?"

"Well, yes. I mean--- I've been so much disappointment to--- look, I'm not exactly in good standing in the temple, now am I? They don't cast priests from the community over minor infractions. I count myself as a pariah."

Keesha sighed. "There are pariahs," she said, "and then there are pariahs. We're all sinners, you know. And since all of us depend on God's mercy, we can hardly treat you any differently than we ask to be treated ourselves. Cast from the temple, yes. But cast from God's sight, no. Not after you've given Him your love. Besides, the temple has received many good reports of you. Some people even rebuke us for having cast you out."

"They do?" Veelos asked in mild astonishment.

"Yes," Keesha answered. "They say we're more concerned with the letter of the law than with the spirit. And that's the milder criticism." She had spoken goodnaturedly. But then, in a tone more subdued, she added, "We had to do it, you know. In truth, you were never called to the priesthood, now were you? Were you?"

Veelos admitted it. "It was only to escape an unwelcome betrothal. It was all a lie."

"The witch's lie," Keesha clarified.

"Have you come to berate me?"

"There would be no point," Keesha said. "But we do keep an interest in you. Even a false priestess is still a priestess, you know. We cannot take the ring from you, until you are ready to surrender it willingly. That's the letter of the law."

Veelos appreciated Keesha's wit.

"I was worried that the priests would hate me," Veelos said, "or even worse, fear me. I know they regard me as someone impure. And in truth, I am impure, entirely unworthy of the silver ring. But Keesha, please try to understand. I can't give up my priesthood. I just can't do it. However tarnished, however impure I am, the ring is still my calling."

"You are a healer," Keesha answered, "a practitioner of the compassionate art. We had hoped that you would find your calling in that."

Veelos nodded. "I have. And that is my calling. But it's not separate from my being a priestess. False though I came to the temple, I don't feel the falsehood anymore. It's the priesthood only that remains."

"Well, I haven't come to quarrel with you," Keesha said, relenting. Then, changing the subject, she asked, "What do you think of this Jagmoor fellow?"

Veelos replied, "He's pleasant enough. He's no longer the miserly cynic he was at first. And the money you sent got me through my apprenticeship with him. I'm so grateful to you. Just one thing, though. I don't understand why you sent me to Jagmoor, of all men. I expected that you would send me to a worshipper of God, someone like the healer Halerd, or the midwife Shamel. I was quite surprised when I met Jagmoor; he's so irreverent. If you wanted my moral regeneracy, why did you send me to an agnostic?"

Keesha answered. "It wasn't to help you. It was to help Jagmoor."

* * * * *

The day fled quickly. While walking and shopping and eating, the pair talked incessantly. Some of their conversation was casual banter, and some of it melancholy. They told jokes, and remembered their homes and loved ones. They laughed, and sometimes shed a tear or two.

Too soon, the sun had begun its descent. Too late, the women realized they had committed a serious error.

"You'll never make it to the temple before dark," Veelos warned. "Spend the night at my place. It's not far."

"I'll walk you to where you stay," Keesha said. "But I really must get back. The brothers will worry over me."

But darkness fell even more quickly than they had thought.

Soon the two priestesses knew physical fear. For no trail through the forests of bandit realms was more savage and deadly than city streets after dark. As the sun went down, people retreated from the open places to their redoubts behind locked doors and barred gates. Sunshine was replaced by shadows, and by shadowy men. White vestments became a beacon.

"Just keep moving," Keesha urged when Veelos lagged. "And keep praying."

Veelos did both. She felt the snake-like eyes from within every dark corner and lair, eyes watching them with predatory intent.

"Alms for the poor?"

The man who suddenly blocked their way was large enough not to need any accomplice. He was stealthy enough to have appeared suddenly as if from nowhere.

Keesha had bumped into him, and found her wrist held tightly in his vise-like fist, clearly able to break bones. Veelos could make out few details in the darkness, but it was clear that this man was no beggar.

"It's too late to rob us," Keesha said. Her voice was full of bluff, but it revealed her fear. "We've already distributed our coins."

The man's reply was gruff. "I'll be the judge of that." Without pause, he began to rifle through Keesha's garb with no regard for her modesty.

Instantly, Keesha began to struggle, and screamed, "Veelos! Run!"

But Keesha might as well have kicked at a mountain. The robber seemed hardly to notice, as he tore at her clothes in search of a purse.

Veelos desperately glanced about for some kind of weapon, whatever might be handy. A rock would do, or a brick, any object heavy enough, or sharp enough, to at least distract the robber. But there was nothing in sight. The only thing to see was Keesha being subjected to crass and violent injustice by an unfeeling brute.

Sudden rage seized Veelos, and without thought for herself, she threw her body against the assailant. She tried to claw at his face, but found only a greasy beard. Veelos kicked, bit, and clawed some more. But the man seemed numb to it all.

Keesha tried to scream, but was so terrified that only a plaintive squeal escaped her throat.

Perhaps it was that sound from Keesha which triggered it. Or perhaps it needed no trigger. Whatever the cause, Veelos felt the rage within her become transformed into something worse than rage. It became hatred. But it did not stop even there. Her rage became part of the night, a slithering shadow, the kind of rage which darkens men's souls.

Veelos no longer hated merely what the robber was doing; she hated the man himself. She was no longer merely intent on stopping the crime. Veelos wanted him punished. She wanted him to die. She wanted the figure before her to die in pain.

The mounting intensity of her emotions conjured form and substance. The hatred in Veelos's heart materialized. Her fist became a claw of flame.

The robber suddenly became aware of Veelos. Some serpentine instinct took over within him, warning him of impending doom. He sensed a menace more sinister than himself. Irrationally terrified, no longer the predator but the prey, the robber felt a desperate urge to escape. In a frenzied attempt to break free, he elbowed Veelos in the ribs with the force of a truncheon.

But all which Veelos felt was heat, a fiery presence in her hand, the embodiment of that which had taken form from within the darkest recess of her soul. Despite the frantic, twisting maneuvers of the robber, there was no stopping Veelos from carrying out the deed she had determined to commit. Her eyes fiercely intense, a vicious snarl on her lip, Veelos pressed her open hand against the man's greasy beard.

First, there was the smell of singed filthy hair; then was heard the crackle of searing skin, and finally, the stench of burnt flesh filled their nostrils. The night suddenly echoed with the howling of a man in unendurable pain, a mortal in unearthly terror.

With an explosive burst of power, the man did break free then. Veelos watched him, as he staggered backward and fell to the cobbled street. She watched as the robber clambered back to his feet; he clutched the scorched side of his face. Then, for an instant, their eyes met.

His were accusation.

In the next instant, the man had turned and was running for his life. For long moments, Veelos listened at the diminishing sounds of his footsteps and his fading cries of agony, listened as if somehow by doing so, she could track him across the dark distance which separated him from her.

The man was not to die of his wound. It would heal. There would remain two scars. The one in his soul would go almost unnoticed, crowded in among his many foul deeds. The scar on his face, however, would be noticed often. For there, for the rest of his life, would be the unmistakable imprint of a bony, clawed hand.

* * * * *

"Veelos? Are you badly hurt?"

"No. You?"

"No. Just shaken. He didn't hit me or anything." Then, drawing closer, Keesha exclaimed, "Veelos! You are hurt. You're doubled over."

"Just my ribs. It's not serious. We haven't much farther to go. Get us to my place."

No further evil impeded their course through the street that night, as Keesha all but carried Veelos. Stumbling side by side, they soon reached the room where Veelos lived. It was a small cube, in a row of similar rooms, where dwelt those who sold cheap goods in the bazaar by day. It was just large enough for a sleeping mat, and a few basic possessions, nothing more.

The floor was not quite level.

There, in relative safety, Keesha and Veelos mended their torn vestments as best they could. And they wept until they fell asleep.

When morning came, Veelos felt a great soreness in her ribs. But there was a deeper wound, an aching soreness deep down in the soul. The robber had not taken any money. But he had stolen something more precious. Veelos hoped Keesha might notice, and offer some soothing words. But instead, she seemed in a hurry to leave without speaking at all.

Veelos felt resentment. "I had no choice, you know. He might have killed you."

Keesha halted her abrupt motions as she dressed, and without looking directly at Veelos answered, "Yes. He might have."

"Well--- you could be a bit more grateful than that."

Keesha nodded. "Very well. You saved my life. Or at least my virginity. Thank you."

Veelos was frustrated. "What else could I do, Keesha? I didn't mean for it to happen that way. I wanted to do the right thing. But I was helpless. Then this power surged into me unbidden. It was there. I had no time to think about it. There was no time. I had to do something, and I had to do it right then, before he killed you, or, or---. What would you have done in my place?"

This time Keesha did look Veelos in the eyes. "I don't know," she answered. "Perhaps I would have done just as you did. Or perhaps not. Maybe I would have fought on until one of us died, maybe until you died. I might have gotten us both killed. But that does not change what you did. It does not make it right."

Veelos remembered how she had felt when she had been on trial before the high priests. Then, she had been cast from the temple. Now she had committed a similar crime, and she feared that Keesha might cast her out again, not from a building, but from their friendship.

And indeed Keesha's words were harsh. "Don't you see what you do?" she scolded. "You did it again, Veelos. Do you never learn? You repeated the very sin that destroys the priesthood, the sin that only a false priestess would unrepentantly commit."

"But this time it was different," Veelos found herself pleading.

"Was it?" Keesha challenged. "The first time, you used the power to heal Shier-Bek--- you did it for good, or so you thought. Then this time, you used the power again--- and once more, you did it for good, at least you say so. Was there any difference? Oh, yes, it was different alright. This time, there was a little evil mixed in, wasn't there? Instead of compassion for a crippled girl, there was hatred of a spiritually crippled man. What will happen next time, Veelos? And unless you change, you know there will be a next time. And another and another. When next it does happen, will there be even the pretense of good? Or will you finally become what Kattaroon became in the end? She was a false priestess too, you know."

Now Veelos became openly angry. "I don't believe you would speak to me like this! I acted out of love for you, and now you call me a witch."

Keesha retorted, "What you did--- do you think that I could not have done that myself, and more?"

"But you would not," Veelos answered, her voice softer than before.

"No," Keesha said. "I would not have done what you did. I would sooner die."

Veelos was on the verge of weeping. "Whatever my crime," she said, "it was not borne of hatred, but of love. Is it a crime to love you?"

"No," Keesha said. "And I am grateful that you do love me. But your crime is this, Veelos: you love me more than you love that robber."

Chapter 13

The Warrior and the Priestess

Somehow, with uncanny stealth, months became years. The incident with the robber was all but forgotten, the sin forgiven. Keesha visited often, shared much, and together she and Veelos crossed from the upper edge of girlhood into womanhood. Yet always, there was this tension between them: that Keesha was walking the highway of priesthood, while Veelos stumbled along its side paths and alleys.

Seven years had passed since Veelos had left Har-Keem, and six years since its destruction. Does time heal? she asked herself. For there were times when she believed herself completely healed of the hurt which lurked within her. Only in the still of night did its ache return. Only in her dreams did it haunt her.

* * * * *

Kl'aarn wandered through the mists of his dreamscape.

He knew that he was lost, hopelessly lost. For this fog-shrouded nether-world extended forever in all directions. It made no difference which way he turned, nor how far he went, nor how fast. And if he went in no direction at all, alas, that would make no difference either. Nothing mattered in this no-place.

Yet still he searched. He wandered across the vast scrubland, unable to see more than a few steps ahead, but taking always one step more along the hopeless journey. For even in hopelessness he had nothing more than the hope, the wish, that perchance within the next misty clump of nothing, he might find her.

But he knew he would not. With an infinity to search, he was wandering in circles, getting nowhere. There was no hope of ever finding her. None. It was madness to continue, he knew. But he could not abandon the search. For he had nothing left now, not her touch nor her kiss, neither her caress. All Kl'aarn could ever have of Miril was the search. And that much, he would not abandon.

"Kl'aarn."

He heard her voice behind him, and turned to face it. Miril stood not far off, a mere infinity away, just barely beyond reach. He could see her clearly, even through the swirling mists.

"Miril!" Kl'aarn cried out. "I've found you. I've found you at last!" Even as he spoke, he wondered how it could be that he had recognized her. For she looked nothing as he remembered her. The softness was gone, replaced by sublime ferocity.

"No, my love." She spoke with a gentleness in her voice that did not belong to her. "You've not found me. It's but a dream, only mere illusion. You shall find me, my dearest, but not yet. Our day is not come. But when it is, we shall have our vengeance. Those who stole from us these priceless years will pay for them. Then we shall regain these six years, and an eternity more."

Kl'aarn stepped toward her. But the distance did not close. Distance was meaningless here. Miril remained as far from him as ever, an endless distance, barely beyond reach. "What is this talk of revenge?" he asked, puzzled. "What do we care for it? Let us have this day, this night, this hour. That alone is worth eternity."

But Miril sadly shook her head. Kl'aarn noticed how long and black her hair had become. "Would that it could be so! But we have enemies all about. This night belongs to them, not to us. Even now I steal these few moments at great peril. Soon, Kl'aarn. I promise you, soon."

Kl'aarn reached for her, but she was infinities away. "Let us awaken together!" he pleaded. Then, his dream becoming more disturbed, he said, "Miril! What has become of you? Your eyes, so narrow and dark. Your lips, your nails--."

"You don't understand yet," Miril said. "But soon you shall. Soon my power will be complete. Then we will belong to each other, once more and forever."

"What talk is this of power?" Kl'aarn asked. "Miril, what has become of you? Have you stepped from your path?"

Then a coldness swept across Miril's already icy face. "Path?" she sneered. "Path, do you say? Oh, yes. The Path! Once I trod that path, the one laid out before me. But now I make my own path. As you shall also make yours."

"No," Kl'aarn replied. "Whatever you are doing, whatever path you are now upon, don't do this foolish thing, Miril. It can only ruin us."

Miril seemed to snarl. "You are as blind as I once was, my love. But see. See your path, see it as it was to have been." She pointed to a place behind Kl'aarn.

He turned, and there before him was a vision. He saw himself, nearly six years younger, in a distant barbaric land. An arrow wound in his leg was swollen and oozing with pus. He saw his image limping upon that leg. In his hand was a rusty sword. Jeering, sadistic spectators surrounded the cage which enclosed him. His friend Trong was also there with him, in that arena, his eyes wide with terror. Trong held up his own corroded sword defensively between himself and Kl'aarn.

"They're demanding that we fight each other--- to the death!" Trong said in horror. "Why are they doing this to us?"

Kl'aarn saw himself reply. "We must not entertain them."

He saw Trong nervously nod in agreement.

"Then let's drop our swords," Kl'aarn heard himself say. "We're dead in any case. Why should we serve those who delight in our pains? At least this much of our dignity they cannot deny us."

"I'm with you," Trong said. "But how can I trust you? You drop your sword first. Then I will, too."

"Agreed," Kl'aarn's image said. Then he casually tossed away the rusty sword.

Instantly, Trong sprang forward and killed him.

The vision became a swirl of mist, and was gone.

Kl'aarn turned back to face Miril.

"Ruin?" she sneered. "That was to have been your fate, Kl'aarn. And mine was to never have known what became of you--- to wonder always whether you might yet live, to imagine you in chains, tortured, demeaned. To hope a false hope, and never be consoled. That, Kl'aarn was our path. I took us from it. I did well, my husband, though you have yet to see the wisdom of it. But you shall, darling. The wisdom of darkness shall be yours."

Even as she spoke, the fog began to surround Miril, and she faded from Kl'aarn's sight.

"No! Miril!" he called out. "Don't leave me!"

The words traveled with him back to the starlit trail in the forest, to the side of the campfire. The others were awakened by his pleas, and reflexively reaching for their swords, noted him sitting upright in his twisted blanket, his arms outstretched to the darkness.

They noted, and as always, they rolled over and pretended to have remained asleep.

* * * * *

One morning, while Veelos was cleaning Jagmoor's infirmary, there was a knock at the door. Jagmoor opened it, but Veelos could not see who had knocked. Then Jagmoor asked, "What brings you?"

A man's voice answered. "I seek the one named Veelos, the priestess. I called for her at the temple. But the priests told me that she is here."

Veelos saw that Jagmoor was taken aback. "Does one such as you ask for a priestess?" he said, as if in disbelief.

Her curiosity aroused, Veelos stepped to the door to see who was this man who asked for her by name. Then she, too, was dumbfounded.

The man was tall and thickly muscled. He wore the armor and sword of a mercenary warrior. Veelos's first reaction was reflexive fear, for this man was obviously a man of violence. But a closer look at him relaxed the fear she had felt. For, unlike others of his profession, this warrior seemed somehow less coarse. His mannerism was more reserved than that of the fighting men who sometimes wandered this far into Shi-Raq. (For most of them remained in the north quarter of the city, among the taverns and brothels.)

His eyes shifted toward Veelos, when she appeared, and he said, "I notice your ring. Are you the priestess, Veelos?" For she was in commoner garb.

Nervously, Veelos nodded. Then, finding her voice, she asked, "How is it that a man of the sword seeks me?"

In reply, he said, "I bear a message for you." Reaching gingerly forward, he handed Veelos a scroll. Veelos noticed that the parchment was of high quality.

The priestess accepted it with trembling hands, for she had not received a letter in six years.

The warrior noted her tremor, and said, "Without meaning to burden you, but I was instructed to await a reply."

Now Jagmoor spoke. "Enter in. While Veelos reads and composes her reply, you may share our food."

The warrior stepped inside and removed his heavy, bronze helmet. He did indeed seem civilized.

"I've eaten my fill," he said, declining Jagmoor's offer. Then, "But before you break the seal, Priestess---"

Veelos paused. "Yes?"

The warrior seemed at a loss for words. Then he spoke strangely. "May I ask you to sit, so that you will not faint?"

Her curiosity more piqued by the moment, Veelos found a floor mat and lowered herself upon it. Jagmoor and the warrior sat before her. "What is this all about?" she asked.

The warrior spoke. "Six years ago, your village Har-Keem was destroyed. You were, then, here in Shi-Raq. And you thought that none had survived."

Veelos felt her heart begin to pound furiously. "But someone did," she surmised.

"Yes," the warrior said.

"Is it--- Miril?" Veelos dared.

"No. Let me speak it right away. May I? His name is Kl'aarn."

Veelos almost fainted anyway. Jagmoor steadied her by the shoulder. He had never seen the priestess react so. And he was totally unprepared when she collapsed into the spasms of sobbing which suddenly engulfed her. She buried her head in her skirt, but the sound of her crying was undimmed.

It continued for some time. Then slowly, Veelos began to gather herself. It was a battle which sometimes turned the other way. Finally, Veelos lifted her head and dried her tears. Then, gently grasping the scroll, almost as if caressing it, Veelos proffered it back to the one who had brought it.

The warrior was confused. "Do you ask me to break the seal?" For that would have been most unusual and peculiar.

"No," Veelos said, her voice barely more than a whisper. "Don't open it. Carry it back to him who sends it. Tell him that Har-Keem is no more, nor its people. And tell him that the one named Veelos died with it."

Jagmoor was visibly astonished by her words. He stared in disbelief.

So did the warrior. "But you said you are---" he began. Then understanding, he spoke more quietly. "For six years he never sent word to you. But---"

"You may go now," Veelos said, averting her gaze.

But the warrior implored Veelos, "Do not judge Kl'aarn harshly. For you do not know what he has been through. He confesses his guilt in this: that before now he never sought you out. He knows he has slighted you, more than merely slighted you, and he repents. But he was under a curse, and now it is lifted. From dishonor he has risen to honor. And now he seeks to rectify all the wrongs he has done."

Then Veelos looked at the warrior with distant, cold eyes. "Tell him I feel no slight. Tell your merchant lord, tell him who sends you, tell him, that I am above feeling offense. And inform him that if he seeks a priestess, to seek her in the temple after all."

The messenger nodded. Then he said, "I notice that you refer to Kl'aarn as my merchant lord. But it is not so. I am not his hireling, but his comrade. He is not a merchant, but our captain."

The words had an effect. Veelos could not ignore them without asking, "Are you saying--- that Kl'aarn has become--- it cannot be."

"He is a warrior," the man affirmed. "And captain of our platoon of twenty-four. But as you say, perhaps he is also a merchant, for he certainly has the talent for such affairs of business as we conduct. But it's by the sword he lives, as do we all."

Veelos inhaled a tremorous breath. "How did this come to be? He never had the body for brawling."

The warrior answered. "He is quite a capable swordsman. But Kl'aarn is no brawler. None of us is. Each man of the platoon is a worshipper of God. I know that must seem a contradiction. But if you would only re-acquaint yourself with him, you would be satisfied that there is none. Lady Priest, won't you at least glance over his letter?"

Again, Veelos shuddered with fear, then regained control. "What is your name?"

"I am Kmir of Sher-Leth."

Veelos nodded. "Sher-Leth." It was not far from where Har-Keem had been. "Indeed. I thought your accent reminded me of the familiar. Has it really been six long years?"

Then, timidly, she accepted once more the proffered scroll, broke its seal, and read. She read it all the way through before, once again, she wept and cried from within the depths of her heart.

* * * * *

Now Veelos could no longer refuse the encounter, and so she agreed to visit Kl'aarn at the Copper Kettle Inn, for it was a place of good reputation, a fit place to meet.

Veelos shed her work clothes, and donning her vestments, was escorted by Kmir to the Copper Kettle.

When they arrived, Veelos at first stood mute in the doorway, hesitant to enter. Her eyes took in a scene to which she was unaccustomed, and which instilled a slight tremor of fear within her. For the dining quarter was occupied by some twenty men, all of whom were clad in leather and bronze, and each of whom was armed with sword and dagger. Veelos felt as a sheep among wolves.

But when Kmir noticed her timidness, he announced her. The men quickly ceased their raucous jokes and rude manners. Moving aside for her, they showed the respect that only men of faith in God would show to His priestess.

As she entered, still not quite sure that she should, Veelos looked discreetly at each man, trying to discern Kl'aarn among them. But there was none whom she could recognize.

Kmir ushered Veelos toward a table, and said, "He is up in the loft. We'll bring him down. He won't keep you waiting."

Kmir need not have been concerned. For Kl'aarn, hearing the men in the room below become suddenly quiet, had guessed Veelos's arrival. So he quickly descended the ladder which connected the loft to the hall below.

When he reached the floor, Kl'aarn turned to face the room, almost hesitantly, as if afraid. Their eyes met.

Although he was very much changed, Veelos recognized Kl'aarn immediately. He was no longer a boy. That was the first impression, and Veelos wondered why it caught her so off guard. His beard was not the wisp she remembered, but the thicker, coarser growth of a man's. He had more muscle than ever he had before, but even so, Veelos could still detect the remnant of frailty in him. Somehow the muscularity and the bones were not a perfect fit. She marveled that little Kl'aarn could ever have become a man of the deadly profession--- and live. Yet there he stood, as unnerved by their encounter as she was.

But what shocked Veelos the most was not what she saw in Kl'aarn, but rather what she felt within herself. The sudden warmth in her breasts embarrassed her. Veelos forced herself to remember her priestly vows.

Kl'aarn approached Veelos humbly and with apology. It was clear that he was master of this company of warriors, and unused to bowing himself. But he did so, a formal and humble gesture very unlike a commander of fighting men.

Veelos was the first to speak. "Let's not be formal, Kl'aarn." The controlled, self-confident tone of her voice surprised her. Veelos was grateful to be able to sound that way, silently grateful that her voice did not waver with the emotions she felt.

Almost as if ashamed, Kl'aarn replied, "You're too gracious, Priestess Veelos. But formality is a refuge to me. I've done you a great wrong, and I am a beggar before you, asking a pardon."

Veelos answered, "You embarrass me. I don't merit your courtesies. Please. Will we publicly apologize to each other? We were never this way before. Let's be children again, at least for a few moments. Now sit, and let's catch up on each other. I'll call you Kl'aarn, not captain, and you'll call me Veelos."

A faint smile of relief showed through Kl'aarn's beard, and he approached the table and sat on the wooden bench across from Veelos. Food and drink were set between them, but neither of them had any appetite.

There was awkward silence.

Then Veelos began it. "Tell me of the end," she said. "You saw it. You were there."

Kl'aarn nodded grimly. "I was there."

Veelos hesitated, then pressed on. "It was surely terrible for you. Can you bear to speak of it? Spare yourself, if not. But if you can recount it, don't spare me. I've lain awake so many nights imagining it. It is better that I have only one death to imagine for them, than the many which my sorrowful visions invent. So please tell me what you can."

"I'll try," Kl'aarn replied. "But I'm in almost the same fog about it as you are. I was the first casualty, you see, wounded and trampled over, being thought dead. Most of what I remember is hearing and feeling. I heard voices speaking a strange dialect, a dialect I've never heard before--- or since. Then there were the sounds of battle--- not a battle, really, but a massacre. Screaming women and children were being treated in ugly ways. Then someone tied my hands and feet and dumped me into the hold of a ship. After that, a storm. What a storm! Something black, malevolent, with conscious intent. No storm ever was like that. I remember almost drowning, then being washed ashore. After that--- it's all a fog for the longest time. I must have stumbled about in a fever for days on end. How I survived I'll never know."

Veelos had listened with rapt attention. Now she shuddered with the fear of asking the next question. It was uppermost on her mind. "Miril?"

Kl'aarn lowered his gaze, and clasped the fist of one hand into the palm of the other, pressing both of them upon his lips. Then he lowered both hands, and said painfully, "The last thing I remember clearly, is asking Shalar to see to her, to make sure she escaped. But I never saw either of them again, that night or since. Veelos, I've searched all east Wirik for her, for any trace of a survivor. Anyone."

There was silence, then Veelos chided, "You knew all along where one survivor was. Did you search all the world and not Shi-Raq? I'm sure you had your reasons, Kl'aarn. But for the life of me, I can't understand how, during six years, you never sent me so much as a note, so much as word that you were alive."

"Perhaps you will," Kl'aarn said. "I'll tell it. Perhaps you'll understand. It won't excuse me, but at least you'll know. Somehow, I made my way back to Har-Keem--- how, I'll never guess--- only to find it burned and looted. There was nothing left but ash and rubble. By the time I stumbled onto the site, a trading caravan had happened along. They had cremated the corpses. They fed and clothed me, but of course they expected something in return. So they put me into forced servitude. I became their slave, setting up their camps when they rested, and loading back up when they broke camp. I was in no condition to object. After all, I had lost everything. And these folk at least fed me and tended my wound."

Veelos reached forward and, gingerly, put her own hand atop Kl'aarn's nestled fists. "At least when I got news of it, I had support. I had all the love and comforting anyone could ask for. But you had no one. I begin to understand a little. But sooner or later you had to think of me. I want to hear what kept you from me."

Kl'aarn continued. "I was on the trail for months, being sold from one merchant to another. You see, whenever one caravan would approach its destination, it no longer needed me. I was sold to the first caravan going the other way. In this way, I remained at forced labor for about a year without rest. There were many chances to run away, but I had no life in me, no hope of anything better.

"Then everything changed. I was sold to a group of men taking spices to Kiriath-Ben-Kovit, a city reached only along the most dangerous trade route in all Wirik. These men were not merely traders. They were trained mercenary warriors. They worked me harder and longer than ever I had labored. I was nothing to them but another pack animal. After a few weeks, I became aware that they would just let me die, rather than ease my burdens. I came to hate them.

"We crossed into the regions where bandit-lords rule the land, where they war against each other, where they exact tribute from all passing merchants. Those who cannot pay, they plunder and massacre.

"Now our captain was willing to pay small tolls to avoid a fight. After all, the value of a warrior is to reduce the amount of tribute demanded by the bandit-lords. The bandits would rather collect tolls than frighten off caravans. There's no profit if the caravan passes through an enemy's domain--- where the neighboring bandit-lord can collect the tribute instead.

"But after we had paid a small tribute, this particular bandit demanded even more. It was clear that his demands would never stop, and so the negotiation erupted suddenly into a full scale battle.

"There were some twenty warriors, but two or three times that many bandits. It was a bloody fight, and the warriors soon began to take casualties. It quickly became clear that we were all to die.

"I hid beneath a wagon, my cowardice complete. A warrior fell dead, his sword within reach of my hand. Then something in me snapped.

"I took up the sword and began fighting like a madman. All those months of hard labor had strengthened me beyond what I had imagined. I got more strength from my fear, and even more yet from my rage.

"Yes, I was enraged. I had no idea why. My hatred for the warriors combined with my hatred for the bandits--- somehow they made me think of the pirates who destroyed Har-Keem. I don't really know. But I had no regard for life, neither mine nor anyone else's. All I could think of was to hack as many people to death as I could, before a sword or an arrow put an end to me.

"Then suddenly it was over. The bandits vanished into the forest and were gone. The warriors who remained were all staring at me, almost as if afraid of me. And scattered about me were the freshly killed bodies of more than a dozen bandits. The sword in my hand was covered in bright red blood.

"Beginning at that moment, I was nevermore a slave but a warrior."

Veelos gently drew back her hand from Kl'aarn's. "You tell a brutal story," she said, "a tale of cruel men and savage deeds. But how can this be? You are not such a man. Nor are these men savage, who call you captain. Yes, they all look rugged, and at first sight one fears them as one fears the brutal mercenaries of which you speak. But among your men, there is not the sense of daggers hidden in boots. One does not fear to hear these men at one's back. They are trustworthy and honorable men. So are you, Kl'aarn. Tell me of these things."

"I got a reputation that day," Kl'aarn continued. "The warrior captain gave me a reward: a sword, and armor of my own, and a pouch of silver coins. I was given the name "Blood-letter." But I had not risen from shame into glory, as I thought I had. Instead, I had sunk even further than one can envision.

"When we got to Kiriath-Ben-Kovit, I quickly spent all my money numbing my pains. Then I hired myself out to another warrior captain. His cargo was salt.

"Salt caravans are never attacked. Who would steal salt? Tribute is cheap for such. But I was not for an easy ride. When bandits did approach, I provoked them, and in a matter of a few days we had fought three needless battles. We lost two men dead, and some crippled besides. The captain dismissed me, fearing for his life. He even paid me my full wages just to be rid of me.

"I didn't care about the money. It mattered to me only to fight. I couldn't get enough of killing, and I cared nothing for the cost, whether the cost to me, or to others.

"After that, I made it a practice to hire myself only to caravans that would travel along the most dangerous of trails. I never did anything to avoid fights. I paid no tribute at all, and the merchants were pleased with that. (For they never cared how many died, only how much money they made.)

"Then one day, after another pointless battle, I saw a mortally wounded bandit lying under a bush where he had crawled away to hide. I walked over to finish him off. I would do it as coldly as that, just pierce him and walk away.

"But as I was about to do that, he looked up at me and spoke. I don't remember the exact words. He was young, only a boy. He had some learning. And he knew that he was dying. He told me his name, and asked that I send word to his family. But he begged me not to reveal to them that he had died a bandit, for he was deeply ashamed.

"You see, he had left his home with bright dreams. But the dreams had gone sour. He had intended to create an honest fortune. Yet bit by bit, he had become transformed from a devout worshipper of the God of angels, transformed from trusting to the Lord's path. Bit by bit he had strayed from the Word. And now, to his shame and astonishment, he found that he had made of himself a common rogue bandit, a thief and murderer, dying ignominiously under a bush in the wild.

"When he died, he died in my arms. I realized then that, like him, I had become what I abominated. Bandits steal money, I was stealing lives. That boy deserved to live more than I. And how many others like him had I killed without knowing their story?

"I gave him a burial and a grave-marker, and sent a letter to his family, saying that he had served loyally and with honor against injustice. During all this, a great darkness was lifted from my eyes, a blindness that had led me stumbling through a long and terrible night.

"It took perhaps another year before I was fully extracted from the evil which had enveloped me. God is patient with sinners, and I required much cleansing. During that year I met Kmir, the man I sent today to the temple to find you. He also has a story; sometime he will tell it.

"All this was concluded about two and a half years ago."

Veelos said, "I can no longer be angry at you for letting me think you dead all these years. As impossible as it seemed to me that I could forgive, now I see that there is nothing that needs forgiveness. You say all this was concluded two years ago, but of course it was not. Two more years you sent no word to me. Why, Kl'aarn?"

Kl'aarn grasped at the tip of his beard, then said, "There is a reason--- not an excuse, mind you. Despite your charity, I do need forgiveness from you for all six of those years. But I beg you, Veelos, before I go on, please tell me of you. I was too timid to face you without a letter going before me. But Kmir sent word from the temple that you were not there. He had been given another address."

Veelos found her own gaze falling to her hands, folded in her lap. "I suppose that does seem odd to you, doesn't it? What did the priests at the temple say?"

"They gave no explanation," Kl'aarn replied. "Don't all the priests live in the temple? I thought that was a strict rule."

Veelos answered, "All the worthy ones do. I was cast out."

Kl'aarn's face showed astonishment. His glance traced the outline of her vestments as if doubting his own eyes.

"Yes," Veelos said. "You see, you are not the only one, Kl'aarn, who has fallen under the dark powers of rage and hate. I also did. But the difference between you and me is that you learned a lesson which escaped me. You learned how to love an enemy. I, on the other hand, was like that young boy who died in your arms on the trail. I had dreams, dreams of healing the infirm, of doing good and noble deeds, of righting the wrongs of the world. Instead of a sword, I had a silver ring, and an Orb of Power. But like that boy--- and worse than you--- I misused that power. I healed by magic instead of by the means God intends. Fortunately for me, I had a mentor, a priestess named Keesha. She kept me from going too wrong. Even so, my sins got me cast from the temple. I am too ashamed to say more. But they still call me priestess. And Keesha and I remain very good friends. Almost as good a friend as I once had in----" instead of Miril's name, a sob choked her voice.

Kl'aarn noticed. "No," he said, "don't hesitate to speak Miril's name. I say it often. Indeed, she is the answer to the next two and a half years I have yet to explain. But how can I begin? Let me do it this way: After I turned away from my wickedness, that was when the dreams began.

* * * * *

"At first they were pleasant dreams. I would sleep, and there would be Miril, just as I remembered her. She was beautiful, gentle, gracious---everything a man could want in a wife. She would talk to me, advise me, console me. I slept well when I had those dreams, and never wanted to awaken.

"I spoke of these dreams to a village elder, an old man, who told me that these were not mere dreams. He said that they were from Miril."

Veelos frowned with concern. "From beyond the grave?"

Kl'aarn shrugged. "At the time, I thought he meant that. But as the dreams continued, I began to think differently."

"Go on," Veelos prodded.

Kl'aarn sighed. "I'm not sure how to say this. Veelos, the dreams had been pleasant ones at first. But then they became disturbing. In them, Miril became less and less the innocent maiden we both knew."

Veelos said, "I'll always remember her just as you described her: gentle, loving. But these dreams disturb you greatly, I can see. If you wish to share them, I am your servant."

Kl'aarn spoke. "In the dreams, Miril counseled me. If I were unsure of which route to follow, she gave advice. When I suspected a merchant of cheating, Miril would reveal him to me--- all in dreams of course. I actually began to pay heed to these dreams, to act according to the counsel given in them. And for a time, the counsels actually proved true."

"Beware!" Veelos warned. "Demons often disguise themselves as loved ones, especially as departed loved ones. They give just enough true advice to ensnare the unwary. But after that, it's ruin and death. And worse."

Kl'aarn nodded. "That is just the advice I was given. And indeed there came evil. For the advice given became advice to steal from my caravans, and to perform treachery against my comrades. In one dream I became so disturbed that I asked Miril why she was speaking so. I said to her, 'Miril, you are using the words by which Kattaroon tried to seduce Tarok into evil.'"

"And?" Veelos prodded.

"And Miril answered me by saying, 'Kattaroon and Tarok are in the land of the dead, but we will always be in the land of the living.' Then she vanished, Veelos. And I have not had the dream since."

Veelos flattened the palms of her hands against each other, and brought her index fingertips up to her lips. She sat in silent contemplation for long moments. Then she shook her head. "I am not an interpreter of dreams. But let you finish the story."

Kl'aarn went on. "After that, Veelos, I began to search in earnest for Miril. I mean, I really thought she might be alive. Men thought me mad. But I arranged our routes to carry us into places we would not normally go. I am speaking, Veelos, of the kinds of places one should stay away from: pirate havens and fleshpot villages. I never did find any sign of Miril, nor of anyone from Har-Keem, but I did discover this. Somewhere, in the hills and forests of east Wirik, although I never could find her, there travels a witch."

Veelos shuddered. "That does not surprise me. The high priests have been warning, for several years now, that some ancient prophecies of upheaval are about to be fulfilled, perhaps even in our own lifetime. To hear you speak of it is terrifying, but I believe you. The hills were never as plagued by bandits as now they are. The seas are infested with pirates as never before. Villages, that once were innocent farming communities, have become dens of gambling and debauchery, such as was not heard of only a decade ago. And the high priests caution us, that a witch will seek to enter into the temple itself, and to corrupt the Great Orb."

Kl'aarn listened, then he said, "When I became aware that something evil is prowling the land, I remembered that Miril had warned me of it before Har-Keem died from us. She knew."

"She could sense danger," Veelos agreed.

Now Kl'aarn became very nervous. He opened his mouth to speak, then closed it again without making any sound.

"Tell me," Veelos prodded.

Finally Kl'aarn answered. "Veelos, I always intended to come to see you here in Shi-Raq. I always intended to send a letter. By the time I decided to do that, so many years had already passed that I thought--- I thought---"

"That another year wouldn't matter?"

"Another day," Kl'aarn corrected. "It was always just another day, another delay--- I'm sorry."

"You needn't apologize anymore. You're here now. I'm glad. So what finally moved you to delay no more?"

Kl'aarn was hesitant to answer. "Veelos, there is within me a feeling about Miril, a feeling so strong and powerful that I simply cannot shake it. Call it what you will--- remorse, delusion, lovesickness--- Veelos, I can't persuade myself that Miril is dead. I've tried, and I just can't. And worse yet, I sense that she is in some horrible danger. I mean, not the kind of danger like drowning or fire, but a steady, constant danger--- and more sinister than I can find words to describe. Veelos, I think that like us, Miril has gotten into something she's lost control over. You and I were spared, but Miril has fallen ever deeper into it. And it's connected with this witchcraft that is corrupting our land from the middle outward. She's in danger, Veelos. And only you can give me the help I need to get her out of it."

Veelos glared at Kl'aarn. "Do you realize what you're saying?" she demanded. "You're accusing Miril of a crime for which there can be only one penalty: death by burning."

"No," he said. "I didn't say---"

"But it's what you're afraid of, isn't it? Kl'aarn, you are sadly deluded. It is not Miril who is under a spell, but you. Now listen to me. I know you love her. I know that your loss is tragic and painful. That can do all sorts of things to one's mind. Look, Kl'aarn, I am glad you came here to ask my help. But I can't. You need to see the high priests."

"No," Kl'aarn replied. "I need to see you. You knew Miril. You loved her. The high priests' answer will give me no hope. If Miril has gotten tangled up in some coven of witches, how much worse will the priests do to her? Even if she's only been enslaved unwilling into their services, the priests will deal harshly. Veelos, if Miril really is alive, she's in desperate trouble. Will you turn your back on her?"

Veelos pushed away from the table and stood. "Kl'aarn, let me ask you this. If it so happened that you did find Miril ensnared in the trap you describe, what would you do? Could you extract her? Or would you yourself become ensnared, seduced into the practice of black arts? For my part, I've learned to trust the scripture. Witches must die, Kl'aarn. Just as they die spiritually upon coming into the sisterhood of evil, so they must die physically when at last the force of good overpowers them. That's just the way it is."

"That's a cold answer," Kl'aarn said, also standing. "You don't live with what I live with. You're persuaded she died. But I am stuck with believing her alive, no matter how much I wish to believe her in heaven with the angels. And if she is alive, Veelos, why hasn't she come to you? It can only be because she knows, as you surely know, that there is enmity between the priesthood and witches."

Veelos calmed herself. "You don't know the half of it," she said. "That enmity is deeper than any other--- even that between warrior and bandit. But that is just the point, Kl'aarn. If Miril were a witch, she would be sworn to kill me--- not the less for being my sister, but more so. And by now she would have carried out her duty. If Miril had indeed become a witch, then by this time, she would have already killed me. But I live. That alone is proof, Kl'aarn, proof that she is no witch."

"You're forgetting one thing," Kl'aarn said. "It takes six years of servitude to make a witch. As soon as that six years is ended, whoever this witch is, she will come hunting. And soon, Veelos, it will be six years since last I saw Miril alive."

Veelos pulled her robe closed about her vestment. "I think we've spoken much this day," she said with cold formality. "Thank God for saving you alive, and for bringing me word of those who died. But now our sweet words are becoming strained, my brother. So let us take respite, and consider apart how we shall speak again tomorrow."

Kl'aarn took in a deep breath, then said, as if hiding behind the formality, "May the love of God be with you, my dear sister. Please do come back tomorrow. I'll send Kmir to escort you home."

Kmir led Veelos to the door of the inn. There, she turned once more, and looked at Kl'aarn. "I really do thank God," she said. "Thank Him forever for saving you."

Chapter 14

Two Priestesses, One Bride

Veelos's room was one among a strip of one-room quarters. The strip was surrounded by a tall masonry fence. Kmir saw Veelos to the gate, and would have quickly departed. But Keesha was there, waiting--- in expectation of what, Veelos could not tell. But clearly, Keesha sensed the great import of what had happened this day.

She greeted them. "Kmir. We meet again. Thank you for seeing Veelos safely back to us."

Kmir returned the greeting. "You are the priestess Keesha, whom I met at the temple. You were with the older one, Jen-Aga they call her. I'll not soon forget the look on her face when I asked for the one named Veelos."

Keesha smiled with amusement. "Nor will I. She has an icy stare that could well deflect your metal sword. But her heart is much kinder than seems her appearance. I do hope her manners were not offensive."

"I was well received by her. Any offense that was given came from me," Kmir answered. Then, "Can I be of further service? If not, I'll be on my way."

"Thank you," Veelos said. "Tell Kl'aarn I'll come by the Copper Kettle tomorrow early. Good day then."

When Kmir had gone, Veelos and Keesha entered her quarter. "My, my," Keesha said.

Veelos allowed herself to collapse onto her bedding with an exhaustion both physical and otherwise. She was hoping Keesha did not wish to engage her with questions.

"What an eventful day," Keesha continued, ignoring Veelos's body language. "When the high priests got word that a swordsman was at the archway, they left aside all their dignified posture and scurried to see what was afoot. I'll confess to being a little unnerved myself."

"We can speak of it tomorrow," Veelos said.

"I just came to see if it went well with you. We were all a bit unsure whether to tell Kmir where to find you. We put him off no little time with our questions. Finally I trusted him. He seems a good man. I hope I did right."

"Indeed, you did," Veelos answered.

"You met with Kl'aarn then. He truly lives after all."

"Yes."

"My!" Keesha exclaimed. "When Kmir mentioned his name, I felt that I'd seen a ghost, no, a man raised from the dead to life. Which is more than I can say of you at the moment. Well, tell of it! You must have something delicious to say."

Veelos raised herself up on one elbow, and leaned her back against the wall by her sleeping mat. "I suppose it's no use trying to send you away without a report."

"Don't think of it!" Keesha said.

The two were seated on the mat, and Veelos began recounting her experience, from the moment Kmir had knocked at Jagmoor's door, until she had departed from the Copper Kettle. She told all, the crying, the reading of the letter, the discussion in the inn.

Keesha had taken in every word of it hungrily. But still she seemed starved for some morsel that had yet to be served.

She hesitated in that way she had, whenever she was embarrassed to speak, but could not contain herself. "You describe him so well that I feel I could pick him from a crowd," Keesha said. "Yet there's something you've left out."

Veelos wondered what Keesha was after, but she had no energy to solve puzzles. "I've told you everything."

"Except---," Keesha said at last, "Veelos--- how do you feel about him?"

Veelos blushed. She remembered the initial warmth she had felt in her bosom upon first sight of Kl'aarn. But that had been only momentary. Must Keesha know every secret?

"But I have told you," Veelos said, hiding her discomfort behind a yawn. "I'm very happy to see him alive."

"Of course you are," Keesha said. "But Veelos---"

"I've been through a lot of different emotions in a short time," she complained. "I haven't sorted them all out yet."

"But of course."

"And stop of-coursing me."

"Of course. I'm sure it was as unsettling for Kl'aarn as for you," Keesha said.

Veelos nodded. "He bears a heavy burden, Keesha. He did not enter Shi-Raq on any mere courtesy call. He seeks help on some very serious disturbance in his soul. And I'm not up to the task. I've asked him to seek help from the temple."

Keesha said, "We'll be happy to provide him with whatever counsel we can. But truth be told, Veelos, from your account of it, it sounds like you've done as well as any of us in the temple could do. After all, you know him very well. Don't you? Or has he changed so much?"

Veelos shook her head. "How can one person change so much, yet be so unchanged? Kl'aarn is so very much as I remember him, yet---. I need time to absorb this."

"I'm sure. But please don't take forever. I look forward to meeting him, too, you know."

Veelos almost gave out a laugh despite herself. "Isn't it the strangest thing, but I've only just now realized you've never met him. Strange. Sometimes I forget that you and I didn't grow up together. Oh, Keesha, you've become so true a sister to me. I would take you to the inn now, if my manners were not departed with my vigor. Shall I take you there anyway?"

"No, you've been through quite enough for one day," Keesha said. Then, she opened her mouth to speak, but thinking better of it, said nothing.

Veelos noticed. "Whatever words could be burning within your throat, Keesha? I've never seen you this way. You're all but bursting with a question, but won't ask it."

"Well--- there is something on my mind. As soon as Kmir made it known to us that Kl'aarn was alive, I felt a great joy rush over me. A very great joy for him--- and a very special gladness for you."

"Yes? And what is this getting to?"

"And," Keesha continued, "I recalled all the times you had spoken of your townfolk through the years. Of Miril, of Valen Elder, of Shalar--- but most of all, of Kl'aarn."

"Well I would not put Shalar among that list, but do go on."

"Veelos, I had always thought that you had a special feeling for Kl'aarn."

Veelos's blush betrayed her.

"Well?" Keesha pried. "How _do_ you feel about him?"

"You ask that again. But I've told you," Veelos said.

Keesha nodded. "You've told me. But you spoke as a priestess."

"Is there something wrong with that?"

"Of course not. But you've been a priestess six years, Veelos. That's a long time to tread a path not meant for one. No, I'm not starting in on you. It's just that, well, when Kl'aarn's messenger showed up--- we took it as a good omen--- which of course it is. But a very clear omen. We sort of thought it was perhaps--- perhaps a way for you to find a path--- is there no delicate way to phrase this? But did you not come to Shi-Raq to escape an unwanted betrothal? Is not that betrothal dead, and are you not a free woman?"

Veelos's eyes widened. "You're not serious! Are you suggesting that Kl'aarn and I could marry?"

Keesha retreated. "The thought came to us. Just the thought."

Veelos shook her head. "Keesha, that's madness. Kl'aarn is Miril's husband."

"She's dead, Veelos."

"It doesn't change it. I just couldn't. He belongs to Miril."

"He'll marry someone," Keesha said.

"As he should."

"Why not you?"

"No," Veelos answered firmly. "Not me."

"I see. I didn't mean to---"

"And you're wrong about me, Keesha. Being a priestess is my path. Even if I broke all the rules and schemed and sinned, even so--- priesthood is my life, Keesha."

"As you say."

"I'm not finished," Veelos pressed on. "If ever I were to renounce the silver ring, it would be not for a man, not for any man. Really now, Keesha, whatever gets into you? Have the priests nothing better to do than engage in romantic intrigue?"

Keesha's embarrassment showed. "We were rash, then. I apologize. We were all so excited when Kmir told us. I guess we already had you married, with seven children, and forgot to ask you first. Oops."

"Apology accepted." Veelos folded her arms, momentarily caught up in her own conjectures. Then, almost sheepishly, she asked, "Keesha? What about you? Don't you ever---? Do you never think about getting a husband? I mean---"

"Sometimes," Keesha answered. "I'm not merely part woman. I'm sure even Jen-Aga has felt the same urge as we all do from time to time. We're not without human desire, you know. Even impure desires. Oh, the scandals we've sometimes had! All for the flesh. But we survive our celibacy and thrive because of it. We are not to be pitied for it. But answer for yourself, Veelos. Is the celibate life for you?"

"I've found it far preferable to the lives I see other women lead," Veelos said. "Simpler. Less binding."

"You've never envied those women?" Keesha asked. "Never lain awake at night, and felt lonely? When you see children playing in the street--- do you never wonder what your own children might look like some day? And forgetting all that, have you never been physically tempted by any man? Never felt attracted to any of them? Never hoped to find one for yourself? Never felt cheated by those other women who lead happy, married lives?"

"No. I've never envied any of them."

"You answer much too quickly," Keesha said. "The scriptures tell us that Eve was given the yearning for her husband, even though he was her master. I think that applies to both of us."

"Well I'm different," Veelos said. "I don't feel that way. Not since I came to Shi-Raq."

"Oh," Keesha said pensively. "Not since seven years ago. Now we're getting somewhere. So you did feel the urge--- in Har-Keem. But if not for Kl'aarn, then for whom?"

"Keesha! You're prying."

"I know it wasn't for Shalar."

"Keesha, stop it. Now really."

"Very well," Keesha said. "I didn't mean to hurt you. I really didn't."

"I'm not hurt. Just drop it, will you? Let's talk about other things."

"Alright. Such as?"

"The priests."

"They're all quite well. All in good health, and growing in spirit. No recent scandals. Blah blah blah and so forth." Keesha restrained a giggle.

"And you?"

"The same," Keesha said.

"Your visits with the crippled?"

"Oh!" Keesha exclaimed. "The most wonderful news. How could I forget? I couldn't wait to tell you, and then all this happened and I completely forgot. May God forgive me. But guess who's getting betrothed? And she asked for you, especially. You! The ceremony is tomorrow evening."

"Who?" Veelos asked impatiently.

Keesha answered. "Shier-Bek."

Chapter 15

Augury of the Demonwitch

The announcement stunned Veelos. "Shier-Bek? Being betrothed?"

Keesha noticed the hesitation in Veelos's voice. "Yes," she said, frowning in puzzlement. "Don't you find that good news?"

"Is it?" Veelos asked.

"Why shouldn't it be?" Keesha responded. Then, perplexed at Veelos's reservation, she said, "Veelos, what are you worried about---?"

Veelos answered, "When I used the Power to heal her legs--- to straighten them--- I know now that I took Shier-Bek from her path. And I did it just for this very purpose, just because I wanted her to be like other girls, to be able to have love, romance, marriage--- children of her own. For this I was rightfully cast from the temple. Because God obviously did not want Shier-Bek to be like other girls. He had a higher purpose for her. And I endangered all that."

Keesha put her hand on Veelos's. "I understand your worry. But you have repented of what you did. Let God take it from there. He has righted many wrongs of mine. Trust Him to repair that which you have damaged."

"Sometimes it's hard to trust God," Veelos said, without rancor. "There are earthly kingdoms in which the ruler punishes wrongdoing, promotes justice, and generally increases the public welfare. One would think that an all-powerful God would do better than any earthly monarch, that He would establish a perfect kingdom without delay."

Keesha nodded. "Actually, He did. We ruined it. With our sins. There will come a day when the scales will fall from our eyes, and we will see clearly that all the reasons we had for doubting God were foolish reasons, sinister deceptions. But while the scales yet blind us, God has not abandoned us. He shines the light of life-giving faith in the darkest of rooms, the chambers of the human soul. And that faith is free for the asking."

Veelos considered, then said, "She asked for me? By name?"

Keesha smiled. "It's been some time since you've seen her. She'll remove all your doubts, I promise you. God has set right whatever you may have set wrong. You'll know that when you visit her. Shier-Bek has set her heart on your officiating over the betrothal ceremony. Tomorrow evening. You won't disappoint her, will you?"

"Well, since you put it that way."

"Good. Then I'll stop by and cheer her up with your acceptance. So I'd best be going. And you'd best be purifying yourself for the service. Oh, and get some sleep. You're exhausted."

Veelos went to bed weary, and despite the excitement she felt, soon fell into a deep sleep, and dreamed.

But this was no ordinary dream. She had fallen into a pit. It was a place of desolation, a place of death. There was something familiar about it. It was the place in which she had found herself that day, long ago, when a marooned pirate had nearly strangled her.

Swirling mists obscured most of the detail, but Veelos made out the gnarled forms of dead trees, and the barren rocks with tortured contours.

Kl'aarn was there with her.

Veelos called his name. "Kl'aarn! Where are we?"

But to her astonishment, Kl'aarn seemed not to see her. He walked right past Veelos, his eyes scanning right and left, trying to pierce the mist. Veelos understood then, that this was not her own dream, but rather Kl'aarn's. She was an intruder here.

"Miril?" he called out. "Miril? Where are you? Please come out. Don't hide from me. I know you're here."

Veelos tried to grasp Kl'aarn's arm, but he seemed always just beyond reach. "How you do love her!" Veelos said to him, although Kl'aarn could not hear. "But she is not to be found. You must understand that. You will never have Miril in this life again. All you will ever have of her is the pain of missing her. Will you cling even to that?"

But just as Veelos finished saying that, the mists swirled between a rock and a gnarled shrub, then parted. And suddenly there, in the space between, was a woman. She wore dark robes, robes so black that Veelos could not have imagined anything so black in all the world. Her face was that of a young and beautiful woman, but there was nothing gentle in her. The features were hard, cruel, and evil.

Veelos shrank in fear from this woman, for she had great power.

The woman in black addressed Kl'aarn. "Over here, my darling. Over here."

Kl'aarn spun to face her. "Miril!" he addressed her. He tried to step toward her, but in this netherplace, he could strive but not reach her.

Veelos shuddered as Kl'aarn called Miril's name. "It's not her!" Veelos said. "That woman is not your Miril!"

But both of them seemed not to hear her at all.

"No, Kl'aarn," the witch said. "It's not yet our time. But soon it will be. Be patient but a little while more, my darling. For we shall have our revenge for these lost years of our life together. We shall have it."

Kl'aarn ceased his futile running toward her, for he could not reach her, however much he tried. "Miril," he said. "I don't want revenge. I just want you. What have you done to yourself? What have you become? Look at yourself."

The witch answered. "I did what I must, my love. You were taken from me. Tarok would not give you back to me. Only the demon would. It did. And soon we will be together again. Soon!"

"Miril!" Kl'aarn said. "You've made it worse for us, not better. This path you're on, it won't lead us to happiness."

"Stop it!" the witch said. "Would you trust to the path Tarok urged us to follow? Here. I will show you where that path led. Look."

The witch pointed with upraised arm, her fingernail but a human claw. Nearby, another cloud of mist formed and parted. There was revealed a vision, a vision of what would have been. In the vision was Kl'aarn as he had been those six years ago, a frail scrawny boy. He was in a distant foreign land, a captive in an arena surrounded by jeering, drunken barbaric men. Kl'aarn's thigh was oozing pus from a recent wound.

In the arena with him was his friend, Trong. Veelos saw that Trong was just as she remembered him, although he too suffered from wounds and mis-treatment. In the hands of both boys were crude rusty swords, weapons not of war but of blood sport.

"They want us to kill each other!" Trong said, his eyes wild with fear.

"Let's not entertain them with our misery," Kl'aarn replied. "If we must die, let it not be in their service."

"I agree," Trong said. "Let's drop our swords. But I don't trust you. Drop yours first."

Without hesitation, the Kl'aarn in the vision cast his sword to one side, well out of reach.

Equally without hesitation, Trong raised his sword and killed his friend.

The mists closed again, and the vision was gone. Kl'aarn turned again to face the witch.

"That," the woman in black sneered, "was the path ordained for us from heaven. For you, it was to die ignominiously in the far corner of Wirik, beyond the Lands of Demi-men. For me, it was to spend all the rest of my life never knowing what had befallen you, never knowing for certain whether you lived or had died, whether you were in comfort or in pain. That was our path, Kl'aarn."

Kl'aarn was shaken. "Perhaps so," he said. "But who are we to judge? What is a path but an escape route through suffering, and into a better world?"

"Don't be a fool," Miril retorted. "What are we asked to do in the name of good but to sacrifice and suffer, in return for some future hope that may never materialize? Far better that we seize mastery over our own destiny. That is the nature of evil, my love. Soon you will understand. For now, I show myself to you, only because this separation has been pain and sorrow to me. But I cannot remain. It is too much risk. So one more time, my love, farewell. Just this one more time. When next we meet, there shall be no more farewells to grieve us."

"No!" Kl'aarn called out. "Don't go. Come back Miril. Please!" But it was Kl'aarn who vanished, leaving Veelos all alone with the woman in witch's robes.

Then the witch turned to face Veelos. "He is mine," the woman warned. "Not even in your dreams shall you taste his kiss."

Veelos was stunned. "No," she stammered. "I have no desire to---"

"Don't lie to me, liar priestess," the witch snapped. "Not even that whore Keesha believes your stupid lies. You're deceiving no one but yourself. You want him. That's why you refuse to believe who I am."

Veelos tried to withdraw from the witch's presence, but she could not. Then she said, "You aren't Miril. You're an impostor. Miril did die in Har-Keem."

"You wish I were dead, Veelos, dear sweet sister. You wish I had died in Har-Keem so that you could take my husband. But whatever power you have, it will never be enough to steal him from me."

Then Veelos dared to say, "If you really are a witch, then why haven't you killed me? For you see that I am a priestess, your very worst enemy. And that enmity is unreconcilable. There can be only one end to it, and that is for one of us to die."

"That's very bold of you," the witch answered. "I would kill you even now, and indeed I could do so this very moment. But I have plans for you, false priestess. Plans. If you are wise, you will serve me well, and turn away from serving your God. If you serve me instead, then perhaps I shall reward you. I could even love you again, false priestess, love you as once, long ago, we loved each other. But know this: Kl'aarn shall never be yours. Never."

Then, with a sudden whirlwind of mist, the witch vanished.

Veelos awoke. Despite it being a warm night, her room was chill. This coldness was no dream. A layer of frost covered the walls. Shivering, Veelos arose and shuttered her window tightly. She lit a candle, and huddled beside it.

"What do you mean?" she whispered into the darkness. "You said you might love me again. But nothing so hideous as you ever loved at all."

Chapter 16

Ceremony of Life, Ritual of Death

The next morning, Veelos arose early. She had slept only in fits, but was too nervous to remain in bed. The priestess moved quickly through her morning routine. Soon, she found herself at the Copper Kettle Inn, unashamedly early for her appointment with Kl'aarn.

But, to her embarrassment, Kl'aarn was engaged in a corner of the lower room, in some animated discussion with Kmir, and two men who wore the garb of rich merchants. Kl'aarn broke away from them only long enough to see that Veelos was served breakfast. Then he begged his leave, explaining, "Business."

As Veelos ate, she watched Kl'aarn from across the room. He was thoroughly engrossed in whatever negotiation was being conducted. One could see that he was talented, and well trained, at the art of barter. L'aarn would have been proud. Veelos noticed something else about Kl'aarn, and wondered why she should find it curious: Kl'aarn seemed well rested. Obviously, he had slept quite peacefully.

When the meeting was concluded, Kl'aarn bade his guests a cheerful farewell, seemingly pleased with whatever deal had been struck. Then he joined Veelos at her table.

"How's the food?" he asked. "If it's not up to your standard---"

"It's far more delicate than my usual fare," Veelos assured him.

"Well then. Where did we leave off yesterday?"

Veelos asked him the question which was plaguing her. "Kl'aarn, did you dream last night?"

He frowned quizzically. "I don't remember any dream."

"I see. Well, never mind." Veelos abandoned the thought. "Before we take up our conversation, I'd like to share some pleasant news. A young lady of the city, a dear friend, very dear, is being formally betrothed today. Keesha and I are to officiate. Since it is the custom, for the presiding priest, to bring his own entourage, I am appointing you. That is, if I'm not presuming upon you."

"I gratefully accept the invitation," Kl'aarn answered.

Briefly, they discussed such matters as the time and place of Shier-Bek's ceremony. The arrangements made, Kl'aarn said, "You asked me if I dreamed last night."

Veelos wished she had not. "Yesterday, we ended on a sour note," she said. "Let's devote today only to sweetness. I'd like to share memories, to reminisce---"

But Kl'aarn saw through it. "You had a reason to ask me if I dreamt. You didn't sleep well last night, though you hide it so well that only forest eyes could detect it. You had a vision, didn't you?"

"It was just a dream," Veelos insisted. "A dream put together by the mind from the raw material of yesterday's experiences."

"Did you see her? What did she say?"

Veelos admitted, "I saw a woman in black. But it wasn't Miril. She pretended to be, but it wasn't her."

"It was her, alright," Kl'aarn said.

"She was a witch, Kl'aarn. A very powerful, very ferocious woman of evil. This was no mere captive, not even a mere sorceress. This one has died the death into evil. You don't want to believe this of Miril, and neither do I. The best I can tell you is that the woman I saw was not Miril. It was not even a convincing impostor."

Kl'aarn turned his gaze slightly away. "I don't want to believe that Miril has willingly become a witch."

"Well she hasn't. She wouldn't. Miril would never sink so low, never."

Then Kl'aarn looked back to Veelos. "For a witch, can there ever be any hope? Is there any way to redeem one?"

Veelos shook her head. "Death."

* * * * *

The house where Shier-Bek had grown up echoed the memories of lost splendor, not only of lavish drapes and furnishings, but of that special kind of grandeur which, once it is vanished, can never be recaptured. The house was the legacy of Shier-Bek's father, whose style was even yet imprinted upon it.

Despite its echoes of tragedy, the house seemed a happy place once again. Shier-Bek's mother and older siblings were hospitable and gracious hosts. Kl'aarn watched them all closely, fascinated by the family bond which animated them, a bond for which there could be no substitute in all the world. He reflected on the years which had passed without his having been in such close-knit, civilized company. In a sad thought, Kl'aarn contemplated how much he had missed during these past six years, separated forever from his own family, unable to begin another one.

But no sooner had he reflected on this, than Kl'aarn immediately began to feel out of place, a ruffian among the genteel. His sword was awkward here. (But it was one of his self-imposed disciplines, that he was never without it.) It insinuated a thought of violence into the merry circumstance. The warrior wondered if anyone else were having that thought. But they seemed to take no notice of his deadly instrument, none at all.

Kl'aarn idly wondered. Had the men who had murdered the master of this house ever paid for their foul deed? Perhaps so. Whether under the sword of a warrior, or by the dagger of treachery, most bandits led short lives. Had they paid? If not yet, then some day.

But one could not dwell long on such thoughts amid this company. There was good food, laughter, true friendship, indeed, love, a very special and selfless love.

When Shier-Bek entered, perfumed and gowned, Kl'aarn found his gaze fixed on her. She was dazzling in her beauty. Every young man in Shi-Raq must have been competing for her, since the very first day she had come of age. Whoever was the man who had won her, Kl'aarn thought, he must be the son of Shi-Raq's noblest family. Even before he arrived, Kl'aarn pictured him. Kind, charming and whatever else made a man deserving of such a bride, he must cut quite a figure.

But just before the lucky fellow did arrive, Kl'aarn felt a strange sense of premonition. It was nothing supernatural. Rather, it was the instinctive awareness that results from long months of living along forest trails. That sense suddenly became heightened. At first, Kl'aarn supposed it must mean danger. He had to deliberately suppress his hand from reaching for the sword at his side. And well that he did, for what he sensed was no danger at all, merely the unexpected, the unexplainable.

When the young groom did enter the room, Kl'aarn became most puzzled. For this man came in on crutches. He needed them, for his legs were so obviously deformed as to make him all but a total cripple.

* * * * *

For the first time in years, Veelos felt safe. The sun was beginning its nightly descent, but there was no need to hasten for the shelter of her abode. Kl'aarn walked by her side, armed and armored, and well versed in the tools of his trade. The mere sight of him sent the stalkers back into their shadows.

"Do you always carry that?" Veelos asked, indicating his sword.

"It's never beyond my grasp," he said. They were making for Veelos's living quarter after the betrothal ceremony.

"The helmet, too? Doesn't it get heavy and uncomfortable?"

"Sometimes."

"Then why do you put up with it? I mean, you don't need to wear them all the time, do you?"

Kl'aarn answered, "Every trade has its discipline, every profession its code. But this business I am in, sadly lacks them. So we are setting some standards. My men are not mere brawlers. For us, the sword is a calling. We do this work not merely as a living--- Lord knows it's more a way of dying. But we do it for reasons that others would scoff at and ridicule us for. Our implements are not merely those things that are made of bronze and leather. They are also things like honor, courage, loyalty. Devotion to justice."

"You seem to have made a priesthood of it," Veelos remarked.

"Not entirely," Kl'aarn said. "Not entirely."

"No? How not?"

Kl'aarn sighed. "We do not eschew marriage."

Veelos nodded. "I see."

"I was talking to your sister priestess, Keesha, today."

"Uh-oh," Veelos said. "I'm not sure I want to hear this."

"She's some lady. And every bit the priestess."

"What did she say?" Veelos did want to know, despite her misgivings about asking.

"We spoke about Shier-Bek. After you told me about the spell you cast on her, Keesha told me how you two had worried that she might come to harm. But she didn't. Shier-Bek stayed true to the path of her life. Not many people would."

"And then," Veelos added, "Keesha managed to entertain you with a speech about love, did she?"

"You know her well."

"And using that, Keesha started talking about----" Veelos was too embarrassed to continue. "About what?"

Kl'aarn chuckled. "It embarrasses me, too. Keesha was very frank about it, though. Is it her habit to be match-maker?"

"No," Veelos hastened to say.

"Well, she bluntly asked me whether I had considered asking your hand in marriage."

Veelos hid her face. "No. She didn't."

"And when I told her no, she asked why. I explained. Miril. I told her I am husband to Miril, and that I believe her to be alive."

"But Keesha didn't give up that easily," Veelos surmised.

Kl'aarn continued. "Then I explained that, well, a man just never thinks about marrying a--- a priestess. The white robes, the blue trim, the hood, the belt--- I mean that garb is designed to have an entirely different effect."

"And it has the same effect upon the wearer."

"But Keesha isn't easily discouraged. She started pointing out little things that might escape notice."

"Like?" Veelos prompted.

Kl'aarn shrugged. "Our language. For six years, neither of us heard our native accents. You had adopted Shi-Raq's manner of speech; I spoke much like the hill folk. Keesha noticed how much more like each other you and I sound, again."

Veelos nodded. "It's true. The old ways are easily revived."

"Then Keesha mentioned other things. Gestures we have in common. The kinds of food we favor. I suppose there is a lot we've forgotten. Do you still cook the same things your mother did?"

"Stop it!" Veelos snapped. She had shed a tear.

Kl'aarn winced. "I'm sorry. What a fool I am."

Veelos dried her eye. "It's alright. I guess I thought I had gotten completely over the hurt. And I had, really--- until you showed up."

Kl'aarn tried to look offended. "How do I answer that?"

Veelos shook her head. "I didn't mean it that way. Perhaps I've had the same effect on you, the reopened wounds, I mean. I must have, or else Keesha's little lecture would not have made such an impression on you. We bring bittersweet memories to each other, don't we?"

Kl'aarn nodded. Then, "In a few days," he said, "I'll be heading for Kagen-Shel-Don. That was what our little discussion was about, this morning, at the inn. Kmir is tightening up the details. We'll be taking a caravan of rare spices."

Veelos walked along silently, a few more steps, absorbing the strangely unwelcome shock with which she heard this news. Then, she said, "You're leaving the city? So soon? I'll be sorry to see you go." Then, after hesitating, she asked, "Will you be returning?"

Kl'aarn nodded. "From now on, Shi-Raq will be my home port."

"Oh?"

"What do you mean, oh?" Kl'aarn asked.

Veelos shrugged.

"Well, my motive is obvious," Kl'aarn admitted. "It's to be near you. Is that?--- am I being---?"

Veelos smiled, "I'll be happy to welcome you home on each return visit," she admitted. It felt comfortable to be able to say that openly. "But I'll also worry over you while you're gone. And if you are delayed, then my worry will become dread. Can't you find a safer trade? You're a merchant by the root of your youth, you know, not a warrior."

Kl'aarn nodded. "It's already occurred to me that, one day, I'll have to hang up my sword and armor for the last time. I've firmly decided that I'm not going to be one of those greying, older men who refuse to admit they've gone too far on the trail, who ride stubbornly into just one more battle until---well, I'm going to retire alive. One learns to become practical."

"And what of your search for Miril?"

There was silence.

"I'm sorry," Veelos said. "Now I'm the fool."

"No, you're not," Kl'aarn said. "Look, Veelos, for six years now I've lived in a world very different from yours. Night and day, in one form or another, my world has been but one thing: a searching place for Miril. Then I sampled your world, just a little bit. I haven't really adjusted to it, but the betrothal ceremony today made me--- well, it made me aware of certain things. If I may be blunt, Veelos, Keesha's lecture did have an effect on me. What if one day I wake up to---?"

Veelos halted. "Don't say it, Kl'aarn. Don't."

Kl'aarn sighed. "I'm glad you stopped me. Sometimes I don't think things through-- personal things, I mean." They resumed their walk, and Kl'aarn said, "I know that Keesha thinks the priestly path is not for you, but even I can see that she's wrong about that. Someday the temple will welcome you back, Veelos."

Veelos shook her head. "That they will never do. Never."

"Really? Is there no appeal? What an injustice! And what dedication it must take for you to live this difficult life all on your own."

"Keesha helps me. So do the others, when I stumble."

"Even so," Kl'aarn said. "Your virtue is certainly more genuine than theirs is. From the root of your own youth, you were always predestined to the holy life."

"You wouldn't say that," Veelos confessed, "if only you knew. And you might as well know. It was no virtue that brought me to Shi-Raq, but only sin. My father had promised me in marriage to--- I can barely speak his name--- Shalar. Yes, him. I abhorred the very thought. I detested Shalar's crudeness and his vulgarity. But I abhorred him even more when I compared him to you, Kl'aarn. You see, in my girlish mind, I had dreamed that I would be wife to someone just like you. And since there was no other just like you--- you stood in his place. I imagined, whether consciously or not, that I would bear your children, that I would know your embrace. Oh yes, I fell in love with you. What girl wouldn't, especially after being held by you and---. But you were given to Miril. So, after your betrothal, I took my mind off those girlish notions of romance. I did so quite promptly, I might add. And I could have endured. I would have enjoyed seeing Miril happy with you. I really would have. But not from Shalar's smithy, I couldn't. I would rather have died. It was all too much, intolerably too much. And so I rebelled, Kl'aarn. I schemed to elude my path. I came to the priesthood, not to serve God, but to hide from Him."

Kl'aarn was astonished at this confession. For long moments he could not believe that Veelos had so abruptly poured out her secrets. "These words come not from you. You are under some spell," he said, when he could speak again.

But Veelos wept, the weeping of a little girl caught in some shameful act. Yet there was also in that weeping a kind of courage unknown to men at arms. "It is no spell but my own," she said, gathering her composure once more. "It is good that you are leaving Shi-Raq, Kl'aarn. I don't mean this unkindly, but now I am sorry you ever came here. You see, I had begun to be content with my lot in life--- perhaps too content. God is punishing me, I know. He is forcing me to a decision: to choose between priesthood and---. You must leave Shi-Raq, Kl'aarn, and not come back. My sin must be my own, mine alone."

But Kl'aarn, still startled by all this, said, "Veelos. I--- I never thought--- I never suspected. Now I think I know why Keesha was so interested in--- it wasn't just idle match-making on her part, was it? I should have given her more credit than to think that." Kl'aarn stopped, then tried to speak again. But for the longest time, it seemed that the words would simply never come forth. When they did, he stammered. "Veelos--- would it be wrong--- for a warrior and a priestess---?"

But Veelos turned away from him. "What would be wrong," she said, "would be for me--- to ever be--- to be in a position--- to be glad that our beloved Miril had died. I could never abide myself in that position, Kl'aarn." Then she faced him once more. "I was meant to die in Har-Keem. I have no right to be alive at all. If I had been there that night, I know that I could have saved Miril, just as you tried to save all the village. And then you would have had her all these years. And the two of you would be happy. Kl'aarn, my sin is so terrible! You can't imagine it."

But Kl'aarn answered her. "If you had been there that night, you would have been overrun just as I was. There was no stopping those evil men. And there was no saving anyone. Now hear me, Veelos. I'll be going to Kagen-Shel-Don in two days. I'll be four months on the trail, and then God willing, back here. During that time, pray with me, Veelos. Just because we've strayed from God's will once does not mean He has abandoned us. Pray with me to discover His will. And when I return, perhaps He will have revealed it to us."

Veelos pondered this a few moments, and then said, "Kl'aarn? What are you saying?"

Then Kl'aarn answered, "In our old age, who will comfort us, Veelos? Who else speaks the language in just the dialect you and I speak? Who else enjoys the same foods, the same customs, the same memories and lore? Only you and I, Veelos. We have no one else in all the world. No one. Is it love I feel, or just fear? Only God can guide us aright."

So Veelos agreed. "We will pray about it, you and I. Each morning at sunrise, wherever you may be, stop and think of me here in Shi-Raq. When you do so, I will know it, and we will pray together on this. And whatever God wills, He will lead us to it."

* * * * *

Fatigued, Veelos soon found herself once more upon her sleeping mat. Physically and emotionally exhausted, she stepped across that misty border which separates wakefulness from sleep.

Stepped and fell.

The priestess found herself once more in the pit where she had dreamt the night before. This time, however, it was less dream-like, more real. Too real. Underfoot was barren rock, a terrain of crevices and gnarled, dead shrubs, the ghosts of which, unmoving, clawed futilely into an airless vacuum. Black, murky smoke swirled about her, sometimes parting to reveal the infinite magnitude of desolation, sometimes enveloping her in a prison of blindness.

Veelos knew of this place. It was not hell, nor any place of the dead. It was that place which the living sometimes inhabit while the body sleeps. It was the place of never remembered.

And once again, the dark-robed woman appeared.

The witch's eyes were empty sockets, empty but for the darkness of fierce hatred. Those dark, empty eyes glared malevolently at the priestess. The lips sneered, almost into a snarl. Behind them were revealed the sharp, pointed tips of fangs.

"I warned you away from him," the witch raged.

But Veelos answered, "Who are you? Do you still pretend to be Miril? And do you think that, by so pretending, you could win Kl'aarn's love? Fool! He would never love so repulsive a thing as you. I command you depart."

But the creature replied, "Do you regard me so lightly? Do you think me but a dream? When you know who I am, then you will respect me and fear me. For I am no mere witch, but the very Demonwitch herself."

Those words struck fear into Veelos. For if ever the Dreaded One Foretold were to appear as anything, she would appear as this one. Veelos felt something cold, like a venomous snake crawling up her spine.

"Yes, liar priestess. I am she, the one whom the high priests do dread. For they know that I am their doom."

Veelos shook her head. "What dream is this?"

The witch spat. "Dream? If you do think me but a dream, then here is a prophecy for you, so that you will know that I am no mere fantasy. When you see this come to pass, then you will know that the Darkmost herself lives. The prophecy is this: the great orb, which is adored in your temple, will be taken from it, just as the lesser orb was taken from Har-Keem. And the thieves will not be mere pirates, but rather soldiers--- the very same soldiers who murdered Har-Keem. Yes, the very same king who took the orb of Harkeem for his own, he is the one who will now steal the Great Orb of Power. His name is Druuk. Remember that name--- Druuk. Together, you and I shall both hate that name. That is my prophecy to you, false priestess, a demonic anti-prophecy, by which you will learn to trust all anti-prophecies."

But Veelos refused to believe the witch. "You lie," she said. "The orb of Har-Keem was destroyed. As for the Great Orb, no king has ever been able to take it."

"When it happens," the witch said, "then you will remember what I foretold. Then will you remember this dream, but not before. Now sleep, liar priestess. Sleep and forget, until the moment this prophecy is fulfilled."

* * * * *

In the morning, Veelos awoke with a mood of dark foreboding. But she did not know why. Nor did she remember her dream of the night before.

Veelos thought to herself, "I am having a premonition. Perhaps it concerns Kl'aarn. His profession is a dangerous one. He leaves soon for a long journey. Will I ever see him again?"

So Veelos did not go to Jagmoor, but instead to the Copper Kettle Inn. There, she found that Kl'aarn was away for the day on the business at hand.

But Kmir was there, with many of his comrades. They were sharpening swords, oiling down their leather straps, and otherwise making the preparations men of war are used to doing before venturing upon the battlefield.

"Priestess Veelos," he said, arising to meet her at the doorway. "You seem worried."

Veelos asked for Kl'aarn, and learning that he was away, meant to excuse herself.

But Kmir insisted that she share their breakfast. Veelos partook sparingly.

"When do you leave?" she asked.

"Two or three more days," Kmir answered. "Kl'aarn is out buying provisions. A shipload of cinnamon is due tomorrow. When it's loaded into wagons, we'll carry it inland."

Veelos asked, "How far away is Kagen-Shel-Don? Is it a dangerous trail?"

Kmir tried to be reassuring. "It's well inland, but not so far into the hills as the fiefdoms of the great bandit-lords. And our best skill is in avoiding battle. There's no reason to worry."

Veelos pretended to be reassured. Standing, she begged her leave, saying, "Kmir? You will take care of him, won't you?"

Kmir nodded. "Upon my very life, Lady Priest."

* * * * *

Far from Shi-Raq, in the central forested hills of east Wirik, lay the small village called Shel-Avak. Not far from it, through a small valley and across a narrow river, was the abode of a man named Trrod.

Trrod sat among his candles in a darkened room. With so many candles burning, the little room should have been brightly lit. But he was conjuring. The darkness which enveloped him was no earthly darkness; it was, rather, a darkness born of sinister power. The candles were no match for it.

Trrod the conjuror was patient. One had to be, if one would practice the deadly art. For the creatures which he conjured from within the eternal night were ancient, crafty, and evil beyond imagining. One careless moment, and they would traverse the barrier, seize the conjuror himself, and inhabit him.

Trrod knew very well the disaster that awaited him should he slip. Many years before, his own mentor had made the fatal error. The demons which he had loosed had sated their appetites upon the master himself, possessing him, befouling him, and tormenting him. Trrod had never forgotten the emaciated man who had finally died, a man reduced to subhuman form by creatures which knew no moderation in their quest for earthly pleasures.

Trrod was patient.

And his patience was rewarded. There finally came to the barrier a spirit more reserved than the wild ones. (The wild ones would find the slight crack which Trrod opened in the barrier. They would lunge for it, dashing themselves against it, in a desperate bid to be unleashed upon the earth. Once, long ago, they had ravaged the world for a time. But they were now isolated from it, impatiently awaiting that day in the future, when once again they might be set loose.)

This one could be reasoned with. Trrod spoke, and the creature replied.

Its tone was sensible. Trrod explained to it what it must do. "I will give you," he offered, "a human host to inhabit. It will be a human, young and healthy. You can gain much pleasure from it. But if you are greedy, you shall do as other demons have done. You shall consume the body in an orgy of lust. Then it will die, and you will find yourself thrust back into the void, there to spend aeons awaiting another chance at freedom, a chance that may never come again. Never. But if you are wise, you will be patient, as patient as I have been these many years. You will assume the identity of your host, and then you will work with me, to establish the reign of evil in the world. If you do as I counsel you, if you wage the war for evil as I do, then your pleasure will be eternal instead of merely fleeting. What say you?"

The demon expressed approval.

"Very well," Trrod said. "Now every day, the girl Valen brings me sweet fruits from her father. She is eleven years old, and she is the one whom you will inhabit. She will soon be here for her daily visit. I will invite her inside, and then---"

Trrod's words were suddenly cut off in a violent eruption of demonic treachery. The demon's patience had been merely a ruse, a trick to get the conjuror to lower his guard, to lower it for but one instant of long-awaited opportunity. Trrod had made the fatal error. Without warning, a reptilian hand had seized Trrod by the neck with lightning quickness. And worse yet, something invisible was seeking to enter inside his body. The tiny rift in the barrier, which Trrod had carefully kept small, was being pried wider, and more demons were gathering at the other side of it, in a frenzy of anticipation. Trrod could hear their delighted squealing and grunting.

With a chill in his bones, and a sensation of ice in his chest, the conjuror remembered his ill-fated master, and was terrified that soon he would join that wretched sorceror in the netherworld of eternal torment.

Trrod realized that, for an instant, just for an instant, he had relaxed his guard. In that very instant, the demon had seized its chance. Why should it wait, its demonic mind had reasoned, even a few moments longer, when prey was at hand? For this was the way of demons. Aeons of waiting, and it could not delay a moment more.

Fury surrounded Trrod. This demon was particularly vicious. It was trying to tear a piece of flesh from him. If it could do so, it would cast it physically into the hell in which it lived. There, the other demons, crowding around, would see it, and would throw themselves upon it, to desecrate it. That would leave the demon all alone with its fresh human host, for just long enough to complete its conquest.

But Trrod had one last hope. He slipped his hand into a pocket of his robe. There, he touched an amulet, and its power fled into him. The demon's grip was suddenly shaken, and before it could seize him again, Trrod had closed the barrier. The last sound he heard from it was a shriek of despair.

The battle had ended almost as suddenly as it had begun. But the aftermath did not as quickly subside. Trrod found himself lying in a tangle, his robes and cords binding him, his candles kicked about, and himself so exhausted that he thought he might die gasping for breath. That had been close, he knew, much too close. Had the demon been but the slightest bit more crafty, it would have seized him entirely, and not just by the neck. Then, Trrod would have died the true death. The mere thought of it chilled him with terror.

But there was no time for the aftershocks of fear. For the girl, Valen, would arrive soon. Her father was the village elder, a holy man named Thrador. She must not suspect anything. No one must suspect, not until that eventual day when Trrod would betray them all. She would be along very soon, now, and she must find the cottage as she always did, tidy and comforting.

Trrod hastened to clean up the mess.

* * * * *

He finished just in time. No sooner had he hidden the candles and the other paraphernalia, than he sensed her near approach. Quickly, Trrod came to the door of his small cottage, stopped, and putting on a casual air, pushed aside the leather curtain which served as its only door. Bright daylight burned painfully into his gaze.

"Good afternoon, Valen!" he called. His voice was just loud enough to reach politely across the distance.

The girl was in his garden, clothed in white, smelling the flowers, and admiring his skillful landscaping. "Oh my!" she said. "You startled me, Teacher."

She always called him Teacher. Trrod daily taught the girl from sacred scripture. Of course, he was always careful to insert just the tiniest bit of falsehood into her lessons. They were the seeds of future harvesting, should Valen grow into adulthood.

"Startled you?" Trrod asked in surprise. "Why, how so?" For surely, she had expected to find him at home.

"I called out for you," the girl explained. "But no one answered."

Trrod frowned. "When was this? I heard no one call. You must have called too quietly."

"I called quite loudly." Her voice was pure innocence. "Just a little while ago." But she was surely clever, Trrod knew. Could she suspect something? "Never mind," she said. "You're here, and so am I. And I am prepared for today's lesson."

"Well, do come in, then," Trrod said cheerily.

The girl walked toward Trrod across the soil of the garden. The old teacher noted that her steps carried her across the graves, which were the secret of his horticultural success. She seemed to be stepping upon each one of them. Wandering strangers fared not well when they chanced upon Trrod's hospitality. But Trrod wondered, was Valen's route a mere happenstance? Could she know what desecration lay beneath her feet?

The two entered into the cottage, and even before they sat at table, the girl was already sniffing. "What's that smell?" she asked.

Trrod chuckled. "What smell?"

"Candles," his young student answered. "I smell candles. But Teacher, you have none."

"Indeed I don't," the old man replied, attempting to maintain his cheery tone. "I'm much too poor to afford candles. You must be smelling some of the spill from my broth. It boiled over into the fireplace."

The young girl shook her head. "I don't think so, Teacher. It smells like candles."

Trrod struggled to conceal his irritation. The child was perceptive, very keen. If she were not careful, it would someday be her undoing. For Trrod could not survive being discovered by Valen's father, or by anyone in the nearby village where Valen lived. Conjurors were always put to death.

"By the way, how is your father?" he asked her. "While I make us some tea, tell me of him."

"As always," the girl answered, "he is very prayerful. And he is very excited about the revelations he has been granted. He is telling everyone that a new Upheaval is soon to occur, a new war between good and evil. He urges all to be vigilant, and to prepare for the coming conflict, once again, between men and demons."

Trrod chuckled as he placed a small kettle over the fire. "Then your father expects the prophecy to be fulfilled literally, does he?"

"Quite literally."

"Well, as we shall see in our lessons, not all prophecies are meant to be taken literally. Why, if one were to believe that, then what about the prophecy which says that all the sins of the world will be drowned in a flood? Surely that refers to a flood of tears, does it not?"

"My father says that, too, is literal. He says that one day, a flood of water shall cover all the earth, even to the highest mountain tops. He says that no prophecy has ever been fulfilled symbolically. They all come true just as they are written."

Trrod faced the girl again. "Well, we shall not argue with your father.

He is certainly a gifted man." He had already planted the spore of doubt in her. Trrod dared not overdo it. "While the tea heats up, shall we begin our study?"

But the girl said, "The pot is already boiling, Teacher. It's boiling over."

Trrod turned away from the girl again. His back was toward her. "Indeed it is boiling over," he said, as he pulled it away from the flames. "My, but that was quick. Very quick. See? I told you that my kettle boils over sometimes. By the way." He continued to fuss over the tea, his attention carefully focused on it, his back still turned to his guest. "That is a very nice white dress you are wearing. I don't think I've seen it before. Was it a special gift? It must have been very expensive. How do you keep it so clean?"

The girl answered, "I don't."

The softness and courtesy had departed that voice, and left it cold. Trrod felt almost as if he had been struck from behind, threatened by some hostile force in that intonation, endangered by those curt and pointed words.

The room went suddenly dark.

For a moment, Trrod wondered if his eyes had not gone bad. Then he recognized the particular character of this darkness. As well he should, for he was well accustomed to it. It was not ordinary darkness. Even the flames in the fireplace seemed to be choked by it. But this time, the darkness had fallen without his conjuring it forth. There was a chill upon his back.

Suddenly recognizing danger, the sort which a hunter feels when stalked by the panther, Trrod spun about to face the young white-clad girl. But she was gone. Innocent, white-clad Valen was nowhere to be seen.

In her place sat another, not a girl but a woman, not innocence but menace. Her garb was the blackest of all blackness, a shadow within shadows. Her features might have been beautiful in another woman, but in this one, they were fearsome. Trrod was startled beyond words. For several moments, he stared at the self-confident woman, and she in turn observed him, but with a casualness that mocked him.

Finally, Trrod sputtered, "Why--- why, you're not Valen at all! What clever disguise was that? Who are you? Who?"

The woman sneered as would a haughty lady to her slave. "Serve the tea, Trrod."

"You're a witch!" Trrod stammered. "An actual witch. But that can't be. All the witches died a thousand years ago. Are you--- are you--- Kattaroon?"

"My name is Miril," she answered. "Miril of Har-Keem. And yes, they all did die. I am the first of a new generation."

Slowly, Trrod began to regain his composure. "Are you really a witch? Or some clever sorceress?"

"Serve us some tea, Trrod. Then I will answer all your questions."

Hurriedly, Trrod set two places at the table, almost tipping the tray and nearly spilling his brew. Nervously, he sat, clumsily pulling the wooden stool beneath himself, taking two tries before he got it right. Then he watched, in cautious silence, as the woman's hand encircled the goblet in which he had served her tea. Her fingernails, long and curved, surrounded the cup. She sipped delicately, then set down the vessel. "That's very good tea, Trrod. Very good indeed. I must commend you. You are quite the herbalist."

"Thank you."

"Too bad your conjury is not half as good."

"What?" Trrod demanded, astonished by the unexpected insult.

The witch glared at him. "You fool. If that girl Valen had come upon you as I did, she would have seen what you do. And what do you think would have happened next? She would have told her father. Even now, Trrod, a band of their fiercest devotees would be preparing your pyre, to burn you to death."

Trrod was incensed. "How dare you speak to me so? You are but a child, while I have practiced conjury these two centuries and more."

"Indeed," Miril said, still sneering down at him. "Practiced conjury, you have, yes. But to what avail? This realm was given you two hundred years ago, to rule. Do you rule it? No. Instead, it is ruled by a holy man named

Thrador, our enemy, a servant of his God. Look about you, Trrod. All the hill country surrounding you is ruled by bandits. Hordes of bandits. But your realm is free of them, free of any who practice evil."

"Bandits?" Trrod spat. "They are worthless scum. All they do is ruin villages and leave them useless. I am cultivating my realm, preparing it for greater---"

"Liar!" Miril accused. "You prepare nothing, Trrod. You sit, day after day, trolling the barrier, seeking some creature that will serve you as slave. Ever timid, you hope for a ghoul to take your risks in your place, and to perform your duty for you."

"But---"

"Be quiet, fool! Listen to me. Those demons will only enslave you, Trrod, not serve you. You have not the fearlessness to master them, to beat them into submission. You have become too complacent, too cowardly. But there is no more time for complacency. You must now develop your courage, and gird yourself for battle. The war has begun, Trrod. A new demonwitch has arisen. The Orb of Power will soon be taken from the priests. And the world, Trrod, the entire world lies naked before us. We have but to take it."

"The Orb of Power?" Trrod asked in amazement. "You are about to seize it from the priests?"

Miril shook her head. "Not I. A sorceror king named Druuk. He is a renegade, once a useful ally, but now an usurper of our power. He uses sorcery, but he uses it for mortal gain, not eternal. We shall defeat him, we shall take from him the Orb, and we shall use it for our eternal gain."

Trrod shook his head. "What can you know? You are young, and but a woman. I'll not submit myself to the counsel of a child."

"I expected you to resist," Miril told him. "So I did not rely upon your acquiescent nature to enlist your service. No, Trrod, I am here to force the issue."

Trrod snorted. "What can you do? You can do nothing against my powers. What will you do? Will you battle me in a duel of sorcery? I think not. You would never dare."

"Duel you? That won't be necessary," Miril answered. "I have a far more potent means of recruiting you."

Trrod raised one eyebrow in suspicion. "What is that?"

Miril's lip curled into the hint of a smile. "Thrador," she answered. Her dark eyes, however, showed no amusement.

Trrod frowned. "Thrador, you say. What riddle is this? Thrador won't help you. He'll burn you. A powerful man is he. And willing to use that power, he is."

Miril nodded. "There is no more time to delay, Trrod. Thrador must be defeated, and he must be defeated today. Not next year, not tomorrow, but this very day. We'll meet him in battle, you and I on one side, he on the other. One side wins, one side loses. Either Thrador dies, or we die. Is that simple enough for you? Today is the day, Trrod."

But the conjuror snorted. "If you are fool enough to duel Thrador, duel him yourself."

Miril took another sip of her tea. Then she set the goblet back down, peered into it, and then glanced upward again at Trrod. "He knows."

"What? What do you mean by that?"

"Thrador knows," Miril explained, "about you. He knows that you have been mis-teaching his daughter. And he knows that you have been conjuring. To be brief, Trrod, Thrador knows everything about you that there is to know."

Trrod shook his head. "Impossible. You are merely trying to frighten me, so that I will stand with you against him. No, Thrador will never suspect me. Forty years I have spent cultivating his confidence. I taught his sons the scripture. Now he has entrusted me with the education of his daughter. Never in a thousand years would he discern my real purpose."

"You're right," Miril answered. "He would never have guessed your secret. One skill you have above all others is cunning deception, I grant you that. Except, of course, for your most excellent tea, which is better. You missed your calling, Trrod."

"My deceptions are lies straight from the snout of Thorgar itself," Trrod boasted. "No mortal could ever unravel them."

"I know," Miril said. Her shadowed eyes glinted with vicious amusement. "That's why I had to tell him myself."

Trrod was perplexed. "What nonsense is this?"

"In a dream," Miril explained. "I revealed your secrets to Thrador in a dream."

"You wouldn't."

"I did. I met him face to face among the graves of your victims, beneath your garden, in that wretched dreamscape which they inhabit. That's why Thrador kept his daughter at home today. Now he has awakened from his nap, Trrod. And is he ever upset with you! All that friendship, of so many years, all that means nothing anymore. Thrador intends to kill you. He is utterly thankless to you for all the kindnesses you have bestowed upon him all these decades. All that effort, gone suddenly to waste. Such a shame. What are you going to do about it, Trrod? Shall I leave you to face him yourself? Or would you prefer me to stand at your side when he arrives? What will you offer me to employ my skills at witchcraft?"

Trrod was visibly shaken. Slowly, he understood that the witch had actually done this treacherous deed. Whether from the foolishness of her inexperience, or from some secretly planned self-interest, she was reckless enough to have risked all. "You fool!" he uttered. "You fool! What have you done? What have you done to me?"

"Settle down, Trrod. Where is your perspective? Let me refresh it for you." Miril lectured calmly, with no sign of worry. "Two hundred years ago, you made a choice. That choice carried many rewards for you, did it not? But it also came with a price, a very serious oath. That price was servitude unto evil--- even at the cost of your very soul. Did you not choose willingly and knowingly, Trrod? You did. And now, now, your soul is demanded of you. Kill Thrador, and your damnation is delayed, perhaps forever. Or else, let

Thrador kill you, and instead of long life, begin your eternity of torment this day. This very day. Now, Teacher, question me concerning this lesson, unless all is clear to you."

Trrod struggled to contain himself. Then he whimpered, "It will be worse for you than for me. Thrador will take especial delight in destroying you."

"I don't care," Miril answered. "I care nothing about what might happen to me. You see, I am not like you, Trrod. You serve evil only for what it can give you. But I, on the other hand, serve evil for its own sake. And that, Trrod, is the difference between a witch and any other mortal."

Trrod swallowed hard. "I have an amulet," he said, almost frantically. "How about you? We will need all the talisman we can get."

Miril shook her head. "I'm no mere witch," she said. "I am the Darkmost herself. I need no amulet. My evil comes straight from the well of blackness. Now. Shall we step outside to greet our guest?"

* * * * *

That day, Thrador led a small band of men from Shel-Avak, followers of his teachings, to confront the evil which had invaded his domain. With him, he carried the tiny orb which had always protected Shel-Avak. Despite the warnings of his elders not to use it for any purpose, Thrador carried it forward into battle. He was no longer content to allow its powers to flow through him. He felt the need to wield those powers. For he was aware what power resided in the witch.

The men arrived in the garden, where Trrod and Miril awaited him. With silence born of contempt, Thrador did not even make an offer of peace, nor did he beseech the repentance of those whom he intended to slay. Confident that his orb would not fail him, Thrador immediately lifted it, and with practiced skill, held it before him and uttered his commands to it.

The battle went well for Thrador. With the orb held aloft upon his upraised arm, he was able to overpower both the witch and the conjuror, and to bind them both to a wooden stake. Then, without ceremony, he set ablaze a bundle of wood at their feet.

Trrod cried out in terror, tearfully pleading for mercy, and promising to do whatever Thrador commanded, if only Thrador would spare his life.

Even Miril knew the foretaste of certain defeat. She was astonished at the intense power of the orb, a power that could overwhelm any talisman she had ever beheld. No wonder that the priests guarded their orb so closely. And if such a small orb as this could so easily overpower her, how much more could the Great Orb do against her?

The burning wood, and the stinging smoke, were a foretaste of what doom and torment awaited her in the place of eternal shrieking.

As Miril began to succumb, as she despaired of being able to kill Thrador, she resigned herself to being satisfied with but one drop of his blood. If that were all she could have of Thrador, a mere drop of his blood, then Miril determined to take that much of him with her into eternal torment. She focused all her might and power on this one task.

Thrador felt a tiny piercing of his flesh, a tiny sensation of fire. It was not much. It was only enough to make him flinch.

But when he flinched, the orb fell from his grasp. It fell to the ground, and shattered into dust. All its power vanished.

Then was Miril able to free herself. What she did next, to Thrador and to his followers, must never be written.

Chapter 17

The Battle is Joined

That night, Veelos tried to sleep, but sleep would not come. For Kl'aarn's caravan was all packed and ready to embark. At sunrise, he would be leaving. She would not see him again, not for a very long time. Veelos was all but obsessed by fear for him--- and indirectly, for herself. What if he never returned? What if he never came back to her? Could fate be so cruel, as to have brought him so briefly back into her life, only to take him away once more, forever? Veelos's feelings of premonition, of dark foreboding, had haunted her all through the day.

The priestess tossed and turned, but slumber eluded her. Try as she might, she could not sleep.

During that sleepless night, late into the silence of darkness, Veelos's uneasy feelings suddenly intensified. They gripped her tightly, causing her heart to pound as it never had before. With a compulsive sense of urgency, the priestess rose from her bed. A cold, clammy feeling encircled her. By this time, it was more than a premonition, clearly more; it was the sense of present danger, as if some sinister peril were in the very room with her. Upon impulse, Veelos glanced out her window.

Although it was midnight, there was a glow in the distance. At first it seemed as sunrise. But the direction was wrong. Instead of sunrise, something was on fire. Veelos suddenly realized that it was coming from the direction of the temple.

Only then did Veelos understand that she had misinterpreted her premonitions.

Swiftly donning her vestments, Veelos ran into the street, frantically ignoring the dangers of the night.

Soon, others were also awakened by the disturbance. People began stepping into the narrow streets of the city. Pushing through the small crowds which had begun to form, Veelos ran as fast as she could, racing toward the increasing glow of fire. "Please!" she begged silently, "don't let it be! Please, not this!"

Just as Veelos felt she would collapse in exhaustion, she heard horses behind her. She turned and looked. Forcing its way through the alleys and streets was a small band of armored cavalry, or so it seemed. They were strikingly out of their element. Horse hooves clattered along the stony pavement. A voice ordered onlookers out of the way. It was a voice that Veelos recognized as Kl'aarn's.

Veelos called out to him, and as he passed, Kl'aarn lifted Veelos up behind him. The horse was unsaddled, but Veelos held tightly to the bronze and leather armor which Kl'aarn wore. And together they stormed toward the temple.

Finally, the party of horsemen emerged from the constricting jungle of city, and found themselves upon the wide, sandy road which lay between them and the temple gardens.

The windows of the temple were bright lanterns, bright except for the smoke which poured from them. Inside, the temple was ablaze.

Veelos cried out in anguish. But Kl'aarn demanded of her, "Where is the entrance? How do we get inside?"

There was only one entrance. It was the wide archway on the seaward side, where the pier was. But Veelos could only choke forth enough words to prompt Kl'aarn onward.

The horses tore through the carefully manicured garden, mangling it as they charged forward. When they reached the burning pier, the horses could go no further. The men dismounted.

Kl'aarn quickly surveyed the pier, and said to Kmir, "I don't think it will burn down. The fire is dying. I'm going to try to make my way along the---"

But his words were interrupted by the unexpected staccato hiss of a score of arrows whipping through the night. They stabbed into the pier, and clattered off the stone facade of the temple. One man fell, groaning in mortal agony.

Reflexively, the men dropped to the ground, securing the nearest available cover. Their eyes searched the night for the source of this surprise attack. Grasping their swords, they prepared to engage the unseen enemy.

"That ship!" someone called out. "It's a war ship."

Kl'aarn looked. By the firelight, he could make out a sailing vessel with oars, its hull lined with shields along its upper edge. It was swiftly making for the open sea. Another volley of arrows quickly confirmed the suspicion: the fire in the temple was the work of raiders.

Kl'aarn called out to his men. "Did no one bring a bow and arrows?" But no one had.

Kl'aarn's next thought was for Veelos. He looked about, but did not see her. "Where is she?" he asked Kmir.

After a moment, Kmir spotted her. "She's on the pier, Kl'aarn. Pray she doesn't get herself killed."

Kl'aarn saw that it was true. Amid flames and breaking timbers, the priestess was picking her way along the precarious planks, toward the temple entrance. Not a few arrows had sought for her, marking her progress with feathered shafts slanted, their tips buried, thankfully, in wood instead of flesh.

Kl'aarn stood.

"Don't," Kmir warned.

"I have to," Kl'aarn said. "Hold the position. Those bastards might turn around and come back." Then he pursued Veelos upon the burning pier, keeping a low profile, mindful of the archers who had already killed one of his men.

He had gotten halfway to the portal when, from within it, he heard Veelos's horrified scream. Abandoning caution, Kl'aarn stood and dashed forward, his sword at the ready.

But it was too late.

For Veelos had not screamed in fear of some straggling enemy soldier left behind. Instead, she had cried out in despair. For inside the temple was such a massacre as Kl'aarn had not witnessed since the last day of Har-Keem.

Veelos had run from the entranceway, into the domed central hall of the temple. There, she knelt over the unmoving form of Keesha. The slain priestess was covered in blood. As Kl'aarn approached, he noted grimly that she had been hacked down from behind by a heavy weapon, probably a battle-axe.

Other corpses were also in the hall, strewn about as if a giant beast had slashed everything in sight with massive, sharp claws. No one had been spared, that much was clear. There were no survivors. The massacre had been carried out with swift, military efficiency.

Soon, Kmir and the rest of Kl'aarn's men were entering into the place of carnage, swords drawn. "Search every corner, every room, every possible place of concealment," Kl'aarn ordered. "I doubt we'll find anyone alive, but try. If it is an enemy, don't kill him. We must discover who it was that did this."

Then, kneeling beside Veelos, he tried to console her. Her grief was unspeakable. She was wracked with sobs, with spasms of anguish so terrible that Kl'aarn feared to touch her. For such grief can kill.

Then, quietly, Kmir approached Kl'aarn and whispered, "Thrake has found one of the priests--- barely alive."

Kl'aarn lifted his head. "Where?"

"There, atop the altar."

Kl'aarn spotted Thrake, and saw that there, before him, was a priest, lying across the altar. He was a large man, black-skinned, and like the others, drenched in blood. It did not seem possible that he was alive. Even if he were, he could not live much longer.

Kl'aarn ran to the altar, and pushing Thrake aside, looked closely into the dying priest's face. The eyes were open, and the lips moved ever so faintly, as if trying to mouthe words. Kl'aarn pressed his ear close to the man's mouth.

He listened intently.

At first, he could only make out a faint hint of breath and no other sound. But after a time, Kl'aarn began to make sense of it. The priest was repeating the same thing, over and over.

"Tell Veelos--- she is Priestess--- of Prophecy--- Orb stolen--- Druuk--- must destroy orb--- beware Demonwitch. Tell Veelos--- she is Priestess--- of Prophecy--- must destroy--- must destroy orb before--- before Druuk masters its power."

Three times the priest laboriously, agonizingly, repeated into Kl'aarn's ear his cryptic message. Then his breathing stopped. It did not resume again.

* * * * *

For a long time, Veelos was wracked by her sobs of grief. But when her tears were finally spent, when her eyes had become drought, then she rose, and made careful motions to arrange her appearance. It seemed madness to make those empty motions, for stains of blood now marred her white vestment. Despite having just emerged from the death grip of abject grief, Veelos seemed so composed that, for a moment, Kl'aarn thought Veelos might indeed have gone mad. He had seen madness before. Often, it was but a mockery of composure.

With deliberate gait, the priestess walked to the steps which led up to the altar. But she did not ascend them. Instead, she sat on the bottom step, her back to the altar, and peered as if into a great distance.

One of Kl'aarn's men brought an arrow to Kmir. "None of us can recognize this," the warrior said. "Even the feathers are of a bird unknown in east Wirik."

Then Veelos seemed roused from her trance. She gazed lucidly at Kl'aarn and said, "The arrow is from a foreign land. The men who did this are not of east Wirik. They are from the west, from a kingdom beyond the Lands of Demi-men."

Kl'aarn approached Veelos, and said, "Your high priest--- him---" he gestured carefully. "His dying words were for you. He said this: 'Tell Veelos, she is Priestess of Prophecy.'"

Veelos shook her head. "No. Lar was not a seer, not a prophet. His words are from the confusion and horror of--- of this."

"But he said more," Kl'aarn continued. "He said, 'Orb stolen.'"

Again, Veelos shook her head. "No one could steal an orb. They vanish upon being touched."

"He said also," Kl'aarn reported, "Druuk. Must destroy orb. Before he masters its power."

This time, Kl'aarn could see that he had gained Veelos's attention. Even through the shock of her grief, Veelos seemed focused. "Say that once more," she told Kl'aarn.

"He said that you are the Priestess of Prophecy. The Orb has been stolen. Then he mentioned the word, Druuk. Then---"

"Stop," Veelos said. "Druuk? Yes, I remember now. Yes. It was in a dream. There was a woman, a horrible woman, in black. Her eyes were empty sockets, but oh what an evil, black emptiness they were. And she prophesied to me. No, not prophesied, because the foretellings she revealed were from no divine source. No. She foretold this very event. She said I would not remember the dream until--- until this. And now it has happened. And now I remember the dream."

Kl'aarn knelt beside her. "What does the word, Druuk, mean?"

Veelos answered. "It is the name of a king. He is lord of all the west, ruler of all Wirik beyond the Lands of Demi-men. And he is a sorceror."

Kl'aarn waited, then asked, "Beyond the Lands of Demi-men? But no one has been able to reach across those lands since the Great Upheaval. Neither by land nor by sea."

Veelos nodded. "Druuk has found a way. Somehow, his ships can cross the Sea of Storms, penetrate the domains of the pirates, and evade the giant creatures of the depths. It signals that the next Upheaval has indeed begun."

Kl'aarn's thoughts raced. "Your priest said that the Orb must be destroyed. How can we do that, if this pirate King Druuk has crossed the sea with it? Are we to take a ship and sail after him?"

"No," Veelos said. "The sea lanes are closed to us. Druuk's sorcerors will have seen to that. But there is another way, a path impenetrable even to the dark powers of Druuk's most potent sorcery. The only way to do this, to carry out Lar's command, is for the Priestess of Prophecy to travel by land to the west kingdom of Wirik. But Kl'aarn--- how can Lar have said that I am the Priestess of Prophecy? I can't be. I'm a false priestess."

But Kl'aarn said, "Veelos, your high priest spoke the name of Druuk, a name only you knew--- and only in a dream. So his words were not the rantings of death's madness. They were a truth revealed to him. He said that you are the Priestess of Prophecy. And how could it be otherwise? Is there any other priestess upon the earth now? You're the only one left in the succession of ordination. Do you think yourself unworthy? Veelos, where in scripture is worthiness a precondition for doing the work of God?"

Veelos took long moments to arrange her thoughts. Then she asked, "What else did Lar say before he died?"

This time, Kl'aarn himself was hesitant to speak. He forced the words. "Beware of the Demonwitch."

Veelos nodded. "She's out there, somewhere. Waiting for us. She knew all about this before it happened."

Kl'aarn frowned. "Did the Demonwitch do all this?"

Veelos shook her head. "No. Not that she wouldn't have wished to do it. For indeed, the Demonwitch seeks to take the Orb for herself. She envies it. She aims to corrupt it to her own use--- and with it, to ravage both the world of substance, and the world of spirit. She is incalculably evil, Kl'aarn, more evil even than this King Druuk. And it was he who destroyed Har-Keem."

It was Kl'aarn's turn to be made attentive. "Destroyed Har-Keem? Him? That can't be! A king? Why would a king destroy a little fishing village?"

Veelos explained. "Because he wanted the lesser orb. He stole it. Yes, before he destroyed this temple, Druuk already had a lesser orb, the one which we always cherished in our clay shrine. It was not destroyed in the raid, as everyone had supposed. That raid was sort of a practice run--- for this. And now he has the Orb of Power itself. If he masters it, even the Demonwitch will fear that man."

Kl'aarn pondered. "Then who is the enemy? Is it the Demonwitch, or King Druuk?"

Veelos answered. "There are two enemies, Kl'aarn, not just one. If either of them prevails, the world will become an unendurable hell. But at least Druuk's evil is only mortal, only physical. Some day it will come to an end. But if the Demonwitch seizes the Orb, her rule will not end, for she will take earth into Hell with her."

Kl'aarn sat. "This is all imponderable. Early today, life seemed to go on as before. Now--- now, are we in a Great Upheaval? I could not have imagined it. But now I cannot deny it. Then what are we to do?"

Veelos spoke. "Not we. I. This is my battle, Kl'aarn. Mine alone."

"Then what are you to do?"

"I am," Veelos pronounced slowly, forcing the words past her doubts, "going to west Wirik. Just as the scripture foretells--- by land."

For a moment, Kl'aarn was dumbfounded. "But what about the Lands of Demi-men?" Even as he said the words, he knew it was a foolish question.

Veelos nodded nervously. "The Lands of Demi-men--- I am going to cross them."

Kl'aarn seemed not to take Veelos seriously. He yet regarded her as maddened by the grief which surrounded her. "Veelos," he said, almost patronizingly. "No one can cross the Lands of Demi-men. No one has ever done so. And pirates control the sea lanes. Wherever this kingdom of Druuk is, there is no hope of reaching it."

But Veelos persisted. "Only death can stop me. And what fear does that hold for me, after all this? First they destroyed our village, Kl'aarn. And now they have destroyed my temple, and murdered all my brothers and sisters. Even Keesha, they---. Why should I live? No, Kl'aarn. This very day I travel only westward, ever westward, until I fulfill whatever destiny Lar commanded."

"Or die," Kl'aarn warned.

"Or die," Veelos vowed.

Then Kl'aarn sighed a deep sigh, and said, "I will go with you, Veelos. My men can fulfill the contract with the caravan without me. If you are gone to avenge Har-Keem, then how can I not go with you?"

But Kmir stepped forward and said, "Wherever you go, Kl'aarn, we will stand beside you. Our contract with the merchant can be sold at a loss, and other men can have it. We'll not be going to Kagen-Shel-Don this day, but to the Lands of Demi-men and beyond."

And so also said the rest of the men, for they had all heard the exchange of words between Veelos and Kl'aarn. And they had all witnessed the evil which was already loose in the world. "What have we to lose?" they asked. "Can we live in a world where sorcery is unleashed? What is our fear of demi-men compared to our dread of demons?"

And so the anti-prophecy had had its initial victory. It had destroyed the temple, which had ruled as would angels of God, ruled for a thousand years. Evil had won a battle. But its victory was not final.

For the priestess was at last upon her path.

Chapter 18

Found and Lost

Kl'aarn sold his contract to another band of warriors. Then, with the proceeds, he bought extra horses, a wagon, and such provisions as he could quickly assemble for a long journey. By midmorning, after a whirlwind of activity, the warriors and the priestess were already leaving Shi-Raq behind them. The abruptness of their departure reminded Veelos of the day she had left Har-Keem.

As they rode through the metropolis, through the city streets, through the neighborhoods and business districts, they attracted stares and murmurs from every class of city-dweller. They, not knowing what was afoot, somehow sensed the great import.

Jagmoor somehow found his way along their route, and having gladdened himself to find Veelos alive, begged her not to leave. But when he saw it useless, he offered her a purse of much silver--- which Veelos refused.

Shier-Bek, and her new husband-to-be, also pleaded with Veelos to stay, and seeing that she would not, promised their prayers and devotions. These, the priestess and her following of warriors would soon need.

Soon, too soon, the city was behind them, and a thought-provoking silence, almost dreamlike, enveloped the band of horsemen. The cobbled pavements ended, and a stony path began.

Suddenly, the dreamlike quality, the rush of events, had given way to the dusty reality of a hot day on the trail. From this, no dream, there could be no awakening. Fate or destiny awaited. Fate or destiny: Veelos could almost sense them, as if they were two combatants squaring off for combat. One of them would not be denied.

When finally, the traveling party had reached the forested hilltop, the promontory overlooking the great city, Veelos turned for one last look. Shi-Raq's distant outlines were framed in the boughs of the trees lining the trail. She paused to take in that view, to see the magnificence, one final time.

"This was the road by which I came," Veelos mused aloud, "seven years ago. This was my very first look at the temple. See it? So polished, so grand, so beautiful. So far away, once more, so very far away. Has it really been seven long years, Kl'aarn? In one way, it seems more like seven thousand. In another way, it seems as if only yesterday I arrived here, a frightened little girl. Here, I grew to womanhood. Now I leave it--- perhaps forever. I would cry, Kl'aarn. I would cry if only I could."

* * * * *

That night, they encamped deep in the forest of the hill country. Veelos had forgotten how wearying a long day's ride could be. Now the aches and pains of it reminded her, as she attended her personal grooming for evening.

Always before, she had seen the forest as if it were a garden, a friendly place inhabited by squirrels and rabbits, and by singing, brightly-plumed birds. But now, for the first time in her life, Veelos began to notice its wildness; predatory animals lurked somewhere in the shadows, she knew. Wolves, or even a panther, might be stalking her even now. But Veelos had greater fears to consider than carnivores. A few more days of travel, she knew, would find them being stalked by more deadly predators yet, the ones known as bandits.

Seating herself in relative security beside one of the camp fires, Veelos confessed to Kl'aarn. "Already, I am attacked by doubts."

Kl'aarn seemed almost a different man to her now, not quite the same one she had met in the city. Here, in the forest, he was in his element, his eyes ever alert. As did his men, Kl'aarn stayed in full armor at all times while on the trail, even wearing his helmet while eating, albeit with face-plate raised, not for comfort, but for better vision.

"Doubts?" Kl'aarn asked. "I would think there could be no doubt at all, that we are on a divine mission. The arrows with strange feathers, the attack, your dream, and your high priest's dying words--- no. There can be no doubt."

Veelos searched for the right words. "It's not our quest which I doubt. It's myself. After all, who do I think I am? I am pretentious, no, arrogant, to think I am fit for the task set before me. My sins have rendered me woefully unprepared for so great a responsibility. Whatever right I may once have had to claim the mantle of priesthood, I have long ago squandered it. And worse yet, I have set you and your men upon a most dangerous, most deadly journey, more dangerous than you have ever faced. Can there be any faintest hope of success?"

Kl'aarn gazed into the fire. "We all have to fend off our doubts, Veelos. During all the years I searched for Miril, with all the dreams I dreamt of her, with every journey I took, I was never without doubts. But I never let them stop me."

"She is always on your mind," Veelos noted.

"I'm sorry if---"

"No," Veelos said. "I think of her always, too. We should. Each, in our way, was so very close to her. What sort of people would we be if we did not think of her always?"

Kl'aarn faced Veelos, the firelight glinting in the hairs of his beard. "Do you remember what we planned to do, together, while I would have been away to Kagen-Shel-Don? We promised to pray at sunrise each day."

"Of course I remember that," Veelos said.

"To pray about a decision," Kl'aarn pressed on. "A decision we would ask God to help us make."

"Yes," Veelos prompted.

"Well---" Kl'aarn stammered, "let's not avoid saying it. You were thinking you might leave the priesthood. I was planning to lay aside my sword for good. We spoke of these things, however timidly, however delicately. We thought--- we thought we might--- might---"

"Might marry each other," Veelos finished.

Kl'aarn seemed relieved to hear it spoken. "Yes. Marry. Each other. And lots of reasons occurred to me why I should desire you as wife. As unthinkable as that had been before, it somehow became an appealing prospect for me."

"And for me," Veelos said. "But now you're having your own doubts. Do you feel guilty? Do you feel that we would be betraying Miril?"

Kl'aarn turned his gaze back to the fire. "Maybe."

"So do I," Veelos said. Then, "But remember, Kl'aarn. It was not to be our decision. It still isn't. Look, Kl'aarn, who are we to try to unravel life's infinite complexities with our finite minds? That is why we need God. That is why we planned to pray on it."

"I know," Kl'aarn said. "I know."

"And God will answer those prayers. Only, while we pray, we won't be separated by the great distance we had planned on. We'll be together. Somewhere, between here and some king's castle beyond the Lands of Demi-men---somewhere, along that great distance, we will find the right answer. I know we will. And when we do, whatever the answer God leads us to, all our doubts will be settled."

* * * * *

Each morning the travelers broke camp quickly. Each day, greater became the distance which separated them from Shi-Raq. Each evening, the territory in which they encamped was more hostile than before. Soon, the safer trails were behind them, and their path grew more perilous.

For several days more, they penetrated ever farther, ever deeper into bandit-infested territory. They had not yet been accosted for tolls or tribute, because they were so many, and because they had but one wagon, a supply cart, which seemed not a very promising item of plunder.

But soon, matters grew more treacherous than before. The warriors clearly recognized that they were more deeply endangered than ever. For they were off the caravan routes completely, a fact which changed all the rules of engagement. Here, there could be no bartering for tribute, because there could be no route of escape. They were entering into the refuges of the mighty bandit-lords. No longer were they mere quarry for would-be looters. They had now become trespassers, invaders of the territories in which only bandits themselves dared venture--- bandits, those who sold to them, and those who were sent to wage war against them.

During those days of travel, Veelos had learned to become as one of the company, no mere passenger, but a worker with specific duties to perform. She helped to set up camp, tended fires, and cooked. Despite her weariness, the priestess drove herself, always the first to rise in the predawn darkness before morning, ever the last to retire in the starlit nights.

During those late hours, when only a sentry kept watch, Kl'aarn and Veelos would sit and pray. And they would talk.

"What do you think is going to happen," Veelos asked, "when we come to the border of the Lands of Demi-men? What do you think we'll do? I mean, the men. You. Myself. Do you think we'll balk? Will fear overcome us? I have heard that it is a fearsome border."

Kl'aarn peered toward the campfire. "It's a fearsome border, yes."

"Have you ever seen it?"

Kl'aarn nodded. "Once. From a very great distance. There is a narrow river. To speak of it doesn't make it sound like much. But it's fearsome to see. It's not the river that strikes fear, but what lies beyond it. The other side of that river is nothing like this side. It's dry, barren, and without any trees. And there's something more, something like a deep, low growl, unheard by the ears, but felt in the tightness of one's chest. Whatever it is, it strikes terror into the hearts of the most dauntless adventurers. The bravest of men have turned back from it. Not even the fiercest of the bandits dares set one foot across that river. They say the land beyond is cursed."

Veelos inhaled slowly, audibly. Already she felt the first tremor of fear. But she dared not say so.

"What do you think?" Kl'aarn asked. "Is it truly a cursed domain?"

Veelos searched her mind for an answer. "The wars of the Upheaval," she explained, "are said to have been fought there. Those were the days when sorcery and witchcraft were practiced as commonly as swordplay is today. Might there yet be a curse upon the land? Yes. But this may be the beginning of another Upheaval. If so, it is time to remove the curse, and to replace it with blessing."

Kl'aarn listened intently, both to Veelos and to the sounds of the night forest. Then he asked, "One always hears about these legends. We hear the stories of Tarok and Kattaroon, of Belchorr and the Ki-Rori. But did these things really happen? And if so, what exactly was the Upheaval?"

Veelos answered. "When the fallen angels were thrown from heaven, they fell to earth. They mingled with men. Their leader had already corrupted the earth with sin, and now his minions tried to establish an earthly kingdom of evil. But the angels of God came down to help our kind. And, with their human allies, they drove the demons from the earth. But not all men were their allies. While some men chose to fight for God, allied with the angels, yet other men sided with the demons. Great battles were fought, a mighty and fierce war. When it ended, the demons and the witches and the sorcerors were all cast from the earth. But evil itself had not been cast from the earth, for it continued to reside in the hearts of men. So, evil does remain in the world. And as long as it does, men will continue to summon forth the demons, again and again. So there will continue to be wars of upheaval, until one day, the final battle of all time will be fought. Then, the demons, and all their evil human allies, will be cast forever into a furnace, never again to threaten men or angels."

Kl'aarn placed a small log onto the fire, and carefully twisted it into a position just so. Then he said, "Even the best of men do evil. So we all bear the guilt of starting these wars."

"Yes," Veelos said. "We are all guilty. But even the worst among us is redeemable by God. Sometimes our sin is to forget that. I confessed to you why I left Har-Keem--- not for love of the priesthood, Kl'aarn, nor for any love at all, but rather because I hated Shalar. I despised him. I never thought him redeemable. Yet, in his final moments, he did do a noble thing, didn't he? He offered to stand at the rampart while you went for help. Then he sounded the alarm. Yet, despite his redeemable qualities, I hated him--- and wrongfully loved you."

Kl'aarn shifted uncomfortably where he sat.

"I shouldn't have said that," Veelos apologized. "Whenever I mention love, your heart aches for Miril."

"Veelos---" Kl'aarn said haltingly. "When I went to Shi-Raq, I went there to search for Miril. I knew she wasn't there. But I knew that you were." He paused, as if reflecting into his own words. Then he continued, "Did I just say something with two meanings? You see, I had failed to find Miril anywhere else in the world. So I tried to find her in a different way. I thought I could find her in Shi-Raq--- in you."

Veelos nodded. "I suppose that, if ever we did decide to marry each other, we'd both be marrying an illusion, wouldn't we? You'd be thinking of Miril; I'd see in you the frail but gentle boy in shining armor."

Kl'aarn tossed another stick into the fire. "I'm really sorry if I'm playing with your emotions, Veelos. I don't mean to. You know, I've been very inconsiderate of your feelings, even cruel."

"We're both in a lot of pain," Veelos said. "We've both lost more than can ever be replaced. Our families, our home, even our language is extinct.

If nothing else, we've lost our childhood. Now, we're trying desperately to salvage what happiness we can from a cold, indifferent world. So if we must be cruel, and if we must be hurt, let us be cruel and be hurt together. At least we can understand each other well enough to forgive. Kl'aarn--- you don't know how much I wish I could believe Miril alive. You don't know how I long to see her, to hear her voice, to laugh with her and share our secrets as once we did. And if somehow we do find her alive, I will rejoice with you. I will. And yes, I'll feel guilty that I ever saw in you a possible--- husband. But for now, all we have is uncertainty--- and each other. I'm not going to feel guilty about that."

* * * * *

Each day thereafter, the men became increasingly aware that they were being watched. Afar among the trees there would be furtive movements in the shadows. Only a skilled eye could detect them. Therein lay the greater danger. Day by day, that danger grew.

"In whose territory are we now?" Veelos asked. Mounted upon her own horse, she was at Kl'aarn's side, and at the fore of the double column of horsemen.

Kl'aarn's faceplate was lifted up, so that it formed a visor, hinged at the forehead of his helmet. "No one's territory in particular," he answered. "There are no clear borders here. These regions are not traveled by traders, except by those who trade directly with the bandits--- slave traders and such. Instead, these forests are a refuge to the various bands of thieves. There are places hereabouts where they can spend their loot. Small villages, here and there, have learned to survive and profit, in the midst of this debauchery."

"Then, if we do encounter any bandits," Veelos asked, "do you think they will let us pass?" Her tone was hopeful. "After all, we've nothing for them to steal."

"That's what we're all praying," Kl'aarn said. "But we can't count on it. They'll take us for mercenaries, perhaps hired to wage war against one or another of their breed. And even though bandits care nothing for rival bandit-lords, there is a natural enmity between their kind and ours. I suppose that's to be expected. Even when we are paying the tributes they demand, for safe passage, even then, there is always a sense of hostility, a tension that could erupt any moment into murder. That enmity is deeply ingrained, just like the enmity between hunter and hunted--- or between priests and witches."

It was midmorning. As Kl'aarn and Veelos spoke, they came to a widening of the trail, and a thinning of the forest. Veelos abruptly halted.

Kl'aarn stopped also, his eyes first upon the priestess, and then scanning the trail ahead. "What is it?" he asked.

Veelos seemed to be listening intently for some sound that only she could hear.

"Why do you stop?" Kl'aarn prodded.

For moments more, Veelos seemed to strain with every sense. "There is danger here," she finally said.

"What is it?" Kl'aarn pressed impatiently.

"A very familiar danger," Veelos replied.

Kl'aarn looked at her quizzically. "What did you see?" For, in all their days of journeying, Veelos had never developed forest eyes.

"I don't see anything," Veelos replied. "But something isn't right. Something is very, very wrong. And for the life of me, I think I should be able to explain it, but I can't."

Kl'aarn surveyed the terrain just ahead of them. "An ambush perhaps," he surmised. "But here? Who would place an ambush here? There is no place to hide in wait. All the advantage is ours."

"Unless," Veelos said, "we would let down our guard. Kl'aarn, please believe me. Something is dreadfully wrong here. Something that we should both be able to feel, but which neither of us can discern."

Kl'aarn's eyes scanned the trees ahead, but still he saw nothing. "It seems quite ordinary to me. But if you sense danger," he said, "then I'll take your word for it." So saying, he lowered the metal visor of his dull, grey helmet, and locked it down over his face. Behind it, only his eyes could be seen, looking out through horizontal slits. And from beneath, protruded his beard.

With a smooth, silent motion, Kl'aarn drew forth his sword. As Veelos glanced at it, she saw its keenly honed blade as she had never seen it before. She saw it now for what it truly was, no mere cutting tool, but an implement of killing. It was heavy, brutal, and deadly. Suddenly, it had become an extension of Kl'aarn, transforming him from the brotherly gentleman she had known, into what he really was: warrior, and all the savagery which that implied.

Behind the faceplate his voice had taken on a different quality, a metallic impersonality. "Take cover in the wagon," Kl'aarn ordered. "And stay there until we're clear of this place."

Veelos hesitated. "Kl'aarn--- be careful." Then she turned her horse and made for the wagon. She noticed that all the other men had also taken on the same look as Kl'aarn. Their faces concealed, swords drawn, and shields hoisted, they had suddenly become an army of formidable, anonymous war machines. The mere sight of them sent a shudder of fright through her. Surely, Veelos thought, their very appearance should deter any attack, even by the most ruthless of bandit hordes.

Then, dismounting from her horse and tying it to the wagon, Veelos took refuge behind its thick wooden sideboards, and hid herself among its cargo. For a moment she felt foolish. Was all this concern for nothing? But as soon as she hoped that, the sensation once again came upon her. There was danger, and there was something about it that was familiar, very much familiar. It was as if the name for it were on the very edge of her memory, but just beyond recollection. Veelos could not discern that elusive name.

She felt the wagon begin to move forward again, and peered out through the spaces between the sideboards. Just as Kl'aarn had said, there seemed no place in which to hide an ambush. The trees were too thin. And the bushes were too low--- then a thought came to Veelos. The bushes were not too low after all. Although mere shrubs, each one of them could conceal a man, if he were clever enough to dig a trough beneath it, and to cover himself with leaves. Yes, Veelos thought. That was where they were hiding. She opened her mouth to sound a warning.

But just as she did, her voice was drowned out by the murderous roar of men leaping into battle. Flinging aside the camouflage of leaves, beneath which they had been buried, they emerged on foot from beneath the shrubs and undergrowth, bearing pikes and spears, long weapons designed to unhorse mounted men. There were some twenty attackers, and Kl'aarn's men could have made easy work of them.

But these bandits were only the snare, only the means by which to gain quick surprise. They were quickly joined by others, the brunt of the attack. From the more distant cover of trees, some twenty or so additional bandits charged into the fray, all on horseback. These were heavily armed with sword, helmet and shield. It took them little time to close the distance, and to completely surround the warriors. The scheme was all but diabolical, and it had worked.

In the space of only a few moments, the quiet forest had become the scene of frenzied battle. The shrill neigh of horses, the curses of men, and the clashing of metal upon metal deafened Veelos's ears. Fear gripped her. For the warriors were heavily outnumbered. Had she brought them all this way to die? she thought.

The bandits did indeed outnumber the warriors two to one. But this advantage was of limited value to them. For each bandit fought only for himself, whereas the warriors fought as a disciplined unit. And for a time, it seemed that the warriors might indeed drive the attackers away.

But that was not to be.

Veelos watched through the space between the sideboards of the wagon as two bandits pressed their attack against one of Kl'aarn's men. Veelos knew that he was the one named Thrake, although how she could know that (for in full armor, Kl'aarn's men all looked much alike), she did not ask. She just knew.

One of the bandits attacking Thrake was on horseback, wielding a sword. The other was on foot, jabbing at Thrake with a pike. The footman found his target, stabbing Thrake's breastplate, and toppling the warrior from his horse. The other bandit, the one on horseback, would have quickly killed Thrake. But the warrior deftly tumbled beneath the wagon, under the floorboard where Veelos lay, and rolled to the other side, where he gained his footing once more.

The mounted bandit maneuvered to pursue. But just as he turned, he found himself facing Kmir. Veelos sensed the sudden terror the bandit felt, knew of the cold pain in his heart as Kmir's sword pierced the man's chest. He fell from his horse, dead. The slain bandit's name, Veelos knew, had been Thantor.

Then Veelos noted a change in the sounds of battle. The clamorous noises slowly diminished into the metallic crashes, clangs and thuds of but one duel, one brutal and awful fight to the death.

One among the bandits was fully armored. This was unusual among bandits, for few of them had the discipline or the complex of skills needed to maintain armor in fighting trim. But this bandit was outfitted in a fashion similar to that of the warriors. He seemed also to have the fighting skills of a formally trained swordsman. Veelos could not see him, but she sensed that he was the bandit-lord, the leader of these who were attacking, with murder in their foul hearts.

The bandit-lord had soon detected that his men could not win this battle cheaply. And he knew that the one wagonload of supplies they escorted would not be worth all this trouble, unless the cargo were indeed some rare and precious metal, as he had hoped.

But the bandit was as clever as he was sinister. From a distance, he had picked out Kl'aarn as the commander of the warriors, and had determined just how to bring this fight to a quick and favorable decision. And that was, to kill the leader of his enemy.

Kl'aarn had seen him also, and had picked out him who was the head of this venomous snake which encircled his band of men in bloody deathgrip.

As the two leaders had fought among the fray, each of them had begun to maneuver his way toward the other. Each had ordered his own men aside, and each had cut his way through any enemy who stood in the way.

It was the custom in those days for opposing armies to line up in formal battle array before, not after, beginning a fight. And although bandits always fought from ambush if they could, they understood the formality of single combat, of a duel between leaders. And they recognized, as did Kl'aarn's men, that the two leaders had chosen each other from among all other enemies on the field of battle. The combat which had begun as an intended swift massacre, and which had disintegrated into a lethal brawl, had now become transformed into a formal, set piece duel.

Each astride his horse, the two armored men collided in single combat.

As soon as the first blows had been exchanged and deflected, it became clear that neither man had a distinct advantage. This duel would be as systematic as already it was fierce. It would be a duel not merely of strength, but also of patience and guile, of tactic and maneuver. And there could be only one end to it: the victory of one man, the death of the other.

As Kl'aarn and the bandit-lord dueled, the other fighters gradually began to disengage. They knew that only this one contest would have any final meaning. It was the only duel among all those on the battlefield that would matter. The outcome of the fight between the two leaders would decide the entire battle. Everyone knew that.

It was thus that Veelos heard the sudden change in the sounds of battle, and lifted up her head to watch. But for Veelos, seeing was horror. For there was Kl'aarn, amid a circle of onlookers, fighting for his very life.

For a time, it seemed an even match, with each man giving as much as he got. One would gain the upper hand, only to have the other take it away. And so it went for a time.

But as Veelos watched, she could see what others could not. Kl'aarn was slowly beginning to weaken. His frailty had been disguised, diminished, but not departed from his bones. Although he was bruising his enemy, Kl'aarn was gradually, imperceptibly tiring.

He was losing the battle.

He could not hope to continue holding his own for very much longer. Unless something dramatic happened, Veelos perceived, Kl'aarn was going to die. Of that, Veelos could have no doubt.

Suddenly cold with fear, Veelos became aware of a warmth in her hand. She glanced at her palm. It seemed almost to glow with a fiery power, a mighty force which she had used only twice before, but with crucial effect each time. The first time it had straightened Shier-Beks's legs. The second time, it had scorched a robber's face. This time, it was stronger yet, fearsomely powerful. This time, it was too savage to merely wound. It could only kill. Veelos knew that with a single gesture, she could hurl a lightning bolt that would instantly disembowel Kl'aarn's evil opponent, and cast the dead soul into the place of eternal shrieking.

Then suddenly, the bandit-lord struck a direct blow, and Kl'aarn fell from his horse. The bandit-lord quickly maneuvered his own horse, causing it to trample the warrior. And although Kl'aarn's armor prevented fatal injury from the hooves of the horse, he was decisively wounded. Worse, his sword had come loose from his grip, and he could no longer retrieve it.

The bandit showed neither hesitation nor mercy. He had no interest in being graceful or ceremonious. All he cared about was to kill the fallen warrior as quickly--- and as dead--- as he could. Leaping from his own mount, the bandit straddled Kl'aarn's helpless form, and positioned the point of his weapon for the kill.

Veelos felt the power of the flame surge within her entire arm. There was no time to think of it. It was now or never, either kill the bandit, or let him kill Kl'aarn. The priestess stood and took aim.

No, Keesha had said. One day, all eyes would see that God's way was best. All else was regret. To use the power was to sink farther each time into the grip of ever darker, ever more malevolent evil, a grip which, sooner or later, would become permanent. Veelos lifted both hands, then, not hands with which to kill, but hands with which to pray. She lifted them up to heaven. And then she cried out in anguish, cried out words not of her own, but words which were given her to call out.

Before the bandit could pierce Kl'aarn's flesh, Veelos leapt to her feet atop the cart and screamed these words: "Don't kill him, Shalar! It's Kl'aarn!"

The words had the effect of freezing every man in his tracks, freezing them all except for the turning of their heads toward the strange sight of a priestess leaping from a horse-drawn cart, appearing, the bandits thought, as if by magic from nowhere.

Veelos jumped down, landing upon her hands and knees in the dust. She quickly came to her feet, and ran between astonished warriors and confused bandits, men who but moments before had been doing all in their powers to kill each other. She ran straight at the bandit-lord, and upon reaching him, threw herself against his armored frame, pushing him backward from his murderous stance above Kl'aarn.

Shalar lifted the face-plate from his helmet, exposing his bewildered expression. "Veelos?" he exclaimed. "Is that you? It is you! What the hell are you doing out here? And Kl'aarn! I thought you dead all these years. Have the gods gone mad?"

Painfully, Kl'aarn struggled to his feet, his faceplate lifted up. And although he was clearly injured, he said coldly, "Shalar, you've killed two of my men. I cannot allow that to go unavenged while I live."

Shalar still had his own sword in hand, and turned its point toward the warrior, as if ready to conclude the duel after all.

But Veelos turned on Kl'aarn. "Oh yes you can allow it to go unavenged. You lost the fight. You were already dead until Shalar recognized you. Besides which, you once swore an oath with Shalar, remember? That neither of you would ever harm the other. The fighting is over, Kl'aarn."

Then Veelos's gaze swept the entire circle of killers standing all about.

"All of you," she commanded. "Put away your weapons. At once!"

For a moment, no one moved. Then Shalar chuckled, and with careful, deliberate moves, sheathed his sword. "Do as the priestess commands," he ordered his men. And when they balked, he prompted them, "Or die by my own hand."

Now the bandits were not of a mind to disarm in the presence of their enemies, but they were clearly afraid of Shalar. One by one, they began to lower their swords and pikes, all the while eyeing the warriors with suspicion and distrust.

Then, cautiously, the warriors also began to do the same. After long, tense moments, everyone seemed to be satisfied that the day's fighting was concluded.

Then Veelos turned again to Shalar. Her glare was disdainful. "Look what you've become, you bastard." Her words dripped with scorn. "A common thief and murderer. How could you, even you, sink this low?"

Shalar's jaw jutted forward as if he had not expected to be treated so insultingly. Then, with sarcasm, he answered, "I see that priesthood has done nothing to mellow your disposition, Veelos. I'm not surprised."

Then Shalar turned toward Kl'aarn. "But merchant boy. Look at you. A fighter! And almost a match for me. Who ever would have thought it? We could still be a team, you and I, just as I once proposed those many years ago. Together, we could defeat Morgrar One-Arm and take over all his territories."

Veelos's voice was icy. "Don't try to make light of this, metalsmith. Men are dead. You are responsible. How could you carry the blood of slain Har-Keem in your veins and use it for such evil? You must answer for that."

"But neither of you has answered me," Shalar retorted. "What brings you into these retreats? Only bandits, slave sellers, and those who would assassinate us venture here."

Kl'aarn's lethal anger seemed to have diminished somewhat. His sword was brought to him, by one of his men, and under Veelos's watchful eye, he sheathed it. Then he replied to Shalar's question.

"The men who destroyed Har-Keem have now destroyed the temple in Shi-Raq. First they murdered all our families, so as to conceal that their plunder was the orb from our village shrine. And now, to further their schemes, they have seized the Great Orb. If they master its powers, Shalar, then Morgrar One-Arm will become the least of your problems. For a great and evil enemy will sweep across from the Lands of Demi-men. More than your life will be forfeit if they do."

Shalar seemed nonplused. "What strange tale is this?"

"It's no mere tale," Kl'aarn answered. "Why else would we be here? The only other reason I could think of would be to hunt you down, and kill you. But we thought you already dead."

Shalar grunted. "By all rights I am dead. The day which dawned upon the aftermath of Har-Keem, I awoke with the noon sun in my eyes; my only shade was from a feather tree growing out of my chest, if you catch my drift."

Hearing those words, Kl'aarn seemed to forget all about the bruises of battle, defeat, and near death. With one hand he grasped Shalar's arm. "What about Miril!" he said eagerly. "Did you get her to safety as you promised?"

Shalar tried to shake off Kl'aarn's grip. "Yes," he said. "I did my part. Miril was running toward the pier. I stopped her. I told her I would rescue you, bring you, to her if she would run to the woods. She argued like hell at first, but she finally obeyed."

"And?" Kl'aarn prompted.

"And," Shalar said, "that was the last I saw of her. I got my sword--- this one!" he showed off its silver-plated hilt--- "and went back to get you. That was back before I had sense. I got arrowshot. I must have been left for dead. When I came to my senses, there was nothing left of Har-Keem, no thing and no person. What happened to Miril, I don't know. But you can't hold me responsible, not after all I went through."

Kl'aarn released his grip on Shalar's arm. "I'm not holding you responsible. Not for that, anyway."

"And what of you?" Shalar asked. "How in hell did you live through it?

They didn't leave you for dead. You weren't there the next day."

"Those of us who weren't killed outright," Kl'aarn said, "were put on a slave ship. There was a storm. I washed up on shore. Everybody else died, everybody."

Shalar nodded. "So it's just us three, then."

"Unless Miril escaped," Kl'aarn said.

"Damn," Shalar said. "I wish I could give you some news of her, but I can't. Surely you've searched for her everywhere and come up empty."

"I have," Kl'aarn said. Then, "Shalar--- have you never wanted revenge? I mean, on the men who destroyed Har-Keem?"

"Sure I have," Shalar answered. "You know me. I'm the most revenge-loving son of a bitch you've ever met. But what could I do? What could anyone do? The bastards are far out to sea. We're no sailors."

Kl'aarn answered. "No. They are not far out to sea. We know who did it. And we know where they are."

"The hell you say," Shalar said. "Who? Where?"

"There is a king named Druuk. His kingdom is a land beyond the Lands of Demi-men. We are going to cross those lands and find him. When we do, Shalar, we will avenge the evils done against us, and destroy his sorcery, by which he threatens to ruin us all."

At first Shalar laughed. "It's a joke, right?" he said. But when he saw that they were serious, his smile vanished and he spat. "This is all too much. Now let's take this slowly. You want me to believe these nonsense stories you speak. I thought the gods had gone mad. But it's no madness of any gods. It's you two. And you think me mad as well."

But Veelos said, "Open your eyes, Shalar. We have not come to all this grief just to pose riddles to you. Unbeliever that you are, you know the legends. Inattentive though you were in your youth, the scriptures were read aloud to you. Well you know the prophecies whereof we speak. Accept the obvious, Shalar. Once before in your life, you accepted your duty and tried to save your village. Then you failed. But now the stakes are much higher.

Even your wretched soul can yet be saved, if you but return to your path. Join us, Shalar. Sojourn with us across the Lands of Demi-men. Succeed now with us, where before you failed alone."

But Shalar was as deaf as ever to pleas to his higher nature. "No one has ever trespassed the Lands of Demi-men," he said, "and lived. No one. And you'll not even get as far as the border. For between here and the Lands of Demi-men is the stronghold of Morgrar. He'll have you for breakfast."

But Kl'aarn urged Shalar. "You and Morgrar are two of a kind. You'll know how to speak to him. If you'll not accompany us, at least do this one little thing for us: tell Morgrar One-Arm that we want only safe passage. If he thinks us madmen, all the better."

But Shalar shook his head, and said, "Morgrar will do no favors in my name. It's because of me that Morgrar is now known as One-Arm. He and I got into a drunken brawl a few years back. I tried to split his skull with an axe. But I missed, and wounded his arm instead. It rotted and eventually fell off. Morgrar's not one to take such insults lightly. He has a great price on my head, a price that turned several of my men against me, rest their souls, and nearly cost my life on more than one occasion. No, I don't think your bargaining position with Morgrar would be improved by my pleading your case."

"Then help us fight our way through," Kl'aarn asked. "Or at least guide us through some secret pathways to elude him."

Shalar shook his head again. "I don't think I'm getting through to you. I'm trying to talk you out of this. It's crazy. Are both of you totally mad?"

Veelos interjected. "We're not crazy, Shalar. Har-Keem was slaughtered. My temple priests were massacred. And those were only the beginnings of the evil conquest about to overwhelm us all, if we don't fight it now, while we can. Will you just stand by like an idiot and let all this happen, while yet you are able to wield a sword for justice instead of for murder?"

"Yes," Shalar said. "Call it what you will. Cowardice or sinfulness, I don't care. At least I have enough sense to avoid both Morgrar and the demi-men."

Then Veelos remarked, "What a cruel thing this is, Shalar: for us to have found you alive after all these years, to have found you in this wretched condition, only to have to leave you in this miserable state into which you have fallen--- to abandon you one more time. Surely this cannot be. Are you indeed so far from God that you cannot be turned from evil at all, not even by the miracle you witnessed this day?"

But Shalar spat, and said, "You are but ghosts, the two of you. Not yet dead, but that little detail will soon be resolved. Go, then. You have safe passage through Shalar's territory. Use it before I change my mind."

Then, without further farewell, Shalar and his men turned away from them and vanished into the forest.

Chapter 19

Evil upon evil

When Shalar finally looked back upon them, the warriors and Veelos were already disappearing from view. He watched as the wagon, and then the rear guard, finally vanished into a bend of the trail, swallowed up once more into the forest from which they had come.

Dimly, Shalar felt something strange, an emotion he had felt only once before in all his life. He was reminded of a day, long before, when he had felt this very same sharp pang in his breast. It had been the day when Veelos had left Har-Keem for Shi-Raq. On that day, Shalar had very nearly acted on this emotion, which now revisited him for only the second time in his life. He had very nearly stepped forward, as he felt compelled once more. But this time, just as he had before, he suppressed that feeling, and allowed the cart to trundle away into the forest.

Shalar purposely reminded himself of the only emotions which could make a home in his heart. They were the emotions felt in battle: bloodlust, frenzy, and sometimes, fear. And apart from battle, Shalar's soul was host to the emotions of greed, and of lust. In company with these, no gentler emotion could long survive.

As to the travelers he had so briefly encountered, travelers from a time past, Shalar put them from his mind. The entire episode might all have been but a dream, just one more among many turbulent and chaotic dreams, dreams eagerly forgotten amid each new day's schemes and plots.

His reverie was broken. It was back to business.

Rith's horse trod upon the forest ground as he approached Shalar. The bandit drew up beside his bandit-lord, and complained bitterly. "Yort lost an eye in this fight. Sigmar and Thantor are dead. And look at Joust and Wolftooth, lying there vomiting blood. They won't live long. And what have we to show for all this loss?"

In reply, Shalar turned a menacing glare toward Rith. "If you dare, chase them down," he said sarcastically. "If you have the courage, challenge Kl'aarn to a duel. He'll be glad to oblige. And however the worse for wear he is, there's still enough man in him to make short work of the likes of you."

Rith scowled. "You think more of your old friends than of your present comrades."

"You're damned right I do," Shalar said. "A hundred of you is not worth one of them. Those are brave men. You saw how they fought. And they had the decency to bury their dead before moving on. By the way, Rith, how many of them did you kill? Did you even bruise one of them?"

But Rith remained bitter. "The men will be very ill tempered after this. They feel cheated. We'll never know what treasure might be carried in that wagon: perhaps a purse of silver, or even a bar of gold. But we do know this much: that they bear a woman among their cargo. The men could have made sport of her."

Rith instantly found a dagger at his throat. It was no idle threat; Shalar was ready to use it. "Speak of her again like that," Shalar growled, "and I'll hand you your tongue."

Rith's thick brow lifted in mild astonishment. He had never seen Shalar slighted over so casual a remark. "Alright," he said. "I won't." Then, "But you know how these men get when they've seen a woman. There will be fights among them, maimings, and maybe a killing. They need something to take their minds off what's happened here, something to salve their disappointed expectations. We gained not so much as a silver coin for our bruises."

Shalar's hand deftly twirled the dagger back into its sheath. For all his deviousness, Rith did have his uses, after all. Even though he could never be trusted, he did have a sense for the moods of the men. And he was right. Keeping a band of some forty murderous cutthroats in line was a tricky, dangerous task, especially when their lusts had been aroused. They needed regular doses of reward.

"We'll dip into the trove," he told Rith. Shalar's long life as a bandit was owed to his secret hoard of treasure. He would store the excess of his stolen booty there in times of plenty, and draw from it in leaner times, such as this. As long as no one but Shalar knew where the trove was, none of his men would assassinate him. "We'll camp outside Shel-Avak," he said. "Then I'll take a pack horse with me, while you wait. When I return, each man will get his share, and we'll turn them loose in the village until it's spent. Then we'll head south a few days and waylay a richer caravan."

This pleased the men. For Shel-Avak had only recently become one of their refuges. A man named Trrod ruled there, and for a price, he provided anything that any bandit desired, be it flesh, drink, or bloodsport. While in Shel-Avak, and while he had money, a bandit was safe. For Trrod quickly punished anyone who raised a hand against his customers. Rumored to be a sorceror, Trrod was respected, even feared by all. And well he was, for his enemies seemed always to die painful, hideous deaths. Not even Morgrar One-Arm would violate the truce while in Shel-Avak.

He would, however, send assassins and snipers into the surrounding forests, wherever he thought he might find any of his many enemies. For this reason, Shalar always sent a scout ahead of his main body. And to ensure that the scout did his job, a runner continually shuttled back and forth between the scout and Shalar, to report that the scout had not been waylaid or run away.

The life of banditry was complicated. Those banditlords who did not appreciate this did not survive.

It was the second day of their journey toward Shel-Avak. The runner had just reported to Shalar that all was well. He was just about to shuttle forward again, when the scout came racing back into the main body. His name was Hathor, and he seemed so frightened that all the men made ready for battle.

Shalar cursed. "Hathor, what the hell have you done? Have you led an enemy straight to us?" Every bandit knew that the scout was to retreat away from the main body, not into it. For a clever enemy would follow a retreating scout, not kill him. But Hathor had fled straight into the midst of his comrades in arms.

Now Hathor was by no means the brightest of Shalar's men. It was for this very reason that he was scout: scouts tended not to live long.

"Who ambushed you?" Shalar demanded. "How many are they?"

But Hathor, his eyes wild with fear, replied, "It's a woman! A woman all alone in the forest."

For a moment, there was silence. Then jeering laughter broke out among the men.

Shalar's anger took on a truly lethal menace. Hathor was in serious danger of being killed on the spot. "What?" Shalar demanded. "You ran away from a what?"

"A woman!" Hathor repeated. "All alone in the forest."

Shalar wanted to know more before he rid himself of the simpleton. "A woman, you say. Some runaway whore from Shel-Avak."

"No!" Hathor said, out of breath.

"Well, then," Shalar said impatiently, "tell us what made you run from her."

Hathor seemed to ponder that question, then answered, "I've never seen such a woman. Suddenly, she stepped from behind a tree, and just looked at me. Just looked right at me, and I got scared."

There was even louder jeering from among the men than there had been before.

Shalar was infuriated. "You got scared of a woman?"

"But she is no ordinary woman, I tell you. There is something terrible about her."

"What was it?" Shalar demanded. "What did she look like?"

"She is young and beautiful," Hathor reported. "And dressed all in black."

"Was she alone? Are you sure?"

"Laugh if you will," Hathor said, embarrassed at last. "Go see for yourself."

* * * * *

Miril did not flinch when the ambush was sprung. Some forty armed men suddenly surrounded her, the air bristling with their arrows, and the forest metallic with daggers, swords and truncheons. She showed no fear at all, but merely froze into a self-assured, dignified posture amid the fierce, brutal murderers who encircled her.

When Shalar saw her, he recognized at once that it was Miril. "By the gods," he swore, dismounting from his horse. "Am I to encounter all the ghosts of Har-Keem in ones and twos? How many more must I exorcise?"

Miril seemed able to both smile and sneer at the same time. "What?" she said in a voice tinged both with sarcasm and menace. "No tender greeting from you, Shalar?"

When the bandits saw that she knew Shalar's name, they were astonished. When they saw that she knew no fear, they became uneasy.

Miril continued. "Why do you not embrace me, and say, Miril! How glad I am to see you alive!"

But Shalar was too astonished to reply.

Miril's eyes glared darkly, burning with mounting rage. "Why do you not say to me, Miril! I did not keep my promise to rescue Kl'aarn for you. Why do you not apologize to me for letting him die?"

But Shalar replied, "He didn't die. Kl'aarn is alive. We saw him just yester---"

"And he travels with Veelos," Miril said.

Now Shalar fell silent for awhile. He carefully looked Miril up and down, trying to make out whether she were truly Miril in the flesh, or merely her phantom. Then he said, with unaccustomed horror, "By the gods, Miril. You've become a sorceress."

"By the demons," she corrected. "And no mere sorceress, you petty thief. Have you never seen a witch, Shalar?"

Shalar stepped backward a pace, still staring at her in disbelief. "A witch, you say?" For he could not deny the obvious. Even so, it seemed impossible. "But you, of all people," he mused aloud. "I would never have believed it."

"You never believed in much of anything," Miril said, "beyond your ability to take what you wanted. You bowed neither to God nor to demons, Shalar, but rather relied only on your brute force."

"No," Shalar said. "I never believed in any of that religion stuff. And truth be told, I still don't. Not enough to care, anyway. So what if you are become a witch. So be it. That's your business. Why trouble me about it? Kl'aarn and Veelos---"

"Never," Miril interrupted him with icy ferocity, "join their names together. Never."

Shalar nodded almost timidly. "Very well. As you wish. But know this, that Kl'aarn has been searching for you. He's all but given up on finding you alive. If you didn't want him to find you, fine. But neither did I. So why did you seek me out, instead of him?"

Miril spat, and her eyes darkened. "You coward. Kl'aarn and Veelos are about their destiny, while you squander yours with drunkards and petty murderers. But you swore an oath to me, Shalar, that you would bring me my

Kl'aarn safe and whole. I am holding you to that promise, Shalar. Take me to Kl'aarn."

Shalar nodded. "Alright. I'll give you a horse, and a man to show you the way. I'll even give you some money, just for old sentiments."

Miril sneered at the offer. "How generous of you, metalsmith," she said with contempt. "But that will not be enough, not nearly enough. Take me to him yourself. Yes, you, and all your men, will accompany me."

"Don't get cocky with me, madwoman," Shalar retorted. "I can see well enough to know what's going on here. You've got yourself tangled up in some war between angels and demons, the same war that Veelos tangled Kl'aarn up in. They tried to involve me, too, and they failed. You'll have no better luck."

As Shalar spoke, he noticed that Rith had dismounted, and with dagger drawn, was stealthily approaching Miril from behind. Shalar carefully kept his eyes focused on those of Miril, so as not to alert her to the treachery unfolding behind her.

"You're already entangled," Miril replied. "Evil has already made its claim on you, just as it has on me. For all these years, we've both been serving the demon, Shalar. You in your pitiful way, and I in a much more fruitful way. Now it's time, Shalar. It's time for you to take a step up, to claim your destiny, as I have claimed mine. Are you on your way to your pathetic trove, to pinch out a few pieces of silver? No, Shalar. You are not. You are on your way to a king's treasury, to scoop out armsful of gold, more wealth than you or your men ever dreamed of obtaining. Druuk's throne is to be yours, Shalar. It will be a fitting revenge for what he did to Har-Keem."

"Kl'aarn is, even now, on his way to Druuk's castle," Shalar said. "So is your sister, Veelos. If you wish to be reunited with them, you are going to get your wish. For very soon, they will both be dead. And so will you." This was Shalar's signal to Rith, who by now was easily within reach of Miril's vulnerable back.

"I think not," Miril answered.

But just then the assassin plunged his dagger deeply into Miril's back. She lurched forward half a step from the force of the blow. Then Rith jerked the dagger back out, and held it aloft for all to see. It dripped red with blood.

But instead of the grimace of death contorting her face, Miril smiled wickedly at Shalar. "The blood on Rith's dagger is red," she said with casual observation. Then she said further, "But as you know, a witch's blood is black. Blackest of all black."

For a moment, Shalar stood in astonishment, not understanding what he saw or heard. Then, as if to solve the riddle, Rith fell forward, collapsing onto the ground beside Miril and Shalar, dead. In his back, a gaping dagger wound formed a pool of red blood.

Shalar stared wide-eyed. By what magic he knew not, Rith had been killed by his own dagger. The wound he had inflicted on Miril had, by some impossible sorcery, been transferred from Miril to Rith. He had murdered himself.

Miril glanced down at the corpse disdainfully, then turned her gaze back to Shalar. "Gather your courage," she said. "You'll need it. For we are all going into the Lands of Demi-men. All of us. You, me, Kl'aarn, and yes---even Veelos. We are reunited, Shalar. Har-Keem has risen from its ashes. And loathsome King Druuk shall know the bitter sting of our revenge."

Chapter 20

Hunter of Men

There was a part of the forest that was far from any trail. It was dense with foliage, and at night, no starlight descended past the thick canopy of leaves and branches overhead. Only a nightcat could see at all in the darkness of such hunting grounds.

In a small clearing, there glowed this night the orange of firelight. Vike sat near its warm protection. He wore leather and fur. His frame was short, but thick of bone and muscle. His beard was bristly. Vike was a man of the forest, a hunter.

Although alert to every detail, Vike was unconscious of the wildness of his surroundings. To him, the clearing was as a parlor would be to a city dweller. The canopy of leaves overhead was as his ceiling, the campfire his hearth. And the rabbit which he roasted upon it was as a feast to him.

The forest was more than merely Vike's home. It was to him what scripture is to priests. For while he could not read written words, he could read in God's handiwork a message few others could.

To Vike, the forest revealed God's glory and majesty, His love and providence, and the depth of His mysteries. With the forest, God provided everything Vike needed: his shelter, his bow, the shafts of his arrows. Through it was given his meal, and the fire which cooked it. From the forest, Vike obtained the furs he wore, the sinews for his bowstring, the feathers for his arrows, the cord for his snares.

But it was not the Garden of Eden, Vike knew. In the forest, one became acutely aware just how terrible was the fall from God's grace. For the forest was also a place of danger and disease, of parasites and pain, and of sudden death.

Of sudden death he was reminded as soon as he noticed the panther.

By the time Vike saw it, it was already in the clearing. Only the glint of firelight in its eyes had given it away. For the creature's fur was exactly the color of forest shadow. Its savage contours were those of forest shapes. And its movements were as stealthy as those of the midnight breeze.

It was death on four silent feet. And it stalked him, openly, in the clearing, unafraid of fire, and unafraid of his puny weapons.

Another man might have panicked and fled in terror, only to be ripped apart by the black lightning which now snaked its way toward Vike. Others would have sat paralyzed with fear, to be pounced upon and crushed by jaws full of tooth and fang. A very few might even have put up some paltry defense against this insurmountable foe, before succumbing to its swift fury.

But Vike reacted as does the forest itself. His movements were so smooth as to seem part of the night. With no visible effort, with no noticeable motions, he deftly reached for his bow and strung it, all in one precise flow of purpose. The arrow might have notched itself, so natural was Vike's manner. And when Vike drew it back, his eye had already aimed along its shaft. He looked down the length of that arrow, and found himself looking into a snarl of fangs which threatened only an arm's length from where he sat. He held the arrow steady, the bowstring taut; it dug sharply at his calloused fingertips.

The panther knew, then. It sensed the power standing ready in that bow.

It knew the feathered wood was merely a bird. But it was a bird made by this man, a bird more swift than the panther's swiftest reflex. The panther knew that that stone beak would need bite but once to complete its deadly mission.

As Vike peered down the length of the arrow, he wondered if the panther felt any surprise. He wondered if it even knew that the tables had been turned on it. For now, Vike was the hunter; it was he who stalked the stalker.

Then, gradually, Vike relaxed the tension. He let the arrow slide slowly forward, its shaft whispering against the straightening curvature of the bow, until at last the bow was drained of its lethal energy. Then he placed the wooden bird back in its nest with its siblings. And having set aside death, Vike unstrung his bow and put it down.

The panther slowly paced the clearing, in an arc before Vike, its snarl a low rumble.

Vike chuckled, and spoke to the cat. "Does a panther bring me death? I think not. Vike would not be caught unaware by one such as you. By no means! I am a hunter of rabbits. But you hunt men. And if you hunt men, then you are no panther, no panther at all, but a messenger. Indeed. So tell me. What message does an angel of God bear to Vike the hunter?"

Chapter 21

Reunion

After the brief encounter with Shalar, the pace of Veelos and Kl'aarn's men had slowed. There were the wounded. Several men had painful bruises, and three had been deeply cut. They needed tending, and could not yet maintain a faster rate. Two of them had been placed into the cart, unable to ride at all. One of the wounded had already died.

"You've lost four of your twenty-four," Veelos remarked, "since you found me in Shi-Raq. I'm bad luck, a curse to you and your men."

But Kl'aarn answered, "Don't lose heart, Veelos. Every man here knows that we are doing what we must."

Veelos shrugged. "Lose heart? One does not fear to fail at an impossible task. There is dishonor only in failing to achieve the possible."

"We won't fail," Kl'aarn said. "Even the impossible yields before us. You've proven that. When Shalar was about to kill me, I was looking straight through the eye slits of his face-plate, and yet I didn't recognize him. All I saw were the eyes of a murderer. But you knew it was him. You called his name, and saved me from death."

"Even that frightens me," Veelos said. "You were spared that time. But there will be other battles, and enemies even more ruthless than Shalar has become. If the outcome depends on me, then we are surely lost."

As they were speaking, there was a signal from the rear guard. Immediately, the men positioned themselves for another fight. Kl'aarn drew his sword and quickly rode to the rear of the column to see what had alarmed the sentry.

"It's your old friend Shalar," Thrake reported, as Kl'aarn pulled up beside him. "It seems he's changed his mind about letting us go, after all."

Seeing the approaching bandits, Kl'aarn shook his head, and sheathed his sword. "I think not," he said. "Look. Those men have no fight in them. They look beaten, scared. Stay here and I'll go find out what they're about."

Spurring his horse, Kl'aarn rode back on the trail along which they had come, until he faced Shalar at the head of the bandit columns.

Shalar did not look Kl'aarn in the eye. But he said, "Fate is a treacherous thief, my friend."

Kl'aarn, puzzled, surveyed Shalar, then glanced up and down the double column of his bandits. Then looking back at Shalar, he asked, "What's come over you?"

Then Shalar did look Kl'aarn in the eye. "A curse," Shalar said. "A curse has come over me. Veelos should have let me kill you while I had the chance. It would have been better for all of us--- including for you. Maybe especially for you."

Now Kl'aarn was more baffled than before. "Have you lost your mind? What are these strange words? Why do you pursue us?"

"Go see," Shalar said. "Go back on the trail, two bends. That's all I can say to you."

Kl'aarn reined his horse backward a step, frowning over Shalar's cryptic behavior. He opened his mouth to speak again. But this time, no words came forth. A sudden premonition overtook him, the feeling one has just before an impending storm, only more powerfully felt. It was a feeling he had not experienced since a day long before, one terrible day in the hold of a slave ship.

Just at that time, Kl'aarn noticed Veelos and Kmir, making their way toward him and Shalar. Without a word, Kl'aarn turned away from them, prodded his horse, and was riding swiftly away as if in retreat, riding the length of the columns of Shalar's bandits.

As he left behind Shalar's rear guard, Kl'aarn came to a bend in the trail, and rounding it, found himself alone on the forest pathway. There was another bend ahead, and soon he rounded that one, also.

Then, suddenly, his horse stopped--- and reared up in sudden terror. With a warrior's reflex, Kl'aarn slid from it, and stepped away. He no longer had any concern about the beast.

She stood in the middle of the trail. A wind that disturbed nothing else whipped the hems of her black robes. The hood slid from her head, and Miril's long, straight black hair fell across her shoulders. The little whirlwind seemed to fairly crackle with energy, as does a dark cloud about to hurl forth its thunderbolt. Then, as Kl'aarn stood transfixed by the sight, the whirlwind died, leaving behind only its passion.

Kl'aarn slowly lifted the helmet from his head, lowered it to one shoulder, and heedlessly let it fall to the ground. His eyes continued to disbelieve. "Miril?" he called softly.

Her only answer was a tender smile, gentle but for a subtle cruelty, a cruelty so subtle as to be all but indiscernible, but so intense that it could not be entirely concealed.

At first, some part of Kl'aarn struggled to deny it. It couldn't be her, the warrior thought. This woman looked nothing like Miril, nothing at all.

"Kl'aarn," Miril whispered. The breeze seemed to surge with her emotion. Her arms lifted ever so slightly from her sides. "My darling."

Hesitantly, the warrior took a step toward her. He shook his head without taking his gaze from her. "Is it you? Is it really you?"

Her hands were now lifted in a summons of embrace. "Come to me," she breathed. "Touch me, and know that this is no longer a dream."

The lips which spoke were not Miril's lips, for hers had been full and innocent, while these were the lips that uttered lethal curse. The hands were not Miril's hands, for hers had been the hands of loving caress. But these were the clawed talons of a murderess. And the eyes. Those dark, piercing, knowing eyes. They were the eyes of a witch. And unmistakably, undeniably, they were the eyes of the woman who loved him, and whom he loved in return.

Kl'aarn found himself standing before her, his fingertips touching hers, his gaze locked with Miril's. Reality melted away as he felt the warmth and moistness of her lips upon his own. Delicate arms rested on his shoulders, soft hands stroked their way around his neck and through his hair.

She felt light and fragile in his hands. The touch of her womanness flooded him with a sense of manhood he had never known but in battle. But in this battle, to be victorious was to surrender, and to triumph was to yield up his life.

Only his armor spoiled it. The bronze-studded leather vest was a wall between his chest and her breasts. He felt her wince, and realized that he had been fairly crushing her against himself. When he relented, their lips parted, and he felt her breath upon his face, passionate as only that of a woman in love. Her cheeks glistened with the trails of tears.

"Miril," he whispered to her. "Look what's become of you." The words had come forth unbidden.

Her hands caressed his bearded cheeks. "And of you?" she smiled through her tears. "A warrior?" She seemed amused.

But Kl'aarn could not dispel the dark storm which had crossed over from Miril's heart into his own. He found his hands involuntarily press her back from him. "You're a witch," he said the words, afraid to speak them. "Have you really done this thing?"

Miril nodded slightly. A flicker of uncertainty revealed itself in her eyes. "Yes. Do you no longer love me?"

Kl'aarn found himself momentarily at a loss for words. Her word, "Yes," and the question with which she had followed it, seemed not to fit together. For he loved Miril, not this.

She answered for him. "But you knew all along. When you washed ashore at Demon Point--- from that moment on, you knew everything. In each dream you knew me. And even now, you have accepted me. For I am your wife, Kl'aarn. I am Miril. I belong to you."

He was holding her in both hands by her shoulders, and looking her up and down. His grasp on her was possessive. But the feel of her was not the feel of ownership. He kept wanting to see an adolescent, girlish woman, a woman who laughed easily and often, who feared snakes and insects, who could be awed by an adolescent display of manly prowess, who would cuddle a puppy or a baby. But this was no such woman.

"I do know," he said. "You are my wife. And when we were torn from each other, you gave away your soul to have me back. All this I know from the dreams you sent me."

"And now we do have each other!" Miril smiled. It was the first hint of girlish exuberance he had seen in her. "We are inseparable now, my darling. We are forever!"

But Kl'aarn replied, "No. Not like this, Miril. Like this you are not mine. You belong instead to some force that will bring us only to grief."

"You speak from unknowing," Miril answered. "For now, just accept me, darling, just accept me for today. We have much time to speak, much time to learn, many years to recapture. And then, if after much time together, if then you command me as is your right, then I shall do all that you bid me do. For how else would a wife love her husband as I love you?"

But Kl'aarn felt his discomfort increase. "I understand," he said, "a frightened, desperate girl doing what you did. But you are no longer that girl. Surely you are aware, that every hour, every moment you spend in witchcraft, puts your soul in mortal jeopardy."

For a fleeting moment, for the scantest portion of time, Kl'aarn saw within Miril a rage, a fury unfathomable. But her voice was soft. "We can settle nothing now," she said. "Do you think I could renounce witchcraft and live? Not until my vow is fulfilled. But this much we can do. We can destroy Druuk. We must! For he seeks to destroy us all."

Kl'aarn disagreed. "Leave Druuk to Veelos. She alone can destroy him."

Miril sadly shook her head. "My dear, precious warrior. Hear my plea. When it is time, I will cast off this garb of evil, and bow down before whatever god you would have me worship. Only do not ask this of me now, for it would surely kill me."

Kl'aarn said, "Then what will you do, Miril? How long will you belong to witchcraft?"

Miril answered. "Only while Druuk lives. Only until he is dead."

"Then go wait for me--- in a safe place--- until he is killed."

Miril wept. "I must fulfill my vow, beloved. Or die. Let it be this way. There are four of us now, four survivors of Har-Keem. Druuk intended that all of us should die. Now let him suffer the four deaths that he inflicted upon us. And let him endure the forty and fourteen and forty deaths that he burdened us with. Let the four of us visit him in his own land, and let him entertain us with his fear, and with his pain, and with his death. After that it will be clear to you, Kl'aarn. After that I will do all that you ask. Only do not destroy me this day with requests that would spill my soul into hell."

* * * * *

Veelos had been swept with a sense of imminent danger, but it had nothing to do with banditry. Kmir had been unable to restrain her, and so he had ridden with her toward Shalar and Kl'aarn. But when Kl'aarn had seen them and fled, Veelos had sensed that the situation was desperate.

She had tried to give chase. But upon nearing Shalar, the priestess had found her avenue blockaded by the bandit-lord and a wall of his thugs. "Leave him," Shalar had ordered.

Veelos had despaired. "What evil have you done now, Shalar? Tell me."

The bandit had replied, "Three days ago, I thought our reunion was but coincidence. It wasn't. It's fate that rules our lives. What's your fate, Veelos? Do you have powers to slay witches?"

Veelos had felt a chill in her spine at those words. But she had put up a brave front. "Yes," she had said. "I have power to slay witches."

Shalar had nodded. "Good. We've brought you one."

"Make sense," Veelos had said. "Are you bewitched?"

"Not bewitched," Shalar had replied. "But held in thrall no less. There is a witch. When she's had her moments with Kl'aarn, you can try your hand against her."

Veelos had felt sweat on her brow. "You've brought a sorceress here? You've sent Kl'aarn into a trap? Damn you, Shalar; have you not even a wisp of honor? Lead me to her now, and let's destroy her."

"You take her," Shalar had retorted. "We've had our chance and failed. Besides," he spoke angrily. "What have I to do with this war between gods and demons? It is your war, not mine. Leave me out of it."

"Very well," Veelos had said, trembling. "Then stand aside. Let me pass."

But Shalar had said, "Not yet. Wait."

"Wait for what?" Veelos had demanded. "What is happening to Kl'aarn?"

Shalar had replied, "His prayers are being answered."

* * * * *

After a time, a raven landed upon a tree top and called out three times. Veelos would not have noticed it at all, except that Shalar glanced up at it, and then at Veelos, saying, "You may pass."

The bandits no longer blocked the path, but Veelos hesitated. Kmir began to move forward, but Veelos stopped him. "Wait here," she said. "This is for me to do."

Kmir objected, but he could see that Veelos knew whereof she spoke, and finally he released her to her duty.

* * * * *

Veelos had never ridden into battle. But as she passed alongside the two columns of cutthroat horsemen, she knew that she was being launched against a foe more fearsome than any bandit horde. At each step, she wished to turn away and flee in panic. Only the faintest courage sustained her.

She came to a bend of the trail, and found herself all alone in the world. A cloud came over the sun. Then Veelos rounded the second bend of the trail, and faced death.

Although she looked nothing like the Miril whom Veelos had known, there could be no doubting it was her. All the details had changed. The hands, the mouth, the eyes: nothing of her resembled any peasant girl of Har-Keem. But the essential Miril was unmistakable. It was her.

She stood half in Kl'aarn's tender embrace, and half at the ready, as Veelos came upon them. For a long, dangerous moment, there was silence. It was a silence filled with terror, filled with anger, and bursting with grief.

"Miril?" Veelos heard herself cry. "Is it true after all? Have you really done this wickedness? Have you sold your soul?"

Miril gently drifted from Kl'aarn's arms, and stood between the warrior and the priestess. Her eyes scanned Veelos's white vestments, and seemed to read each inscription embroidered into the blue trims. Then her gaze met Veelos's.

"Sold my soul?" she said, shaking her head so very slightly, ever so curtly. "On the contrary. I have regained it, my sister. At long last, my soul is my own--- my very own. It belongs neither to any god nor to any demon. I have become--- truly--- my own mistress, Veelos."

Now Veelos recognized that what Miril was saying was that with which the serpent had tempted Eve in the garden. But the forbidden fruit of which Miril had eaten grew in no earthly orchard.

Veelos trembled. "You see that I am a priestess," she said. "Then why have you not struck me dead, as you have struck others dead before me?"

Miril stepped closer to Veelos. "I could ask you the very same, dear soulmate. What stays your hand against me? Is it fear? Or is it, dear love, that the enmity between our separate garments is suborned by some higher bond?"

Veelos shook her head. "No. What stays my hand is weakness, Miril. My soul weeps for you, and cries out to kiss you. But you are death to me. It is weakness and fear which overwhelm me. But you are not weak, Miril. Nor are your sentiments for me gentle ones. Then why do you let me live?"

It was Kl'aarn who answered. He stepped forward. "I made her swear never to harm you," he said. "And I ask the same oath of you. Swear never to harm her, either. Swear it, Veelos."

Veelos saw Kl'aarn through a well of tears. "And do you trust her to honor that oath? Do you think she can alter her nature, Kl'aarn? You might as well ask the stones underfoot to cast off their hardness, as for her ever to cast off her blackwoven robes."

Kl'aarn was silenced by this. But then he did say, "Veelos, what would you have me do? Slay my own wife? You know how I love her."

"It is not a question," Veelos said, "of what I would have you do."

Kl'aarn pleaded. "Give us a chance. I have wrested from her all that can be gained for now. But she is redeemable. She is, after all, Miril. She will cast off this witchcraft."

But Veelos said, "I can ask no more of you than I ask of myself. And I find myself more wanting than you. For I cannot perform my duty, either. Would I attack my own sister? My heart fails me. Would I do battle with the Demonwitch? She would slay me in the blink of an eye. And if she could not prevail, if I could slay her, then surely your sword would come between her and me, and then what would I do? Could I bear to battle even against you? Has every weakness of my soul conspired against me to bring about this day? Why do not the angels themselves descend to my rescue?"

Now Miril turned to Kl'aarn, and said in a quiet voice, "See? Did I not assure you? Veelos and I will not let our enmity come between us. All that will clash is the truth--- her truth against mine. And the stronger truth will prevail. For is Veelos so much a priestess that she cannot love me? Her truth is not strong enough to raise her hand against me. Her truth gives way whenever it is opposed. Did she not lie to escape betrothal? Did she not lie to obtain her silver ring? Did she not lie and say that I was dead--- because she wanted to obtain you?"

Then Kl'aarn grasped Miril's hand. "Don't say hurtful things of Veelos. She did weep for you all these years."

"As I did for her, Kl'aarn. Know that! Would I wish her harm? Why would I do such a thing?"

But Kl'aarn was afraid, and said, "Miril. Don't harm Veelos. What would I feel if I knew you had killed her?"

Miril lightly pressed one finger to Kl'aarn's mouth. "Of course I'll not harm Veelos, my dearest. Is she not more than a sister to me? And so we will become, sisters, once more, I swear it. For Veelos is wise. And she, too, will embrace the starlit night."

But Veelos stood down from her horse and uttered, "No, Miril. You and I will never stand together. You have won this day your victory against me. But do not think it is your strength which prevails. It is my weakness upon which you feed, and that alone nourishes you."

Then Kl'aarn struggled to bring peace between them, and said, "Veelos. Druuk is too much for us. We'll need Shalar's men. We'll need all the help we can get. Veelos, make a truce with Miril. There will be plenty of time to sort things out later."

Veelos looked to Kl'aarn, and asked, "Is it true? Are you allying yourself with the Demonwitch?"

Kl'aarn showed his frustration. "Damn it, Veelos! This was to have been a joyful day for me. For six years I searched for her. For six years I imagined her a slave. For six years I prepared myself to find her a concubine, a harlot, a toothless diseased hag, or worse. In all that, I swore that I would love her as my wife, no matter what. Yes, I hid from the truth. But now I have her, Veelos. Don't ask more from me than I have to give."

"And don't ask of me," Veelos said, "to surrender to the Demonwitch the trust which Lar placed in me with his dying breath. Good never gains from evil, never--- and I'll not lay myself open to Miril's treachery by allying myself with her."

But Miril merely laughed in derision. "Such bold words from trembling lips. Veelos, you have no authority to make such pronouncements. And you have no choice in the matter. Kl'aarn and Shalar are coming with me. And so are you. We four are destined to kill Druuk, or else, to die trying. Do you think Shalar has come along willingly? No noble sense of duty guides him. But you will be one among us, Veelos. Because to do otherwise would be to leave me with all the destiny to myself. And you won't relinquish that to me."

Veelos tried to gather her courage. She tried to imagine herself in mortal combat against this dread which now outwitted her. But she might better have tried to hold a burning coal on her tongue than to hold that thought in her mind.

Veelos struggled to say no. She fought within herself to refuse any connection with Miril. She wanted to deliver an ultimatum, and if necessary, to strike out on her own, leaving Shalar and Kl'aarn to Miril. But in the end, she could not.

I am alive, she said to herself. Expecting to have died, I find my life spared. But is that blessing or curse? It will come to a duel between us, between Miril and myself. Today, I excuse myself and say to myself, oh yes, I will fight her when I am stronger. I promise myself that I only await some advantage. When I gain it, then will I confront the Demonwitch and slay her. So I claim.

But inside me, I know that it is exactly the opposite. By facing her now I would gain strength, for she has none. By facing her now, I would slay her, even though I myself should die, or worse: I might slay her and live, and face Kl'aarn. But I dread it, and cower instead.

It is Miril who gains with time, and I who lose. What madness has overtaken me, that I surrender a present victory for a future defeat? What wretched curse this sinful nature of mine, that it turns me against myself?

Men must always fail in their quests. Thank God that He never fails. Forgive me, dear Lord, and guard me against that day when finally I perform my penance, when finally I offer up my sacrifice, and when at last I duel, as I must, the Dreaded One Foretold.

And slay her.

Chapter 22

Uneasy Alliances

Kmir was not normally headstrong.

But as the main party of warriors was discovering that Kl'aarn had brought a witch among them, he argued bitterly with Kl'aarn. Kmir's arguments resembled those which Veelos had posed. They were arguments of strength, strength of reason and logic, arguments of right, which Kl'aarn could not refute. But in the end, Kl'aarn's decision hinged not on logic, nor on questions of right and wrong. He could not be swayed by arguments of any sort.

Then Kmir and the other warriors turned to Veelos for guidance. They urged her to stand against the witch. They promised to stand with her, even against Kl'aarn himself.

But Veelos answered them, saying, "How I envy your zealotry for the cause of rightness. Would that I were as bold. But do not despair at my weakness, for if the Lord were willing, he could strike down the witch with my little finger. So if he has not done this, shall we doubt? Then we would be like those who disbelieve in the Lord because He allows evil in the world. We shall not despair in our present weakness, but depend upon deliverance in its time. Look for a sign, for I believe that the Lord is already sending strength to us."

When the warriors saw that Veelos would not stand against the witch, they were disappointed. But when they heard her words, the warriors were encouraged, and put aside their dread of the woman whom Kl'aarn loved.

In this way, those who traveled turned their thoughts once more to the task which had set them upon their path: it was their purpose to cross the Lands of Demi-men, to pursue King Druuk to his lair, and to remove from his possession the Great Orb of Power.

The party now numbered sixty-seven. Kl'aarn's warriors numbered nineteen plus Kl'aarn. Shalar's bandits numbered forty-four plus Shalar. And there were the two women. Altogether they were sixty-seven.

Now they arranged themselves as before in double file. But this time, although Veelos rode at the front of the column, she rode alongside Shalar. His bandits followed close behind. After the bandits rode Kl'aarn beside Miril, and his warriors last.

"Why didn't you kill her?" Shalar asked, keeping his voice down. "I thought you priestesses had power over witches. Or is that just the way it was told in priestly scriptures?"

"Are you taunting me?" Veelos asked.

Shalar shrugged. "Sorry. Hey, I tried myself to have her killed. The man I sent put a dagger in her back. But the wound was made his, and he fell dead of his own act of murder. I was just hoping that you could do better."

Veelos looked intently at Shalar. "Do you always speak so casually of taking a life? I would really rather die than harm a hair of Miril's head. She is precious to me. But she is already dead in spirit, and it is my duty to oppose evil. Yes, I must stand against her. But I'll not do it casually, Shalar."

Shalar returned her gaze. "Now you're taunting me, in your priestly way."

"No," Veelos answered. "I'm just trying to stir your conscience. I admit I was uncharitable toward you. I never liked you. Alright, I hated you. I hated you as much as Miril hates all that is sacred. How strange--- that I no longer hate you now, when you are worse than you were before. Not long ago I honored your memory, Shalar, thinking that you had died in doing some noble deed. But now, I find you alive--- alive and despicable. And yet, I can no longer hate you anymore."

"Being despicable," Shalar said, "has its uses. There was a time when you were glad of my murderous nature. Do you think it was Kl'aarn who saved your virginity from that pirate on the bayshore? It was me. So come off your high horse, Veelos."

"Well," Veelos said. "How nicely we're getting along. After all these years. And we have a long ride ahead of us yet to go."

Shalar shook his head. "No we don't."

"What?" Veelos asked.

"We're not going to get very much farther than we already have. We won't even make it as far as the Lands of Demi-men."

"Why not?"

"Because," Shalar answered, "with every step, we draw closer to the domain of Morgrar One-Arm. If you think I'm despicable, you'll have to make up a new word to describe his nature."

"It was mentioned," Veelos said, "that Morgrar has a price on your head."

"But only," Shalar supplied, "if I'm brought to him alive. At least I kill my enemies. Morgrar takes delight in keeping his captives alive for days. I've watched him torture men before. He enjoys it. And if he ever takes me alive, my howls of pain will fill these forests for weeks. You can be sure of it."

"Then we should go around his domain," Veelos said.

"There is no around. He rules all the interior hills from the north sea to the south. And he collects tribute from vassals in every realm. He's more than just bandit-lord. He's all but a king. He has hordes of fighting men at his call."

Veelos drew a deep breath. "Very scary. But you don't sound very frightened."

"One can always twist things to advantage," Shalar said. "When we battle Morgrar's horde, as we must, then Miril will have her hands full just staying alive. That will be my chance to get away from Miril. If we're lucky, Morgrar will do your work for you and kill her himself."

"How much farther to his domain?" Veelos asked.

Shalar chuckled. "There won't be a border. Bandits rule as far as their sword reaches. One day the border is here, the next day somewhere else. As soon as Morgrar's scouts see us, they will---"

Both Shalar and Veelos halted, and the columns stopped behind them. "Well, speak of the devil," Shalar spat.

Ahead of them on the trail, just more than fifty paces, three horsemen had emerged from the trees and showed themselves. They were positioned side by side, and their posture was clearly hostile.

"Morgrar's men?" Veelos asked.

"Not exactly," Shalar said. "These men are woodsmen, hunters. There must be more of them in hiding, or else they would not be so bold."

Veelos informed him, "There are none in hiding. These three are alone."

"That would not make sense," Shalar said. "Unless they intend to run off and report us to Morgrar for some reward."

"They intend no such thing," Veelos said. Just then Kl'aarn rode up between them. Veelos continued, "These three men intend to do battle with us."

Kl'aarn took in the sight. "Hunters," he said. "We don't often have trouble with them. Even if they wanted a fight, what chance would they have against us?"

"Every chance in the world," Veelos answered. "These three are men of God. And they have no fear of death."

"How do you know so much?" Shalar asked.

But Veelos said, "Never mind. They mean no harm to any man here. They're here to kill me."

"What!" Kl'aarn said, drawing his sword. "Get back to the wagon---"

"Not this time," Veelos said. "Put away your sword. We'll not take up arms against God's people. Let me go speak to them. Whatever they do, it will be of God. For this is the sign I told your men to look for. These men are strength to us. Put away your sword and never draw it against these men."

But Kl'aarn said, "Veelos, you'll be at their mercy. They can escape us in these forests and they know it."

"Put away your sword," Veelos said. "I command it."

Kl'aarn sighed, then obeyed. "Be careful, Veelos."

But just then Miril pushed her way among those at the fore. "What delays us?" she asked.

But Kl'aarn replied, "Go back, Miril. We'll handle this."

Miril sniffed in the direction of the three hunters ahead. "Has your God rejected you, Priestess?" she asked. "Do even the godly seek your death? Then rely on me. I can make swift work of these---"

Then Kl'aarn grasped Miril's wrist. "I told you to get back," he said, both angered and embarrassed.

Miril glanced haughtily at Veelos, then back at Kl'aarn. "Very well, my husband. I was only trying to spare Veelos's life. But I leave it to you." Then, with one last taunting look at Veelos, Miril turned her horse and prodded it back the way she had come.

Veelos said to Kl'aarn, "Her purpose was to unnerve me. She succeeded. I suppose we'll have to get used to that."

"I'll see to her," Kl'aarn said. "Now about those three---"

"And I'll see to them," Veelos said. "Wait here." Then she leaned forward slightly, and her horse carried her onward.

Veelos tried to reassure herself with the thought, I am a priestess. These men will recognize my vestments; surely they will honor me.

But when she stopped, a pace from them, the hunters looked upon her with an icy, hostile gaze.

"I am Veelos of Har-Keem," she said. "Priestess of the temple in Shi-Raq, and sadly, the last survivor among them. I am sent forth by the dying command of my high priest, Lar, to take the Orb of Power from the hand of him who abducted it."

The hunters were all independent men, loners. Each was clad in fur garments of his own making. Each bore weapons of his own design and craftsmanship. Even so, one among these three seemed to be the acknowledged leader. He spoke.

"My name is Vike," he said. "My companions are Belgar and Valmark. We too, are sent forth, because the forces of Upheaval are gathering for battle. We have been chosen to serve God, and are pleased to obey Him."

Veelos looked each man in the eye, then said, "I would think us to be allies, then. But you come to me as an enemy. Will you kill me?"

"Though you are a priestess," Vike said, "yet you travel with a witch. Your duty is to slay her. If you refuse to do this, then you will be seduced into witchcraft yourself. Then the world will suffer not one witch, but two. So we must stand against you, even though you wear the robes of priesthood."

Veelos answered them. "You speak correctly. I should have the courage to do what is right, and not be doing what is cowardly. But in truth, if I face down the witch, she will kill me, and take with her these men to their doom. And I am too afraid to engage her in combat. Now you have heard my confession. Will you then kill me? If so, please be merciful and swift. For since I will not oppose the witch, then neither will I oppose you three."

The three hunters glanced at each other. Then the leader among them said, "Your words reveal you for what you are: a woman of weakness and doubts and fears. Yet you stand before us at our mercy, and all but invite us to kill you. This is a great paradox."

Veelos answered. "You speak truly. For I know what I should do, and do it not. I know what I should put aside, but I embrace it instead. Why is it I who leads this quest? Why is not another appointed, one more worthy than I am?"

Vike said, "You do wrong to allow this witch among your men unchallenged. It is a craven error. But we are not your judges, rather your servants. We are sent not to slay you, but to guide you. Allow us, then, to serve as your guides, and as your hunters."

Veelos was encouraged that God had anticipated her need and provided for her. So she brought the three men with her to the front of the column and introduced them. Once they had assessed them as allies, Kl'aarn and Shalar agreed immediately to admit these men to their company, for indeed there was need of their skills.

But when Kl'aarn rejoined Miril at her place in the column, she objected. "Why do you allow these witch-burners among us?" she complained. "We need no scouts. Nor do we need hunters. My talents are sufficient to warn us of danger, and to find food. Send these barbarians away from me."

But Kl'aarn and Shalar had already decided the matter. Thereafter, Miril kept silent before them.

The travelers now numbered seventy.

Chapter 23

They Confront Morgrar

As the sun began to set, the three hunters led the group off the trail and found campsites for them. Soon, campfires were burning, and rations were distributed.

Kl'aarn had been eager all day to be alone with his wife. They bedded down together in a secluded place. Their embraces were impatient. But intimacy was strained in such circumstance. So the pair contented themselves with kisses and caresses, which lasted long into the night.

"I've waited six years for this," Kl'aarn said. "I had hoped for more privacy than we can expect here. But neither will I complain. Six years! But it's almost as though it were yesterday I saw you last."

He was surprised by the passionate energy of Miril's kiss, a passion that was so intense as to be violent. Hers were kisses not merely of lips, but also, of teeth. When at last she took breath, Kl'aarn stroked the outlines of her face. By starlight, she was more beautiful than by day. "In the dreams, you looked so fierce," he said. "But now, only your kiss is fierce."

Miril pressed her cheek against Kl'aarn's bare chest. "I sometimes thought this moment would never come," she said. "But it has."

Kl'aarn hesitated to speak, then said, "You know how I spent those years. Searching for you. But you spent them hiding from me."

Miril lifted her head, and gazed pleadingly into Kl'aarn's soul. "Please forgive me for that," she begged. "It was never my wish. As soon as you were freed from Druuk's men, I wanted nothing but to rush down upon you, to nurse you and care for you--- even to die with you if it came to that."

Kl'aarn said, "I know you did. I knew you were nearby. And I could think of nothing but you, nothing. You were my first and only thought, then. Somehow I knew--- I knew you were with me, in some mystic sense. But even then--- even my knowing--- that, too, was your witchcraft at work, wasn't it?"

Miril nodded. "It was the witchcraft of love."

Kl'aarn hesitated again, and then said, "You know how horrified I am."

"Yes. But it's only because you don't know."

"Or because I do know," Kl'aarn said. "For six years you've been reminding me of the price we would have paid, had we done God's bidding. I'd be dead. You'd be a widow, not knowing my fate. I know."

"But we have defeated that fate," Miril said.

"We have disobeyed God," Kl'aarn answered.

"Yes. Just as the demons did. Just as Adam and Eve did. We have shared the fruit of Knowledge. Only one forbidden fruit remains, the fruit of Life itself. And we shall eat of it and live forever."

"You speak evil," Kl'aarn said. "It pains me. Miril, do you think evil will repay you with good?"

Again, Miril rested her head against Kl'aarn's chest. "Let's not be theological tonight. We have time. As long as we love each other, that is what counts. Even Shalar was right about one thing. What have we to do with this war between angels and demons? Just sleep with me, my love. Dream with me."

* * * * *

The next morning, camp was broken early. Shalar seemed to have some difficulty stirring his men. Veelos watched from a distance as he argued bitterly with a pair who seemed to have the backing of most of the others. They mentioned something about a feast they had been promised in Shel-Avak.

Just as it seemed Shalar would come to blows with them, Miril wandered in among the bandits. It was an intentional happenstance. She spoke in undertones between Shalar and those who disputed with him. The would-be rebels seemed suddenly cowed, and after that, Shalar had no more trouble with them. As if having successfully concluded a routine detail of business, Miril strode away from them, to attend other matters.

Later that day, as they rode along the forest trail, Veelos asked Shalar about the incident. "Does Miril have a spell over your men?"

"Only the spell," Shalar answered, "of their own cowardice. I hate to admit it, but bandits are at heart a cowardly lot. Oh, they can be brave enough in battle, some of them. When it suits them. But each one lives with a dread fear of some kind. That's how I rule them. I find out what each man is afraid of. Miril just gives them one more thing to fear."

* * * * *

For a time, the travelers managed to elude Morgrar's lookouts. Veelos began to hold forth hope that Vike, and his companions Belgar and Valmark, would lead them between Morgrar's sentries.

But it was not to be. Vike returned from a scouting foray and reported, "There is a wide break in the forest just ahead, some kind of ancient riverbed, dry now, but with no trees, no concealment of any kind. On the far side of it, where the forest begins again, we can see that a large force of men lies in wait. They hardly bother to conceal themselves."

"That will be one of Morgrar's roving bands," Shalar said. "If any of their spies have recognized me, they've already sent their swiftest messenger to him."

Vike found himself pressed on all sides by questioners. "How many are there?" Kl'aarn asked.

Vike replied, "We can be sure of at least twenty. But they could easily have a hundred more near at hand. I won't know much more until I cross the clearing and try to sound them out."

"No," Veelos said. "That would be suicide, Vike."

"Better to risk one man," Vike said, "than the entire party."

But Shalar interjected, "Veelos is right, Vike. Morgrar's men would be sure to kill you. We're stuck with making a choice. Either we all cross the clear-cut together, or else we turn back--- before Morgrar moves a large force behind us. If Morgrar's men are fewer than we are, they'll turn and run from us. They're not used to being outnumbered."

"Then," Kl'aarn said, "we've got to press ahead. Our only hope now is decisiveness. Let's form a battle wedge. My men will take the lead."

"Not so fast," Kmir said. "Shalar's men are not keen for this fight. Look at them; their demeanor is one of fear. They'll turn and run at the first show of enemy force."

"No," Miril injected, "they won't. You leave Shalar's men to me."

But Shalar quickly rejoined, "Why turn your curse against my men? It's Morgrar's men you should hate. Test your powers against them."

But Kl'aarn forced himself between Shalar and Miril, and glared at the bandit. "Never!" he spat. "Never again tell my wife what to do. For your part, know this. I have forbidden Miril to call upon any evil powers."

"What?" Shalar exclaimed. "This is a hell of a time to tell her that. After she's already used witchery to kill one of my men."

But Kl'aarn retorted, "You'll not be hiding behind Miril's skirts, Shalar. If you're afraid to fight, then run away. Bandits always do, when they're outnumbered."

Shalar turned angrily to Veelos. "And what about you? Are you as afraid to fight Morgrar as you are of Miril?"

But once again it was Kl'aarn who answered. "Still looking for a woman to fight your battles? That silver hilt on your sword was supposed to make you something special, as I recall. You're no better than Morgrar."

Shalar elbowed Kl'aarn away from him. "Go to hell, Kl'aarn. I fight when it suits me. The only thing I stand to gain from this battle is a promise of looting the treasure vaults of some king we'll never live long enough to find. As for your wife not cursing, tell her to lift the curse she holds over my men, and we'll leave now."

Kl'aarn roughly returned Shalar's elbow thrust, and said, "Done. Miril, whatever curse you've---"

But before he could finish, the hunter Valmark rode up swiftly among them, out of breath from a hard gallop. "We're cut off," he said. "At least fifty have taken up positions behind us, with more arriving by the minute. Belgar is looking to see if we've any escape route. He'll be along soon. But I hold no hope."

"Well, damn! That settles it," Shalar said. "We've got to pick a direction and move fast, or we're finished."

"The direction," Veelos said, "is forward."

"Veelos is right," Miril agreed.

Veelos angrily turned her gaze to Miril. "Don't try to wedge your way into authority here. I don't need your ingratiating approval."

"Authority?" Miril sneered. "We'll see whether your authority is still intact after Morgrar---"

"Shut up," Kl'aarn ordered. "Both of you. Everyone. While we stand here bickering--- Shalar, my men will form the point of the spear. Your men will be the shaft. We'll ride in formation through the clear-cut. If Morgrar's men run away, fine. If there's a fight, we'll form a circle around the cart and stand our ground. Women--- as hard as this is to do, put aside your grievances long enough to hide in the cart. There will surely be arrows, even if Morgrar's men turn and run. The cart is your only armor. Don't argue, just do it. Now."

* * * * *

When they reached the edge of the forest, and surveyed the expanse of open terrain before them, Kl'aarn's courage wavered. "This is worse than I thought," he confessed to Shalar and Kmir. "This is a killing ground. We'll be easy targets for their archers. And if we try to assault their position in the treeline, we'll have to worry about being attacked from the rear by reinforcements."

Shalar cursed. "This is a fine fix you've put us in."

But Kmir said, "We can't curse our way out of it, either, bandit. Now hear me. Tell your men to look cocky, confident. The farther along we can bluff our way, the fewer of us their archers will pick off." Then to Kl'aarn, Kmir said, "Let's not delay."

With that, all those with helmets lowered their visors and face-plates. And drawing their swords, the men forged ahead into the clear-cut, marching as a spear.

With every step, Kl'aarn felt his heart pound faster. No arrows had arced forth from the opposing treeline. Not yet. That might be a sign, that the bandits ahead were cowed by the sight of nearly seventy men riding straight toward them. Maybe they feared more were to follow. Or, maybe, they had set a trap, and were merely waiting to slam it shut.

Veelos and Miril found themselves cramped among the cargo in the cart. At first, neither had spoken to the other at all. But now Miril said, "There is going to be a battle. You know it as well as I do."

"Maybe not," Veelos said.

"Well if there is," Miril said, "what will you do?"

"What do you mean? There's nothing I can do. I'm no warrior."

"Oh, yes you are," Miril replied. "You once put quite a mark on the face of a robber. You have the power, Veelos."

"How did you know of that?"

"I know all about you," Miril said. "You fascinate me, dear sister. You'll make a good witch, some day."

"Never," Veelos retorted.

But Miril replied, "That's what I once said."

Just then, they felt the cart stop.

"Oh my God," Veelos uttered. "What now?"

* * * * *

The mixed party of warriors and bandits had reached the halfway mark across the open expanse, when suddenly the treelines before--- and behind them--- bristled with the arrows of more than a hundred archers.

The trap had closed.

But no arrows flew. It was a show of force only, at least for the moment. The reason for it soon became apparent. For, emerging from out of the treeline, accompanied by two armored men, one on each side of him, rode the infamous Morgrar One-Arm himself. Seeing his great size, and seeing that he was missing his left arm, there could be no mistaking him.

"Shalar," the bandit called out. "My brother! I come to greet you."

"Oh, shit," Shalar swore. "Damn it all to hell. Son of a bitch. Damn, damn, damn! The bastard has been tracking me all along. Kl'aarn, promise me one thing right now. Don't let him take me alive. If you have to kill me yourself, don't let him have me alive. Promise it!"

"He won't take you alive. I promise. Now listen, go back near the cart, and stay in the center of the formation, so that no archer can single you out. Hurry. I'll go see what I can talk Morgrar into."

Shalar turned, and did as Kl'aarn had told him. As he took his position beside the cart, he saw Veelos and Miril. They had clambered over the sideboards, to the ground, and were mounting their horses. Shalar thought it odd that they would leave the only place of protection they had.

"Kl'aarn said for you two to stay in the cart," he told them.

But Miril spat, "How nice of you to share his concern for us. But no thanks."

Shalar glanced at Veelos, but without a word to him, she turned away, and drove her horse toward Kl'aarn.

Shalar wondered aloud, "What gets into women?"

* * * * *

The bandit at Morgrar's left (the armless side) had murdered so many men that a new name had been given to him: Slayor. He was almost as large and as fierce looking as Morgrar, and was obviously Morgrar's chief lieutenant.

The one named Slayor said to Morgrar, "Why do we taunt them? We've enough archers to halve their number in the first volley. Let's be done with them."

But Morgrar answered, "I'll kill every archer who lets fly an arrow this day."

Slayor did not understand. "We'll lose more men than we need to, if we fight them sword to sword."

"So what?" Morgrar replied. "It's a price worth paying, to take Shalar alive. I'm going to have his arm. And then, I'm going to take his other arm, his leg and then his other leg. And then I'll only have begun to torture him. Any man who kills Shalar, and ruins my sport, will take Shalar's place on the rack."

"But see that," Slayor said, pointing. "Shalar's gone back among them, to hide from us. And now, two women are riding into his place, at the front. What is this strange thing?"

Morgrar saw it, too. "The spies did mention," he said, "that there were two witches with Shalar. These must be them. Of course. They could not have survived this deep into bandit realms without sorcery. No matter. We've fought before against conjury. The secret is not to run away from it. Once their magic is spent, once their power is depleted, sorceresses are but mere women after all. We'll make sport of them, too."

"One of them is not a witch," Slayor observed. "She wears white. A priestess of the Orb."

Morgrar spat, "Priestess, witch, they're all women. Keep your eye on that warrior. He's the one we need to watch. There's something about him, something I don't like."

"Now the three of them are coming forward under truce," Slayor said. "We can cut them down without risk of hitting Shalar. Shall I signal the archers?"

"No," Morgrar said. "Not yet. I would test them first. Follow me."

With that, Morgrar prodded his horse forward into the clear-cut.

Having the luxury of superior numbers, Morgrar had decided to indulge his curiosity. Riding into the clear-cut with his two personal guards, under truce, he met Kl'aarn, Miril and Veelos halfway.

Morgrar was the largest man Kl'aarn had ever seen. So large was he, that even Morgrar's horse seemed to strain under his weight. The bandit's beard was thick and greasy, his brow huge beneath the bronze skullcap which served him as helmet. Where his left arm should have been was a small, round shield made especially to cover the wound. But the one arm he did have wielded a blade that lesser men could not have handled with two.

Morgrar spoke first. "What treasure do you transport into Morgrar's domain? And what tribute do you offer for safe passage?"

Kl'aarn answered. "We bear no treasure. We are only seeking a path into the Lands of Demi-men. Beyond those lands, to the west, we will carry war to an evil king. If we lose that war, he will master the Great Orb of Power, which he stole from this priestess's temple. With it, he will launch an army of demons into this land. The witch and the priestess are the only two who can defeat him."

Morgrar shrugged. "Why not? Why not believe that? Why else would two such women be found together?"

"Then let us pass," Kl'aarn said, "and you will see us no more."

But Morgrar said, "What tribute do you offer, warrior?"

Kl'aarn held out his hands, palm up. "We have very little to offer. A few silver coins at most, but nothing you would count as a worthy price."

Morgrar shook his head. "I can see that. But you do have something of value to me. And his name is Shalar."

Kl'aarn refused. "I have sworn an oath of brotherhood with him."

Morgrar leaned forward. "Let it be clear, warrior. This day, Shalar is mine. That is already decided. The only question is, how many men will die for him?"

But Kl'aarn added, "And how slowly. We know you mean to torture Shalar. We would hear his shrieks all the way to the west kingdom. You would have attacked us already, but you fear he would die too easily in combat."

Morgrar chuckled. "If you will not think of yourself, nor of your men, then what of these women? You seem a civilized sort. Think of their safety."

Now Miril spoke to Kl'aarn. "Consider. If it were you that Morgrar wanted to torture, Shalar would already have handed you over to him. When you measure his worth, weigh that on the scale, too."

But Veelos replied to Miril, "If you offer up Shalar to appease this man, then how many more of us do you intend to spend along the way?"

Miril ignored her, and glanced at Kl'aarn. "What is your answer?"

Kl'aarn replied, "You know my answer, Miril."

Seeing that Kl'aarn agreed with Veelos, Miril then spoke to Morgrar. "I admire a man with a sense of vengeance, bandit. Your skill at retribution is much to be respected. You make a high art of revenge. But so do we. It is vengeance which drives us, also. For we have much to repay this king, against whom we war. So we understand your desire to avenge yourself against Shalar. But consider this: there is also a time to think of higher gain than revenge. And that higher gain can be yours, Morgrar, wealth unlike any you have ever dreamed of. This king--- his name is Druuk--- he has treasuries beyond your wildest imagining. His very throne could be yours, Morgrar, and all that goes with it. You are just the man to take it from him."

But Morgrar replied. "Many a sorceress has tried to seduce me with her magic. I killed them all. And if you truly are a witch, then you know what your choices are. For if you oppose me, take care only that I take you not alive, either."

Both Kl’aarn and Veelos were taken aback by Morgrar’s blunt, and threatening, refusal of Miril's proffer. For surely, he was not a man unaware of what powers a witch could summon forth. But Miril was not impressed. "Don't dare to offend me further," she said. "Accept my generous offer while it stands. For I am no mere sorceress, and no mere covenwitch. You know not against what dark powers you contend, if you are so careless of your life as to defy me."

Morgrar scowled an ugly, insulting scowl. "Words. They are your only power. For the only power any woman has is but to give life and nurture it. But witches are barren, able only to destroy life, and to spell out words, albeit words of death. Yes, you are a fit opponent for me, woman of evil. But I am more evil than you, and my power is the power of sword. Accept my offer, proud woman. For what I ask is cheap to you, and pleasure to me. You'll not deny me, for no evil motive would spare Shalar."

Miril answered. "If I could torment Shalar for you myself, I would do so, only because as you say, no evil motive could spare him his wretched deserts. But vengeance against Druuk is our first concern, Morgrar. Nor can you stand between him and us. Wealth, Morgrar. Wealth and power, beyond your vainest hope, can be yours. Seize it."

But Morgrar had but one purpose. "Give me Shalar," he said, "or suffer with him on the rack. This is my final word. Deny me this, and I will do worse to you than to him. No--- do not utter again your empty promises of wealth. Just give me your answer, either yes, or no."

Miril sneered. "Is your hunger for revenge so mindless? Then I will drag you into Hell, Morgrar. There, amid the unquenchable flames, you will discover what revenge truly is. For you will feel its never-ending torment, day and night, without rest from it. Today, your eternity there will begin. This I prophesy."

Morgrar surveyed the other two, then spat. "Is this your final word? Very well, then. I do not abide fools. You have sealed your doom, you three, and all who follow you."

Kl'aarn became nervous. For were Morgrar not wary of the hunters, now atop the wagon, posted as archers, Morgrar would already have cut through the three adversaries facing him, killed them with a single slice of his sharp, heavy sword.

"You outnumber us," Kl'aarn told Morgrar. "But these women have a power you cannot fathom. Let us pass."

Morgrar sneered. "You threaten me? You threaten me with a witch? I laugh at your threat. The earthly evil of a ruthless man is more than a match for any evil from Hell. Let your witches cast their spells. In the end, the curse of my sword will prevail." And having taunted them this last, Morgrar turned and sped back to his entrenchments.

Kl'aarn, Miril and Veelos lost no time in retreating also. For Morgrar's archers had no respect for truce.

While Morgrar's men jeered, to fix their courage, Kl'aarn and Shalar quickly followed their earlier plan. With curt orders, they assembled their men in a circle around the wagon. Miril and Veelos hid once again within it, while the hunters kept their positions atop the cargo, as archers. Of the remaining archers, that is the warriors and bandits with bows, they formed an inner ring within the outer circle of swordsmen.

This was all the plan Kl'aarn had, a formation of circles, one within the other, a circle which, if broken at any point, would give reality to Morgrar's fearsome threats.

"Why do you tremble?" Miril taunted Veelos, in their cramped position. "Are you afraid? You should be conjuring up your fire. We will have need of it soon."

But Veelos replied, "When Kl'aarn sees your conjury, he will know the true nature of your soul, Demonwitch. And you fear that. That is why you obey him when he commands you to abstain from sorcery. You don't want him to see what you truly are."

Then Miril scowled. She began to reply. But in the next moment, there was a fearful roar from all about them. A flood of savage cutthroats poured from behind their entrenchments, and raced toward the defending travelers.

A storm of arrows ripped from the inner circle of defenders, and a rain of blood fell from the attackers.

Seeing this, Slayor spoke angrily to Morgrar from their concealed position. "I warned you this would happen. Why haven't we thinned their ranks with our own arrows? We are losing good men for naught."

But Morgrar snarled back, "What is the loss of a few men? If the first arrow kills Shalar, then I am denied my entertainment. We can always get more men. But just as I had only one left arm, so also there is only one Shalar to pay for it. And indeed, his screams shall be heard, even among the demi-men themselves. That is why I ordered no archery, no slings, no javelins, but only swords. And the order stands."

Despite the well-aimed arrows, despite the trail of their dead and wounded lying behind them, Morgrar's men poured forth into the attack. Soon, the combat was hand to hand.

Immediately, Kl'aarn realized that Morgrar's bandits were more fierce than any bandits against which the warriors had ever fought. They wielded pikes and truncheons, swords and maces, and every manner of weapon, except those that flew or were thrown. Beneath the fierce onslaught, it was not long before the circle of defending swordsmen began to collapse inward.

Shalar found himself standing shoulder to shoulder with Kl'aarn, as the two of them fended off four bandits at once. Shalar grasped the shaft of one's pike, and before the other had sense to release it, impaled the enemy with his sword. But as soon as the bandit fell mortally wounded, another more fearsome opponent stepped into his place.

"We're losing men!" Shalar shouted at Kl'aarn.

But Kl'aarn was too engaged in the desperate struggle to reply.

"We've lost men," Shalar shouted again. "How many must die before you turn Miril on them?"

With his shield, Kl'aarn fended off a battle-axe. But the blow was so mighty as to leave his arm bruised. The axeman lifted his weapon for another strike, this one, better aimed than the last. But before he could bring the axe to bear, an arrow from Vike's bow pierced the man's throat, and he staggered backward to die.

"He's got over a hundred men on the field!" Shalar shouted, "and hundreds more will soon arrive. Without magic, we are doomed!"

The warrior named Kelric was at Kl'aarn's other side, and as Shalar spoke, Kelric fell dead, the victim of a well placed pike-thrust. As he writhed in the throes of death, Kmir shouted to Kl'aarn, "The archers have spent all their arrows!"

Kl'aarn dared to glance toward the hunters. Valmark and Belgar had cast aside their bows, and were struggling to wield clubs which they found at hand. Untrained in combat, they were sure to be the next ones to die.

"Miril!" Kl'aarn called out.

He could sense that she heard him. He could sense a sudden energy flow forth, from where she lay in the cart. There was a darkness to it, and Kl'aarn felt a sudden loathing for what he was about to speak.

"Miril!" Kl'aarn shouted again.

She understood. His wife would need no more explicit instruction than the mere calling of her name. Neither of them doubted what he wanted her now to do.

It was then that Miril clambered atop the wagon, and with a vicious curse, forced Vike and his men to the ground. Then Miril turned her venom upon Morgrar's men.

Daring enemy archers, Miril stood tall above the fray, stood atop the bundled cargo among which Veelos yet hid. She briefly surveyed the battlefield, and then lifted up one arm. There could be no doubt, to any observer, that that arm was itself a lethal weapon. But before she sent forth destruction, Miril glanced downward at where Veelos huddled. "Arise!" she said. "Arise and behold the power of evil!"

But Veelos only cowered more deeply.

Miril sneered, then turned her attention from Veelos to the battlefield. She straightened her uplifted arm, and aimed it at the enemy. A brilliant blue shaft of light erupted, leaping forth from Miril's hand. Where it struck, the ground exploded with flame, and half a dozen of Morgrar's men were dismembered.

The battle fell silent, as men were seized with fear. Morgrar's fighters stepped backward a pace, disengaging from their combat, and staring at the malevolent, defiant witch. Amid the silence, Miril glared about her. "Leave us!" she commanded. "Or you will all die."

For a moment, it seemed that the attackers would indeed run. For they had never seen such potent witchcraft. But just as they might have retreated, Morgrar's voice boomed loudly from his redoubt. "Kill her!"

Instantly, the attack resumed, if anything, more fiercely than before.

Miril's face contorted with rage, and she launched yet another bolt. Another six men plummeted from life into Hell.

Now Slayor protested to Morgrar. "She is indeed a witch, Morgrar. And no virgin at the black art. This one is too much for us. We'll all be burned to ashes by her."

But Morgrar elbowed Slayor aside. "Take heart. It is daylight. She'll soon have spent her poison, and have no more until nightfall. Before then, we'll have done with her."

"And what of the other? The priestess--- she'll need no darkness for her spells."

"That one is weak," Morgrar said. "I looked into her eyes and saw only doubts and fear. She'll be a medal for whomever I award her this day. After, of course, I've tasted her for myself."

The battle had turned. With Miril hurling her bolts one after the other, Morgrar's men dared not close ranks, for wherever they closed, there Miril struck death.

Yet even so, Morgrar's men feared their lord more than they feared the witch. And the battle continued.

After a time, Miril's curses began to weaken. They became fewer in number, and more widely spaced in time. Finally, Miril could not constrain them to Morgrar's men alone. One of Shalar's fell with her bolt.

Then Kl'aarn shouted an order to her. "Hide yourself, Miril. You're killing our own men!"

And Miril collapsed onto the bed of the wagon, exhausted and weak. She glanced skyward. Darkness, with its renewal of her venom, was yet far off.

Then Morgrar said to Slayor, "Enough of this. The witch has spent her magic. Her warriors are weary, wounded and weakened, by now. It's time to settle scores. Let's go."

With that, the two bandits mounted their horses. Both Slayor and Morgrar One-Arm charged into the fray.

There was no stopping them. For Morgrar cut through defenders with but one stroke of his massive sword, first one of Shalar's men, and then one of Kl'aarn's. Tmarsk the bandit and Vantor the warrior both lay dead, without having even slowed Morgrar down. One final arrow from Vike was aimed at the bandit-lord. But instead of hitting Morgrar, it struck the man's horse and felled it. Morgrar found himself on his hands and knees at the foot of the cart. Quickly, he stood, and peering between the sideboards, was staring Veelos full into her terrifed face. "Your turn soon," he said to her. "But first things first."

And then he leaped astride the wall of the cart, and rolled inside it. All of this had happened so quickly that, in the fury of battle, none had opposed him and lived, save for Vike, who was no longer armed.

Morgrar had vanished into the cart. With his one arm, he threw Veelos from it; with a crash, she broke through its gate at the rear, and fell to the ground. When Morgrar arose again, he stood leaning backward against the baggage. And leaning backward against Morgrar, a dagger to her throat, was Miril.

She screamed. "Kl'aarn! Help me!"

Kl'aarn turned, and saw. Without hesitation, Kl'aarn lifted up his voice above the din. "Disengage!" he ordered. "Cease battle!"

Silence fell across the battle plain.

Even Morgrar's men, unsure of whether the order came from one of their own leaders, stepped back, their breath heavy; many of them were stained with blood. All eyes turned upon Morgrar and the witch, whom he held hostage. All eyes, that is, except Kl'aarn's.

Morgrar glanced about at his attentive audience, and announced, "Warrior. Warrior captain! Where are you? Is he still alive?"

"I am," Kl'aarn said. He had moved quickly behind Shalar, and with a deft movement, pressed the blade of his own dagger to Shalar's throat. Shalar's bearded chin lifted upward to avoid the razor sharp bronze which now shaved his neck hairs. His eyes strained downward, trying to see the death which toyed at his jugular.

When Morgrar saw what Kl'aarn had done, he chuckled. "Don't dream of it, warrior. It's a nice try, but it won't work. Well I know your kind. You'll not sacrifice your woman. I've seen many a man in love with a sorceress, and not one of them could loose himself from her claws. Now this is the deal: hand Shalar over to Slayor. Then take your men and these two women from my land, and never come back."

But Kl'aarn answered by speaking to Shalar. "Don't worry, my friend. He'll never take you alive."

Now Shalar squirmed. "Kl'aarn! I didn't mean it. I release you from your vow. Don't kill me! At least give me a fighting chance!"

Then Kl'aarn spoke to Morgrar. "Even if I trusted you to release us, even then I would not do it. I cannot release Shalar to you while yet I live. As soon as I do, you'll betray us. But even if you were a man of your word, even then I would not hand Shalar over to you, until first you had killed me. So there is only one thing for it, Morgrar. And that is a duel. You and me, Morgrar. A duel for full measure or none. Shall we stand off like this all day? All night?"

Now Morgrar seemed amused. "You?" he laughed. "You? Fight me?"

And then a roar of laughter erupted among Morgrar's men.

When it died down, Morgrar said, "You mean to cheat me, warrior. For after I kill you, Shalar will fall on his own sword. Coward that he is, he'll not let himself fall alive into my hands. Have him bound hand and foot. Then we shall duel, little man."

Kl'aarn hesitated a moment, then gestured to one of his own men and to one of Morgrar's. "We've no choice. Bind him and hold him between you. Let the loser's fighter run for his own life, while the winner's man presents Shalar to his captain."

Shalar protested. "You can't do this to me, Kl'aarn. Not after all I've done for you. You can't tie me up like a lamb on the altar. You can't do this to me! Damn you to Hell, Kl'aarn!"

But Morgrar nodded his agreement, and the two fighters held Shalar as mortal collateral for the contest about to begin.

Morgrar slowly released Miril, pushing her out the back of the cart. Miril, exhausted and terrified, fell to the ground, and crawled beneath the cart, where Veelos also had taken cover.

The men surrounding them cleared away, as Kl'aarn and Morgrar assumed their fighting stances.

Then Miril peered from beneath the cart where Veelos also hid. And Miril grasped Veelos's collar, and showing teeth, she hissed, "What are you waiting for? Morgrar will kill Kl'aarn. You know that. You know what you must do. Act now! Do something to save him!"

But Veelos trembled in fear, and answered, "I am doing something, Miril. I'm praying to God. That's all we have left now. All of us."

But Miril spat, "God is not here, Veelos. He did not spare Har-Keem. He will not spare Kl'aarn. Or you, either. Now kill Morgrar, and do it quickly. Kl'aarn won't last beyond the first blow. He couldn't even beat Shalar, you stupid bitch!"

But Veelos replied, "Were I able to do so, it is you whom I would kill, and Morgrar whom I would love. But I can do neither."

Morgrar quickly assessed his opponent. He knew that Kl'aarn was not to be taken lightly. Here was not only skill and swiftness, but moreover, a kind of courage rarely seen. "He is neither foolhardy nor timid," Morgrar thought to himself. "So I shall be careful and patient. For my strength shall wear him down, and then he will die. And I'll forget him, as I forget all those whom I have killed."

Kl'aarn felt that he was fighting a mountain. Morgrar was even larger than he had first seemed. And the bandit knew how to keep size in his favor. Even the swiftest maneuver would not succeed against Morgrar. Indeed, there seemed no way to defeat him at all man to man. Kl'aarn hoped that somewhere, an archer was taking aim. But there was not.

The battle began. The first thrust of Morgrar's sword snapped forward. Kl'aarn parried it, but was surprised at how heavy Morgrar's sword was. To deflect it was like parrying a log. And Morgrar's thrust had only been a feint, one to test Kl'aarn's reaction. Then the bandit slashed, once again merely to measure his opponent. But the slash nearly knocked Kl'aarn off his feet.

Another thrust came, more powerful and more swift than the first. It was followed by another slash, more dangerous than before. Then came more---slashing and stabbing and thrusting. After some time, Kl'aarn felt himself growing weak. He had already been wearied from the battle. This was even more demanding than that. He knew it would not be long, now. Morgrar's plan was obvious, and it was working. Morgrar would do nothing foolish.

There remained but one hope. Kl'aarn knew he would have to act soon, and decisively. Carefully, he planned what he would do: a slash, a step, and a feint. Then, in the tiniest moment while Morgrar would be off balance, he would thrust his sword to Morgrar's chest, and hope to find an opening in the studs of his armor. It was little hope, but now was the only chance for success.

Morgrar thought Kl'aarn was only testing him in return. Kl'aarn slashed, Morgrar parried. Kl'aarn stepped, and Morgrar pivoted. Kl'aarn feinted. But Morgrar was not fooled. He would not lose his balance. He would not be moved by the feint.

But Kl'aarn's feint to Morgrar's throat was not a feint. It was an all or nothing gamble. Morgrar could easily have disemboweled Kl'aarn on the spot, had he known that Kl'aarn would really strike full force. For it was a foolish strike, one which left Kl'aarn fully exposed to Morgrar's lethal counterstrike. But Morgrar thought it was only a ruse. He thought Kl'aarn would not deliberately lay himself so open to death.

But just as Morgrar realized Kl'aarn was doing exactly that, he tasted cold bronze in his throat. The blade pierced both jugulars, and filled his throat with blood instead of air.

Morgrar stumbled backward a pace.

His massive sword, the sword which so long had terrorized so many, which so recently had murdered gallant men, that blooded sword slowly dipped to the ground in a morbid, unintended salute. Morgrar's face was a mask of terror. The sword fell from his grasp into the dust. Then, like a giant tree, the once-mighty bandit-lord tumbled backward, and landed on the ground with a thud.

His helmet came loose, and with the force of its impact, rolled across the dry, hard ground like a kettle. When it came to a stop, it tipped upside down.

A murmur swept the crowd of men around them. There was a time of silence, the silence of disbelief. That lasted only a few moments. Then it was quickly broken by Shalar's irreverent whelp of joy. "By the Gods Kl'aarn! You did it! By the very gods of all that is sacred, you killed him!"

Now for a moment, the bandit who held Shalar wondered whether to kill him anyway. For he held a dagger at the ready. But then Slayor's voice was heard by all, as he announced, "I am lord of this realm now. I, Slayor! Does anyone challenge me?"

No one did.

"Who is Shalar to us anymore?" Slayor roared. "Is he worth even one more death from among our number? And who are these mad, bewitched people who yearn for death in the Lands of Demi-men? Leave them to their wretched fate. As for the rest of us, let all who aspire to treasure worth fighting for, follow me."

And soon, only the dead of Morgrar's men were left to attend him on the plain.

Chapter 24

Into the Lands of Demi-men

They had numbered seventy. Now, another of Kl'aarn's men lay dead, and two more were too wounded to ride. Four of Shalar's men had been killed, and two more wounded. So their number was now reduced to sixty-five living souls, with four of those who lived being injured.

While Veelos tended the wounded, Shalar was untied from his bonds. The bandit, happy to be alive, grasped Kl'aarn and danced about him for joy. "By the very gods themselves, Kl'aarn, you're a fighting man of renown, now. Wherever you go, men will say, 'There is the man who slew mighty Morgrar.'"

But Kl'aarn shrugged him off and turned his attention to Miril. "Are you hurt?" he asked her.

"Only bruised," she replied. Her eyes were downcast.

Kl'aarn placed one finger under Miril's chin. "You seem angry," he said. "What a strange emotion in such a moment as this."

But Miril turned her head away. "That bastard touched me," she said.

"May the demon find a special torment for him."

Kl'aarn said, "You are only embarrassed. You thought that your powers would awe them, and carry the day. They didn't. You underestimated a ruthless enemy."

Then Miril spun to face him so that her hair whirled as if tossed by a storm. "My powers did carry the day," she spat. "Without them, none of us would be alive now."

But Vike was nearby, and he said to Kl'aarn, "It was not the witch that preserved us, but the priestess, and her power alone. For she relied not on herself, but upon God."

Then Miril turned on Vike, to curse him. But Kl'aarn grasped her wrist, and turned her from him. "Let it be, Miril. I have seen the working of magic this day, and it is a sight I would rather never see again. Especially from your hand. Look at you, Miril. The evil you wield is consuming you. Where is your softness, your mirth, your joy? Your innocence? I love you, dear Miril. But are you yet the Miril I fell in love with?"

Now Veelos, returning from attending the wounded, spoke to Kl'aarn. "Our wounded are in the cart. We can't leave them here. But what of Morgrar's wounded? There are too many. I can't possibly tend them all before nightfall. And we can't take them with us."

Kl'aarn glanced about, then said, "They are Slayor's responsibility, not ours. Let's be on our way. Some of Slayor's men will be scheming against us if we delay. For they know we are few, and that we have women."

* * * * *

It was mid-afternoon when they reached the shallow river. It marked the border of Morgrar's (now Slayor's) domain. But more than that, it marked the border between two worlds. For there, at that shallow river, the world of men came to an end, and the Lands of Demi-men began. There, a stone's throw away, was the feared, fabled, and cursed land from which no man had emerged alive in centuries. The travelers halted in awe.

"Just look at it," Shalar remarked. "Nothing but desolation and death.

They say that any man who sets foot there is cursed forever. None have ever stepped across that river and lived very long. No one. And I've no mind to join them in their graves. I'm not going any farther."

Miril sneered with contempt. "You coward. Five of our men lay dead on your account. And now, do you think of running off? Then think of this, Shalar. My curse is already upon you. If you do run, my curse will run with you. You will die of a hundred boils, each a separate torment. You will count them off with your shrieks of agony. Morgrar would have been more merciful to you than I will be."

But Shalar replied, "I have seen your power today, Miril. And I have seen its limit. Morgrar had you at his mercy, and there was nothing you could do. Besides. What do I gain if I follow you? Only more curses, and a more hideous death."

Miril knew that she required Shalar, but knew also that she could not bewitch him to obey. So she turned instead to Veelos. "And what says the priestess? Is her power so strong that she can afford to release Shalar from his duty? We are all that is left of Har-Keem, we four. Did they not teach you this nuance of prophecy in your temple?"

Then Veelos gave it some thought. And she spoke to Shalar. "Of course I would rather you ride with us. But it is clear that you will not. And who is to say that you are wrong? Has any one of us been guaranteed to live another day, another moment? No. So each of us must decide for himself.

"But your choosing is such a sad one, Shalar. For, only once in all your life have you done any noble deed at all. Only once. And you did that one, as you say, only because you had no sense. Is that what you call being sensible, Shalar? To be noble only when there is no price? But many a man has accepted that price--- to perform one noble deed, and then to die. You refuse to accept that bargain. But think what price you pay instead.

"Across that river lies death, Shalar. But more than mere death. There, Shalar, stretched out before you is the one thing you fear more than death: the unknown."

Then Miril scorned Veelos. "You fool! What do you think you're doing? With sixty we are strong, and with twenty we are weak."

But Shalar said to Veelos, "I know what you're doing. You're being clever, Veelos. Miril should know that, for she used to be like you. But now, she's forgotten how you two used to get us boys to do things. And it's almost working. Oh, I can feel your words tugging at my heart, Veelos. What kind of coward would turn away from destiny, and let women ride to their death? Is that it? Do you think me still a little boy, that I would fall for that? Do you think I still care about impressing you with my pretended courage, with feigned valor? Sorry, Priestess. I care nothing for valor, and nothing for your opinion of me.

"But do listen to me, for once," Shalar continued. "Because you're right about one thing. Death lies across this river. And if you cross it, death is exactly what you are choosing. Veelos, I know nothing of your war, and I care nothing. It's all shit. We are born to this earth for only a short time, and then we rot. All that we have, is that little space in between. I've enjoyed my space, Veelos. And I'm going to enjoy what's left of it. Now think. Turn away from this foolhardiness, and let's go back to the east land. Let's laugh again, like we used to."

But Veelos answered, "Your brief moment of joy is only illusion, Shalar. Life is even shorter than you think. Should you live a thousand years, and a thousand times that, the end comes before you are ready. And how will your death come? One night you will lie down drunk. One of your men will have a score to settle. Even the man riding next to you, right now. He'll cut your throat. And then, what will your life have been? Will your momentary joys sustain you after they are no more? Will there be any dignity in your final breath? Any rest in your eternity?

"Oh, Shalar. You are so able to ward off the curse of a witch, but you curse yourself more horribly than ever she could. So now it is your choosing, bandit. And mine, also. You choose the moment, but I choose eternity. Goodbye, then, Shalar. I shall weep for you, but I'll not share with you the needless misery in which you live. Goodbye."

Then Veelos turned her horse, and with a firm jolt to its flanks, and before Shalar could reach out his hand to stop her, she prodded it across the stream, to the other side. Then Kl'aarn and his men, with Miril, followed after.

Shalar watched them. "Damn her," he said. "Damn that woman. She's done it again," he said. For the briefest instant, he remembered a cart disappearing from view, and the indefinable feeling he had felt only twice before in his life. This time, that feeling would not, he knew, depart easily from his heart.

"I'm going with them," he announced.

Then he, too, splashed across the stream. And more out of habit than courage, Shalar's men followed him.

Chapter 25

Nightfall in the Lands of Demi-men

The land was cursed. That much was obvious. Nothing seemed to grow except thorns. No creatures were seen, but for those which crawled and had poison stings. Even the air seemed stale.

Kl'aarn wondered if their food would hold. For Vike and his two hunters, Belgar and Valmark, could find no quarry.

In their weariness, they decided to make camp early. For they had found a small pool of water, and might not again for many hours.

As the sun began to set, Kl'aarn took up watch at a post. Miril came to his side, and they sat apart from the main body of men.

Miril wrapped both her arms about one of Kl'aarn's, and rested her cheek against his shoulder, in a pensive, half-embrace. "It's getting dark," she said.

Kl'aarn glanced inquisitively at her. "Has that a special meaning?"

"Indeed it does," Miril replied. "It will be our second night together as man and wife. And this day you have proved yourself to be my hero. Manly deeds can have an arousing effect on women. And women take especial joy in rewarding such deeds. Don't you know this? But why do you squirm, Kl'aarn?"

"I'm not."

"We are man and wife, are we not? Do not the vows of betrothal stand?"

Kl'aarn nodded. "They stand. But Miril. There is no privacy here for us. We'll not have any for a long time to come."

She laughed delicately. "Why, whatever were you thinking, my dear? I only said that---"

"I know. Miril. We hardly know each other anymore. And I'm afraid of you--- afraid for you. Dear woman! This black art you practice will turn against you, against us both. You're shrewd enough to know that. You know the legends. Look what happened to Kattaroon. And what of the worshippers of Thorgar? When they debased themselves in worship of it, it betrayed them. Do you think it will deal with you any differently?"

Miril replied. "You are wise to ask this, my beloved. But then hear my answer. Every sorceress, since Kattaroon died, has defiled herself with indulgence. Yes! They welcome evil as their servant, and call upon it to satisfy their every whim. And when they have filled themselves with its pleasures, they are horrified to find that it has become their master. And a cruel master evil is, just as any master must be. These women are the toothless, emaciated hags we have seen gone mad in the caves.

"But I did not come to evil in this way. For me, it was no dalliance. I had no illusions. I came with eyes open, knowing that evil is treacherous, even to its practitioners.

"A witch does not serve evil for only what it can give her. She goes one step more. She makes the commitment. When I had lost everything, Kl'aarn, I knew that no half measure would heal our wounds. And I knew what I desired. I demanded it. And that is you, Kl'aarn, nothing less. I knew that I would either lose you forever, or have you forever. There was no half measure.

"So I made my choosing, Kl'aarn, not for a day or a year, nor even a lifetime, but for all eternity. I chose to be your wife forever--- death will never part us. Not even death!

"And the evil which I serve has but one purpose, Kl'aarn. Its end is to destroy all that is good. No half measures suffice! Evil's destiny is to conquer, to destroy, and to rule. There can be no timidness in its march. It seeks all or nothing. That, Kl'aarn, is the soul of witchcraft."

Kl'aarn was silent for a time. Then he said, "Your eyes are veiled, Miril. You seem wise only to yourself. That is part of the deception of evil. How can I awaken you?"

Miril answered. "Evil is a stranger to you. In it, you see only an abhorrent thing, as I once did also. But soon, you will see its beauty. Even Veelos will. Yes! She will become a witch, Kl'aarn. She, too, will embrace evil. And when she does, then I shall give her the choicest realm of my queendom--- of your kingdom, my lord."

But Kl'aarn answered. "I know Veelos. She'll never turn to witchcraft. She would die first."

And Miril said to herself, "Indeed. And she will do both."

Chapter 26

Demi-men in the Night

That night, they heard sounds in the wilderness. Shadows moved in the darkness, and footsteps clattered across the rocks.

Veelos shivered despite the warmth of the campfire. "What is that noise, Vike?"

The hunter placed another stick of wood on the flames, as his eyes scanned the shadows surrounding them. "Whatever creatures inhabit this strange land, they seem clever. They know to come only close enough to count us. For tonight, they are too few to attack so many. But if they are truly clever, they will know how to send for help."

At sunrise the travelers, both warriors and bandits, broke camp hurriedly, and continued westward, ever deeper into the cursed domains. The terrain became more hostile, strewn with large boulders, each of them as tall as four or five men. The horsemen had to maneuver their way between them, as if along the lanes of a village.

Shalar tried to hide the worry in his eyes, as he said, "If I were to plan an ambush, I would want it in just such a place as this."

Kl'aarn nodded his agreement. "There are perches for archers above us, and clefts for swordsmen below."

Then Shalar showed his worry. "You don't think these monsters practice archery, do you? If so, we are doomed."

But Kl'aarn did not answer. For, after all, this was the very land of doom.

For a time, they saw no sign of the creatures which had unsettled them. But by midmorning, men began to glimpse movements behind, and atop, the huge boulders, between which the caravan made its way.

A few of Shalar's men grumbled. "We've no qualms about fighting human enemies," they complained. "But we're being stalked by beasts which carry swords. And they seek not our silver, but our very flesh to devour!"

Shalar tried to quiet them. "You sound like a gaggle of women. Keep your wits. Can an animal be more dangerous than we are? Are we not more evil than they? Remember who you are, and be ready to fight."

And Kl'aarn spoke to Miril. "If they do attack, I want none of your magic. Fighting is for men and swords, not conjury."

But Miril began to protest. "These creatures themselves are the product of ancient magic---"

"I've made my order clear," Kl'aarn cut in. "No witchcraft. Will you obey, or will you turn against me?"

Miril seemed visibly wounded. "My husband! I would never turn on you. Not ever!"

"I'm depending on that," Kl'aarn replied.

But Veelos overheard them speaking, and she said to Kl'aarn, "Do you think that you can de-fang the nightcat? Do you think she'll not ply her sinister craft? Kl'aarn, Miril cannot help but betray you. You know better!"

Then Miril glared at Veelos. "Who speaks but a liar priestess? And with what motive? You've your own devious schemes, Veelos. And they have nothing to do with priestly purity, now do they?"

"Stop it," Kl'aarn commanded them. "Shalar and I are trying to gird up the courage of these men, and you two are causing dissension. If they see even you two quarreling, then how will we keep order? Now keep near the wagon, and keep silent."

Obediently, the two women fell silent. Veelos turned away from Miril, her face flushed with both anger and embarrassment. But she knew that Miril was enjoying their battle of words. She could feel the witch's burning stare upon her back.

Without warning the attack erupted. From every place of concealment, there sprang a demi-man. With howls both too beastly and too human, combined into a single, fearful roar, the creatures launched themselves into a frenzied rampage.

In appearance, they were short, squat and furry. They ran on thick hind legs, and in their forepaws they carried truncheons and pikes. Their ears were pointed rearward, and their snarls revealed curved, yellowed fangs. Across their chests, many of them wore a studded leather sash, which served as a crude breast-plate. The mere sight of them was enough to unnerve the bravest man.

Kl'aarn regretted that he had no lance. For the creatures were too swift to engage in duels. They would close from behind, strike a blow, and be off in another direction. Often as not, the demi-men would not even use their crude clubs, but slash with claw or fang instead.

Because the horses panicked, the men soon found themselves dismounted, and forming squads of four. In this way, the creatures could not attack a man from behind, for the men stood back to back.

But neither did the demi-men shrink from frontal attack. And when they did engage, their blows were like sledgehammers against the mens' shields. It was fortunate that they seemed to have no plan of battle. For, no human could long endure the sheer ferocity of these beasts.

Veelos had hesitated to crawl beneath the wagon for shelter. For she had worried over the four men inside, who would be helpless should any creature leap upon them. So she stayed with them, inside the cart.

But leap the creatures did. And when Veelos found herself in close quarters with the ferocious predators, all her physical courage suddenly left her. Confronted with their raging snarls and savage claws, Veelos shrieked in terror and fled, abandoning the wounded men she had intended to comfort and protect. She did not consider her retreat, but ran blindly, without thought.

It was then that one of the beasts seized her. Its claws dug into her arm, and the demi-man began quickly to drag Veelos from the battle.

When the priestess saw its red eyes and smelled its wretched breath on her neck, she fainted as if dead.

At this moment, all the attackers were withdrawing, with whatever sort of loot they had managed to seize. For they had torn open the saddle bags of nearly every horse. Their purpose had been not to murder, but to raid and plunder. And that they had done.

When Kl'aarn saw that Veelos was being carried off, he felt but a moment of indecision as he sought how best he might rescue the priestess. The creatures were too swift for him to pursue on foot, and no horse was at hand. An arrow would be too uncertain, as likely to strike Veelos as to wound the demi-man which carried her. And so, in the heat of the moment, Kl'aarn settled on the only action he deemed available.

"Miril!" he shouted out. "Save her! Quickly!"

Just as before in the battle against Morgrar, Miril needed no further instruction. Assuming the same stance she had against Morgrar's men, Miril straightened her arm. And with a vile curse, the witch flung a firebolt of death at the retreating demi-man.

There was flame and smoke, a loud crash of thunder, and in the next instant, the hapless demi-man was but a smouldering heap of bones, and burning clumps of bloody fur.

In the following moment, all the demi-men had vanished into the wilderness, and an unearthly silence fell like a cloud over the field. Kl'aarn watched as Vike and Belgar ran toward the place where Veelos lay unconscious. She would be alive, Kl'aarn knew--- injured and blooded, but alive. He thought that he should have felt comfort in that much, at least.

Instead, the warrior felt a darkness in his heart. Although his decision had spared Veelos from some horrid fate, he knew that he had enlisted the service of evil to save her. For, it was by his own command, not hers, that Miril had launched her death bolt. And had Veelos herself not warned him against this? Had she not cautioned him that evil always requires a tenfold payment in kind?

The warrior glanced uncertainly at his woman.

Miril met his gaze with hers, and, with none of the uncertainty that plagued Kl'aarn, said, "That was but a taste, my love. And like the taste of strong drink, it burns. Oh, how it burns! But that is only because it is potent medicine, my dearest, most powerful indeed. Fear it not! For soon, you will discover its sweetness, its intoxicating delight. And when you do, then the bitterness will vanish away."

Without answering her, Kl'aarn turned away to watch the men bringing Veelos back to the wagon. (He could see a patch of bright red on the sleeve of her white vestment.) The priestess had tasted it, too, Kl'aarn knew. She had tasted the strong drink of evil, first in Shi-Raq, and now here, in the wilderness. He wondered if Veelos also felt the same darkness, the same doubt, the same remorse, which now burdened him.

Somehow, he knew she did.

Chapter 27

The Wounded Priestess

It was twilight when Veelos awoke. She vaguely remembered being in a semi-conscious state, in which she had been painfully jostled by the wagon at every bump in the terrain. But what awoke her now was the fierce sting of cool water on her open wounds. She tried to cry out, but her voice was hoarse and dry.

"Don't worry, I won't drown you." The voice was Miril's. She was lowering Veelos into a shallow pond. They were alone together, bathing. But the sounds of the mens' camp was nearby.

Veelos tried to resist, to clamber out of the water. But Miril's hand was firm upon her shoulder. "Now, you can't go running about," she chided Veelos, "clothed only in your bandages. Imagine the scandal that would cause." Her tone was a mockery of innocence, a satire of concern and sincerity. Even so, it reminded Veelos of a day long since passed, a day when Miril had been able to speak with a gentleness that had not masked her motives, but revealed them for what they were: true concern, and sincere compassion. For just a moment, Veelos imagined Miril as once she had been.

That thought quickly fled.

Veelos gasped at the shrieking stings in her wounds. Soon, the unbearable pain would subside, she knew. But there was another kind of pain also, far deeper than any physical wound.

"You're very badly bruised," Miril said. "I haven't seen you this bloody since our little scuffle with that greasy pirate that Shalar killed for us. Of course, you were a bit braver then. Are all priests such cowards as you?"

They were both immersed up to the neck, now, and Veelos shook herself free of Miril's grasp. "I was more willing to kill, then," Veelos replied angrily.

Miril sneered. "And I was more revolted by killing then. We've gone far since that day--- and in opposite directions."

Then Veelos began to peel her stuck dressings from her wounds. The violent stinging pains were renewed, but Veelos could see that the wounds were not dreadful. They would leave scars, but she would live. "It's not possible to converse with you, Miril. You are full of lies. And you say only what serves you."

Miril sneered. "You loathe me, don't you?" she said. "You think yourself too holy to even share this water with me."

Veelos winced in pain, and then answered, "There is only one possible end to our enmity, Miril. One of us must kill the other. There can be no other outcome. You know this as surely as I do. So why don't you just kill me now, Miril? Why not be done with it?"

But Miril replied, "I saved your life today, you silly little bitch. Why do you speak of killing me?"

"Yes, you did," Veelos answered. "No doubt you summoned up your dark power, and spread a little more Hell in this already fallen world. But don't expect gratitude from me, Miril. You did this for your own good, not mine. Perhaps you even summoned forth those creatures from their lairs to attack us. But the worst of it is that, now, I've been made a part of whatever evil scheme you have concocted. The ache in my soul tells me that much."

Miril replied, "Don't flatter yourself, priestess. You are not that important to me. I can kill Druuk without your help. The reason I spared your life was because Kl'aarn commanded me. He is my husband, after all, and I must obey him."

"Then obey him in this," Veelos said. "Renounce your demon."

Miril laughed at that. "You think yourself so clever. But I was delighted to save your life, Veelos. Truly I was. You think that the evil cannot love, but we do, Veelos. Does not your own scripture confess that, that even the evil love their own kin? You are more kin to me than anyone. And I really don't want it to happen as you say: I really don't want us to be enemies. I certainly don't want to kill you. Can you believe that?"

"In part," Veelos answered. "I'm sure you would choose the pleasant way, if that were possible. But when you find it not possible, you'll not be deterred from your evil goal, regardless of the cost. To that end, you will drag all your loved ones into eternal agony. Your kind of love is poison, Miril. You have even gone so far as to trick Kl'aarn into calling for your conjury. That is why he asked you to rescue me. You are slowly bewitching even him."

Miril scowled angrily. "At least I did not try to seduce him from another woman. You think I don't know your feelings for him. But I do. You thought that, with me out of the way, you would get him to marry you. Didn't you?"

"That's a very twisted version of the truth, Miril."

"And you still do think that," Miril said. "It still does occur to you that, somehow, I will die before you do--- whether by your hand, or by some danger along our way. You still hold some hope to take my place in his bed."

Veelos spat. "Better for him to marry a whore than you."

Miril laughed again. "The scorpion still has a sting, does she not? Very well, then. It's plain to see that there is no reasoning with you, at least for now. The arrogance of telling everyone else right from wrong--- that is the curse of priesthood--- it makes you unable to deal with the real world. But guess what, Veelos. We still have a long way to go. And if you live to see Druuk, you are going to confront a reality for which your godly teachings have never prepared you. When you confront his power, his wrath, his evil--- then you will listen to my counsel, Veelos. And you will understand the wisdom of witchcraft."

Chapter 28

Burnt Offering

"Have some," Vike offered.

Kl'aarn looked up from where he sat at his watchpost. The hunters had killed a deerlike animal, and the meat was a welcome treat. "Thanks."

Vike sat down near him. "Keeping an ear out for the women," he noted.

Kl'aarn shrugged. "My wife is down there."

Vike studied the warrior for a moment, then said, "Your wife. You are bound to her by a sacred oath, then."

Kl'aarn nodded. "An oath of betrothal. But it stands, after all these years, as an oath of marriage."

"Holy matrimony?"

The warrior looked angrily at Vike. "Make your point, hunter. She has departed from the way of God. She has taken on the garb of witchcraft. And she has powers of destruction. I oppose all those things, Vike. I have given my life to the service of God. But Miril is still my wife. I still do love her. And yet, I cannot change her. So tell me, Vike. Have you some sage counsel to lift all this from my shoulders? But if you tell me to forsake her, then forget it. I can't do that."

Vike shook his head. "Who am I to tell you anything? I am no priest."

"But Veelos is," Kl'aarn answered. "She does wear the silver ring. And her counsel would be just the same as yours. Or worse. Did you know that witches and priests are sworn to kill each other? You do know that. So tell me, Vike. Whose side am I supposed to take?"

Vike did not answer.

So Kl'aarn filled in, "You would say to take God's side. You would say to forget all about the love I have for Miril. You would have me let her die. You'd have let Morgar kill her. Truth told, Vike, you would kill her yourself."

Then Vike stood as if to leave.

"I'd have to stand against you," Kl'aarn said to him. "I'd never let you harm her."

"Truth told," Vike said, "I'll never be the one to harm your woman. But she will harm herself. All evil is ruin, even to the evil themselves, warrior. And to the ones they love. When Tarok refused to kill the demonwitch Kattaroon, Kl'aarn, he thought he was doing her some great good."

Then Kl'aarn stood also. "Enough, hunter. This talk is going to no good conclusion. This day, we are bonded, you and I, by the blood of battle, having fought on the same side against the same enemies. Just remember, some day, we may fight another battle. And when we do, we might no longer be on the same side."

Vike looked into Kl'aarn's eyes, and saw that he meant it. Then the hunter turned and walked away.

Chapter 29

Echoes of Doom

Of the four wounded, whom Veelos had tended, only one lived beyond a few days. He was Thrake, one of Kl'aarn's men, the one who had found Lar still alive in the temple after the massacre. The others all died of infection, in horrible agony.

The travelers numbered sixty-two, all counted.

For a time after the attack of demi-men, the rocky wilderness had given way to increasing greenery. There had been ample game, and so the hunters had kept the camp supplied with fresh meat. For a time, it seemed as if the dry, rocky wilderness were completely behind them, and that all the remaining distance would be across green meadows and abundant fields of fruit and game.

But if the men had hoped for easy passage through the Lands of Demi-men, those hopes were too soon met with disappointment. For, just as the land seemed to become a Garden of Eden, all that changed with a vengeance. Suddenly, there was a dry riverbed. Beyond that, lay a land of such desolation that even the horses seemed averse to crossing over, into it. The entire company of travelers came to a halt, surveying the bleak barrenness before them.

"Can you hear it?" Miril asked Kl'aarn. She sat high in her saddle, as if attentive to some distant sound.

Kl'aarn listened intently. There was only silence, a silence so intense that it made him imagine how the deaf must feel. "Hear what?"

"The echoes," Miril answered. "The ancient echoes of a thousand men, a thousand chariots, and ten thousand more besides. A great battle was fought here, a mighty battle to shake the very foundations of the earth."

Kl'aarn surveyed the scene. There was no sign of life, not even of insects. The only things resembling trees were gnarled stumps.

"No battle of mere horsemen and chariots wrought all this desolation," he said. "No earthly force did all this."

Miril nodded. "You are correct," she said. "The great sorcerors fought here. But that was a long time ago. Their magic is gone now, gone forever. All we need fear is starvation and thirst. For this wilderness stretches many days of travel."

But there was no turning back. And so, the travelers crossed into a land that they would not soon forget.

* * * * *

It was as Miril had said it would be. For days, the travelers forged westward, day after weary day, through a dry and sterile landscape. It took all the skill of Vike, Belgar and Valmark together just to find water. When they did, it was always in stale, stagnant pools. The only greenery was scrub grass that barely fed the horses. The men went on half rations to conserve food. It seemed that the journey might never end.

Then, one afternoon they crossed a ridge and, atop a distant crest of land, saw a castle, if a castle it was. For its architecture was of a style none of them could identify. Its edges were not straight, but curved, in the shape of flame and fang. At its base were the signs of what once had been an overgrowth of vegetation, but was now only dead vines.

"Druuk's fortress?" Shalar wondered aloud.

"Hardly," Veelos answered. "We have far to go before we reach the west kingdom. No, that is no longer a castle of the living, Shalar. It is only a skeleton of what once was."

At the sight of the castle, the men broke out of columns and formed abreast of each other to see it. For it had once been a work of splendor. It was built of great stones, cut and fit. The outer walls stood the height of five or six men. Those walls enclosed towers, the tops of which were visible from far away.

"Deserted ruins," Kl'aarn said. "Who would have thought there could be anything so grand in the midst of this forsaken wilderness?"

But Veelos answered, "By no accident."

"What?" Kl'aarn asked.

Veelos explained. "The closer we have come to that place, the more barren and void the land has become. Whatever curse has kept this land so forsaken all these centuries, it emanates from within that castle. We would be well advised to steer wide of it."

Miril was at Kl'aarn's side, and she also spoke. "In the wars of the Great Upheaval, there was a demon named Thilgol. Betrayed by its ally (the demon Thorgar), Thilgol took refuge here, and fought its final battle against the followers of Tarok. It lost, and was cast forever into Hell, along with its demonwitch, Kattaroon."

Kl'aarn turned to Veelos. "Do you sense the same?" he asked her. "Can you two know such things?"

But Veelos answered, "I have never served Thorgar. It is the betrayor of all who do."

Miril understood the taunt, and replied, "Thorgar would betray me, too, if only it could. But it cannot."

Kl'aarn sensed the mounting hostility between the women, and feared as always that, unchecked, it would infect the men. "Well, we've no time for sightseeing ruins," he said. "Everyone. Form up. We'll be well past this place before sundown."

But Shalar said, "Not so fast, warrior. What sort of plunder might there be?"

Kl'aarn answered impatiently. "Probably none. But even if there were gold, Shalar, we've no time for it. The only treasure that will do us any good out here is food and water. Gold would be far too heavy to carry. And there is certainly none of it there."

But Shalar persisted. "I've no thought for gold," he said. "To be sure, it would be too heavy to carry, and it won't buy anything out here. When it comes time, we can plunder Druuk's castle for gold. But I've another thought."

"Which is?" Kl'aarn asked.

"Helliron," Shalar said.

Kl'aarn spat. "I never thought that you'd be the one to believe in old wives' tales."

But Shalar looked to Veelos and Miril. "Is it really just an old wives' tale? When we were children, did not Valen Elder tell of the ancient wars? I thought them foolish stories, at the time. But now, here we stand, with that castle to bear witness. Did not the demons give their soldiers swords and shields of helliron? They were swords which could pierce any armor, and shields which no enemy could breach. Yet they were light as feathers. Now if any such weapons are to be found, they lie within the walls of that castle."

Miril spoke. "You need no such weapons, Shalar. The anti-prophecy is our sword and our shield. We need nothing more."

"That may be true for you," Shalar replied. "But the only weapon I trust is one I can hold in my hands. When we come to Druuk's palace, we men will have a right to some magic of our own."

"Demonic weapons," Veelos warned, "are not wielded by men, Shalar. Rather, those weapons wield men. As soon as one touches a demonic sword, it possesses him. It sends that man to fight its own battles, not his. If you take up such a sword and shield, Shalar, you will become a slave to them. Nor can you put them down until they have drained the life from you."

But Shalar glared at Veelos. "And how is that worse than my present state? It was you who talked me into this land. You bewitched me with whatever magic your God gives you. Are you not using me exactly the way you warn me against being used by helliron? At least Miril's magic has done us some good. It killed our enemies."

"As it will continue to do," Miril said. "But, Veelos is right for once, Shalar. Helliron would master you, and not the other way round. You have not the evil to conquer it."

But Shalar spat. "You're afraid of such weapons, Miril. For what is a demonwitch against a demon warrior? No, I'm not facing Druuk's sorcery without some of my own. Nor will I forego magic enough to defend myself against your treachery."

Miril laughed. "No weapon will make you invincible against me."

Veelos tried one last time to dissuade the bandit from his intentions. "Think of it, Shalar. Thilgol's men had such weapons. But then, if those weapons were so potent, why were they defeated?"

But Miril's spell was upon Shalar, and none of them knew it. They tried to dissuade him, but could not. Shalar insisted upon exploring the castle, and finally even Kl'aarn agreed to it.

Chapter 30

Venom of the Dead Serpent

They found the gate locked.

It was a wooden door, but the wood, though very ancient, was yet strong. And when Shalar tried to hack through it, the wood dulled his sword without giving up so much as a chip.

The bandit vented his frustration on Miril. "Why didn't you say it was magic-locked? Did you think me too stupid to know? Open it."

But Veelos warned, "Others have come this way and gone inside. They've never come out."

Even so, Miril looked to Kl'aarn. "What shall I do?"

Kl'aarn's expression was one of disgusted resignation. "Do it," he said.

Then Veelos spoke angrily to Kl'aarn. "What is becoming of you? Do you now give in so easily to evil? At least before, you yielded only reluctantly, and even then, with remorse. Is there no more fight left in you?"

But Kl'aarn ignored her. "Let's get this over with," he told Miril.

So Miril cursed the gate, and with a dull, grating sound, it opened.

* * * * *

Within the castle walls was a courtyard. Though open to the sky, it seemed in shadows, like those of a forest. But that was only what seemed. For what darkened this place was the shadow of evil. Here was a darkness not of space, but of the soul.

The ground was littered with dust and debris, with garbage and filth. Whatever once had lived here had been something unclean. A broken down cart lay crumbling near the gate, and just beyond that were large fragments of a barrel. Leaves and branches rotted underfoot. There was a cracked trough, and some sort of wooden chest, forced open long ago and now empty but for decay. A kettle, rusted through, lay on its side. Numerous other items were strewn about, which no one had considered valuable enough to carry off when the fortress finally had been abandoned, lifetimes before.

In the center of this ghostly courtyard was a very large blockhouse. It was four storeys tall, and wide enough to dominate the space within the castle walls. There were no windows. It seemed to form part of a giant cube, a gambler's die, come to rest after a last, desperate bet, a bet that had been lost---the cost having been both the wager, and the gambler himself.

All this, the men could see when the gate fell open to Miril's curse.

While the others hesitated, Miril stepped through the gate and into the courtyard. Warily, she cast about with cat-like eyes, half expecting some unseen danger to leap in ambush from the shadows. Then, satisfied that no immediate danger lurked nearby, Miril faced Shalar. "Well?" she prompted.

Shalar seemed taken aback for a moment, and said nothing.

Miril pressed him, saying "Either get on with it, or let's abandon this scheme of yours."

Then Shalar seemed to remember his quest for the swords of helliron. He, too, stepped into the suffocating gloom of the courtyard, his eyes as furtive as Miril's had been, his hand tight on the hilt of his sword.

The bandit swallowed hard. He had not expected the fortress to look so much more forbidding inside than out. Here, the darkness was not so much a shadow, but rather a pallor, the pallor of death seeking a corpse.

There was silence and stillness.

Next Kl'aarn, then Veelos and Vike, and finally the other men, began to step warily through the gateway and into this dark world within cold, stone walls.

Veelos shuddered as she looked about. She could feel the evil. It hung heavy in the air, cold and ruthless and--- and hungry. It was the evil of a demon. The menace in this place was overwhelming.

"If Thilgol is still here," Veelos said to Miril, "it will kill us all. Nor will it spare you."

Kl'aarn thought Miril had never looked more a witch than now. It disturbed him, that she seemed not a bit out of place amid such wicked surrounding. He wondered how much more at home she must have been within Thorgar's crypt. "You're sure it's dead?" he asked.

Miril herself seemed to remain cautious. "Thilgol is dead," she said.

"True," Veelos spoke. "It's dead. But even a dead serpent has venom enough to kill."

Now Shalar forced himself to find his nerve. "The blockhouse," he said. "The weapons must be in there. Let's find a door."

Recessed within the wall, the men found an alcove which ended in a door. And the door gave way easily.

Beyond it was a narrow corridor with a low ceiling. It was a tunnel of blackest midnight. No one dared venture inside.

"Bring torches," Shalar ordered. Several of his men eagerly made for the castle gate, as if afraid that it might suddenly shut, sealing them inside forever.

When finally the torches had been prepared, the first of them were lit, and holding one aloft, Shalar pushed forward into the blackness. For a moment he hesitated, for even the torchlight seemed to be swallowed up in the dark confine. But once again he girded himself, and pressed onward.

One at a time, the others followed, both terrified and fascinated, as children walking at midnight through a graveyard on a dare. But this was no prank. For all of them knew that in such a place, their wildest fears could become reality. In such a place, the corpses of the dead could grope for them with hands of putrefied flesh.

Then they saw the skeletons.

Kl'aarn moved beside Shalar to see, for here the corridor widened slightly. The skeletons were upright. They lined both walls, facing the center of the tunnel, as would sentries standing guard. But they were not the skeletons of humans.

"What sorts of creature were they?" Shalar asked.

Kl'aarn peered at them. They were the more frightening in that they resembled humans so much, and yet were so distinctly beast-like. "Demi-men," Kl'aarn answered. "But much more like men than the ones we have fought. Still, look at those fangs and claws."

Nor were these skeletons naked. Their bones were glued together by mummified flesh. Upon them, they wore armor of leather, with metal helmets not quite turned to rust.

"They bear no weapons," Shalar noticed.

"Perhaps plundered," Kl'aarn said.

"Or removed to an inner vault," the bandit countered. “Weapons of helliron.”

Kl'aarn sighed briefly. "Very well. Then lead the way."

They resumed their steps, walking between the macabre sentries, carefully avoiding their touch, not daring to disturb the dead.

Timidly, the others followed.

They had to tread carefully past the skeletons, to suffer their obnoxious stares, to endure their obscene gaping jaws, and to smell their cold breath. But these were ghosts without wrath. If one listened, one could hear from them not curses, not threats, but warnings. Escape while you can, strange creatures. Escape, and drag my bones with you, so that I may at last be freed from my centuries-long vigil. Do not ignore me, as these others did, who now stand beside me. Or else you will surely join our regiment of the damned.

The column proceeded forward, torches aloft, a snake with many orange eyes along its body, the living intruding into the domain of the dead.

The corridor came to an abrupt end. Another door, wooden and frail with age, gave easily to Kl'aarn's kick. It fell from its hinges, and crumbled into dust. He knew then that no one before him had ever survived this far. Those who had tried were those whom he had left behind him, whose warnings he had ignored. Whatever evil inhabited this place, it was feeble with age, he reassured himself. It was too weak to harm him. Or else, the thought came to him, it was unable to challenge the witch who now clutched his elbow.

"To the right," Miril said. The door which now lay in ashes had revealed another corridor running left and right. It was no tunnel, but a much wider thoroughfare. It was, however, just as dark and forbidding as the smaller one.

"And what's to the right?" Kl'aarn asked her.

But Miril answered, "To the left is certain death."

* * * * *

In this larger corridor, the floor was covered with a fine, powdery dust. It was ankle deep, and when the men walked, they stirred it up. Its stale, musty odor made them cough. Kl'aarn ordered, "Move slowly. A panic now would choke us all."

Even so, the dust billowed up waist high.

After a time they found another door. But this one was no frail wooden shell. It was a massive stone portal, nearly twice as tall as a man, and as wide as the corridor itself. Upon it were strange inscriptions, in a language none of them had ever seen written.

"What does it say?" Shalar asked of Miril.

But the witch shook her head. "Ask the priestess."

Veelos said, "It is no human language, Shalar. But rest assured, it does not mean, 'Welcome.'"

At that, Shalar drew his sword, and asked again of Miril, "You have the eyes of darkness. What do you see beyond this door?"

Miril again shook her head. "My vision does not penetrate it. But you might as well store your paltry sword. For if anything is there to be fought against, it will wield a sword forged in hell. You'll stand no chance. Nor can I help you. You're on your own, Shalar. If you haven't the nerve to risk your soul for whatever lies inside, then you are not the sort of man who could master a demonic weapon."

Slowly, Shalar slid his sword back into its scabbard, his eyes pondering the barrier before him. His courage wavered. "This door," he gazed up at its height, "looks made for the passage of a sizable creature." He hesitated, then finally said, "What the hell! If I'm to die, let it be for something worth the dying." He stepped to the door and leaned his weight against it. When it did not budge, several of his men joined in the effort.

Finally, and as if protesting its disturbance, the massive portal gave way, and of its own momentum, opened fully.

As it swung wide, the men's eyes were wide with fear, with dread of what might set upon them from within. But their fear was soon turned to awe, and stupefaction. For instead of facing their darkest fears, the men were looking upon their wildest dreams come true.

The room was fully two storeys tall, much wider, and as long. Embedded in the walls from bottom to top were glittering gems, precious stones of every color, sparkling as if afire with the light of the torches. Rubies as large as a man's fist were set in the stone, along with emeralds such as any king would envy for his crown. There were jewels of every description, and some which none could describe at all except to say that they would buy a kingdom, an empire.

The bandits continued to stare for a time as if bewitched. Then, the movements of their feet began to stir up the choking dust. Kl'aarn's warning to them fell upon deaf ears. The men in the rear began demanding access to the demon's trove, and with the scuffling of their feet the noxious cloud, which they kicked up, began to overwhelm them all. Men began coughing and choking in the dust. Its foul, musty smell drove them from the corridor into the jeweled treasury upon which they had stumbled.

In the maddened rush, Kl'aarn reached out and groped for Miril. He tried to call her name. But his breath was heavy with the noxious storm of dust.

Veelos also was blinded in the greedy rush of men. At first, she tried to retreat, to retrace her steps and leave the corridor for the tunnel entrance. But the dust behind was even worse than before her. Veelos knew that if she retreated, she would not be able to find her way. Nor could she hold her breath much longer. So she made for the vault, where at least the air seemed breathable.

But as she did so, Veelos felt someone bump into her, and push her aside. It was someone going the wrong way. Veelos tried to reach for whomever it was. But the figure eluded her and was gone. She tried to call out. But then, out of breath and blinded, Veelos ran into the demontrove.

The air was clear there.

Kl'aarn grasped Veelos by both arms. "Where is Miril?" he demanded.

"She was with you." Veelos replied. "Isn't she in here?"

Kl'aarn pushed Veelos to one side. "She must have been trampled. I've got to find her."

But Veelos quickly took Kl'aarn's hand. "She's not been trampled," the priestess told him. "It must have been her who pushed past me, going the other way, and eluding my grasp. She knew what she was doing, Kl'aarn. And where she's going, you cannot follow."

Kl'aarn sensed the truth in what Veelos said. "What more do you know about where she's gone? What is she doing?"

"I know only this," Veelos said. "That Miril is about her business. She is a demon's witch, Kl'aarn. And this is a demon's lair of long ago. Miril alone knows what she is about."

* * * * *

Shalar walked about the center of the great hall, holding his torch aloft as if in salute, his eyes scanning with fascinated attention the jeweled walls. He had entirely forgotten about magic weapons and helliron shields. He was held now in the grip of another spell, one cast centuries before Miril had cast hers. The legendary wealth of a once mighty kingdom surrounded him. He had found it. And now, he swore to himself, now it would be his, and his alone.

All around Shalar, men were engaged in an orgy of greed, not only the bandits, but the warriors also. Some were breaking open ancient chests. Others pried with sword tips to loosen sapphires and diamonds from musty stone walls and columns.

Shalar was content to let the men do for him this work. He would allow them to collect the booty and load it for him into the wagon. But after that, he schemed, any man who dared touch Shalar's treasure would stand guard forever in the corridor which had led them to this place. It was Shalar's trove, and no one would ever have so much as a single tiny flake of it.

* * * * *

Miril moved quickly through the hidden, secret corridors. She glided swiftly through their blindness with the sure-footedness of one well accustomed to evil abodes. The witch required no map. She was a nightcat, guided by instinct, lured by scents which others could not detect. Those scents directed her every step, and instructed her every turn. Like a deadly sea creature at the bottom of a deep, black ocean, Miril homed in on the scent of blood.

But there was danger for her as well, danger so mindless and sinister that, even for a witch, this was a place of dread.

One needed not be a witch to have sensed the ruthless, malevolent evil, which ruled this eternal midnight. There was no subtlety to it. It did not disguise itself here, as it did in the world of men. Here, it was shamelessly naked and raw. It made no pretense of reward for those who served it. The evil here promised nothing, nothing that is, except what could be taken from it by force.

Miril paused. She heard something. It was not a sound heard by ears, but of the spirit. It was the sound of wails and shrieks. Within the very stones she trod, were trapped the spirits of those who once had been loyal to Thilgol. In its moment of final death, the demon had damned all within its reach.

The witch sensed something more. A trap. She was being lured into it. The bait was an evil power. A lesser offer might not have impressed her. She might have turned back. But something particularly potent lay ahead, something exceptionally evil. There was an amulet. It would make Miril more powerful than ever she had imagined possible.

But the bait was offered only as a lure, only as something by which to trap her. Miril knew that. There was no intention of actually letting her escape with it. The evil here would never surrender that amulet. Never.

Miril hesitated. Then she cursed. "I will take it," she swore. "I will take it, or die."

But worse than death awaited should she fail.

Miril continued forward, stalking the vapors which drew her ever deeper into the trap. Whatever lusted for her murder seemed to laugh.

Thick cobwebs ensnared her, and for a moment, Miril could not move. Their touch made her skin crawl. But instead of fear, Miril felt a seething hatred well up within her. The cobwebs were burned away.

She took another step. And stopped. A sudden, cold chill gripped Miril. It was the fear the damned feel, when they realize too late, that they have woven their own doom. It was that sick feeling they know, in that moment, just before being hurled into the bottomless pit, never to return.

There was the presence of a demon.

Miril cursed. "Thilgol! It yet lives, after all!"

"Are you sure it's dead?" Kl'aarn had asked her.

"Even a dead serpent," Veelos had warned, "has venom enough to kill."

There were movements in the blackness. Evil dead were staggering toward Miril, attracted by the warmth of her living blood, and thirsting. They were only empty corpses, animated not by life, but by evil alone. Yet, they were predators, hungry, and on the hunt.

This was a form of evil that Miril had never encountered. Her mind struggled to find a way to combat it.

Lies! she thought. Lies, all lies. Thilgol is not alive. It is no longer able to enter the world of substance. It forever falls, ever deeper into a pit in which the only direction, every direction, is down. For if Thilgol were yet alive, then Tarok the holy warrior could never have escaped it, could never have appeared to Miril in the shrine in Har-Keem.

Miril's failing resolve had returned with a vengeance. For an instant, a near fatal instant, she had succumbed to the demonic lie, which yet infested this castle. But Miril had pierced the lie. The power, which these evil dead had held over her, now vanished. They would not devour her flesh.

The mummified remains of Thilgol's conjurors moaned in their disappointment. Their laborious scheme had failed. A thousand years of meticulous planning, planning and patient waiting, had come tantalizingly close to fruition. Their cold, maggot-eaten tongues had already been anticipating the delicacy which had been brought before them. Their diseased fangs had already been bared to pierce Miril's soft, moist flesh. But just as their dried, crusted lips had drawn close to her, the witch had proven more evil than them. The walking corpses withered before her punishing curse. The witch's wrath was not content to merely drive them off into their misery. She ground them to dust, and cast the dust into hell as fuel for the fire. Then, undaunted, she continued along her way.

As Miril pressed relentlessly forward into the oblivion, she sensed the growing smell of power, an ancient, malicious force. She knew that she must challenge it.

The darkness swallowed her up, and Miril did not permit herself to fear again until, at last, she stood before the fabled Doors of Nothing.

Chapter 31

Sword of Hell

Kl'aarn and Veelos, with the hunters, were the only five in the vault who had not fallen under its spell. The others all seemed maddened, wealth-maddened men who rummaged violently through the false delights of stolen booty. But for Kl'aarn, the inability to control his men was no longer his worst fear come to pass.

"Where could Miril be?" he asked Veelos, worriedly.

Only steps from where they stood, Thrake used his sword to smash open an ancient, wooden chest. When he found it empty, Thrake broke it into pieces, and hurled the fragments apart. A shard of wood slammed into the wall by Veelos's head.

Kl'aarn's men had become indistinguishable in behavior from Shalar's.

"I don't know where Miril is," Veelos answered. "But be assured that she knows exactly where we are. It was she who led us here, after all. And clearly, she did not do this for our good."

But Kl'aarn said, "You're not saying that she's left us here to die. Miril would never do that."

"Wouldn't she? You don't know her, Kl'aarn. You thought you knew your own men. But look at them now. This is what evil does to a man. Do you think it does less to a woman who embraces witchcraft?"

"You're wrong about Miril, Veelos. You're a priestess. You have to feel a certain way. But Miril loves me. I know she does."

Thrake walked away in disgust from the chest he had ripped apart. But his eyes were alert, and they scanned the room with some purpose only he knew. He ignored the shimmer of diamonds and rubies. They were not what he sought. He cared nothing for the jade idols and sparkling emeralds. He desired something more. With an inaudible summons, heard only by Thrake, it was calling to him, tempting him, luring him.

His eyes fixed upon another chest in a far corner of the room. Attracted, Thrake walked directly to it, absently pushing aside any who stood in his way. After what seemed a long journey, he reached the place where it was. Using his sword as a pry, he lifted up its lid.

When he saw what was inside, Thrake's jaw fell slack. For a moment, he could only stare at the golden beauty he beheld. It was a shield. But such a shield Thrake had never imagined. For this one seemed made of purest gold. And the workmanship was unearthly. Across the entire face of it were graven the images of demons and sorcerors. They were locked in a fierce orgy of torture, death and debauchery. Thrake reached forth and grasped it.

As soon as he did so, Thrake felt its power surge through him. With one hand, he lifted it up and admired its compelling beauty. No woman could ever look so alluring, Thrake thought.

Hathor, the bandit, was nearby, and his eye was also caught by the exquisitely crafted, shimmering object of beauty. He wandered toward it, and asked in bewilderment, "Warrior, how did you come by such strength as to hoist so much gold? Not a dozen men could bear that much weight."

Thrake's eyes seemed to gaze through the shield, into some distant horizon. "It's not heavy for its master," he said. "And though it is indeed of gold, it is not the soft gold of mortals, which can be bent into shape. No, this gold is harder than the Orb itself, and as light to my arm as a thought." His eyes remained captured, still focused on the images carved in relief on its surface. The eternal, mutual massacre fascinated him.

But Hathor scoffed. "If it is weightless, then of what use is it? A heavy weapon will break the arm that bears a shield so light."

Thrake glared at Hathor. "This is no ordinary shield, bandit. Can't you sense its power? But I'll cure your doubt. Watch."

So saying, Thrake set down the prize, balancing it precariously against the chest, so that it seemed a breath might topple the shield. Then he drew his sword from its scabbard. He said to Hathor, "This sword is heavy enough to bruise your arm, whatever shield you carry." Grasping its hilt with both hands, Thrake swung it with such might that it could have severed the trunk of a small tree.

The blade was shattered. But the brutal force of the blow did not so much as dent the shield, nor move it even a hairsbreadth off its delicate fulcrum.

Hathor's eyes widened in amazement. "The witch spoke the truth, then. Why, this shield could stop a falling mountain!"

Thrake nodded. "No harm can ever befall me while this shield is mine."

"But look," Hathor said. "You have broken your sword. What will you do?"

Thrake smiled knowingly. "Indeed I have," he answered. "Then I shall have another, the mate of this shield. It is close by. Help me search it out."

* * * * *

The Doors of Nothing were set within arches that spoke of the curvature of fangs. They loomed menacingly before Miril, sealing her (and the rest of the world) from a bastion of demonicry long forgotten by men.

"Even Thorgar itself does not know," Miril smiled to herself. "It thinks this place destroyed these many centuries. Nor can its mind penetrate into the depth of this dungeon. So--- I have a knowledge which even the demon is denied. And in that, I have power over Hell itself."

Miril could not see the doors with her earthly eyes in this unearthly darkness. But she could see them clearly with her blindness, with that part of her soul that stared with hatred from empty sockets.

That blindness revealed to Miril this massive portal, imposing itself between her and that which she sought.

She had come this far. But the Doors of Nothing intended that Miril go no farther. They intended that she never reach what lay beyond them.

But Miril could sense that, whatever did hide behind those doors, it had a power that she coveted. It was so powerful that even the Doors of Nothing could not hold back the reverberations. For it was a power so evil that it had laid waste a kingdom a thousand years before. Nor had that power faded in all this time.

These doors had no soul. But even so, they had intent, purpose, intelligence. "Barrier," they said in silence. The single thought was unmistakable.

Miril struggled to sense what was beyond. She listened. And with thought tendrils from her mind, she probed the Doors of Nothing. Something other than mere echo inhabited the other side. There was something which yet moved, moved and waited patiently. Whatever it was, it was more evil than anything Miril had yet encountered in the mortal world. The taste of it! Miril's tongue licked her teeth. There was a familiar taste behind those walls. It was the taste of the Well of Blackness.

Something other than Miril had soiled its lips at that trough.

Miril smelled it and thirsted. It was the scent of the darkest of all earthly evil, the very source of abomination. She drank it in deep, thirsty gulps, reveling in its wrathfulness, and savoring its unrelenting hatred. She knew the pleasure of its pain, the joy of its horror, the fearsomeness of its ruthless, mindless cruelty. It was the taste of doom.

"Open to me," the witch commanded the doors.

They defied her, and scorned her command.

Miril's rage slashed at the doors with a tangible wickedness that could have made them bleed, had she desired it.

But the doors cast her curse back in her face.

Miril winced at her reflected pain. But her vengeance only intensified. "Open now, Doors of Nothing," she hissed. "Your Darkmost Demonwitch commands you. Guard no more the corpse of Thilgol. Open now, or else I will curse you with life."

"You cannot give us life," the doors rebuked her. "For nothing evil can give life, but only take it."

Miril retorted, "The kind of life I can give you is life by which to feel the torment you contain. Do you put me to the test?"

Not even the unliving doors could endure so terrifying a threat. For if anyone could carry it out, surely this woman could. Very slowly, the Doors of Nothing, for the first time in a thousand years, parted.

Miril stepped through the opening.

* * * * *

Hathor watched with the fascination of idiocy as Thrake continued his methodical search for a sword.

All around them, bandits and warriors were occupied in the prying loose of impossibly large gems from the walls in which they were embedded. They would cooperate for a time in extracting whatever particular brilliance was their obsession of the moment. But then, as soon as they had freed it, they would quarrel violently over it. But again, just as they would have shed each other's blood over the jewel, yet another one would lure them, this one more desirable than the last. So they would cast aside the one for which they had stood ready to kill, or to die, and would pursue the successor as raptly as they had the castoff.

Kmir had broken the spell which, for a time, had obsessed even him. Now, he struggled to restore order. But he was steadily losing ground. It was clear that before long, a general melee would erupt, from which few would emerge alive. So Kl'aarn joined Kmir in his effort. Finally, even Shalar realized that his men could not carry treasure for him if they killed each other arguing over it.

But although Shalar proved able to separate dueling men with violence of his own, it was becoming all too clear that this place was infested with self-destruction. Soon, none of them would be able to contain it. Indeed, none would be able to avoid infection themselves.

"Look!" Thrake boasted to Hathor. "I told you it was nearby. And here it is, a sword unlike any other. Was this weapon not made as mate to this shield? It was! Could any man fail to conquer a kingdom with armament such as these? Admire this sword, Hathor. It is a feather in my hand, but death to any who stand in my way."

"Let me hold it," Hathor begged.

Thrake's eyes iced over with menace. "No one touches my sword and lives. Only I."

Even in idiocy, Hathor knew better than to repeat the request. "But I haven't seen it tested. Can it cut through your bronze shield?"

Thrake glanced at his discarded shield, and with a mere flick of his wrist, sliced it in half, with his golden sword, as if the shield were mere parchment. "Indeed," he said to Hathor, "it is truly magic. I am invincible. But one more test to impress you, bandit."

So saying, Thrake walked up behind his friend Kmir, the Kmir who had saved Thrake's life in combat. Thrake casually severed the other's head.

* * * * *

As Miril stepped through the opening, she heard behind her the muffled thud of the doors--- the Doors of Nothing--- sealing shut. Whatever trap had seized her, there was no escape. But Miril's attention was focused on what lay before her.

She found herself in the shrine of the vanquished demon, Thilgol. The interior seemed to be of no specific size or shape, much as in a dream. Its many corners were obscured behind shrouds of smoke. The source of that smoke was a human skull, its top lopped off, and its eye sockets glowing red with whatever smoldered where its brain once had been.

The ceiling came to a point high above, in the shape of a horn, twisted and curved.

At the farthest visible wall was an altar. A semicircle of steps led up to it. They were not a smooth semicircle, but rather jagged and rough. The altar itself was cut from stone and bone in ancient demonic fashion. Its lines were the contours of flame and fang.

There were witches.

Four of them knelt on the jagged steps, their backs turned to Miril. A fifth one stood on the top step, also facing away from Miril toward the altar, her attention riveted to the skull of the sacrificed human whose remain now served as censer.

The four who knelt, all had their hoods over their heads. But, in contrast, the one atop the altar steps had let her hood rest upon her shoulders, a sign of authority and power. Her arms were stretched out wide and at a slight angle upward. She seemed to lift the smoke by some unseen force, for it poured copiously from the skull.

Miril sensed that somehow, the man whose skull it was, was not nearly as dead as he wished he were. His eye sockets glowed not only with fire, but with terror and torment.

With the thud of the doors sealing shut, the witches turned in startlement. For it was a sound unheard in a thousand years.

First, the four witches on the lower steps turned, for their attention to the demonic ritual did not absorb them as properly as it did their mistress. They turned on one knee each, all at once, and faced Miril.

As accustomed as Miril was to horror, even she was revolted by the sight of these hideous faces. She wished to look away from them. Their features were grotesque distortions of human form. Eyes, unequal in size, glowered above cleft lips. The tips of their leprous noses had rotted off, and what remained were swine-like snouts. Their skins were an oozing, peeling paste, pocked with craters and warts. Within their hoods, their heads seemed to be barely more than skulls with wisps of tangled, stiff hair. But worse than even this physical appearance was the murderous hunger which glowed in their asymmetric eyes. For nothing could be more fearful to a witch than the bloodlust of another witch.

Miril had been revolted by the repugnance of the four lower witches. But a moment later, the other turned to face her. Miril gasped in horror and took a step backward.

For this witch had turned so suddenly that her hair whipped into serpentine contours. And her eyes met Miril's with a force that struck like a hammer-blow.

What made Miril gasp was not repugnance, but beauty. Miril felt the stab of jealousy. For as intensely ugly as the four lower witches were, this one was every bit as intensely beautiful. Miril had never envied any woman's appearance. She had never worried that Kl'aarn would find another woman more attractive than herself. But she had never imagined that a woman could appear as beautiful as this witch now did.

Her hair was black as coal, her features clean and sharp, yet delicately feminine. Even the terrible cruelty of that face was subtle, seductive and deceptive. Her narrow brows were perfect frames for her almond eyes. The nose was small and precise. And her crimson lips could be described only by a word which meant both sensual and wicked without separating the two meanings. For this woman made them one.

Without doubt, here was a woman who could command the love of any man, even despite the fangs which those artful lips could not conceal.

"How dare you intrude?"

The words were a predatory hiss, lubricated with acid venom. Her green eyes were bottomless pits of outrage. An unseen menace sprang from within her, lethal as a hurled spear, so that Miril had the impulse to dodge. She knew then, what the moment just before death felt, just before sudden, violent murder.

But just as Miril felt that, she resolved to fend off whatever daggers of fear this other had attacked her with.

Quickly, Miril estimated this opponent. "Like me, she is a demonwitch. But her demon is dead. She can draw no power from it. Yet she might not need to, for this one is well practiced in the craft. Look how sly she is. For even in her startlement, she had presence of mind. She did not flail wildly at me with some killing spell. If she had, I would have turned it against her. She knows better than to challenge an enemy of unknown powers. Even now, she is seeking in me some weakness. She will find none."

Miril spoke aloud, then. Her voice flowed with easy authority, clear and confident. "I am a witch," she said unpretentiously. "I carry forth the Evil Quest. I call to obtain a favor."

If Miril had expected the fanged beauty to be intimidated, she was wrong. Instead, Miril felt evil thought tendrils. Snake-like, they explored her, not frantically, not desperately, but with the practiced skill of routine. If those projections of mind found so much as the slightest weakness, it would mean death, instant death. Miril knew that if she betrayed the slightest tremor, the panther would pounce with the quickness of lightning. She would tear out Miril's black heart so quickly that Miril would live just long enough to see it pump out its lifeblood.

The groping stopped.

The ancient one spontaneously laughed. It was a laugh of genuine amusement, almost childlike. "A witch you say? You?" Her head rocked backward in laughter, but this time it was derisive laughter, that of a spider finding a fly tangled in its web. When her head rocked forward again, the eyes had narrowed, become lamps of red fury, the eyes of murder. "You are a mere kitten, stumbled into a lion's den. Do you seek a favor, housecat? Then serve me a thousand years, as these four have. Shed your pretentious beauty, and help us retrieve Thilgol from the void. And then, when we succeed, ask Thilgol for favors. For I grant none."

Miril felt a powerful temptation to cowardice. It would be the most natural thing to fall down before this mistress in obedience. But Miril resolved to die rather than serve this witch.

"Why should I give you my youth, as these four have, merely to preserve yours?" Miril spat. "Did you persuade them that their sacrifice was for Thilgol? I see they believed your lie. But their sacrifice was futile. Thilgol is dead forever, covenwitch. Where Thilgol is, there is no upward direction, but only ever downward. Escape from the void is a self-contradiction."

The fanged one sneered. "Look about you, housecat. Has evil vanished from the world? No. Thilgol yet sends forth its curses. It will return."

Miril replied, "It is not Thilgol which curses the earth, but Thorgar. It lives."

"You lie," the other said. "Thorgar is dead."

"What can you know?" Miril taunted. "You are imprisoned here in your windowless tomb. If Thorgar finds out that you are alive, it will destroy you, just as Thilgol was itself destroyed. Do I lie? Then look at me. Who taught me so recently the craft? Only a demon could. Do you know who I am? I am the Dreaded One Foretold. I am Darkmost Demonwitch. The end of cycles is at hand, and only those who serve me will escape Thorgar's trampling hooves, once I loose it from its cage."

The fanged witch's sneer turned to rage. "You arrogant bitch! Have you the audacity to suggest that I might ever serve you? I have toyed with you too long, housecat. Now you will regret that ever you dared invade this domain. Now you will know the anguish of eternal torment." Then she turned to the nearest underwitch. "Grollush," she called her name. "Kill her."

The witch named Grollush crawled to her feet. The mere mention of her name made Miril feel a clammy touch of memory, the memory of a name long buried in legend, a memory forgotten only because it had been too terrible, too painful to keep alive. But the name itself yet lived. It evoked repressed instincts of dread.

"Don't be a fool," Miril said to Grollush. "You were once a mighty princess of Hell, beautiful beyond description. But now look at yourself---see what's become of you. You are loathsome to behold. Even so, your days of glory can return. You can become once more, what once you were. All you need do is to serve me."

But Grollush was already consumed with the lust for blood, the bloodlust and jealousy of a once proud woman who dared not admit to herself that she had squandered all for nothing, and instead had been betrayed by that which she now served.

Grollush's lewd, lustful smile contorted her cadaverous lips. Her grating voice began grinding forth an ancient, brutal curse, one which could turn its victim's very blood to poison.

For the first time in her life, Miril knew what it is to be in the grip of pure malice. Unseen thumbnails gouged at her eyes, intent on popping them from their sockets one at a time. At the same time, something tried to pull the entrails from her body. Conjured spirits sought to violate her womb.

Grollush's touch was masterful. She had done this before, many times, and had done so gleefully. Grollush knew of agony and despair, and delighted in inflicting them.

Miril's rage left no room for fear. Hatred and malevolence exploded from within her cold heart. Unlike Grollush, Miril required no incantations to unleash her spell. Her power sprang directly from the cauldron of evil which was her self. And she was more evil than Grollush could ever become.

Miril reached forward with one hand. Its long, curved nails clawed in the direction of Grollush. From them, an unseen force was projected across the distance, a vile curse not to be found in any demonic underscripture ever memorized by Grollush or her sisters.

Too late, Grollush understood what was about to happen.

The talons which Miril's fingers had formed began to close. Grollush contorted in the invisible, relentless crush. Her desperate struggles for escape became a macabre dance of agony. One by one, her bones began to crunch dully beneath the foulness of her flesh.

Grollush began squealing pathetically. "I beg you for mercy, dear child. Don't do this to me."

But Grollush's pleas for mercy fell on ears more deaf than her own. The invisible fist crushed her still further, slowly crumpling her into a ball. Her head was forced downward into her torso, and her legs were pushed up into her abdomen. Her shattered ribs pierced her viscera.

Miril did not stop until Grollush was a writhing clump of tortured flesh that labored to die, but could not yet do so.

The living, dying mush that had crawled to its feet now gurgled and squealed with untold agonies, and made wretched squawks in the desperate quest for just one more breath. For although the body yearned to die, Grollush's soul well knew what awaited it in the eternal, hopeless void. She struggled to delay every possible instant that final moment, which would see her cast into the place where she would shriek forever without cease.

Miril released the spell. "I warned you," she taunted the vanquished witch. "Now look at you. You can never utter another curse. And do you remember all those spirits, which you've conjured so many times? They are gathering about you, Grollush. They have a lot of vengeance to celebrate. So take your time, and die slowly."

Thilgol's demonwitch had observed the duel without expression. Now, as Grollush slowly drowned in her own fluids, the fanged witch raised one eyebrow ever so slightly. It was a subtle--- and unintended--- sign of grudging admiration. Then, she descended the steps, ignoring the bloody, squirming mush that once had been Grollush, taking care only to step around it. She moved toward Miril with the cautious confidence of a master snake handler approaching his deadliest serpent.

Miril replied to the fanged one's approach with a posture that showed the same respect. For although she had easily killed Grollush, she was under no illusions about the demonwitch. The black terror, which slinked toward her now, was vastly more powerful than Grollush had been. Vastly. And whereas Grollush had struck with ample warning, this one would deal out death with the quickness of a nightcat. There could be no relaxing of guardedness, especially so, now that the demonwitch regarded Miril as dangerous.

The fanged witch's eyes revealed a mild curiosity. Her lips formed a precise hint of smile, meant to be seen but not noticed, a smile which flickered with heartless cruelty. It revealed just a bit more of her vampirous fangs. Slowly, but boldly, her face came close to Miril's in mock affection, her eyes searching diligently for any sign it might have missed from a greater distance. The slightest twitch, the tiniest bead of sweat--- either of these would mean instant death, and eternal torment.

"You are no mere sorceress, dear child. You nurse directly from the breast of nightfall."

Miril recoiled one step backward. But it was not fear, rather disgust, which moved her. For as the other had spoken, she had reached forward and stroked Miril's own breast with her clawed fingers. That hand now also lurched backward from Miril's sudden indignation, in rightful concern for its safety, and then retreated more slowly with a graceful, dignified motion.

Miril scowled, and said, "The favor which I ask is not for myself. Nor is it yours to deny."

The other's eyes glowered. "You were able to slay my daughter," she said just above a whisper. "But do not toy with me, Miril of Har-Keem. You cannot imagine the evil which I command."

Miril glared back with equally deadly menace. "I'm not impressed that you know my name. I speak it freely wherever I go. No one can use it against me, not even you. Nor do I care to know your name. I won't need it if I must duel you."

The fanged one smiled with a deadly amusement that suggested she had discovered a harmless prank against herself. "Not know my name? Surely you must. For neither do I hide it, but rather boast of it. Or perhaps, on the other hand, you really do not know who I am. That would explain why you do not fear me more than you do."

Miril sneered. "If you are so proud of your name, blackwitch, then speak it. Else, we have other business."

The other laughed. "Do you really not recognize me, Miril? Can you possibly fail to recognize the most powerful demonwitch ever to curse creation?" The smile vanished, to be replaced with dangerous scorn. "I am Kattaroon. I am seducer and slayor of Tarok himself."

"You lie!" Miril countered. "Kattaroon is long dead, vanished with Thilgol to its bottomless grave."

The other, once again smiled in earnest humor. "You really don't believe me, simpleton. But I am she. And I still own Tarok's corpse to prove it. His soul has escaped, but only after I had vented my wrath upon him. Even now I abominate his corpse. Still you doubt? Then see for yourself."

The witch pointed, with one dagger-like fingernail, toward a corner, to Miril's left, and slightly behind her. From the edge of one eye, Miril saw a misty blue glow, where before there had been a blackness even she could not penetrate. Cautiously, she turned her head slightly to the left, not daring to allow the black-robed danger entirely from her sight.

There, where the other had pointed, Miril saw the tortured corpse of a man whom Miril immediately recognized. It was the earthly husk of Tarok. The body was fastened securely to a large, almost vertical slab of wood. The board was studded with long, barbed spikes, each of which pierced the mummified cadaver. None of the wounds was a fatal one, but each was calculated to inflict maximum torment. The body was frozen in a gruesome contortion, the face twisted with pain, the kind of pain which Miril could only begin to understand.

For its lifeless eyes were those of a man betrayed. As unendurable as the physical agonies had been, the anguish of betrayal had been even worse for Tarok.

"He loved me," Kattaroon explained. "Then he made the mistake of trusting me. It was his last. It took him six years on that rack to die. For six years I offered him a throne of evil, but he would not accept it. Then his soul escaped into death. Do the legends still speak of him, Miril? Do they still recount his dying words? Even then he loved me. 'Kattaroon,' he gasped at the end. 'My beloved Kattaroon!'" But Kattaroon's expression was a sneer.

Miril suddenly spun to face the witch of legend once more. "It is a good proof. So I believe you. You are indeed the ancient dread. But I have no time to be impressed. You, of all people, should know that we two have no profit in opposing each other. On the contrary, the gathering clouds of war force us into alliance."

But Kattaroon seemed in no mood for conciliation. "You fear the angels, don't you? But I don't. I have already tested them in battle and defeated them. Even in their moment of seemingly final triumph over evil in the world, I seduced their leader and killed him. They sent their legions of priests and soldiers against me to no avail. All that remains of the forces of good is one, faltering false priestess. Her only legion is a dwindling band of cutthroat scum who even now are turning against each other. And you have delivered her to me, housecat. The Priestess of Prophecy now belongs to me. For, whatever power this Veelos has over you--- in that you spared her life--- she has no power over me. It is I who will kill her, and it is I who will inherit her destiny to rule."

"If you kill her," Miril warned, "you condemn us both. For I have spared the priestess only because we need her to defeat Druuk."

Then Kattaroon hesitated. "Druuk. I know of him. But he is only a petty tyrant. Why should we fear him?"

"Because," Miril answered, "he has stolen the Orb of Power. Until we win it away from him, we cannot defeat the angels. And for that, we shall require the assistance of the Priestess of Prophecy."

Kattaroon's brow arched in uncertainty. "You lie," she said.

But Miril knew she had finally breached Kattaroon's defenses. There could no longer be any denying it. "You do know," Miril said, "that what I speak is true. I speak according to demonic prophecy. You have studied them. You understand, as none other can, that we are in peril of our lives, unless I achieve my quest."

For long moments, Kattaroon struggled to disbelieve. But at last she relented. "Then it has come to pass," she admitted. "The angels have let their power slip into the hands of men. A new cycle begins, a new opportunity to win the final victory."

Miril sighed with relief. "Then you will join with me."

But Kattaroon replied, "You have it backward, housecat. You will join me. For you are too young, too inexperienced for the task at hand. Only I have enough evil to do what must be done."

Miril scoffed. "The anti-prophecies no longer even mention your name, Kattaroon. It is now I who command the winds of fate."

"Do you?" Kattaroon asked. "Then let me put you to one little test, Miril. It is only a simple question. If you answer it correctly, then I will bow to your authority."

"What question is that?"

Kattaroon spoke it. "Are you evil enough to do, to your precious Kl'aarn, what I did to my Tarok? If he refuses to occupy the throne of evil with you, what will you do? Will you gladly sacrifice him, as I did Tarok? Answer carefully, Miril. For there is only one correct answer."

Miril shifted nervously. "He will accept," she answered. "Already, he is beginning to understand the beauty of darkness."

"But if he does not? Then what?"

Miril answered. "Kl'aarn and I will drink the blood of the priestess from her own skull. When the time comes, he will savor the taste of it."

Kattaroon's poise was haughty. "You are too soft, woman. If Kl'aarn were mine---"

Miril snarled, "He is not yours. He will never be anyone's but mine. Don't test me, witch, for you already failed your own test when you were driven from the light of day. Now it is my reign. You need take care only to grant the favor for which I come. If you provide it, a realm of the earth will be made yours to ruin. If not, then you will remain sealed in this tiny hell of yours forever."

Kattaroon took a step backward, her eyes flashing with anger. But hers was the anger of defeat. "If you are Darkmost Demonwitch as you claim, then what can you need from me?"

Miril replied, "Give me that dark weapon which turns good against good. Give me the Amulet of Doom."

"I don't have it," Kattaroon spat. "I used its power long ago to turn Tarok against his priests."

Miril's eyes narrowed, and her gaze focused on Kattaroon. "You lie," she said.

"I don't have it," Kattaroon repeated. "Even if I did, you could not wield it. It was forged in Hell's hottest furnace."

Miril paced closer to the evil figure before her, daring to invite attack. "The priestess must ask me to destroy a great good. This is demonic prophecy. It must be fulfilled. And only the Amulet of Doom can bring that about. Else, you and I are destroyed."

"Then we are destroyed," Kattaroon said. "For indeed, I do not have the amulet."

Miril's reply was a silent, burning stare.

Kattaroon glared back. But gradually, she weakened her gaze. Then slowly, grudgingly, she withdrew from a pocket of her vestment a small black, horn-shaped amulet.

"I remind you," Kattaroon said. "Its price is a realm of the earth, just as you offered. No less."

Miril reached out her hand for the treasured talisman.

But Kattaroon suddenly lurched it backward. "I warn you," she said (her voice had the quality of a nightcat's growl), "if you try to cheat me, the price will go higher. For remember that I have one power which will always be greater than yours. By the power with which I seduced Tarok, I can also seduce your Kl'aarn from you forever."

Now Miril felt anger well up within her. But she decided that Kattaroon's threat was merely that of a cornered animal, a sign of desperation. All that mattered now was the amulet.

Miril felt it pressed into her hand by Kattaroon's. Its cold, greedy power sucked the warmth from her flesh. Miril recognized the familiar touch of evil, its dark emptiness, its bellowing rage. The craftsmanship was unmistakably demonic.

"It turns good against good," Kattaroon said. "That is in itself the most primitive evil, and the most lethal."

The demonwitch Miril slipped the evil device into her own pocket. Miril then turned her attention once more toward Kattaroon.

But Kattaroon laughed. "Well I know the murderous impulse you now feel toward me. Now that you have the amulet, you think it is safe to kill me."

Miril nodded. "I could do it, you know. And why shouldn't I?"

Kattaroon answered, "Because, Miril. You admire me. You almost envy me, don't you? And who in all the world will admire you--- if you succeed in casting all of earth into Hell? Who, but I, will understand the art of your craft? If you kill me, Miril--- that is, if you could hope to defeat me in battle--- even if you kill me, you'll find eternity a very lonely thing without me."

Miril felt the seething lust for murder slowly ebb. "There is no profit in our enmity," she told Kattaroon. "I will even award you the soul of Tarok, to torment once more and forever. Just one last thing. Never again mention the name of Kl'aarn. Never."

* * * * *

A moment earlier, the treasure room had been filled with the sounds of jubilant men, men drunk with the fantasy of newly achieved wealth. Until a moment before, the men had forgotten all fear, and had abandoned every sense of right and wrong.

But now the silence of death had sobered the plunderers. For in their midst stood a madman who had casually decapitated his best friend with as much thought as one might swipe at a mosquito.

Kmir's headless body lay crumpled in the dust, his neck a diminishing geyser of red. Nearby, the head stared grotesquely up at them from amid the debris of the floor.

Only Thrake, alone among all present, was unperturbed. He seemed not even to notice that the others were dismayed by his mindless, murderous act. "It's a magic sword," he commented. His attention to the golden weapon was rapt. "I am invincible."

No one dared move. Indeed, no one dared draw Thrake's attention at all. For they believed him, when he said he was invincible. And since it was clear that Thrake was in thrall to some demonic power, no one wanted to be his next victim. Whatever power was embodied in that awesome sword, it struck fear into the hearts of all.

The first one to speak was Veelos. "This is not a room of treasure," she said, to everyone, "but a room of mirage. Even the very jewels you gather are mere illusions, pieces of dung, placed here as bait. And the weapons which promise to make you into invincible warriors are instead cruel masters which wield men. There is nothing here for us but death. We must leave this place."

Shalar looked downward into his arms, which cradled as many large jewels as he could hold. He eyed them with awakened suspicion. "One sees in them," he said dryly, "only what one wishes. But in the light of day, they rot." He opened his arms, and let fall an emperor's ransom into the dust.

Thrake alerted to Veelos. Holding the sword upright before him, his head turned, he eyed the priestess. "No," he said calmly. "This sword is not evil. It makes me strong. See? And there are other such weapons in this room. We must use them. Otherwise, we cannot hope to survive the battles we have yet before us. But with them, we can conquer all creation."

Veelos did not reply. For there was nothing in Thrake to reason with. Instead, she turned to both Kl'aarn and Shalar. "Quietly, get the men out of here. Do it now."

Shalar did not hesitate to relay the order to his men. But the bandits obeyed only reluctantly. Loath to unburden themselves of their illusory treasure, they moved slowly for the doorway.

"Call them back, Priestess," Thrake implored. "These jewels were stolen long ago from sacred temples, plundered by evil warriors. It is only right that we return them to the purposes of good."

Veelos now turned her eyes to Thrake. She spoke. But as she did, she spoke as if into a mist. "I know you can hear me, Thrake," she said, "even though your soul is buried deep within your body. So do not despair. I will not abandon you. Listen closely, and make good your escape from the spirit which has murdered Kmir. Do not fear. I will not be deceived by the words spoken through your mouth."

Thrake stepped slowly toward the priestess. "There's nothing wrong with me," he said. "I am not possessed, if that's what you're thinking. Look. This sword can kill even the witch. Here is the chance you've been waiting for. If you don't kill her now, she will surely kill you. Take up the sword, Veelos."

"Your tone is smooth, and convincing, demon of Hell," Veelos told it. "But your bloodlust gave you away. Kmir's corpse puts the lie to your words."

Thrake's expression changed to a scowl. His voice became noticeably more hostile. "You have no choice, woman. Do as I say. For otherwise, you will never leave this place alive."

Veelos felt the cold touch of fear. She knew that she must stand her ground. For if she did not, then the sword would cut through the men to get to her. It would not allow her escape. The others it would not bother with; the real prize was the priestess. If it could not seduce her soul to evil, it would at least destroy her body.

She felt Kl'aarn at her side. The warrior was reaching for his own sword.

"Don't be foolish," the priestess warned Kl'aarn. "He'll slice you in half without a thought. Your sword is nothing against his."

"Then run for it," Kl'aarn said.

"No," Veelos said. "You leave. Save yourself."

"Not while Miril is still in this castle."

"Miril is no victim of this fortress," Veelos snapped impatiently. "Can't you see that she is at home here? Now get out, before you get all your men killed with you."

"Veelos. I can't just---"

"I know what I'm doing," she said urgently. "Go."

Kl'aarn let his half-drawn sword slide back into its scabbard. There was no time for debate. Kmir's bloody corpse was proof enough of that. And Veelos did indeed seem to know what she was about. Despite her terror, she was sure of herself. Some inner strength gave her resolve. So Kl'aarn stepped away from her, then disappeared into the corridor.

Only the two of them remained, Thrake and Veelos, in the room. "You're making a very bad mistake," the demon said through him. "Order the men to return."

But Veelos' rejoinder was, "Release the sword, Thrake."

"You have not the magic to make me do that."

"Release the sword, Thrake. Release its grip on you. Free yourself from it. It has no real power, but only deception. Its power is a lie. Do not hold to it."

Thrake's face began to scowl. "If you don't bring them back, Priestess, then I will get them back myself. I'll kill you, and then I'll hunt them down. For they will not disobey me, as you have."

"Release the sword," Veelos repeated. "By the power of God's angels, I command you."

Thrake's face contorted with rage. He raised the invincible weapon for the deathblow. "This is your final warning," he roared.

Veelos cowered in dread. For she knew now that she was completely powerless to stop what was coming. "I forgive you, Thrake," she said. "I know this is not your will."

Infuriated, and casting aside his enchanted shield, Thrake grasped the sword with both hands, and sliced downward with a savage blow aimed for Veelos's head. The sword would have sliced completely through her, splitting her in half. But it slipped. As Thrake swung it downward, it slipped from his hands, and was instead hurled forward by the force. The magic sword hit the wall just above the priestess. It buried itself to the hilt in stone. As it did, it made a sound like a shriek. Somewhere, a demon hurtled into a bottomless pit.

Veelos had winced in expectation of death. Now she breathed a sigh of relief, and held Thrake's hands in her own. "Only God is invincible," she said to him. "And that is all the invincibility any of us ever needs."

* * * * *

When Kl'aarn had retreated from the treasure vault, it had been at Veelos's command. He knew that he was abandoning the priestess to some terrible danger. It could not be helped. It would have been futile to simply die with her, even though some sense of duty within him required that. Veelos's command had freed him from that duty, but not from the inner sense of guilt.

But as he groped his way along the dark, cold corridor, Kl'aarn's thoughts turned from Veelos to Miril. She had deliberately evaded him, he knew. And however much danger Veelos was in, Miril surely was in even greater peril than that. For she had forayed alone into this cavern of death.

Dust choked him. Kl'aarn felt his strength ebb as he struggled for breath. Then, with no warning, a terrible chill engulfed him. It was no mere feeling; something physical had seized him, something dark and sinister. For a moment, Kl'aarn thought himself in the claws of some ravenous beast. Evil swirled palpably around him.

"Kl'aarn!" she said. It was Miril. She had collided with him in the blindness of the corridor. "Why is everyone in rout? Why are they empty handed?"

Kl'aarn seized Miril's shoulders, and demanded, "Where the hell have you been? Why did you run off?"

"I had to," Miril replied. "I'll explain later. Right now, we have to get our hands on the magic weapons."

"We did that," Kl'aarn answered. "Thrake found one and it possessed him. It caused him to kill Kmir. Veelos is in there now, trying to free Thrake from its thrall. As for us, we have to get out of here while we can."

"I'll free Thrake," Miril said. "And win the weapons to boot."

"No!" Kl'aarn commanded. "You're leaving with me. And now." With that, he began pulling Miril with him.

"Kl'aarn please! I can rescue both Veelos and Thrake. We can't just leave them there."

They had turned into the smaller corridor which led to the outdoors. Miril had continued to plead with Kl'aarn, but to no avail. Shortly, they found themselves between the two lines of skeletons which stood as mummified sentries. Most of them had been knocked down by the fleeing men who had preceded them in retreat. Bones lay scattered on the floor in disarray. Daylight was a jewel afar.

Suddenly, Kl'aarn stopped.

Miril fell silent, then asked, "What is it?"

Kl'aarn drew his sword, and pushed Miril toward the daylight. "Get behind me," he said. "Something is coming, from inside the castle."

Miril felt a tremor of fear, then, and stepped backwards, away from the danger she sensed in the dark.

The sound of footsteps quickly approached them. There was the sound of coughing and gagging.

"Veelos?" Kl'aarn called out.

"It's us," she answered. "Thrake and I. Help us out of here."

Miril trembled. Despite the powerful amulet secreted in her robe, she felt fear. For although she had been alert to every kind of danger in the fortress, she had not expected that Veelos also would find there a weapon, and one suitable for a priestess.

But, to Miril's surprise, she had.

Chapter 32

Scripture and Anti-scriptures

Not until Thilgol's demonic fortress was far behind them did the chill at last leave their bones.

A shadow had seemed to follow them, haunting them, calling them to return, to return, to return. Indeed even now, some of the men looked back, longing for the dreams of riches and power they had so fleetingly realized, held in their very hands, and then lost.

When at last the castle disappeared from view, one could sense the wail of despair of demons, ghosts of evil spirits, which had invisibly pursued these men, pursued them until the demons had come to the end of the leash which chained them to their castle prison, a leash which now jerked them back into their dungeon, lest they, too, escape whatever master held them in thrall. The men, for whose flesh the demons lusted, had now slipped forever from their hellish, predatory grasp. Their wails of despair echoed silently to the horizon.

But even though the demons had finally been eluded, Thrake was haunted just the same. For, strapped to his side was the sword of Kmir, the sword of the man he had murdered. It was sheathed where Thrake's own sword once had rested, before he had shattered it, squandered it, against a demonic shield.

Never, Thrake knew, would this unfamiliar sword become truly his own. It would always remember that its true master was Kmir, not the one named Thrake who now bore it. And although Thrake would wield this sword (unlike the demonic blade, which had wielded him), he would also be obliged to carry Kmir's blade wherever Kmir himself would have carried it, and to wield it just as Kmir always had. For the sword no longer served the man, but rather, served the cause for which its owner had died. The warrior Thrake was bound to the weapon, by a code of honor which only men-at-arms can fully understand.

Engrossed in his melancholy thoughts, Thrake rode silently.

"Pray that you be rid of this poison," Veelos said to him.

Thrake was surprised to find the priestess riding at his side. For the others had avoided him.

"Pray that you rise from this gloom," she continued. "The guilt of Kmir's death is not yours alone to bear. We all bear it equally, I no less than you. There was evil in the sword you uncovered, a very great evil indeed. It was possessed. And when you touched it, the evil in that sword possessed you, also. But the guilt belongs to all of us. For we were all in a place we knew better than to venture into. None of us should have gone inside, least of all, me."

Thrake seemed to stir as if from a dream. He looked toward Veelos with a mixture of gratitude and shame. Then he said, somberly, "You say we all share the guilt. But I find no comfort in your saying that. For my guilt is no less than if I had acted alone. It was not because of the demon that I killed my friend and comrade. For even though the demon did indeed take hold of me, it knew exactly where to find its grasp. It had not far to search, to find a dark corner of my soul. The ghoul used not only my hand to murder Kmir, but it used also my evil."

Veelos replied, "So you discovered within yourself a dark nature. Welcome to the human race, Thrake. For we are all creatures fallen from God's grace. We do have a dark nature, and there is no limit to the evil into which we would descend, if we were without God's protection. But he provides that protection to those who trust in Him. So let's be thankful that God created us in His own image and likeness, a higher nature which preserves us from our corrupt instincts--- if only we allow it to."

"Don't preach to me," Thrake said despondently. "I appreciate your concern, but it doesn't help."

"But I must make you understand," Veelos said. "You must not be consumed by this guilt, but rather nourished by repentance."

"And you must understand," Thrake said, "that a short time ago I was preparing to kill even you. Even when I knew that you were ready to sacrifice your life for mine, even then, I had murder in my heart for you--- for you, personally. I'm not fit company for a priestess. For now that this terrible evil is awakened within me, I will never again feel safe from it. It could return at any time, and possess me once more."

But Veelos persisted. "Then all the more so, you must be told what really happened back there," she said. "When you held that blade over my head, your soul was flooded with darkness. It was your nature, stripped bare of all pretense. Only the slightest flicker of good remained within you, only a candle as against a dark, clouded sky, a candle placed in your soul at conception by God. But its tiny flicker was enough. You could have chosen to snuff it out, to darken your soul for all eternity. But instead, you allowed it to remain, and to shine. And when you did, you allowed its power to prevail. That is all any of us can do in the war between darkness and light. The only power any man has is the power to choose--- to choose between good and evil. And you chose to let the good prevail. That sword slipped from your hand not by accident, but because that tiny flame of Godliness drove it from you. You allowed the light within you to flourish. And it overcame what you could not: your own nature."

For a few moments, Thrake seemed to ponder what Veelos had told him. Then he said, "I am not a learned man, Priestess. All I know is the sword. All I know is that Kmir would have laid down his life for mine. Indeed, he often did. Yet by my hand he died. I am no longer worthy to be called a warrior. I am as base as any of these bandits we have allied ourselves with. I have become one of them."

It was Veelos's turn to ponder. She answered, "It is true that we have allied ourselves with bandits. But we have not allied ourselves with banditry. That may seem a minor point, but it makes a very big difference. Shalar and his men have done great evil. God will judge whether it was by their choosing or not. But as for you, Thrake, you have not chosen to do evil. God is a merciful judge."

"Then what of the witch?" Thrake challenged. "Can you say that she has not chosen evil? She has. So why do we ride with her? Is it not written that a witch must be burned?"

"It is," Veelos answered.

"Then why do we allow her among us? She has poisoned this entire quest. Surely you can see the venom she has injected into us. And while we grow fewer and weaker, the witch grows ever stronger. You also are a warrior, Priestess, a warrior against evil. Why do you not oppose Miril?"

Veelos trembled. "Now you are preaching to me, Thrake. No, do not apologize. You speak the truth. I should have opposed Miril from the very first. Just as Kl'aarn was prepared to find her a toothless hag and love her still, so I should have been prepared to find her a witch and to slay her. Because I did not, she grew more powerful, and I became weaker. Now, she is fearful to behold. Even so, I have a duty to do combat with her, to do it now. Had I more faith, I would do as you say. But if you are unworthy to be called warrior, Thrake, how less worthy am I to be called priestess. At least you released your demon. I have yet to let slip mine."

* * * * *

A few days journey carried the travelers ever farther from the demonic fortress which cursed the landscape. They had used up the last of their food, and the barren land provided none. The men began to despair, and to dread the prospect of starvation.

But, just as their fears became dire, they reached a new land, a land rich with well-watered meadows and abundant game. There, amid the lush greenery they had come into, food was plentiful for man and beast.

Vike's men scouted out a small lake, a small body that nourished them not only with clean water, but also, with an abundance of very large frogs, which the men gleefully speared, for a feast of frogs' legs. There, the party camped and rested for a night.

In the cool morning that followed, no one was in a hurry to start upon the journey again. Even Veelos, always urgent to hasten forward, took respite in the shade of the trees at the lake's edge.

"It is truly a garden of providence," she said to Vike. The priestess and the hunter strolled together by the water. "Look at all the delicious plants which grow here. I've never seen these kinds of fruits before, nor tasted their sweet flavors until now."

"Indeed," Vike agreed. "I've never seen the like. There are no such trees elsewhere but here, in this gentle and generous land. I think the entire world must once have been very much like this place, before the fall of Adam and Eve."

After awhile, they stopped walking, and found a resting-place. There, the two of them, hunter and priestess, sat close together at the edge of the lake. Veelos removed her sandals, and soaked her feet in the cool water, resting her back against a tree that shaded her with a canopy of broad leaves.

"I had always assumed," Veelos said, "that the reason no one ever returned alive, from the Lands of Demi-men, was because they all met some horrible fate. But perhaps that isn't so. Do you suppose that some might have found such places as this? Maybe they found places so beautiful that they could not bear to depart from them. I'm tempted myself to end our quest right here, and to live out my days at the edge of this lake. We could, you know.

The thought of returning to our own, maddened world could easily keep me here. The only thing that forces me to depart from this paradise is Druuk. His armies will trample this garden and destroy it--- unless we succeed against him."

"It is indeed a good land," Vike said. "Let's be thankful that no angel guards its entrance from human foot." He referred of course, to the angel who guards the entrance to the Garden of Eden, forbidding anyone to enter.

Veelos replied, "But, there is indeed, an angel here. He's not a sentry, though, but rather a gardener of sorts, one who tends and manicures this domain. I can sense his presence. Can you?"

"Then where is he?" Vike asked. "Why does he not show himself, as the angel showed himself to me, in the form of a panther?"

* * * * *

In another part of the shore, out of sight of the others, Miril and Kl'aarn also sat together in the shade. They looked across the shimmering beauty of the wind-rippled surface, and sensed the innate gentleness of the being which tended it, the gardening angel.

But the angel also sensed. He recognized Miril, and also the demonic power in her vestment, the amulet which preyed upon good. The angel took refuge in his lake, not in fear, but in obedience to a command from God.

Kl'aarn rested his head in Miril's lap, and looked up into her face, framed as it was by blue sky and billowy white clouds. But his mood was not one in which to appreciate beauty, not even beauty such as Miril's. "I just can't believe he's dead." Kl'aarn's tone was dreamlike, tinged with the aftershocks of recent mourning. "How suddenly a life can end. One moment, Kmir had plans, a future, a destiny for which he had been preparing all his life. And then--- it all came to nothing."

Miril combed through Kl'aarn's hair with her fingers. Silently she thought to herself, Kmir had escaped the hell which Miril had prepared for him. Else, all of Kl'aarn's and Shalar's men would even now be marching with vacant eyes, obedient to Miril's every command. The priestess had won a small victory in that. But it was a minor setback, all things considered. There would be time, later, for retribution. For now, it was enough that Kmir was no longer around to influence Kl'aarn against Miril, as he had. He had really, Miril thought to herself, become more than a mere nuisance. Were he yet alive, Kmir would already have become a threat. He and the priestess, together, might already have overpowered the demonwitch. But none of that mattered, now. Kmir was dead.

"I shouldn't have let Shalar take us in there," Kl'aarn said. Remorse permeated his words.

Miril replied consolingly, "Now, don't blame yourself. There was nothing you could do. If anyone's to blame, I am. I should have blinded Shalar with a spell to force his obedience to you."

Kl'aarn lifted his head. "No," he said. "You shouldn't. You should never cast spells. That only points out another mistake I've been making, Miril. First, I bound you to cast no spells, and then I went back on my word. When I asked for your magic, I hoped that evil means might have good results. But they can't. I see that, now. Evil deeds can have only evil results."

Miril smiled softly, and said gently, "Were it not for my spells, dear, we would all have been killed by now. You know that."

Kl'aarn relaxed back into Miril's embrace. "Yes," he said, "I can't deny that. But still--- the result of good must always be good, however difficult the immediate moment, however awful it seems at the time. But the result of evil only seems good, and only for a time. Then it turns out worse than the problem it promised to solve."

Miril laughed her gentle, soothing laugh. "So--- now you fancy yourself a philosopher, do you? But, dearest husband, when it comes to questions of good and evil, philosophy is not adequate to answer them. It is not even adequate to ask the right questions. Even you, with all your learning, confuse the word 'bad' for the word 'evil.' How can you puzzle out the difference between good and evil, when you cannot even perceive the difference between bad and evil?"

Kl'aarn frowned. "Bad, evil," he said. "They mean the same. Don't they?"

Miril shook her head, smiling. "No. Everyone thinks they are the same. But evil and 'bad' are not at all the same."

"Alright. How do they differ?"

Miril was happy to instruct. "'Bad' means--- well, unpleasant. Like a bad taste, for example. But 'evil' is never bad. 'Evil' means power, the power to force a desired result."

Kl'aarn thought about that. "All evil may be power," he allowed. "But not all power is evil. For there is also the power of Good. What about the Orb of Power?"

Miril laughed sweetly. "That just proves my point, beloved. The orbs are so delicate as to be vanishing from the earth. Soon there will be none--- all destroyed by evil."

"And," Kl'aarn asked, "if evil is not bad, then what of Good? Is good--- bad?"

Miril smiled tenderly. "You perceive keenly, my dear. The word 'good,' as men use it, is commonly taken to mean pleasant. But--- but the scriptural meaning has nothing to do with pleasantry. Good, as opposed to evil, is not at all pleasant, Kl'aarn. Good has to do with submission and self-denial. These are what divine scriptures mean, by the word, 'Good.' But, can this goodness--- this submission and self-denial--- can they ever bring pleasure? Of course not! The mere suggestion is a cruel prank. Oh, Kl'aarn! If men could only see the true nature of good and evil, they would choose evil. They would understand that evil is merely a way of fulfilling themselves, a way of achieving a prosperous world. Then, the things we mistakenly call evil would cease to exist: murder, robbery, rape and all the other terrible injustices. They would be no more."

"Now wait," Kl'aarn said. "Are you saying that evil men do not do those things?"

"Are you saying," Miril asked in return, "that good men don't? Of course they do, no less so than evil men do. Have not wars been waged in the name of Good? Oh, the bloodiest of wars they were, too. Kl'aarn, the forces of evil want only to free everyone from the slavery--- from the bondage--- which inhibits men from achieving their highest destiny. Oh, darling, I wish we had time to explain it all. But we don't, not yet. All I can ask of you for now, my love, is to keep an open mind. Be patient. The true natures of both good and evil will unfold before our eyes in the days to come. You will see, you will see that difference, and you will be able to make the sensible choice between them. Your blindness will vanish in the darkness."

"But," Kl'aarn said, "I believe that it is you who are blind, Miril."

"Am I?" Miril returned. "I have read the divine scriptures. You haven't. I know them more thoroughly than even Veelos does." A subtle rage began to erupt in her words. "But, unlike Veelos, I have also read the underscriptures of the demons. My dearest Kl'aarn, you have sampled only the morsels, the scraps cast from heavenly tables. But I have tasted the wines of both good and of evil. The wine of good is bitter, my love, though you are drunk with its remorse. I know, for I was once as you are. Then I tasted the wine of evil, and found it both sweet and strong, a welcome deliverance from the tyranny of what is called by the name, 'good.' You will taste it, too, when you are ready. And you will be ready. You, too, will gain the vision of darkness, which empowers me. Such power! Then, darling, then you will you make your choosing, just as I made mine. The light will no longer blind you. The darkness will free you to see. When you drink from the well of darkness itself, as you shall, then you will become as I am, and we will be together forever. Forever!"

* * * * *

Veelos shuddered, as if the cool day had suddenly become chill and stormy.

Vike noticed it, and asked with concern, "What is it? What's wrong, Priestess?"

Veelos nervously replaced her sandals onto her feet, and bringing herself to a standing position, said, "We must go now, quickly. For a horrible curse has been uttered on this sacred ground."

Vike stood also, but without the sudden fear Veelos felt. He intended to reassure her, to help her settle her frayed nerves. It was just her imagining, he wanted to say. Nothing was amiss. No curse stained sacred ground this day.

But just as Vike began to speak, his eyes caught a glimpse of a fish nearby in the lake. It was floating belly up, dead.

Chapter 33

The Handiwork of Evil, the Craft of a False Priestess

The road, which had led them from the castle, continued westward through a land of bounty. Its terrain became increasingly beautiful, and more friendly, with each passing day. The touch of God was easy to behold in the land through which they were passing. Nature was sculpted in its most gentle expressions, harmonized and balanced. Food was plentiful; fruits and wild grains were all about. Water was abundant and pure.

Even the air was so clean that Veelos remarked to Vike about it. "We shouldn't even be building this fire," she said to the hunter, as they made camp. "Its smoke is an affront, like wearing muddy boots into a palace."

Vike agreed. "I, too, feel guilt. The men demand meat, and so I hunt. But, these animals we cook, were less hunted than slaughtered. We are as sinners in a sinless land."

Miril had ventured near them, and as usual when she did so, both Veelos and Vike felt exceeding discomfort. But Miril had heard them speaking, and she said to them, "Enjoy this while you can. Even the bandits would receive scripture in times such as these, times of ease and leisure. But this won't last. Before we reach Druuk's kingdom, we must first cross the land which swallowed up a legion of his elite soldiers. There, against we know not what, we will do battle. It will be combat such as no man has ever seen, not seen and survived."

Both Veelos and Vike glanced uncomfortably at each other, expecting Miril to leave her cryptic words behind, for them to ponder..

But the demonwitch stepped even closer to them, insulted by their unease at her presence. And with anger at the edges of her eyes, she said, "So. You two deem yourselves too good to carry on conversation with me. We'll see how you feel about that when, once again as before, you have need of my powers."

Then, releasing pent anger, Veelos retorted, "We have never needed your powers, Miril. For what you call power is only ignorance."

"How dare you lecture me?" Miril sneered in reply. "How dare you presume to be wiser than me? You eat the forbidden fruit just as I do. You savor the fruit of evil when it serves you, and when it has done so, you spit out its seed. But I plant those seeds, Veelos. In my soul they grow, to bear yet more evil fruit, ever more. I'm no hypocrite as you are."

Veelos turned to walk away.

But Miril called after her. "Hear my prophecy," she said. "For I prophesy this: Before we reach Druuk's kingdom, you shall once again call me sister. The next time my powers are called upon, and my might is summoned forth, the pleading words shall come not from Kl'aarn, but from your own mouth, Veelos, and from your own heart. Yes! You, O holy and pure priestess: you shall call upon my evil sorcery to destroy a great good. This I prophesy."

Then Veelos turned and faced Miril once more. "Then hear also my prophecy," the priestess said. Her voice was a burning ember, subdued but fiery. "I know you found, in Thilgol's fortress, whatever charm you sought against me. And you have placed your faith in it, and in yourself. But in the end, Miril, in the end, evil destroys not good, but destroys only itself. Enjoy your evil while you can, Demonwitch. For the moment is fleeting, but eternity is forever."

Then Miril lifted her chin, and said, "Excellent! It is a contest then. We shall see whose prophecy is the stronger." With that, she turned and walked away.

* * * * *

Early the following morning, they embarked again upon the journey. At mid-morning, Shalar peered ahead on the road and said, "That's Valmark. He's reporting back early from the scouting foray, alone--- and he seems in a hurry. I knew this respite couldn't last."

Valmark indeed was in a hurry, and his horse reached the front of the columns at nearly a full gallop before he could rein it to a sudden halt near to Shalar.

"Well?" Shalar asked Valmark, "what obstacle lies now in our path?"

Valmark did indeed have something unusual to report. But as to whether it was bad news or good was a question yet unanswered. "There is a city," he told the priestess.

By this time, Kl'aarn and Miril had joined Shalar and Veelos at the fore of the double column.

"It's a city of polished stone," Valmark continued. "It is inhabited, by perhaps five hundred to a thousand--- but not by men."

"By demi-men, of course," Kl'aarn supplied. "Describe them."

Valmark replied, "I saw them only from a distance and cannot supply detail. But they walk upright, and have a slender shape. And they ride upon beasts that look much like deer, but large and broad. When we first saw the city, Vike commanded Belgar and me to remain, while he rode forward to show himself, to test what reaction there might be to his presence."

Veelos was alarmed by this. "He did what? And you let him?" For she was reminded how Vike had offered himself up as bait to Morgrar's men.

"We gave in to his demand," Valmark said, "for from the looks of the city, these creatures do not appear to be wild and savage, but clean and civilized. Belgar remains at a distance to keep watch, and I was dispatched to report to you."

Veelos asked, "How did the demi-men respond to Vike's advance?"

"Three riders came out from the city," Valmark replied. "They wear flowing robes, so I could not see if they were armed. Nor could I see enough to know whether they are fanged and clawed. But if their demeanor can be interpreted, they seemed peaceful and curious, although I am sure that they must also be suspicious and fearful. The three demi-men dismounted from the beasts upon which they ride, and Vike dismounted from his horse. As I left Belgar to report to you, I saw the four sitting at the roadside, looking as if they were trying to communicate."

Veelos absorbed all of this, and remarked, "A city of polished stone--- in the midst of the Lands of Demi-men! We had feared much worse than that indeed!"

But Kl'aarn said, "Don't raise your hopes just yet, Veelos. We've met nothing friendly in these lands so far."

"Perhaps not," Veelos agreed. "But we have seen beauty in them. Even amid the wilderness, we have seen that once it was a garden. So let's do nothing hostile unless provoked. And let's hope for the best. For behind us is no safe retreat."

* * * * *

By noon, the party reached the crest of a ridge overlooking the city. They saw. And indeed, a city it was, no mere village. A wall surrounded it, providing fortification. Outside the walls lay a number of dwellings and farms. Inside the walls, one could make out what were unmistakably stone buildings, buildings of a size that confirmed a civilization dwelt here, and one capable of elaborate architecture.

But what caught Veelos's eye, before anything else, was the largest of all the edifices, the one in the center of the city. For its architecture was distinctly different from that of the rest of the city. Only in one other place had Veelos seen such a magnificent, gleaming dome.

"It's a temple," she breathed. "A temple built by God's angels."

Kl'aarn nodded. "A double to the one in Shi-Raq."

Veelos tried not to weep. "Is it possible that, even among demi-men, the priesthood might yet live?"

"Let's hope so," Kl'aarn said. "But keep your caution, Veelos. That thing was built more than a thousand years ago, before the Upheaval."

Just then, Veelos scanned the roadway ahead, and afar her gaze found Vike. He was in a half-kneeling squat, drawing in the dust with a stick. The three demi-men, whom Valmark had reported upon, were attentive to what Vike was drawing. They were as Valmark had described them, slender of frame, somewhat shorter than Vike, and distinctly not human in appearance, even from this distance.

But if Veelos had welcomed the sight of a temple among them, her spirits now rose even higher. "That one," she pointed. "He wears white with blue trim! The cut of his robes are as mine. Kl'aarn, I think he is a priest."

"I hate to be a damper," Kl'aarn said, "but I warn you against over-optimism. Let's hope for good, and prepare for evil."

"They burn witches," Miril said.

Kl'aarn and Veelos were both startled at Miril's sudden appearance behind them, for they had not noticed her approach. For a long moment, both of them, even Kl'aarn, felt too awkward to speak.

Then Kl'aarn looked to Veelos. "You say they might be priests. If they are, then what do you think they'll do--- when they see Miril?"

Veelos hesitated, then stammered. "I don't know."

But Miril scoffed, "Don't you? You won't avoid the issue that easily, Veelos. Tell the truth for once. These creatures are the descendants of a race of demi-men who once allied themselves with Tarok against Kattaroon."

"Only in legend," Veelos replied. "The scriptures make no mention---"

"Nor denies them," Miril said. "But it's plain to see that these animals will kill me on sight--- if they can."

Then Kl'aarn looked again at Veelos. "Is that true?"

Veelos glanced first at Miril, then at the demi-men, the city, and finally at Kl'aarn. "If they are priests," she replied, her voice slightly tremorous, "then surely, they know the prophecies, just as the priests in Shi-Raq, who feared that the Demonwitch would come among them and destroy them. Scripture warns of this. So. Instead of asking what these priests will do to Miril, ask her what she will do to them."

Uncertainly, Kl'aarn turned to Miril. "This enmity between priests and witches: will it turn your hand against these demi-men?"

Miril answered. "No. I have no quarrel with these beasts. Let them live. Let me live."

"She lies," Veelos said.

Miril seemed to snarl, "Who accuses, false priestess?"

But Kl'aarn immediately forced his way between the two women. "Now look," he said. "If these demi-men are indeed as docile as they seem, then we can avoid a confrontation. Veelos, you and I will go down there and join Vike. Perhaps we can find a way to ask safe passage. That's all we'll need---safe passage, nothing more. Miril, you are to stay completely out of their sight."

"Yes, my dear," Miril answered. "But of course."

* * * * *

Vike had never seen such creatures as these. They seemed almost as deerlike as the large beasts of burden upon which they rode. But whereas the beasts were clearly beasts, the demi-men were far more than that. Despite that they looked nothing like humans, their appearance conveyed a distinctly manlike impression.

Their faces were elongated like that of deer, and the eyes were not set all the way to the front, but angled off slightly to the sides. The ears were set high on the head, pointed and somewhat mobile. Their hair was sparse, but even, all over, wherever the clothing did not conceal. The hands had four fingers and a thumb, but the index finger was the longest of all.

Vike did his best to read their mood. But whereas one could read the expressions and gestures of any human, however foreign, the mannerisms of these creatures could not be interpreted. How nervous were they? How suspicious? How might one tell if they were on the verge of panic or violence? And how were they interpreting Vike? He tried to sort through these questions.

All along, the demi-men had been aware that Vike was not alone. This had not seemed to alarm them. But when they saw the top of the ridge fill with some fifty humans and their horses, Vike noted a change in their mannerism. They glanced repeatedly back and forth between each other, Vike and the ridge. Their ears seemed to strain for any sound.

Finally, when Kl'aarn and Veelos began to descend the ridge, the deerlike demi-men stood up, and carefully positioned themselves near their large, antlered beasts of burden.

When Veelos saw the demi-men rise, her first impression was that she was being formally greeted. But then it occurred to her that their act was one of prudent suspicion. They seemed ready, either to flee, or to fight. However gentle these creatures themselves might be, Veelos knew, they lived in a land where surely there were more enemies than friends. If need be, they could well defend themselves.

The priestess instructed Kl'aarn, "It's better that you stay back here. They're nervous enough as it is, and your armament won't make things better."

Kl'aarn replied, "I don't like the looks of this, Veelos."

"What else can we do?" Veelos pointed out. "Let me go forward alone. Here, hold my horse while I approach them on foot."

Hoping to soothe any fears the demi-men might have, Veelos dismounted and slowly walked the remaining distance, trying to appear as meek and docile as she could. Kl'aarn's warnings to her had been with effect. Veelos felt the unwelcome stirrings of fear, fear that was a pale reminder of the terror she had felt when the short, squat brown demi-man had abducted her, no doubt intending to make a meal of her. And although these demi-men appeared more vegetarian than the others, they were demi-men no less.

As Veelos stood among the group of them, Vike and the demi-men, she made out the final details of what sort of creatures she faced. They were not of human stock. Any similarities were only as those of a whale to a fish, a matter of form, but not of ancestry. Veelos wondered if they had souls.

She was comforted at least in that they appeared not to be carnivores, more like deer by far than like wolves. Their slender appearance did not, however, speak of frailty.

But after noting all the ways in which the demi-men were different from her own kind, Veelos suddenly felt a sense of kinship with them, a kinship she had not in many weeks felt with humans. For upon the robes of one, inscribed in blue trim, were words in the ancient language of scripture. Veelos could read them, not only read them, but even recognize the very passages of scripture from which they were drawn. All those long hours of midnight study in the temple, under Keesha's stern tutelage, had carved those words in her mind.

She hoped the robed one could as easily read the words inscribed upon her own vestments. The thought of being able to communicate with creatures so alien filled her with excitement.

"Wo ken jee tar," she said. It was an ancient greeting, a blessing between priests.

The demi-men had clearly taken notice of her white garb. Their gazes had fixed upon the blue trim and white lettering. But they seemed not to understand the words she spoke.

Veelos's hopes sank. Imitators, she thought. More complex than parrots, more clever than the cleverest animal, but nothing more. These creatures had once been pets, perhaps even beasts of intellectual burden, owned by human beings. After the humans had died out, the animals which survived had continued to mimic their former owners. Monkey see.... but only outwardly. The interior was hollow.

Veelos remembered that the demi-men which had attacked the travelers had wielded the weaponry of humans. But their real weapons, those to which they had resorted in the frenzy of battle, had been their claws and fangs. The rest had been but mere imitation. They could use a weapon, but not fashion one. They kept alive ancient human customs, but only in form, not in substance.

And these deerlike creatures could copy inscriptions, but not understand them.

Finally, one of the two demi-men, wearing what Veelos deemed to be commoner garb, spoke to the one in priestly vestments. The voice was fluid, and the language seemed to be tonal, with few consonants. The sounds were staccato and clipped. It was surely no human language, and Veelos wondered if translation were even possible. How does one translate the sounds of a rushing brook?

The one with seeming authority, in priest cloth, looked carefully at Veelos, turning his head slightly first to one side, then to the other, as if letting each eye take her in separately, as if each eye served a different visual function.

Veelos decided to try once more, this time by words written. Slowly, she knelt, and with a stick, scratched out four symbols on the ground, so that to the demi-men, they were right side up. Then, pointing at each symbol in turn as she pronounced them, Veelos repeated, "Wo ken jee tar."

The one in priest cloth then knelt also, and pointing to each symbol, spoke. To Veelos, it sounded something like, "Wah gen jeh dah."

Alas, nothing more than mere imitation, Veelos thought.

The creature then scratched out four more syllables. "Or zeh nah dib."

Veelos pronounced the syllables in the way she had been taught. "Ur see no tib." It meant, "Woman wearing priest cloth."

Veelos wondered at this. Were they merely describing what they saw of her, or were they questioning what they saw? If the latter, they might be sentient. Perhaps. Just perhaps.

She scrawled out the words which meant, "I am priestess."

Again, the creatures fell silent. Veelos prompted them further, by writing a question. "Do you not ordain women?"

The reply formed on the soil, a quote from scripture. "Let all be ordained who are called."

Veelos was dissatisfied. Were they responding to her question, she wondered, or merely reciting a repertoire, however impressive, of scripture without understanding?

"Yet you have never seen a priestess," Veelos scrawled.

"Until now. The ring is upon your finger."

Veelos breathed a sigh of relief. Perhaps these beings had souls after all.

"My name is Veelos," she said. Throughout, both she and the demi-men had been speaking as they wrote. Already, Veelos could detect their pattern of speech. Perhaps soon, they could understand each others' pronunciation of the ancient script.

In writing: "I am Shay-Toom, high priest of the Land of Ki-Rori. Wo ken jee tar. Is your arrival here an omen?"

"If so, a good one we hope," Veelos answered, as she wrote. "For though we bring no material gift, we are upon an urgent pursuit which concerns all who worship the one true God."

Shay-Toom responded, scrawling in the dust. "Tell us of this pursuit. For indeed, our visionaries have seen visions of great import. What brings humans into the land of Ki-Rori?"

Veelos laboriously explained to Shay-Toom who she was, and the task upon which she had been set. She mapped out as best she could the East Land, from Har-Keem, to Shi-Raq, to the domains of the bandit-lords. She described the crossing of the river, the attack by the squat, brown-haired demi-men, the castle of Thilgol, and the garden beyond it. And she emphasized the need to retrieve or destroy the Orb before Druuk subverted it to evil.

"And that is why," she concluded, "we beg of you that we may pass through your domain, and be swiftly upon our way."

Shay-Toom had been attentive, frequently interrupting with questions which Veelos answered. As Veelos's narration had progressed, there had become less and less need for writing every syllable. Gradually, they had become accustomed to each others' separate corruptions of the sacred tongue.

When Veelos had done, Shay-Toom stood, contemplating the matter in silence. After a time, he turned to his two companions, and spoke to them in their infathomable language. Veelos strained at trying to intimate any trace of what they were saying. Were they suggesting means to help her, or plotting some sudden treachery? But there was no more of guessing their mannerisms than of deciphering the meaning of their (perhaps?) wordless language. Did they even believe any of Veelos's story? She did not know.

Finally, the high priest again spoke to Veelos in the ancient tongue. "You have told us who you are. Now we know to whom we speak. We will also tell you who we are, so that you will know who speaks to you."

Veelos found herself impatient. She wanted to get these talks over with and be quickly away. But obviously, the Ki-Rori did not do things in any great hurry. Their minds did not work in the way of human minds. And Veelos dared not be abrupt with them.

"We are the Ki-Rori," Shay-Toom began. "We have lived in these lands for ages beyond memory. Your kind also once lived here, among us, and in harmony with us. Behold our temple. It was built in the days of Tarok, Warrior of God. It was he who taught us as the angels had taught him. We accepted him, a human, as our king and prophet. He ruled wisely, and we prospered.

"When the forces of Hell conspired against creation, the demons raised a mighty army, first from among those you call demi-men, and then also of men. These marched against us. Against this fearsome host, Tarok led us into battle. We followed. We fought. We prevailed. The demonic armies were vanquished. Defeated, the demons took to fighting among themselves, seeking to exploit the weakened state of other demons. To what advantage?

Only a demon could imagine. But after all, is not treachery their very essence?

"But just when it seemed that Tarok had won a total and complete victory, he was undone by a woman. Her name was Kat-Tar-Hahn. Tarok loved her. But she had given her soul to evil, and so she was forbidden to him.

"The witch seduced Tarok. He listened not to the truth, but rather to her sweet lies. He fell under her power. Only too late did he awaken to his fatal error. For when Kat-Tar-Hahn found she could not turn Tarok to evil, she killed him.

"Leaderless, Tarok's human legions quickly fell beneath the witch's thrall. She turned them against us, the Ki-Rori, and attacked. For the witch wielded the Amulet of Doom, a talisman which turns good against good.

"It was not our wish to battle our human brothers. We had come to recognize them as our superiors, as beings destined to survive the coming flood. But we fought. It was the bloodiest battle Wirik had ever seen. Fewer than one of us in a thousand survived. But in the end, the last of Kat-Tar-Hahn's forces had been annihilated, and she was no more.

"Tarok, who had brought the world so close to Eden, had failed. Evil had not been vanquished from the world. That day had been pushed far into the future.

"The forms of demi-men which surround us degenerated into their animal natures, keeping of humanity only the worst which they had learned from men. Except for our faith in God, we would be as they are.

"It is us to whom you speak, Priestess Vee-Los. Wah ken jeh dah."

At first, Veelos had been impatient with the telling of the story. She had heard it many times before, first at the knee of Valen Elder, and later in the studies in the temple. But this was different. This time, Veelos had heard the story told in the ancient tongue, from one who lived in Tarok's native land, and upon the very battlefield where the legendary war had concluded.

It was as close as one could come to having witnessed it. Veelos could almost picture the catastrophic scene, the clashing of thousands upon thousands of swords, the sky darkened by clouds of arrows raining down their lethal burden, and that same sky pierced by the deadly lightning bolts hurled by sorcerors. The din of battle must have been deafening. And the terrain, Veelos visualized it, the soil soaked with the blood of all those thousands of fierce warriors.

It had happened. To stand upon this hallowed ground was to know that.

Veelos shook herself from the vision. A thousand years had passed since that day, fifty generations. The millennium had come full cycle. Once again, another Upheaval was under way. Veelos wondered, would civilization once more be reduced to rubble? She knew that could be averted. But the outcome depended upon her. The fate of Wirik rested in her trembling hands.

Veelos spoke. "As it was in the days of Tarok, so also is it again in our day. That is why our pursuit concerns you as much as it does us. We haste. I beg safe passage through Ki-Rori."

"No." Shay-Toom said the single word.

Veelos was shaken. For a moment she did not believe her ears. Or perhaps Shay-Toom had misunderstood. Veelos knelt, and with hands unsteady, traced out the symbols to convey her question once more.

But Shay-Toom had neither misunderstood the question nor misspoken his answer. "You are not," he said carefully, "granted passage through our domain."

Veelos stood. "But," she asked, "why not?"

Shay-Toom answered, "As it was between us and Tarok's men, so it is between us and your men. None of you shall pass."

Veelos was baffled and angry. "Is that it? Do you carry on the bloodfeud, begun those centuries ago by Tarok's men, who turned against your kind?"

"You misunderstand," Shay-Toom said. "Tarok was seduced by the demonwitch. As it was with him, so is it with you. We recognize and honor you as a fellow worshipper of the one true God. But you are not whom you say you are, though you believe it yourself. You are not the Priestess of Prophecy."

Veelos tried to restrain her frustration. But she found it difficult to comport herself with priestly dignity. "I am set upon this task," she said, "by my slain high priest, Lar of Shi-Raq. It was he who named me the Priestess of Prophecy."

But Shay-Toom said, "You travel in companionship with a witch, a most powerful and terrible witch. Your task is hopeless while yet she lives. Worse, it is her plot to turn you to evil. You cannot begin to imagine the fate which awaits you among her schemes. Why do you not destroy her, straight away? Is your desire for her husband so strong?"

Veelos was grateful that neither Vike nor Kl'aarn could understand the ancient language. Even so, her face turned red with embarrassment. "I desire not the man."

"You do. It is plain. If you do battle against the witch, then he will do battle against you. You deem it would harden his heart against you. But even him you lead to ruin. Cast aside this forbidden lust which nests in the dark, secret places of your heart. Challenge the witch once and for all. End it here and now."

"I can't," Veelos said. "She would kill me."

Shay-Toom considered this, then said, "Then lead me to her. I will do it."

Veelos trembled at Shay-Toom's single-minded, persistent, devotion. "She would slay you also, high priest."

Shay-Toom seemed to nod. "Perhaps. That is of no concern."

"I respect your convictions," Veelos said. "Please respect mine. There will come a moment when I have become equipped to duel the witch. Then I will. But not before. Entrust me as Lar did."

But Shay-Toom replied, "There will indeed come a moment. But by then, it is not you who will have become equipped, but the witch. I tell you, it is better to die this moment against the witch than to live a single instant in a world she rules."

"Just let us pass," Veelos begged. "We ask nothing more. You must not deny us this request. At least let me try."

"You alone may pass," Shay-Toom said. "But not the witch. Nor any man who loves her, or serves her, or follows her. In their place, we offer our hundred best warriors."

"I can't leave any of my men to her," Veelos pleaded.

"Your refusal," Shay-Toom said, "speaks for itself. But in no wise will we ever permit our land to be trod by any witch. These words are final, this resolve is unbending."

For a moment, Veelos's faith encountered the brick wall of doubt, and could not surmount it. Shay-Toom's wisdom was subtle, she knew, his perceptions keen. And he was more right than she cared to admit. Perhaps there was, after all, a residue of forbidden desire in her heart for Kl'aarn. Perhaps. If so, then what paradox this emotion called love, she lamented, as she had once before, long ago in Har-Keem, so necessary for good, yet so handily the instrument of evil?

"Very well," Veelos said stiffly. "We shall retreat from your domain at once, as it is your right to command. But your intransigence has not defeated our task. You merely exact a more severe price from among the lives of noble men. For we will go around your land, not through. The cost in time, and in lives lost, is upon your conscience, not mine."

Shay-Toom seemed to sigh. "I do not dictate your path," he said. "It is of your own choosing. But the only detour around Ki-Rori is traced by the footprints of Thilgol. For to our north lies a great sea of boiling mud. Its surface swirls with the movements of monsters which dwell therein. And to our south is a land of insects the size of men, who live in great swarms, and who sometimes wage war against us, for they savor warm-blooded flesh.

"No, Priestess Veelos. Your only path is through Ki-Rori. As for the path of the demonwitch--- it must end, either here, or else--- or else upon a throne of power too terrible to contemplate."

Veelos turned away from Shay-Toom, and angrily strode a few paces toward where Kl'aarn stood with her horse. Then, stopping, and turning once more to face Shay-Toom, Veelos said, "I make one final plea. Do not visit this travail upon me. I have enough to bear as it is."

Shay-Toom answered, "We do nothing against you, but for you. Our lives we offer freely in your contest with the witch. Merely abandon her, and we offer you the throne of high priestess in our temple. Choose good, Veelos, while yet you can."

* * * * *

Miril already knew.

"Another failure," she sneered when Veelos, Vike and Kl'aarn returned to the camp which had been set up. "So far, your record of achievement is unblemished by success. Oh, I could understand your failure to persuade the likes of Morgrar. He was evil. But you cannot persuade even your fellow worshippers in the slightest thing. When will you learn, Priestess? There is no power in good. There is power only in power itself."

Kl'aarn was as dismayed as Miril was vindictive. "Is there no way to reason with these creatures?" he asked in frustration. "Surely they know, we mean them no harm. Then why do they oppose us?"

Veelos could not answer. She could not bring herself to tell Kl'aarn that Shay-Toom had sensed the presence of a witch. She could not bear to tell him that a high priest commanded her to kill the woman whom Kl'aarn loved. And most of all, Veelos could not speak of the shameful feelings which somehow kept resurfacing whenever she began to believe herself free of them.

Only Shalar's timely intervention spared Veelos from embarrassment. "The question," the bandit said, "is not why, but rather, how. How do we get through?"

Kl'aarn turned his attention to Shalar. "And does the metalsmith have an answer to this puzzle?"

Shalar replied. "My scouts have surveyed the city. There are many among the demi-men who carry swords. And in the forests to our south are many more of them, sentries with bow and arrow. So that leaves the northern path."

"We'll try that way, then," Kl'aarn suggested.

But Veelos was forced to reveal the distressing truth. "The north offers no passage at all. Shay-Toom says it is a sea of boiling mud, in which great monsters swim."

"A tale to force tribute from us," Shalar scoffed.

But Veelos retorted, "His motive is not so crass. Nor would he lie to us. Whatever else, he is high priest, a servant of God."

Miril interjected. "Even if there were a long way around, why should we suffer it? Nothing so far has been able to stand against us. Nor can these creatures."

"Kl'aarn," Veelos implored, "we can't do anything violent against these folk. They are the gentlest inhabitants of all Wirik. Even in opposing us they mean us no harm."

"Liar," Miril accused. "They mean you no harm. As for me, and as for the likes of Shalar, they stand in judgment. Admit it. They urged you to kill me, did they not? Why don't you answer, Veelos?"

"Very well. They did." Veelos felt her face turning red.

But Kl'aarn did not react angrily. "I have a thought," he offered. "Miril and I can move at night by stealth. The rest of the party can travel openly. If the Ki-Rori see you without the witch, they would give you passage, no?"

"No. It would never work," Veelos answered. "Oh, at first it would. They would offer us food and supplies. But they would also want to know what became of the witch. And when I could not answer them---"

"Then lie to them," Shalar suggested.

But Miril sneered, "The priestess is too pure to lie. Except, of course, when it suits her own purpose."

"Even if I did lie," Veelos said, "they would know. The ruse won't work,

Kl'aarn. No trick will deceive them."

Kl'aarn turned back to Shalar again. "These sentry archers to our south. We might be able to elude them under cover of darkness."

Shalar nodded. "I know what you're thinking. Yes, my men can get past them."

Then of Vike, Kl'aarn asked, "Can one of your men map a path through the south forest, before darkness, without being detected?"

"Belgar can search one out," Vike said.

"No!" Veelos objected. "Vike, you can't cooperate in this. We cannot take up arms against these creatures. We just can't!"

But Vike replied soothingly. "I don't think Kl'aarn intends that. If sentries watch the southern border, their concern must be to watch for invaders from the south. We will find a path behind them, where their attention is not focused. Then we'll move at night. Warriors and bandits have skill at stealth and maneuver. What better hope have we?"

Miril remained dissatisfied. "Why all this skulking about? We have nothing to fear of any archer or swordsman among them."

Kl'aarn ignored her. "It's decided then. Belgar will report back before sundown with a map that gets us past the city. At sundown, we'll move out. Once we have the city to our back, it will be daylight. By then, we can rely on speed to elude these demi-men. Veelos, have you a better idea?"

"She does," Miril said. "But it involves burning a witch. Say so, Priest-ess."

"Are you challenging me?" Veelos dared to say.

Miril laughed. "You would welcome that, wouldn't you? Win or lose, you would be delighted to have the choice thrust upon you. And you would lose, Veelos. You know you would."

Veelos turned away from her enemy. "We still have a few hours before nightfall," she said to Kl'aarn and Shalar. “Let those who can, get some sleep."

* * * * *

The hand which nudged Veelos awake belonged to Vike. "The men are ready," he said.

Veelos was instantly alert, and quickly shook off whatever bad dream had troubled her brief nap. It was twilight. At the time when camp was normally being settled, it had been broken. A number of bonfires burned, but these were meant to deceive.

"Would you like a moment of prayer?" Vike asked.

Veelos pulled on the hood of her vestment. She asked, "Is it wrong to pray insincerely?"

Vike frowned. "Why such a question?"

Veelos shook her head. "I don't know," she answered, "what to pray for. Success? At what? My life is becoming like Shalar's, a web of schemes and plots. Just as he runs from the law, so I've become a fugitive from a high priest. Like Thrake, I'm finding the dark places of my soul. For what success should I pray?"

"For the quest," Vike answered.

But Veelos replied, "It's no longer the quest that propels me along the path, but only the cadence of the steps. All these little distractions have taken over. The details dominate my hours, not the purpose. I've lost sight of the one goal that matters."

Vike helped lift Veelos to her feet. "Those little distractions matter, too. How you handle them determines how you will handle the main event. They are preparation."

Veelos was not encouraged. "Shay-Toom says that I am not the Priestess of Prophecy, Vike. What if he is right? What if I have not her destiny? Then all this is for nothing. Then none of us will emerge alive from these Lands of Demi-men. All is futility."

"Only in the end will we know that," Vike answered. "Failures will abound, of that we can be sure. But God never fails. Of that, we can be even more sure. Let these words we have just said serve as our prayer, then, and let's be on our way."

* * * * *

Kl'aarn allowed Shalar to take charge. The bandit was master of evasion. He had seen to it personally that the axles of the wagon were well greased. He had personally inspected every man's armor to ensure that no metal object would rattle against another, and that no glint of bronze would betray them. Even the horses seemed to understand the necessity of stealth.

Lastly, Shalar divided the party into small groups, so that no large number would be trapped if anything went wrong. Each group began its maneuver as soon as Shalar gave it the signal.

Before anyone could have second thoughts, the invasion had begun. There would be no turning back.

Inside the forest, blackness ruled. Only an occasional star, glimpsed through the treetops, made sense of direction possible. The blackness was now become an ally.

As Kl'aarn led Miril through the forest, he could not see her. She blended into the night as if inseparable from it. He could be sure of her nearness only by that ineffable sense that lovers have for each other.

Nervously, he felt for his sword, although it would provide no protection from any arrow which might be launched against them. Sudden death could impale any moment. Helpless. Miril wore no armor. Kl'aarn discovered himself unable to protect her, as helpless as he had been that night so long ago, when Har-Keem had died. He began to pray, but as suddenly as he began, stopped. What prayer could one say for a witch?

Then, a moment of madness, just a very brief moment. It passed, and Kl'aarn breathed a sigh of relief. For the briefest moment, he had questioned the entire venture. For a flickering instant, Kl'aarn had felt hot anger. What was he doing here? How could any man come to a state in which he escorted his wife forward into battle? One night, six years gone, he had sent Shalar to turn Miril away from battle. He had sent her into the forest, into the night.

She had never returned from it.

* * * * *

Somehow, the long night had passed without incident. No sound had reached Kl'aarn's ear, no battle-cry of sentries, no clash of swords, no rush of hooves. Silence had ruled in collusion with the darkness. Almost too soon, Kl'aarn thought, the stars grew more dim. The night sky had begun its daily transformation into dawn.

Glancing to his right, Kl'aarn became alarmed. For not many arrowflights distant, the walls of the Ki-Rori city could be seen. They were only just now passing it. The price of stealth had been paid in lost speed. Together the sun, the thinning forest, and time, had conspired against the creeping humans.

Then the conspiracy was sprung. There was an outcry not quite human. A relay of voices took up the call.

Kl'aarn turned to Miril. "They're on to us," he began to say. He had expected to see her startled. He had thought to find in her eyes the fear of witch-burners.

But Miril was composed, assured.

Women, the thought occurred to Kl'aarn, don't react like that.

"It's too late," Miril said to him, "for stealth. We can't afford to slow each other down. We'll rendezvous."

"No," Kl'aarn replied. "We'll stay together."

"It's death if we do," Miril insisted. Then without a further word, she kicked her horse's flanks, and disappeared into a twilit thicket of trees.

Angrily, Kl'aarn raced after her. But in the trees, his horse could not maneuver with anything like the speed of Miril's mount. Recognizing that she was using more than mere horsemanship to elude him, Kl'aarn cursed. Then, selecting a more open trail, he made for the rendezvous.

* * * * *

Thrake found himself at the edge of a break in the trees. Through the dim light of dawn, he saw that there was a wide swath of partially cleared land, beyond which the forest resumed. The warrior paused, wondering whether this land had been cleared as a gallery for archers.

A movement to his right caught Thrake's attention. It was Hathor, arriving at the edge of the forest, also hesitating to venture any further. Soon after, Thrake recognized a warrior named Larek afar to his left. Slowly, more riders appeared beyond these two, all equally suspicious of what might well prove to be their killing ground.

There were the sounds of approaching hooves, but not of horses. The hoofbeats came from the direction of the city. The local militia were responding quickly to the alarms sounded by their watchmen.

Thrake felt time slipping swiftly. If the humans waited any longer to risk the open, there would soon be a wall of Ki-Rori cavalry before them. Archers or no, the only choice was between attack and death. Thrake chose attack.

As soon as his spurred horse had carried him into the open, Thrake heard the whistle of an arrow whip past him. He was unused to keeping his back to an attacker. The thought of running from an enemy was contrary to his nature. But all that mattered was to reach the other side of the clear-cut.

Thrake was grateful that no volley of arrows sprang from the forest before him. Nor was there an ambush of cavalry awaiting him. A quick scan to the right and left revealed that the other men had followed his lead. And since no horse was riderless, it meant that no men had been killed.

Thrake re-entered the forest at the other side, and comforted by the cover of trees and bushes, he breathed a sigh of relief. But no sooner had he begun to feel safe, than a Ki-Rori rider, atop his large, deerlike beast, emerged from beside the path. He looked much more fierce than Thrake could have imagined such a demi-man appearing. His arm wielded a blade that curved in three dimensions, almost as if cut from a coil. The deftness with which it was held put Thrake on notice that here was a skilled artisan of death.

Reflexively, Thrake drew from its scabbard the sword which had been Kmir's. As he did, Thrake felt as if Kmir were displeased. Enmity had no place between men of God. And was this demi-man not obeying the command of his high priest?

Yet it was with clear determination that this creature blocked Thrake's further advance, making impossible the thought of passage without a fight. Despite having no desire to kill, Thrake felt duty bound to break through to the rendezvous. And he knew, as he surveyed the enemy swordsman, that this creature was equally duty bound to stop him.

With a sudden lurch forward, Thrake attacked. He met his opponent head on, and swung Kmir's sword with as much force as he could put into it. As the demi-man raised his shield, Thrake made no attempt to find a lethal spot. Merely striking the shield might dismount his opponent, and if so, Thrake would be well gone before the wounded demi-man could recover for battle.

But the demi-man used his shield as Thrake had never imagined possible. Instead of fending off the blow by matching its impact, the shield seemed to absorb the blow. It was in some small way like striking a heavy blanket.

Then the Ki-Rori blade came swiftly around.

Thrake used his sword to parry the slash, and sensed the well designed cutting action of that blade, wielded as no human arm could have used it. This foe was truly dangerous. Thrake knew he could no longer hope merely to dismount his opponent. This was a fight to the death.

The human warrior gripped the hilt of his weapon with both hands. He aimed with lethal intent, not allowing the Ki-Rori fighter to use his shield, but forcing him to parry with that coiled blade. Thrake's strike landed near the hilt of the enemy sword, with both force and leverage, enough to dislodge it from the demi-man's long-fingered grip.

The Ki-Rori blade fell to the ground.

Thrake turned his horse to lunge into the forest. But if he had expected the demi-man to relent, he was mistaken. Before Thrake could fully penetrate the Ki-Rori position, the demi-man leaped from his own mount onto Thrake's back and pulled him from his horse.

The two landed on the ground with a thud. But Thrake was nimble despite his armor, and well trained in close combat. Before his opponent could get any better advantage, Thrake had broken free, and brought his sword to bear. For a moment, the two of them stood. The tip of Thrake's sword was poised at the demi-man's throat.

The Ki-Rori drew a dagger.

Thrake was stunned by the other's audacity. Any human would have given up the fight, grateful to have been allowed to live. But this demi-man knew the universal code of all principled warriors: be no more ready to kill than to be killed. His paltry dagger demanded a final, decisive end to their combat.

Thrake took a step backward, but the Ki-Rori soldier matched him step for step, refusing defeat.

"I am sorry," Thrake said, though he knew that the other could not understand. "But I must kill you now."

Fearless Ki-Rori eyes comprehended, and waited.

Thrake tensed his arms for the kill, mindful of whose weapon it was he bore. He pressed forward. But his arms refused. Loosening his grip, Thrake allowed Kmir's sword to fall to the ground.

The Ki-Rori warrior understood. He waited for help to arrive. When it did, a number of demi-men bound Thrake as their prisoner, and took him into their city.

There, Thrake was to live to an old age. But that is another story.

* * * * *

Veelos had become aware that her vestments were ill suited for concealment. Their whiteness seemed to her as a beacon, inviting attack. The foliage tore at them, slowing her progress.

She was glad that she had insisted on traveling alone, instead of burdening Vike with her clumsy progress.

When sunlight came, Veelos was grateful for it, heedless of the danger it posed. Upon reaching the open swath of ground, she welcomed its openness, not understanding the vulnerability it imposed.

As her horse galloped across the clear-cut, arrows tore the air about her. Before she reached the other side, a platoon of enemy footsoldiers was taking up a position between her and safety. Only then did the priestess begin to appreciate the full magnitude of the danger she was in.

Veelos reined her horse sharply to the right. The maneuver carried her safely past the swift-footed infantry which had rushed her. Without a mind for tactics, Veelos thought she had evaded the Ki-Rori force. But the rightward maneuver was undefended by the Ki-Rori for a reason. It carried her into the maw of yet another squad of soldiers.

This time escape was more narrow. Sharp tipped lances nearly found their mark. In horror, Veelos recognized that the Ki-Rori warriors were trying to kill her. To kill her! These, whom she had deemed the gentlest folk in all Wirik, now they sought her blood.

Another frantic turn saved her. But it, too, was to the right, in the direction from which more enemy were flooding into the fray. Then yet another group of Ki-Rori appeared, and once again Veelos veered rightward.

Before she knew it, Veelos had departed from the clear-cut. But she had not reached the forest on the other side, nor the cover of trees and scrub. Rather, she found herself upon the open roadway.

For the moment there were no soldiers posted against her. So, without considering what might lie ahead, beyond the twists and turns of the road, Veelos urged her horse full speed forward. Struggling to remain mounted as the horse negotiated the curves of the roadway, Veelos did not notice when the beast took yet another rightward fork in the road.

By the time she did recognize the error, it was too late.

The barrier which stopped Veelos's horse, this time, in its tracks was no band of cavalry, but only a single mounted Ki-Rori. Nor was he an armored swordsman. He wore white, trimmed with blue. He wore a silver ring. None other than Shay-Toom himself stood now against Veelos.

For a moment, the two faced each other in silence, Veelos's face a mask of astonishment and fear, Shay-Toom's one of immovable serenity.

Veelos found her voice. "Let me pass," she said, hoping that her pronunciation in the ancient language would be understood. Then, knowing what Shay-Toom's answer would be, she added, "The others have already escaped. There is nothing to be gained by resisting me."

Shay-Toom slowly lowered himself from his deerlike mount, and stepped with deliberate strides to the center of the road. His eyes seemed to Veelos both angry and sad at the same time.

Veelos could not bring herself to simply trample him, and there was no way around. She decided to turn and retrace her steps.

But when Veelos attempted to rein her horse about, it reared up and shook her from its back. She landed painfully on her side in the dust. Aware that Shay-Toom could now seize her, Veelos ignored the wrenching pain she felt, and quickly lifted herself upright, making ready to escape on foot.

But Shay-Toom had made no move toward her. He had not needed to. His imposing stance in the road was sufficient by itself to give Veelos pause. She sensed power unseen. Veelos had last been so keenly aware of mute potence only during her days in the temple, and only when the high priests had stood in judgment over her.

When Shay-Toom spoke, his voice was heavy with an emotion that not even his alien intonations could disguise. "You deceived me," he said.

"No," Veelos replied. "I concealed from you. I had to."

"You had to," Shay-Toom repeated. "Since when do the servants of God deal with each other in this manner? Do we not share in all things at all times?"

"Now look," Veelos said. "I know you think you're in the right. But you're mistaken. The others have already made their rendezvous. And the witch is surely among them. You can't leave those men in her hands. You must allow me to pass."

"You will not pass," Shay-Toom said. "By the authority of the silver ring, I command you to confess, to repent, and to obey the law of this land. Surrender--- or die."

The final three words shook Veelos. For a moment she stared at Shay-Toom in disbelief. "Are you saying that you would kill me?"

"You have much power," Shay-Toom answered. "But you have not mastered it. If my soldiers arrive, and attempt to bind you, they will be in great peril from you. The power within you, you will turn against us. You would kill us all."

Veelos shuddered. "This is madness. We are priests. We kill no one, least of all each other. If I must die, let it be at the hands of your soldiers." So saying, Veelos turned to run.

But an enormous force threw her backward, back toward where Shay-Toom stood, implacable in his determination.

Veelos spun again to face him. Her astonishment this time was greater than before. "You've used the power against me!" she uttered. "You cast a spell. That is forbidden!"

"I did no such thing," the demi-man answered. "This power you do not understand. It is not magic, but a natural force, invisible to your eye, but as ordinary as the power which pulls you ever toward the bosom of the earth. And it is much more merciful. Surrender, Veelos. Surrender. For I can in no wise allow you to continue your alliance with the Dreaded One Foretold."

"You have no authority over me!" Veelos screamed in frustration more than anger. "I am the Priestess of Prophecy. Don't you understand? My mission cannot fail. It must not. It is I who command you, High Priest. Relent!"

"You are not her," Shay-Toom insisted. "You are not the Priestess of Prophecy."

Again, Veelos turned to run. Again, an unseen barrier hurled her backward. And once more, she turned her anger against Shay-Toom. "I cannot raise a hand against you," she said. "But neither can you stop me. Would you kill me? Then do so, Shay-Toom. For I will not meekly lay aside all that I have suffered so long to accomplish. I will not betray the good men who have already died in this cause. Nor will I leave unavenged the murder of a priestess named Keesha. Kill me, Shay-Toom, if you must--- if you can. But you cannot."

Then, yet another time, Veelos turned, and threw herself against the invisible barrier. This time, she felt it weaken. Another effort, and it broke. The invisble wall had crumbled, and not even Shay-Toom could rebuild it again.

Veelos stepped past it.

But just as she did, she discovered that Shay-Toom had one last weapon in his arsenal. Veelos felt a sudden heaviness in her chest. It became difficult to breathe. She found that Shay-Toom had moved close beside her.

"This is my final plea to you," he told her, standing near at her side. "I have placed this coil about your heart. Once I remove it, I will have no power over you anymore, except for your word of promise. Now give me that word, Priestess. Upon the scriptures writ in your vestments, make a vow that you will obey me, as a priestess obeys her high priest."

Veelos struggled to speak. "Shay-Toom! You are--- killing me!"

"Quickly," Shay-Toom replied. "Promise your obedience. I will accept your word on it. Make the vow."

But Veelos shook her head. "Release me!" she said. "I am dying."

A tear streamed from Shay-Toom's eye. "Must it be so?" he begged. "Must it be me who does this to you? But I swear to you, Veelos, as surely as I live, I will not release you into the witch's claw. Death is preferable for you. And I, who will gladly die for you in combat against the witch, I, will slay you. Better that, than to slay you later, after you have become her ally, her underwitch. Do not doubt it. Quickly, Priestess! Relent!"

Veelos found herself upon her knees, inhaling deep, swift breaths. The crush was becoming unbearable. "I will not," she said. And suddenly Veelos knew it. She really would not relent. Nor would Shay-Toom. She could not. And he was unable to.

Lie to him. Give him your promise. He will believe you. He will release you. And then he will have no power over you.

Veelos heard the words, but knew that they came not across the dusty air, but rather across the medium of her soul. And certainly they had appeal. A simple lie, and Shay-Toom would release her. He would have to. And then Veelos could run from him.

Veelos opened her mouth to speak. But she could not. It was too late. Already, the coil which constricted her heart had tightened her throat as well. Speech had become impossible. Soon, breath would likewise elude her forever.

Dimly, Veelos knew that she was upon all fours. Vaguely, she knew that Shay-Toom was saying final prayers for her. An angelic escort was marshaling, heavenly beings to escort a false priestess into eternal safety.

But Veelos raged. Defeat. Its taste was bitter. To have come so far, only to meet so ignominious a fate. For a brief instant, she knew that Miril must have felt this same rage in the grip of Morgrar One-Arm.

It is indeed how I felt, Veelos. Welcome to the club. But whereas you stood by, ready to watch me die in Morgrar's deathgrip, I am not so callous toward you. I can save you, Veelos. Merely call upon my power, and you are released. Oh, I know. You'd rather die, right? Except that now, it is not an abstraction anymore. It's real. It's here. Death is right now, Priestess. This very minute. So haste, my dear! Unleash me, ask me to help you, and I will save your life.

Veelos struggled to ignore the voice. But she found its argument irrefutable. Indeed, death awaited, not death in its glory, not in its natural role of concluding life. This was death in its horror, its pain, its grim finality. And in the last possible instant, in the final moment of conscious decision, Veelos did the unthinkable.

"Miril! Help me!" she squawked. Then the priestess felt consciousness slip from her.

The mist swirled about them. Gnarled, dead trees surrounded them. For Veelos was not alone here. Shay-Toom was there also. Veelos was astonished to see him. "What happened?" she asked him.

Shay-Toom's response was spoken in great sadness. "The tragedy," he said plainly in Veelos's own language, "is not that I died, but that I failed to save your life. Beware, Veelos. You are now in debt to a witch. And she has no forgiveness. She will be paid every last measure. For even a debt to a witch must be paid in full. The tragedy, Veelos, is that I failed you."

Then, suddenly, the mists turned to dust. The gnarled corpses of trees had vanished, replaced by the greenery of a Ki-Rori forest. Veelos found herself once again upon the road. The coil which had nearly squeezed the life from her was no more. Slowly, the dimness which blinded and deafened Veelos lifted like a veil, and she could see and hear clearly.

But as suddenly as sunlight had appeared, Veelos just as suddenly found herself inside a dark shadow. A horse stood beside her. From her crawling posture, Veelos looked upward at the rider. It was Miril. The hood of her robe was a blackness which pierced the morning sun.

The witch offered her hand. "Ride with me," she said. "The soldiers will be here at any moment. And when they see what you've done, they won't be in any mood for taking prisoners. Nor will there be magic enough, between us both, to deny them their revenge."

Veelos had pulled herself upward, clinging to Miril. She heard herself gasping in exhaustion. "Shay-Toom. Where is he?"

"No," Miril said gently. "Don't look behind you. Really. You won't handle it well if you do. Now hurry, dear. We really must be away from here."

Veelos closed her eyes and wept. Imagining what Shay-Toom's corpse looked like was horror enough. To look upon it would be devastating. The Priestess felt herself pulled upward. She felt her arms close about Miril's waist. Her legs straddled the horse's back. With a violent jolt, the animal raced away with its painful burdens.

Veelos opened her eyes then, and looking backward caught a distant glimpse of Shay-Toom's bloody, charred corpse, the handiwork of evil, the craft of a false priestess.

Chapter 34

Escape into Peril

Horrified by the evil she had done, Veelos wished she could have crawled into a hole and pulled it in over herself. For, Miril's prophecy, her hideous anti-prophecy, had proved powerful. And it was the more powerful in that, Veelos herself had fulfilled it. She had asked Miril to destroy a great good. The result had been Shay-Toom's murder. Unable to confront the reality of her foul deed, her craven failure, Veelos withdrew into a state of mind more dreamlike than wakeful. For the remaining hours of daylight, she made no conscious actions, formed no decisions, but only reacted blindly.

Miril had delivered her to the rendezvous point where, in the presence of all who had survived, she had dumped the priestess unceremoniously onto the dusty ground, showing all that she had rescued the helpless priestess from the hand of her own spiritual kindred. Humiliated, Veelos had remained where Miril had let her fall, on her hands and knees in the dust, her face in the dirt.

One of the warriors had retrieved Veelos's horse for her, and timidly had lifted her up onto it, sparing Veelos the added humiliation of having to ride further along the trail clinging to Miril. For Veelos, hugging Miril for dear life had been the worst of it, more shameful even than being cast like refuse onto the dust of earth. Upon her own horse, she had at least some remaining semblance of dignity.

Mercifully, there was no time for anyone to inquire as to what had happened. For the rendezvous point was merely a staging ground for swift retreat. As soon as Veelos was mounted, it was a matter of blinding speed, a retreat ignominious to the warriors. With the demi-men in hot pursuit, sometimes within arrowshot, the ride lasted all the rest of the day.

Not until the sun neared the western horizon did the demi-men break off their determined pursuit, and turn back toward their city. It became safe, at last, to take a desperately needed rest.

Without having slept all the night before, and having pressed their retreat all day, both man and beast were weary to the bone when finally, beyond the border of Ki-Rori, they stopped to make camp.

And indeed, they knew all too well that they had crossed into another land, a land foreign to Ki-Rori. For here, the terrain was decidedly harsh. Once more, the Lands of Demi-men had become savage.

Four had not made it that far.

"What became of Thrake?" Kl'aarn asked anxiously when at last they stopped for the night.

But no one knew. "I saw Eron arrowshot," a warrior named Larek offered. "Whether it was a fatal wound I could not tell."

Two missing bandits made the casualty count four, but Shalar seemed unconcerned. "Either dead," he said dismissively, "or headed the wrong way."

Turning his attention to the women, Kl'aarn said gratefully, "Well, at least you two made it safely."

Without answering, Veelos slipped quickly from her horse to the ground, and with her head bowed, led the beast away from the main body of men.

"What's with her?" Kl'aarn asked his wife.

"She's in mourning," Miril explained, also dismounting. "Shay-Toom died."

"Oh?" Kl'aarn gave Miril a look. "How did that happen?"

"It wasn't me," Miril said, as dismissively as Shalar had shrugged off his missing men. "You can ask the priestess. She killed him herself. I saw it."

Kl'aarn turned his head to Veelos, but she had withdrawn as if behind a wall. Turning back again to face Miril, he asked, "Exactly what happened?"

Miril hinted at pouting. "Are you so concerned for her?"

"Shouldn't I be?"

"Oh. I see. Very well, then. I'll tell you of it. What would you like to know first?"

Together, they began making a place to bed down. As they did, Kl'aarn spoke. "When the two of you made the rendezvous together, on the same horse, that was quite an unexpected sight. I knew something extraordinary must have happened. But of course there was no time to think about it then. Besides that, we could all see that Veelos had gotten injured. We all knew she had done combat of some sort, and survived. It must have been one hell of a fight for her. Now we discover that she was fighting Shay-Toom himself. How did she manage to survive a battle against him? And what was your part in rescuing her?"

"So many questions," Miril said. "Where to begin? I found her," she paused, then continued, "lying on the road beside the dead Ki-Rori holy man. They had used some kind of powers against each other, something I had not seen before. Obviously, Veelos won. But I suppose priests don't rejoice in their victories, so it's doubtful we'll get much more of the story."

"And you," Kl'aarn said, his eyes searching Miril's expression, "rescued her. Risking your own life to save hers, you brought her to the rendezvous."

"Yes," Miril replied simply. "Yes. I did both of those things. I put her on my horse, and I brought her out of the battle."

Kl'aarn glanced again in Veelos's direction, then once more he faced Miril. "There is something more to this than all that. She doesn't seem angry about it. Not even at you."

"Why should she be angry at me?"

"Because," Kl'aarn said, "whenever things go wrong, she blames you. Why not this time?"

"I think she and I are closer now," Miril answered. "Much closer than before."

* * * * *

When Veelos awakened, dawn had not yet lightened the sky. But despite her weariness, she could not sleep further. Arising, she dressed and made her way to a dwindling campfire. There, Vike sat, staring into the dying embers.

Veelos positioned herself beside the hunter, but he seemed to take no notice of her.

"Are you angry at me?" Veelos asked him.

Vike shook his head. "No."

"Yes you are. If not angry, then something worse. Disappointed. Disillusioned."

Vike sighed. "My mood has nothing to do with you, Priestess. You haven't failed me. It's just that--- in the brief time I spent trying to know Shay-Toom, to bridge the--- well, he's dead now."

"Murdered," Veelos supplied. "By me."

"You did not kill him," Vike said. "We all had a part in it. We all delivered death to his door."

"It was me alright," Veelos insisted. "I could have stopped it. I should have listened to him."

"It was the witch," Vike said. "All of us live in fear of her. It is not for nothing that she is called the Dreaded One Foretold. This witch has powers we do not even suspect. None among us is strong enough to face her."

"No, we're not," Veelos agreed. "But we don't have to be strong enough. God is. And that's all the strength we need."

"But we have a role to play," Vike said. "And we're not doing our part.

We're all hoping that things will work out in the end. But that hope is simply a way of abdicating our---"

"No. Things will work out," Veelos said firmly. "Not because of us, but in spite of us. This is not our mission we are upon. It's God's. He knows us. He knows that we are weak, too weak to succeed. Our part in this is not to win the victory, but only to participate, to share with Him in the effort. We are like little children trying to help father build a house. We only get in the way. But I remember how my father used to love letting me help him, even when I only slowed things down for him. And I remember how much I loved him for that. That is how my father and I shared our love for each other. And that is how we share our love with God--- the same way children help their parents, even when it means getting in their father's way. It may be a poor way of putting it, but that's how it is."

Vike nodded. "Your wisdom is growing, Priestess. Even in the short time I have known you, I can see that. A good omen indeed. And if you are increasing, despite all our failures, then there is surely hope for our success."

With Kl'aarn asleep at her side, Miril lay awake. The hint of a smile curled the corners of her mouth. "You owe me, Veelos," Miril whispered. "You can't imagine the debt I shall collect from you, my dear sweet priestess. For the collateral is your very soul. And after you have paid that debt, paid it in all its terrible fullness, then will my husband serve me your blood, in the cup of your own skull." Her eyes closed, and Miril dreamt.

* * * * *

"I've never seen such gloom," Shalar complained. "Nothing but brown and grey everywhere you look. Even the sky seems always dull and overcast. How many more days of this can we take?"

The bandit rode with Kl'aarn and Miril at the fore of the column. Veelos no longer challenged Miril for the lead position. Ever since Shay-Toom had died, Veelos had kept to herself, ashamed.

"It won't be much longer," Miril told Shalar. "We've nearly crossed the Lands of Demi-men. The next land we reach will be Druuk's kingdom."

"How do you know that?" Shalar asked. "Do you have a map?"

"I don't need one," Miril said. "The ghosts of Druuk's lost legion are all around us, watching us."

"Lost legion?" Shalar asked.

"That fool, Druuk," Miril mused. "He sent a thousand men into this wilderness, hoping to find a way across it, an invasion route to Shi-Raq. But none of them lived, not one man. Now, their spirits wander around, unable to break the curse of these lands, unable to find graves in which to hide, unable to recover their flesh from the bellies of the demi-men who devoured them."

Shalar did not seem pleased to hear all this. "He lost a legion of a thousand? All of them? What manner of creature killed so many? And what about us? What exactly are we getting into?"

"Relax," Miril said. "I got you this far, didn't I?"

"Got us into what?" Shalar demanded.

"Don't be such a coward, bandit. After all we've been through, do you still fear death? How absurd. Death was the life you were leading, before I lifted you from it. Admit it. Your life had become nothing more than a dead end."

"Yes," Shalar answered. "Dead. But it still had a few years left in it. More life than I'll have left in this land."

"A mere few years? You have to learn to think big," Miril said. "Not in terms of years, but millennia, aeons, and finally, forever. Little men fear little losses, and so they lose all. But with me, Shalar, you risk much more than merely your paltry life. You stand at the precipice of Hell, either to rule it, or to fall in."

Shalar spat. "You think you sound so grand. But it's all crap. You and Kl'aarn had easy lives as children. I didn't. I faced fear every day, and won. I've always stood ready to put everything on the line. Even that pirate that I killed. I was only a boy, but I stood toe to toe, face to face with him. It didn't bother me that he might kill me. I stood at the edge of your Hell, Miril, and stared him in the eyes. When he flinched, I killed him. The first man I ever killed, and the last one I'll ever forget."

"It was a brave thing you did," Miril said, her tone mildly sarcastic. "Even your father was impressed."

Shalar nodded, but there was a frown on his brow. "That he was," the bandit said, pausing to reflect upon it. "Impressed. Funny, that. Because, at the time I killed the brigand, I thought--- never mind."

"Thought what?" Miril asked.

"Nothing."

"Now don't tease me. You know I won't stop until I've gotten an answer."

Shalar glared at Miril. "You already know, don't you?"

"Know what?"

"That when I killed that man," Shalar growled, "I thought he was my father."

* * * * *

After a few more days of travel, they came to a fork in the road. The path split into two courses, each of them seeming to be the twin of the other. The double column, mixed of warriors and bandits, halted, not knowing which way to turn. Shalar and Kl'aarn both looked to Miril for an answer. But the demonwitch remained silent.

Shalar turned next to Kl'aarn. "Which way?" he asked.

"They both look the same to me," Kl'aarn answered. "Pick one."

But Shalar replied, "Oh, no. You think I am fool enough to take this as a matter of minor import. But it's plain to see. All along our way, every decision we've made has either been our salvation, or has haunted us evermore along the path. Now this. One route leads to Druuk's treasury. The other leads to death. I need no sorcery to divine that truth. But we may need sorcery to choose wisely."

Kl'aarn shifted nervously in the saddle, then turned to Miril. He said nothing.

But Miril merely returned their gazes, Kl'aarn's and Shalar's, and said,

"How should I know? Must I do everything?"

Shalar scowled. "You're always the one taking credit. You're the one with powers. You see the ghosts of a dead legion. But now, are we to believe that you can't choose between left and right?"

"Very well, then," Miril said. "Left."

"You just flipped a mental coin," Shalar sneered.

"Then rightward," Miril answered.

Shalar scowled even harder. "Let's ask Veelos."

"Oh, yes," Miril said sarcastically. "Surely, she will choose wisely."

Kl'aarn pushed his way between the two, Shalar and Miril, aborting any further confrontation. "We'll wait here for the hunters to return from their foray," he pronounced. "They'll have a report on which route is the best."

By this time, Veelos had ridden forward to see why they were delayed. Miril had just turned to say something to the priestess, when Kl'aarn announced, "Here comes Vike now. What timing! He knew exactly when we'd get to this point."

When Vike drew near, he reported. "I took the left fork by myself, and sent Valmark and Belgar to scout the rightward fork. The path I took seems very level and straight, at least for as far as I followed it. But there's little food or water in that direction. I told the other two to be cautious, and to come straight back here if they saw any hazard on their path. Let's hope they've found the better path. But now I worry for them. They should have met us here. I'll go search them out and return."

"Wait," Veelos said. "Let us send a few men with you, just in case."

"No need for that," Vike answered. "If it's something the three of us cannot handle, I doubt a few more will make any difference. Give me until sundown tomorrow. If I'm not back by then, assume the worst, and take the leftward path." The hunter turned to depart.

But Veelos called out to him again. "Vike. Wait here. Belgar and Valmark might be along any time, now."

Vike turned back to face Veelos. "Or they might be depending on me to go look for them, as I told them I would, if they weren't here when I got back."

"But you said it yourself. If they cannot--- I mean---"

"You've some premonition?" Vike asked her.

Veelos stammered. "Yes."

"What is it?" Vike asked.

By this time, Kl'aarn was interested. "Veelos? Can you sense what lies ahead?"

But Veelos shook her head. "Not exactly. I'm not a seer. But I don't feel good about this. We should wait."

"I can't," Vike said. "I made them expect me. Sundown tomorrow. Expect us back here before then. If not, then you'll know what to do."

Veelos impulsively rode forward and took Vike's hand. "You will come back to me," she said.

Vike nodded. "I promise it."

"No," Veelos replied. "I promise it."

* * * * *

But he did not.

The sun had gone down, risen, and gone down again. There was no sign of the three hunters.

As the campfires burned, Kl'aarn found Veelos alone, and sat beside her.

"If you've come to console me," Veelos said, "there is no need. There is yet a long night before us. Vike and his fellows can find their way in the dark."

Tossing a small branch onto the fire, Kl'aarn said, "You've been leaning on Vike ever since--- well, basically, ever since we found Miril. I sort of deserted you after that, didn't I?"

"One can hardly blame you. You found your lost love after all these years. You---" seated, Veelos pulled her knees up, and rested her forearms across them.

"It wasn't right of me," Kl'aarn said. "I should never have let it be a matter of my making a choice between you and Miril. I just lost my head, that's all."

Veelos looked into Kl'aarn's eyes as she replied. "How could you not choose, Kl'aarn? You had to. But yours is not a choice between Miril and me. It is one between good and evil. Miril has made her choice. And sadly, so very sadly, she has made the wrong choosing, Kl'aarn. She has chosen evil. And now--- now she's leading us all upon the same tragic pathway, the one that she has decided to follow. Do you worry that you merely lost your head? We've all lost our minds, Kl'aarn. Pray that none of us loses his soul."

"It must be nice," Kl'aarn said, "to see the world in black and white like that, right versus wrong, good against evil. It makes everything so simple and straightforward. But I'm beginning to discover it's not like that. The real world has shades of grey."

"You're right," Veelos quipped. "You have lost your head."

"I lost my head," Kl'aarn said, "over you. We both knew it. I was starting to fall in love with you."

"No."

"And you with me."

"Stop it, Kl'aarn."

"But when Miril showed up--- well, everything--- look, I dropped you like a hot coal. I was wrong. I apologize."

"Is that it?" Veelos angrily lifted her chin from its resting place on her forearms. "Is that what you think? That I'm reacting like a woman scorned? That I'm jealous?"

"No---"

"Then what? Alright, you and I did mention the idea of marriage once or twice. We got confused for awhile. But at least we did agree to let God make that decision for us. And now we know what that decision would have been: No. However lonely we had become, marriage would have left us even lonelier and worse, embittered--- each expecting from the other something neither of us could deliver. And we know that, now, because Miril is lawfully your wife. We didn't know that before. We thought her dead. Or at least I did."

Kl'aarn sighed. "You're a difficult woman to apologize to, Veelos."

Despite her anger, Veelos heard herself chuckle. "Apology. You're such a gentleman, Kl'aarn. Here we are, in a savage place, uncharted, unmapped, perhaps to be eaten by creatures we had only heard of in legend, and you speak of apology. But don't you see? The real danger is Miril. Not the demimen, not Druuk, not whatever else lies before us. Kl'aarn, how can I say it gently? Your love with Miril is doomed, and perhaps you with it."

Kl'aarn nodded. "Good. Let's get that said. You're a priestess. You have to say that."

"No!" Veelos insisted. "No. I don't have to say that. And if Miril has her way, the time will come when she has both you and me in her thrall. Do you think it any easier for me to turn my back on her than for you to do it? I loved her differently than you do, but not less."

"But you are, in fact, a priestess. You have become as much an enemy of Miril as I had of Shalar that day, when I fought him in that ambush. He stood ready to kill me. And even after I discovered it was him, I stood ready to kill him or to die trying. Enmity. The world is defined by it. But, Veelos. As much as Shalar and I had become enemies, we've patched things up. We've put a lifetime of conflict behind us. We're friends."

Veelos put her head in her hands. "How I hate to hear you speak so," she said, almost as if in pain. Then lifting her gaze once more, she said, "Are you trying to say that Miril and I can somehow become friends? Do you think that our enmity is comparable to any other? This isn't about Miril and me. It is--- is, black and white. It is--- is, right against wrong, good versus evil. Life or death. You have not read the scriptures concerning the Dreaded One Foretold. They speak of her marriage feast. They speak of drinking the blood of the Priestess of Prophecy from her own skull. And you, Kl'aarn, you are to pour that drink and gulp it down with her."

At those words Kl'aarn suddenly stood and faced Veelos in barely suppressed rage. "That's a lie," he said. "Miril would never do that to you--- or to me. I don't know what scripture you're using--- or misusing, but I do know Miril, and I do know myself. Neither of us, neither of us would ever---"

"And I," Veelos interrupted him, "I never thought that I would ever sink so low as to murder a high priest."

* * * * *

When the sun rose, Veelos awoke suddenly. She knew instantly that Vike, Belgar and Valmark had not returned during the night. Her temptation was to weep, to wail, in loud lamentation of that which, she now knew, she had lost.

But instead she prayed.

"Oh dear God," she began. "We have come to a fork in the road. And now is come a time of choosing. I beg you guide me."

But already there was the noise of camp being broken. Shalar and Kl'aarn were urging their men to haste. Clearly, they had already made their decision, prayer or no prayer.

Veelos rushed through her morning routine, refusing the breakfast rations that had been offered to her.

When she was prepared, she confronted Kl'aarn. "I'm taking the rightward path," she announced.

"What?" he asked, puzzled.

"You heard me. I'm going to follow the path from which the three hunters failed to return."

Kl'aarn tried to sound patient. "I know," he said. "I know how you feel."

"No, damn you," Veelos retorted. "You have no idea how I feel. And besides, what difference do feelings make out here? A thousand men died not far from here, a thousand souls were lost. Their feelings counted for nothing."

"Whoa, slow down," Kl'aarn said. "Look, I know you get premonitions. I trust them in you. Just give me a good reason for taking the rightward path and we'll do it."

"This is not a premonition," Veelos said. "It's something anyone can do. We all know that Vike, and Belgar, and Valmark, have been loyal servants to us. Every step of the way, they repeatedly offered up their lives for us. They found food when there was no food. They found water in a dry wilderness, and grass for the horses. Does anyone think we could have survived this far without them? Now it is our turn. Their lives may depend on us. In any case, we simply cannot turn our backs on them, and leave them forever vanished in this cursed wilderness."

Veelos's emotional outburst had attracted the attention of the entire camp. And more than a few of the men seemed shamed by it. Especially among the warriors, there was sympathy for the priestess's call to honor.

But Miril quickly delivered a rejoinder.

Stepping between Kl'aarn and Veelos, her black witch's robes an emptiness in the dawning sunlight, she sneered. "Why your sudden concern for human life? Where was that concern when these men were fighting and dying, and you withheld your power? While others were looking to your safety, your only concern was that things be done according to scripture. Well, this too has been done according to your scripture. I warned you of it, did I not? The power of Good is to use men, and then to cast them aside when no longer needed, to demand sacrifice, but to offer nothing in return. So it was with these three hunters, whose deaths you mourn, but refuse to accept. So it will be with all who serve Good."

"That's not true," Veelos shot back. "You twist the truth."

"No!" Miril spat. "It is you who twist the truth, False Priestess. It is you who preaches mercy but withholds it. It was you who refused to strike down Morgrar to save me, and then begged me to kill Shay-Toom for you. You are full of hypocrisy, woman. Look at yourself. The scriptures you spout are empty, hollow, meaningless symbols. When the chips are down, even you abandon them. What do they offer but suffering and death? What have they brought any of us but misery? The strong need no gods. The only happiness you will ever find is what you take for yourself by the might of your own will. Your religion provides none of that, nothing but false hope. So don't ask these men to follow you."

Veelos felt her cheeks burn with Miril's stinging accusations. She glanced about at the faces of the men who, but moments before, had begun to murmur in her favor. Now, after Miril's tirade, those very men had suddenly become strangers to her, no longer moved by her exhortations to honor. Like Veelos, they too had come to a fork in the road.

Veelos addressed them. "Very well," she said. "You might as well know. I am a hypocrite. There's no point in denying it. You've all seen it for yourselves. And the worst hypocrisy I've committed is to have allowed the witch to walk among us while yet I live. At first, all of you were horrified by her, both warrior and bandit alike. But as time passed, we all grew more accustomed to her. Now, we even listen, attentively, to her counsel. And that is my fault, not yours.

"But we have come to this fork in the road, a place of choosing. And the choice will be to follow me, or to follow the witch. You know what a wretch I am. But what of this witch? Who is she? Destruction. She is the curse you utter when you curse, the dread you feel when your skin crawls.

"She claims to share a common goal with us, the noble goal of dispossessing Druuk of the Orb. But her reasons for that are not our reasons, no more so than her methods are our methods. She intends not to aid us but to destroy us. We must reject her counsel. We must reject evil."

There was silence.

Finally, Shalar spoke. "Our main concern now is to survive," he said. "Failing that, it is Druuk who wins this argument. The only reason we are here is because otherwise he will destroy us. At least that is what you two women have preached to us all along. As for the hunters, we are already decided. They are dead."

Veelos glanced at the faces of the men. She knew then that she had lost her debate with Miril. "Very well," she said. "The witch has power over you.

But not over me. You follow your paths. I will follow mine."

Kl'aarn stepped before her. "How would Vike counsel you now?" he asked.

"He's not here to do that," Veelos replied.

"Look," Kl'aarn said, "We can't stop you. Do as you will. But it is Vike's instruction we are following, not Miril's. He told us what to do. It was he who told us, that if he and his men could not handle what lies in wait along the rightward path, then more of us would only die as well. If we ignore that, Veelos, then his death has been in vain."

It took Veelos a long time to think about that. But after she had prayed yet another prayer, and wept a tear for Vike and his men, the priestess struggled for an answer. No sign came to guide her. She felt abandoned now, more alone than ever she had felt. And she began to imagine what sort of creature had prevented the return of the hunters.

It was with embarrassment that she capitulated. She reassured herself that she was doing as Vike had instructed. But some small part of her knew that Miril had won yet again.

* * * * *

Hathor was all the scout the travelers had, after that. Which was little. He would barely pass beyond sight of the main party when back he would come at a full gallop, to report that a possible ambush site lay ahead. But when the party came to it, there was no sense of ambush anywhere to be seen. More than once Shalar nearly killed Hathor in rage. One time, it took the best combined effort of Veelos and Kl'aarn to stay Shalar's hand.

To this, the combined effort, Miril reacted angrily, once she found a private moment with her husband. They had stopped at a watering hole, and the two had drifted away together.

"I notice that you and Veelos seem to act very well in concert," Miril accused.

"It was just to save Hathor's skin," Kl'aarn explained.

"And Veelos's. You were quite the chivalrous knight when Shalar's temper turned on Veelos. Don't you think you've become a bit too protective of her, lately?" Miril complained.

Kl'aarn's brow lifted slightly. "Protective? Is that what upsets you?"

"That may be too weak a name for it," Miril snapped. "I'm assuming there's nothing more to it than that, mere chivalry. And I'm assuming you feel the same way. You do feel the same way, Klaarn. Don't you."

Kl'aarn's hands reached for Miril's shoulders, but she shook him off. "Ever since Vike died," she said bitterly, "it's been poor Veelos this, and poor Veelos that. It wouldn't bother me if I did not already know how seductive that woman can be."

Kl'aarn laughed without humor. "Seductive? Veelos? Miril!"

But Miril said, "Lower your voice." Then, "It's no secret. All your men know about what went on in Shi-Raq, between you two. I've forgiven---"

"Miril, nothing went on---"

"Don't interrupt me. I'm not finished. I forgave you that. I never brought it up until now, because I thought it was over. But now I can see that there's still a bit of flame there, isn't there? Not so much with you, but certainly with Veelos. That's why she was so glad when she thought Morgrar was going to kill me. And that's why she did not set out on her own at the fork in the road. Don't you see, Kl'aarn? She's coming between us."

"Miril, you've got it all---"

"Don't deny it," Miril said. "Even Shalar's men talk about you and her."

Kl'aarn shook his head. "This is crazy."

"Oh! Crazy!" Miril sneered. "I see. So now I'm crazy. What other names has your priestess been calling me behind my back?"

"Look," Kl'aarn said. "If you think I've been too--- well, too friendly with Veelos--- I'll treat her more as a priest and less like a friend. Will that satisfy you?"

Miril softened. "I'm sorry, my love. I didn't mean to snap at you like that."

"It's alright," Kl'aarn responded. "We're all buckling under the pressure out here. But you say that we're almost through these lands. How much---?"

Shalar's loud curse broke in on their privacy. "Aw shit! It's that damned Hathor again. I swear, this time, if he doesn't have a good reason---"

Kl'aarn pulled himself away from Miril. "I'd better go see to this. And I'll do it without Veelos this time."

Hathor's retreat seemed even more urgent this time, if that were possible, than any of the times before. Before his horse had fully stopped, the bandit scout had already half fallen, half dismounted from it. He half ran, half stumbled toward Shalar and Kl'aarn. "Dead men!" he shuddered. "Dead men everywhere, as far as the eye can see. All dead. All of them!"

Despite these words, no one was overly impressed, not coming from Hathor.

As Hathor groveled, Kl'aarn noticed something. "What's that in your hand, Hathor? Let me have it."

Hathor proffered it as if eager to be rid of it, something like a seashell, the size of a man's hand. "I picked that up before I saw them," he explained. "I must have forgot to drop it."

Kl'aarn held it up, using sunlight as a backdrop. "It seems to be a scale," he mused. "A fish scale, or---"

Shalar prompted, "The scale of a serpent. A snake or lizard. How came you by this, Hathor?"

Hathor shivered despite the warmth of the day. "I saw some--- some things--- like this one atop a ridge. I got off the horse to examine them. Then they--- the dead men--- they caught my eye. A hundred dead men or more, their bones white, just on the other side of the ridge. One of those toothy skulls was grinning at me not two paces away, just staring at me with those empty, terrified eye sockets."

Kl'aarn turned to Miril. "Druuk's lost legion?"

Miril nodded. "They lie in our path."

"Killed by whatever shed such large scales," Shalar said. "Giant, lizard demi-men. It is against just such beasts as these that we need swords of demonic hell-iron. And we don't have them."

"We won't need them." The voice was Veelos's. "No demi-men lie in our path. Vike has distracted them from us."

All eyes turned to the priestess.

"Well," Miril said. "Look who's come out of her shell. And what more, pray tell, does your special insight glean for us?"

"Just that," Veelos answered. "Nothing more. We are safe if we do not tarry."

Kl'aarn nodded. "Then let's not tarry any further. Mount up." Conscious of Miril's glare, he returned her gaze. "Unless you've got some better advice."

Miril's glare softened. "The priestess is right. It's not wise to tarry near so many massacred corpses."

* * * * *

When they reached the ridge, the men found it just as Hathor had reported. There were a number of the serpentine scales lying about, as if a very large number of the beasts had been in the area at one time. And beyond the crest of the ridge, spread before their view, was a battlefield in its terrible aftermath. The bones of hundreds of men littered the land.

As the travelers made their way across the site of carnage, Shalar kept a running commentary, nervously venting his fear. "They didn't leave much plunder," he said. "Not many of these skulls wear helmets, nor do many of these arm-bones bear shields. From what armor is left, we can see that this was a professional army, not a wandering band, but a garrison. Look, there's a helmet, not plundered of its red plume, some high-ranking commander no doubt. Nor many swords lying about, either. If these beasts attack us, they'll be wielding those swords, and wearing that armor. And look at those bones. Crushed. After the demi-men won this battle, they feasted, feasted on human flesh, flesh as human as ours."

"Stop frightening yourself," Miril chided.

"And one more thing," Shalar said. "These bones. Every one of them is human. Not a demi-man bone among the lot. That means the creatures took no casualties, not any."

"Yes they did." Again, Veelos had interjected.

The bandit faced the priestess. "What?"

"The demi-men did take casualties," Veelos affirmed. "Not many. But some. Some died here."

"Then where are their bones?" Shalar asked. "Where are their corpses?"

Veelos answered. "These creatures are not like you, Shalar. They bury their dead."

* * * * *

It was nearing nightfall, before the travelers had passed beyond the corpses of Druuk's vanquished legion. But even where they camped, the men could imagine hearing the clashes of swords, the roaring of mighty beasts, and the howls of ghosts. They got little sleep that night.

For two days more, the travelers forced themselves ever westward, along a path which, for so many others before them, had been a journey into oblivion.

The ambushes they imagined never came. They feared that the very earth might open up to swallow them, but it did not. No ancient spells sprung from the soil to curse them; no creatures from their nightmares materialized to attack them. For two days more they pushed onward, westward, eager to leave behind them this last of the Lands of Demi-men before, at the very last moment, it might change its mindless mind, as it were, and claim them after all.

Early on the morning of the third day, they saw trees, trees utterly unlike the harsh vegetation which grew in the Lands of Demi-men.

There was a small, shallow river, much like the one which they had crossed over to bring them into these lands. Like the other, it was an understated border, too small for its importance as the demarcation line between curse and blessing.

When the men saw the trees, and discerned that they had reached the end of the Lands of Demi-men, they cheered, and almost bolted for the forest which lay before them.

Both Kl'aarn and Shalar resorted to threats to keep the men in line. "That land, which you see before us, which we have traveled all this distance to reach, is after all, a foreign country," Kl'aarn reminded everyone. "The only thing we know of it, is that it can field a legion of trained, professional infantry. If that nation can so cheaply spend a thousand infantry, it can produce thousands more to fight against us. There could be an ambush ahead. Who will go first to see if there is one?"

That quieted the men down. For indeed, the forest ahead was well able to conceal an army.

"I'll go," Veelos said.

Kl'aarn snorted. "I think Hathor can handle this."

But Veelos said, "I was the first to cross into the Lands. I should be the first to cross from them. Unless, of course, Miril has decided that there is some kind of prophetic significance to claim for herself."

Miril hesitated. "We are leaving a land of ancient curse," she said. "But the land into which we are about to enter is neither any safe haven. Even so. No one has ever crossed these Lands alive. I would wish that honor for myself, of course. But since the priestess has been so gracious about it, I must suspect her intention. Go ahead, Veelos. Claim your prophecy. It's about time one of them proved better than a lie."

Veelos did not reply. She turned her horse, and at a casual trot, splashed across the river. Once on the other side, she disappeared into the trees, for a brief time, and then emerged again onto the bank of the river. "There is no one here," she announced.

Then, in orderly fashion, the double column of men and witch departed, at long last, from the Lands of Demi-men.

* * * * *

"It seems that we should be celebrating," Shalar told Kl'aarn, once they were all across the river.

Kl'aarn replied. "It feels that way. A thousand-year curse has been broken. A thousand years, and a thousand of Druuk's men. All that cursed them, has been defeated by two women."

Shalar nodded. "You make a deep point there, merchant's son. It was the women, wasn't it? We were just along to do the labor. It was them all along, wasn't it?"

Kl'aarn glanced at the women, who were watering their horses a short distance away. "Actually," he said, "I misspoke. It wasn't both of them. Just one. It was either Miril, or Veelos, whose power brought us through. Not both. Only one of the two of them has any real power. But the hell of it is, I can't say which."

Shalar shrugged, and turned his attention to the forest. "Something tells me," he said, "that we've stepped from the snake pit into the lion's den."

Kl'aarn scanned the trees uncertainly. "I surely do miss Kmir, and Vike's men. But we're on our own, now."

Miril overheard the two men speaking, heard them mention the names of Kmir and Vike. But Miril gave no hint that she had overheard. Kmir and Vike had been minor obstacles to her, one an influence on Kl'aarn, the other had bolstered Veelos. Fate had rid Miril of both of them, fate not by mere accident, but by her power to guide that fate.

Instead, Miril approached Veelos. "So. Priestess of Prophecy. Did being the first to emerge from the Lands of Demi-men give you some newfound power?"

"Get away from me, Miril. I don't want to get into it with you right now."

"I hope it did," Miril continued, ignoring the rebuff. "I hope it did empower you, and mightily. Because we're going to have need of that power. And soon. You can feel him too, can't you? Druuk is nearby."

"I won't discuss it with you."

"Your skin crawls just like mine does, just knowing that he rules this land. Does he know we're here? What do you think?"

"I think," Veelos said, "that I loathe you. Do you imagine that I'm going to plot with you against Druuk?"

"You have no choice. It's time now, Veelos. It's time for you to throw your lot in with mine. He's powerful, Veelos. We both sense that awesome power. He's much stronger than either one of us alone. We'll have to take him together. Just as we did that pirate in the---"

"I wish he had killed us both," Veelos snapped. "I wish that cursed pirate had raped and murdered both of us. And I wish Kl'aarn and Shalar had never interfered."

"Oh, how touching," Miril sneered. "Then you and I would be in heaven, together, sharing our sweet happiness for all eternity. Or so you think. But I wouldn't have liked heaven, Veelos. What I've done here on earth, I'd have done also in heaven. Even the demons started out in heaven, you know. No. It would have done you no good, Veelos. I'd have left heaven. And I'd have taken Kl'aarn with me, never to return. As for you, why, you would be Shalar's wife in heaven, Veelos. Was it not your path? Think upon that! If you think heaven is so wonderful, ponder it for awhile. What would eternity be like as Shalar's wife? You'll change your mind about heaven once you've thought that through."

But Veelos squared off against Miril. "You think this through," she said. "Only one of us can kill Druuk. My scripture says he must be slain by the Priestess of Prophecy. Yours says by the Demonwitch. So we cannot collude on this, as we did in crossing the Lands of Demi-men. If you kill him, you get all the power and all the destiny that comes with spilling his blood. If I kill him, I restore Tarok back to power, power to intervene in the world of men. And you know what he'll do to you once he has that power, don't you?"

Miril laughed. "So. Do you think you can slay Druuk without me?"

"No," Veelos answered. "I did not say that. All I said was, I won't help you. If that means we both die, and Druuk wins, so be it."

Miril sneered. "You say so. But by your own words you lie. Because you know what Druuk will do if he masters the Orb. And not even Tarok will be beyond his reach then."

Veelos turned away.

"You know I'm right," Miril said. "That's why you cannot answer. Face it, Veelos. You never had any choice. You needed me to cross the Lands of Demi-men, and you need me now to kill Druuk. And we will kill him, Veelos. We'll either kill him together, or else we'll die together. Because however much you hate me, you know that if Druuk wins, we'll both have hell to pay."

Veelos still did not answer.

"It's time," Miril said in parting. "The time has come. You must pay your debt, Veelos. Even a debt to a witch must be paid, and paid in full. But, then, you always did know that, didn't you?" Then, Miril mounted her horse, and rode into the forest.

* * * * *

The forest canopy was thick overhead. As the double column of riders made its way along the trail, Shalar grew increasingly nervous. "I don't like the smell of this place," he said.

"You should feel right at home," Kl'aarn answered. "This forest is made for hiding in. Just the sort of place a bandit would call home."

"It gives me the shivers," Shalar answered. "We've been moving along this trail for two days now, and it gets eerier all the time."

"The scouts have seen nothing," Kl'aarn said.

Shalar nodded. "There you have it."

"Have what?" Kl'aarn asked.

"Just what you said," Shalar replied. "Nothing. Not a sign of life anywhere. A forest such as this should be full of hunters and--- and bandits. Yes. That's it, Kl'aarn. We know we're in the land of a mighty tyrant now. This trail used to be well traveled; one can easily see that. But it's begun to grow over again. Soon it will be gone. This Druuk, whoever he is, is a real bastard."

"I'm told," Kl'aarn agreed.

"I mean," Shalar said, "that he killed all the bandits. All of them. The women were right about him. He needs to be removed from the face of Wirik. I just hope we can do it."

* * * * *

That night, they made camp in the style of bandits, finding a place where the light of their fires would be hidden by surrounding high ground.

When everyone had settled, Kl'aarn and Shalar drew away from the others. "We have to change our tactics," Kl'aarn said. "We're too predictable."

"Go ahead," Shalar prompted. "Speak of it."

"Today," Kl'aarn continued, "when Hathor was late in reporting--- while some were fearing he was dead, I caught myself fearing he was alive--- that he'd been captured by one of Druuk's patrols."

"He just got lost for awhile," Shalar said. Then, "But I do catch your drift. He would have told everything. He would have led them right to us."

"Any of the men might do that," Kl'aarn said. "Miril says that Druuk can torture anything out of anyone. It's said he can even make a rock cry out in pain."

"But if it's soldiers you fear," Shalar said, "then it makes no sense to travel without scouts. We could all blunder into a garrison."

"We could," Kl'aarn admitted. "But at least we might arrive unexpected, catch them by surprise, and have a chance. And we can move faster when we aren't waiting on reports."

"You sound like you're in a hurry," Shalar said. "I still have my doubts about meeting this Druuk."

"I'm in no rush," Kl'aarn said, "to face him either. But in talking with Miril, I take it that Druuk might be expecting us, and making preparations. He has sorcerors of his own, to be sure. For the moment, he's expecting us to arrive by sea. Some kind of prophecy involved in that. But if he's watching the sea ports, we just might be able to surprise him from behind."

"Spoken like a true bandit," Shalar said.

"Yeah," Kl'aarn said. "I'm becoming more like you all the time."

"And?" Shalar prompted. "You make it an insult."

Kl'aarn sighed. "It's Miril," he said. "At first I thought that this witchcraft was just some--- some infantile thing she'd gotten caught up in. I thought I could make her change. But I haven't. She's more into it than ever. Veelos warned me about this, but I wouldn't listen. And now, I find myself getting more and more comfortable with what she's become."

Shalar shrugged. "Witch, priestess. They're all the same, Kl'aarn. One wears white, the other wears black. But you do have to admit, Miril put a lot of Morgrar's men out of action. And she did kill that demi-demon that was dragging Veelos away. And while she did all that, what good was Veelos doing any of us?"

Kl'aarn replied, "You half answered your own question, metalsmith. Everything that Miril has done for us has involved killing. Sometimes she killed evil men, and sometimes good men. It seems to make no difference to her. But who among our number has not had a wound bandaged by Veelos? Not one among us has come down with disease or fever that she could not heal. While Miril incites men with threats, Veelos appeals to their sense of honor. Even your men, Shalar, have asked her to pray for them on occasion. It seems that Veelos is the only one left who has not been touched by Miril's darkness. You know, Shalar, I sometimes fear Miril."

Shalar scoffed. "A good slap across her face will remind her that you're her husband. Witch or no witch, no man should ever fear any woman, let alone his own wife."

"Are you really such a dullard?" Kl'aarn complained. "To you, there are no profound questions, no eternal principles. Every problem has but one solution: kill somebody. Like Miril says, most men think of good as that which they like, and evil as that which is unpleasant. But there is more, Shalar, so very much more. Good and evil are the only two powers of the universe. One must conquer in the end. The other must vanish forever into oblivion. And Miril and Veelos are locked in that struggle, Shalar. One of them must kill the other."

Shalar scoffed. "They won't do that. Hell, look at us. We've got more reason to kill each other than they do. And I trust you behind my back. I can't say that about my own men."

Kl'aarn's frustration grew into agitation. He grabbed Shalar by the shoulder strap of his chest plate and shook him. "There is death between them, Shalar," he said through his teeth. "And however it ends, it's going to be unbearable."

"Alright," Shalar said. "I've never been a good listener, but sure, I sympathize with your plight. Hell, we all grew up together. And after all we've come through lately, I can't help but have sentiments, too. Yeah, Miril has changed, and for the worse. It's like some disease she's got. It's not that I don't give a damn. It's just that there's nothing anyone can do about it. So I don't waste myself in worry over it. Kl'aarn. This thing has got to run its course. Nothing we do can make any difference. None."

"There is too much at stake," Kl'aarn said, "to not worry."

"What's at stake? A brief thousand years from now we'll all be dead and forgotten. Nothing any of us has done will make any difference. Oh, I know, you're talking about the saving of souls. Well even if I did believe in any of that, it wouldn't change my view. Because if men do have souls, no one can save it for them, no one can lose it for them. Each man chooses his own eternal destiny. Isn't that what we were taught by Valen Elder? The damned damn themselves."

"But the saved," Kl'aarn said, "are saved by God alone. And to be evil is to reject God, to reject salvation."

Shalar sighed. "Look at me, Kl'aarn. Do I look like a priest? Why are you asking me, of all people, about things like this? I'm a bandit."

Kl'aarn nodded. "Let's get some sleep. Tomorrow's another long day."

Shalar turned away, then turned back again. "Look," he said to Kl'aarn. "When I made that vow of friendship to you, I meant it. But I'm not cut out for being that kind of friend. I just want you to know."

Chapter 35

Toothless Hag

At midmorning the next day, Shalar commented to Kl'aarn, "Do you notice how the forest seems to be thinning out, the farther we go? The trees are smaller, farther apart, and if a tree can look sickly, these do."

Kl'aarn nodded. "It reminds me of the wilderness in the lands of demi-men. It got worse and worse as we approached the demonic castle. Now, we're approaching Druuk's castle."

"Or perhaps," Shalar guessed, "the demi-men have crossed the river just as we did, and raided hereabouts. It's said that, once an animal has tasted human flesh, its appetite cannot be satisfied by anything else."

* * * * *

Just before noon, they came within sight of a village.

It had taken them all by surprise. For no sounds had warned them of it, nor had they seen any smoke, which usually marked any human habitation from afar. But aside from that, at first view, it seemed to be much like any ordinary village of the east land of Wirik. Only its deathly silence gave the men pause.

"Ambush?" Shalar asked Kl'aarn.

"If so, we very nearly stumbled into it. Perhaps we should reconsider whether to employ scouts."

"It's awful quiet for a forest village," Shalar said. "There should be the sounds of a smith at the forge, or children playing in the street, or something."

As they drew closer, Kl'aarn was taken by how much the village resembled those of his native land. Small wooden cottages were scattered in haphazard fashion. Between them, a road snaked its way toward the other side, disappearing around one of its many turns. Each cottage sported a clay chimney, and each ruled over a small garden plot fenced in by thick wooden rails. Here and there were the shops of craftsmen and artisans, a smithy here, a cabinetmaker's shed nearby.

But nothing grew in the untended gardens save weeds. The metalsmith's forge was cold. No sounds of chipping wood emanated from the cabinetmaker's. But the deafest silence of all was that of no children.

Shalar stopped his horse and peered at the deserted scene. "Not good," he said. "It was like this when we raided Gol-Ret. The villagers had set a clever trap for us. We lost men, for no booty gained."

"If it's a trap," Kl'aarn said, "it's a poor one. Doors and windows are open everywhere. We'll send a scout. He will be able to search very quickly, with little risk. I don't think anyone is there."

"Why not?" Shalar asked. "Why is no one there? If it's deserted, where did everyone go, and why? Was it a plague? What if this place is diseased? We might all die."

"There would be graves," Kl'aarn said. "We've seen none. Nor corpses."

Shalar inhaled nervously. "I guess there's only one way to find out. I'll have a look around. Keep watch for me." With that, he nudged his horse forward and rode into the village.

When he was amid the ramshackle houses, Shalar called out. "Is anyone here?"

There was no answer.

The bandit dismounted, and walked to the nearest cottage. Its door was closed. But when he pushed it, it fell from its leather hinges. Shalar stepped inside, and for a few moments was out of sight. When he emerged, he announced, "Nothing here. Not even an arrow sticking in a door."

Kl'aarn had joined him in the survey, trotting his horse back and forth among the cottages. "No sign of a massacre," he said. "Nor of famine. The wells are full. And the garden fruits withered ripe on the vine. So why is the place deserted?"

The other travelers had drifted in, suspiciously looking about, when suddenly they were all startled by a loud noise, and a sight that sent a momentary wave of panic through them.

The door to a nearby hut crashed open. From within, there all but leaped a black clad figure, that of an old woman. She stormed into the middle of the roadway where all could see her. Scrawny white hair, darkened only by dirt, snaked from her mangy scalp in chaotic tangles. Her grimace was toothless but menacing. Despite her emaciated look, or perhaps because of it, she appeared fierce. Before the stunned men could even draw their swords, she had pointed her bony finger, weaponlike, at the nearest of them. Her cracked, dry voice froze everyone in their tracks.

"I am a witch!" she cackled with menace. "Don't try to harm me. If you do, I'll boil your eyes in their sockets. All of you!"

For a moment there was confusion, as even the horses cast about for some means of escape.

Then Miril nudged her horse confidently forward, and looked down upon the hag, into the old woman's defiant stare.

"Stop right there!" the hag commanded. "One step further, and I'll turn you into a spider, a hairy brown spider as you live."

"No need for that, witch woman," Miril replied calmly. "We come as friends. What toll do you ask of us for safe passage?"

The old hag's eyes squinted as she leaned sideward to peer at the cart behind Miril. "My spells tell me there is food there," she said in her rusted voice. "Am I right? Don't lie to me, or else I'll---"

"Your spells serve you well," Miril said. "Indeed we have food, much food. But it's too fine fare for the likes of you." As Miril spoke, she withdrew from her pocket a strip of dried meat, trail jerky. "Here. Gnaw on this."

The hag glared evilly. "Give me the entire cart, I say. Or else I'll turn you all to spiders, ugly squat spiders, all of you."

Miril tossed the jerky onto the dust at the hag's feet.

The famished woman was instantly on her hands and knees, greedily scooping up the morsel to cram it into her mouth. But just as it came to her crusty, dried lips, the woman found that she was holding not a strip of meat, but a double handful of spider, brown and furry and huge.

With a dry, raspy shriek that seemed would tear out her throat, the old hag flung the arachnid away. Shrinking with abhorrence, her eyes filled with sudden dread.

"By the demon's fang," she wailed. "You are a real witch!"

Miril tilted her head slightly backward in laughter, amused at the old woman's horror.

The hag spoke quickly. "I meant no harm, my lady! I am but an old and helpless widow, scrounging for life as best I can. I meant you no harm, I swear it."

"It seems," Miril taunted, "that in your wretched state, you would fare much better as a spider."

"No! Please!" the hag pleaded, nearly convulsed by the threat. "Please don't do that to me, I beg you!"

Miril's horse lurched as Veelos, now on foot, pressed herself between Miril and the old woman. The priestess reached down to the kneeling woman. "Don't fear her," she said. "She is a witch, but she'll do you no harm. Not while I live. Stand up, now, and tell us where we can prepare a broth for you. You cannot chew such food as we carry."

Miril sneered above them. "Are we to stop and cook for every old hag along the way? I say kill her now and silence her treacherous tongue. Or else, she'll sell word of what she's seen to the first patrol that happens through here."

Veelos ignored Miril as she helped the old woman to her feet, and spoke instead to Kl'aarn. "While I speak with this lady, please make a fire and a broth. There may be much she can tell us in return."

Kl'aarn answered doubtfully. "Even if she does know something useful, we can't trust anything she might say, Veelos."

Veelos glared back at him. "Do you intend to follow the counsel of the witch? Have we become murderers of helpless old women? I tell you, warrior, you'll kill me before you touch this woman."

Kl'aarn seemed angry for a second as he wavered. Then he gave in. "Alright. This one time. See what you can learn from her. But we're taking an awful chance. We won't be tending to every beggar in this kingdom."

Veelos took the old woman's hand and led her to the porch of the nearest house. There, she sat her upon a chair, and tried to reassure her. "You won't be harmed," Veelos said. "We'll give you a broth and some food, and then we'll be on our way. You'll owe us nothing. All I ask is that if you do wish to answer our questions, that you speak only the truth. But if you wish to keep silent, we'll still not harm you."

The old hag looked at Veelos incredulously, her feeble eyes straining to see what kind of woman could utter such strange words, and in so strange an accent, so foreign in its tones.

"Where are the other villagers?" Veelos asked.

The old hag's face frowned with renewed suspicion. At first, it seemed that she would refuse to say anything helpful. But when the old woman happened to glance in Miril's direction, a change of heart quickly expressed itself upon her demeanor. For among so many possible enemies, she clearly preferred to deal with the woman in white. Besides which, she noticed, the men were already filling a pot with water to boil. Perhaps they were going to feed her, after all.

"I'm the only one here," she finally answered. "The others are all gone."

"Gone where?" Veelos asked.

The hag shrugged. "Who knows? First, it was the young men. One by one, they went off to the wars. The conscriptors promised them good pay, you know. But even the ones who did not want to go, they were taken anyway. Soon after, the young women followed too." Her thin lips contorted into the mockery of a lurid smile, as if amused by an obscenity. "After all, soldiers spend their pay on women, you know."

"And what of the others?" Veelos asked.

The black clad woman shrugged again. "After that, who was left? Only the old, and the lame, and the children. No one was left to care for us. Oh, we managed for awhile. We eked out a living. But one by one, we began to die off. We caught fever, or were bitten by snakes, or carried off by wolves. Some went mad. With none of able body, what could we do for ourselves? The old were too old, and the young were too young."

"Are you saying," Veelos asked, "that the young were left behind, abandoned?"

"But of course," the old one said. "What use is a child to a soldier, or to a whore?"

Veelos shook her head grimly.

The hag continued. "It didn't matter. There weren't that many children anyway. Most of the women had already become barren of womb, and most of the new mothers were dry of breast."

"Why?" Veelos asked.

The old hag looked suspiciously again at Veelos. "You sound as if all this were new to you. My eyes are not so good anymore, but you haven't the look of one from hereabouts. My ears are going deaf, but your manner of speech is unheard in this region."

"Why did the women become barren?" Veelos repeated.

The hag gazed past Veelos, her eyes losing their focus. "Who knows? Some say it was the sorcery. Druuk--- our King Druuk His Majesty, that is---

he sends sorcerors to root out all those who are disloyal to him, all those who might plot rebellion. I would help King Druuk, of course. I'm very loyal to His Maj---"

"We are not in the service of Druuk," Veelos promised. Then, "How do you survive here, all alone?"

"How do I survive? But by my wits, of course. How else? When soldiers patrol through here, I threaten them, just as I threatened you. I tell them I'm a witch. They always believe me, and give me food and drink. I do look like a witch, don't I?"

"Quite like one," Veelos said. Then, "How often do the soldiers come here?"

The hag shook her head in disgust. "Not often enough anymore. I've scared them away, I'm afraid. Maybe I look too much like a witch."

"Is it necessary to threaten them?" Veelos asked. "Are none of them kind enough to feed you?"

The hag scoffed. "Kind? What is kindness? You're the most compassionate soul I've ever met. And even you might be merely clever, performing some treachery against me. Not that I'm afraid, mind you. I'm a goddess, you know. I'll avenge myself if you kill me."

"I'll do no such thing. How long has this fiefdom suffered these trials?"

The hag peered closely at Veelos. "You don't know? Where indeed are you from, woman?"

"From far away. How long has all this been going on?"

"Ever since Druuk--- King Druuk His Majesty--- got the Orb of Power. They say it draws power. Draws it to King Druuk. He gets it all, and leaves little for anyone else. Even the forests seem to be dying out. You are very far inland, you know. How could you have got so far inland and not know these things?"

Hathor brought the bowl of soup. Veelos took it from him, and handed it to the old woman. The priestess watched as she hungrily slurped it down.

"We can't spare much more than this," Veelos said. "We have barely enough for ourselves. But we'll leave you with enough for a few more bowls of broth. Perhaps by then, more soldiers will come. If they do, try to urge their compassion. Sometimes, all it needs is a chance, you know. But when you pretend to be a witch, you only invite their evil. And there seems to be too much of that already. Perhaps it's worth a try."

The woman eyed Veelos intently for long moments, as if weighing the risk of speaking what she was thinking. Finally, she said in a tone almost as low as a whisper, "You wear white."

"Yes."

"Then truly, you are not in the service of that viper Druuk."

"I'm not."

"Then get yourself into some decent garb, woman. If the soldiers catch you in white, your head will soon decorate the point of one of their pikes."

"Why so?"

The hag scoffed her reply. "Fool! Have you not even so much as heard the sorceror's proclamation? Druuk's death comes cloaked in white. Get you out of that garb, for great is the reward of the man who slays the woman in white. No white cloth touches woman's skin in all the kingdom."

Veelos nodded. "Thank you. I'll change out of these vestments immediately."

* * * * *

The hag watched suspiciously until the last of the strangers had left her village. She was still half expecting some treachery to be unveiled. When it did not materialize, she shook her head and hobbled back to the porch, wondering whether or not she should alert the next patrol of soldiers that she had seen a woman in white. But no, she decided, they would never believe her. They probably did not even believe she was a witch.

"Giving away food," she clucked. "Such a fool as that one does not deserve to live." Then she reconsidered. "No," she decided. "No fool is that one after all. For she is wise enough to travel with a witch."

Chapter 36

Savage Beasts

Lesser forest dwellers might never have been able to find concealment in the sparse forest. But the eyes which peered from behind the bush were well practiced in the finding and use of cover. And now the skill of those eyes focused on the unsuspecting riders who approached the hidden man as they rode toward him along the trail.

Those eyes saw much that another might have missed.

At the head of the column rode Veelos, in brown commoner garb. Riding at the fore as she did, a less discerning eye might have thought her the leader. But this observer could sense that she was more fleeing from those behind, than leading them. Though her back was straight, it was only to conceal a spirit that was bent, bowed beneath the burden of past mistakes and sins. Her eyes betrayed a weariness that reached to the bone, even to her very soul. Less keen observation would never have detected that this woman was set upon a noble task. Rather, she seemed engaged in some dull, monotonous chore. Only by very astute inspection would one notice the iron will beneath the disillusionment. Only by noticing the barely noticeable could one sense the stubborn determination, the endurance of continual setbacks, the endurance of doubts, and even, the endurance of confusion.

Not far behind the brown-clad woman rode Shalar. It was easy to pick him out as a bandit, a murderer, the perpetrator of foul and violent crimes, the weight of which he was unconscious. The eyes of that one were almost as keen as the eyes of the hidden observer. But Shalar's eyes, long since blinded to truth, beauty and love, were accustomed instead to searching out victims, and in finding places to hide from justice. The bandit furtively glanced into the trees and bushes, but he searched them less with alertness than with worry and fear. Nor were his glances confined to the trees. He would now and then glance, first at the brown-clad woman, and then backward toward the other woman, the one in black.

Were it difficult to understand what Shalar could fear from Veelos, there was no such difficulty regarding his distrust of the other. A blind man could have seen that she was a witch, most wicked in her evil, most treacherous in her designs. She rode near the rear, as if to keep her eyes on the men, and especially upon the brown-clad woman, as if keeping them all bewitched. She drove them toward whatever unfathomable evil plot enwrapped her being. This one had no confusion, no doubts, nor any regrets whatever. This one ruled.

It showed in everything about her. The cut of her robes was in the contour of flame and fang. Her long black hair, unadorned, lay proudly across her shoulders, tracing out serpentine lines. Her eyes, beautiful and fierce, were calculating and ruthless. Those eyes had seen sights upon which no ordinary mortal could bear to gaze. And they saw into a future which none would dare envision. Her slender hands rested gently on the rein of her horse. Yet something in those delicate hands threatened instant death, the sudden and unprovoked ripping out of one's throat before any sound could escape it. This woman could kill in a single, casual motion, with neither hesitation nor remorse.

Yet, for all her poise, despite her physical beauty, with all her power, yet there was within the witch a terrible void, a black, empty hollowness. The only life within her was the turbulent, searing whirlwind of an empty soul, a spirit which long since had been sapped and emaciated by the poison of hatred, and by the malevolence of unearthly horror.

How then, could it be, the observer wondered, that at her side was a man who loved her, not with the love of self (as she loved him) but with a form of desire entirely alien to the object of his affection. The futility of this doomed relationship had obviously taken its toll on Kl'aarn. It took little examination, to see that he was a man who once had been able to face uncertainty with resolve, to risk death with steadfast calm. Now his loyalties were torn between the ideals of his youth and the realities of his adulthood. Well he knew that his love was forbidden. Yet he could neither tear himself from her, whom he loved too well, nor surrender this woman to his God, whom he knew too little. He dared not ponder very deeply the inevitable doom, unto which his misguided love was taking him. Like a man who had sold his soul, he took what pleasure he could while it lasted, attempting vainly to compress his eternity into what few days yet remained.

And finally there were the others, men forming a double column from the priestess to the witch. They were a curious mixture of disciplined men-at-arms mingled with ruffian thugs. They formerly had been natural enemies, but now were bonded in an alliance sealed by the blood of many battles, one of them a battle they had fought against each other. Upon this alliance depended one more battle yet to be fought. Despite all that, however, the basic enmity between them had never completely died, but become merely dormant. The men themselves seemed to know that. All that they really had in common was that none of them were men of transcendent wisdom. The quest upon which they were embarked surpassed their ability to understand. They merely rode, their minds upon marching when marching, upon fighting when fighting, and rarely reflecting on the inevitability of their deaths.

All these observations the hunter made with a single scan. For his eyes were well practiced in looking not for what appeared to be, but rather for what was. And even though he saw that, he knew that the course must be run to the end. Girding up his courage, and resigning himself to his fate, Vike stepped onto the forest trail before Veelos.

* * * * *

For a few moments, Veelos sat frozen upon her suddenly halted horse. The shadows of overhead leaves, mixed with jewels of sunlight, raced erratically back and forth in unison across the fur-clad shoulders of the husky figure which had surprised her. It was only that mixture of light and shadow that lent the credence of reality to the otherwise incredible sight which presented itself to her. But for that, Veelos would have been persuaded she saw a ghost, either a ghost, or else an illusion spawned by aching affection.

The weariness melted from Veelos's expression. It melted into one of radiant joy, a euphoria she had not felt seemingly for ages. She had all but forgotten the sensation. Now it rejuvenated her, and enlivened her with a vigor that bordered on passion. Spritely as a child, Veelos slipped from her saddle and cast herself upon Vike's welcoming embrace. She hugged him so tightly as to both astonish and embarrass the hunter. Only when her arms grew weary with the exertion did Veelos loosen that embrace enough to smile tearfully into Vike's weathered face.

As Veelos kissed the hunter on his cheek, Shalar jumped from his horse to celebrate the unexpected encounter. "You lousy rascal!" he laughed in rejoicing. "You took a shortcut and left us to rot, did you? If I weren't so glad to see you, I'd give you a good pounding about now. Alright! Now tell us, where are you hiding those other rascals, Belgar and Valmark?"

Vike answered somberly. "They are both dead."

Shalar winced. "Oh. Terrible news, that. They were good men, both. You had a rough go of it, then. I'm sorry."

Veelos's delight was cruelly dampened. "How awful, Vike. We share your sadness."

Vike spoke reverently of them. "They died as hunters should die. I am over the worst of my grieving for them. May my own death come as theirs did. But there is no time for mourning now. Nor is this the time to tell you their tale.

"But," he continued, "as Shalar said, I did find somewhat of a shortcut. I've spent a few days scouting about, eavesdropping on conversations of the natives, spying you might say. As I'm sure you've discovered, this land is even more cursed than the Lands of Demi-men. And we are now not far from the seaport city of Gur-Molkn, which Druuk's castle overlooks from its mountaintop redoubt. It's a wonder you've not been detected, for Druuk's army patrols these trails frequently. Speaking of which, follow me. I'll show you a place where we can camp, safe from discovery."

As the column followed Vike along a winding forest trail through thick cover, Miril spoke to Kl'aarn. She had drawn up her hood. Her eyes peered sideward from behind an edge of blackest cloth, as she glanced at her man. "This is very fortunate for us," she said. "Just as we had run out of resources, Vike shows up alive and well. How very provident."

"You're being sarcastic, Miril."

"No, I'm not. But you're being very reticent. You're thinking to yourself, 'I wonder what Miril's thinking now. She had thought Vike dead, but her occult cognition failed her.' You're thinking that the winds of destiny are now upon Veelos, not me."

"What I'm thinking," Kl'aarn said, "is that I wish we weren't here, that we had no part in this. I'm dreaming of living on a small farm, quiet and peaceful, just the two of us--- and our children, of course. That's what I want. To raise our children, to grow old, and to die in bed."

Miril laughed gently, with barely more sound than a smile makes. "You'd soon grow bored with the domestic life," she said. "Adventuring is in your blood. You've become a leader of fighting men, now, my lord. Once drunk upon that wine, no man surrenders it and finds contentment in anything else. And now that we draw near to Druuk's castle, you shall soon have greater power than ever you imagined, my love. Armies will snap to attention at your presence, march upon your orders, and attack upon your signal. Kl'aarn shall conquer, and no man will be able to stand against him."

When Kl'aarn did not reply, Miril turned her gaze confidently forward. Only one man could stop her now, she knew, and that was Druuk. Only one woman could hinder her, and that was the Priestess of Prophecy. The time had come.

* * * * *

After nightfall, small bonfires burned from where their light would not reach curious eyes. Beyond the next tall hill lay mighty Gur-Molkn, the very westernmost tip of Wirik, beyond which lay only infinite ocean. Its harbor was crammed with flotillas of warships, according to Vike, preparing for invasion.

"Not for a thousand years have ships been launched on so long a journey, nor in such numbers," Vike said. "Druuk has learned the secret currents and winds, and how to avoid leviathan creatures which rule the waves offshore the Lands of Demi-men.

"But Druuk himself hides in his castle, atop a specially fortified spire. For his recurring dreams of doom grow more frequent. In them, he sees a foreign woman, dressed in white, who bears upon her head a silver crown."

Miril snickered, and said to Veelos, "So. In Druuk's dreams, it is you whom he sees bringing his death. You. He believes that you are going to kill him. Are you? I'm trying to picture it, but I just can't. You, killing someone. Ha! Not unless you worked up a very unpriestly rage."

"The city itself teems with refugees," Vike went on. "Farmers continue to abandon their fields for the flowing riches of Gur-Molkn. Druuk's debauchery has infected everyone, it seems. And indeed the city does flow with wealth. But the greatest riches are reserved for those who enlist in the armies and navies. So many men seek entry into the ranks that enlistment itself has become contingent upon winning death duels in blood-soaked arenas. These are packed with crowds of cheering spectators. And every military unit keeps its own brothels and slaves.

"The streets are bazaars that never close. Those who arrive there with gold have soon spent it all. Afterward, to survive, they must either steal, or else trade that which they never thought themselves base enough to sell. Murder and suicide are commonplace. One requires either a ruthless sword-arm, or demonic cunning, in order to live out a single day and night in that chaotic city.

"Yet for all its wealth, the city is filthy. Amid the frantic seeking and selling of pleasure, none has either the time--- or the inclination--- to tend the overflowing sewage ditches."

Even from their wooded refuge topped by the stars, those who listened to Vike could almost smell the stench that wafted inland from the city. The sky to the west was aglow with the flames of countless torches.

But they also sensed a cold, clammy touch. And that chill came not from the city, but rather from the castle which ruled over it.

* * * * *

Vike had not finished telling all that he had seen. Nor had he told his listeners all they must know, to lay their plans. But while he paused to let them reflect on what he had already revealed, Hathor's attention was caught by a bronze medallion, which Vike was wearing, hung upon a leather cord about his neck. It was a crudely shaped disc, corroded by age. But when Hathor called attention to it, none could remember having seen it before.

"It bears an inscription," Hathor said, examining it at the end of its tether, "but in no writing I've ever seen."

Shalar scoffed. "Ever seen. You can't even read."

Hathor turned it over. "And on this side is carved the head of a creature I've never seen." Then to Shalar, "I can read likeness." Returning to Vike, he said, "It's a charm, isn't it? Is this what brought you the luck to escape from the Lands of Demi-men?"

"Perhaps," Vike replied, "it is luck which brought me the charm, and not the other way around."

"What sort of creature is on the face of it?" Hathor asked.

The hunter hesitated, then said, "I give them the name, Sauroid. What they call themselves, I cannot guess."

"Call themselves?" Hathor pondered. Then he exclaimed, "Demi-men! You got this away from the demi-men. You must tell us your story. How did you escape? Did you have to battle these creatures? How did Valmark and Belgar die? Tell us of their courage. What magic is in this medallion that saved your life?"

"It did save my life," Vike said. "But not by magic. You ask so many questions. Where shall I begin? Shall I start from the end and tell it backward?"

"No," Hathor said, accepting the mild rebuke. "Tell it from the beginning. Last we saw of you was at the fork in the road. The three of you had gone forward to scout. What happened then?"

* * * * *

Vike began. "Priestess Veelos had a premonition that some tragedy awaited. I knew she was right. I hoped that I might intervene before it caught Belgar, and Valmark. So I raced as swiftly as my horse would carry me. But I was too late, as I was soon to discover.

"After two or three hours, I stopped to rest my horse, and that was when the creatures sprang their attack on me.

"They are as tall as a man but much heavier. Their appearance is much that of a lizard, though they are more apt to stand on their hind legs alone than to fall on all fours. Scales cover their body from snout to tail, an adequate armor indeed. They carried weapons fashioned by men, but resorted to using their teeth and claws.

"Before I knew it, my horse had been killed, its throat ripped out by the jaws of these fierce creatures. I was clubbed by another creature, and as I sank into unconsciousness, I counted myself dead.

"My next memories are a fog. I became aware that I was not dead, but rather, bound hand to foot, unable to free myself. I was being carried across the shoulders of one of the sauroids, as were the quarters of my butchered horse being carried by other sauroids.

"The ground across which they took me was a treacherous maze of boulders and gorges, a rock-land of gullies and canyons. But the creatures were strong and nimble-footed. They were also clever, for across the canyons they threw ropes, which caught upon poles that had been set for that purpose on the other side. They crossed these precarious rope bridges by walking upright, balancing the whole way, seemingly without a thought that a misstep--- or a broken rope--- would plunge them to their death at the distant, jagged bottom of these canyons.

"I have no sure idea how long the journey lasted. When it ended, we were carried across a particularly wide and deep canyon, from the bottom of which jutted fangs of rock as fearsome to look upon as were the jaws of these creatures.

"We arrived atop a tall column of rock, one of many such natural formations. In this one was a cave, their den. Here were many sauroids of all sizes and ages. I remember one old one in particular. He seemed to be the unchallenged leader. His scales were not smooth, like the others', but rather rippled, as if drying out with age, and with bare spots aplenty. There were also many hatchlings which nipped at me hungrily. These were rebuked by the stern discipline of their elders.

"I was taken into the cave, and literally thrown to the floor at one side, where there was a shallow pit.

"It was then that I became fully aware of all my pains. The leather and twine which bound me dug deeply into my wrists and ankles. They drew blood, and numbed my fingers and toes. Then I noticed that Belgar and Valmark were there, too, similarly bound.

"Belgar was groaning in a painful nightmare of torture. But Valmark was already dead. I remember vividly the feel of his icy corpse against me, and that I could not squirm free from it.

"I noticed also that bones littered the shallow pit in which we lay. Some were those of animals. Others were bones of demi-men, but not of sauroids.

And finally, some were unmistakably human. Even in my half-conscious state, I knew then that we were in storage for being eaten, kept fresh, so to speak, by the salt of our own breath.

"At the mouth of the cave, I heard the crackle of fire, and smelled the odor of roasting horseflesh. All the sauroids were outside the cave. I could hear their hissing and snarling, what passes for them as language. I heard the sickening sound of joints being torn apart, and bones being crushed.

"Belgar began to regain consciousness. I tried to explain to him what was happening, but he understood little. I suppose that was a mercy.

"I discovered that I still had a dagger in my coat. What great fortune! I supposed. I tried to work it loose, hoping that I could roll over and get my hands on it. But just as it fell out of my coat, the demi-men, finished with feasting, trooped into the cave--- and found the dagger, which I had hoped would save me from them.

"I expected some terrible retribution for this futile escape attempt. But the sauroids simply took the dagger, and forgot about us.

"We lay there helpless for hours. Then at nightfall, the demi-men became hungry again. They took Valmark's corpse. I shall not describe the feasting on him that soon took place. Knowing that we were next, I said my farewell to Belgar. Too quickly, the demi-men had done with the first portion of their supper, and returned to the pit for more.

"There seemed to be some discussion as to which of us to take. In the end, they noticed that Belgar had not much more life left in him. In horror, I watched as they seized him with their murderous claws, without the slightest regard for his terror and agony, and dragged him away. At least I did hear them kill him before putting him on the fire. It was a grudging gratitude I felt for that.

"Then a strange thought came upon me. I thought, how fitting a death this was for three men who had all their lives lived by the hunt. We had, in the end, died as we had lived. Had not these creatures stalked us, and snared us? Were they not, then, entitled to their reward, a meal for themselves and their offspring? A very strange thought, I'll admit, yet somehow, it remains with me yet.

"After they had done with Belgar, the sauroids came once more into the cave, and I knew that they came for me. I heard their guttural snarls and hisses, and imagined their conversation something along these lines: Let's eat him now, I'm hungry. No. Let's save him as breakfast for the hunters, that they do not set out on empty stomachs in the morning.

"In any case, the sauroids finally left me, and retired to the depths of their cave, lying down to sleep, but not so far away that I could not see them.

"There was a small bonfire inside the cave. It filled the upper half of the air space with a layer of smoke, which drifted out the entrance. When it began to die down and smoulder, I guessed that there was no sentry at the door. It occurred to me that if, by some chance, I could get loose, there would be no one to miss me until morning. But it was only the vain hope of the doomed, for I had no means of getting loose.

"At first, all was quiet. But after a time, the hatchlings began to stir. The adults must have been accustomed to their nocturnal play, for they did not awaken.

"Their play was very rough. I think they must sometimes kill each other in their games. They threw rocks, and struck each other with makeshift clubs, in mock battles. I remember being afraid that they might decide to snack on me! But I simply lay on my side and watched them, resigned to my fate.

"One of the hatchlings found my dagger, the one which had been taken from me. They played with it as roughly as they did with their less lethal weapons, and I was sure that one of them would be killed or maimed by it. I knew also that if one of them were to cry out in pain, he would be sure to rouse the adults, who might awaken very hungry.

"Suddenly the knife was thrown, and whether by design or accident, it hit me and fell. One of the little ones ran toward me to recover it.

"I reacted by reflex. Without thinking, I rolled onto the blade and found a grip on its hilt. As soon as I had done that, I expected an immediate outcry from the hatchlings to alert the adults.

"But neither did they cry out, nor dared they approach me, once they had seen that I could yet move. I began clumsily hacking at my bonds, terrified that my unresponsive fingers could not do the work, and fearing that at any moment, the hatchlings would awaken the adults. Indeed, I began to fear that their very silence would arouse suspicion. But eventually they began again to play, unmindful that my curt, repetitive movements had any significance.

"After what must have been hours of feverish effort, my hands were finally free. The hatchlings gawked in fascination when I sat up to saw through the bonds about my legs and feet. My hands and feet were needles of sensation, but at last I managed to work enough blood into them that I could dare to try escape.

"Too soon, I dared to stand, and stumbled. The noise did not arouse the adults. However, it frightened the hatchlings, and they scurried noisily away from me in all directions. One of the adults did stir, then, and uttered a rumbling snarl, then a hiss, and rolled against another. There was a brief commotion among them as they repositioned themselves. Then, once again, I could hear their even breathing as they slept on.

"More carefully now, dagger in hand, and my eyes smarting with the last of the smoke, I made my way toward the starlit cave entrance. I proceeded, step by careful step, being especially careful to allow the hatchlings to get well out of my way, and never stepping directly toward any of them. For, I did not want to provoke them into making an outcry, which would awaken their parents.

"As I plodded slowly forward, the young sauroids parted before me, pressing themselves against the cave walls, all the while staring at me in what I could only guess was a mixture of fright and fascination. I continued forward, toward the beckoning starlight, until only one sauroid, a very small one, still retreated before me in fright. Now it stood at the mouth of the cave, the only obstacle between me and freedom. But it dared not take the one step more that would have carried it outside the cave and into the darkness beyond. It was trapped between me, and the darkness.

"I could sense freedom, now, tantalizingly close, the only barrier a frightened and helpless hatchling. Behind me, a crowd of its siblings and cousins watched in mute wonderment. I could hear adults again. The protracted silence was beginning to penetrate their sleep. All I could think of, then, was how good it would be to disappear from view, so that the hatchlings would play once more, and the adults dream on.

"Carefully, I squeezed my way forward and to one side of the little creature, which stared up at me with a scaled face incapable of expression. But it remained frozen where it was, and my only hope was that, as I got within reach of it, it would move away rather than cry out.

"I got one foot outside the cave before its ear piercing shriek shattered the night. It was a sound much too loud to have come from so small a body.

"Without knowing what I had done, or why, I found myself clutching the noisy hatchling as a shield. My only weapon, the paltry dagger, was pointed not at the bristling fangs and claws of the onrushing carnivores, but rather rested at the throat of the helpless, terrified hatchling.

"It was, after all, the only one of them I had any ability to kill.

"The sauroid attackers suddenly halted. I realized that I had a hostage, and that as long as it lived in my grip, so would I. For the elder, wrinkled sauroid, their leader, issued what unmistakably were stern commands, accentuated by a whip-like, forked tongue much like a snake's. He could see that I had not yet killed the hatchling, and I think he had notions of rescuing it."

"Time was not in my favor. I could not stand there forever. And the wriggling hatchling seemed unaware of the death at its throat as it whined and squealed its pleas to the adults. It struggled to escape from my grasp, and surely would have succeeded had I relaxed for even an instant.

"A plan quickly formed in my mind. It was a slim chance, but my only one. I backed slowly toward the rope-bridge that spanned the canyon. The sauroids followed me, step for step, being careful not to close the distance between us too thinly. All the while, they eyed me with merciless eyes which promised murder at the first glint of opportunity.

"When I reached the rope-bridge, I could not simply walk across it as they were able to do. I could never keep my balance, especially with the hatchling squirming and struggling.

"So I sat, as if astride a horse, facing my enemy, and moving backward. Only desperation made me think I could keep my balance, and soon I lost it. I tipped sideward and spun upside down, my legs still wrapped around the rope. But somehow I held on, not only to both the rope and the hatchling, but also to my dagger. I was no longer able to threaten cutting the young one's throat, but I could certainly drop it into the abyss below, and the sauroids knew that.

"But now I was in a terrible fix. With my hands so occupied, I could not move along the rope. I thought, what next? The thought occurred to me that I could cut the rope and swing to the other side. It would almost surely kill me, once I hit the opposite canyon wall. But my prospects seemed bleak at best, no matter what I did. Of course, to cut the rope, I would first have to drop the hatchling, to its death.

"As these thoughts flashed through my mind, however, I noticed that in my frantic loss of balance, my dagger had already nicked the rope, and it was already beginning to separate. But on the wrong side! If I did not act quickly, I was going to swing to the canyon wall just below the sauroid cave, on their side of the divide.

"I released the dagger and let it drop. It seemed to take forever to vanish into the darkness below. Momentarily, I wondered whether I should follow it, and spare myself whatever horror awaited me in the claws of the demi-men.

"But just then, the rope suddenly broke, and I reacted, once more, purely by reflex. I threw their hatchling at them.

“Why? I can only guess. I couldn't hold onto it any longer. I could have simply dropped it to its death. After all, it had partaken of the flesh of my two slain comrades, and now I was sparing it so it could feast on mine. Call it a hunter's instinct, but it just never occurred to me to kill a cub.

"At the short end of the rope, I swung back to the canyon wall, where my feet cushioned the impact. I now had a choice, either to try to climb down the canyon wall without falling, or to try to climb up and fight to the end.

"Before I could even begin to weigh these alternatives, I felt razor sharp claws close around my arm. Somehow, the old sauroid had nimbly descended the rope and caught me in his grip, probably acting as reflexively as I had. In any case, I was unable to free myself from his grip, though I got in a good kick or two in trying.

"Next I knew, the old sauroid had pulled me back up to the top, and there I was, unarmed, fighting for my life, surrounded by the fiercest carnivores I had ever faced."

Vike paused, and glanced about at his listeners.

But Hathor was beside himself with impatience. "What happened?" he asked. "Did you kill them all?"

"I killed none of them," Vike said. "As I kicked and punched at them, I noticed that they were not fighting back. Not only that, but my arm, by which the old sauroid had pulled me up the rope, was not bleeding. Not at all. He could have easily disemboweled me, but instead, had handled me without inflicting any wound.

"When I ceased my pointless combat, the old sauroid approached me. He stood before me, and spoke. I could understand none of it, of course. There seemed no words, only hisses and raspy, guttural sounds. And its tongue flickered like a whip as it did so.

"I was deeply moved, then. By speaking to me, these creatures had for the very first time acknowledged that I was something more than a meal to them. Until then, they had never taken note of our intelligence as humans. The fact that we rode horses, the fact that we carried weapons, that we spoke to each other--- none of this had made any impression upon the sauroids that we were sentient, thinking, feeling creatures."

"Then what," Hathor asked, "was it that changed their minds?"

"It could only be," Vike answered, "that I spared the life of their hatchling. I saw it cradled snugly in its mother's cherishing arms. This, more than anything else, is to these brutal creatures, the mark of a creature with a soul.

"The old sauroid brought forth this medallion, then, and tying it to this cord, placed it about my neck. At sunrise, they carried me to the border of their land, and passed me off to other sauroids, who relayed me until finally I was at the river which marks the end of the Lands of Demi-men. There, they gave me provisions, and this horse, though how they came upon the horse I don't know.

"After that--- well, here I am."

Chapter 37

Rumors of War

Miril had listened attentively to Vike's account. But his tale had ended without her learning anything that would serve her purpose. Unlike the others, who had found the recital fascinating, Miril had become impatient with it. "Enough of idle story telling," she said. "We have more pressing matters to consider. We are now within striking distance of Druuk's castle. Our greatest task is now at hand, the very reason and purpose for all we have endured. We must discover how we may penetrate his defenses--- which, we can surely assume, are formidable, and many layered. He has a powerful army to man the castle walls. And within those ramparts, we can expect all manner of sorcerors, pitfalls, and untold horrors of every kind. You have spied, Vike. What are we up against? How can we penetrate to the king's most inner chamber?"

Vike glanced awkwardly at the witch, clearly reluctant to answer her. For here was a predator more savage than the hungriest of sauroids. She would kill without need, and would delight in inflicting pain. Her war against

Druuk was prelude to her war against Veelos. Vike felt that, by answering Miril, he was also arming her against the priestess.

But regardless of his apprehensions, there was no avoiding it. He had to tell everyone what he knew.

"First," he said, "the city abounds with rumor, so that correct information is difficult to obtain, and more difficult yet to judge. One of these rumors is that an army of priests--- from the east of Wirik--- is about to invade Gur-Molkn, in retaliation for the massacre of the temple. It is said that this army will be led by a powerful priestess, who will come to steal back the Great Orb from Druuk. Surely, these rumors were used to justify the conscription of so many into the armies and navies. But it may be that Druuk himself believes some version of the story, for indeed he has fortified himself deep within his castle defenses."

Shalar scoffed. "Rumors. What do we care of them? Give us facts, not rumor."

But Miril interjected, "Let him speak, Shalar. Rumors have great power. If the people have war jitters, this can be used against them."

Shalar dismissed the thought. "Rumors, jitters. Rot," he said to Miril. Then, to Vike: "Tell us of their soldiers, hunter. Just how good are they?"

Vike replied, "Their discipline is very strict, but sometimes arbitrary. There is corruption. Promotions can be bought, or attained by assassination. But, despite the moral decline among the ranks, there remains an old line of disciplined professionals, men who form the core of military power. These are the men who fought and won Druuk's wars of conquest, and made his kingdom so large. These men are not to be underestimated. They are masters in the art of war: skilled, equipped, and brave. If they lead the invasion of Shi-Raq, they will quickly overwhelm all of east Wirik. We do well to fear them."

Kl'aarn asked, "What of the castle itself? How tall are the walls? How many men patrol the catwalks? What lies inside?"

Vike answered, "I could not get very near. The walls are ringed with archers, who have standing orders to kill any approaching man--- or beast. And these archers never miss."

"Then," Kl'aarn asked, "how does anyone get in or out of the castle?"

"There is one lane of safe passage, such as it is," Vike answered. "A long, straight, open road leads to the castle gate. The road is flanked by a long gauntlet of soldiers. Upon the slightest suspicion, they summarily kill anyone on that road. So, you can imagine, that only those very few, upon the king's urgent business, come to the castle."

Miril asked, "You have not seen the inside of the castle. You could not approach more closely. But you may have heard some description of it. What do people say is inside its walls?"

"There are only rumors," Vike said. "Monsters, traps, conjurors, ancient spells, magic weapons, whatever wild story you can imagine--- and more."

"Beyond rumors," Miril pressed, "what have you learned as fact?"

Vike shook his head. "Nothing."

"Oh come now," Miril insisted. "Surely a man of your skills---"

"He's told us all he knows," Veelos injected. "Why would he hold back?"

Miril turned to Veelos. "Perhaps he's saving a little something for you, just between him and yourself."

"Such as?" Veelos challenged.

"Such as," Miril answered with quiet menace, "the location of the Orb."

"I see," Veelos said. Then, to Vike, "It's alright to tell what you know. If the winds of fate are upon Miril, then she will discover its location anyway. But if the prophecy holds, then only the Priestess of Prophecy can take the Orb. So speak openly, Vike."

Vike nodded. "It is said that Druuk had a special vault built, constructed in the very center of the courtyard. It is also said that, after it was finished, Druuk killed all those who did the work, not only the laborers, but also the designers, and, moreover, curiously, a great number of sorcerors."

Miril affirmed, "That makes sense. If Druuk were to build a vault to safeguard the Orb, it would be a magic vault. Any sorceror who had placed spells and curses to protect the vault, would also be able to remove those curses. So, of course, Druuk would foreclose that possibility--- by killing all the sorcerors. But if he is able to kill sorcerors--- if he has that much power--- this can only mean that he has even more potent conjury among his inner circle of counselors. This is sorcery in its might and power indeed!"

Shalar suddenly stood, and paced angrily about. "Spells? Curses? Sorcery indeed?" His tone was sarcastic and irate. "Garbage! This is all hearsay," he said. "We have nothing firm to go on. Nothing! How are we to go about looting Druuk's treasury on rumor? We have no way of getting past the first soldier, and here we are discussing magic vaults. I want to hear something that makes sense. You women brought us here on the promise that, once we arrived, you would have matters in hand. Now, here we are, and all you can do is to ask Vike what rumors he's heard. Well now, how is this for a rumor? I'm getting the impression that, with all your mystic powers, you've run up against a power far greater than you bargained for. I think we've come all this way for nothing."

"Shut up," Miril retorted, "and sit down. I got us across the Lands of Demi-men, and I can handle this, too."

But Veelos also retorted. "No, Miril. You did not. You merely made everyone believe it was your power that got us across. In fact, you were our greatest hindrance."

Miril sneered. "Tell that to the brown, hairy demi-man who nearly made a meal of you, but for my killing curse. I saved your life."

"Liar," Veelos said. "He had no intention of harming me and you know that. He wanted a prisoner. We were invaders in their land, and they its defenders. Had they abducted me, we could have made peace with them. They would have helped us. Lives would have been saved. You know that now, and you knew it then."

Miril was quick to retaliate. "You whore of Tarok. How dare you call me a liar? If you have such powers as you boast, show them. But no, you can't. Your powers are, as you say, only passive. You do not use them, but rather, they use you. Then, what good are they to us? Your powers are nothing, Veelos, neither against me, nor against Druuk. You are no longer even in contention against him. This has become a duel strictly between Druuk and me. And I will win. I, not you, will slay Druuk. Your stubborn refusal to join with me will only doom you, and all who follow you. Give up, Veelos. Surrender to me while yet you can. Embrace the powers of witchcraft. For only in them can you ever find refuge from the horror we are sent to attack. Only witchcraft can destroy Druuk. Join me, Veelos. Don the robes of witchcraft, kiss me on the cheek, and let us be as one in the eternal night of evil."

"Never!" Veelos retorted. "And if you have no need of me, then slay me now, as surely you must in the end." So speaking, the priestess stood as if to strike Miril.

But Shalar stepped between the two women, and threw out his arms in a gesture of anger and frustration. "Great!" he stomped. "This is just what we need: the two of you still at each others' throats." He stopped his pacing, and squared himself against both of them. Then he said in a low, even voice, "Let me tell you. I have power also. However I fit into your schemes, I have power. I know this, because both of you wanted me to make this trek. You both need me. Now, we're all facing a common enemy, one who is going to laugh while we turn against each other and kill ourselves. But not Shalar. Not me. I'm having no part of this. Neither of you can win without me. And I'm not going to get killed by your bickering. It's going to take all we've got to beat Druuk. And if we're not all of one accord on this, then you can count me out."

Miril had lowered her eyes while Shalar spoke. When he had finished, she said softly, "Shalar is correct. Whatever our differences, we must act in unison against Druuk. Let there be a pact between us."

Veelos answered flatly. "No. I'll go it alone."

Before Miril could retort, Kl'aarn rose and spoke. "Veelos, be reasonable. Shalar is making sense. We can't have come all this distance only to fight each other, instead of Druuk. He's the one who killed our families. We must never forget that, not until he lies cold in his grave."

Veelos looked at Kl'aarn and answered him. "Shalar is wrong, Kl'aarn. You don't understand the prophecy. Only one of us can get to Druuk. Only one of us can get to the Orb. Whichever of us does these things, fulfills her prophecy--- or her anti-prophecy--- and thereby defeats the other's. Whichever of us does that---" Veelos hesitated before finishing, "whichever of us wins, will rule the world."

Kl'aarn glanced at Miril, then back at Veelos. "And what of Druuk's destiny? Who is your worse enemy, Veelos? Is it Druuk, or Miril? Which will you fight, or if both, in which order?"

Veelos did not answer.

But Kl'aarn persisted. "Which one, Veelos? Druuk? Or Miril?"

Veelos's face reddened, but she said nothing.

Angrily, Kl'aarn spun to face Vike. "You reason with her, then. You're the only one she seems to trust anymore. She certainly doesn't listen to me."

Quietly, then, Vike stood, and gently taking Veelos's elbow, said to her, "Let's take another of our walks."

* * * * *

The pair made their way a short distance into the trees, away from where the others sat. The night was cool, and the stars were bright and multi-colored overhead. Veelos felt an ironic sense of peace in these surroundings, sandwiched though she was between two dreaded and powerful enemies, the Demonwitch on one side, and Druuk on the other. But she might have been in another world, apart from them, separated by aeons. Here, there was only the peace of the forest, the jeweled night sky, and the close presence of Vike, who nourished her soul with comfort. For a few long moments, Veelos spent an eternity of rest in the earthly heaven she had found.

Too soon, it was time to return to the terrifying reality of life or death, of victory or defeat, of destiny or fate.

"Vike," she said, her voice trembling. "I'm so afraid. Miril has some horrible plan. I can sense it more strongly than ever. She has victory in her grasp, Vike. And it's my fault. My faithlessness has made her strong. I should have battled her at the very beginning, or else fled her, as the scriptures command. Now is my last, final chance to do so. I've got to take a stand against her. I must do so now. She is ready to spring her trap, and I can no longer be party to it."

Vike put his hands on the priestess's shoulders, and spoke quietly, calmly. "If you had battled Miril at the outset, she would have killed you. Had you fled her, she would have run you down, just as she pursued Kl'aarn and snared Shalar. And if you fight her now, you will be attacking her strength. If you battle her tonight, she will kill you, just as surely as she would have slain you at the first. And still there is no fleeing her."

Veelos felt despair. "Then what can I do on this blackest of nights? Is it totally hopeless? Are we lost already? Is there nothing at all I can do?"

"You can only follow your own path," Vike said. "Let Miril follow hers. And, Priestess Veelos, this is very important--- let Kl'aarn follow his path. Miril took him from it once. He will fare no better if you do the same to him now. That is the test you are facing. You must pass it."

Veelos cast her gaze downward. "I can't, Vike. I can't just do nothing. That would be the same as forming a pact with her. If I do nothing, then Miril will continue using me, just as she's used me all along to her own evil end. The Demonwitch consumes people, Vike, and then discards their empty husks. She'll do it to me, and she'll do the same to Kl'aarn."

But Vike counseled her, "You're making this too complicated, Priestess. Don't concern yourself with all that. Only walk your path. Don't fear Miril. Don't fear evil. And most of all, don't fear making mistakes. None of us can do good; we can only choose it. It is God who does good, not us. We can only choose to let Him work through us. Miril taunted you tonight about that passive power, but she has no idea, the power of letting ourselves be the instruments of God."

Veelos looked up at Vike. "Are even you saying that I should make a pact with the witch?"

Vike sighed. "No! As you yourself told the others, you must go it alone. Do your part. Miril will be there, working against you, trying to distract you. But walk your own path. For as long as evil exists, it will always walk where there is good."

Veelos clutched Vike's hands. "But what if I fail? So very much is at stake. So very much is now at risk! I'm not strong, Vike. I am weak. Yet upon my success so awfully much depends. Vike, what will happen if I fail?"

Beneath his beard, the hint of a smile showed on Vike's face. "You will fail, Veelos. We all fail. But God does not. Take heart in that, Priestess. Though we shall fail, God will never."

Veelos gazed at Vike a long time before speaking again. Then she said, "Vike, my dearest friend. Can I trust even your counsel?"

Vike shook his head. "No," he said. "You can't. You can trust only God."

* * * * *

The two of them returned to the clearing, where the campfire illuminated the faces of those who waited, as if for a verdict. Miril's eyes stared into Veelos's with sinister threat.

With a composed demeanor, Veelos seated herself upon the fallen log, upon which she had sat before, and with her hands, swept the wrinkles from the brown garb which covered her lap. She said calmly, "Let's make our plans."

There was a collective sense of relief.

Miril's glare relaxed into an expression of composed self-satisfaction. It will be oh, so much more convenient this way, she thought to herself. And the victory will be all the sweeter. Indeed it will. Things might have gotten messy if Veelos had tried to ruin it all now. But messy for Veelos, too. Perhaps she knows that. Perhaps that is why she is unable to work up the nerve to do, in defeat, that which she could have done long ago in victory.

Perhaps Vike has consoled her with some nonsense, like, "Bide your time." But Veelos's time has long since passed. It's no longer her, I worry about, so much as Kl'aarn. He's not yet given himself over to evil, not quite yet. He's not ready to share with me that cup of priestly blood, the blood of the Priestess of Prophecy. But he will be.

Soon, as do I, he also will belong to evil.

* * * * *

Veelos glanced at Kl'aarn, then at Shalar, in a manner much more serene than when she had left to speak with Vike. "The two of you seem to know the most about matters of fighting," she said. "So devise a plan for us. And whatever that plan be, let us follow it, and rely upon God's blessing."

Shalar replied, "I'm glad to see you've come to your senses, Veelos. But how can we make plans with no facts? How do we get into the castle? Once inside, how do we deal with whatever we find there? And most important of all, how do we escape? There were once over sixty of us. We now number thirty-five. With such losses as we can expect to take in Gur-Molkn, there won't be enough of us left alive to get back to our native land."

Kl'aarn studied Veelos's face, and then Miril's, pondering some deep and disturbing question which troubled him greatly. Finally, he spoke to Shalar. "It seems we've gotten all the information we're going to get. We'll have to make do with it. Here is my plan. We'll divide into two groups. My men and I will take care of the castle. We'll get inside, do what must be done, and get out. You, Shalar, with your men, will see to our escape. That does seem to be your main concern."

Shalar looked inquisitively at Kl'aarn. "Escape is indeed the secret to all success. But it will involve a journey of months."

"Not so," Kl'aarn replied. "Since there are too few of us to ride back to Shi-Raq, as you pointed out, our escape will be by ship. There is an abundant supply of them in the harbor."

Shalar scoffed. "By ship? We're no sailors."

"True," Kl'aarn said. "But we can row. It's our only hope. Now listen.

In a harbor the size of Gur-Molkn, there are places where ships are docked for repair of their rigging. These ships cannot sail. But they can be rowed. Any such ships will be the most lightly guarded of all. You will steal one for us."

Shalar looked to Veelos. "Doesn't Druuk command the sea monsters? Won't he block our escape?"

Veelos answered. "If we succeed inside the castle, Druuk's powers will be finished. And we will have the Orb of power. We will need fear no sorcery."

Shalar turned back to Kl'aarn. "I have only seventeen men plus myself. There are thousands of sailors. And warships will be all over the harbor. How do we get past them?"

"Panic," Kl'aarn replied. "Vike says they're expecting an invasion, aren't they? Good. If we move at night, set fires, spread rumors, we just might be able to incite chaos. If the people believe an attack is under way, an attack by priests with mystic powers--- that would give us the cover we need. I'm sure you can embellish the plan, enough to make it work."

Shalar grunted. "That's not much of a plan, merchant. But it looks like it's all we're going to come up with. What about the gold?"

"I told you," Kl'aarn said. "My men will take care of the castle. Unless, of course, you'd rather do that yourself."

Shalar glanced about among his men. None of them seemed eager to challenge Druuk in his lair. "What do you think, Hathor?"

Hathor replied worriedly, "We're better at escaping than anything else."

Shalar nodded. "We'll steal a ship, then. What the hell. It's the only thing we've never stolen before." Then, "So tell me, Kl'aarn. How do you plan to get into the castle?"

Kl'aarn answered, speaking to both Miril and Veelos. "Our part of it will be much simpler. We'll make some grapples, and use them to scale the walls. Once over the walls, we simply jump inside, and deal with whatever we find, as we find it."

Miril jerked her head to stare at Kl'aarn in disbelief. "That's it?" she said in astonishment. "That's your plan? What kind of plan is that?"

Kl'aarn shrugged. "It'll be nighttime. If Shalar does his part, the docks to the west of the castle will be on fire. We'll climb the east wall, from the dark side. Hopefully, attention will be toward the west, especially if Druuk's men believe they are being invaded. From there, Miril, and Veelos, we'll have to rely on the strength of whichever of your two prophecies is, in fact, Druuk's undoing. It will be a fitting way for the two of you to vie against each other. Instead of a battle between you, you both will get a chance to battle the real enemy, Druuk himself."

Miril did not look particularly happy. "And what of the archers on that wall we are so blithely supposed to climb?"

Kl'aarn looked squarely into Miril's eyes. "As Vike pointed out, my darling. They never miss."

* * * * *

It was one thing to have made the plans. They were necessarily ambiguous. There was no map of the city. The rigging repair docks were only an assumption. Surveillance was impossible. And although Vike had tried to be useful, his spying had been of scant help.

But if the planning had been perfunctory, carrying out the plans was anything but that. They had decided they must act the very next night, fearing any delay. There had been much to do. The supply wagon was destroyed and cannibalized to make the grapples. These were padded for silence, and attached to long ropes. Torches were fashioned, and a thousand, minute details attended to. These preparations kept them occupied all night, which in turn, made it possible for them to sleep throughout the daylight hours of the following day. If nothing else, they were at least able to preoccupy themselves enough to keep their minds off the dangerous raid they were about to attempt, and the overwhelming prospect of disaster which awaited them.

By the time Shalar began to reflect on the absurdity of it all, the plan had already been set into motion. As darkness once again enveloped the forest, his men donned their disguises, clothes with hoods to conceal their faces.

This made them look much like a column of sorcerors. They hoped that no one in the crowded city would dare challenge a band of conjurors. But as Shalar observed them, he thought his men looked nothing like sorcerors. They looked to be exactly what they were, a collection of thugs. He wondered who would panic first, the west landers, or his own, nervous men, who were well aware of what would happen to them if they were discovered.

Despite his doubts, Shalar found himself caught up in the workings of Kl'aarn's almost fatalistic faith that destiny would somehow ensure their success. As to whether it would be Miril's destiny or Veelos's, Shalar had little faith in either. But at least it was fairly certain that Kl'aarn's plan was their only hope of survival. For, trying to subsist in this land would be as futile for Shalar and his men as it had been for all the bandits who once had roamed the west Wirik forests. And if anything went wrong with Kl'aarn's raid, at least Shalar and his men had the best prospects of escape.

These thoughts carried Shalar through the streets of Gur-Molkn, and all the way to its harbor.

Setting the fires, he knew, would not be difficult. Torches abounded on the docks. There was plenty of fire to be spread. What made Shalar hesitate was the sudden realization that, at long last, this was it. This was really, really, it. After all they had been through, after all they had survived, after all the dead and vanished they had left along the long trail--- they were here. They were on the opposite edge of the world from Har-Keem. Having finally reached their goal, they were about to fulfill the purpose of their journey, a purpose which often had been forgotten, amid more immediate concerns. Now that purpose was the only thing remaining.

This was it.

As Shalar crouched in the darkness of a boat shed on the dock, he tried to remember the words of Veelos. She had used magic words to persuade him to cross that first river, that watery borderline which separated his homeland from his destiny. He couldn't quite remember exactly, but they had been words such as, "One noble deed in a lifetime."

"One noble deed," he breathed, "and then to die."

Then, inhaling deeply, Shalar uncovered the lit oil lamp which he had brought into the boat shed with him. It bathed the interior of the dirty, rat infested shed with brilliant light. Now. He raised the lamp, and without further thought, smashed it against the dry, wooden wall.

"Invasion!" he shouted as he ran from the inferno. "Pirates! Seamonsters!" Other sheds along the dock also erupted into flame, and from them, hooded men jumped onto the dock crying out with similar calls.

It had begun.

The rumors were being spread. Everything now depended upon how easily panicked the west landers would be. For rumor could spread very quickly in a crowded city.

But from somewhere in the back of Shalar's mind, the thought occurred to him that, sometimes, rumors were quickly crushed.

* * * * *

In the darkness, Kl'aarn saw that the east wall of the castle faced an expanse of open meadow in which was the castle dump. Beyond the meadow was forest. Within that forest, Kl'aarn and his men found that they were not alone. Other people besides themselves skulked through the trees.

Scavengers. There were scavengers in the forest. Unable to survive in the city, they lived off the rotting refuse of elegant banquets eaten wastefully within the castle. The uneaten portions were discarded, and the meadow was littered with the leftovers of fine feasts. There was enough thrown away to sustain a good number of scavengers.

But by starlight, Kl'aarn could see that even to be a scavenger was a dangerous occupation. He could make out the forms of several corpses, in various stages of decomposition, lying unburied in the meadow. Each had an arrow in it. Either the archers who guarded the walls were very protective, of even the castle dump, or else they made sport of their job. For some of the corpses were pierced by several arrows, more than enough to kill.

Kl'aarn's thoughts dwelt not, however, on sympathy for the scavengers.

Positioning his men along the tree line, he became concerned that one of the wretched west land scavengers would take note of the fully armored swordsmen moving through the trees. Any one of them might report them to the castle guards, in hopes of some reward. And there were too many scavengers for Kl'aarn's men to kill them all.

But the scavengers stayed well away from Kl'aarn's men. None approached closely enough to identify the warriors' faces as foreign. They did not even come close enough to note that the armor belonged to no regiment of Druuk. All the scavengers knew was that armored swordsmen were slipping through the trees. Could they be other than Druuk's soldiers, hunting for scavengers?

After understanding this, that the scavengers thought his men to be Druuk's, Kl'aarn turned his attention to the meadow. Getting across that open expanse, even under cover of darkness, would be no easy matter. Darkness would not stop an arrow.

But he knew that they had to be at the foot of those walls when Shalar started his fires. There was no time to wait. They had to move immediately, and hope that if seen, they would be counted as mere scavengers.

The signal was given, and slowly, Kl'aarn and Miril began snaking their way through the darkness of the garbage-strewn meadow. As he moved, crouching almost to a crawl, Kl'aarn glanced about to see the movements of other figures in the dump. Whether they were his own men or indigents, he could not tell. That was good, he decided. For if he could not tell, then neither could the archers.

The whistle of an arrow made him pull Miril close. He covered her, for there was no other protection. The arrow skidded onto the ground nearby. He tensed, waiting for a volley. The number of arrows he had seen in a single corpse told him to expect more than one missile to follow the first. Nervously, he glanced at the top of the castle wall. He thought he saw the silhouette of an archer unstringing his bow, then turning and disappearing from sight.

It had been a random shot, perhaps intended to panic any scavenger nearby, causing him to run. That would certainly be fatal. But whatever the intent of the shot, it was clear that Druuk's men had arrows enough to waste.

They continued on, crouching and crawling, moving like thieves. Indeed, Kl'aarn mused, this was work more suited for Shalar's men than for warriors. Only inside the walls would the skills of disciplined fighters become necessary. And even that might not be enough.

Kl'aarn and Miril continued on, trying to keep a steady, even movement, stopping only when another arrow whistled overhead or landed nearby. Once, they surprised a scavenger. The hapless man saw Kl'aarn and, assuming himself about to be attacked by a soldier, shrieked loudly and ran for the trees. He got not so many as a score of steps before half a dozen arrows ripped into his back and felled him, to become bait for the four-legged scavengers which also stalked this meadow.

They were by this time close enough to the castle to hear the laughter of the archers. Kl'aarn could make out the phrase, "Must have been snake bitten," then the words, "flying snakes," and more laughter.

Grasping Miril's hand, he continued on with her, in a journey that seemed to be as long and as dangerous as the trek from Shi-Raq had been. When at last they reached the foot of the castle wall, they crouched in its night shadow, and felt the cold hardness of its massive stones at their backs. Kl'aarn felt a strange sense of relief, even though their position was infinitely more dangerous than in the meadow. He sat, leaning his back against the castle wall, not daring to breathe audibly, and hardly believing that they had made it so far.

Then Kl'aarn began coiling the rope he carried, to prepare the grapple for throwing.

"Not yet," Miril whispered in his ear. "Give the others a chance to get to the wall. Maybe Shalar will draw some attention."

Kl'aarn whispered back, his voice barely louder than a thought, "I hate plans which depend on timing."

"I only hate depending on Shalar," Miril said softly. "He has no loyalty. He might even set sail without us."

Kl'aarn answered, "If he does wait for us, he might have a very, very long wait."

"Speak more quietly," Miril cautioned. "Any louder and they might hear you."

Kl'aarn nodded. Then, his voice so low even he could only barely hear it, he asked, "Is there any spell you can make, which will help conceal us and the men?"

Miril shook her head. "I'm going to need every smallest measure of my power to fight Druuk. If I squander a single grain of it, it might be the difference between life and death for all of us--- wait." She stopped. Then, "Listen. Can you hear it?"

Kl'aarn listened. "Nothing that sounds like panic," he said.

"No, not from the city," Miril said. "Sleeping. Can you believe it? The guard directly over us is asleep."

"I can't hear it. Did you bewitch him?"

"No. I told you. My powers tonight are stored up for Druuk, and for him alone."

Kl'aarn turned himself to face Miril fully, momentarily forgetting the danger. "Miril."

"What?"

"Don't kill Druuk."

"I must!" she answered in astonishment.

"Miril. I know this sounds crazy. But I don't want you killing anymore. I want you to become gentle again, as you once were. Do you remember when Shalar killed that pirate in the inlet? The man had tried to kill you, and yet you felt only sympathy, for the pirate. Can you remember what it was to feel that? That was the real you, Miril, the woman you truly are. I want you to be like that, be her, once more."

"Kl'aarn. Druuk must die. Throw your grapple. The sentry is asleep.

This is our chance."

"Then let me kill him," Kl'aarn said. He held Miril's shoulders with both hands. He felt a sudden, surprising emotion within himself, an absurd urge, to abandon the entire venture, then and there. For an instant, he believed they could do just that, simply walk away from it all, and not look back.

But Miril burst the fantasy as soon as it formed. "Don't lose your nerve, not now," she whispered impatiently.

Kl'aarn felt a sense of desperation mounting within himself. "It's you I'm losing, not my nerve," he said. "If you go through with this, if you actually do succeed--- I'll have lost you for all time."

"You're not going to lose me, my love. This will be our hour of final victory over those who sought to separate us for all time."

"I've never had a premonition," Kl'aarn said. "But now I am, and it's no mere feeling. It's real. I know it."

"Then you kill him," Miril said. "But we must hurry. Throw your grapple, before it's too late."

Kl'aarn stood then, and arranged the grapple and rope for throwing.

But Miril stood also and touched his elbow. "If you do kill Druuk," she said, "make sure of one thing. I want him to die slowly, Kl'aarn. Very, very slowly."

* * * * *

Akmeb was practiced in the dangerous art of sleeping on duty.

Like the other guards in his regiment, Akmeb had begun his career as a vigilant observer, eyes carefully scanning every shadow and movement while at his post. Diligently obedient to orders, he had shot arrows at every target, however questionable, just in case it were a clever enemy come to harm the empire. He had been warned that such an enemy might come magically disguised, seemingly harmless, but mystically powerful and dangerous. And so the sentry had obeyed. Even such innocuous targets as rabbits and squirrels had died beneath his meticulous watch.

But after a time, as had been the case with the other sentries, Akmeb had wearied of the dull routine of sleepless nights, followed by the often-disturbed day-sleep of garrison life. The frequent awakenings had kept him pale and fatigued. Boredom had eaten away at his initial dedication. The glowing promise of life as a royal guardsman had once been alluring. But no more. That empty promise had been broken by snarling superiors who cared more about the polish of his armor than the accuracy of his aim. The arrogant men with authority were, for the most part, hypocrites and drunkards, who would upon any pretext find him in violation of the least of their endless regulations. And having found a trifling violation, they would extort from him as much of his pay as they could.

Even all that might have been ultimately bearable, were it not for the utter meaninglessness of it all. For of all Akmeb's dissatisfactions, his greatest resentment was the pointlessness of what he did. Nothing he had ever shot an arrow into had remotely resembled a threat to the castle. That knowledge had dawned on him but slowly, and had become a festering wound in his soul. Those whom he had killed, all of them, had been but pathetic garbage-pickers, scavenging the dump for bones to gnaw. Akmeb's comrades had made sport of the senseless killing, sometimes by day even setting fine meals upon banquet tables, complete with linen and silver, expressly as bait for the scavengers. It had worked. At night, the table would lure half a dozen or more vagabonds, who would be cut down in volleys of inerrantly aimed arrows. Akmeb abhorred these sadistic perversions. Yet, he had come to regard depravity as just another of life's many sad facts about which he could do nothing. With the passage of time, he had become numb.

Akmeb had not volunteered to be a sentry. He had sought assignment to one of the legions. He had respect for true soldiers. They fought the enemies of the empire not from a distance, not from behind garrison walls, but rather toe to toe, face to face. They fought not feeble beggars, but instead against fierce pirates, or murderous bandits, or against organized rebel armies. True soldiers fought enemies who fought back. Akmeb had wanted to be one of those soldiers, a swordsman, not an archer. But the sword which was strapped to his side was only another item to be prepared for inspection, not expressly a weapon of his trade, but little more than a ceremonial ornament. He had not even been trained in its use.

Beneath the weight of his rancor, Akmeb slept on duty.

He had mastered the art. And it paid handsomely. Having slept at night, he had time and energy during the daylight to visit the farm girl who lived across the hill. They were in love. She was not like other women. She did not debase her body. She made him know what it was to feel like a man, and not a mere stud animal. They had made plans for a future together. Whereas before, Akmeb had planned to desert and become a fugitive, he had decided instead to serve out his enlistment, marry the farm girl, and settle down with her to raise a family. They had such plans as these.

Akmeb slept skillfully. Even asleep, his ears were alert for the sound of the approach of the sergeant-of-the-guard. To be found asleep was to die without awakening. Those were orders. Of course, as with anything else, there was an intricate code of unwritten rules. If the sentry awoke before the sergeant could kill him, the sergeant would pretend not to have caught the sentry asleep. To make an issue of it, with the sentry's life at stake, could be fatal for the sergeant.

Of course, the skillful sleeper would not press his luck. He would not arouse any suspicion. Every so often, he would arise, make a show of walking his post, launch an arrow, and then return to his niche on the catwalk and steal another period of sleep.

Akmeb awoke from his sleep as soon as he heard the military cadence of footsteps marching smartly toward him on the catwalk. He was on his feet in a single, smooth action, at the rigid posture of formal respect. He was safe, he knew, awake in plenty of time. And from the rapid cadence of the footsteps, it was just the officer of the watch eager to be finished with his tour, probably eager to get back to sleep himself.

"Post number eight," the sentry recited as the armored silhouette marched up before him. "Corporal Akmeb reports that all is---"

He felt the blade in his heart just after he saw, to his horror and bewilderment, that his killer was not a west lander.

* * * * *

Kl'aarn eased the corpse into a half sitting, half leaning position, so that the man appeared to be sleeping. The lie was given away by streaming blood which pooled beneath the dead sentry on the catwalk. But for the moment, it would work.

Kl'aarn felt mild astonishment that he had been able to get onto the cat-walk unseen, and to kill a sentry without hearing an alarm. Clearly, the reputation of these men was overblown. Perhaps the rest of Druuk's army was not so formidable after all. He hoped.

Moving swiftly and silently, Kl'aarn continued the charade of appearing that he belonged where he was. He pulled up the rope, which was weighted by Miril on the other end, hoping that while she was vulnerable, no one would challenge him. Miril finally reached the top edge of the wall, and deftly rolled across it, keeping a low profile. Kl'aarn quickly concealed the rope and grapple, then hid with Miril, huddling in a notch near the corpse of the archer. There, they awaited the signal flames, which they hoped would arise from the port before any other sentry arrived.

Miril glanced at the corpse. "You're good at this," she said, admiringly. "You pierced his heart from the side, at the joint of his armor."

"He was just a kid," Kl'aarn said. "He thought I was his---"

"Have we been seen?" Miril asked.

"If we have, we've not drawn any suspicion. I don't think it ever occurs to them that anyone could breach their outer defense. My worry isn't about us, but Shalar. I don't hear any panic from the city. Let's hope nothing has gone wrong for the bandits."

Miril carefully peered around the notch of wall into the courtyard below. "I think I see the vault," she said. "It's right in the center, just where Vike said it would be. At least that much is going right."

"It could be only a barracks," Kl'aarn said.

"Not with magic-lock," the witch replied. Then, "And look up there," she gestured.

A hundred paces from the vault loomed a tower, a tall spire, which ended in a turret. From its windows glowed the bright, yellow light of many candles. "Druuk's refuge," Miril uttered. Her voice had become venomous, icy with contempt. "His sleeping quarter." Her nostrils flared in anger. "I can smell the bastard."

As she spoke, there arose a commotion on the catwalk, not far from where they hid, the sound of metal armor scraping against stone.

A voice called out with urgency. "Post number ten! Attempted intrusion!"

"Damn!" Kl'aarn cursed. "They must have seen us!"

From the courtyard below, another voice bellowed back. It was a voice accustomed to authority. "What is it, Chalert? You'd better not be calling out the guard for another scavenger again."

"It was no scavenger this time," Chalert answered back. "It was an intruder. His grapple is right here on the wall, if you want to look."

"Only one?" the voice called back.

"That's all I saw."

"Did you kill him?"

"Of course."

"Chalert, are you sure about all this?"

"Hell, I'm looking right down the wall at his corpse. The bastard is wearing armor."

Kl'aarn muttered, "Oh, hell, they've killed Sheldak. That was his position."

Despite all this, the voice from below remained skeptical and impatient. "What sort of armor? Can you recognize the regiment?"

"No. It's too dark."

"Must have been someone sneaking back in from a night on the city. See if you can identify the regiment. We'll have to notify his commander."

Chalert's voice became direly defensive. "Well, nobody had told me to let anybody back in." Then Chalert augmented his case. "Besides, for all I know, it still might be an intruder. And until I know better, I'm calling it an attempted breach."

"Alright, alright," the officer below replied with irritation. "Let's do a post check. Post eleven. Password."

"Lancer!" came a distant reply.

"Post nine."

"Chariot!" The reply was much closer.

"Post eight."

Kl'aarn whispered urgently to Veelos. "Post eight, that's us. And the password is lying dead."

"Post eight! Password!"

Kl'aarn turned in near panic to Miril. "Make yourself invisible!" he urged.

She whispered back, "No! It doesn't work that way."

"Akmeb, damn you! Answer up."

"What do you mean it doesn't work that way?"

"I'm spelled for killing," Miril answered. "I've put all my energies into that alone. Other than you, I have no defense whatever."

"Alright, then, post seven!"

"Amber!"

"Post seven, Charinok, go on over to eight and check on Akmeb. If he's asleep, kill him."

"On the way, sir."

"Miril, get out of here," Kl'aarn urged her. "We've been caught."

"Not without you."

"You have to."

Miril was insistent. "I got you into this. If they kill you, why would I want to live? I'm staying with you."

By then, Kl'aarn could hear Charinok's footsteps drawing close. "Hell," he hissed. "This is it. We've had it."

Chapter 38

Valley of Death

Shalar was discovering that west landers did not easily panic. For a long while, it seemed, his men had been racing up and down the docks, waving torches and swords, and making as much commotion as possible. Added to all this, they were starting as many fires as they could. But for all their efforts, they were attracting little attention. The natives seemed apathetic, lethargic. For all the locals seemed to care, Shalar's men were a band of drunken sailors, perhaps madmen, celebrating drunkenly on the docks.

Even after the fires had actually burned some people to death, there was no more panic than a small, ordinary fire would evoke. As if this were some common occurrence, people merely ran toward the nearest place of safety, as one might sidestep a runaway horse--- in fear at most, but nothing approaching panic or dread.

"East landers!" Shalar shouted at a group of retreating drunks. "Invasion! Dragons!" But the ruse was not working, not at all.

A drunkard stumbled past Shalar, bumping into the bandit's flailing arms. "You'd better get out of here," the drunkard advised Shalar, with exaggerated solemnity. "The pier's on fire."

Shalar grabbed the man by the shoulders. "Go find the army," he shouted into the west lander's face. "The east landers have invaded."

"They have?" The west lander stared at him in wonderment.

"Yes!" Shalar bellowed. "With magicians and monsters. Go tell the army. Go tell everybody."

The drunken man nodded somberly. "I will. This is very serious, you know." Then he turned and began stumbling away. Suddenly he stopped, and turned again toward Shalar. "Your face. I've never seen such. Say, you're an east lander yourself, aren't you?"

"Yes. But never mind that, now, you idiot. Find the army. Tell everyone that we're being overrun."

Confused, the man nodded and hurried away, trying to remember what it was he was supposed to tell, and to whom. In another few moments, he had forgotten completely.

Shalar turned to see that a small group of naval sailors had stepped from a warship onto the pier. One of them, an officer, called out to Shalar. "What's going on here?"

Shalar replied in near exasperation, "An invasion!"

The officer looked about. "Invasion, hell," he scoffed. "This is some sort of trick. You look like pirates, to me." With that, he drew his sword, and his sailors did likewise. "Whatever you're up to, I'm going to scuttle your little invasion right here and now."

With a quick rush, the seamen and the bandits became locked in battle on the weathered planks of the dock. In short order, men were lying dead or wounded in the firelight. The clashes of swords and curses of pain filled the night, mingling with the roar of flames. Other denizens of the docks ran past to escape. These ran, some into the city, and some aboard various ships, reporting what they had seen: foreign swordsmen battling Druuk's sailor's, and defeating them. Upon more distant ships, there were also witnesses.

After that, it did not take long for word to get around. With only a few retellings, the imagined invasion was underway in the minds of thousands.

* * * * *

Charinok walked right past Miril and Kl'aarn without seeing them. His eyes were fixed on the form of Akmeb, lying slumped against the wall. He reached down and whispered urgently, "Hey, Akmeb, wake up! They're---"

Charinok withdrew his hand from Akmeb's shoulder, stared at the blood on the catwalk, and then called down into the courtyard. "Was Akmeb caught sleeping?"

"What do you mean?" came from below.

"He's dead. Stabbed. Sword."

For a few moments, there was silence. Then came the words, "Sound the alarm! Intruders over the wall! There's been a breach!"

Sentry seven drew his sword and cast his eyes nervously about. The courtyard below began to fill with sound, the noise of armored men rushing to stations. Charinok's eyes alerted to the shadow where Miril and Kl'aarn hid. "Who's there? I can see you. Come out."

Slowly, Kl'aarn stood.

The sentry took a step closer. "Who are you? I don't recognize your armor. What's your regiment?"

"My name is Kl'aarn, of Har-Keem. Sorry about your friend, there." Kl'aarn did not feel nearly as composed as he sounded. But he was trying to stall for time.

The archer was clearly unused to handling a sword. He was as clearly confused by Kl'aarn's casual demeanor. And Akmeb's dead body did nothing to settle Charinok's state of mind. "Har-Keem?" he asked. "I've never heard of the place."

"It's east of here."

"Your accent. Your face. I've never seen or heard the like." Then Charinok's face became a mask of dread. "By the gods! You're an east lander. You killed Akmeb!"

"I'm afraid I have to kill you, too," Kl'aarn said.

Charinok braced. "Do you realize where you are? What you've done? If you think you can escape alive, you're a madman!"

"Am I?" Kl'aarn stepped menacingly toward Charinok. "Then take a look in the direction of the harbor. It's all aflame with the fire of war. My countrymen have invaded. We are as many as the sands of the sea, and invincible. It is you who should worry about escape."

By then, in the courtyard below, bells were being rung, and torches were being lit. The entire garrison was being roused, and sleepy men were stumbling into the night, fastening on their armor as they went.

From the direction of the city came the bright glow of fires raging out of control.

Charinok saw this, and then did exactly as Kl'aarn had intended. He virtually threw himself down the ladder to the ground below, informing all who heard him that an east land army had invaded, and had already breached the castle walls.

* * * * *

Kl'aarn and Miril quickly ran in the direction of the newly vacant post seven, which Charinok had abandoned. There, they found another ladder, and quickly descended to the ground below. They had no choice. For, from other ladders, the catwalk was quickly filling with soldiers, not mere archers, but swordsmen wearing the uniforms of fighting legions, veteran warriors expecting to do battle.

Once on the ground, Kl'aarn faced the rush of a platoon, and expected to die. But he had lowered his faceplate, and the platoon ran right past him and Miril, climbing the ladder which he and the witch had moments before descended.

In disbelief, he turned to Miril, whose face was concealed by her hood. "Have you made us invisible?"

"No," she replied. "But look at how many different kinds of uniform they wear. And they're expecting to confront regiments, not lone warriors.

With your faceplate down, we don't look like invaders to them at all. Put away your sword, and let's walk."

Incredulous, Kl'aarn did as Miril suggested. They made their way into the thick of scrambling formations, which were rushing around uncoordinated, without plans, and unable to locate the columns of enemy they were being told to defend against.

"Damned drills," Kl'aarn heard one man say.

Kl'aarn grabbed the soldier's arm, and in a voice muffled by his face plate said, "This is no drill, soldier. This is the real thing. East landers have overrun the city. Make sure everyone understands that."

The bearded west land soldier looked Kl'aarn and Miril up and down with a fierce, no nonsense expression. "Says who?" he demanded. "And who the hell are you two, anyway?"

Miril parted the hood which had concealed her face, and stared with contempt at the man. "I am a witch. This man is escorting me to the king. And you'd better inform everyone that this is no drill."

The west lander saw Miril's teeth show, and witnessed the savage fire of Hell in her fierce eyes. He knew then that this woman was truly the mistress of a demon, and that as midnight approached, her powers were reaching their zenith. "I'll tell them," he said quickly, and ran off.

Miril closed her hood again. "He'll tell them I'm an east lander," she said. "But all the better."

Kl'aarn and Miril continued to bluff their way forward. They came upon the figure of a dying, west land soldier, an arrow piercing his abdomen--- an east lander's arrow. "Good," Kl'aarn said to himself. "Others of us got through."

* * * * *

Vike had spent all his arrows into the crowd below, leaving enough dead and wounded to make credible the growing rumor that a full scale attack upon the castle was in progress. That the soldiers had seen few of the enemy, and had killed but one, only added fever to the chaos. The words "ghost army" had begun to be heard and repeated many times.

The hunter, out of arrows, used his rope to drop to the castle floor, and held it while Veelos quickly followed him down, her robes a brilliant flutter of white. Soon, two of Kl'aarn's men had joined them, and soon after, three more.

Everyone had quickly discovered the ease with which they could infiltrate in the confusion, and they walked boldly toward the vault. Only once were they stopped, by a burly officer who challenged them. "Who are you?"

Veelos replied smoothly, "I am the priestess Veelos of Har-Keem. These men escorting me are mercenary warriors."

The officer seemed baffled. Then he nodded. "Alright." And proceeded on his way.

"This is too easy," Vike told her.

"I know," Veelos said. "Druuk has neglected the power of sword. He now relies on a much more powerful force, something much more sinister. I can feel it."

By the time Veelos and her companions reached the vault, the military discipline of the west landers had eroded into chaotic frenzy. Many of them had begun to desert over the walls, spurred on by the outcries they could hear from the nearby burning city. A platoon of elite archers, under the direction of an infuriated officer, was launching arrows at those deserting, in a desperate effort to put an end to the senseless rout. But the sight of dead comrades, and the absence of any visible enemy, only made the panic worse. Soon, there was no order left to be restored.

Finally, Veelos and those with her reached the door of the vault. "This is it," she said. "The Orb of Power is inside. But the door is sealed by magic."

"What can we do?" a mercenary asked. "Can you open it?"

"No," Veelos replied. "I can't."

The mercenary was astounded by her answer. "Then what do we do?" he asked, stupefied.

Veelos looked into his eyes, and revealed to him her fear. "I don't know," she said. "By all that is sacred, I really don't."

* * * * *

Kl'aarn and Miril found themselves all alone at the base of the tall spire.

"He's up there," Miril said.

Kl'aarn answered, "I don't think so, Miril. He has fled by now. Druuk wouldn't still be here after his army has deserted."

Miril shook her head. "He has other armies. The one we got past was just for show, a parade army. He's up there, alright."

"No he's not," Kl'aarn replied. "He has sorcerors who can fly."

"Druuk is not afraid," Miril said. "On the contrary, he is eager to fight this battle. He thinks he is about to fight the Priestess of Prophecy. And he senses her weakness. Little does he know; fate has sent him a witch, instead."

"Why don't we get to the vault, first, and destroy his power?" Kl'aarn asked.

"Leave that to Veelos," Miril answered. "I want Druuk. And I want him now."

"But I thought---"

"Never mind," Miril said. "I don't want the Orb anymore. I don't care about its power or its prophecy. Druuk is our only enemy. I know that, now that we are here. If we don't strike now, then he will strike us all. We can't lose this chance, my love."

Kl'aarn gave in. "As you say, then. Let's go inside."

"Not you," Miril said. "The spire staircase is guarded by enchanted warriors, zombies whom Druuk has beghouled. If we had the magic swords--- but Veelos prevented our taking them. So now I must do this alone."

"Like hell," Kl'aarn replied. "I'm going in there with you."

Miril's eyes showed real fear, then. "It's dangerous, Kl'aarn. You could be killed."

"And so could you. I can see it in your eyes. You're afraid, as afraid now as you were of Morgrar when he held you at his mercy. Shalar was right when he said you'd bitten off more than you can chew. And now you know it. This Druuk fellow is a monster. You can't take him alone."

Miril hesitated. "There's no turning back now," she said. "Open the door."

* * * * *

"Well?" the mercenary demanded. "Is this the end of it? Do we give up the quest at the last door?"

Vike silenced him. "We'll get through the door," he said. Then to Veelos, he urged, "We must."

"I can't," Veelos said. "Not without magic. And I must never yield to that temptation again. Never. To do so now would surely defeat us forever."

The mercenary fumed. "Where is Miril? She'll open it soon enough."

But Veelos turned on him angrily. "I can't use magic of myself. How much worse, then, to draw it from a witch?" Then she softened her tone. "No good can come of magic, warrior. I know by sad experience."

Vike looked at the door. "There must be a way to open it," he said, "and without using any dark power."

"You're right," Veelos said. "Why did I not see that before? Of course!"

Vike was puzzled. "See what?"

Veelos answered with confidence. "Vike. Kick the door open."

Vike scoffed. "It's solid granite."

"No," Veelos said. "It's not granite. It's not even sandstone. It's nothing. And you have the power, Vike. Just as Shay-Toom had powers we do not understand, but which demi-men do, so now do you have that power. The sauroid high priest ordained you, Vike. Instead of a silver ring, he gave you a medallion. But you are no less a priest than I am! Vike. Kick open the door."

Vike looked at the priestess quizzically. Then, with determination, he said, "I will do it." Then, positioning himself, Vike raised his foot and kicked.

There was a thud. Vike was pushed backward. The door had not budged. The magic lock had held as firmly as a mountain.

Vike set his foot back down. "It's hopeless," he said.

"Try again," Veelos said. "The magic which holds shut the door is strong. But, that very magic, it has consumed the granite, of which that door was built. Only the magic remains. Don't try to break the stone, Vike. Break the magic. Break the evil. And not of your own power, but by the power which moves through you."

Vike touched the medallion. Then, looking at the door, he kicked it so hard that it crumbled into dust.

* * * * *

Druuk's personal guards were whirlwinds of fury. And they filled the twisting stairway which led up the spire. Not a step of the winding stone slabs was yielded without blood. The human forms which blocked their path were devoid of fear, devoid of pain, devoid of human soul. They were controlled by ravenous ghouls such as not even Trrod could hope to conjure in faraway Shel-Avak. And their sole lust was for killing.

With his shield overhead on a straining arm, Kl'aarn hacked and thrust with his sword at legs and loins, while a rain of death pounded at him from above. His shield was already dented by the brutal hammerblows, and it threatened to crack with each thunderous strike ceaselessly ramming into it. His arm was sore from the fatigue of holding the shield aloft, and it ached as if about to break from the constant, bone wrenching shocks.

Even the bodies of those he killed were a weapon against him. They fell forward onto his shield, and Kl'aarn had to lift them up and over Miril, so they would not crush her as they tumbled down the helix. At times, it seemed that the mere weight of those above him on the stairway would become a flood, washing all of them to the bottom in a pile of death.

Miril had been correct. There was awesome power here. No mere men could fight as these men fought. No sooner had one died, than the next would take his place, attacking even more ferociously than the last.

Kl'aarn longed for the strength that had come to him when he had fought Morgrar. But it did not come. He had been a different man, then. He had been able to receive such energy. Now he was a lesser man, and he relied upon a different woman than when he had relied upon Veelos. He had set out upon a quest of good. And now, even as he struggled each second to stay alive, he knew in a part of himself that, somewhere, he had departed the path of good. His quest was now an evil one. And it was too late to turn back.

He fought on for as long as he could. Then he felt his knees begin to buckle. He knew then that he was not going to make it. Like Kmir, he knew that his life was about to come to an abrupt end, and that death cared nothing about his concerns of the moment, nor about his plans for the future. Amid all his hopes and dreams, this was the end. He was facing death, and not even the death into glory he had faced so often. This was a death of the soul he was confronting, a death into darkness and anguish, a death beyond which lay only the emptiness which agnostics and atheists ascribe to it. Kl'aarn began to feel the light being extinguished from within his spirit. And when at last that light would be all gone, he knew that nothing of himself would be left.

Miril saw Kl'aarn's weakening stance, and cursed with fear. She could see that the man she loved was about to die, unless she used up some of the death within her, death reserved for Druuk. She cursed Veelos then, cursed her for foiling her plot to gain the weapons of helliron by which Miril's own beghouled men could have swept up this corridor of death with impunity.

Angrily, Miril cast forth one of her spells, Blinder. It was a weak curse, but the only one she could summon under the circumstances. It would have to do.

Kl'aarn found it suddenly easier to fight. His enemies could no longer see him. Yet, they fought anyway, and they remained deadly adversaries. They continued to wrack him with pain, and their dead bodies continued to roll over him, one at a time.

He was weak, exhausted. The body which rolled over him next, forced him down, against bloody stone. He was unable to protect Miril from it, and unable to protect himself from the next fighter. In agony, he awaited the death-blow, awaited the wrath of judgment, and the fire of hell.

"We're at the top," Miril said.

Kl'aarn lifted his head and looked. There were no more ghoul-men. The stepway ended on the flat landing of the turret. Struggling, he allowed Miril to help him to his feet, and found himself leaning against the curved wall of a small, interior, circular area. It was fashioned from polished stone, and elegant in its regal splendor.

Opposite where he stood, there was a door, studded with priceless jewels.

Kl'aarn heaved for breath. Sweat dripped profusely from his beard, while a trickle of blood came from one nostril.

Miril waited for him to marshal his last reserves of strength.

When he could speak, Kl'aarn said, "I can't believe it, Miril. We've killed an army. How many were there? In all my days, I've never killed as many as I've killed this one day."

Miril replied, "You are gaining in power, my love. For the first time, I could sense it within you."

Kl'aarn noticed the darkness within himself. "I liked it."

"I knew you would," Miril said.

"You don't understand. I liked it. But I don't admire it. This power, it consumes. Even its sweetness is death."

"It consumes one's enemies," Miril said. "You've tasted that sweetness now, darling. You'll not let go of it. Soon, you will master it."

Kl'aarn waited until he had caught his breath. "What next?"

Miril gestured toward the jeweled door. "He's in there. Cocky, confident, waiting for the Priestess of Prophecy to enter his trap."

"Do we just go in?"

"Oh, of course," Miril smiled. "It's midnight. I'm at the height of my power. Whenever you're ready, my love." Her eyes seemed to gaze beyond the door, into a far distance.

"What are you thinking?" Kl'aarn asked her.

"I was just musing. The winds of destiny: Druuk rode them for so long.

They carried him so far, across his kingdom, across his years. For so long, he was the most powerful man in the world, the most powerful man in all worlds. Now, those very winds of destiny have capriciously dropped him, abandoned him like a leaf in a gutter. He is nothing anymore. Only an ignorant fool, unaware that death is at his very door, not death in the form of a priestess, but rather in the armor of a warrior, and in the robes of Demonwitch."

Kl'aarn looked at Miril. "You seem very confident. But so does he."

"The winds of destiny are ours, my love, ours not just for today or even a lifetime, but ours forever. Push open the door, my love. It's unlocked. Our eternal rewards await us."

Kl'aarn stepped to the door. "You're sure about this?"

"Do it."

Kl'aarn carefully lifted one foot, and placed it against the door. It began to give way easily. Druuk had no need of locks. "Someone," Kl'aarn thought to himself, "is overconfident."

Then, violently, he kicked open the door.

Instantly his eyes took in a horrifying scene.

There was a bed near the center of the floor. Its headboard was to Kl'aarn's left, its footboard directly in front of him. Beyond the bed stood the man who was Druuk.

The king wore a nightrobe laced with threads of gold, and sprinkled with the dust of diamonds. His chin sported a thick beard, perfectly squared and trimmed. His hairy brows formed a wedge which pointed downward at the bridge of his nose. Those brows framed eyes which glowered ruthlessly, hideously, with murderous power.

Between Kl'aarn and the bed, there stood three blackrobed sorcerors, their cadaverous eyes filled with evil, their arms stretched outward, poised to launch magical murder.

All this Kl'aarn saw in the very first instant. There was no time to see anything more. For the fire which erupted from those outstretched arms blinded him with soul searing agony.

Kl'aarn felt himself plummet downward into a place in which there was no upward direction.

* * * * *

Beyond the crumbled granite door of the vault was an anteroom. Vike stepped through the curtain of dust which rose from the shattered door. Veelos followed him. One by one, the five warriors followed.

Inside, a dull blue light suffused the air, and a misty blue smoke, which seemed to glow of its own, swirled about them. Although the anteroom was just large enough to hold the seven without crowding, the eerie light and swirling mist seemed to give it a size of no particular dimension. The result was a dreamlike disorientation, obviously an intent of the architect.

The anteroom had no door but for the one through which they had entered. There was no way to proceed any further into the vault.

Carefully, Veelos reached forward with one hand, and touched the bare, featureless wall. It was colder than ice. She withdrew the hand, and said, "The magic within is not as powerful as the magic that locked the vault. I wonder why that should be."

Vike replied, "It smells of a trap. Whatever the design, I think we are about to get an answer to your question."

His meaning became clear, as the wall of the anteroom opposite the entrance began to thud with the impact of a battering ram.

Vike spoke again. "The rumors of monsters were true. There is something alive, on the other side of that wall, caged in there, trying to get out. It seems to be a sizable beast."

"The Orb is also in there," Veelos said. "I recognize that familiar---"

Another thud drowned out her words. This time, slivers of granite slid from the wall, leaving shallow gouges.

The warriors drew their swords. They were brave men, ready to fight, whatever the odds. But in the face of the incredible power crashing itself into the wall, even they stepped backward a pace.

Vike also drew his sword. But instead of stepping away from the wall, he stepped toward the sounds of brutal impact. Another massive thud sounded from inside, and a flake of stone fell to the floor, this one larger than before. Vike stood his ground, and the warriors behind him held their swords in both hands. Whatever was coming at them, though they could not hope to stop it, would not have to pursue them to do battle.

Vike spoke to Veelos, his tone suddenly urgent. "Hear me carefully," he said. "This is for you alone to understand, for I cannot. My words to you are these: the Orb must destroy the Orb. That is how it must be done. The age of Orbs is soon to end. When it does, it must be ended by the Orb itself."

Veelos was confused. "Vike, I don't understand."

"Not now you don't," Vike said. "But when the time comes, remember my words. The Orb must destroy the Orb. The age of---"

"Vike! Get back!" Veelos screamed. A mighty thud jarred the vault to its foundation, and the wall began to crack open where Vike stood. Veelos stepped forward, intending to pull the hunter away.

But she was too late. The crack in the wall burst open with explosive fury. Vike raised his sword to fend off the monster which charged forth. An enraged, guttural snarl reverberated in the anteroom, and a clawed hand smashed downward with a leaden club.

Vike tried to block the strike with his sword. But the immense weight of the creature's weapon, and the awesome force which propelled it downward, were too much for any man to withstand. Vike was killed before Veelos's eyes. He lay face up, his back broken, his legs folded grotesquely beneath him. And he was surrounded by his own blood.

Veelos was too horrified to scream, too terrified to move. She stood, paralyzed, her eyes fixed on Vike's corpse. Sudden and unexpected grief competed with her fear of death, for control of her torn emotions.

The warriors were also frozen where they stood, knowing the futility of trying to withstand the terrible killing force which had effortlessly crushed Vike. They would have run. Only their discipline, long since become instinct, held them at their post in expectation of imminent death.

The beast which had killed Vike looked down at his body, still holding in its serpentine claw the bloody instrument of destruction. The creature's fangs were bared in a snarling hiss, and its forked tongue whipped rapidly downward, deftly tracing the medallion which lay atop Vike's unbreathing chest. Then, slowly, the sauroid turned its head toward Veelos, its savage eyes burning into hers.

Veelos could barely see through her tears. The reptilian face seemed distorted through the rainfall in her weeping eyes. But even so, she could see in the harsh, carven features of that savage face, an inexplicable appearance of remorse. Veelos's voice trembled weakly as she spoke into the fierce monster's glare. "You could not have known," she said, "that he was your priest. Himself unknowing, he knew what he must do to save the rest of us. But do not slay yourself, as your custom requires. For Vike died as he wished to die, at the hands of a creature of the hunt. You are not the perpetrator of this wicked crime. You are, as we, its victim."

The sauroid uttered a low, rumbling snarl, punctuated by a sharp hiss. Then its tongue lashed across Veelos's face, barely touching it, tracing her outline with a dry, frictionless brush that felt light as air. Then it traced also, the silver ring upon her hand. Veelos heard the thought which projected from the demi-man's savage heart. It told her something for which there are no human words, no human thought, no human emotion. She understood.

Then, followed by several of its kind, the sauroid stepped through the anteroom, between the warriors, and into the courtyard beyond the curtain of dust. Just as the last of the demi-men disappeared from view, those inside the vault could hear the panic-stricken death cries of west land soldiers. Whatever doubt had remained among Druuk's men concerning invasion, the sauroids were erasing it in a tornado of claws and teeth.

Veelos addressed the warriors. "The Orb must be destroyed."

* * * * *

Kl'aarn stopped falling. He had reached the bottom, though at the bottom there was no direction other than ever downward. He was blind. But though he could not see, he could hear. All about him, he was surrounded by the shrieks of the damned, screams of all encompassing agony, howls of unearthly terror. Merely to hear those wails was unbearable. He could not endure the sound. Dimly, he wondered if one of those shrieking voices were his. He could not tell. The pain had thus far reached only his ears.

Kl'aarn felt the icy hardness of hell. It surprised him. He had always thought that hell would be on fire. Now he discovered that it was not. Hell was not aflame. It was frozen, frozen with the cold of absolute darkness.

At first, he thought he had been spared the torment of being able to see. But slowly, even that mercy was withdrawn from him. He was afraid to look. But the shrieks of pain grew sharper, less distant, and he could no longer block them out. He knew that he would also be unable to block out sight. For his eyes, although blind, were already open, and beginning to see.

Slowly, the horror of vision was forced upon him. He saw that he was lying among ashes. Ashes. Hell had indeed been aflame at one time. But Hell had long since burned itself out. All that was left of it were ashes, now. Hell had consumed itself.

There were bones, human bones. A charred skull, minus its lower jaw, bit the floor beside Kl'aarn's face. The shrieks which tormented his ears might be coming from within that voiceless skull. Kl'aarn knew that they were not his own screams, not yet.

They were not the screams of the blackened skull, either, he realized. The skull was empty of life, staring at him with empty, hollow sockets. Charred fragments of black cloth lay around it on the stone floor.

He was not in Hell.

Not, at any rate, in the hell of afterlife. But the air was thick with agony nonetheless, pervaded by unearthly torment such as had been a stranger to all human flesh until now. The agony being suffered was too much for one body to contain. As a result, it was filling the room, making Kl'aarn's teeth ache with every shriek.

He found himself struggling to his feet. As he climbed upward, a direction which he had thought vanished, his field of vision widened. He saw that there were not one, but three blackened skeletons, those of the three sorcerors he had seen for but an instant before their fiery spell had nearly killed him. They had intended to do to Kl'aarn what Miril had instead done to them. Now they were dead.

But someone else was yet alive, erupting with those unendurable screams. "Miril! Where are you?" Kl'aarn tried to speak the words, but nothing came forth. He groped for his sword, for it had occurred to him that she must be in the merciless clutches of Druuk. Willing himself to regain his balance, Kl'aarn lifted his head, and saw the two of them, Druuk and Miril.

He saw, but could barely recognize, either of them.

Druuk no longer had human shape. He had been crushed into a mass resembling the form of a hen's egg, squashed by an invisible fist. He had been broken at every point of pain, scorched and scalded over his entire surface. The torture had been skillful, methodical. For although he hovered near his inevitable death, he could not yet die, however much he struggled to achieve the death for which now he yearned. For Druuk, the pain grew worse with each new joint twisted loose, with each new groan that tore itself from his scalded throat.

But if Druuk were all but unrecognizable, Kl'aarn was even more unnerved by the sight of Miril. The abomination which she was performing against Druuk had twisted her, also, but in a different way. Her face seemed to be staring into a fiery whirlwind, contorting her features and reddening her complexion. Her claw-like hands stroked the air above Druuk's hideous form like blood-drenched talons, projecting hatred from the bottom of hell. She was caught up in the glee of wreaking long-awaited vengeance. The witch was lost in the obsession, the passion, the infliction of cruelty. Her obsession was so complete that, in order to more fully savor it, she herself sampled some of Druuk's unspeakable agonies, making them her own, so as to enjoy all the more his torment. The demonwitch delighted in Druuk's terror, reveled in his incomprehensible torture. She extracted from his mangled, living corpse, every pain which raw nerves could conceivably suffer.

Kl'aarn stood in mute shock. He could hardly bring himself to believe that this was Miril. She was totally different, now. Her features were distorted into angles of uttermost cruelty. Her eyes were aflame with hellfire, her lips a maddened smile of abominable lust. Her hair was whipped by an invisible, fiery whirlwind.

She was utterly absorbed, Kl'aarn knew. She could not even hear him, as he pleaded with her to stop. All her attention was directed at Druuk. The witch had once warned Trrod, never to let down his guard while conjuring. Now, Miril herself was completely vulnerable. She was utterly defenseless.

Having escaped one hell, Kl'aarn had found himself in another, equally unendurable. He drew his sword.

Then he began to step forward. It was an effort, as if he were climbing a very steep hill with a great weight in every vein of his body. It was like approaching a hot furnace, a cauldron of evil, which lay open before him. But he approached. And when he was near enough, Kl'aarn raised his blade. Then, with all the might he could bring to bear, he hacked in half the quivering jelly which had been mighty Druuk.

The shrieks stopped instantly, ended forever by the clack of metal on the marble floor, a clack muffled by the ground flesh which he had severed. Kl'aarn felt the blade cut completely through the man with sickening, disgusting ease.

Miril lurched, as if she herself had been cut. For an instant, the agony which had been released into the air, had had no place to go. She had had no place to project it. She and Kl'aarn both felt it for the briefest particle of time. Then, Miril was suddenly able to see again, to see into the material world about her, instead of the unearthly world in which she had been delighting.

She whirled fiercely to face Kl'aarn. "Why did you do that?" she screamed. "Why did you kill him? I was not finished with him. How dare you!"

Kl'aarn replied angrily. "You said you'd let me kill him. I did. But, you--- why did you torture him like that? How could you have done that, Miril? No one could have deserved what you put him through, no matter what they had done."

But Miril snarled in rage. "Oh, yes he did. He deserved it all, and more besides. There was still life left in him, Kl'aarn, and many more agonies yet to be suffered. But now, you've given him to Thorgar. He was mine, Kl'aarn. Mine!"

"Look at you," Kl'aarn shouted. "Look what you've become. Everything I hate."

Miril sneered. "Do you hate me? Do you? Then whom do you love, Kl'aarn? What is her name?"

Kl'aarn stepped closer to her. "I fear you, Miril. You are full of killing. And you're not done, not yet. Who's next on your death list? Is it me?"

Miril shuddered. "No," she said. Her voice was suddenly subdued, her entire manner collapsed. "Of course not. Never. Never in all eternity. Kl'aarn, I'm sorry. I never meant for you to fear me. Please. I'm just--- it's just that--- Kl'aarn, he killed my mother, my father, my brothers. And yours. And Shalar's. And Veelos's."

"He can never pay for that," Kl'aarn said. "But you weren't just trying to make him pay. You were--- Miril, what in hell were you doing? I never saw you like that. I never thought you could become like that. You scared the hell out of me. Or into me."

"I'm sorry. I never wanted you to--- look, Kl'aarn, it's over. He's dead. It's done. I got him, and he's dead. I'll never--- I'll never be like that again. I promise. Never."

"Good."

"Kl'aarn, please hold me. Tight."

Putting away his sword once more, Kl'aarn embraced his wife. He was surprised at how frail she felt. The battle had weakened her. He spoke. "As you said, Miril, it's over. You came to kill Druuk, and now he's dead. You got what you came for. Let's go home, Miril. Let's go back to where Har-Keem once stood. Let's rebuild it. Please."

Gently, Miril pushed herself slightly away from Kl'aarn, and looked up into his eyes. "We will," she said. "There is just one thing."

"What's that?" he asked.

"I came for two things," she said. "One of them was Druuk. The other? Look behind you, my dear."

Kl'aarn looked. Only just then did he notice it. He had not seen it before. Up until then, much else had occupied him. But now, although he had never in his life laid eyes upon it, he knew instantly, without a doubt, what it was.

From its corner in the room, glistening with a light all its own, there sparkled the Great Orb of Power itself.

* * * * *

Beyond the opening, which the sauroids had broken through the wall, Veelos saw a long corridor. It seemed to stretch an infinite distance into the vault, a distance measured not only in the familiar units of paces and cubits, but also in that otherworldly span, that dark misty realm, which Veelos had known only in her dreams.

There was magic there, a magic not of the brutish sort which had locked the outer door of the vault. This magic was more subtle, less like a sword, and more like the venom of a dead serpent. Here was not the magic of raw force, but rather, the evil magic of lies. And of the many doors which lined the corridor, a seemingly infinite number of them, all were doors of deception, every one.

Into this valley of death's shadow, Veelos stepped. And within it, she trembled. At the very first door, she paused. It beckoned to her. Its promise was that of riches, and all that they could buy. Veelos had never thought herself susceptible to promises of wealth. But already, she felt tempted. Even knowing that what the door promised was a lie unto death, for an instant Veelos felt the urge to open it.

But instead, she pressed on, trekking farther along the illusory corridor. The next door promised delights of the flesh, and once again, Veelos felt shamed by her curiosity. Another portal offered power, unbridled power. Veelos no longer disbelieved the lies. They may as well have been true, so persuasive were they. Only some small part of Veelos knew that, behind each door, lay a separate doom, a unique hell, an ingeniously devised torture.

Veelos fended off the deceptions. She refused their offers, focusing her effort not on disbelief--- the lies were too convincing to disbelieve--- but focused instead only on rejecting the promises, as if they were indeed true.

She forced her way along, deeper into the trap, ever more deeply into the lair of whatever waited. At each door she paused, stopping only long enough to seek the sensation which only the Orb could evoke from her. And not finding it, Veelos moved on, farther into the depth of the vault. For an endless distance, she continued onward. The anteroom was vastly far away, and yet Veelos pushed forward.

The doors grew more powerful. At first they had promised earthly pleasures, power, and the satisfaction of raw lusts. But having passed these by, Veelos found the remaining deceptions more diabolical yet. She paused at a door which promised knowledge. Then another offered wisdom, sublime and complete. Yet another door beckoned her, holding forth to her the attainment of holiness and sanctity.

She knew, then, that she was drawing near to the Orb. For only such wishes for spiritual attainment would stop anyone who had survived this far into the vault. But there was yet one more door to confront.

This one promised the love of any man she wished. Any man. And to make its seductiveness all the more compelling, this door was not a lie. Veelos knew then, without deception, that she held in her hand the key to Kl'aarn's heart, the guarantee of his undying love. All she needed do now was to turn around, return into the world of substance, and claim him. Miril could do nothing to stop her. That for which Miril had sold her soul could be taken from her, with but a smile from Veelos's lips, with but a gentle caress of her hand, indeed, merely by wishing it to be so. Kl'aarn's devotion to Veelos would be irreversible. And none of this was a lie. It was all within the grasp of the priestess.

But Vike's admonition came to mind. He had counseled Veelos to allow Kl'aarn to walk his own path. Miril had taken him from it, and the consequences would be, must surely be, tragic. Any satisfaction the witch had hoped to achieve would eventually be crushed by that tragedy. And for Veelos to do the same as the witch had done could not undo that catastrophe, but only worsen it.

Veelos continued onward. Kl'aarn was behind her now. She released him to whatever path he chose to follow, to whatever destiny--- or fate--- he embraced.

Coming to the next door, Veelos's heart quickened. She placed the palm of her hand flat against the door, and pressed her cheek against it. She closed her eyes. "The Great Orb," she breathed. "At last, at long last, I have found it!"

But then a moment of doubt engulfed her. What if it were a trap? Would not this be the cleverest trap of all? Could any trap be so devious as to counterfeit the mystic fragrance of the angels, the sweetest innocence of their purest jewel? Surely no darkness could imitate light?

And to be sure, the emanations Veelos felt were not strong. The Orb should radiate greater power than she felt. Perhaps the door was weakening those emanations. Or perhaps, as lead weakens the luster of gold.... perhaps it was a trap after all.

For a moment the priestess wavered. For a moment, she decided to turn and run, to escape this place of doom before it sealed her inside forever. For surely, the Orb was not in the vault at all, but somewhere else. Surely Druuk would never have let it be far from his immediate grasp. Surely he---

But Veelos suddenly pressed against the door with all her might. Trap or no trap, the time of decision had arrived. Many had died along this quest. Why not, she thought to herself, the priestess? Why should she flinch from danger? Why should she not take risks, perhaps even a fatal risk, in the cause of good? Had not she urged Shalar to cross the river? It was time.

A second time she threw herself against the unyielding portal, and then a third time, and a fourth. She gasped, out of breath, and in pain. The door was locked, locked twice. One lock was that of Druuk's magic, an evil stronger than her weakened virtues could overcome. But the second lock was even stronger. Veelos recognized it. It was that she had squandered the strength of her prophecy, squandered it long ago. To open the door was a hopeless hope. She could not.

There was a sound. Although Veelos had never heard such a sound before, somehow she instantly recognized it for what it was. It was the muffled clack of a sword against a marble floor, the death of a man, and the end of his magic.

The door moved upon its hinges, as if by a wisp of air. Veelos put her hand upon it. Granite grated against stone as her effortless touch pushed open the portal. As it swung wider, the emanations from within grew stronger yet. If this were deception, it was potent deception indeed.

Then, impatient to be done with it, the priestess gave it one final, firm impulse, and the door came fully open.

The priestess looked, and could hardly believe her eyes. This was not the Great Orb. The Orb of Power was not, alas, kept in the vault, but in Druuk's chamber. That much became clear to her in an instant.

Instead, within the tiny chamber before her, Veelos laid eyes on the small, round crystal she knew so well, pure sparkling, and undamaged after all these years, after all it had endured. Gingerly, she approached it, as if having found a long lost friend, a dear loved one. Standing adjacent to it, she caressed it gently, carefully, with hands that knew how not to destroy so fragile a thing.

Behind her, one of the warriors suddenly stood in the doorway. The long corridor, which Veelos had traversed as if upon a great journey, was no more. It never had been. There was no corridor, only the wall of the anteroom, the opening within its wall, and this tiny chamber. There had not been any corridor at all, at least not in this world.

"Is that it?" the warrior asked. "Is that the Great Orb?"

"No," Veelos answered.

The mercenary's voice was full of disappointment. "A fake?"

Veelos replied, her voice gentle and tearful. "No. No, it's not a fake at all. It's real alright. It's a genuine orb of the angels, not the Great Orb, but even so, a lesser orb, the one which once rested in Har-Keem. All these years, we had thought it destroyed. But fragile as it is perfect, it has endured. It has triumphed."

"We must destroy it," the warrior said.

"Yes," Veelos said sadly. "We must. But there is only one way, one method of destruction, which will destroy but not desecrate. Our task now has become more difficult than ever."

* * * * *

Kl'aarn stared at the Great Orb for long moments, before finally tearing his gaze from it. He turned back to Miril, whose expression seemed suddenly gentle, relaxed, and triumphant. "It was here all along," he breathed. "But of course. We should have known. Druuk would never have trusted it to be beyond his reach. A careless breath could have destroyed it. A clever sorceror could have stolen it. Why didn't we think of this?"

Miril's lips hinted at a smile. "I knew," she said.

"You did?"

"Of course, my love. Did I not tell you all along? Destiny is mine. It was my destiny to defeat Druuk, and it was my destiny to take from him the Orb. And I have achieved it, Kl'aarn. I have achieved it all. The final battle has been fought. We won, my dear. We have won at last! All Wirik is ours. Our enemies are vanquished and in full retreat. We rule. It is time to celebrate, my dear, time to have the grandest feast this world has ever seen. Our wedding feast, the very one which Druuk ruined for us, will now be completed. And nothing can ever again separate us. Nothing!"

Kl'aarn noted that Miril's voice had been dreamlike, full of rejoicing throughout all she had said, all except the final word. With the word, "Nothing," she had punctuated her meaning. She had said it vindictively.

Kl'aarn felt a cold chill in his spine. "Is that true? Do you now have all power over the entire world?"

But Miril answered, "We do, my love. We. I would never reign over you. You have become my king, and it is you whom I worship. We shall rule as one, with one mind, one purpose, one power."

"And," Kl'aarn said, "what about Veelos?"

"Oh. Her."

"She told me one time," Kl'aarn revealed, "that--- that at our wedding feast---"

"There would be demons?" Miril filled.

"Yes."

"They will be our humble guests. And well behaved, Kl'aarn. For in the world of substance, only the Darkmost has any power. We shall share that power as one."

"She also said," Kl'aarn continued, "that--- that---" he could not bring forth the words.

"That we would drink her blood," Miril completed for him. "From her skull, I think she said."

"You're making light of this."

"Of course not."

"I've heard no denial."

"I deny it, then."

"You were in no hurry to disavow it. Your denial is not very persuasive."

"Kl'aarn, Kl'aarn, my dearest! Why all this fretting and worry? Do you think I would betray the sweetest friend I ever had in life? Do you think I have no love in my heart for Veelos? Why, then, did I save her life so many times? Why did I dress her wounds, those smelly disgusting pockets of pus, after she was injured? And why did I risk my own life when she battled Shay-Toom? Kl'aarn, I want Veelos to be our closest confidant. Blood? We shall make our blood her own. She will become as a daughter to us."

"You will cause her to become a witch."

"But of course. And now that our conflict is at end, she will gladly reconcile with us. You'll see."

Kl'aarn shook his head. "Veelos will go to her death before she ever dons the robes of black."

Miril turned, and walked slowly to the window, and looked out at the suddenly deserted courtyard below, deserted but for the many corpses in it. Many of those corpses had been ripped to death by sauroid fangs and claws.

"Veelos is in danger," Miril said. "But not from me. She's down there in that vault. I worry for her, Kl'aarn. She's no match for the treachery of Druuk's magic."

Kl'aarn rushed to Miril's side, and stared out the window toward the vault below. "You're right!" he said. "Miril, I've got to warn her."

"Go, then," Miril said. "Rescue her. And when you have, invite her up here. Bring her to me, Kl'aarn. I'll wait for you."

Kl'aarn hesitated.

"It's safe for her here," Miril said. "I promise it."

Then Kl'aarn turned, and leaving the turret of the spire, made his way down the helix of steps, past the rotted corpses of enchanted warriors, corpses long since dead, dead long before he had killed them. Reaching the bottom slab of stone, Kl'aarn stepped into the courtyard.

Fallen torches lit the night like so many ghosts, casting long, grotesquely flickering shadows across motionless corpses. For a moment he stood frozen, appalled by the carnage. Then a movement caught his eye, shadows slinking in the darkness with unhuman motions. Nor were they human, but serpents, giant lizards walking upright. There could be no doubt of it. The figures found a ladder, and snaked their way to its top. Finding ropes there, they quickly disappeared across the wall, and into the night beyond.

Suddenly he remembered Veelos, and hurried across the courtyard toward the vault.

As he reached the door, Kl'aarn found several of his men there. "She's found something," Larek said. "Not the orb, but---"

Kl'aarn pushed the warrior aside and, looking into the anteroom, saw no one.

"I'm not hurt," Veelos said. She stepped through a gaping fissure in the opposite wall, into the anteroom. She reverently avoided a smear of blood on the floor. "Vike is dead," she told Kl'aarn.

"He is? Where? I don't see---"

"They came back and took him," Veelos said, "after they had cleared the courtyard of enemies. The sauroids, that is. He'll get a proper burial." As she spoke, she was bundling something into the white, hood cloth of her vestment, from which she had fashioned a carrying pouch. "But Kl'aarn. The Great Orb is not here. It's not in the vault. We have to find it, before Miril does. Or else---"

"We did find it," Kl'aarn announced.

Veelos stopped in her tracks; a cloud of apprehension shadowed her eyes. "Miril?"

Kl'aarn nodded. "We killed Druuk. He was keeping the Orb in his sleeping quarter."

Veelos seemed about to collapse. Larek steadied her. "Are you saying," she asked, "that Miril defeated Druuk?"

"It's alright, Veelos. She---"

"And that she has the Orb in her possession?"

"That's what I'm trying to tell you. There's nothing to fear. She won't harm you. She promised. Come, I'll show---"

Then Veelos did collapse, almost dropping the lesser orb from its bundle. Larek and Kl'aarn lowered her gently to the floor, where the priestess sat, her back against the wall, her face buried in her hands. "All is lost," she lamented.

"No, Veelos. She promised me. Let me take you---"

"You fool!" Veelos screamed. "You pathetic, witch-loving fool!" Veelos cried out. "Do you realize what you've done? Do you understand what she has accomplished?"

"Veelos, I---"

"She lied to you, Kl'aarn. How could you have believed her? Did you think that, once she had fulfilled her anti-prophecy, she would become any less evil? Any less of a witch?"

"Veelos, it's not like that. Go see for yourself. Go see Miril."

"Go see her?" Veelos sneered. "See her? That we shall do, Kl'aarn, that we shall do. Indeed, we have no choice but to see her. But we won't find her in Druuk's lair, warrior. Instead, she will be in Thorgar's abode. There we will find her, in the demon's crypt, at Demon Point. There, in that unholy place, her wedding feast is being prepared."

"No!" Kl'aarn said. "She's in Druuk's---"

"See for yourself, Kl'aarn. Take a good look. Do it now."

Kl'aarn released his grip from Veelos's elbow, and stepped the few paces into the night air. Once outside the vault, he looked toward the tower, his gaze tracing upward to the turret which topped it.

The light of many candles had illuminated it. But now it was dark up there, utterly black.

Dimly, Kl'aarn felt Veelos step to his side. "Now do you understand?" she asked him. "She tricked you. She lied. Miril has taken the Great Orb. And she is on her way to Demon Point, to present her trophy, in exchange for her throne. There, Kl'aarn, she will marry you once more, in a ceremony not sacred, but desecrated. There, Kl'aarn, you will serve to Miril my skullcap of blood."

Kl'aarn's gaze was fixed solidly on the turret. His arm was cold with sweat. Suddenly, he tore himself from Veelos's touch, and ran back into the tower, raced back up the spiral path of rotting corpses, and finally into the dark, empty chamber of Druuk's refuge. His corpse was a mush of crushed flesh and ground bone. His gold adornments and jewels lay scattered throughout the room. But one jewel was missing: the crown jewel. The Great Orb was gone, and with it, Miril.

Then did Kl'aarn cry out with a great cry of anguish from the depths of his soul, and kneeling, wept bitterly.

Chapter 39

Return to Demon Point

At sea, a storm-tossed ship skimmed the waves. Of itself, the swift current gave great speed to the ship it bore. But there was also a mighty wind, which propelled the ship even faster, as fast as it could move without coming apart.

The winds of destiny, Miril mused with satisfaction. They were upon her, now. They were at her command. Soon, all the world would be at her command, as well. The journey by land, across the Lands of demi-men, had taken weeks. The return trip would take but three days. They would be three days unspoiled by sunlight. The storm cloud would see to that. Those three days without light would also be three days without Kl'aarn. But he would arrive safely, Miril knew. Fate would see to that.

The demonwitch paced about the deck of the ship, glancing at the sailors. They mindlessly carried out their work, trimming the sails for maximum speed, keeping the rudder straight, and attending to the many details needed for the voyage. There was food aboard, but only enough food for one.

Miril had bewitched them. For the three days remaining of their lives, the men would neither eat, nor drink, nor sleep. They would be consumed, their bodies wasted by their ceaseless labors. And then, when no longer needed--- well did they know what awaited them. But they were helpless to avoid it.

The witch relaxed on the deck of the ship, and stared into the darkness. Although triumphant, yet there was one matter over which she brooded. Three days without Kl'aarn. This would have been their first long span of togetherness, of privacy. Veelos had ruined that. She had managed to keep Kl'aarn just barely beyond reach of the final darkness, just barely away from the edge of the abyss. There would have to be some adjustment made for that. But, no matter, Miril had an eternity in which to persuade Kl'aarn to accept evil, to seduce him into embracing it as his own. And a pleasant seduction it would be, for both of them.

During that future time, Miril pondered, Veelos would endure an agony so intense that even she would beg Kl'aarn to serve that cup of blood, to serve it just so that at last, Veelos could die. And die she would. Miril smiled. But after Veelos did die, she would discover, to her horror, that her sufferings had only just begun.

As the sailors worked feverishly about her, ignoring their injuries, enduring their terror, Miril leaned back against a railing and gently whispered into the storm, "Veelos, my dear. Bring him to me. Would you be so kind?"

* * * * *

Shalar threw the last of the dead west land riggers from the deck of the ship to join, in the waves below, the bodies of the two bandits who had died in the brief struggle. Hathor had already launched the first, flaming signal arrow into the night sky, an action he would repeat at regular intervals, to attract the mercenaries, if they were still alive.

Shalar peered through the darkness along the street which led away from the dock. "They'd better get here quickly," he muttered. "Because there'll be a real invasion soon enough. It won't be long before pirates get word of the situation here. By tomorrow night, Gur-Molkn will be a plundered city."

"And what of our plunder?" Hathor asked him. "We were supposed to have broken into Druuk's treasury and had all we could carry."

Shalar spat across the railing of the ship, still peering into the street between rows of squat, clay buildings. "You weren't so eager to cross those walls before," he said. "If you've had a change of heart, go into the castle, and see if any of Kl'aarn's men are still alive."

Hathor looked across the burning city, and up the hill atop which Druuk's castle loomed over it. "It's best if we wait for them here," he concluded.

* * * * *

Shalar had paced about impatiently for what he thought were hours. "I've got a bad feeling about this," he told Hathor.

Hathor tried to be reassuring. "I don't think it could have gone bad," he said. "Not with both the witch and the priestess on our side."

Shalar glared at Hathor. "That's just what I'm worried about," he said. "Just last night, Veelos and Miril seemed to have gotten as mean with each other as I'd ever seen them. There was something about this being the final conflict between them."

"Yes," Hathor said. "I remember that."

Shalar huffed. "Well. I've got a feeling that Miril won."

Hathor, seeing Shalar's mood turn foul, was hesitant to ask. "Is that bad?"

Shalar nodded. "If Miril has killed her, that's very bad. Damn. Maybe I should have--- well, what the hell could I have done? Dammit anyway. If Miril went through with this--- damn, and me and Kl'aarn were starting to be a real team, too. But if Miril has killed Veelos--- this is going to---"

"There!" one of the bandits said. "I see what looks to be white robes. Nobody wears white, we've been told."

Shalar fairly jumped to the railing of the ship for a better look. "By damn!" he smiled. "She did it! She beat Miril. She killed the witch! But wait. Is that Kl'aarn I see with her? That doesn't make sense. If Veelos has killed Miril, then Kl'aarn would not be---. Send up another signal flare, Hathor."

"They seem to be running very lightly," another of the bandits said. "Not weighed down by very much gold, I'd say. Maybe the witch is bringing it. But, then, who can trust a witch?"

After a time, Hathor's flares had attracted the small band of warriors, and Veelos. They seemed as frantic to escape as did the west landers who fled in the opposite direction.

As she approached within calling distance, Veelos's first words told a story not of wealth gained, but of misfortune. "Miril betrayed us," Veelos said breathlessly. "She has the Orb of Power. She's taking it to Demon Point. Shalar, we've very little hope of stopping her, but we must try. Will you please help us? Please, Shalar, this is no time for---"

But one of the bandits demanded, "Where is the plunder we were promised?"

Veelos answered, "Everything is at stake, now, everything. If the Orb touches the demon's feet--- won't you please trust me? Shalar, I need you desperately."

"Come aboard," Shalar said. "We didn't settle for just any ship, mind you. This one is the admiral's flagship. And we've taken prisoner a few of his men, who suddenly claim to have taken a dislike to navy life. Very convenient timing for them. Perhaps we can persuade them to sail us home."

* * * * *

There were twenty-seven aboard, plus four west land sailors. Kl'aarn and Shalar each left behind three of his men, dead or missing.

The ropes which moored the ship were cut, and as the galley drifted out into the bay, the men began to row, in an effort to get to the open sea.

But seamanship proved to be a far more difficult art than any had imagined. Rowing a full sized war ship was nothing like rowing a small fishing boat. Oars cracked against each other chaotically, and uselessly splashed in the water. The vessel drifted out of control, colliding against other ships with fearful, splintering sounds.

The west lander petty officer was eager to ingratiate himself with the victors, but even he spoke discouragingly to Veelos. "This will ney ever do," he said. "No man among ye has the skill or talent for this. We'd best be taking aboard a full crew."

"Like hell," Shalar retorted. "Four of you are as many as I'll trust."

"Ye've ney any choice for it," the sailor retorted.

But Veelos intervened between them. "Put up the sail," she said to the west lander.

The petty officer all but laughed. "There ney be any wind in the bay. It's for rowin tonight."

But Veelos said, "Lift the sail. Four of you can do that. Just hoist it up, and then we'll see."

The sailor shrugged resignedly. "As ye say it, m'lady." He had never seen such a woman, but neither was he any fool. This one wore the forbidden white garb. And all the foreign fighting men (the likes of which he had never seen in all his travels) paid her great respect. The west land petty officer did know, when the chips were down, how to pick a winner.

No sooner had the sail been fastened at full mast, than it filled with a strong breeze. The sailors rushed to steady the rudder. "By the gods!" the petty officer said. "It's a miracle."

Veelos shook her head. "Not by the gods," she said, "but by the one and only God. Let me tell you of Him...."

* * * * *

The wind carried them to the open sea, and raged furiously behind them. The mast could not have withstood any more power than that which pressed against it. The sail seemed about to tear at any instant. And the hull hissed loudly against the waves, as the ship all but skimmed over the water. Every measure of speed which the ship could endure was being forced from it.

Veelos stood at the bow, staring off into the empty blackness which lay ahead of them, mindful that somewhere, in that dark tempest, raced another ship. But this one drew its power not from any miracle, but rather, from a curse. The men aboard it, manning the deck, were no longer men. They had become mindless slaves, doing evil labor, and killing themselves in the service of their doom.

"Khormar says---"

Veelos flinched, startled at the sound.

"Sorry," Shalar said. "Didn't mean to sneak up on you that way. A bandit's habit I guess. This sailor fellow, Khormar, he says that we're in something called the demon's lane. Sailors supposedly know about it. It's a very strong eastward current with a very strong eastward wind. But it's a rare event. It arises only once every seven years, and lasts for three days and three nights. Khormar says that in that time, it will carry us all the way to the opposite end of Wirik. Just one little problem, though. No ship ever survives the demon's lane. It's very violent."

"So," Veelos said, facing forward again. "Khormar doesn't believe in miracles, does he, but rather in demons? But he's wrong. Our speed is not because of any demon's lane."

Shalar shrugged. "If it is, it's funny how we happened to show up on the exact night that the lane begins. Could one hope for such a coincidence? Or is it an omen?"

"Well, let's hope that it's a better omen for us than it is for Miril."

"You seem certain she's out there."

"She's out there, alright."

"How do you know?" Shalar asked. "How can you be so sure of things unseen?"

"This was all prophesied," Veelos said, "both in holy scripture, and in demonic foretellings. It all becomes clear, now."

Shalar grunted, and moved to the railing, where beside the priestess, he leaned forward against it. "Scripture," he mused aloud. "And anti-scripture.

I know it must sound ignorant of me to ask, but, what does it all mean? They are only scrolls that somebody wrote down. What useful purpose can they have?"

Veelos explained. "The purpose of holy scripture is to reveal those truths which the mind of man could never discern otherwise. The purpose of demonic scripture is to confound the human soul, to deceive and destroy. The two scriptures compete. Only one can prevail. And it seems that Miril's scripture has won. You see, the demonic foretelling is that the demonwitch would recover the Orb of Power from the human usurper. But the holy scripture says that this would be done by the Priestess of Prophecy."

"Who is you," Shalar said.

"Was."

"Huh?"

"I was the Priestess of Prophecy," Veelos said. "But I failed. The prophecy was that I would follow my path, and do God's will. But that prophecy could not force me to do those things. It removed neither my free will nor my frailty. And I made my choosing. I chose wrongly. And now, I'm afraid, many will pay the penalty for my sins."

"So," Shalar said. "Let's see if I can make sense of this. It was Miril's prophecy that proved true, and not yours. Is that what you are saying? But--- then why are we still vying against her? Is there yet any hope?"

Veelos nodded somberly. "There is hope."

"You don't sound very sure of it."

"If somehow--- somehow, we can prevent the Orb from touching Thorgar's feet--- alright, I don't see how. But we have to try."

"And if it does touch the demon's feet?" Shalar prompted.

Veelos shuddered. "Then I die. And Miril lives."

"And she rules the world."

"She rules it even now," Veelos said.

"Huh?"

"Don't ask me to explain, Shalar. I can recite to you a hundred volumes of prophecy. But prophecies are not merely revelations of the future. They reveal not only what will be, but perhaps more importantly, what is here and now. For, while the future opens its blossoms into tomorrow, its stem is today, and it sinks its roots into yesterday. And looking at today, can we say, Shalar, that good rules the hearts of men? Is that the present state of being? I think not, Shalar. I think that evil rules this world already. But however deeply rooted evil may be, the sacred prophecies do offer us hope of a better future."

"But," Shalar pointed out, "as you already said, your prophecies have failed."

"No," Veelos corrected him. "It is I who failed, not the prophecies." Her tone revealed unfathomable disappointment.

Shalar tried to console her. "Defeat is a crushing thing," he said. "But you're not the first one, Veelos, not the first one to fail in a noble deed. I've had men among my band, who once had been men of great faith. One had even been a candidate for priesthood in the temple. Another had become an honored village elder at a young age. They, and others just like them, became ruthless bandits, every one. I hate to say it, Veelos, but there comes a time, in the life of every believer, when he realizes that he was wrong. It's a terrible thing, when that crushing realization hits. I wish I could soften the blow for you. But now that you've discovered your god is false, you can at least hope that Miril's demon is also false. And maybe, in the end, maybe there are neither gods nor demons, neither good nor evil, and no life after death. And perhaps even life itself, Veelos, is but a cosmic practical joke, allowing life to discover that it is doomed to extinction. Then, when we die, we just vanish, as if we never had been."

"Is that what you believe?" Veelos asked. "That all is absurdity?"

Shalar chuckled, and then fell silent. For a time, he leaned upon the railing, and stared with Veelos into the darkness that was swallowing them up. Then, after reflection, he spoke again. "You fought well, Priestess," he said at last. Coming from him, it was a salute, a tribute of admiration rare in

Shalar. Veelos had never heard him commend anyone in so gentle a tone. But he had spoken as if from the gallows. "You have fought better than any man among us," he continued. "For although your power is quiet, subtle, and goes unnoticed in the noise and clamor of battle--- yet no one can say that you did not do your share. You did most of our shares, as well."

Veelos opened her mouth to speak, but Shalar continued.

"You need not fear, Veelos. There is no damnation for you. Your soul is incapable of burning. You are one of those valorous warriors I have sometimes seen, men for whom defeat is impossible, however much it may seem from the outside that they have lost a battle, a war. Such warriors never lose--- never. For from within, they always find one final reserve of strength upon which to draw, some final courage, some ultimate power to sustain them. And they win. As for the rest of us, all mankind, we may spend tomorrow in hell. But its flames will not so much as smudge you, Veelos. Rest assured of that."

Veelos felt a wave of emotion wash over her, an emotion no man had ever evoked from her, and an emotion utterly unlike anything she had ever associated with Shalar. She was astonished to see him gazing directly into her eyes as he spoke. Never before had she noticed, that his eyes had never met hers, never in all the time she had known him. She detected something else also, something new in him: a tinge of fear in his voice. Fear, long accustomed to concealment, hidden within Shalar's shell of insulation, hidden within his bravado and bluster--- Shalar's fear was now, for the first time, unmasked. His was the fear of imminent doom, of inevitable extinction--- once taunted from a distance, but now it had been met at close quarter. Death was no longer someday, but now.

Veelos noticed something more in Shalar, also. She was not certain what it was. Was it something newly created within him? Or had it been there all along, and only just now emerged? Or, Veelos wondered, had it always been in plain view, and she had never cared to look upon it, preferring instead, to see only his ugliness. Whatever it was, this ineffable quality, it was nothing sinister, but quite the opposite. Of one thing Veelos was certain. Only one other woman had ever seen Shalar the way she now saw him--- his mother, Lev-Wan.

Veelos was almost at a loss for words. When they came, they astonished even her. "I had never thought I'd hear," she said, "a sincerely kind word, for me, from you. Certainly not such words from your heart."

Shalar slowly took his gaze away from Veelos's, and looked forward again, across the spray of water fanning from the bow of the creaking ship. "One should always give one's enemy respect," he said. "This is my last chance to pay you that due."

"I'm not your enemy, Shalar."

He chuckled grimly. "Don't insult yourself. If you knew me, then you would know that we are indeed enemies, you and I. It's not just your being a priestess and my being a bandit--- although that should be enough to make us enemies forever. But it goes much deeper than that. To the end, you will remain a priestess. And in that, you will not outdo me, woman. For on my dying day, I will yet be a bandit. We are opposites, you and I. And even though I hate the witch who damns me, yet in many ways, I am closer to her than I am to you. It is a fitting thing that, even the evil, hate the evil."

Veelos answered softly. "You have done evil," she said. "But there is forgiveness. There is a place in heaven for you, as much room as for anyone."

Shalar snorted cynically. "What can you know of forgiveness, Veelos? All you know of it, is what you have read on carefully written parchments, in a temple of polished stone. But the real world lives in mud. It's easy for you to speak of forgiveness for sins you have not seen committed. It's easy for you to forgive what minor infractions you have seen. But some deeds are too brutal for forgiveness. No forgiving heart could ever endure those deeds. You can have no idea what I've done.

"Even though you've seen killing, woman, you have never seen me kill for money. And I tell you, I have killed everyone. I have killed people I've forgotten killing, leaving them not even the dignity of a remembrance. The strong and the weak, the noble and the common--- I've cut down brave men in battle, and murdered cowards hiding under tables. I've killed everyone.

"Forgive? Yes, it's easy for you to forgive. You have not seen. You haven't seen their blood foaming in their mouths. You haven't had your face pressed against theirs as their lifeless eyes rolled back up into their heads. You have not smelled their vomit. You haven't heard their women scream and their children cry as husband and father were hacked to death before them.

"And it's even worse than that, Veelos. For one can never murder only one man. Every murder is many murders. I have left behind me more than a trail of dead and maimed victims. I left a trail of survivors. I've left a trail of tears, of ruined lives and shattered hopes, of romances snuffed out in tragedy, of nightmares and fear, and a trail of bitterness and hatred. Yes, the survivors who live even now, live murdered. I have murdered everyone.

"Perhaps worst of all, I have murdered trust. For what is it that a thief really does steal when he steals? He steals away trust. Whether I was taking a copper coin or a life, I stole away the ability to trust. I made everyone see in everyone else a bandit, a murderer."

As Shalar had spoken, Veelos had carefully searched his eyes for a tear of remorse. But Shalar shed no tears. His heart was much too hard for that. Eyes which had seen what his eyes had, could never have seen them through tears. And Shalar had seen clearly, even as now, he saw through tearless eyes.

Veelos also saw what Shalar had done. They were horrible deeds, crimes which the world of men could never forgive, no matter what penance Shalar might ever do thereafter. For no penance on earth could ever make up for those abysmal, inexcusable crimes. Shalar had done far more evil than ever he could undo, even in a hundred lifetimes, a thousand.

She spoke. "I must confess something to you," she said. "I, too, once stole something. I stole it from you."

Shalar was amused. "You did?" he chuckled easily. "What was it? Let's see if I can remember. Was it in Har-Keem?"

"It was," Veelos answered. "But you'll never guess it."

He shook his head. "No, I can't. So tell me, then. What was it that you stole from me?"

And Veelos told him what it was that she had robbed him of. "A wife."

* * * * *

Shalar seemed confused for a moment. But as it quickly dawned upon him what she meant, he laughed out loud, so audibly that the men, huddled about the lamps on the deck, wondered what could be funny at such a dark hour.

"Yes," he nodded. "I know about that. Our parents were going to engage us. So you ran away, instead."

"And stole the ring of ordination," Veelos added. "I stepped from my path, which was to marry you. Yes, you are right, Shalar. When one steals, one steals many things. When I deserted you, I deserted you to banditry. And in having done that, I share in all your crimes. My hands are as bloody as yours. It's lucky for me that mortal eyes cannot see truth. For if they did, widows and orphans would hunt me, as filled with hatred of me as they feel against you."

Shalar shook his head. "Escaping from marriage to me was the smartest thing you ever did, Veelos. Do you think you would have prevented me from becoming a bandit? Ha! Do you regard yourself that highly? Don't be so vain, woman. You couldn't have changed me. I was worse than my father. If you had married me, I would have beaten you ugly. And I would have beaten the children, also. My only teaching to them would have been, to teach them, to bring you grief. And after I had done all that, then it would have been me who deserted you. I would have left you pregnant and impoverished, and gone off to become a bandit, after all. Your life would have been wasted. All your efforts and devotion would have come to nothing."

Veelos answered. "You are correct, in some ways. All that you say, it would all have come to pass. It would indeed have been just as you describe it. I know so. But it would not have been for nothing, Shalar. We will never know, now, what the final result would have been, could have been, if the path had been followed to the end. But it would not have been for nothing. I know that, also."

Shalar shrugged. "It doesn't matter. We were fated to lead miserable lives, you and I, whether together or separately."

"And they have been made the more miserable," Veelos said, "because we led them separately. For nothing, you say? Look at me. Look at what my life has come to. I fear it has come to far worse than nothing. Compared to what I have, I would prefer nothing. If you could have left me with nothing, Shalar, what a blessing that would have been. I'm sorry, Shalar. I owe you a wife, and cannot pay my debt to you."

They both fell silent, again, and for a long time they were simply together, one man and one woman, facing an empty darkness. For a long, long time they did not speak, did not move, did not even look at one another. They stood together, were together, on the bow of the speeding, creaking, west land warship, standing together in their separation from each other.

"You know?" Shalar's voice finally broke their trance. "I've never looked back. I've never wished I could go back in time. I've never wished I could change any part of my past. But now that I think of it, there is one thing that, if I could do it over again, I would do differently. If I could go back to that day you left Har-Keem--- I would prevent you from leaving. Even if I had to drag you from that carriage and fight off the entire village, I would do that, if I had it to do over again. You are the only thing I ever surrendered without a fight, the only thing I ever owned that I gave away." He grunted forth a laugh of self-ridicule. "But why am I saying this? There is no going back, no changing the past."

Veelos lifted her sleeve and wiped the moistness from her eyes. "No," she agreed. "There is no undoing what's done. That is what damnation is--- forfeit opportunity."

"And we are damned," Shalar said. "However it goes, this war between angels and demons, our lives are damned."

"But there is a life after this one," Veelos said. "There is a world after this one. And in it, we will once more have a path. All the evils of this world will have been undone, and all our crimes forgiven, erased. Whatever happiness we have squandered in this life, it will be restored to us by the loving God who created us. If not marriage, there will be something even better. There, Shalar, in that never-ending bliss, we shall love each other perfectly. I will love you then as I should have loved you in Har-Keem--- and as I do love you now."

Shalar frowned, and moved sideward away from her. But he said, "Looking to that will make death from this world more easy for me, when it comes." Then he turned to walk away.

Veelos grabbed his arm. Shalar stopped in surprise. Veelos leaned forward, and gently kissed his lips.

Shalar glanced aftward, to see if anyone might have noticed. Then he looked at Veelos again, and his expression had become stern. He spoke in careful tones, making certain that no one but Veelos could possibly hear. "When we catch up with Miril," he uttered, "kill her. Be sure of it. Kill her as quickly as you can, and do it however you can. Do it as I would do it, if I had your power. Do it without pity, without scruple. For these next two days, Veelos, train your mind, and think of nothing else. However you must do it, destroy the witch."

He did not wait for her reply, but quickly returned to the lower deck.

* * * * *

Before Shalar spoke again, he had sat by the lantern with his men for a long time. With hawk's eyes, he had observed the despondent figure of Kl'aarn leaning against the rail, enveloped in his empty confusion, drained of spirit.

Without reluctance, Shalar arrived at his decision.

He spoke it to his men with the same concealed bandit's voice with which he had warned Veelos as to what she must do to Miril. "He's a broken man," Shalar said to his bandits. "He is betrayed by his lover, abandoned by her, broken. But do not let down your guard. Despite all that, he loves her yet. He still yearns for the wine of her kiss. For he loves a witch. And once a man has loved a witch, he is seduced by her forever. He will love her forever, whatever may happen. He will always desire her, above all else. That makes him dangerous. As soon as it can be done--- but not where the priestess can see it, mind you--- I want him dead. I cannot do it myself, because I have a pact with him. Nor can you let me know who did it--- I would have to avenge him. But as soon as one of you can, he must do it, swiftly and without a thought. It's our death if he eludes us."

* * * * *

The storm continued to propel them steadily eastward throughout the endless darkness. The ocean current, which Khormar called the demon's lane, raced with the wind to see which could lend more speed. The long night continued on as if forever, even by day hiding the sun, as if in prelude to eternal darkness.

Veelos did as Shalar had suggested. She kept her mind on the battle to come. Any moment, Miril's ship might appear suddenly before her. Any moment, the snarl of the demonwitch might be heard. Her bone-chilling curse might reach Veelos's ear. The Dreaded One Foretold would be at the height of her power, and in the frenzy of a killing rage.

Veelos shuddered. Each time she envisioned it, each time she tried to imagine killing Miril, she could not endure the thought. Each time, just as Veelos imagined putting the stake through Miril's heart, she saw not a witch, but a peasant maiden, sweet and gentle. Then did Veelos begin to understand what had stayed Tarok's hand when Kattaroon had lain beneath his power. Even knowing that Kattaroon had then murdered Tarok, even that made it no easier to imagine killing Miril.

"But I must," Veelos reminded herself over and again. "One of the two must die. The world cannot long contain both the Darkmost Demonwitch and the Priestess of Prophecy. One must die. And moreover, she who dies must be slain by the other. She who lives must slay the other."

Veelos wept.

* * * * *

The darkness seemed to have lasted far more than the three days it had. The first sign that it was ending was a misty twilight appearing about them. The first sign that they were nearing Miril's ship was the sight of a dead sailor in the waves, a west lander's corpse, past which the ship raced.

After what had seemed the doorstep of eternal darkness, the first glint of daylight began to brighten the sea. And as the black fog lifted, a watch was posted for any sign of the ship which bore Miril.

By the time they saw it, the wind had diminished, the current had weakened, and full daylight had returned.

It could have been any ship. But there could be no doubt that it was the one Miril had bewitched. It was a west land warship. And it lay wrecked and broken on the rocks which jutted into the sea from the foot of a tall cliff. There was no mistaking that cliff. Even though they had never seen it, all recognized it as Demon Point, the realm of Thorgar.

In and around the wreckage, strewn about, lay the corpses of dead sailors. Even from a distance, they could make that out. Amid that wreckage there was no sign of Miril, but they were rapidly closing in.

The wind, which had carried them at an impossible pace, now pointed their ship at those same brutal, jagged teeth of rock, which had devoured countless ships before. Men scrambled for handholds as the ship which they now rode threatened to become their coffin.

The cliff began to loom taller and taller above them, growing impossibly huge. It seemed to cover the sky as might the opening mouth of a giant sea serpent. This, for so many before them, had been the last earthly sight seen. Through wide, terror-stricken eyes, the men watched that giant, towering mass of rock rise above them, and then, watched it finally arrive at the prow of the ship.

Then they crashed.

For an instant they heard the crunch of shattered beams of wood, which erupted with a deafening roar. The mast snapped with an ear-piercing crack. Men were thrown about like leaves in a gale. The mast toppled like a felled tree, and its rigging swirled downward like heavy vines.

And then it was over.

* * * * *

Shalar cut his way from beneath the sail.

Water was rushing up into the ruined ship, leaping upward in white-crested waves through the smashed keel. But the ship was not sinking. The wreck was wedged firmly between two massive boulders. It would be long before the waves would work loose the creaking planks of wood.

Dazed, but not seriously injured, Shalar struggled to regain his senses. He stumbled onto the treacherously angled and distorted surface of the deck, his dagger still in hand. Others around him were extracting themselves from the tangle of ruin. None of them seemed much injured beyond bruises and scrapes. Finally, when all struggling motions beneath the piles of rubble had ended with freedom, the bandit took a quick headcount, and came up only two short.

But the two who were missing were Kl'aarn and Veelos.

Shalar cursed angrily above the noise of wind and waves. "Where is she?"

Hathor pointed. "Up there."

Shalar looked. Along the face of the cliff there ran a sloping, diagonal path, a fissure in the cliff, which provided a tenuous foot and handhold. Veelos was climbing swiftly up that precarious gouge, with seeming disregard for the ease with which she could slip and fall to her death. She was virtually running on all fours. She was nearly to the top of the cliff when Shalar spotted Kl'aarn.

The warrior was well behind her, about halfway to the top, struggling along under the clumsy weight of his armor and sword. He was shouting words which the wind whipped away, leaving only meaningless bursts of sound to reach Shalar's ears.

Shalar turned to the men on the ship and demanded, "Does anyone here have a bow and arrows? That man is our doom!"

But no one could find any such weapon.

"Then follow me," Shalar demanded. "If the man in front of you is too slow, then push him off the cliff and speed to the top. Catch up to Kl'aarn and kill him before he kills the priestess. Stop him, or die."

With that, Shalar began the long climb.

Chapter 40

The Priestess Unmasked

Within the darkness of Thorgar's crypt, a damp, clammy chill clung to Miril's skin. For here was no serpent dead, as in Thilgol's castle, but rather one alive. It fouled the air with its noxious breath. In this earthly hell, the living demon awaited its release from the prison which, for so many centuries, had entombed it. Finally, release was imminent.

The Orb of Power was unable to glow within this damnation. The winds of fate had suffocated its light in the lethal darkness. Miril herself had executed that curse. For the eyes which saw in this shadow of hell would not tolerate the slightest luminosity, would regard any glimmer as a blemish of impurity. Miril had seen to it that the gift would be perfect.

The doors had sealed shut behind her, and she held forth the spherical object in her hands. It felt to her like so much air, seemingly weightless, but with a powerful presence nonetheless. Nothing of earth could be so large and yet so easily carried. Now Miril carried it, slowly, ceremoniously, toward the feet of the impatient demon, which hungered for the power within that which had been stolen from the very angels themselves.

The moment of destiny was, at long last, at hand, snatched from the grip of the priestess, just as the demonic scriptures had foretold. Miril stepped slowly forward, savoring each moment of the ceremony.

Thorgar rumbled and growled at the few moments of delay, delay that was intentional, almost taunting. Miril heard its greedy rage tearing in her breast. But her approach toward the idol's feet remained unhurried, deliberate. After all, she knew, the demon had already waited a thousand wasted years. She could make it wait a few moments longer to receive its final freedom. She could tease it, and in doing so, tease not only the demon, but also the angelic beings. For they knew that once the Orb touched the idol's feet, their jewel would be lost to them forever.

Miril continued, until finally she stood before the idol, stood holding the Orb of Power above its feet. Then, still unhurried, she let it begin its gradual descent toward the awesome talons of Thorgar. Slowly, gently, the witch lowered the Orb ever further, ever closer, toward the foulness of the cold, stone claws. It came to within a hairsbreadth of touching the idol's feet.

Miril inhaled in anticipation. The instant of destiny, for which she had labored so long, had at last arrived. Just another hairsbreadth of space, and the anti-prophecy would at long last be fulfilled. Then nothing, nothing at all, could ever stop her from ruling the world.

With a sound barely heard, the Orb touched the feet of the idol. The witch released it into the demon's greedy grasp.

Miril's heart raced with exultation. She had done it. She had defeated the prophecy. The good within the Orb struggled and choked. When it finally died, nothing was left in it but raw power.

The witch could almost hear the angels weep in anguish, and tremble in terror.

* * * * *

Kl'aarn struggled up and over the top of the cliff. Then, a step away from the precipice, he raced from it, toward Veelos.

She was already at the doors of the demonic shrine, pressing her weight against the massive, slimy portal. The putrefaction stained her white robes as if to mock her futile efforts. And the smudges with which it insulted her face were washed away only by tears of anguish.

Kl'aarn drew his sword as he reached her. "Let me try it," he said.

Veelos was surprised to see him. But she stepped back, exhausted and aching, and watched Kl'aarn kick against the doors until it seemed the impacts would break his leg. When he could bear that no longer, he tried to place the point of his sword between the doors, to pry them loose.

But all his efforts mocked him. He turned pleadingly to Veelos. "What can we do?"

Veelos's eyes were globes of fear, and her voice trembled as she cried in answer. "We can do nothing but keep trying. When the final instant arrives, let it find us having tried to the end."

* * * * *

Miril let the Orb settle between Thorgar's feet. She had released it into the demon's possession. Rising from it, she stepped back, to the center of the floor, and stood triumphantly before the victorious demon.

"Now," she proclaimed. "Now it has come to pass. The anti-prophecy which opens the gates of hell is fulfilled. The prophecy which spoke against our victory is smashed in defeat. Now does the demon rule the world of spirit. And now does the Darkmost Demonwitch of all ages rule the lands of men, with invincible curse. Now is the rule of evil unleashed into the twin worlds, to scorch them both, with darkness and doom.

"Bring forth, then, the final cataclysm, Demon of Rage. Sink your fangs into the heavens, and exhale your fiery breath into the skies. Let me hear the screams of the angels fall from the clouds, and let their blood rain down upon a ravaged earth."

Thorgar gloated in ecstasy at the power which lay at its feet. It glowed redly with greed at the object of its lust. For then it knew, that its witch had served it well. It spoke. "Is there not also another gift which you bring me,

Demonwitch?"

Miril's smile was pure wickedness. "There is indeed," she said. "The angels themselves have delivered to our door their final sacrifice unto us. She is their last, desperate tribute, Demon of Vengeance. Open wide the doors and give me back my husband, who was stolen away from me. Open them wide, for he brings with him the Priestess of Prophecy. Let us drink her blood. It is a time for feasting. Let us devour her tortured flesh, and let her soul writhe upon your talons forever."

Thorgar was pleased by the gift, and also by Miril's powerful curse. It granted her demand, and allowed the doors to part.

* * * * *

Kl'aarn kicked once more, in such violent desperation that, had not the doors given way, he would indeed have broken his leg.

Just at that moment, Shalar's head appeared above the top of the cliff, a dagger in his teeth, and a sword in the hand by which he pulled himself over the precipice.

The bandit saw the entrance to the demonic shrine come open before Kl'aarn's mighty kick. He saw Kl'aarn grasp the terrified priestess by the arm, pulling her inward.

With murder on his mind, Shalar raced with fury as the two figures became framed by the hellish contour of the doorway and the blackness beyond. He knew he could not reach Kl'aarn in time to prevent the warrior from killing Veelos. So as the two of them began to vanish into the demonic darkness, Shalar took his dagger and hurled it with all the might which any man has ever put behind a weapon of death.

The whirling dagger whipped in a long, shallow arc, slicing the air from its path. It reached the shrine just as the doors once again sealed shut. The dagger clattered uselessly off the stone, and fell onto the dusty ground beneath.

Veelos had vanished from Shalar's sight. Then did he know with a terrible certainty that he had seen the last of her.

* * * * *

Thorgar's voice rumbled in raging delight at the imprisonment which Miril had wrought upon the two mortals. "It is done," it rejoiced. "The final detail is fulfilled. The victory is total and complete. You are Queen of Darkness, Miril. You are Queen of Hell and eternal tormentor of earth. Take unto yourself your chosen husband. Perform the Damning Seduction, and then assume your throne."

Miril glanced backward to where Kl'aarn and Veelos stood. Their eyes were vacant and blind. Their bodies stood helpless, overpowered by an evil which had grown so powerful that neither of them could resist it.

Miril turned her eyes back to Thorgar. "It is time," she said, "to pour priestess blood into her skullcap and drink it. This can be done only by him whom I have chosen as husband."

"Yes!" Thorgar rumbled. "It is time!"

Miril glanced once more at Kl'aarn, then back at the demon. "But that ceremony can be performed later. He is not yet ready to serve that cup. Let the coronation proceed."

For a moment Thorgar was silent. Then it said, "Well know you what must be done."

Miril answered. "I know it very well. I have studied the matter most carefully. Only my husband can serve that cup. And he will. He has come a long way in his journey into evil. And he loves me, truly loves me. After a time, he will see how I desire it, and he will willingly take that final step into utter evil. But for now, we can set aside that ceremony. It is not essential."

Thorgar rumbled deeply, then said, "If he does it not of his own accord, you can see to it. Bewitch him. Then will he gladly obey you."

But Miril objected. "You and I discussed this matter once before, long ago. Kl'aarn's love for me is not to be suffocated by edict. It has value to me only because he gives it freely. Absent that, it would not be love. Enough of this. I am impatient to wear my crown."

"Indeed we did discuss this," Thorgar said. "And as a consequence, we formed a pact. I told you then, what it is that you truly desire of Kl'aarn: his looks, his mannerisms, his charm. These are yours, Miril, nor do I deny them to you. Take them. Nor deny me what is mine."

Miril frowned. "I deny you nothing that is rightfully yours. But Kl'aarn is rightfully mine."

"Only that of him," Thorgar said, "which it is that you love. His physical self is yours, for you do rule the world of substance. But the realm of spirit has been conquered by me, witch. And that of Kl'aarn which you love not---is mine. His soul, Miril. I demand his soul."

Miril spat. "You lie. You speak not from power but from greed. Kl'aarn is mine, both in body and in soul. This I know quite thoroughly. This is writ in much blood upon the parchments of anti-scripture. Do not test me, Thorgar. Never have you found in me any weakness by which you can betray me, as you have betrayed all others who served you. And never you shall."

Thorgar's idol glowered in murderous rage. "Only through me are you loyal to evil, Demonwitch. Hold nothing back. Six years ago it was I which gave you the black robes you now wear. Six years past, it was this one which taught you, nurtured you, empowered you, and set you upon the path which for centuries so many other women sought in vain, but instead fell to their doom in pursuing. It was I which made it yours, not parchments or scrolls, nor anti-prophecies of any kind. Thorgar! I, Thorgar made you Darkmost. In six years, Miril of Har-Keem, you had much time to learn. And well you did learn, that you could not both have evil, and have any love other than self-love. Surrender his soul, Miril, and command only his love."

Miril retorted defiantly. "You chose me, Thorgar. You chose me for my power and for my evil. Now feel its smarting sting. I did not labor these many years to betray Kl'aarn, but to bring him into evil. That I shall accomplish, not by removing his soul, but by darkening it. Of his own free will he shall love me and rule in evil. Nor can you oppose me. I have power of my own, demon, power which not even you can take from me. Remember, demon, without a demonwitch you are nothing. Unless I rule the world, you cannot conquer heaven. For they are twin worlds. Enough of all this. Let us proceed with my coronation."

"His soul is nothing, Demonwitch. Do not lust after nothing."

"If it is nothing, then it is nothing to you as well. The crown! Shall I take it from you by force?"

For a few moments, the demon was as silent as death. Then, beginning very quietly, there came forth cruel laughter, demonic laughter. "So. You think you can dictate to me, do you? Fool. You utter, utter fool."

Miril fairly snarled. "How dare you! How dare you address me in that way. I am your equal now, Thorgar. But you are in my domain, not yours. This world I rule, with your acquiescence or without. Give me not the crown, then I shall wrest it from you. Dare not to trifle with me, demon."

Thorgar replied, "I call you fool, and a fool you are. For this day you have forfeited all that you sought, both your throne, and your beloved, beloved Kl'aarn. You have lost it all, foolish girl. You have lost everything."

Miril sneered. "And what are you, without a demonwitch?"

"Ah, without a demonwitch I am indeed nothing, as you say," Thorgar said. "But I have seen to that little detail."

Miril's eyebrow raised. "What can you mean, demon? What detail?"

"Behold," it said.

For another few moments, there was again the silence of death. Then Miril noticed a movement from beneath the idol, between its legs. It was a blackness in the blackness, the motion of a shadow at midnight. But it was an imposing presence.

As soon as Miril could make out any form, she heard the voice of this sinister shadow speak to her. "Thorgar is right. You are an utter fool, house-cat."

Miril was astonished, but not afraid. "Kattaroon! You devious snake."

Kattaroon laughed. "You are a monumental fool, a kitten in the lair of the nightcat. Did you really think you could put me aside so easily? You should have killed me while you had the chance. Now you are truly lost.

And I will not overlook the necessity of being rid of you forever."

Miril answered in a voice that needed no bluff. "It is you who are the fool, Old One. Thorgar toys with you. It sends you to your death, merely to test my resolve, just as you sent your own daughter, Grollush, to her death in your place. It is you who have squandered what you could have had. I would have gladly given you a share of earth to ruin. I would have loved you in place of Veelos. But instead, you shall have your share of Hell."

Kattaroon laughed with fierce derision, a laughter which bared her fangs. "Seven years, Housecat, are too few to have gained for you the wisdom which you sought. They are too few, kitten, to have learned the intricacies, the subtlety, of underscripture. Even the most simple lesson you missed, Miril of Har-Keem: evil is deceptive. Its very nature is falsehood. And you, silly child, you are utterly deceived. You fell for it, Miril. And for that, you will die a vermin's death."

"Not I," Miril answered, "but you are deceived."

"Am I? Then ask yourself this, childwitch. Did you really think that Thorgar could surrender a single soul more than it must? Idiot. It was Thorgar itself that took Kl'aarn from his godly path. Thorgar itself sent Druuk on his vainglorious quest. Druuk was deceived, and you were utterly deceived. The demon played you all against each other, fool against fool. And now, do you ask the deceiver to return to you that which it stole from you? Sooner can the nightcat change its color, Miril! And because you refused to yield this one more soul unto it, it is now I who shall rule in your place. And add this to your agonies, Miril: it is now I who shall command Kl'aarn's love."

Miril was enraged at this last. "Deceiver!" she screamed at Thorgar. "I worshipped you. I served you. I regarded you as the salve for all my woes, the satisfaction of all my desires, the banishment of all my troubles. But during all that time, it was you who were the source of all my pains, the inflicter of all my grief, and every arrow which wounded my soul. You! You took all my efforts in service of you, and then turned them against me, to bring about my doom!"

From Thorgar there came only a growl of amusement.

Miril spat in fury. "But it is not yet finished, serpent of Hell. Your ancient demonwitch shall soon lie dead. And then, demon, then shall we test my evil against yours, my power against your power." Almost before she had finished speaking, Miril hurled a firebolt of hatred against Kattaroon.

The ancient demonwitch grimaced. Pain and surprise were hers. But she fended off the worst of the firebolt with magic of her own. "You have grown even stronger, since last we met," she said. "But alas! The winds of destiny have abandoned you. It is now I who wield the Orb of Power. You brought it to me so that I should kill you with it. Taste, then, your own death."

But Miril was unbowed. "Then use it if you can," she sneered. "Learn it quickly. For I slew its last possessor. It did him no good. Nor will it save you." Then yet another violent spell exploded from Miril's wrath.

Kattaroon writhed at the awesome force of Miril's power, and worry showed itself on her face. She had known that Miril was strong. But even so, she had underestimated her foe. It was all the ancient one could do, even with her own awesome powers, to survive Miril's onslaught of chaotic hatred. Seeking every advantage she could get, Kattaroon desperately clawed at the Orb of Power, the darkened lens which was now her only hope.

Miril did not relent. Even in her turbulent rage, she was methodical, directing her spells one at a time to break down the other witch's defenses. Bone by bone, she inflicted increasing agony on her enemy. Both witches knew that it was only a matter of time before Miril would find in Kattaroon her fatal weakness.

Kattaroon groaned in pain and desperation, cursing the orb which was proving so surprisingly difficult to overpower. Even the winds of fate now stood neutral, swirling about them in the dark, odorous enclave, awaiting the outcome of this battle.

Miril slashed and cut with projections of murder across the space which separated them. And at last, she drew blood. A black trickle streamed down from the outer corner of Kattaroon's eye, forming a line like a scar down her cheek. The stolen beauty of Thilgol's ancient demonwitch had, for the first time in centuries, been insulted with injury.

But Kattaroon was not conquered yet. Alone, her powers against Miril's had proved less than sufficient. But Kattaroon gouged from the Orb a measure of its power, and adding that to her malevolent unholiness, was able to strike back.

Miril felt it slowly, at first. Kattaroon's power was not wild, not a flailing of spells, but a careful, deadly groping, patient and deliberate. The icy hand of a skeleton snaked its way between Miril's breasts, seeking a route to her heart. It was in no hurry, for it knew that it would get but one chance. It would have to make that one kill.

Miril chose to ignore the threat. She refused to allow her assault to be diverted by any thoughts of defense. Instead, Miril intensified her attack against the object of her hatred. Miril knew that at any moment, long before Kattaroon's conjured skeletal hand could succeed, the ancient one would be dead, her body a mass of crushed putrefaction, and her soul tortured by the very evil she now served.

But Kattaroon's power grew swiftly stronger, aided by the magical Orb. Miril felt bony fingers wrap around her heart. They had found their way between the atoms of her flesh. Now they gained their hold, and slowly began to squeeze. Kattaroon had found Miril's fatal weakness. And as Kattaroon's power increased, so did Miril's fade.

Still, Miril was not done. In agony, she twisted downward to her knees. But even as she did, she continued the struggle, continued to fight back with deadly spells and lethal curses. Her venomous rage continued unabated to buffet Kattaroon with invisible blows.

The skeleton's hand squeezed harder, not merely crushing against Miril's heart, but even gouging at her very soul. The pain began to grow unendurable.

Miril felt herself begin to die.

She felt the first, preliminary pangs of inevitable defeat. However powerful Miril was, she knew now that Kattaroon was winning. The cataclysmic battle had entered its final stage. Miril knew she would soon be dead. In a very short time, Miril, who had never in her life lost a battle, would meet her doom. And well she knew what awaited her. Damnation would soon begin. If this pain were unendurable, Hell would be unimaginably worse. And it would never end. Throughout all eternity, it would never relent for so much as a single instant.

Miril's only thought then was to inflict as much pain as she could on Kattaroon in the final, few moments which were left. With the same unreasoning, vengeful hatred she had used to wound Thrador, Miril again drew blood from Kattaroon.

Kattaroon winced. The Orb tottered precariously in her grasp. If, like Thrador, she were to drop it, it would be her doom. But Kattaroon's hatred was every bit as unreasoning as Miril's, also vengeful, also whirling into being from the well of blackness. And although Miril had wounded her again, Kattaroon did not flinch from her resolve to crush forever the weakened, vulnerable witch who knelt dying before her.

Miril could bear it no longer. The prospect of immediate damnation, which now stared her hungrily in the face, robbed her of all the evil pleasure of inflicting pain. Miril learned of hopelessness. She realized how futile it was to torture herself by torturing Kattaroon. There could be no point in pricking Kattaroon's skin when, in short order, Miril's very flesh was about to be seared by hellfire.

Miril felt the emptiness of utter helplessness. She had spent the energies of her life in creating her own doom. The hell into which she was now sinking was a monster of her own creation. There was no avoiding the inevitable outcome of her own folly. She had no energy remaining with which to crawl from the pit before it swallowed her up forever. There was no hope left within her empty, desecrated soul.

"Veelos!"

Miril cried out the name in terror and agony. "Veelos, save me!"

But as the inferno raged about her, Miril knew at last that it was too late.

* * * * *

Kl'aarn watched from his helpless paralysis as the flames of Hell enveloped the woman he loved. He watched as they tore at her breathless lungs. Nor could he help her. He could neither move, nor avert the disaster which was taking place before him. He could only watch, and catch a foretaste of his own doom.

He knew that Veelos stood beside him, equally helpless, drained of all her prophetic powers, unable to overcome the overpowering furnace of evil which was fueled by the double measure of evil being poured out before them.

But Miril's outcry seemed to free Veelos, seemed to recant the curse with which Miril had imprisoned the priestess.

Yet even though Veelos could now move, there was nothing she could do. Her efforts to help Miril were puny, restricted to a pathetic effort to pull Miril by her hands from the flames of Miril's own making. It was an impossible task.

Kl'aarn watched as Veelos stepped into the flames. For a moment he dared to hope, for he saw that Veelos was not burned in the fire. He saw her grasp Miril's hands, saw her pull, saw her try to extricate Miril from her own evil. But the flames swirled around Miril into an even tighter deathgrip, holding her fast, refusing to release the witch who had damned the world for love of him. Then he knew why the flames did not burn Veelos. For their rage was reserved for Miril alone.

Veelos released her hold on Miril's hands, tearing herself from the witch as if repulsed by the repugnance of her touch. Veelos staggered backward from the fire.

Kattaroon laughed at Miril's despairing death throes. "She cannot save you, housecat. Her powers are squandered. You saw to that little deed yourself. She cannot even save herself. Look! Death is even now writ upon her forehead. Even she herself knows it."

Veelos heard Kattaroon's words, and her eyes went wide with terror. For she knew it was so. She was about to die. Indeed, it was so written.

But Kattaroon added one final taunt to Miril's torment. "Soon," she said, "your beloved Kl'aarn will serve me a drink of blood from her skull. We shall gulp it down together, he and I. And then--- then I will make love to him on your corpse. But I'll not be greedy, Miril. His soul shall I gladly hand over to Thorgar. And in Hell, your beloved Kl'aarn shall curse you forever."

Veelos reached into the pouch, which was tied at her waist.

Kattaroon paid no attention, for she was by now savoring Miril's final, squirming torment, about to end in death. She was unconcerned about the mortal who would forever owe a debt to the dead witch. Let her pay it in hell.

Veelos extracted from her pouch the small object within, round and clear and weightless, the lesser orb of Har-Keem. In her hands it was frail, a mere whisper against the now corrupted Orb of Power.

Kattaroon paid no attention, until Veelos raised the tiny orb above her head, holding it in a two handed grasp, and stepped forward. It glowed.

Kattaroon spat a curse, not at Miril this time, but at Veelos. "Stop, Priestess!" were the words of that curse. Then Kattaroon returned her attentions once more to Miril, who was now crouched in her prelude to death.

But the curse of anti-priest had no effect. Veelos took one step more.

Kattaroon glared at Veelos in astonishment, for surely, she thought, this priestess had no power to fend off such a curse. Not even with a lesser orb could her power be so great. Yet here she was, unhindered by a curse prepared especially for the priesthood.

Even the demon Thorgar noticed it. And itself rumbled forth an even mightier curse. "By the silver ring," it blasphemed, "I command you freeze!"

But again, Veelos took yet another step forward.

Kl'aarn watched with disbelief. For though he knew little of witchcraft, he could not understand why the potent curses of anti-priest had no power at all against Veelos. None. Surely the lesser orb was no match for the greater, the demon, and its demonwitch, combined. Yet all three together, now had no power against Veelos. None at all.

Veelos continued forward, and it had become clear that she was challenging not only Kattaroon, but the very demon itself. Veelos, who for so long had dreaded Miril, had now not a tremor of reluctance to duel both the ancient of witches and the mightiest of demons. But from whence this resolve, and from whence this power?

Kattaroon's exultant expression of triumph quickly turned into a scowl, and then the scowl quickly faded into a look of terror. For she saw then that not even Thorgar, not even the very demon itself, could defend itself against the woman in white. Shades of recognition crept into the horror which now contorted Kattaroon's face. She began to understand. "Wait," she said to Veelos. "Wait! I will share the throne with you."

But Veelos continued forward, not with boldness, but rather with fearful resolve.

"Alright!" Kattaroon offered. "I will give you the throne. I will make it yours! I will make you more beautiful than myself. And you will have this warrior as your own. His soul as well. I swear it!"

By this time, Veelos stood directly before Kattaroon. Kattaroon looked directly into Veelos's eyes, unable to curse her. And knowing what Veelos was about to do, she screamed, "No! No, you fool! You'll kill us both!"

But Veelos knew now what Vike had meant when he had said, just before his death, that the age of orbs must be ended by the Orb itself. And without further thought, with a sudden downward thrust, Veelos smashed the lesser orb into the greater, the pure into the corrupt.

There was an immediate explosion, a thunderous roar and a flash of brilliant white light. In that instant, Kl'aarn felt fall from his body the invisible shackles of curse which had paralyzed him. The explosion threw him against the wall with such force that it momentarily jarred his soul loose from his body. For a brief moment, he found himself in the world of spirit. It was there, that he saw a great demon tumbling end over end, into the vertical tunnel of a black and bottomless pit, a pit in which the only direction was ever downward.

Then once again, Kl'aarn had returned into the world of substance. He saw Kattaroon, still standing, but consumed from head to toe in ferocious flames. It quickly burned away all her flesh, until nothing was left but bone. Even then, the flaming skeleton did not fall. Its arms flailed, and it stepped backward a pace. Then, its skull tilted backward, the jaw fell open, and there erupted from within it a piteous shriek. Then the flames grew yet more intense, a tornado of fire. Then the flames suddenly vanished, and the smoking skeleton collapsed in a rain of ashes.

Kl'aarn fell to the floor, and there was silence.

* * * * *

He became dimly aware of a repeated, rhythmic thumping sound. At first, Kl'aarn thought it was his heartbeat. But it was much too slow for that, and much too loud.

Kl'aarn opened his eyes. They were flooded with daylight. Daylight! he thought, and lifted his head, to see that there were cracks in the wall of the shrine, and gaping holes in the ceiling. Blue sky and white clouds were clearly visible overhead. The crypt, which before had seemed so strongly built, now proved its age and decay. An ocean breeze was forcing out the stale and noxious air, reclaiming for purity this bastion which for so long had refused it.

The slow thumping continued. Kl'aarn recognized it, now. It was the sound of impact a log would make, an improvised battering ram, forcing open the shrine doors from outside. A vertical slit of light sliced through the shrine from a narrow, hard-earned opening in the doorway. The slit grew ever so slightly wider with each new thud.

The blade of light from the door fell upon the black-robed figure of Miril. She was lying in a crumpled heap in the center of the floor. The hood of her garment was pointed to the place where, but a short time before, had stood the idol of a fierce and malevolent demon. Kl'aarn briefly recalled the vision of it, tumbling into the oblivion.

Unsteadily, the warrior sought to gain his footing amid the rubble which surrounded him. He tried, but was unable, to call out to Miril. His voice was paralyzed by a cold fear, a fear that Miril could never again answer him.

But then he saw within her black garb a movement. Almost spiderlike, one hand emerged into the light, struggling to gain a hold in the world from which she had so nearly been forever cast. Miril did not try to stand. Instead, impatient to move toward the object of her search, she crawled, not toward Kl'aarn, but toward the place where the Great Orb had been, but was no more.

Kl'aarn staggered after her. But by the time he could stand, Miril had already reached that toward which she had crawled. Still on her hands, Miril knelt beside the rumpled robes of white, which contained the form of Veelos, who lay face down in the center of the blast area, which had rent the shrine. Veelos seemed untouched. Not a drop of blood stained her, nor was there so much as a rend in her vestment.

Gingerly, Miril reached forward with one hand. Her fingers trembled, their long, jagged, broken nails a stranger upon the alien fabric of white and blue. Miril expected to recoil from the touch. But she brazenly grasped Veelos by the shoulder. Then, slowly, she rolled the limp figure toward her. Veelos's face was turned upward, toward the sky which peeked through the gaping cracks above.

Miril turned her face toward Kl'aarn. He knelt beside her. Miril spoke. "She's dead."

Kl'aarn felt a shudder. Only one time before had he ever imagined Veelos dead. That time, it had not been so. But this time, there was no denying it. Her soul had fled her mortal husk. His eyes welled forth with tears. He understood then the grief which had paralyzed Veelos when, in the temple that terrible night, she had mourned Keesha.

Miril's lip quivered slightly. "She's dead," she repeated. This time, the tone was that of complaint, an angry but sad complaint.

Kl'aarn turned his gaze toward Miril's face for the first time, then, and felt a jolt of horror. Her hair was tangled and knotted, her skin dark with receding death. Her eyes were blackened with witch blood.

The relentless thumping continued. The crack had grown nearly wide enough to admit a man.

Kl'aarn stood, and being very gentle, hoisted Miril to her feet. "Let's get out of this place," he said.

Miril glanced downward at the corpse of Veelos. "Are you going to leave her here?"

"We must. Let Shalar carry her out. Let us---"

"Shalar comes," Miril said, "to kill you. When he sees Veelos dead, he will kill us both."

Even as she finished speaking, the massive door finally gave way, swinging wide open. A flood of daylight coursed into the shrine, carrying with it Shalar and all his men. They poured in through the wide-open doorway, swords at the ready.

Miril's eyes fixated with dread horror upon what she saw. The scream she uttered then was of such terror and despair that the invasion of bandits was stopped, frozen in its tracks. For they, too, saw what had transfixed Miril, and they too, were afraid.

For the nightmare Miril so dreaded was not the bandit Shalar, but rather, a warrior most fierce. At the sight of him, Miril collapsed to the floor in a huddled, black, ball of terror.

With a single, practiced motion, Kl'aarn turned as he drew his sword, prepared instantly for combat. Before, he had expected to face Shalar. But instead, he found himself facing none other than Tarok.

* * * * *

The ancient warrior, long accustomed to living in the world of spirit, was now completely at home in the world of substance. He was of solid flesh, tall, and wide-shouldered, with thick, sinewy arms. His musculature was that of a man who could fight for days on end without rest, large yet agile. Here was the man who once had stood victorious against an army of sauroids.

His armor was of the ancient style, consisting of two sashes of thick leather crossing his torso, studded with nuggets of grey bronze. A beard of long bristle concealed much of his face, but it could be seen that his square jaw was thick. From beneath his simple helmet there showed a wide, broad forehead, thick brows, and fierce eyes. Those eyes glared with earthy authority. But despite that, one could not miss seeing the wisdom behind those eyes, a wisdom greater even than his thousand years could give account.

Despite all this, Kl'aarn stood fast, both hands gripping the hilt of his sword, its tip pointed directly at Tarok. "Leave her," Kl'aarn said. "She is no longer the demon's. She is mine."

The warrior raised a brow at Kl’aarn’s audacity. "Irreverent mortal!" Tarok accused. "Do you take up arms against heaven?"

Kl'aarn did not answer.

Tarok stepped toward Kl'aarn a pace. "Those who do so face inevitable defeat. Do you doubt it? Then ask the witch. Well does she know the futility of opposing God."

Kl'aarn had already begun to waver, but his resistance was finally broken by Miril. "Don't fight him, Kl'aarn," she wept. "Go. It's over now. Just go."

Even then Kl'aarn tried to force himself to strike. But his flesh rebelled, unwilling to perish beneath Tarok's invincible might. Despite his love for Miril, he might sooner have stepped into fire to rescue her than to face Tarok in battle. As if swept aside by an unseen force, Kl'aarn abandoned Miril to her fate.

When Tarok stepped forward into the space vacated by the mercenary warrior, Kl'aarn could do nothing but watch.

* * * * *

Miril huddled in a mass of black, bent forward so far that her face was pressed against her bent knees. Her hands covered the back of her head, her fingers seeming to claw at her hair, as if somehow she might hide herself within herself. The once dreaded demonwitch was now but a clump of frenzied terror, shuddering uncontrollably.

Tarok stood triumphantly over her and reminded Miril, "There was once a time when you stood in my presence, bold and defiant, cursing me by name. I prophesied to you, then. I warned you, that when next we met, there would be no demon to protect you from my wrath."

Miril wailed from within her black robe. The demonic cloth muffled her outcry.

The invincible prophecy had come true, as all divine prophecy must. Miril knew then the utter emptiness of total defeat, the madness of self-inflicted tragedy. She anguished at the recognition of how avoidable it all had been. Too late, she saw that she had devoted her life to destroying her life.

Tarok bent down, and with massive hands clutching Miril's shoulders, lifted her forcefully to her feet.

She tried to cower from his piercing gaze behind the tangle of her matted hair. Her hands would have gone so far as to gouge out her own eyes, if that would spare her from having to look into that fearsome countenance, to spare her from facing truth.

But Tarok would not permit that. He gripped her wrists, and forced them apart, leaving Miril with no place to hide. Her face had already been stained by near death, her eyes dark and hollow, her lips nearly black. As she stared, unable to avert her gaze from Tarok's, Miril was wracked by shudders so violent that Kl'aarn wondered what kept her from literally dying of fright.

Even Shalar, standing at the doorway, wished to look away. Unbeliever though he was, there could be no doubt in his mind that the warrior who now stood in total and final victory over the witch was the fabled Tarok, who dwelt among angels. As much as Shalar wanted to see Tarok cast Miril into Hell, yet he found it difficult to look. For Tarok carried unseen the sceptre of justice. And nothing so terrifies the unjust.

Tarok spoke. Glaring into Miril's face, his tone was low, yet as forceful as thunder. "Tell of your fears, Miril," that voice commanded.

Miril wished not to reply. But despite that, the words spilled from her mouth, for Tarok's command would not be disobeyed. Lips long unaccustomed to speaking truths were now forced to utter them. "You have won," she said. "I have warred against the One True God of heaven, Whom even the angels themselves do worship. And I have lost. As all who war against God must do in the end, I have lost, defeated by my own denial of truth, by my own rejection of God's love, by my disobedience to His command. I departed from the path He set before me. Now He sends you to punish me. And I fear His terrible retribution."

Tarok seemed unsatisfied. "Speak more," he commanded.

Miril shuddered and cried out. "I am forced to see myself as I am, as I have made myself to be. I was created pure by God. But I replaced beauty with ugliness, innocence with guilt, and godliness with demonicry. I have heaped desecration upon myself, when God had prepared a joyous mansion for me in His home. No longer can I hope to enter into His kingdom. For there can be no forgiveness for a witch."

"Then so be it," Tarok said. "Death to the witch, as the prophecy foretold. Death by the hands of the Priestess of Prophecy herself."

Miril closed her eyes, anticipating the wrenching of those mighty arms, arms which would disjoint her every bone in flinging her across the oblivion into the abyss.

"Veelos?" she heard herself ask. "Is Veelos arisen to slay me?"

Tarok grunted. "Veelos is in a far better place than this. Nor will she return here."

Miril opened her eyes, glanced at the white robes, and then back at Tarok. "But I don't understand. How will she slay me?"

Tarok's grip on Miril's shoulders relaxed. "Prophecy," he said, "is not mere fortune telling. Its purpose is not merely to reveal the future, but also, to reveal the present."

Miril shook her head. "Do you taunt me? Must I be cast into Hell puzzling over riddles?"

"No." Tarok shook his head. "You are not going to Hell, Miril. Though you have wrought much evil, you have repented. Fortunate you are, that the Holy One against whom you warred, would rather take prisoners than slay His enemies. And by your words, Miril, you surrendered to Him. By your words, you slew the Demonwitch."

"But I am the Demonwitch. And Veelos did not slay me."

"Veelos did not slay you," Tarok said, "nor could she. Only the Priestess of Prophecy could do that, and Veelos was never a true priestess, but only an impostor."

"Then torment me no more with these strange words," Miril pleaded. "Who is the Priestess of Prophecy? When will she slay me? Let her do it quickly, for I am ashamed."

"It is you," Tarok said. "You, Miril, are, and have been all along, the Priestess of Prophecy, as well as the Demonwitch. You were both of them, the choosing between them. The battle between them was never a battle between two women, but between two forces. The battlefield was your soul. And God won that battle, Miril, won it for you, because you yourself could never have succeeded in winning it. God is merciful."

Kl'aarn's sword clattered where it fell to the stone floor. He did not notice that he had dropped it.

Miril shook her head. "I have not the power to believe this."

"Then look," Tarok said, holding up Miril's hand before her face. "See. The silver ring. When you were in the whirlwind of fire, Veelos removed it from her finger, and placed it upon yours. That is why the curse of anti-priest had no effect upon her. She knew, then, that she must return to her path, wherever it might lead. And it led her to heaven, Miril, where all godly paths lead."

Tears streamed from Miril's eyes. "She gave her life for mine. After all I had done against her. Through it all, she never hated me, though I grieved her very soul. She died in my place. Why?"

"Because," Tarok said. "She loved you. And at the last moment, she saw the truth. She saw the prophecy. She saw that you, not she, is the one destined to wear that ring."

Miril shook her head. "A ring. This silver does not change who I am. It does not erase what I have done. I am no better now than when I meant to damn you."

Tarok nodded. "Nor am I any better now than when I yielded my love to Kattaroon and betrayed my own armies. But being good is not what grants us favor in God's eyes. We can never be that good by our own effort. We are forgiven sinners, Miril, sinners no less, but forgiven, because we allowed God to forgive us. By yielding to Him, by allowing Him to perform the work of our redemption, we are saved, but only by Him. And there will come a time, Miril, when God will erase all the evil we have done. We will become worthy, and pure, even to perfection--- by His works, not our own. Miril, all who are damned are no worse than we are. But they refuse to be forgiven. So died Kattaroon, so died Morgrar, so died Druuk. And their tragedy is that, had they repented, God stood ready to forgive them, to erase their sins, to bring them into His family."

"But what if," Miril asked, "I choose evil again? I might, you know. For its shadow remains within me."

Tarok shrugged. "No prophecy takes away one's ability to choose. But you know, now, the folly of choosing evil, as none other knows it. You had destroyed yourself, damned yourself, and could not save yourself. It was only love which saved you, the love which your greatest enemy has for you. Choose, then, Miril. You remain a mortal, incapable of doing good, capable only of allowing God to do it through you. You will yet be tempted. And you will yet continue to fail.

"But God never fails, Miril. Never. Be thankful of that."

Miril's hands, held by Tarok, were suddenly in vacant air. For Tarok had vanished as if never had he stood there.

---EPILOGUE---

Shalar slowly approached the rapidly cooling husk of Veelos's mortal remain. He knelt over it.

The room was deafness itself as he tenderly stroked her face with callused fingertips. For a long time, a very long time, he knelt over her in quiet, tearless mourning, a mourning from depths of his heart which never he had encountered. He could shed no tears, show no emotion. But the air itself was heavy with his grief. No one dared move, nor did any dare speak. None dared disturb in any way his moment of yearning, his savage yearning, for the woman he had lost in this life.

After a time, Shalar slowly seemed to return from his journey through whatever spiritual land it is that the inconsolably grief-stricken visit. Slowly, Shalar brought himself up to a standing position. Slowly, he turned and faced Kl'aarn and Miril. And he showed them the murder which lurked within his eyes.

Kl'aarn and Miril stood motionless. The one they had known since childhood stalked them openly. Yet Miril was without a spell for him, and Kl'aarn would not leave Miril's side only to lose a race for his fallen sword, which still lay where he had unconsciously dropped it. There was nothing anyone could do. There was no stopping Shalar anymore.

The seething rage within the bandit carried him ever closer to Kl'aarn and Miril, a rage the more savage for its silence. It carried him to within easy striking distance of his sword.

Kl'aarn looked down at Shalar's hand, and only then did he notice, to his astonishment, that Shalar's fist was empty.

Shalar spoke to Miril. "You wear the ring she put on your finger. Wield it as she would have. See to it."

* * * * *

Veelos was returned to the dust. They buried her as far from the ruins of Thorgar's realm as they could properly carry her. There was no need, of course. Demon Point had been cleansed of its stain. It might even have been a fitting tribute to Veelos, to have made it her grave site. But Shalar would have none of that, and no one disputed his wish in the matter.

The ceremony was one of great sorrow, not only for the three survivors of Har-Keem, who bade farewell to their fallen kindred, but for the others as well. They regretted words never spoken to her, words which would have meant so much to the beleaguered priestess who, stumbling all the way, had followed her faith, even when lost, despite doubt, despite failure.

"The demon had placed its mark upon her," Miril said. "It had chosen her to be its witch. Yet she chose God. Kattaroon would have given her throne to Veelos. Veelos knew that. But instead, she chose to die in my place, despite all that I had done against her."

Miril turned her gaze sideward and upward at Kl'aarn. "And after all is said and done, that was what it was all about, in that last moment. Simple love. Whatever lofty things the sages might say of her in legend, and however true they may be, but in the end, all that mattered to Veelos was a love that knew no limit, a love not of self, but of an undeserving---" she turned then to face Shalar. "You know it too, don't you? That is why you did not kill us in the shrine."

* * * * *

They all drew away from the mound, to leave Shalar bid his solitary farewell to Veelos. While they waited at a distance, Kl'aarn spoke to Miril. "What next? Are we free to live on that farm you promised me? Are there children in our future?"

Miril nodded. "I promised you. I will keep it."

Kl'aarn said, "Which means you must remove the silver ring. But before you do, there are some important things to do first. Who else but you will ordain new priests? The sauroid high priest? He might eat them instead."

Miril allowed a faint smile upon her face. "Me? Ordain others? They might sooner burn me. But let them. I deserve it."

"I won't allow that."

"Kl'aarn, I've been a fool, the penultimate fool. In that, even Kattaroon was correct. But I'm still a fool, still able to slip and fall--- there are other demons, you know. There always shall be, until men stop summoning them. Greed, lust, hatred, perversions--- they will abound until the end. And I am no less human than any who sin."

Kl'aarn said to her, "Let tomorrow's worries wait until tomorrow. Today, let us serve God. If we can serve Him but one day before reverting again to evil, let's at least give that one day to Him. If we do, I'm sure he'll take care of our tomorrows for us."

* * * * *

They all walked together until sunset, along a deserted trail through the forest. No one had used it in many years, save those rare few who had sought the demon. And those few each had walked this trail but once, save Miril alone.

They walked, Kl'aarn and ten warriors, Shalar and fourteen bandits, all that were left alive of the seventy who had taken part in the long adventure, plus the four west land sailors.

When it was almost dark, and Miril had become weary, Kl'aarn selected a campsite. They had no provisions. They would rest the night in destitution, and hoped to find a village the next day.

But Shalar and his men, with the four sailors, did not stop in the clearing where Kl'aarn's men began to unshield themselves. Wordlessly, they continued to walk into the forest. It was clear that they intended to walk until daybreak.

It was a parting of ways.

"Where are you off to?" Kl'aarn asked.

Shalar paused, then turned and shrugged. "You have a place to go. And a reputation to assure your good fortune. Me? I have a trove, well hidden."

Miril spoke. "And from there--- to where?"

Shalar shrugged. "Who knows? Somewhere to spend it, maybe. Perhaps I'll come back this way, now and again, just to keep the grave as it should be."

"To be a bandit again?" Miril asked. "That would be more disappointing to me than you could know. I've taken so much from you. I hope you won't try to take it back from others."

Shalar laughed a despondent laugh. "A hundred ropes await my neck, Miril. They hunger. My name is well known by many, who have good reason to hunt me down and kill me. God may have sent Tarok to deliver forgiveness to you. But, men who were boys when I killed their fathers--- they do not forgive. What am I to do but hide? I have no courage to face the gallows."

Miril stepped forward, and took Shalar's hand in her own. "That final night in Har-Keem. You saved my life. I've never thanked you for that, have I? I thank you now."

But Shalar said, "I didn't do that for you. It was for Kl'aarn. He's thanked me often enough." Then he turned and walked away.

Kl'aarn stepped to Miril's side. "Shalar," he said.

Shalar turned once more. "Yes?"

"I will continue to escort caravans."

Shalar knew what Kl'aarn meant by that. He nodded. "We will meet again--- as enemies, perhaps."

"We may," Kl'aarn agreed.

They faced each other in farewell.

Kl'aarn added. "And as brothers also."

Shalar acknowledged. "Yes. That, too."

THE END

www.ingramcontent.com/pod-product-compliance
Lightning Source LLC
Chambersburg PA
CBHW030823310726
48980CB00006B/607/J
* 9 7 8 0 6 1 5 1 3 9 4 8 7 *